The
Bachelor
List

The
Bride
Hunt

Also by Jane Feather

The
Bachelor
List

The
Bride
Hunt

Jane
Feather

BANTAM BOOKS NEW YORK

Bantam Dell
A Division of Random House, Inc.
New York, New York

Copyright © 2004 by Jane Feather
ISBN 0-7394-4055-1

Contents

The
Bachelor
List

Chapter 1

Constance Duncan nodded at the doorman as he held open the glass doors to Fortnum and Mason. The buzz of voices greeted her from the wide marble expanse of the tearoom, all but drowning the brave strains of the string quartet on the little dais at the rear of the polished dance floor.

She stood for a moment at the threshold of the tearoom until she saw her two sisters sitting at a coveted table beside one of the long windows looking onto Piccadilly. The windows were streaked with rain, however, and offered little view of the street beyond or Burlington House opposite.

Her sister Prudence saw her at the same moment. Constance raised a hand in acknowledgment and hurried between the tables towards them.

"You look like a drowned rat," observed Chastity, the youngest of the three, when Constance reached them.

"Thank you, sweetheart," Constance said, raising an ironic eyebrow. She shook rain off her umbrella and handed it to the morning-coated attendant who had appeared as if by magic. "It's raining cats and dogs."

She unpinned her hat and examined it ruefully. "I think the ostrich feather is ruined . . . At the very least it's going to drip all over everywhere." She handed the hat to the attendant. "You had better take this too. Perhaps it'll dry off in the cloakroom."

"Certainly, Miss Duncan." The attendant received the dripping hat, bowed, and glided away.

Constance pulled out a spindly gilt chair and sat down, spreading out the folds of her damp taffeta skirts. She drew off her kid gloves, smoothed them, and laid them on the table beside her. Her sisters waited patiently until she was comfortably settled.

"Tea, Con?" Prudence lifted the silver teapot.

"No, I think I'll have a shooting sherry," Constance said, turning to the waitress who now stood at the table. "I'm so cold and damp I might just as well be on a grouse moor, even though it is only July. Oh, and toasted tea cakes, please."

The waitress bobbed a curtsy and hurried away.

"Prue and I didn't get caught in the rain at all," Chastity said. "It started just as we arrived." She licked her finger and chased pastry crumbs around her plate. "Do you think we can afford it if I have another one of those delicious millefeuilles, Prue?"

Prudence sighed. "I don't think we'll go bankrupt on your sweet tooth, Chas. It's the least of our worries."

Constance regarded her sister sharply. "What now, Prue? Something new?"

Prudence took off her spectacles and wiped the lenses on her napkin. She held them up to the light, peering shortsightedly. Deciding the smudge had gone she replaced them on the bridge of her long nose. "Jenkins came to me this morning looking even more mournful than usual. Apparently Father has instructed Harpers of Gracechurch Street to lay down a pipe of port for him and replenish his cellar with a dozen cases of a very special Margaux. Mr. Harper sent a very large and very overdue bill to Father with a polite request that it be settled before he filled the new order . . ."

She broke off as the waitress appeared with a silver-lidded salver and a glass of rich dark sherry. The waitress placed them before Constance and lifted the lid on the salver to reveal a fragrantly steaming stack of toasted tea cakes studded with plump raisins and oozing golden butter.

"Those look delicious." Chastity stretched a hand and took one of the tea cakes. "You don't mind, Con?"

"No, be my guest. But I thought you wanted another millefeuille."

"No, I'll just share these, it'll be cheaper." Chastity took a buttery bite and wiped her mouth delicately with a fine linen napkin. "So how did Father react to Mr. Harper's bill, Prue?"

"Guess . . . I'll have a slice of that decadent chocolate cake, please." Prudence leaned back in her chair and pointed to the confection on the cake trolley. "He started thundering around, threatening to take his business away from Harpers . . . *This family's been customers of Harpers of Gracechurch Street for nearly a hundred years* . . ." She took a forkful of cake and carried it to her lips. "The usual diatribe . . . oh, this is *very* good."

"Perhaps I'll have a slice too." Chastity nodded to the waitress. "What about you, Con?"

Constance shook her head and sipped sherry. "This is all the sweetness I need."

"I don't know how you can resist all these luscious goodies," Chastity observed. "But I suppose that's how you stay so slim." She glanced down somewhat complacently at her rounded bosom contained beneath the bodice of a white lace blouse. "Of course, you're a lot taller than I am. That gives you an advantage."

Constance laughed and shook her head. "To revert to the previous topic of money . . . I took some copies of *The Mayfair Lady* to a few newsagents this afternoon and asked if they would display them. Just one or two to start with to see if they would sell."

"This edition?" Prudence reached beneath the table for her capacious handbag and drew out a broadsheet, which she laid on the table.

"If that's the new one." Constance leaned forward to look. "Yes, that's the issue with the article about the new pub licensing laws." She smeared a piece of tea cake in a puddle of butter on her plate and ate it with relish. "I pointed it out to the newsagents as something that their customers might find interesting. You know . . . how they can't drink themselves silly at any hour of the day or night anymore; whether it'll reduce drunkenness and increase productivity and stop men beating their wives. People must have *some* opinions on the subject, wouldn't you think? It's something that will affect your average Londoner."

"Did you get any interest?" Prudence inquired, leafing through the three printed sheets.

"Well, two of them agreed to carry it for a week and display it with the other magazines. We're only charging twopence, after all."

"Twopence a copy won't tow us out of the River Tick," Chastity observed.

"Well, that's just for the man on the street," Prudence pointed out. "We're charging sixpence a copy for Mayfair folk." She gestured eloquently to the elegant, chattering throng of tea drinkers and cake eaters around them. "I managed to persuade half a dozen hairdressers on Regent Street and in Piccadilly to display it on the counter by the till and Chastity laid siege to the modistes and milliners on Bond Street and Oxford Street."

"With some success, I might add." Chastity sat back in her chair and regarded her empty plate somewhat regretfully. "I rather fancy myself as a saleswoman. I was very persuasive from beneath my veil."

"Well, it's a start," Constance said. "But I think we need to offer more . . . more in the way of services . . . if we're going to charge for it." She leaned forward over the table, dropping her voice. "I have an idea that might turn out to be really lucrative."

Her sisters leaned forward, elbows on the table, copper-colored heads close together. "You know those cards people put in shop windows," began Constance. "Well, I saw—" She broke off at a pointed cough just behind her.

"Oh, Lord Lucan!" Prudence said, sitting up straight and smiling without too much warmth at the young man who had approached the table. "Good afternoon. We didn't hear you creep up on us."

The visitor blushed crimson. "I . . . I . . . Forgive me. I didn't mean to creep up . . . or interrupt . . . I just wondered if Miss Chastity would give me this dance." He gestured rather weakly towards the dance floor, where couples were moving to the strains of a leisurely waltz.

"I should be delighted, David." Chastity gave him a radiant smile. "How kind of you to ask me." She stood up as he drew back her chair, then she raised an eyebrow at her sisters. "I won't be long." She went off on Lord Lucan's arm, the emerald green wool of her skirt flowing gracefully with her step.

"Chas is so patient with these poor young men," Prudence said. "They hover around her like wasps at the honey jar and she never shows the slightest irritation. It would drive me insane."

"Our baby sister has a very sweet nature," Constance declared with a half smile. "Unlike us, Prue dear."

"No," Prue agreed. "Positive ogresses, we are. We'd eat 'em alive given half a chance."

"But remember how Mother always used to say that Chas, for all her seemingly amenable disposition, is no one's fool," Constance pointed out.

Prudence made no immediate response and for a moment the two sat in silence, both occupied with their own memories of their mother, who had died three years earlier.

"Do you think she'd turn in her grave at the idea of our making money off of *The Mayfair Lady*?" Constance asked after a while as the strains of the waltz came to an end.

"No . . . she'd applaud it," Prudence said stoutly. "We have to do something to keep this family afloat, and Father's not going to help."

After a little while, Chastity returned to the table on the arm of her partner, whom she dismissed with a sweet smile that was nevertheless firm.

She took her chair again. "So, where were we?"

"Moneymaking plans," Constance said. "I was asking Prue if she thought Mother would be horrified at the idea of selling *The Mayfair Lady*."

"No, of course she wouldn't be. She'd have done it herself if there'd been any need."

"Not that there would have been. If she was still alive Father wouldn't have thrown his money away on an impulsive gamble." Prudence shook her head in some disgust. "What could have possessed him to invest every sou in some chimerical venture? Who ever heard of a railway line across the Sahara?"

"The Trans-Sahara Railway," said Constance with an involuntary chuckle. "If our situation wasn't so dire, it would be funny."

Prudence was betrayed into a choke of laughter as reluctant as her elder sister's and Chastity tried not to smile but failed miserably. Their mother, Lady Duncan, had instilled in all three of her daughters a frequently inconvenient and always irrepressible sense of humor.

"Don't look now, but my ears are burning," Chastity said casually, picking a fat currant off the salver. "I'd lay any odds we're being earnestly if not salaciously discussed at this moment."

"Who by?" Prudence leaned back in her chair and swept her myopic gaze around the salon.

"Elizabeth Armitage has just sat down with a man I've never seen before."

"Interesting," Constance said. "A stranger on this scene is certainly a rare sighting. Where are they?"

"Behind you, but don't turn around, it'll be too obvious. I know she's talking about us, I can almost read her lips."

"She's such a gossip," Prudence declared.

"There's nothing wrong with gossip," Constance responded. "I write it all the time." She gestured to the broadsheet still lying on the table. "Look at the column I wrote on Page 2 about Patsy Maguire's wedding."

"That's not real gossip," Chastity said. "That's just Society chitchat. Everyone loves that. It's not malicious."

"I could imagine writing something malicious if I thought it would serve a useful purpose," Constance said thoughtfully. "Mother was all in favor of exposing people's hypocrisy if she believed it would do some good."

"Then it wouldn't be simply malicious gossip," Chastity stated. "But I wish I knew what Elizabeth is saying about us. I must say, that man is an attractive specimen. Far too attractive to be gossiping with Lady Armitage. Let me see if I can disconcert them." She propped her elbow on the table, rested her chin on her palm, and gazed steadily and serenely across the room at the table where an angular lady in her middle years was discoursing with a tall man whose hair waved luxuriantly across a broad forehead.

"Chas, you're so bad," Prudence said even as she imitated her sister's elbow-propped pose and steady stare. Constance, whose back was to Lady Armitage and her companion, could only hide a grin and wait for a report.

"Ah, that got to her. She's looking through her handbag," Chastity said with satisfaction. "And he's gazing around the room everywhere but here. He seems to be taking an inordinate interest in the dance floor. Perhaps he likes to tango."

Constance could resist it no longer. She dropped her napkin to the floor, bent to pick it up, and as she did so, turned as casually as she could to look over her shoulder. "Oh, you're right. A very handsome specimen," she said. "Distinguished-looking, I would have said."

"Bit arrogant, *I* would have said," added Prudence. "I suppose we should stop by the table on our way out?"

Constance nodded solemnly. "It would only be polite. Elizabeth is a family friend, after all." She raised a hand towards the waitress and signaled for the bill.

"But you haven't told us what your other idea is," Prudence reminded her.

"Oh, I'll tell you while we dress for dinner." Constance picked up the copy of *The Mayfair Lady*, smoothing the sheets with her flat palm, while Prudence counted coins onto the table.

The three women rose as one, gathering gloves, scarves, and handbags, then they strolled together through the tables, greeting occupants with a smile or a bow, pausing to exchange a word here and there. In this manner they arrived at the table occupied by Lady Elizabeth Armitage and her mysterious companion.

"Elizabeth, how are you?" Constance bowed politely. "Terrible weather for the middle of summer, isn't it?"

"Yes, indeed, terrible. How are you all, my dears? You look charming." Lady Armitage had recovered her poise and greeted the younger women with a dowager's smile. "You're out of half mourning now."

"Lavender and dove gray grew a little boring," Constance said. "And Mother was never a stickler."

"No, indeed. Poor woman." Lady Armitage allowed a small sympathetic sigh to escape her, then remembering her companion, turned in her chair.

"My dears, allow me to introduce Max Ensor. He just won the by-election for Southwold and is newly arrived to take his seat in Parliament. His sister is a dear friend of mine. Lady Graham . . . so charming. I'm sure you're all acquainted with her. Mr. Ensor, may I present the Honorable Misses Duncan." She waved a hand between the gentleman, who had risen to his feet, and the ladies.

He was taller than she had expected, Constance thought, and his rather powerful frame was set off to great advantage by the formality of his black frock coat, black waistcoat, and gray striped trousers. She found the contrast between his silver-threaded black hair and his vivid blue eyes set beneath arched black eyebrows most striking. "Constance Duncan, Mr. Ensor," she said. "My sisters, Prudence and Chastity." She smiled. "We are certainly acquainted with Lady Graham. Do you stay with her at present?"

Max Ensor bowed in both greeting and assent. "Until I can find a suitable house in Westminster, within hearing of the division bell, Miss Duncan." His voice was surprisingly soft, very rich and dark, emerging from such a powerful body.

"Of course, very important," Constance agreed with a knowledgeable nod. "You couldn't risk missing an important vote."

"Quite so." His eyes sharpened as he wondered if he had heard a slight hint of mockery behind the apparently solemn agreement. Was she making fun of him? He decided he had to have been mistaken; a man's devotion to duty was hardly cause for ridicule.

"Do sit down again, Mr. Ensor," Chastity said. "We only stopped for a minute to greet Elizabeth. We have to be on our way."

The gentleman smiled, but remained on his feet, his gaze still sharp.

"Have you ever seen this publication, Elizabeth?" Constance laid the copy of *The Mayfair Lady* on the table.

"Oh, it's a dreadful thing!" Lady Armitage exclaimed. "Lord Armitage won't let it in the house. Where did you get it?" She reached a hand towards it with an eagerness she couldn't disguise, although her mouth remained in a moue of distaste.

"In Elise's Salon on Regent Street," Chastity responded promptly. "She had three copies on sale."

"And I saw several in Helene's," Prudence put in. "She had the most delicious straw bonnet in the window. I couldn't resist going in to try it. Quite impractical in this rain, of course. But there were copies of the broadsheet right there."

"For sale?" exclaimed Lady Armitage. "It was never for sale before."

"No, but I think there's more in it now," Constance said thoughtfully. "Some of the articles are really quite interesting. There's something in here about the Maguire wedding that you might enjoy."

"Oh, really, well, I . . ." Lady Armitage's hand hovered over the sheets. "Perhaps I could just take a peek."

"Keep it," Constance said with an airy gesture. "I've read it already."

"Oh, how charming of you, my dear, but I couldn't possibly take it home. Ambrose would have a fit." She folded the sheets carefully during this protestation.

"Leave it in the retiring room when you've finished with it," Prudence suggested casually. "No one need know you'd read it."

"Oh, I shall tear it up and throw it away," Elizabeth declared, deftly tucking the sheets into her handbag. "Such a scandalous rag, it is."

"Quite so," murmured Chastity with a tiny smile. "The Maguire article is on Page 2. We'll see you at the Beekmans' soirée this evening. They have an opera singer, I understand. From Milan, I believe."

"Oh, yes, I shall be there. It's not dear Armitage's cup of tea, but I do so adore singing. So charming." Elizabeth patted her throat as if preparing to break into an aria.

The sisters smiled, murmured their farewells to the Member of Parliament for Southwold, bowed again in unison, and left the salon, their heels clicking on the marble floors.

"How are we going to make any money if you give the broadsheet away?" Prudence demanded as they waited for Constance's hat and umbrella.

"It's one way to create demand," Constance pointed out, regarding her somewhat sad-looking hat with a grimace. "I knew the feather would be ruined." She peered into the mirror as she adjusted the pins. "Perhaps I can replace the feather and keep the hat. What d'you think, Prue?"

Prudence was diverted by the question that appealed to her highly developed fashion sense. "Silk flowers," she said. "Helene has some lovely ones. We'll go there tomorrow. Then we can see if she's sold any *Mayfair Ladys*."

"So what did you think of the Right Honorable Gentleman, then?" Constance inquired as they went out onto Piccadilly. She laid gentle stress on Max Ensor's official title as a Member of Parliament. It had stopped raining and the pavements glistened under the feeble rays of the late-afternoon sun.

"Certainly distinguished, and quite possibly pompous," Chastity pronounced. "We're bound to meet him if he's Letitia Graham's brother."

"Mmm," murmured Constance, looking up and down the street for a hackney cab. She raised her umbrella and a carriage clattered to the roadside beside them, the horses' wet flanks steaming in the now muggy summer air. "Ten Manchester Square, cabby," she instructed the coachman as she climbed in, her sisters following.

If Prudence and Chastity noticed their sister's reluctance to impart her own impressions of Max Ensor, they said nothing.

Max Ensor gazed thoughtfully after the three sisters as they left Fortnum and Mason. He was convinced now that not only he but also Elizabeth Armitage had been exposed to a degree of gentle mockery. He wondered if Elizabeth had noticed it. Somehow he doubted it. It had been so subtle, he'd almost missed it himself. Just a hint in the voice, a gleam in the eye.

They were a good-looking trio. Redheads, all three of them, but with subtle variations in the shade that moved from the russet of autumn leaves to cinnamon, and in the case of the one he guessed was the youngest, a most decisive red. All green-eyed too, but again of different shades. He thought the eldest one, Constance, with her russet hair and darkest green eyes was the most striking of the three, but perhaps that was because she was the tallest. Either way, there was something about all three of them that piqued his interest.

"Are they Lord Duncan's daughters?" he inquired.

"Yes, their mother died about three years ago." Elizabeth gave a sympathetic sigh. "So hard for them, poor girls. You'd think they'd all be married by now. Constance must be all of twenty-eight, and I know she's had more than one offer."

Tiny frown lines appeared between her well-plucked brows. "In fact, I seem to remember a young man a few years ago . . . some dreadful tragedy. I believe he was killed in the war . . . at Mafeking or one of those unpronounceable places." She shook her head, briskly dismissing the entire African continent and all its confusions.

"As for Chastity," she continued, happy to return to more solid ground. "Well, she must be twenty-six, and she has more suitors than one can count."

Elizabeth leaned forward, her voice at a conspiratorial volume. "But they took their mother's death very hard, poor girls." She tutted sorrowfully. "It was very sudden. All over in a matter of weeks. Cancer," she added. "She just faded away." She shook her head again and took a cream-laden bite of hazelnut gâteau.

Max Ensor sipped his tea. "I'm slightly acquainted with the baron. He takes his seat most days in the House of Lords."

"Oh, Lord Duncan's most conscientious, I'm sure. Charming man, quite charming. But I can't help feeling he's not doing a father's duty." Elizabeth dabbed delicately at her rouged mouth with her napkin. "He should insist they marry—well, Constance and Chastity certainly. He can't have three old maids in the family. Prudence is a little different. I'm sure she would be content to stay and look after her father. Such a sensible girl . . . such a pity about the spectacles. They do make a woman look so dull."

Dull was not a word Max Ensor, on first acquaintance, would have applied to any one of the three Duncan sisters. And behind her thick lenses he seemed to recall that Miss Prudence had a pair of extremely light and lively green eyes.

He gave a noncommittal nod and asked, "May I see that broadsheet, ma'am?"

"It's quite scandalous." Elizabeth opened her bag again. She lowered her voice. "Of course, everyone's reading it, but no one admits it. I'm sure even Letitia reads it sometimes." She pushed the folded sheets across the table surreptitiously beneath her flattened palm.

Max Ensor doubted that his sister, Letitia, read anything other than the handwritten menu sheets presented to her each morning by her cook, but he kept the observation to himself and unfolded the papers.

The broadsheet was competently printed although he doubted it had been through a major press. The paper was cheap and flimsy and the layout without artistry. He glanced at the table of contents listed at the left-hand side of the top page. His eyebrows lifted. There were two political articles listed, one on the new public house licensing laws and the other on the new twenty-mile-an-hour speed limit for motorcars. Hardly topics to appeal to Mayfair ladies of the Elizabeth Armitage or Letitia Graham ilk, and yet judging by its bold title, the broadsheet was addressing just such a readership.

His eye was caught by a boxed headline in black type, bolder than any other on the front page. It was a headline in the form of a statement and a question and stood alone in its box, jumping out at the reader with an urgent immediacy. WOMEN TAXPAYERS DEMAND THE VOTE. WILL THE LIBERAL GOVERNMENT GIVE WOMEN TAXPAYERS THE VOTE?

"It seems this paper has more on its mind than gossip and fashion," he observed, tapping a finger against the headline.

"Oh, that, yes. They're always writing about this suffrage business," Elizabeth said. "So boring. But every edition has something just like that in a box on the front page. I don't take any notice. Most of us don't."

Max frowned. *Just who was responsible for this paper?* Was it a forum for the women troublemakers who were growing daily more intransigent as they pestered the government with their demand for the vote? The rest of the topics in the paper were more to be expected: an article about the American illustrator Charles Dana Gibson and his idealized drawings of the perfect woman, the Gibson girl; a description of a Society wedding and who attended; a list of coming social events. He glanced idly at the Gibson article, blinked, and began to read. He had expected to see earnest advice to follow the prevailing fashion in order to achieve Gibson-girl perfection, instead he found himself reading an intelligent criticism of women's slavish following of fashions that were almost always dictated by men.

He looked up. "Who writes this?"

"Oh, no one knows," Elizabeth said, reaching out eagerly to take back her prize. "That's what makes it so interesting, of course. It's been around for at least ten years, then there was a short period when it didn't appear, but now it's back and it has a lot more in it."

She folded the sheets again. "Such a nuisance that one has to buy it now. Before, there were always copies just lying around in the cloakrooms and on hall tables. But it didn't have quite so many interesting things in it then. It was mostly just the boring political stuff. Women voting and that Property Act business. I don't understand any of it. Dear Ambrose takes care of such things." She gave a little trill of laughter as she tucked the sheets back into her handbag. "Not a suitable subject for ladies."

"No, indeed," Max Ensor agreed with a firm nod. "There's trouble enough in the world without women involving themselves in issues that don't concern them."

"Just what dear Ambrose says." Elizabeth's smile was complacent as she put her hands to her head to check the set of her black taffeta hat from which descended a cascade of white plumes.

She glanced at the little enameled fob watch pinned to her lapel and exclaimed, "Oh, my goodness me, is that the time? I really must be going. Such a charming tea. Thank you so much, Mr. Ensor."

"The pleasure was all mine, Lady Armitage. I trust I shall see you this evening at the Beekmans' soirée. Letitia has commandeered my escort." He rose and bowed, handing her her gloves.

"It will be a charming evening, I'm sure," Elizabeth declared, smoothing her gloves over her fingers. "Everything is so very charming in London at the moment. Don't you find it so?"

"Uh . . . charming," he agreed. He remained on his feet until she had billowed away, then called for the bill, reflecting that *charming* had to be the most overworked adjective in a Mayfair lady's vocabulary. Letitia used it to describe everything from her young daughter's hair ribbons to the coals in the fireplace and he'd lost count of the number of times it had dropped from Elizabeth Armitage's lips in the last hour.

However, he would swear that not one of the Honorable Misses Duncan had used it.

Women taxpayers demand the vote.

It would be both interesting and enlightening to discover who was behind that newspaper, he reflected, collecting his hat. The government was doing everything in its power to minimize the influence of the fanatical group of headstrong women, and a few foolish men, who were pressing for women's suffrage. But it was hard to control a movement when it went underground, and the true subversives were notoriously difficult to uncover. Unless he was much mistaken, this newspaper directed at the women of Mayfair was as subversive in its intended influence as any publication he'd seen. It would definitely be in the government's interest to draw its teeth. There were a variety of ways of doing that once its editors and writers were identified. And how difficult could it be to uncover them?

Max Ensor went out into the muggy afternoon, whistling thoughtfully between his teeth as he made his way to Westminster.

Chapter 2

So what was this plan of yours, Con?" Prudence poured sherry from the cut-glass decanter on her dressing table into three glasses and handed two of them to her sisters before sitting down in front of the mirror. Her bedroom windows stood open to let in a slight breeze that refreshed the damp air of the long summer evening, and the shouts of children and the thud of cricket ball on bat drifted up from the square garden.

Constance was repairing the torn lace edging to her evening gloves, setting tiny stitches into the cream silk. She didn't reply until she'd tied the end of the thread and bitten it off. "That'll have to do," she observed, holding the glove up to the light. "I'm afraid these have seen better days."

"You could borrow my spare pair," Chastity offered from her perch on the worn velvet cushion of a window seat. "They were Mother's, so they really belong to all of us."

Constance shook her head. "No, these have a few more evenings left in them." She laid them down beside her on the bed coverlet. "Do you remember, I was talking about those cards you see in newsagents' windows? People advertising things to sell, puppies or chests of drawers . . . those kinds of thing."

Prudence swiveled on the dresser stool, a powder puff in her hand. "And?" she prompted.

"Well, I went into two newsagents on Baker Street this morning and they each had cards on their doors. Not the usual advertisements but people wanting people."

Chastity wrinkled her forehead. "I don't follow."

"The first one had a card from a man wanting to find a woman. A widow preferably, he said, around forty with or without children, who wanted to find companionship and security in her later years and would be willing to keep house and see to his creature comforts in exchange . . . I'm not quite sure what the latter would embrace," she added with a grin.

"Anyway," she continued, seeing her sisters' continued puzzlement, "the second one, in the next newsagent's, was—"

"Oh, I see it!" Chastity interrupted. "A woman who fit the bill, asking for her own companion."

"Precisely." Constance sipped her sherry. "Well, I couldn't resist, of course. There were these two separate cards in two separate windows and never the twain would meet unless someone did something about it."

"What *did* you do?" Prudence dabbed the powder puff on the bridge of her nose where her glasses had pinched the skin.

"Copied each one of them and paired 'em up, so both newsagents now carry both cards. When the advertisers go to check on their cards, that's what they'll see." She chuckled. "They can take it from there, I think."

"I agree you've done your good deed for the day," Prudence said. "But I don't see the relevance to our own somewhat dismal affairs."

"Don't you think people might pay for a service that puts them in touch with the right mate?" Constance's dark green eyes darted between her sisters, assessing their reactions.

"You mean like a *matchmaker*?" Chastity crossed and uncrossed her neat ankles, a habit she had when she was thinking.

Constance shrugged. "I suppose so. But I thought more like a go-between. Someone who facilitates meetings, carries messages, that sort of thing. Like what I did this morning."

"And we'd charge for this service?" Prudence caught up her long russet hair and twisted it into a knot on top of her head.

"Yes. I thought we could advertise in *The Mayfair Lady,* have a poste restante address to preserve privacy—"

"Not to mention our anonymity," Chastity put in, going over to help Prudence with her hair.

"Yes, of course."

"It's certainly an original idea," Prudence said thoughtfully, holding up tortoiseshell hairpins for her sister. "I vote we give it a try."

"Me too," Chastity agreed. "I'm going to take the next issue to the printer tomorrow. I'll add the advertisement to the back page. Do you think that's the right spot?" She teased a long ringlet out of her sister's elaborately piled hair and stood gazing intently at her handiwork in the mirror.

"I think it should go on the front page," Constance stated. "At least for the first couple of times. Just to draw the most attention. What should we call the service? Something eye-catching." She frowned in thought, tapping her lips with a fingertip.

"What's wrong with 'Go-Between'?" asked Chastity. "Since that's what we're offering."

"Nothing wrong with it at all. What d'you think, Prue?"

"I like it." Prudence turned her head this way and that to get the full effect of her sister's hairdressing efforts. "You're so good with hair, Chas."

"Perhaps I should open a salon." Chastity grinned. "Where's the curling iron? You need to touch up your side ringlets."

"Oh, I have it." Constance stood up. "In my room. I'll fetch it." She paused on her way out to examine her own reflection in the long swing mirror by the door. Her evening gown of cream silk chiffon fell in rich folds, the hemline brushing her bronze kid shoes. Her bare shoulders rose from the low neckline edged in coffee lace and a broad satin ribbon of the same color spanned an enviably small waist that owed nothing to the restrictions of whalebone.

"I think the coffee ribbon and lace really do transform this gown," she said. "I almost don't recognize it myself and this is its third season."

"It doesn't seem to matter what you wear, you always look so elegant," Chastity observed. "You could be in rags and heads would still turn."

"Flattery will get you everywhere." Constance whisked out of the room in search of the curling iron.

"It's true," Chastity said.

"Yes, but part of Con's charm is that she doesn't seem to notice it. Once she's dressed and checked herself she never looks in a mirror again for the entire evening." Prudence put on her glasses and peered at her own reflection. She licked her finger and dampened her eyebrows. "I wonder if Max Ensor will be at the Beekmans' this evening."

"Why would you wonder that?" Chastity was curious; her sister rarely made purposeless remarks.

"No reason, really." Prudence shrugged. "But Con is looking particularly lovely this evening."

"You don't think she was attracted to him, surely?"

"He *is* an attractive man with that silvery dark hair and those blue eyes. You must admit he commands attention."

"Well, yes, but Con hasn't been seriously interested in any man since Douglas died. She amuses herself a little but her heart's not in it." A frown crossed Chastity's countenance, a shadow of sorrow that was mirrored in her sister's eyes.

"Surely she can't grieve forever," Prudence said after a minute. "She doesn't show her grief at all, not anymore, but it's still there deep down. It's as if she believes no other man could measure up to Douglas."

"When I look around at who's on offer, I tend to agree with her," Chastity observed with unusual tartness.

Prudence laughed slightly. "You have a point. But I just felt some stirring in the air this afternoon around Mr. Ensor."

"Oh, that was just because Con loves teasing Elizabeth Armitage."

"Yes, probably," Prudence agreed, although the tiny frown remained in her eyes. "Dear Elizabeth, such a *charming* woman."

Chastity laughed at this remarkably accurate imitation of the lady's fulsomeness and let the subject of Max Ensor drop. "Is Father dining in this evening?" she inquired. "I'm sure we won't see him at the Beekmans'. Opera singers are not quite in his style."

"The ones who go to Mayfair soirées, you mean," Prudence responded with a judicious nod of her head. "I'm sure the more euphemistic opera singers are very much in his style."

Chastity raised an eyebrow at this caustic comment. "He is what he is," she said pacifically.

"Who is?" This from Constance, who had just returned with the curling iron. "Oh, you mean Father."

"Prue was accusing him of dancing attendance on opera singers."

"I'm sure he does. Mother wouldn't begrudge it, he's been a widower for three years." She set the curling iron onto the trivet over the small fire in the grate, lit for just this purpose, although it also helped to keep at bay the residual dampness in the air from the afternoon's downpour.

"I don't begrudge him anything but what it costs," Prudence said with the same acidity. "We go without new gowns while some opera singer or whatever she is wears the latest fashions and is all hung about with jewelry."

"Oh, come on, Prue. You don't know that," Chastity chided.

"Oh, don't I?" her sister said darkly. "There was a bill from Penhaligon's the other morning for a bottle of perfume from the House of Worth, and I don't smell it on any of us."

"Ask him about it at dinner, if he's in," Constance suggested. "See what he says."

"Oh, no, not I." Prudence shook her head vigorously. "I'm not risking one of his tantrums. You know how he resents any suggestion that I might be looking over his bills."

"I don't mind the shouting so much." Chastity took up the now hot iron and twisted her sister's ringlets around it. The smell of singeing hair rose momentarily. "I can't bear it when he looks sad and reproachful, and starts talking about *your dear mother,* and how she never would have dreamed of questioning his actions let alone his expenses." She set down the curling iron.

"Quite," Prudence agreed. "You can ask him if you like, Con, but don't expect me to back you up. It's all right for me to manage the household accounts, but to pry into his own personal business? Oh, no!"

"I shall be silent as the grave," Constance assured. "Are we ready?" She went to the door.

As they descended the wide curving staircase to the marble-floored hall the stately figure of Jenkins the butler emerged from the shadows as if he'd been waiting for them. "Miss Prue, may I have a word?" He stepped back into the gloom beneath the curve of the stairs.

"Yes, of course." They moved towards him into the shadows. "Trouble, Jenkins?" asked Constance.

"His lordship, miss. It's the wine for tonight."

Jenkins pulled at his long, pointed chin. He was a tall, very thin man with a rather spectral appearance enhanced by his pale face, his black garments, and the shadows in which he stood. "Lord Duncan ordered two bottles of the '94 Saint-Estèphe to be brought up for dinner tonight."

"And of course there's none in the cellar," Constance said with a sigh.

"Exactly, Miss Con. We ran out some months ago and Lord Duncan instructed me to order replacements . . ." He spread out his hands palms up in a gesture of helplessness. "The price of a case is astronomical now, miss. When Lord Duncan bought the original to lay down it was quite inexpensive, but now that it's drinkable it's quite another matter." He shook his head mournfully. "I didn't even attempt to put in an order to Harpers. I hoped his lordship would forget about it."

"A fond hope," Constance said. "Father has the memory of an elephant."

"Couldn't you substitute another wine? Decant it so he can't see the label," Chastity suggested, and then answered her own question. "No, of course not. He'd recognize it right away."

"Why don't we tell him that Harpers didn't have any more of that vintage but you forgot to mention it earlier?" Prudence suggested. "What could you substitute for tonight that would console him?"

"I brought up two bottles of a '98 claret that would go particularly well with Mrs. Hudson's chicken fricassee," Jenkins said. "But I didn't want to mention it to his lordship until I'd discussed it with you."

"Forewarned is forearmed," Constance said with a grimace. "We'll tell him ourselves. We can say that you mentioned it to us."

"Thank you, Miss Con." Jenkins looked visibly relieved. "I believe his lordship is already in the drawing room. I'll bring in the sherry."

The sisters moved out of the shadows and crossed the hall to the great double doors that led into the drawing room at the rear of the house. It was a delightful room, its elegance only faintly diminished by the worn carpets on the oak floor, the shabby chintz of the furniture, and the shiny patches on the heavy velvet curtains.

The long windows stood open onto a wide terrace with a low stone parapet that ran the width of the house and looked over a small, neat flower garden, glistening now with the afternoon's raindrops. The red-brick wall that enclosed the garden glowed rosy and warm beneath the last rays of the evening sun. Beyond the wall the hum of the city buzzed gently.

Lord Duncan stood before the marble-pillared fireplace, his hands clasped at his back. His evening dress was as always immaculate, his white waistcoat gleaming, the edges of his stiffened shirtfront exquisitely pleated, the high starched collar lifting his rather heavy chin over the white tie. He greeted his daughters with a smile and a courteous bow of his head.

"Good evening, my dears. I thought I would dine in tonight. Shall we take our sherry on the terrace? It's a lovely evening after the rain this afternoon."

"Yes, I got caught in it," Constance said, kissing her father's cheek before stepping aside so that her sisters could perform the same greeting. "I was drenched when I got to Fortnum's."

"Did you have tea?" Arthur Duncan inquired with another benign smile. "Cream cakes, I'm sure."

"Oh, Chas had the cream cakes," Constance said.

"And Prue," Chastity exclaimed. "I wasn't alone in indulgence."

"Well, you all look quite handsome tonight," their father observed, moving towards the open windows just as the butler entered the room. Jenkins raised an inquiring eyebrow at Constance.

"Oh, we ran into Jenkins in the hall," she said swiftly. "He was concerned because he'd forgotten to mention that Harpers has no more supplies of the wine you wanted him to bring up for tonight."

Prudence stepped out onto the terrace beside her father. "He's suggesting a '98 claret," she said to him. "Mrs. Hudson's chicken fricassee will go very well with it."

A pained look crossed Lord Duncan's well-bred countenance. "What a nuisance. It was a particularly fine St. Estephe." He turned to Jenkins, who was following him with a silver tray bearing decanter and glasses. "I hope you told Harpers to let us have whatever they can lay hands on as soon as possible, Jenkins."

"Indeed, my lord, but they were doubtful of finding another supply. It was a small vintage, as I understand it."

Lord Duncan took a glass from the tray. He frowned down into a stone urn on the parapet planted with brightly colored petunias. There was a short silence in which everyone but his lordship held their breath. Then he raised his glass to his lips, muttered, "Ah, well, these things are sent to try us, no doubt. So what are you girls planning for this evening?"

The crisis had been averted. Jenkins moved back into the house and Lord Duncan's daughters breathed again. "We're going to the Beekmans' musical evening," Chastity informed him. "There's to be an opera singer."

"I don't imagine you'll want to escort us, Father?" Constance asked with a touch of mischief.

"Good God, no! Not my kind of thing at all!" Lord Duncan drained his glass. "No, no, I shall go to my club as usual. Play some bridge . . ." He regarded his daughters with a suddenly irritated frown that indicated he was still put out by the loss of his St.-Estèphe. "Can't think why none of you is married yet," he said. "Nothing wrong with you that I can see."

"Perhaps the problem lies with potential suitors," Constance said with a sweet smile. "Perhaps there is something wrong with *them*."

There was something in that smile and her tone that caused her father's frown to deepen. He remembered Lord Douglas Spender's untimely death. He didn't care to be reminded of unpleasant things, and Constance had rarely exhibited an excess of emotion over the loss of her fiancé . . . at least not in front of him. But he was astute enough to realize that with this oblique reminder she was taking him to task for his thoughtless comment.

He cleared his throat. "I'm sure it's only your business," he said gruffly. "Let us go in to dinner."

Dinner passed without further incident. Lord Duncan drank his claret without complaint and made only a fleeting reference to the rather limited selection of cheeses presented before dessert.

"Jenkins, would you ask Cobham to bring the carriage around in half an hour?" Constance asked as she rose with her sisters to withdraw from the dining room and leave their father to his port and cigar.

"Certainly, Miss Constance." Jenkins poured port for his lordship.

"Ah, I meant to tell you. I have it in mind to purchase a motorcar," Lord Duncan announced. "No more of this horse-and-carriage business. We can be at Romsey Manor from the city in less than four hours with a motorcar. Just think of that."

"A motor!" exclaimed Prue. "Father, you can't be serious."

"And why can't I?" he demanded. "Keep up with the times, my dear Prudence. Everyone will have one in a few years."

"But the cost . . ." Her voice faded as she saw a dull flush creep over her father's countenance.

"What is that to you, miss?"

"Why, nothing at all," Prudence said with an airy wave. "How should it be?" She brushed past her sisters as she left the dining room, her mouth set.

"He is impossible!" she said in a fierce undertone once they were in the hall. "He knows there's no money."

"I don't know whether he really does know," Chastity said. "He's denied every fact of life since Mother's death."

"Well, there's nothing we can do about it at present," Constance said. "It always takes him a long time actually to do something, so let's wait and see." She hurried to the stairs. "Come on, we don't want to miss the opera singer."

Prudence followed her upstairs with a glum expression that did not lighten while they collected their evening cloaks and returned downstairs, where Jenkins waited by the open front door. A barouche stood at the bottom of the shallow flight of steps that led down to the pavement. An elderly coachman stood on the pavement beside the carriage, whistling idly through his teeth.

"Evening, Cobham." Chastity smiled at him as he handed her up into the carriage. "We're going to the Beekmans' on Grosvenor Square."

"Right you are, Miss Chas. Evening, ladies." He touched his cap to Constance and Prudence as they climbed in beside Chastity.

"Did you hear that Lord Duncan is talking of getting a motorcar?" Constance asked him when he had climbed somewhat creakily onto the driver's box.

"Aye, miss, he said something to me the other morning when I was taking him to his club. Reckon I'd make a poor chauffeur. I'm too old to learn new tricks . . . no time for those newfangled machines. What's going to happen to all the horses if there's no call for 'em? Are we going to put 'em all out to grass? Put me out to pasture, that's for sure," he added in a low grumble.

"Well, if he mentions it again try to persuade him that it's a very bad idea," Prudence said.

Cobham nodded his head as he flicked the whip across the horses' flanks. "Expensive business, motors."

The Beekmans' house on Grosvenor Square was brilliantly lit both within and without. A footman stood on the pavement directing the traffic and a trio of underfootmen held up lanterns to light the guests' way up the steps and into the house.

"Ah, if it isn't the Honorable Misses Duncan," a familiar smooth voice declared from the steps behind them as they went up. "How pleasant to meet you again."

Constance was the first to turn and the first to realize that she had responded to the greeting with more than ordinary alacrity. She disguised this beneath a cool smile and offered a small bow of her head. "Mr. Ensor. A pleasure." She turned unusually enthusiastic attention to his sister beside him. "Letitia, you look wonderful. Such an elegant gown; is it Paquin? The gold trimming has her look. We haven't seen you for several weeks. Were you in the country?"

"Oh, yes, Bertie insisted we fetch Pamela from Kent ourselves. She spent a few weeks in the country but she gets bored so quickly. Children do." Lady Graham smiled fondly. "Her governess gets quite distracted trying to keep her occupied."

Constance inclined her head in acknowledgment but she couldn't help the slightly disparaging lift of her mobile eyebrows that frequently betrayed her true responses. It was an involuntary reaction she thought she had inherited from her mother. She smiled in an effort to counteract the effect of the eyebrows and continued up the steps.

"May I help you with your cloak, Miss Duncan?" Max Ensor moved behind her when they reached the majestic pillared hall and with a calm and seemingly innate confidence reached around her neck to unclasp her silk cloak.

"Thank you." She was taken aback. Men did not in general presume to offer her such attentions unasked. She saw that Letitia was in animated conversation with Prudence and Chastity and clearly no longer in need of her brother's escort.

Max smiled and folded the cloak over his arm, turning to find a servant to take it from him. "I have a feeling you disapproved of my niece's inattention to her governess," he observed once he'd divested himself of his own black silk opera cloak, its crimson silk lining a jaunty flash of color against the black and white of his evening attire.

"My wretched eyebrows," she said with a mock sigh, and he laughed.

"They do seem rather eloquent."

Constance shrugged. "I have very strong feelings on the education of women. I see no reason why girls should not be expected to learn as well as boys." She noticed a twinkle in Max Ensor's blue eyes as she spoke that disconcerted her. Was he laughing at her? Mocking her opinion?

She felt her hackles rise and continued with an edge to her voice, "I can only assume your niece has a poor governess. Either she's incapable of making her lessons interesting, or she's incapable of making her charge pay attention."

"The fault I fear lies with Pamela's mother," Max said, and while his eyes still contained that glint of humor his tone was now all seriousness.

He offered Constance his arm to ascend the wide sweep of stairs leading to the gallery above, from whence the strains of a Chopin waltz drifted down. "She will not have the child subjected to any form of structure or discipline. What Pammy doesn't like, Pammy doesn't do."

Constance looked up at him. His mouth had now acquired a rather severe twist and the amusement in his eyes had been replaced by a distinctly critical expression. "You don't care for your niece?"

"Oh, yes, I care for her a great deal. It's not her fault that she's so spoiled. But she's only six, so I have hopes she'll grow out of it."

He was speaking with the level certainty of experience. Her antagonism died under a surge of curiosity. "Do you have children of your own, Mr. Ensor?"

He shook his head vigorously as if the question was absurd. "No, I don't even have a wife, Miss Duncan."

"I see." How old was he? Constance wondered. She cast him a quick upward glance as they stood together in the doorway to the large and brightly lit salon waiting for the butler to announce them.

He looked to be in his late thirties, perhaps early forties. Either way, a little old to be beginning a parliamentary career, and certainly of an age where one would expect a wife by the fireside and a nursery full of children. Perhaps he had had a wife once. Or some grand illicit passion that had ended in disaster and disappointment. She dismissed the thought as pure romantic nonsense. Not something she indulged in as a rule.

"The Honorable Miss Duncan . . . the Right Honorable Mr. Max Ensor," the butler intoned.

They stepped forward to greet their hostess, who regarded Max Ensor with sharp, assessing eyes. She had two marriageable daughters and every single male newcomer was possible husband material. To Constance, whose own unmarried status made her a possible rival, she merely nodded. She then began to question Max Ensor with artful ease.

Constance, who knew Arabella Beekman's tactics all too well, smiled politely and moved on to greet other friends and acquaintances. She took a glass of champagne from a passing tray, then found herself watching Max Ensor. To her amazement, he managed to extricate himself within five minutes from his hostess's formidable investigative curiosity. Something of a record in these circumstances.

He paused, looked around, and made a beeline for Constance. Constance, embarrassed that he had probably sensed her own interested gaze, turned away, and began to address a lanky youth whose spotty complexion and hesitant manner generally kept him on the social sidelines at such functions.

"I feel as if I've been subjected to the third degree," Max Ensor declared as he came up to her. "Oh, you've finished your champagne." He took the glass from her suddenly inert fingers and handed it with a firm smile to the young man. "You should always make sure that your companion has everything she needs, you know. Fetch Miss Duncan another glass of champagne."

Constance was about to protest but the youth stammered an apology and almost ran away with her glass. "I have no need of another glass," she said, not troubling to hide her annoyance.

"Oh, nonsense," he said carelessly. "Of course you do. Anyway, how else was I to relieve you of your companion?"

"It didn't occur to you that perhaps I didn't wish to be relieved?" she said tartly.

He raised his arched black eyebrows in incredulity. "Oh, come now, Miss Duncan."

And despite her very real annoyance, Constance could not help but laugh. "The poor boy is so shy it's only charitable to engage him in conversation. Did you realize that Arabella Beekman was sizing you up for one of her daughters?"

"I thought it might be something like that."

"And are you in the market for a wife?" she queried before she could stop herself.

He took two glasses of champagne from a tray proffered by a footman and handed one to Constance. He caught sight of the lanky youth out of the corner of his eye. The boy had halted a few yards off with a refilled glass and a nonplussed air.

"I've never given it much thought," Max answered finally. "Are you in the market for a husband, Miss Duncan?"

"I suppose one impertinent question deserves another," she responded after a second's hesitation.

"And one honest answer deserves the same." He regarded her over the lip of his champagne glass.

Constance could not deny the truth of this. She had foolishly started the conversation and she had to finish it. She could not bear to continue such a potentially painful topic. She said carelessly with an air of dismissal, "Let's put it this way, Mr. Ensor. I am not *looking* for a husband, but I'm not actively against the idea."

"Ah." He nodded slowly. "And are your sisters of the same opinion?"

"I wouldn't presume to speak for them," she retorted.

"No . . . well, perhaps that's laudable. It strikes me as unusual, though, to find three attractive sisters . . ." He let the sentence fade as if aware that he was about to say something offensive. It had occurred to him that this particular reader of *The Mayfair Lady* might well share that paper's political opinions.

Constance took a sip of champagne. "Three sisters happily facing the prospect of a husbandless future, you mean." Her voice was perfectly calm and even, but her spirit was dancing at the prospect of a battle. This was much safer ground.

"Spinsterhood is not generally a sought-after goal among women of your age." He shrugged with seeming carelessness, although he was very curious now to see what he could flush out about Constance Duncan's views. "Women are not equipped to manage their own affairs. Indeed, I would say it's most unsuitable for them to do so."

For a moment Constance, despite her delight in the challenge, was breathless. Of all the presumptuous, pompous, arrogant male statements. Utterly unequivocal, without entertaining the slightest possibility of there being another opinion on the issue. She stared at him. "Unsuitable?" she demanded, no longer able to pretend nonchalance.

"Well, yes." He didn't seem to notice her outrage. "Women are not educated to handle financial matters or business affairs. And that's how it should be. There should be a division of labor. Men take care of the business side of life and women are best suited to household management, nursery matters, and . . ." Here he laughed. "Amusing themselves, of course."

"And cosseting their husbands . . . waiting upon them hand and foot, of course," Constance said, a dangerous light in her eye.

"It's only reasonable for a man to expect a little pampering in exchange for providing security and all the little comforts women find so necessary to their well-being."

The man was beyond the pale. He wasn't worth doing battle with. "I think it's time for the music to begin," Constance declared. "I see your sister gesturing to you. I imagine she would like your protection during the arias."

Max saw the glitter in the dark green eyes and he had the uneasy sensation of being in a cage with a tiger. Perhaps he had gone too far. "I can see we don't share the same opinion," he said with a placatory smile.

"How perspicacious of you, Mr. Ensor. Excuse me, I must find my sisters." She walked off in a swirl of cream silk chiffon, and her dark red hair that had struck him as richly colored but scarcely fiery now seemed to Max to be suddenly aflame.

Definitely a woman to be handled with care. He pursed his mouth thoughtfully, then went to obey his sister's summons.

Chapter 3

Constance seethed throughout the opera singer's performance, oblivious of the soaring perfection as the soprano's glorious voice hit every high note. Her sisters, sitting on either side of her, were acutely aware of her distraction. Prudence gave her a quick sideways glance and saw how tightly Constance's hands were clasped in her lap.

At the end of the performance Constance remained seated on the little gilt chair, until Chastity nudged her. "Con? Con, it's over."

"Oh." Constance blinked and looked around as if she were awaking from a deep sleep. "It was wonderful, wasn't it?"

"How would you know?" Prudence asked. "You didn't hear a note."

"I most certainly did." Constance gathered up her evening bag and rose to her feet. "But I've had enough for one evening. Let's make our farewells."

"Are you quite well, Con?" Prudence asked with concern.

"Just a headache," Constance replied. "Nothing much but I'll be glad of my bed. There's Arabella by the door. We'll catch her before the crowd." She moved forward swiftly, aiming to reach her hostess before the rest of the guests took their farewells.

Prudence exchanged a knowing glance with Chastity and followed on her elder sister's heels.

"Are you leaving so soon, my dear Constance?" Arabella exclaimed. "There's supper in the yellow salon."

"I have a slight headache." Constance touched her brow with a fingertip in emphasis and offered a smile that she hoped was convincingly wan, although she felt remarkably robust. Anger was a great energizer. "But it was a delightful evening, Arabella."

"Isn't the singer wonderful, utterly charming? A sublime voice . . . just sublime. I was so fortunate to be able to catch her." For all the world like a butterfly in a net, Constance thought, but she smilingly agreed.

They moved away towards the doors to the gallery and the stairs leading to fresh air and escape.

"Miss Duncan, Miss Prudence, Miss Chastity . . . leaving so soon?" Max Ensor pushed through the crowd towards them. "Allow me to call for your carriage."

"There's no need, Mr. Ensor. One of the footmen will call him." Constance gave him her gloved hand. "I bid you good night."

"At least allow me to collect your cloaks, ladies," he protested, tightening his hold slightly on the silken fingers. He dropped them immediately when their owner gave a sharp tug.

"There's not the slightest need, I assure you," Constance said firmly. "I know you're looking forward to your supper."

"If you know that, you know more than I do," he said. "I've never felt less like supper."

"Oh." Constance was silenced, then repeated firmly, "Well, I bid you good night." And turned away towards the head of the stairs.

"I trust I may call upon you ladies?" Max said, addressing himself to Prudence since he didn't feel inclined to talk to Constance's rapidly retreating back.

"Of course," Prudence said. "We are At Home on Wednesdays from three o'clock. We should be delighted to see you." She gave him her hand and a somewhat speculative stare, before following her sisters.

"So what was all that about?" Prudence asked as she and her sisters stood on the steps outside waiting for Cobham.

"All what?" Constance scanned the street intently.

"You know perfectly well. Why were you giving Max Ensor the frozen treatment?"

"I wasn't. I don't know him so I'm hardly going to treat him like a bosom friend." She glanced at her sisters and read their skeptical looks. "If you must know, he's the most arrogant, pompous, stuffed shirt of a man it's been my misfortune to talk to."

"Oh, sounds interesting!" Chastity said. "Whatever did he say?"

Constance didn't reply until they were in the carriage, and then she treated her sisters to a succinct account of her conversation with the Right Honorable Max Ensor.

"Mother would have made short work of him," Chastity observed with a chuckle.

"We'll have some fun with him if he comes to an At Home," Prudence said, her eyes gleaming under the streetlamps. "We'll ambush him."

"You didn't invite him, did you?" Constance asked.

"He asked if he could call."

Constance grimaced, then said, "Well, if he comes, he can expect a less than enthusiastic welcome."

"Oh, I think we should try to convert him," Chastity said. "Mother would have done."

"I don't think he's worth the effort," Constance responded. "Not even Mother wasted her time on lost causes."

"He *is* a Member of Parliament," Prudence pointed out. "Just think how useful a convert he could be."

Constance regarded her sisters, a light dawning in her eyes. "How right you are," she said slowly. "The Right Honorable Member for Southwold is about to discover that there are some women in London society who don't quite fit his stereotypes. Perhaps he'll come this Wednesday."

"You don't really have a headache, do you?" Chastity asked.

"It was a headache called Max Ensor," Constance responded. "And curiously it has quite gone away."

"Good," Chastity said. "Because we need to draft the advertisement for the Go-Between, and check the final layout for next month's issue. I have to take it to the printer tomorrow morning."

"We'll do it before we go to bed."

The barouche drew up outside the house on Manchester Square and Jenkins had opened the door before Constance could get out her key. "You must have seen us coming," she said.

"I was watching out for you, Miss Con."

"Is Lord Duncan in?" Prudence drew off her gloves as she stepped into the hall.

"No, Miss Prue. He went to his club. He said there was no need to wait up for him."

The sisters nodded. It was not unusual for their father to return to the house in the early hours of the morning, and sometimes not until dawn. Where he spent the night was not a question they cared to examine.

"You had a pleasant evening?" Jenkins closed the heavy front door.

"Very, thank you," Prudence replied with a quick grin directed at her sisters. "At least Chas and I did. Not so sure about Con. Good night, Jenkins."

"Good night, Miss Prue." He watched them up the stairs and then extinguished all but one small lamp on a console table before taking himself off to his pantry in the basement.

The small square sitting room at the front of the house on the second floor had been Lady Duncan's private parlor and was now used exclusively by the sisters. It had a pleasantly faded, lived-in air. The furniture was worn, the colors of the upholstery and curtains bleached by years of sunlight and laundering. But there were bowls of fresh flowers on every surface amid a cheerful clutter of books, magazines, and sewing materials. As usual, a pan of milk stood on the sideboard ready to be heated over a small spirit stove.

"Ham sandwiches tonight, and Mrs. Hudson has made her luscious macaroons again," Chastity announced with satisfaction, peering beneath a linen cloth on a tray beside the milk. She struck a match and lit the flame beneath the milk. "While that's heating we'll look at the draft pages. I think I put them on the secretaire." She rummaged among a stack of papers on the overcrowded desk. "Ah, here they are."

Constance tossed her cloak over the back of the chesterfield and perched on one of the broad arms. She took the sheets her sister handed her and glanced through them. "You know what might be fun . . ."

"No," Prudence supplied the required answer.

"Why don't we write a review of tonight's performance? There were . . . what? Less than a hundred people there. Not a grand crush but everyone who is anyone in these circles was there, and the only newcomer that I could see was Max Ensor. And as Letitia's brother and an MP he's hardly an unknown quantity." She chuckled. "It'll really set the cat among the pigeons. It will have to have been written by a guest. Can you imagine the speculation about who could possibly have written it?"

"Great publicity," Prudence said, turning the heat down under the milk. "The details of a private party are much harder to get hold of than those of a Society wedding or . . . or, say, a grand ball. There are always gate-crashers and newspeople at those do's anyway. But tonight was very different."

"People will be desperate to get their hands on a copy," Chastity said. "We should double the print order, I think. Who's going to write it?"

"I will," Constance stated. She had a tiny smile on her lips that hinted of secrets. "I have it roughed out in my head already."

"I'm not sure you can be totally accurate when it comes to the arias," Prudence observed. "You weren't listening."

Constance waved a dismissive hand. "I'm only going to touch on that anyway. That's not what's going to interest people. It'll be the intimate details, the kinds of things only an insider could have gathered."

Chastity regarded her thoughtfully. "You've got something up your sleeve."

"Maybe," her eldest sister agreed with another little smile. "Let's get on with this Go-Between advertisement."

"Do you want chocolate in your milk, Chas?" Prudence broke a square off a bar of chocolate.

"Yes, please."

"How can you two drink that sickly stuff?" Constance said. "I shall have some cognac instead."

"Each to his own." Prudence dropped two squares of chocolate into the saucepan, stirring it with a wooden spoon. A few minutes later she brought two wide-mouthed cups filled with dark, fragrant liquid over to the sofa, where Chastity was laying out the sheets of closely written paper.

Constance poured a small measure of cognac into a glass, took a ham sandwich, and then carried the plate over, holding the sandwich in her mouth. She set the plate down on the low table in front of the sofa and reflectively chewed her sandwich. "Why don't we have a banner headline for the advertisement? Just under the title. It'll draw the most attention."

Chastity took a clean sheet of paper and a sharpened pencil. "What shall we say?"

"*Are you lonely? Craving companionship? Do you spend long evenings with your own thoughts?*" Prudence began, helping herself to a sandwich. "*Can't find the right match . . .*"

"*You need a Go-Between.*" Constance chimed in. "*The Go-Between service will help you find your match. We guarantee discretion; we guarantee security. All inquiries personally vetted and personally answered. Send us your—*"

"Not so fast," Chastity protested. "I'm trying to write this down." She paused to drink some of her hot chocolate.

Her sisters waited patiently until she took up the pencil again. "All right. *Send us your . . .*" She looked up inquiringly. "Your what? *Requirements.* No, that sounds a bit clinical."

"Desires?" suggested Prudence, settling her glasses more securely on her nose.

Constance choked on her sandwich. "We're not advertising a brothel, Prue."

Prudence grinned. "I suppose it might sound a little suspect."

"How about something really straightforward? *Send us a brief account of yourself and a description of the person you would like to meet. We will do the rest.*" Chastity scribbled fiercely as she spoke.

"Bravo, Chas. That's perfect." Constance applauded. "Now we need an address."

"Why don't we ask Jenkins if his sister would mind getting this mail? She has a corner shop in Kensington and I know she acts as a poste restante for people in the neighborhood who don't have a proper address for whatever reason. It would be easy enough to fetch it from her." Prudence brought over the basket of macaroons. "Jenkins is on our side in all of this, after all."

"Just as he was on Mother's." Chastity took a macaroon and bit into its gooey depths with a little murmur of pleasure. "He used to run her errands for *The Mayfair Lady* if one of us couldn't do it."

"I'll just run down and ask him. He won't be in bed yet." Constance went to the door. "That way we can get this finished tonight."

Jenkins, ensconced in the butler's pantry with a tankard of ale, listened to the request with his customary imperturbability. "I'm sure my sister will be agreeable, Miss Con," he said, when she'd finished her explanation. "I'll be seeing her on Sunday evening, as usual. I'll explain the situation to her then. You'll be wanting the address." He took a sheet of paper from the dresser and wrote in his meticulous hand.

"That's wonderful, Jenkins," Constance said warmly as she took the paper. "Thank you so much."

"No trouble at all, Miss Con."

Constance smiled, bade him good night, and hurried back upstairs to the parlor. "That's all settled," she said as she closed the door behind her.

"Did he think it was a strange request?" Chastity asked.

"Not particularly. He's used to the eccentricities of this family," Constance replied with a grin. "Here's the address." She handed them a scrap of paper. "Now, I'm going to write my piece about this evening while you two finalize the layout." She sat down at the secretaire, pushed aside a toppling pile of papers, and took up her pen.

Her sisters settled companionably to their task while their sister scribbled behind them. It was the usual division of labor, since Constance, as the most fluent writer of the three, penned the majority of the longer articles.

"I've had another idea," Chastity said suddenly. "Rather on the same lines. Why don't we provide a personal column . . . you know, if someone has a problem they write in and ask for advice. Then we publish the letters and give advice."

Constance looked up from her work. "I don't see myself giving advice," she said. "I have enough trouble organizing my own life."

"That's because it takes you forever to make up your mind," Prudence said. "You always see both sides of every question, and then a few extraneous aspects as well."

" 'Tis true," Constance agreed with a mock sigh. "At least until I do finally make a decision. Then I'm constant as the evening star."

"That is also true," Prudence conceded. "I'm not good at dispensing advice either, most of the time I can't see what people are worrying about. I think Chas should do that column, she's so intuitive."

"I'd like to," Chastity said. "And to get the ball rolling I'll make up a problem letter. We'll only use initials to identify the writers so people will feel secure about making their problems public." She sucked the tip of her pencil. "What kind of problem?"

"Love's always a good bet," Constance suggested. "Torn between two lovers, how about that?"

She blotted her paper and reread the three paragraphs she had written. "There, I think that'll do. What d'you think?" She carried the paper to the sofa and took up her glass again, taking a sip as she watched her sisters' reactions.

Chastity gave a little choke of laughter. "Con, this is scandalous." She began to read aloud. " 'This evening, the Right Honorable Max Ensor, newly minted Member of Parliament for the county of Southwold in Essex, made his social debut at the delightful musical soirée given by Lady Arabella Beekman in her charming mansion on Grosvenor Square. Mr. Ensor is the brother of Lady Graham of 7 Albermarle Street. The Right Honorable Gentleman turned quite a few heads as an eligible newcomer to Society, and several anxious mamas were seen jockeying for a chance to introduce him to their daughters. It is unknown whether Mr. Ensor is a fan of the opera, but he certainly made fans of his own this evening.' "

Prudence whistled softly. "Declaration of war, Con?"

Constance grinned. "Could be."

"Well, it's outrageous," Prudence said, chuckling. "It's not really about the soirée at all."

"Oh, it goes on," Chastity said. "Descriptions, lavish praise for the singer, some faint disapproval of the Gluck aria . . . so you were listening, Con . . . and a nice little tidbit about Glynis Fanshaw and her new escort." She looked up. "Was Glynis really escorted by that old roué Jack Davidson? She's really scraping the barrel."

"I didn't say that," Constance said piously.

"No, and I suppose you didn't imply it either." Chastity shook her head. "People are certainly going to have some fun with it."

"That is the idea, after all. Where shall we insert this?"

"Inside the back page. We'll save the fluffy stuff for that page and hope that readers will be distracted by Con's serious pieces on their way to the cream."

"On the nursery principle of bread and butter before cake," Prudence mused. "How's the problem letter coming along?"

"I've kept it very simple," Chastity replied, "but who should they be writing to? Dear *who*?"

"Someone grandmotherly," Prudence said. "Smelling of gingerbread and starched aprons."

"Aunt Mabel," Constance said promptly. "No, don't laugh," she protested. "It's a very fine name denoting stability and wisdom and all the coziness of a favorite aunt. You couldn't imagine ever being led astray by an Aunt Mabel."

"Aunt Mabel, it is," Chastity said. "I'll read the letter to you. 'Dear Aunt Mabel—'" She broke off at a knock on the door. Lord Duncan called, "Are you still up, girls?"

Constance swept the papers off the table and stuffed them behind a cushion. "Yes, we're still up," she called. "Come in, Father."

Lord Duncan came into the parlor. He carried his black silk hat in his hand and his tie was crooked. His gaze was benign but bleary. "I saw the light under the door as I was passing," he said. He leaned against the door, his eyes wandering around the parlor. "Your mother loved this room." He frowned. "It seems very shabby. Why don't you replace the curtains, and surely some new cushion covers would improve the look of it."

"We like to keep it as Mother had it," Constance said, her tone soothing and reasonable.

He nodded and coughed into his hand. "Oh, yes, I see. Of course . . . of course. A nice sentiment. Did you enjoy your evening?"

"Yes, it was delightful. The singer was magnificent," Prudence said. "We were just chatting about it over our hot chocolate before going up to bed."

"Good God! You don't want to be maudling your insides with that pap," he declared. His eye fell on the cognac glass that Constance still held. He said with a nod of approbation, "At least one of you has an appreciation for the finer things of life."

"I consider chocolate to be among the finest things in life," Chastity said, smiling at him.

He shook his head. "I suppose such solecisms are only to be expected with a house full of females." His gaze fell suddenly on a sheet of newsprint that had fallen to the floor. "Good God! What's that disgraceful rag doing in here?" He stepped forward and bent to pick up the fallen copy of *The Mayfair Lady*. "There was a copy of this in the club this evening. No one could imagine how it got through the door." He held it by finger and thumb as if it might be infected.

"I wouldn't expect to find it in an all-male establishment," Constance observed serenely. "But it's a more substantial newspaper than it used to be."

"Your mother used to read it," Lord Duncan said with a grimace. "I tried to forbid it . . . all that nonsense about women's rights." He shrugged. "Forbidding your mother anything she'd set her heart on was a futile operation at best. I don't imagine it would do much good with you three either. Oh, well . . ." He shrugged again as if the recognition didn't much disturb him. "I'll bid you good night. Don't stay up too late: you need your beauty sleep if you're to—" The door closed on the silent end to the sentence.

"Catch husbands," the three chimed in unison.

"You'd think he'd get tired of singing that song," Constance observed. "Well, beauty sleep or not, I'm ready for bed." She retrieved the papers from behind the cushion. "Thank heavens he knocked. I didn't hear him come up the stairs."

Prudence yawned. "I think we've done enough for one evening. I'm for bed too." She took the sheets from her sister and locked them in the secretaire. "I confess to being intrigued as to how people are going to receive this edition. I think it might well bump up our circulation considerably."

"Just as a matter of interest, how did a copy get into Brooks?" Chastity inquired, taking the dirty cups to the tray. "Any guesses?"

"Oh, I think it's possible that your Lord Lucan accidentally discovered a copy in his overcoat pocket," Constance said airily. "He was on his way to Brooks yesterday morning when I bumped into him inside Hatchards. We chatted for a while. His coat was just hanging over his shoulders and he was very animated, flinging his arms around, and the coat fell to the floor so I picked it up—*et voilà*. I expect he abandoned it in the cloakroom at Brooks without even knowing what it was. He's not the brightest bulb in the chandelier."

"Poor soul. He's very good-natured," Chastity said kindly.

"Yes, sweetheart. And so are you." Constance kissed her cheek as she held the door for her sisters. "Prue and I should take a leaf out of your book."

"I can be nasty," Chastity said with a touch of indignation. "As nasty as anyone, in the right circumstances."

Her sisters laughed, linked arms with her, and went up to bed.

Chapter 4

W hat are we to do about these suffragists?" demanded the Prime Minister, seating himself heavily in a large leather armchair in the Members' Lounge in the House of Commons. Sir Henry Campbell-Bannerman had a perpetually preoccupied, worried air that was not diminished by the large goblet of post-luncheon cognac in front of him and the fat cigar he drew on with obvious satisfaction.

"The Pankhurst woman has started up her Women's Social and Political Union in London now. At least while they stayed in Manchester we could ignore them for the most part." He examined the ashy tip of his cigar critically. "Now we can expect petitions and delegations and excitable meetings right on our own doorstep."

"Appeasement," one of his companions suggested. "We'll get nowhere by provoking them. Promise them a steering committee; it doesn't have to come to anything."

Max Ensor leaned across the glossy surface of the low table in the square formed by the armchairs of the four men who were digesting a particularly substantial lunch with an equally fine cognac. He pushed a copy of *The Mayfair Lady* towards the Prime Minister, and indicated the black boxed headline: WILL THE LIBERAL GOVERNMENT GIVE VOTES TO WOMEN TAXPAYERS?

"This seems to be a particularly sensitive issue. We could announce that we're establishing a committee to discover how many women taxpayers and ratepayers there are in the country. That would quieten them down, at least for the moment."

Sir Henry picked up the newspaper. "A copy of this found its way into the Cabinet Office," he said. "How the devil did it get in there? I've asked all the staff but no one will admit to it."

"You see it everywhere . . . they'll be wrapping fish and chips in it next." One of the four gave a sardonic laugh as he reached for his goblet on the table.

"Does anyone have any idea who writes it?" the Prime Minister asked.

"Not a clue." Two of his three companions shrugged in agreement. "Perhaps it's the Pankhurst women."

"No, they're too busy organizing meetings and protests. Besides, it has its lighter side. I don't see Mrs. Pankhurst indulging herself in society gossip and fashion news. And in the latest edition they're offering some marriage broker service. The Go-Between, they call it. What with that and this Aunt Mabel, who'll wrestle with your love problems, I doubt the Pankhursts would sully their eyes or their hands with it."

"But it's a clever strategy," Max said. "Most ladies wouldn't be in the least interested in a political tract, but they are interested in the other stories on offer—"

"I notice you're mentioned in this one," one of his fellows interrupted with a deep chuckle. "Quite complimentary, really."

Max looked less than gratified. "It's arrant nonsense," he said shortly. "But my point still stands. Women who wouldn't ordinarily think about these issues will have their attention drawn to them the minute they leaf through the paper."

"If we're not careful, we'll have our wives and daughters waving placards on the steps of every town hall in the city," muttered Herbert Asquith from the depths of his armchair.

"Whoever wrote it had to have been present at the Beekmans' soirée," the Chancellor of the Exchequer continued. "No one could have written this commentary on Ensor without having been present. What d'you think, Ensor?"

"I think that's obvious, Asquith." Max tried to keep the irritation from his voice but barely succeeded. He had been stung by the underlying mockery of the piece. As a politician he thought he had developed a thick skin, and yet those little darts had somehow managed to penetrate. "At least we know the paper's written by a woman . . . or women."

"How so?" The Prime Minister held a long curl of gray ash over a deep marble ashtray, waiting reflectively for it to drop from the cigar tip of its own accord.

"It's obvious," Max said with a dismissive wave at the newspaper. "Only women would write of trivialities in that mischievous way. Gossip is not a man's forte. Neither is idle chitchat, not to mention this matchmaking service. It's a women's newspaper."

"A Society women's newspaper," Asquith stressed. "So who could be responsible?"

Max was silent and his companions regarded him with interest. "Max, you have some idea?"

"Perhaps," he said with a careless shrug. "Just a hunch. But I wouldn't bet the farm on it."

"Well, I certainly wouldn't mind knowing who's behind it." The Prime Minister yawned. "What is it that's so soporific about steak and kidney pie?"

It was a rhetorical question. Max stood up. "If you'll excuse me, Prime Minister . . . gentlemen . . . I have an engagement at three o'clock."

He left them dozing peacefully amid the soft snores and discreet conversational buzz of the Members' Lounge and made his way to Albermarle Street to collect his sister. He was looking forward to the rest of the afternoon. A little cat and mouse with Miss Constance Duncan.

"I can't think where Constance is. Did she say when she would be back?" Chastity asked her sister as Prudence came into the drawing room with a large crystal bowl brimming with heavy-headed, deep red roses.

"No, but since she was only going to Swan and Edgar's for some ribbon, I assumed she'd have been home long since." Prudence set the roses on a round cherry wood table and wiped a drop of water from the tabletop with her sleeve.

A worried frown crossed Chastity's face. "Surely she would have said if she wasn't going to be back for three o'clock?"

"Normally she would have said if she wasn't going to be back for lunch," Prudence declared, trying to dissipate her sister's concern with a briskly cheerful mien.

It worked to a certain extent, diverting Chastity's anxiety for a minute. "Well, she didn't miss much," Chastity responded, plumping up cushions on the sofa. "Last night's warmed-over fish pie." She wrinkled her nose. "There's something about second-day fish, particularly cod, that's more than ordinarily unappetizing."

She caught her elder sister's expression and said, "Oh, don't look so disapproving, Prue. I can make a comment, surely. I know perfectly well we can't waste food, heaven forbid, but I don't have to like old cod, do I?"

Prudence shook her head ruefully, wondering why she so often felt responsible for the shifts they had to make to manage some degree of solvency. It was true she made these sometimes disagreeable choices for them all, but someone had to. "No, you don't," she agreed. "And neither do I. But we can only eat up leftovers when Father's not at the table."

"So we must take the opportunity when it arises," Chastity responded with a wry grimace. She glanced up at the handsome Italianate gilt clock on the marble mantelpiece. "Look at the time. Where *is* Con? It's almost half past two. People will start ringing the bell at three." The worry was back in her voice.

Prudence tried another diversion. Once Chastity started fretting, she would soon be imagining every kind of disaster. "I wonder if Max Ensor will beat a path to our door this afternoon?" She went to the French doors that opened onto the terrace. "Should we open these?"

Chastity forced herself to concentrate on the issue. "Why not?" she said. "It's a lovely afternoon, people might like to stroll on the terrace." She repositioned a group of chairs into a conversation circle. "If he does come I'm sure it'll be in pursuit of Con. You could tell how interested he was that night at the Beekmans'. Tactless but interested," she added with a chuckle, forgetting her concern for a moment. "He can't have any idea what devil he's aroused in Con. I can't wait to see her demolish him, or rather, his pompous arrogance." Then she demanded again, "Where *is* she?"

Prudence stepped back from the now opened doors. She said soothingly, "She can't have had an accident, Chas, we would have heard. A policeman would have been here by now . . . Oh, Jenkins . . ." She glanced at the butler, who entered with a tray of cups and saucers. "No sign of Con yet?"

"No, Miss Prue." He set the tray on a console table. "Mrs. Hudson has prepared two kinds of sandwiches, cucumber and egg and cress. She could make tomato as well if you want more variety, but she was hoping to use the tomatoes for the soup this evening."

"Keep them for our soup, by all means," a voice chimed in from the door. "We could always give our guests potted meat paste or jam."

"Con, where have you been?" Prudence demanded, ignoring her sister's joking suggestion. "We were getting really worried. Or at least Chas was," she added.

"I wasn't really," Chastity said a mite defensively. "But you might have sent a message, Con."

Constance removed the pins from her wide-brimmed felt hat. "I'm sorry," she said, instantly penitent. She knew how quickly Chastity became anxious. "I didn't mean to worry you. I would have sent a message, only I couldn't. I have had the most invigorating day." Her cheeks were flushed, her dark green eyes asparkle; energy seemed to flow from her with every long-legged stride as she crossed the room. "I'm sorry," she said again. "I've left you with all the work."

"There's not much to do," Chastity reassured. She was now smiling, her relief at her sister's reappearance visible in her eyes and in the relaxation of her mouth. "Mostly you were fortunate to miss the old cod pie."

"Last night's?"

"Mmm."

"Oh, and I had a Cornish pasty and a glass of sherry," Constance said with a stricken expression. "But mostly it was food for the mind."

"Well, what were you doing?" Prudence regarded her with curiosity.

"Do you remember Emmeline Pankhurst, Mother's friend?"

"Oh, yes, Mother worked with her on the Women's Suffrage Committee, and the Married Women's Property Committee. I thought she was in Manchester."

"No, I knew she had moved to London but I haven't had a chance to visit her. But I bumped into her this morning. She and her daughter Christabel have formed a London branch of the Women's Social and Political Union. They're lobbying for votes for women, but of course you know that." Constance was rummaging in her handbag as she spoke. "I went to a meeting this morning and joined the Union afterwards . . . See?" She held up a purple, white, and green badge. "My official emblem in the colors of the WSPU."

"So you go out for ribbon and come back with a political badge," Chastity said. "How did that happen?"

"I didn't even get through the door of Swan and Edgar's. I bumped into Emmeline on the pavement outside and she invited me to this meeting. She was speaking at Kensington Town Hall. It was electrifying. You can't imagine what it was like."

Her words tumbled over themselves as her mind still raced with the details of the meeting she had attended. The excitement and enthusiasm of the audience still rang in her ears. She had grown up with the sentiments that had been expressed and the issues that had been aired at the Women's Social and Political Union but she had never participated in a group discussion before. Her mother had been convincing when she'd talked to her daughters about women's suffrage, but the surge of jubilation, the sense of a group of women in harmony, prepared to fight for a just cause, had been a new experience for Constance.

"I can't say it surprises me," Prudence said. "You've always been passionate about women's suffrage. Not that Chas and I aren't too, but I'm not a great one for soapboxes and joining associations."

Constance shook her head. "I didn't think I was either, but something happened there. I felt . . . well . . . inhabited by something suddenly." She shrugged, helpless to describe the overwhelming sensation any more clearly.

"Well, whatever you do, don't flaunt the badge," Prudence said seriously. "If it becomes common knowledge that you've joined the Union, it won't be long before someone puts two and two together with the political views of *The Mayfair Lady*. And the cat really would be among the pigeons then."

"You have a point," Constance agreed. "I'll be as discreet as I can. I'm sure I can attend meetings and even speak at them in parts of London where no one we know would be seen dead.

"Anyway," she continued in the same breath. "Since I was in Kensington, I stopped afterwards at your sister's shop, Jenkins, and picked up the mail. Four letters for *The Mayfair Lady*." She took white envelopes from her bag and flourished them gleefully.

"You haven't opened them?"

"No, I thought we should open the first ones together. But that's not all," she said with a significant little nod. "Before I went to Swan and Edgar's I visited all the shops on Bond Street and Oxford Street that had agreed to carry *The Mayfair Lady*. And guess what?" She paused expectantly, then when her sisters declined to guess, continued, "They had all sold out. Every last copy in every shop. And they all told me they would order three times the quantity next month."

"Well, something's working, then," Prudence said. "Is it Aunt Mabel, or the Go-Between, or your wicked gossip, Con?"

"It could be the politics," Constance suggested, then shook her head ruefully. "No, of course it's not. Not yet. But I live in hope. Chas will have to don her heavy veil and widow's weeds and go and collect the proceeds of all those sales. Shall we open these letters? Just quickly to see if they're for the Go-Between or Aunt Mabel."

"We don't have any time now," Prudence, ever practical, said reluctantly. "You need to change, Con, the doorbell will ring any minute now. You may be dressed for a political meeting but it's a bit severe for an At Home."

"Do you really think so?" She looked down doubtfully at the soft gray skirt and black, buttoned boots.

"Yes," Prudence said definitely.

Constance yielded as always to her sister's infallible sense of what was appropriate dress for any occasion. "I'll be back before the first guest."

"We were thinking that Max Ensor might be ringing the doorbell," Chastity said with a mischievous glimmer.

"And it's for him that I should change my dress?" Constance asked, arched eyebrows lifting in ironic punctuation.

Her sisters made no response. Constance, aware of Jenkins's suddenly rather interested glance, brought the topic to a close. "I'll be no more than ten minutes." She whisked from the room and hurried upstairs to find a suitable afternoon gown for the sisters' weekly At Home. Not, however, that she intended to make any special effort on the off chance that the Right Honorable Member for Southwold might decide he was in need of a cucumber sandwich and a slice of Mrs. Hudson's Victoria sponge.

She examined the contents of the wardrobe as she pulled free the narrow tie she wore with her gray and white striped shirt and gray serge skirt. A very businesslike outfit that had, serendipitously, been exactly suitable for her unexpected activities of the morning. She selected a crêpe de chine blouse in pale green and a green and white striped silk skirt with a wide band that accentuated her tiny waist.

She sat on the dressing stool to fasten the buckles on her heeled green kid shoes and then turned to the mirror. The heavy chignon had loosened and wisps of dark red hair clustered on her forehead. She debated the need to undo the whole elaborate construction and start again, but decided she didn't have the time, instead placing a pair of tortoiseshell combs strategically in the mass piled on top of her head.

Her face struck her as a trifle flushed so she dusted her cheeks with powder. Her hand hovered over the tube of lipstick, a birthday present from a friend whose natural coloring was rarely seen beneath rouge, powder, and lipstick. The new cosmetics were wonderfully convenient; they could even be carried in a handbag for running repairs. Or could if Constance ever bothered with them. She despised lipstick; it was more trouble than it was worth, leaving smudgy mouth-shaped imprints on glasses and white table napkins. So why was she considering it now? She wasn't trying to impress anyone this afternoon. She snatched her hand away from the lipstick as if the tube was red-hot. She simply intended to put Max Ensor firmly in his place if he darkened her door this afternoon and she could very well do that without artificially reddened lips.

The doorbell pealed through the quiet house and she jumped to her feet, smoothing down her skirt, checking that the tiny pearl buttons at the high neck of her blouse were all fastened. She hurried to the door and headed for the staircase as Jenkins's dignified tones drifted up from the hall below.

"Lady Bainbridge, good afternoon," she said as she corrected her speed and descended the stairs with rather more decorum. She held out her hand to the rigidly corseted dowager in the hall and greeted the two younger women who accompanied her. They both wore spotted veils that they lifted in response to Constance's greeting. Two identical pairs of pale eyes were demurely lowered to the hems of their stiff bombazine gowns, bodices as firmly underpinned as their mother's.

Lady Bainbridge raised her pince-nez to her nose and subjected Constance to a critical stare. "You look a trifle flushed," she declared. "I trust there's no fever in the house."

"It's a warm afternoon," Constance said, maintaining her smile with some difficulty. The woman was a distant cousin of Lady Duncan and had been the bane of her life with her constant carping criticism. Her twin daughters were pinched and pale as if they lived in the shadows and rarely saw the light of the day. Their mama considered sunlight ruinous to the complexion.

Lady Bainbridge sniffed and sailed ahead of Constance into the drawing room, where she scrutinized Prudence and Chastity with the same stare that clearly searched for something wanting. Apparently she failed to find it in either of the sisters' smiling countenances and very correct afternoon attire, because she gave another audible sniff and inclined her head in a stiff bow before turning her attention to the drawing room.

"You've allowed this room to become sadly shabby, Constance," she declared. "Your mother always took such pride in her house."

Since the sisters could well remember diatribes on the lack of beeswax and silver polish directed at their mother, they allowed this remark to pass over them. Lady Bainbridge seated herself on a sofa, then frowned and began to pick at what Prudence realized was a very faint coffee stain on the upholstered arm.

"Sit down, girls. Sit down. No need to stand there like gabies." Her ladyship waved her fan at her daughters and Mary and Martha obediently perched on the edge of the opposing sofa.

"Tea, Lady Bainbridge?" Chastity brought a cup to their visitor while Jenkins proffered the plate of sandwiches.

Her ladyship peered at the offering on the platter and waved it away. She accepted the tea, however. Her daughters dutifully declined sandwiches and held their own teacups on their laps.

"So what's this I hear about Letitia Graham's brother coming to town?" Lady Bainbridge demanded. "I wasn't at Arabella Beekman's soirée last week, but I hear that he was there, causing quite a stir."

"We met him briefly," Chastity said. "Just an exchange of civilities. I didn't notice him causing a stir, did you, Con?"

"No," Constance responded with a delicate little frown. "As I recall, he seemed perfectly insignificant, madam."

"That's not what I read," her ladyship declared, sipping her tea.

"Oh? Did someone write about him?" Prudence leaned forward, her lively green eyes wide behind her spectacles.

"Did you receive a letter, Lady Bainbridge?" Chastity asked, her own eyes, more hazel than the pure green of her sisters, fixed with rapt attention upon the visitor.

"Oh, Mama found a copy of that newspaper," whispered Mary. "In the ladies' cloakroom in Swan and Edgar's, of all places."

"That will do, Mary," Lady Bainbridge declared. "You're always chattering."

The three Duncan sisters exchanged a glance. Mary spoke so rarely, the sound of her voice was a novelty.

"What newspaper?" inquired Prudence with an innocent smile.

"Oh, you must have seen it. A disgraceful thing." Lady Bainbridge set down her cup on the small table beside her. "It's called *The Mayfair Lady*. A dreadful misnomer if ever I heard one. There's nothing ladylike about it at all."

"Lady Letitia Graham and the Right Honorable Mr. Ensor, Miss Duncan."

Jenkins's voice from the drawing room door startled them all. No one had heard the front doorbell.

"Oh, Lady Bainbridge, I do so agree with you," trilled Letitia, wafting into the drawing room on a cloud of lavender water and a rustle of silk and lace. "It's quite shocking. My poor brother was quite dumbfounded to be the subject of such an article. So embarrassing, don't you agree? When one is but newly come to town, it's no way to be introduced to Society."

"Curiously, Letitia, I consider it quite flattering to have attracted such notice." Max Ensor's voice was as mellow as Constance remembered it, but she could detect an edge to it and guessed with satisfaction that he was not quite as sanguine about his appearance in the pages of *The Mayfair Lady* as he made out.

"Mr. Ensor, how nice of you to honor us with your company." Constance came forward with outstretched hand. Her smile, though polite, was cool, disguising the prickle of anticipation, the slight thrill in her blood at the prospect of engaging in battle with him.

"The honor is mine, Miss Duncan." He bowed over her hand.

"Not attending the Prime Minister's Question Time this afternoon, Mr. Ensor?" Chastity asked brightly.

"Apparently not, Miss Chastity," he replied, taking a cup of tea from Jenkins.

"Oh, but surely as a responsible Member of Parliament, Mr. Ensor, Question Time must be very important," Constance said. "Will you have a sandwich? Egg and cress or cucumber?" She extended the platter in invitation.

Max found three pairs of eyes of varying shades of green fixed upon him with smiling attention. But there was more than pleasantry in that attention. He felt a little like a mouse under the intently malicious gaze of a trio of felines. "If there are any questions of earth-shattering importance, you may rest assured that I shall be informed," he said, to his annoyance hearing a defensive note in the statement. "As it happens I lunched with the Prime Minister and left him in the Members' Lounge less than an hour ago." He took an egg sandwich.

"Oh, I see." Constance's smile remained constant. "You have a direct route to Sir Henry's ear. An unusual honor for a new MP, is it not?"

Max said nothing. If she intended to make him sound like a boastful coxcomb he wasn't going to play a duet.

Constance regarded him quizzically. "So I gather you were the focus of a piece in *The Mayfair Lady*. You found it complimentary?"

Max looked at the overstuffed sandwich in his hand and regretted his choice. Cucumber was a much tidier filling than mashed egg and strands of cress. "I barely glanced at it, Miss Duncan."

"Really? But of course you would have little interest in a women's newspaper. Women are rightly concerned only with trivialities. That is your view, Mr. Ensor, as I recall." The smile didn't falter; the dark green eyes never left his face.

He became aware that her sisters had rejoined their other guests on the far side of the drawing room and he was at an acute disadvantage facing this woman who was all armor while he stood there holding two soggy pieces of white bread from which white and yellow interspersed with green strands threatened to tumble to the carpet. He looked for somewhere to put it since he couldn't eat it and conduct any reasonable conversation—or rather, respond credibly and confidently to what was undeniably an attack. He had come prepared to play his own little game but now he realized Miss Duncan had her own basket of tricks. He must have touched a nerve the other evening.

"Ah, I see you need a plate, Mr. Ensor." Constance moved to the sideboard and took a bread and butter plate from the stack. "How remiss of me."

He suspected it had been an intentional lapse but accepted the plate with relief. "I know nothing of the newspaper, Miss Duncan. You gave Lady Armitage a copy the other week. As you say, it seemed mere uninformed babble to me. The kind of flippant insubstantial discourse that women like." He watched her face and noted the clear flash of chagrin that crossed her eyes. His point, he decided. That made them even.

"There was an article in there about the new licensing laws," Constance said with a casual smile. "You consider that to be the subject of insubstantial discourse, Mr. Ensor? I would have thought a Member of Parliament would have an opinion of his own and be interested in the opinions of others."

"Informed opinions, Miss Duncan, yes." He was enjoying himself now and sensed that Constance was too. Her eyes were flashing and dancing like fireflies.

"And women's opinions are not informed?"

"I didn't say that, Miss Duncan. There are many areas where women's opinions are both informed and vitally important."

"Those involved with hearth and home, kitchen and nursery. Yes, you made that clear the other evening."

"And it offended you?" He raised a quizzical eyebrow. "Indeed, it was never my intention. I have only respect and admiration for your sex."

"And my sex is suitably complimented, Mr. Ensor. Allow me to introduce you to Lady Bainbridge and her daughters, Lady Martha and Lady Mary." She turned and the battle was over, for the moment. He was not entirely sure which of them had won that round.

Jenkins announced a trio of guests and the buzz of conversation filled the drawing room. Constance and her sisters were kept too busy taking care of their visitors to linger in any particular conversation, but Constance was aware of Max Ensor's hooded gaze following her as she moved around the room. He looked bored, she thought. He was standing behind his sister's chair, having abandoned both teacup and sandwich, taking no notice of the conversation around him. In fact he seemed oblivious of everyone but Constance.

Constance cut a slice of Victoria sponge and carried it over to him. "Mr. Ensor, our cook is renowned for the lightness of her sponge cakes." She handed him the plate before he could refuse. "Is there anyone I can introduce you to?"

"No, thank you," he said. "I came here to talk to you, Miss Duncan. No one else interests me."

The sheer effrontery of this took her breath away. "You're saying you find no one in this room worthy of your attention?"

"That was not what I said, Miss Duncan." He looked at her, both challenge and question in his steady gaze. Constance felt a warmth creep over her cheeks and with an effort dragged her eyes from his. She searched for a swift comeback and for once was at a loss. A satisfied smile lingered at the corners of his mouth. He knew he had nonplussed her.

Max broke off a small piece of cake with his fingers. Constance couldn't help but notice that he had unusually long and slender hands for a man. She said coldly, "A person with such restricted interests can hardly expect to be considered interesting to others." She felt the snub barely began to express her true feelings but for once she was at a loss in the face of this supremely indifferent arrogance.

He pursed his lips on a soundless whistle. "Touché, Miss Duncan." His smile broadened. "I'm sure every one of your guests is most worthy," he said. "I daresay my lack of interest reflects poorly upon my own social skills." He gave an offhand shrug.

"I would have to agree with you," she retorted.

"I tell you, my dear Lady Bainbridge, I am seriously considering giving the woman her notice." Letitia's voice rose suddenly above the generalized buzz.

"I most strongly advise you to do so, Lady Graham. Waste not a moment." Lady Bainbridge snapped her fan against her hand. "One cannot entrust one's precious children to such women. They will corrupt those young and unformed minds. I wouldn't permit Martha or Mary to listen to such sacrilege."

"What sacrilege is this, Letitia?" Constance inquired, grateful for the opportunity to withdraw from battle and regroup.

"Oh, my dear, you won't believe it. But I was going through Miss Westcott's bedroom this morning—Miss Westcott is Pammy's governess, you know. One must keep an eye on things. I consider it my maternal duty to inspect her room periodically." Letitia nodded her head virtuously. "But what should I find?" She paused for dramatic effect and now had the attention of all within earshot.

"I can't guess," Prudence said.

"One of those pamphlets from that organization, the Women's Union, or something."

"The Women's Social and Political Union," Constance said without expression.

"Whatever it's called. She'd hidden it away in a drawer. Of course she knows perfectly well that I won't have such scandalous nonsense in my house. I mean, what is the world coming to when you can't trust your own daughter's governess."

"What indeed?" Constance murmured. "Your vigilance does you credit, Letitia. I'm sure that the right to privacy is well sacrificed on its altar." She glanced at Max Ensor, and the light in her eye would have given a sensible man pause. "Are you of your sister's opinion, Mr. Ensor?"

It hadn't taken her long to renew the attack, he thought. But since he was extremely interested in what she might be persuaded or provoked to reveal about her own views of the WSPU he chose to disregard the warning flash in her eyes. "I haven't given it much thought," he said, then added deliberately, "There's some logic, of course, in saying that women who pay taxes should have a vote." He thought he detected a flicker of surprise cross her countenance. Watching her carefully, he continued with a dismissive gesture, "But it's such a small share of the female population that it hardly matters."

He had hoped to provoke a response but he was disappointed. Constance turned aside to pick up the teapot, offering it to Martha.

"Men can vote perfectly well for us," Letitia said. "I'm sure dear Bertie knows exactly the right things to vote for. But I don't know what to do about Miss Westcott . . . Pammy is so fond of her, and we've had so many difficulties with governesses. They so often don't suit Pammy."

"I doubt Miss Westcott's political opinions could mean much to a six-year-old, Letitia," Prudence pointed out.

"Oh, you'd be surprised, Prudence. The tricks these females use to corrupt the young," Lady Bainbridge said with a direful nod.

"No, well, I'm sure I don't know what to do," Letitia said. "I can't talk to her about it because then she'd know I'd searched her room." Letitia pouted in a manner that Constance thought would look more appropriate on her daughter.

"Yes, that is inconvenient," she murmured, catching sight of Chastity's outraged expression. Chastity's views on snooping and prying were akin to her views on theft and murder.

"I would think," Chastity said, "that you might remember the adage: *What the eye don't see the heart don't grieve over*, Letitia. How much more comfortable you would be if you hadn't discovered Miss Westcott's political interests."

"I have my daughter's welfare to consider," Letitia announced a shade stiffly, setting down her teacup. "Well, I must be on my way. I promised to take Pammy to call upon her great-aunt Cecily." She rose from her chair. "There's no need for you to escort me, Max, if you'd prefer to stay. Johnson is in the square with the barouche. He can very well convey me home."

Max gave the matter barely a second's consideration. He had come to see Constance Duncan and test the waters a little. It had been for the most part an amusing and enlightening engagement, once he'd recovered from the initial ambush, but he sensed that nothing further would be gained this afternoon. It was time to retreat and regroup.

"My dear Letitia, I escorted you here, I will escort you home," he said with a smooth smile. "Miss Duncan, ladies . . ." He bowed to the sisters in turn. "Delightful afternoon."

Constance gave him her hand. "I was afraid you were bored, Mr. Ensor. I'm so glad I was wrong."

"I cannot imagine how I gave such an unfortunate impression," he returned. His hand closed over hers, applying a faint but definite pressure. If she noticed it she gave no sign, merely offering him a purely social smile.

"Perhaps I may call upon you again and correct any wrong impressions," he continued, increasing the pressure of his fingers infinitesimally.

Constance, to her chagrin, was disarmed by this sudden change . . . the frank smile, the glow in the blue eyes, and the humorous tilt to his mouth. There was nothing bored, indifferent, or arrogant about Max Ensor at this moment. "If you think it's possible," she found herself saying.

"Oh, I think it is," he responded, his confident smile growing. "I think I deserve the chance at least." He raised her hand to his lips with old-fashioned courtesy, then offered his sister his arm as he escorted her from the drawing room.

Chastity and Prudence exchanged significant glances and Constance felt herself blushing slightly, something she never did. She shot her sisters what she hoped was a dampening look.

"Personable enough gentleman," pronounced Lady Bainbridge, rising to her feet with a creaking of whalebone. "Nothing to cause a stir about, though. Can't think what that dreadful paper could have meant."

"Harmless gossip, Lady Bainbridge," Chastity said with a soothing smile. "It was lovely to see you . . . and, of course, Martha and Mary." She smiled warmly at them as they gathered up gloves and fans. "We must walk in the park one afternoon."

"I trust you'll walk with me one day, Miss Chastity." Lord Lucan, a late arrival, hovered beside her, reluctant to take his leave with everyone else.

"We're going into the country this weekend. We would love it if you would join us. Just a small house party," Chastity said. "We're going to have a tennis tournament and I know how good you are at the game."

Lucan blushed and stammered his thanks, murmuring something about having to ask his mother since she made all such arrangements and he didn't know if she had made other plans for him.

Chastity mercifully interrupted his stumblings. "Well, let us know. We should like to see you if you can make it."

"It's to be a Friday to Monday," Prudence said. "If Lady Lucan would care to accompany you, we should be happy to see her." The invitation was pure form since the Dowager Lady Lucan rarely left her bedchamber, although she kept a fearsome eye on her only son's activities and allowed only those of which she approved.

Lord Lucan made his farewells in some disarray. Finally Jenkins closed the front door and the sisters were alone again.

"That went well," Constance said, piling dirty plates and cups on the tray.

"The ambush of the Right Honorable Member for Southwold or the party in general?" Chastity inquired through a mouthful of sponge cake.

"Both," Constance said, handing the tray to Jenkins. "I would like to think we'd seen the last of the gentleman."

"Oh, that I doubt," Prudence said with a shrewd glance at Constance. "I think he's picked up your glove."

"We *all* ambushed him," Constance said, catching the glance and not liking it.

"Only to get things started. You carried on solo," Prudence pointed out.

"And I can tell you that you definitely piqued his interest. I could feel it from across the room," Chastity said with a chuckle. "I'm very good at sensing such things."

Constance shrugged with apparent carelessness. "If I did, then I shall put it to good use. If he really has the Prime Minister's ear, then who knows what little whispers can be planted."

"You might find it an amusing exercise," Prudence observed with an exaggerated wink.

Constance gave up the battle. She could never fool her sisters. "I might at that." She walked to the open doors to the terrace. "Let's walk outside for a little and read our letters."

"Oh, did you bring them down?" Chastity set down the teapot she had been carrying to the sideboard.

"In my pocket." Constance drew the envelopes from the deep pocket of her skirt and flourished them.

They went outside into the tranquil garden where the early evening air was perfumed with the heavy scent of roses. The clatter of iron wheels and the clop of horses' hooves reached them from over the wall. They sat on the low parapet and Constance slit the first envelope with her fingernail.

Chapter 5

To the Go-Between:
The Mayfair Lady, July 14, 1906

I am interested in using the above named service advertised in the June edition of your newspaper. My situation is both delicate and complicated and I am reluctant to set down the details in writing since I suspect that my employer is in the habit of searching my room and personal papers. If it would be possible to meet with whoever provides the above service I would explain the full nature of my requirements at that time.

I am presently employed as a governess in Mayfair and am able to take time from my duties on Thursday afternoons between the hours of three and six, when my charge pays calls with her mother. If a meeting could be arranged at that time it would be most convenient. I must stress the urgency of my situation and of course I rely upon your utmost discretion. Please send the favor of a reply to Miss Amelia Westcott, care of the Park Lane Post Office. I am able to collect my post most mornings when I walk in the park after breakfast with my pupil. You didn't mention in the advertisement what charge you levy for this service. I should state at this point that that would be a consideration for me, but I am of course prepared to pay an initial consultation fee. I trust this will be satisfactory and I look forward to our meeting.

"Amelia Westcott," Constance murmured, regarding the sloping signature from every angle. "It's too much of a coincidence, surely?"

"Not necessarily," Prudence said. "May I see?" She took the letter from Constance and read it again silently before handing it to Chastity. "It has to be the Grahams' governess. Her employer searches her room; she has these niggardly hours off. It fits to a tee."

"Well, I feel a great need to help that poor put-upon woman," Chastity declared, folding the letter.

"Her situation is hardly unusual," Constance pointed out. "You might even say she's fortunate. Think of the cook-generals, the maids-of-all-work, who rise at six and don't see their beds until midnight. Ill-fed, overworked, underpaid, with two hours off a week . . ."

"Con, get off your hobbyhorse," Prudence protested. "We know the facts as well as you do, and you know we sympathize, so we don't need a lecture."

"Sorry," Constance said with a ready smile. "It's just that after this morning's meeting I'm full of fire and brimstone."

Her sisters laughed tolerantly. "Save it for Max Ensor," Chastity advised.

"I feel a bit guilty actually," Constance said with a frown. "I was rather acerbic about Miss Westcott, before I knew how grim her situation is, of course. And actually Max . . . Mr. Ensor . . . defended her."

"How so?"

"I made a rather hasty judgment when Letitia was saying how her daughter was always bored and her governess was at her wits' end to keep her amused." Constance shrugged. "I commented to Max Ensor that the governess obviously didn't know her job. Either she didn't know how to interest a child in her lessons, or she had no influence over the girl. He said it was Letitia's fault. She wouldn't allow anyone to impose discipline or structure on her dearest Pammy."

"Well, that's a promising piece of insight," Prudence observed. "Perhaps he's not as black as he paints himself."

"Then why would he give that impression?"

"Perhaps he has some ulterior motive," Chastity suggested thoughtfully. "I mean, you have one in cultivating him, so why shouldn't he have?"

Sometimes Chastity's intuitive observations only served to complicate matters, Constance reflected. Although her sister was frequently and uncannily on the ball. "I'll think about that later," she said, and hauled the subject back on course. "Let's see what the other letters are about. You open the next one, Prue."

Prudence took the envelope and slit it, then removed the sheet of paper and unfolded it. "Oh, look at this. Our first finder's fee." She held up a crisp banknote that had been enclosed in the fold of the letter.

"Another Go-Between letter?" Chastity leaned forward to look over her sister's shoulder.

"Yes, from a gentleman who prefers to remain anonymous," Prudence said. "He writes that he's looking for a young lady of good family but not necessarily possessed of an inheritance . . . or even of beauty." She looked up from the letter and raised her eyebrows questioningly.

"Interesting. What does he want her for?" Constance inquired.

"Marriage, of course."

"Then what's wrong with him?"

"You're such a cynic, Con," Chastity declared. "Why shouldn't he simply want to find a soul mate without fussing about money and looks?"

"No reason, really. But he's a very unusual man, in that case."

Prudence impatiently waved her sisters into silence. "He says here that he's a bachelor of reasonable fortune, doesn't like living in Town, so he's looking for a quiet young lady who likes country pursuits."

"But he wants to remain anonymous?" Constance frowned. "I wouldn't like to recommend some unsuspecting young woman to someone we haven't had a chance to vet in person."

"We'll suggest he meet us somewhere. At Jenkins's sister's post office, for instance. It makes sense to meet at the poste restante address. We'll be veiled just in case he might know us," Prudence suggested.

"I think just one of us should go in this instance," Constance said. "Chastity. She has the ability to analyze people. She'll know at once if there's anything suspect about him."

"I think you two should be there, even if you stay out of sight," Chastity said. "I'll be more comfortable."

"Yes, of course," Constance agreed instantly. "We'll make an appointment for . . . oh, it'll have to be after the weekend. Wednesday morning, let's say. We can fit it in easily before the At Home. We need to meet with Amelia Westcott tomorrow since that's her afternoon off and we don't want to wait another week, and Friday we have to go into the country."

Her sisters nodded their agreement and Chastity opened the third envelope. "It's for Aunt Mabel," she said with a chuckle. "Oh, this lady really liked my response to the woman with two lovers. We have to publish this letter. Listen . . ." She adopted a tone of syrupy flattery. " 'Such an intelligent understanding response. Such wisdom and sagacity . . .' " She looked up. "I thought they were the same thing."

"They are," Constance said. "Go on."

"Well, she says she had a similar problem and if only someone had been able to advise her in such fashion she wouldn't be in the situation she's in now."

"Which is?"

"Stuck with the wrong one," Chastity said succinctly. "I'd better write a response and we'll publish it underneath her letter."

"This one's another Aunt Mabel." Constance waved the fourth letter. "A married lady is having terrible problems with her mother-in-law, who dictates her every move, controls her son by keeping a close hand on the purse strings, and is now threatening to move from the dower house back up to London because the daughter-in-law doesn't seem to be managing the household adequately."

"Any signature?"

Constance shook her head. "It just says, 'Desperate in Knightsbridge.' "

"Well, I can think of several women that might apply to," Prudence observed.

Chastity leaned forward and took the letter from Constance. "I'll think of some creative solution, but I think it's probably best if we don't speculate over any of the letters. We'll soon be looking at all our acquaintances suspiciously."

Constance laughed. "You're right, Chas. But it seems that Aunt Mabel is a definite draw." She became serious again. "But how shall we respond to our first client?"

"Oh, yes, first things first. Amelia Westcott is top priority," Prudence stated. "We must write an answer at once. Jenkins will take it to the post when he has his evening constitutional."

"Down the pub," Chastity said in a passable cockney accent. "Very partial to his pint of mild-and-bitter is Mr. Jenkins."

"So we'll say we'll meet her tomorrow afternoon." Prudence was already moving back into the house. "The letter will go by the first post tomorrow morning and be at her post office by breakfast time. Where should we rendezvous?"

"Not Fortnum's. She'd be uncomfortable there," Chastity said swiftly, following her sister.

"Yes, of course she would." Constance nodded. "Oh, I know, what about the Lyons Corner House at Marble Arch? No one we know would be seen dead there. But it's perfectly respectable, very middle-class."

"With the added advantage of being relatively inexpensive," Prudence added. "I don't know what the etiquette is when it comes to having tea with clients, but if she's going to pay her way it's considerate to keep it reasonable, and if we're paying for clients then the same thing applies."

"Don't tell me a cream tea at Fortnum's would break the bank. Don't forget we're getting paid for this service," Constance pointed out.

"Something we haven't discussed at all," Prudence said over her shoulder. "Should it be a sliding scale? The rich pay more to subsidize the less well off?"

"Definitely," Constance said with emphasis, following them up the stairs. "Of course, it's easier when someone sends in his fee with his request, but they're not all going to do that."

"Also," Prudence said, opening the door to their parlor, "the nature of the services themselves could require different payments. Expenses, for instance . . . supposing we have to take trains, or hackney cabs?"

"Since we have no idea exactly what kinds of services are going to be required, I don't see how we can anticipate." Constance went over to the secretaire. "I think we have to charge a sliding scale hourly rate with expenses on top, and have a provision for extra cost if the job needs something extraspecial." She took a sheet of writing paper from a pigeonhole. "This has Father's crest on it. We need plain paper." She rummaged at the back of the secretaire.

Prudence considered. "I think we can all meet with Miss Westcott. We know who she is and she has no idea who we are, and even if she did she has to be as interested in discretion as we are."

"With other clients we're going to have to do this cloak-and-dagger business," Constance said. "Heavy veils and disguised voices." She sat down at the secretaire and dipped her pen in the inkwell. "Stop laughing and concentrate. I'm being very serious. Now, what shall I write?"

They had just tucked the letter into its addressed envelope when a knock brought in Jenkins with a letter of his own. "This was just brought for you, Miss Con. The boy's waiting for an answer."

Constance turned in her chair, hand extended. "Thank you, Jenkins. And we have a letter that needs to go to the post this evening. Would you be able to take it?"

"Of course." They exchanged envelopes.

Constance looked at the handwriting on hers. It was unfamiliar but definitely masculine. Dark ink, strong downward strokes, no curls or flourishes. She knew immediately, instinctively, who it was from. The handwriting proclaimed the man as clearly as did his voice. Out of the blue she felt a jolt in the pit of her belly. She tried to ignore it and with an assumption of calm slit the envelope with the silver paper knife on the desktop and unfolded the single sheet. The bold signature was as she had expected.

"Well?" her sisters demanded.

"It's from Max Ensor. An invitation for dinner tonight." Constance reread the short letter, relieved to find that her voice was as steady as ever and that novel sensation in her belly had disappeared. "If I have no other pressing engagements . . ."

"Which you don't."

"No, I don't." She tapped the sheet against her mouth. "To go or not to go."

"That is indeed the question." Prudence took a fresh sheet of paper, this one engraved with Lord Duncan's crest, and laid it in front of Constance. "The boy's waiting for an answer."

"Why would he want to have dinner with me?" Constance questioned. "An intimate tête-à-tête so soon is rushing things rather, don't you think? Particularly after we did our level best to make him uncomfortable this afternoon."

"If you don't go you won't find out," Prudence pointed out, in her practical fashion.

"I suppose so. And it might be useful to prod him a little about the governess," Constance said with the same considering frown. "He must know something about her."

Prudence regarded her sister with a half smile. "It will be very useful," she agreed. "So write your acceptance and then we'll go upstairs and dress you."

"I wonder if he'll take you to the Savoy Grill or the Café Royal?" mused Chastity.

"Café Royal," Prudence stated, shaking the ink dry on Constance's message as she took it from her before she could change her mind. "I'll lay odds. Although," she added thoughtfully, "he is a Savoy kind of a man. Something about his dress and the way he carries himself just shouts it out. But then, the Café Royal is more suited to a quiet, intimate dinner. The Grill, on the other hand, is best for lunch."

Her sisters allowed her to consider the issue without interruption. Prudence was always right about such things.

Prudence made up her mind. "We'll dress you for the Café." She folded the sheet and handed it to Jenkins, patiently waiting for the second letter. "There, Jenkins. Make sure the right one goes to the messenger."

"Miss Prue!" he protested in dignified indignation.

"I jest, Jenkins." She gave him a quick kiss that produced a dull flush and a hasty exit.

Max Ensor inserted diamond studs into the high wing collar of his evening shirt. They matched his glittering cuff links. His valet hovered near the door with his crimson-lined opera cloak and black silk hat.

"That will do, I believe." Max gave a quick tug to the tails of his coat and held up one black-shod foot to the light. It gleamed with Marcel's champagne polish. "Another triumph, Marcel." Max was willing to admit to himself and his valet that he possessed a streak of vanity but he was also capable of making mock of both himself and Marcel's obsessive regard for the niceties of dress.

"Yes, sir." The man bowed, admiring as only a valet could the set of the coat across his master's broad shoulders. Reverently, he draped the cloak over the shoulders, smoothing the line with a fussy little pat. "Should I summon a hackney cab, sir?"

"No, it's a lovely evening. I'll walk to Manchester Square and hail a cab there." He took up his white gloves. "I doubt I'll be later than one o'clock."

"Very good, sir." The valet bowed his master from the bedchamber.

Max strode down the broad hallway of the Graham mansion towards the main staircase. As he passed the foot of the narrower flight of stairs that led to the nursery floor above, the sound of a large crash followed by a high-pitched wail of fury gave him pause. A tired voice said, "If you don't want it, Pamela, I'll take it away. There's nothing to cry about."

The wailing continued unabated, then ceased abruptly. The silence in its wake had a curious suspended quality. Then again the wearily patient voice. "Please, Pammy, don't do that."

Max had never really noticed Miss Westcott. He supposed he'd passed her several times a day, and certainly run into her when she brought her charge to the drawing room to visit with Lady Graham every afternoon, but he was hard-pressed to picture her features. That weary resignation in her voice, however, caught his attention. After what he'd heard this afternoon about Letitia's treatment of the governess, and from what he knew of his sister's indulgent attitude towards her child, he could guess at the hell that was the life of the governess in this house.

It was no wonder, he thought as he climbed the stairs to the nursery floor, that educated women like Miss Westcott should find appealing the agenda of the Women's Social and Political Union. Downtrodden as they were, powerless to change their lives in any meaningful fashion, the idea of a vote could offer a smidgeon of hope, some possibility of influencing their working conditions. It was a novel thought, and one that until this afternoon in the Duncan sisters' drawing room had never disturbed the peaceful surface of his view of the social structures of his world. A wry little smile touched his mouth as he thought that Constance Duncan was entirely responsible for his present trek up the nursery stairs.

The door to the day nursery stood open, giving him a perfect view of its inhabitants. A small girl, with pigtails sticking out from either side of her head, stood beside an upturned chair in the middle of the brightly painted room, her face purple to the point of apoplexy, her eyes bulging. She was clearly holding her breath. A slightly worn woman in her early thirties stood regarding the child with an air of resigned exasperation. The young nursemaid who assisted the elderly Nanny Baxter, the grande dame of the nursery who had cared for both Max and his sister and was now past the age for the more active aspects of child care, stood wringing her hands, murmuring, "Oh, do breathe, Miss Pammy, do!"

Max lifted the child off the floor and held her high between his hands. In surprise, she took a gasping sob of a breath and her eyes returned to their sockets. He noticed that she didn't seem to have shed a single tear. He held her until her face had taken on a more normal hue and then set her down again.

"It seems something's not right with your world, Pammy," he observed amiably. His niece remained for the moment bereft of speech. She gazed up at him, her thumb finding its way into her mouth.

"I'm so sorry if you were disturbed, Mr. Ensor," the governess apologized. She brushed a limp strand of hair from her forehead where it had escaped the pins. "There was no need for the tantrum. She didn't want her buttered toast so I took it away immediately, but she still . . ." She shrugged, expressing a world of helpless frustration in the gesture.

Max regarded the child. "It must be so unsatisfying when opposition just crumbles at the first objection," he observed. "There's nothing like a well-justified tantrum for testing limits, but in the absence of limits, what's a small person to do?"

A glimmer of appreciation appeared in Amelia Westcott's gray eyes. "Lady Graham, sir, does not encourage limits."

"No," he said. "So I understand. Poor child . . ." He smiled at Miss Westcott. "And poor governess. You have my sympathies, ma'am."

"Thank you, sir." Color touched her rather faded cheek. "I think it's over for this evening. In general, once a night is all she can manage."

He shook his head. "I'll have a word with my brother-in-law."

She took a sudden urgent step towards him. "Oh, no, Mr. Ensor. That's very kind of you, but I wouldn't like Lady Graham to think I'm complaining about Pammy."

He slapped his gloves into the palm of one hand. Letitia might for the sake of convenience and her daughter's good humor put up with a governess with suspect political opinions, but she would never tolerate even the hint of disapproval about the child from anyone, let alone someone in her employ. Besides, privately he didn't think it would do any good to talk to Bertie. Lord Graham hated disharmony and kept his eyes firmly closed to anything that might cause it.

"Very well." He nodded and turned to go.

"Uncle Max." Pamela finally spoke. She tugged at the tail of his coat. "Where are you going? Can I come?"

"I'm going out to dinner," he said. "With another lady. I don't think I should put her off at the last minute, do you? It would be most dreadfully rude."

Pamela considered this. Her one protest of the evening over, she was perfectly prepared to be reasonable. "She might think I was . . . I was a rival for your affections," she declared with a triumphant clap of her still-dimpled hands.

Max stared at the governess over the child's head. "Where on earth . . . ?"

"Nanny Baxter is very fond of romances, Mr. Ensor," she said, her face as straight as a die.

"Oh, I see."

"Lady Graham and Nanny Baxter are in the habit of discussing the love stories when her ladyship visits the nursery."

"Oh," Max said again. "Oh, I see." He gave his niece's pigtails a gentle tug, said, "I bid you good night, Miss Westcott," and left the now peaceful domestic scene with a swift step.

He encountered his brother-in-law in the hall. "Ah, Max, going to the House?" Bertie asked jovially, the words wafting on a whisky breeze. "Just came from the Lords . . . some cursed boring discussion about agriculture. Can't be bothered with it m'self. As long as the tenant farmers pay their tithes, let 'em alone, say I. What?"

"I represent a rather more urban constituency, Bertie," Max said. "As it happens, nothing that affects my constituents is on the agenda this evening. I'm taking Miss Duncan to dinner."

"Oh?" Lord Graham's bleary eyes struggled to focus. "The oldest one. Deuced attractive girl, reminds me of her mother, but she'll soon be on the shelf if she don't take some man . . . plenty after her. Shame about that chappie she was engaged to, can't remember his name now . . . killed in the war. Mafeking . . . or some other godforsaken part of the veldt. In the dragoons, I believe."

"That was what, five or six years ago?" Max mused. Constance Duncan would not have struck him as a tragic figure pining for a lost love.

"Something like that." Bertie waved a dismissive hand. "Caused the devil of an upset in the family. Mother took the girls to Italy for six months, hoping Constance would get over it. Expect she has by now. Girl that age . . . can't weep forever."

Max absorbed this in silence, then headed once more for the door. "Well, have a good evening, Bertie."

"Oh, meant to ask you . . ." Lord Graham laid a hand on his brother-in-law's sleeve. "You think there's a cabinet post for you in the Prime Minister's reshuffle? Heard you were very tight with Campbell-Bannerman."

"No," Max said with a laugh. "I'm too new at the business for such an honor, Bertie."

"Pity." Bertie sighed. "Cabinet Minister in the family could be useful."

Max shook his head and left his brother-in-law to the whisky decanter and his reflections. It was a beautiful evening and he walked briskly through the Mayfair streets towards Manchester Square. His brother-in-law's question had not come totally out of the blue, although he had laughed it off. He was very much in the Prime Minister's confidence, but he was still too new a member of the House of Commons to achieve such a promotion. If he played his cards right it would come at some point sooner rather than later during the Liberal Party's reign. And he had every intention of playing his cards right. He had found the issue that would keep him in the forefront of the Prime Minister's mind. Campbell-Bannerman and his Cabinet were not in favor of women's suffrage but they could not afford to alienate those members of the Liberal Party who were. Finding a suitable compromise was going to be Max Ensor's route to the Cabinet. There were many covert ways to draw the teeth of the Women's Social and Political Union without angering its more influential supporters. And what better way to start than by cultivating the acquaintance of an active and passionate member of the Union.

He didn't know that Constance Duncan was a member, but she made no secret of her strong views on women's equal rights. He didn't *know* that she had something to do with *The Mayfair Lady,* but he suspected it. Either she was actively involved or she knew who was. If that newspaper was going to cause trouble, then it would be very useful to know exactly who was behind it. So he was very happy to combine business with pleasure in the cultivation of Miss Duncan.

He had thought hard about issuing tonight's invitation, wondering if it was too soon to suggest an intimate evening, but he'd decided that a full-frontal attack could well surprise her into an acceptance that a more measured approach might not achieve. He would be charming, a little seductive, disarm her. And then, he thought, he would pull back, leave her alone for a few days, and let her wonder about his intentions. It was a tactic that had worked for him before.

But he had to admit that he wasn't totally confident of success in this instance. Constance puzzled him. She didn't seem to fit into any category of woman known to him. She had all the bristly attributes of the bluestocking, the sharpness of the shrew, the face and form of the beauty, the savoir faire and dress sense of the Society woman. And yet she defied all categorization. She and her sisters. And now there was a dead fiancé to throw into the mix. Some bright and heroic scion of a noble family, killed while fighting for his country. If she still carried a torch for him, a pedestrian politician would find it hard to match up in the hero stakes, he reflected as he mounted the steps to the house.

The door opened at the peal of the bell and the butler he remembered from the afternoon bowed him within. "Will you wait in the drawing room, sir? I'll inform Miss Duncan that you're here."

"Thank you. And would you send someone to summon a hackney, please?" Max followed Jenkins into the drawing room and was taken aback when the butler announced him. "Mr. Ensor, my lord. He's waiting for Miss Con."

Lord Duncan turned from the open doors to the terrace. "Ah, I didn't know my daughter was going out this evening." He came towards his visitor, hand outstretched in greeting. "No one tells me anything in this house," he said. "Sherry . . . or would you prefer whisky?"

"Sherry, thank you."

"Daughters never tell you anything," Lord Duncan reiterated. "Rather like wives." He laughed and handed Max a glass. "So, where are you taking her? Don't mean to pry, nothing too paternal about the question . . . Con's more than capable of taking care of herself." He sipped his sherry.

"The Café Royal, I thought," Max replied.

"Oh, splendid choice. I took her mother there the night after our wedding . . . must be thirty years ago now." A shadow passed across Lord Duncan's countenance and vanished as swiftly. "You're the political chappie, aren't you? One of Campbell-Bannerman's protégés?"

"Hardly a protégé, sir."

"Up-and-coming . . . up-and-coming," declared his lordship with a conspiratorial wink. "Cigarette?" He flipped the lid on an engraved silver box.

"Thank you, no."

Lord Duncan lit his own and inhaled deeply. "So where did you meet my daughters? I assume that if you met one you met 'em all."

"Yes, indeed, Lord Duncan." Max looked restlessly towards the door. "I met them at Fortnum's, when I was having tea with Lady Armitage. She's a friend of my sister's, Lady Graham," he added in case his host needed further enlightenment.

"Oh, yes, I know that, dear boy. Well, you must come down to the country this weekend. We're having a small house party. The girls want to play tennis . . . not a game I care for. Give me croquet any day, much more vicious . . . just when you think you've—"

"Oh, Father, you'll bore Mr. Ensor to death with your croquet obsession." Constance made her entrance with a carefully executed swish of her black taffeta skirt. "Mr. Ensor, I hope I didn't keep you waiting long."

"Not at all, ma'am." He couldn't take his eyes off her. The black taffeta skirt had a bodice of a deep red that almost exactly matched the color of her hair. The neckline curved low to reveal just a hint of creamy breast, accentuated by the stunning jet collar that circled her neck. Her collarbone stood out in a way that lured his mouth and his tongue, so that he found himself curling his toes in his shoes. She was wearing heels that added at least an inch to her already noticeably tall and willowy frame. Her hair was piled high, dressed over pads, adorned with tiny jet black butterflies, and it begged to be loosened, each pin withdrawn, each lock and strand gently teased from restraint to fall to those perfect sloping shoulders.

He could not take his eyes off her.

"Con does look particularly beautiful tonight, Mr. Ensor." Prudence spoke from behind her sister and Max mentally shook himself free of enchantment. He saw that both of Miss Duncan's sisters were regarding him over her shoulder with knowing smiles. They had read his reactions to their sister as if he'd shouted them aloud.

"Miss Duncan is lovely as always," he said with a slight bow. "As, indeed, are her sisters."

"Oh, prettily spoken, Mr. Ensor." Chastity smiled and although he looked sharply he could detect no hint of mockery. "So, where are you taking Con?"

Max thought that of the three of them, Chastity was probably the most benevolent. A man needed to be a little wary of the other two, they both had a wicked edge. As it happened, he found that edge, particularly in Constance, both challenging and perversely compelling. "The Café Royal, I thought. If that pleases you, Miss Duncan?"

"Greatly," she said. "Did I hear Father invite you to Romsey Manor for the weekend?"

Max bowed his acknowledgment and demurred, "But I'm not sure that I . . ." He let the sentence fade, watching her carefully for a flicker of hesitation. She would be duty bound to second her father's invitation, but he'd made one bold move and had not intended making another one. He was not prepared to risk his mission by accepting an invitation to which she showed the slightest hint of aversion. Better to go slow now and get there in the end than rush matters and scare her off.

Constance considered for only an instant. She could handle Max Ensor and he wouldn't even know he was being handled. A three-day country weekend would give her plenty of time to work upon him. By Monday she'd have him wearing the colors of the WSPU.

She bit back the chuckle that bubbled in her throat and said warmly, "Oh, I do so hope you can join us. I know it's short notice but we would all enjoy your company." She turned to her sisters for confirmation and they both acquiesced with the same enthusiasm.

They sounded convincing, but Max nevertheless felt a certain wariness. He could not, however, identify its cause, so he said simply, "Thank you. I should love to."

"Good, then we'll talk about it over dinner. You do play tennis?"

"Indifferently."

Constance regarded him through narrowed eyes. "False modesty, Mr. Ensor," she accused.

He laughed. "I'm not coxcomb enough to praise my game when I don't know the standard of the competition." He turned as Jenkins announced the arrival of the hackney. "Shall we go, Miss Duncan?" He offered her his arm.

"Enjoy yourselves," Chastity said.

"We'll see you in the country at the weekend, Mr. Ensor," Prudence called after them.

"You don't keep a carriage in town?" Constance inquired as he handed her into the cab.

"I have a motor," he said. "But I don't drive it in town."

"A motor, how dashing." Constance was genuinely impressed. "I've never ridden in one."

"Perhaps you'd allow me to drive you down to the country at the weekend."

Constance made no immediate response and he looked at her expectantly. "Did I say something wrong?"

"No, not at all." She sighed. "It's a little awkward."

He waited for her to explain and when she didn't, he let the subject drop.

Chapter 6

The hackney drew up outside the restaurant and Max escorted her inside, handing their cloaks to an attendant. They followed the maître d'hôtel up the wide flight of gilded stairs and were seated in a quiet alcove, from where Constance had an excellent view of the dining room and its occupants.

Max ordered champagne and opened his menu. He regarded his companion quizzically. "Do you like oysters, Miss Duncan? I see they have Breton oysters tonight."

"I do," Constance said. "But I'm not sure I feel like them this evening."

"Ah, then perhaps the quail eggs in aspic," he murmured, almost to himself. "And then the turbot in hollandaise, followed by the pigeon breast aux truffes." He looked up with an air of decision.

Constance laced her fingers. If there was one thing she detested it was a man presuming to order for her. And this man barely knew her. She opened her own menu, glancing up with a smile as the waiter poured champagne into her glass. "You make up your mind quickly, Mr. Ensor," she said. "I for one like to linger over the menu. It always takes me at least fifteen minutes to decide what I want to eat."

Max heard the tincture of acid in her voice and hid his chagrin. He was accustomed to women allowing him to make choices for them; indeed, it had always been an infallible arrow in his seduction armory. Now it seemed if he was to preserve his dignity he had to pretend it was his own selection. He particularly detested turbot, was not overly fond of pigeon, and had been looking forward to the saddle of lamb, for which the Café Royal was justly famed.

He turned his attention to the wine list, determined that there she should have no input.

Constance sipped her champagne and watched him. "I always think a

Sancerre goes well with turbot," she suggested. "And then a good burgundy with the pigeon, to bring out the truffles."

Max closed the leather-bound volume. He took up his champagne glass. "Perhaps, Miss Duncan, when you can tell me what you intend to eat, I can make some more informed choices."

"Oh, yes," she said, turning her attention back to the menu. There was an undeniable sparkle in her eyes, a distinct rosy tinge to her cheeks.

Max turned his champagne glass around between his long fingers. She was radiating smug satisfaction at having bested him. Should he yield the point? Disarm her with a frank apology for being overbearing? Or simply ignore her complacency and eat his turbot and pigeon even if they stuck in his craw?

The former, he decided. It would catch her off guard and he had the feeling that if he was going to get anywhere with Constance Duncan he needed to keep the advantage of the unexpected. He laughed ruefully. "I hate turbot," he said. "And I'm going to have the saddle of lamb."

She looked up, surprise clear in her eyes, and then she laughed with him. A warm, open chuckle that for once seemed to carry no underlying mockery. "I didn't mean to snub you."

"Yes, you did."

"Well, forgive me. It was very rude when I'm sure you were only being kind."

"*Kind,*" he exclaimed in disgust. "I was not. I was being charming."

"Oh," she said. "Was that what it was? It always surprises me that men seem to think women find it appealing to have their decisions made for them."

"You are an unusual member of your sex," he said dryly.

"Perhaps not as unusual as you think," she responded. "I think there are probably quite a few of us around."

"Let us call a truce, Miss Duncan." He stretched a hand across the table.

Constance could see no reason to refuse the offer. At least for the duration of the evening. She shook his hand in a businesslike fashion. "Let us also dispense with formalities, Max. My name is Constance."

"Constance," he said, holding her hand for a moment longer than a simple handshake warranted.

She became aware of a sensation in her fingertips akin to pins and needles and caught herself contemplating his hands, thinking that she liked them, had liked them from the first moment of their acquaintance. Firmly she took back her own hand, dismissing the irrelevant and distracting reflection.

"What are you going to eat?" he asked into the moment of silence that threatened to become awkward.

"The lamb," she said. "Smoked salmon, lobster soufflé, and the lamb."

He nodded gravely and returned to the wine list. "Sancerre, you think?"

She raised her hands, palms towards him. "Please, I would not presume to guide my host."

"Oh, wouldn't you just?" He grinned and his vivid blue eyes crinkled at the corners. It gave him an almost boyish air and Constance was once more surprised. She was willing to acknowledge that he was an attractive man, but until now she had not found his appearance particularly appealing. Perhaps she hadn't given it a chance.

Another distracting thought. She sat back and allowed her gaze to roam around the dining room while he talked with the sommelier.

Constance was aware that they were drawing some interested glances. A new tidbit for the gossipmongers. It occurred to her that she could write a little squib for the next edition describing the dinner enjoyed by Max Ensor and Miss Duncan. An involuntary choke of laughter escaped her and Max turned back from the sommelier.

"Something amusing?"

"Oh, just a stray thought," she said carelessly, waving her fingertips at an acquaintance across the room.

Max proved a deft conversationalist and Constance was content to follow his lead as he discussed Bernard Shaw's latest play, *Man and Superman,* the recent death of the artist Camille Pissarro, and the design for the new Liverpool Cathedral. The range of subjects that seemed to interest him struck her as unusual. The depths of his interests went way beyond the ordinary social demands of skillful small talk.

"Let me guess," he said, as the waiter removed their plates with the remnants of saddle of lamb. "You're a cheese-before-dessert person."

"You're close but not quite close enough," she said, regarding him over the rim of her wineglass.

"Ah." He nodded his comprehension. "Cheese, no dessert."

"On the nose."

"Well, I can see the virtue, but I can't resist the crème brûlée here."

"My sister Chastity would tell you that the napoleon is the best in town. She is something of an expert."

"It's unusual to find a woman who has no sweet tooth," he observed.

Constance raised an eyebrow. "Another stereotype, Max?"

"An observation from experience," he retorted.

Constance turned in her chair towards the cheese trolley. It was her turn to be placatory, she decided. "As it happens, I think it *is* unusual. I inherit the lack from my mother . . . Some of the Epoisses, please." She pointed to a round cheese that was in the process of fleeing its board. "And a little of the Bleu d'Auvergne."

"A glass of port?" suggested Max, as he pointed to the wheel of Stilton. "In lieu of dessert."

"Lovely." An involuntary little sigh of pleasure escaped her as the waiter snipped off a bunch of green grapes and laid them on the plate beside her cheese. "Port, cheese, and grapes . . . a ménage à trois made in heaven. Who could possibly want cake when one can have that?"

Max consulted once more with the sommelier and then leaned his elbows on the table, his hands loosely clasped. "So, will you permit me to drive you to the country on Friday?"

Constance shook her head. "No, I'm afraid I can't."

He looked disconcerted. "I'm a very safe driver, I assure you."

"I don't doubt it." She considered for a minute, then said in the low tone of one sharing a confidence, "My father, however, is not. His eyesight is not what it was but he's dead set on getting a motorcar. We're doing everything in our power to dissuade him, and if he sees me merrily aboard one our arguments are going to look somewhat hypocritical."

"Oh, I see." He nodded. "He could have a chauffeur."

"Yes, but he'd say that would be pointless—a case of keeping a dog and barking oneself. Besides, Cobham, our coachman, has already said he couldn't get used to these newfangled machines and he's been with us far too long to be put out to grass . . . to use his own expression." She shrugged and gave him a what-can-one-do? smile.

"Awkward," Max agreed. "Perhaps I should take the train myself."

"I hardly think such a sacrifice is necessary."

"Perhaps I'd choose to make it," he said, taking the scent of his port. He nodded at her glass. "Tell me if you approve."

Constance did so. "Why would you choose to forgo your drive? I hear it's very exhilarating," she added, unable to hide a wistful note.

"It is. But I would readily exchange it for your company on the train."

Did he really think she was so naïve as to be disarmed by such a piece of naked flattery? "You are a very smooth talker, Mr. Ensor," she observed, disappointed by such an unsubtle approach, although she supposed that a man who saw women in terms of generalizations would probably see nothing wrong with tried-and-true seduction maneuvers, however hackneyed.

"That implies insincerity, Miss Duncan," he said as he cut into his Stilton.

"If the shoe fits," she responded, then changed the subject before the exchange could become any sharper. "We usually take the noon train from Waterloo. It gets to Southampton at three, and connects with the branch line to Romsey, arriving at half-past. Someone will meet us with the trap."

"May I take that as an invitation to meet you at Waterloo?" He sipped his port, determined to persevere even though Miss Constance Duncan was the most prickly dinner companion he'd ever encountered.

"Please do." She raised her own glass and smiled at him across the ruby contents. Antagonism wasn't going to advance her cause at all and she could see how put out he was. She needed to blunt her tongue a little.

"I felt guilty this afternoon about what I'd said about your niece's governess," she said, peeling a grape with her knife.

"Oh?" He was instantly alert. "Why so? What has Miss Westcott to do with you?"

Constance began to peel another grape. It gave her an excuse for not meeting his eye. "Nothing, of course. And that's why I feel bad about what I said at the Beekmans' soirée. I had no idea of the woman's situation when I presumed to pass judgment on her skills."

"Since she's unaware of your lapse in judgment I think you can safely lay your guilt to rest," he said aridly, still as sharply watchful as before. It seemed wise to assume that she had just delivered an opening salvo designed to distract him before the main attack.

Constance raised her eyes and gave him a disarming smile. "It's a little awkward. By apologizing for casting aspersions on the governess I am indirectly criticizing your sister."

"Yes," he agreed. "I confess myself fascinated to know why you're digging yourself into this particular hole." He had no faith in that disarming smile at all.

Constance met his steady gaze and dropped the pretence. "You were the one who defended the governess. I'm merely saying that after your sister's comments this afternoon I take your point."

He pursed his lips slightly but asked only, "Coffee?"

"When you've had your crème brûlée."

"I think the port has spoiled me for pudding." He nodded to the ever-hovering waiter. "So you feel a mother should not concern herself with the political and social opinions of those in charge of her children?"

"I think she has no right to invade her employees' privacy," Constance retorted. "If they keep their opinions private, then surely they are no one's business but their own. Is Miss Westcott able to stand up for herself?"

"Probably not," Max said, his expression carefully neutral.

"How long has she been with your sister?"

"Oh, I believe she's lasted almost ten months," he said. "At least six months longer than any of the others."

Constance suspected that he was trying to provoke her with his light insouciance. She refused to be provoked. "Is she very young?" She poured coffee into two cups from the delicate china pot set reverently at her elbow. The waiter took one cup and placed it in front of Max.

"Well above the age of discretion," Max said, taking a sugar lump from the bowl with silver tongs. "Why does she interest you so much?" He dropped the lump into his cup.

"She doesn't really," Constance said.

He looked at her askance. "Oh? I was assuming that as a downtrodden member of the exploited female classes Miss Westcott held a most particular interest for you."

Constance drank her coffee. "I won't deny that. My sisters and I were educated by a woman who felt very strongly about such issues."

He leaned across the table, his gaze intent. "And you would deny that children are influenced by the views of those who are responsible for forming their minds?"

"No, of course I wouldn't. I never said any such thing. I simply said that a woman is entitled to keep her opinions private if she's made it clear she wishes to do so. Is there any evidence that this Miss Westcott has attempted to press her own political views on the six-year-old?"

"I doubt Pammy has the concentration span to take in anything so complex," Max said. "Like most—" He broke off.

"Like most women," she finished for him. "Was that what you were about to say?"

He sighed. "Must you put words into my mouth?"

"You've made your views quite clear."

He leaned forward, resting his forearms on the table. "I do not understand why women should need the vote. They wield a powerful influence on their menfolk at home. Why, I know more powerful women than men, I can tell you. Their husbands and brothers do exactly what they're told."

Constance stared at him. "I can't believe you'd trot out that old saw," she said in disgust. "*Women are the power behind the throne.* And even if I concede that some lucky women do have influence over the men who make decisions for them, what about all the women who have no such power? Who's going to make decisions that would improve their lives? Who's even interested in them?" She shook her head, her eyes glittering with angry conviction, her cheeks flushed.

Max toyed with the idea of commenting that she looked beautiful when she was angry but decided that he'd provoked her enough for one evening. He was fairly certain now that she was a card-carrying member of the WSPU and would serve his purposes very well. It was time to retreat, offer a sop, and plan the next step. If he played his cards right she would spill all the information he needed.

"Maybe the WSPU has some merit," he said calmly. "But these women need to consider the far-reaching effects of such a social change. It must be considered from every angle."

Constance's angry flush died down. She couldn't argue that point. When she spoke, it was as calmly as he. "But we need some assurances from the government that they would consider the issue." The candle on the table flared in the breeze created by a waiter's coattails as he hurried past and Max saw golden light flash against the intent dark green of her eyes. He also heard the inadvertent *we*. She was showing her true colors.

"As I understand it, the issue is on the table in Cabinet," he replied.

Constance examined his countenance and could read no dissembling there. Presumably he would know if he lunched regularly with the Prime Minister and the Cabinet. "That's something," she said neutrally.

He inclined his head in acknowledgment and firmly closed the subject. "Would you like a cognac?"

"No, thank you. I need a clear head for tomorrow. But don't let me stop you."

"I too need a clear head." He caught the hovering waiter's eye and when he brought the bill asked him to summon a hackney. "Perhaps next time, if you'll do me the honor of dining with me again, we can take a drive in the motor. I could pick you up out of sight of Manchester Square and we could drive out along the river. There's a very pleasant spot near Windsor, good food, pretty view . . . ?"

"It sounds delightful," Constance said in the same neutral tone. She gathered up her evening bag. "If you'll excuse me . . ."

Max rose to his feet as the waiter pulled back her chair and she extricated herself with a graceful twitch of her skirts. Max watched her as she moved through the dining room towards the ladies' retiring room, pausing at a number of tables en route. He couldn't decide whether the evening had been a success or not. He'd discovered what he wanted to know, but he didn't think he'd succeeded too well in disarming the lady. She showed no inclination to respond to either flattery or overt seduction. And for his part, while she was a lovely woman and a stimulating companion, he found her passionate wrongheadedness and her constant sparring utterly exasperating. But perhaps it was a way to hold him at bay. If it was, it succeeded all too well.

And now his interest was truly piqued. He would topple the castle one way or another. There had to be a woman beneath the intellectual shell. It was all very well to be possessed by the passions of the mind, and he was more than happy to pay all due respect to her mental prowess, but there were other passions that even such a single-minded woman could learn to respect and enjoy.

Constance emerged from the retiring room, having discreetly left a copy of *The Mayfair Lady* in the basket of linen towels, out of sight of the attendant. She wasn't sure what she'd accomplished this evening. A few details about Miss Westcott, but nothing significant, and the possibility that the government was at least examining the women's suffrage issue. It wasn't much to take away. And she didn't think she'd made a dent in Max Ensor's Neanderthal views on a woman's place. *Power behind the throne, indeed.* But she had an entire weekend ahead of her. A weekend under her own roof. If she couldn't make some headway with the man, she wasn't the woman she believed herself to be.

Max was on his feet as she approached the table. She wore a little half smile, a secretive and rather complacent Mona Lisa smile, and a certain gleam in her eye that fascinated him even as it put him on his guard. *What had she been up to in the ordinarily innocuous confines of the ladies' retiring room?* He said only, "The cab's waiting."

Constance became aware of her smile as she caught his slightly speculative look. She realized that she had been smiling for the entire walk across the dining room and now hastily composed her features and murmured the correct pleasantries.

They sat in silence in the darkened interior of the hackney, but it was a suspenseful silence. Constance wondered if he would make a move, and wondered how, if he did, she should respond. It wouldn't be unusual at the end of such an evening for her escort to offer a discreet if not hesitant kiss. She waited, but not for long. Max laid a hand gently on her knee. She did not react. She let the warm pressure soak through the thin silk. He turned on the leather bench and with his other hand cupped her chin, turning her face towards his. She could see his eyes in the gloom, glowing and yet dark, the shape of his nose, the full sensual curve of his mouth. She remained still and silent, still unsure as to how she wanted to react.

Max ran a finger over her lips, wondering how to interpret her silence, her immobility that was neither rejection nor resistance. Then she parted her lips and lightly touched his finger with the tip of her tongue. The bold assurance of her gesture surprised him even as he realized that it was time he ceased to be surprised by Constance Duncan. He bent his head and kissed her. Her response told him clearly that she was no tyro in these matters. So much the better, he thought. Her mouth opened beneath his, her hands moved to encircle his neck, and as his tongue moved deep within her mouth she met him thrust for thrust. He had thought to offer nothing more than a chaste peck, but she had taken matters into her own hands. Perversely, he wasn't entirely sure that it pleased him.

The coach drew to a halt. "Manchester Square, guv." The cabby's lilting call broke the silence and they drew apart. Constance brushed her lips with her fingertips, smoothed her hair. "Thank you for a lovely evening, Max."

"The pleasure was all mine, Constance." His teeth gleamed white as he returned her formal farewell and the very polite smile. He stepped out to the pavement and gave her his hand to help her alight. He walked her to the top of the steps, pulled the bell rope, and raised her hand to his lips. "À bientôt."

"Friday, Waterloo, at noon," Constance responded.

"I look forward to it."

Constance raised a hand in a gesture of farewell and turned away as Jenkins opened the door for her. "You had a pleasant dinner, miss?" he inquired.

"I'm not entirely sure," she responded. "Are my sisters in bed?"

"I hardly think so, Miss Con," Jenkins said with a knowing smile. "I believe you'll find them in the parlor upstairs."

"Then I'll bid you good night." Constance gave him a wave and hurried up the stairs, holding her skirts clear of her feet. She couldn't avoid this tête-à-tête with her sisters, who would be eagerly awaiting her return, and she wouldn't want to anyway, but she wasn't sure how much she was prepared to reveal about the carriage ride home. She had intended to offer a light and playful good night kiss that would merely tease him. Somehow that was not what had happened. Not at all what had happened. She opened the parlor door.

Prue and Chastity were playing backgammon but they jumped up as she came in. "So, tell us all," Chastity demanded. "Did you squabble all evening, or did it become wonderfully romantic?"

"Oh, you are impossible, Chas." Constance drew off her gloves. "As it happens we squabbled almost nonstop and the only romantic moment was when he kissed me good night in the cab."

"A good kiss?" Prudence asked with raised eyebrows.

"I'm still trying to decide." She flung herself inelegantly into the depths of the chesterfield and kicked off her shoes. Her sisters were gazing at her with all the fixed attention of lions waiting to be thrown their food.

"On a scale of one to ten," Prudence demanded.

Constance pretended to consider the matter. She stretched out her hands and examined her nails. "Bold," she said thoughtfully. "Strong . . . warm . . . lips and tongue well plied . . . Since I don't think it's possible to give a ten because you never know what else you might experience, I'll say an eight."

"Pretty high praise," Prudence judged.

"Sounds a little forward for a first kiss," Chastity observed, beginning to gather up the backgammon pieces.

"I suppose it was," Constance agreed. "But it wasn't entirely his fault."

"Oh, really?" Her sisters regarded her intently. Then Chastity asked simply, "Was it at all like with Douglas?"

Constance didn't immediately reply. "I don't know," she said after a minute. "It's awful, but I can't really remember anymore what it was like with Douglas. It's hard enough to see his features clearly in my mind. But when I think of him buried under some South African kopje I want to tear my hair out, scream and hiss and spit at the whole damned injustice of it all." She stared down at the carpet, but her eyes were unfocused. "I'm over it, of course I am, but I'm in no hurry to bury his memory in some new passion."

"So Max Ensor isn't getting under your skin," Prudence stated.

"No," Constance said definitely. "His opinions are. He's positively Neanderthal. But I very much like the idea of working on him." She looked up, her expression once more relaxed, the shadows gone from her eyes. "I intend to give Max Ensor a radical education, and before I'm done with him he'll be wearing the colors of the WSPU."

"And he's definitely coming to Romsey for the weekend?"

Constance nodded. "Yes. He'll meet us at Waterloo."

"And you've already made some plans for him?"

"They're in embryo at present but they're coming together." A grin flashed across her countenance. "I'll tell you when I've sorted them out properly. Oh, by the way, he wanted us to drive down but I managed to dissuade him. I told him father's eyesight was bad but he still wanted to get a motor and we didn't want to encourage him."

"Nicely saved." Prudence yawned involuntarily. "Anything useful about Miss Westcott?"

"Not really. She's not some ingenue, that much I did discover. Past the age of discretion is how Max put it. She's managed to stick it out at the Grahams for longer than any other governess, so the child likes her. That's about it."

"Oh, well, it's something. I wonder what it is that's so delicate about her situation." Chastity went to the door.

"No doubt we shall find out." Constance extinguished the lights and followed her sisters up to bed.

Amelia Westcott hurried across Park Lane from Hyde Park, clutching the hand of her protesting charge, and entered the Park Lane Post Office just as a shower of rain gusted across the street.

"My hat is wet," Pammy complained. "It's my new straw hat. Mama just bought it, and now it's wet and spoiled."

"It will dry, Pammy," Amelia said. "See, we're out of the rain now." She let the door bang behind her. "Let's have a race with the raindrops on the window." She encouraged the girl over to the glass and pointed out two drops trickling slowly from the top. "The one on the left is mine." She indicated with her finger.

"I want that one."

"Very well. Then I'll have the one on the right." Suppressing a sigh, Amelia went to the counter, where the clerk gave her a sympathetic smile.

"Mornin', Miss Westcott. Got a letter for you . . . arrived in the morning post." He turned to the wall of pigeonholes behind him and took out a long envelope.

"Mine won! Mine won!" Pamela danced over to the counter. "See, Miss Westcott. Mine won!" She grabbed her governess's hand, tugging her back to the window. Amelia pocketed her letter, smiled her thanks to the clerk, and allowed herself to be dragged to view the triumph of the anonymous raindrop.

"See!" Pamela jabbed at the bottom of the window. "That was mine. Let's do it again. I want to do it again." Her voice rose slightly as if she was anticipating argument.

"Which one is yours?" Amelia said quickly.

"That one!" The child pointed. "And that one's yours."

Amelia reconciled herself to a tedious quarter hour playing this game. The letter itched in her pocket but nothing would be gained by rousing the devil in Pamela. She thought wearily that she had always liked children. She had told herself that becoming a governess wasn't the worst fate to befall an educated woman without means. Now, regarding this spoiled and rather sad child, she thought that a life on the streets might be considerably more congenial.

Finally, however, Pamela tired of the game and the rain stopped. They walked back to Albermarle Street, the child in great good humor, having secured herself a win in every raindrop contest. She prattled nonstop, skipping through puddles, heedless of the splashes to her smocked pinafore and white stockings. Nanny Baxter would grumble from the comfort of her armchair all afternoon, Amelia reflected. But this afternoon it wouldn't trouble her. She had a few short hours of liberty and a letter in her pocket.

In the day nursery she installed her charge at the lunch table under the supervision of the nursery maid, and went to her own bedroom conveniently situated next to the night nursery, in case Miss Pammy awoke with a nightmare. She withdrew the envelope from her coat pocket and slit it with a fingernail. She took out the single sheet and sat slowly on the narrow bed. The handwriting was feminine and the core of the message made her heart leap. *Lyons Corner House. Marble Arch, at four o'clock this afternoon.* Whoever or whatever constituted the Go-Between, she or they were prepared to help if they could.

Amelia lay back on her bed, still in her damp coat and hat. When she'd seen the advertisement in *The Mayfair Lady* it had seemed like the answer to a prayer. Her situation was impossible; it had no feasible solution; and yet it would inevitably be resolved one way or the other. She had no one to turn to. And then the advertisement. The service had to be offered by women; no man would advertise in *The Mayfair Lady*. For the first time she saw a smidgeon of hope on the bleak horizon. And now, as she read the response a second time and her eyes dwelled on each feminine stroke of the pen, she felt a strange but sure comfort. The only women friends she had known had been in her school in Bath. When she left there, sufficiently educated for a life as a governess, she had known only her employers, and there were no cozy female relationships to be developed there. Letitia Graham was about the worst Amelia had encountered.

"Miss Westcott? Your lunch is getting cold."

"I'm coming right away," she called back to the nursemaid, who'd accompanied her call with an imperative rap at the door. She discarded coat and hat, combed her hair, and returned to the day nursery to eat macaroni pudding with her charge.

Three o'clock came at last. Pamela went off with her mother and Amelia left the house. She walked quickly to Marble Arch. Gusty showers swept leaves from the trees and dampened the pavements and pedestrians scurried under umbrellas, sheltering in doorways or under awnings whenever they became particularly threatening. Amelia was unperturbed.

The Lyons Corner House was on the corner of Marble Arch, its glass windows steamed up with the rain outside and the warmth within. She went in, glancing at her watch. She was half an hour early. She selected a table in the window and took a seat facing the door so that she would have a clear view. She set her copy of *The Mayfair Lady* on the table in plain view and ordered tea. The letter had said that the Go-Between would be carrying a copy of the newspaper; it made sense to Amelia that she should do the same.

Her tea arrived, with a hot buttered crumpet. She took her time, enjoying every bite. Apart from her late-night supper, which was always cold meat of some description and sliced tomato or beetroot, she ate every meal with her charge, and Pamela's tastes were monotonous. She kept her eye on the door and precisely at four o'clock, three women walked in. They wore hats with delicate little veils that covered only their eyes—neat hats—and subdued clothes that nevertheless shouted both money and elegance. Amelia felt her optimism fade. Then she saw the distinctive badge—purple, white, and green—that the tallest of the women wore; and she saw the copy of *The Mayfair Lady* that she carried. Her spirits lifted. This woman was a member of the WSPU.

The three women paused, looked around the restaurant, and Amelia hesitantly lifted her copy of the newspaper. They came towards her, putting back their veils as they did so.

"Miss Westcott." The woman wearing the WSPU badge held out her hand. "I'm Constance. Let me introduce my sisters. This is Prudence . . . and Chastity." She indicated her companions, who shook Amelia's hand and sat down.

"So how can we help you, Miss Westcott?"

Chapter 7

"I need to find a husband," Amelia Westcott stated.

"Well, that's to the point," Constance observed, taking off her gloves and putting them in her handbag.

"It is what your service offers?" Amelia said, her heart fluttering, her gray eyes expressing uncertainty and anxiety.

"Certainly it is," Prudence said. "Let us order tea."

"Those crumpets look delicious," Chastity declared. "We shall have a plate of those and four cream slices." She smiled at the elderly waitress in her starched cap and apron.

The waitress made a note on her pad and went away with the weary flat-footed tread of one who spent far too many hours on her feet.

"So what kind of husband did you have in mind?" Constance asked.

"Well, I don't know exactly. I assumed you'd have a list . . . a register or something . . . of men looking for wives."

The sisters glanced at one another and Amelia's anxiety increased. The return of the waitress with tea prevented further discussion but once she had gone and the thick china cups were filled, crumpets passed, Prudence took off her glasses, rubbed them with her handkerchief, and carefully replaced them on her nose.

"That is what we hope to achieve, Miss Westcott," she said. "But as of this moment we don't exactly have a register." She blinked once behind her glasses. "You see, you happen to be our first client."

"Oh." Amelia looked as confused as she felt. "How . . . how could that be?"

"Well, there has to be a first," Chastity pointed out, spooning sugar into her tea.

"Yes, we've . . . or rather, *The Mayfair Lady* has just started offering the Go-Between service," Constance explained, cutting a crumpet into neat quarters. "But I'm certain we can help you. You said something about a delicate situation. If you could tell us something about yourself and your position, we could make a start."

Amelia regarded the three sisters doubtfully. She had nerved herself to confide her wretched situation with a businesslike and efficient agency. She had not expected to take tea with three society ladies and discuss the matter as if it were mere social chitchat.

Constance saw her hesitation and said, "Miss Westcott, we understand something of your situation. It can't be pleasant to be subject to Lady Graham."

Amelia flushed. "How could you possibly know . . . ?"

"This is awkward," Prudence said. "We know Letitia. And we happened to discover that her daughter's governess was a Miss Westcott." She shrugged a little defensively. "It's inevitable in our position." She shrugged again.

Amelia reached for her gloves on the table beside her. "I cannot see how you could help me. I had assumed this would be a businesslike arrangement; I could not possibly confide my situation to people who would be in a position to betray my trust." Her hands shook as she struggled with her buttoned gloves.

There was a moment of silence, then Chastity leaned forward and laid a hand over Amelia's quivering fingers. "Listen for a minute, Amelia. We would not under any circumstances betray your confidence to *anyone*. We have a pledge of utter discretion. What we know of Letitia simply makes us all the more anxious to help you. You need a husband to escape her service. Is that the situation?"

There was such sincerity and sympathy in her voice that Amelia felt some of her earlier hope trickle back. She looked at the three women and read the compassion in their eyes. There was compassion but there was also strength and determination in all three faces that somehow imparted confidence.

Amelia made up her mind. *What did she have to lose, after all?*

"It's not as simple as that," she said, a dull flush creeping over her cheeks. "If it were, I would simply find another situation."

She had their complete attention. Tea cooled in cups, butter pooled beneath crumpets. "Two months ago I was in the country with Pamela. Lord and Lady Graham wanted her to spend the summer out of London in their country house in Kent."

The three sisters nodded. Amelia toyed with the spoon in her saucer, her eyes on the white linen tablecloth. "There were to be no formal lessons since it was a holiday, but I was to take her for instructional walks, supervise her riding lessons . . ." She paused and the flush on her cheeks deepened. "And supervise her music lessons. Pamela is always very reluctant to practice on the pianoforte. She is, I'm afraid, an impatient pupil in most areas."

"Her mother is not an advocate of education for women," Constance said.

Amelia gave a short laugh. "Indeed not. But it's hard to blame Lady Graham since her own education was so sadly lacking. Indeed, I believe she considers it to be a disadvantage in a woman."

"I'm sure she does," Prudence said, pushing her glasses up the bridge of her nose with a forefinger. Her eyes were shrewd as they rested upon Amelia Westcott. "The music teacher . . ." she prompted.

Amelia took a deep breath. "Henry Franklin," she stated on a swift exhalation. "The youngest son of Justice Franklin, the local magistrate and owner of the local brickworks. Henry's a musician; his father does not approve. He wants him to do the accounting at the brickworks. His two brothers work there and Mr. Franklin expects Henry to join them."

"And Henry refuses." Chastity took a cream slice from the plate and thoughtfully licked a dab of raspberry jam from her finger.

"Not exactly . . . he . . ." Amelia shrugged helplessly. "He goes into the office and tries to do what his father wants but it's killing his soul. His father said that if he could make a living at teaching music then he would cease his objections, but Mr. Franklin knows perfectly well that Henry couldn't survive as a musician without his support, and in exchange for that support he must do as his father says."

Constance thought that this Henry Franklin lacked strength of character if not conviction but she kept her mouth shut. She had the sense that this was only the beginning of Amelia Westcott's problem.

"I'm getting the impression that you and Henry Franklin developed an understanding while you were in Kent," Chastity said delicately, breaking off a piece of flaky pastry from her cake.

Amelia finally raised her eyes from the tablecloth. "Yes," she said bluntly. "Rather more than an understanding." She met their gaze without flinching. "As a result I now find myself in a delicate situation."

"Oh," Prudence said. "That's very awkward."

"A husband is the only solution," Amelia said. "Once my condition is known to Lady Graham she'll cast me out without a reference, and I'll never be able to find another situation. No self-respecting house would employ a fallen woman." She met their eyes again. "Would they?"

"No," Constance agreed. "You'd be blackballed."

"And besides, you'll have a baby to care for," Chastity said, frowning. "Even if you boarded the baby—"

"Which I would never do!"

"No, of course not," Chastity said quickly. "I wasn't really suggesting it as a possibility."

"So I need a compliant husband," Amelia stated. "I was hoping you might have one on your books. A widower, perhaps . . . someone who'd be willing to give me the protection of his name in exchange for everything else. Child care, housekeeping . . . whatever was necessary."

"That seems like exchanging one form of servitude for another," Constance said.

"What choice do I have?" Amelia laid her hands palms open on the tablecloth. "I am not a woman of independent means." There was a bitter note in her voice that drew the comparison between an impoverished governess and her present companions.

"Oddly, neither are we," Prudence said. "We're trying to keep our father out of debtors' prison and ourselves off the streets."

"Hence our venture with *The Mayfair Lady* and the Go-Between," Chastity said.

Amelia was silent for a minute. Then she said in a flat voice, "But none of you is pregnant."

"That is certainly true," Constance agreed. "So let's look at your options here. Have one of these before Chas eats them all." She offered the plate of cakes to Amelia.

"I've developed the most dreadful passion for sugary food," Amelia confided, taking one of the creamy confections. "Fortunately Pammy is kept well supplied with such things." She took a healthy bite, aware that she was feeling stronger, almost lighthearted. These three women had somehow managed to take the desperation out of her situation. She had no idea how, since they didn't appear to offer the salvation she had hoped for.

"It seems to me that Henry would be the best candidate," Chastity suggested somewhat tentatively. It was such an obvious solution she assumed there was a problem that Amelia had not divulged.

"Unless he's already married?" Prudence ventured.

Amelia shook her head and dabbed pastry crumbs from the corner of her mouth. "No, he's not. He can't afford to marry without his father's consent, and Justice Franklin would not consent to his marrying an impoverished governess. Even though my family is every bit as good as the Franklins," she added with a flash of fire.

"But what if Henry earned his living independently of his father," Constance mused. "Could he get a job in a school as a music teacher? I believe some of the better prep schools even provide housing for their teaching staff."

"I could suggest it if I could get in touch with him," Amelia said, and now her voice lost its vibrancy. "I've written to him several times, although I couldn't tell him the situation. I couldn't risk writing something like that. Lady Graham probably reads my blotter in a mirror."

"I doubt she's clever enough," Constance said acidly.

A wryly appreciative smile touched Amelia's lips but her expression instantly returned to gloom. "I haven't heard a word from Henry. He's not answered a single one of my letters. He must have received them; the post is perfectly reliable. I can only assume he doesn't want to hear from me."

"There could be other explanations," Chastity said. "Perhaps he's not at the address anymore."

"In that case why wouldn't he write and give me his new address?"

"There you have me." Constance drummed her fingers on the table. "I suggest we find out."

"How?"

"Pay him a visit."

"But I could never get even a day's free time."

"Not you, Amelia, us."

"Yes, we'll go and make a reconnaissance," Prudence said. "We won't necessarily tell him anything specific; we'll just see what the situation is."

"It's a start, at any rate." Chastity touched Amelia's hand again. "Don't worry. We have plenty of time to sort this out. When do you think the baby's due?"

"Oh, not for another seven months." Amelia smiled, clearly making an effort to respond to Chastity's optimism.

"Then you won't start to show for another two or three months," Prudence stated. "And you can always loosen your gowns. You'll be able to cover it for quite a while."

Amelia nodded. "But I must make provision. I can't wait until the last minute."

"No, and we won't," Constance said firmly. "We'll start with Henry, and if that proves a dead end, then we'll find another solution."

Amelia glanced at the clock on the wall and gave a little cry of alarm. "I must get back, it's almost five-thirty. I must be back by six when Pammy gets back with her mother." She began to fumble in her handbag. "What do I owe you for the consultation?"

"Nothing," the sisters said in unison.

"And you won't owe us anything ever," Chastity declared, ignoring a slight twitch from Prudence.

"Oh, but I must pay you. You're providing a service for hire. It says so." Amelia tapped the copy of the newspaper on the table.

"It's all right," Constance said with blithe exaggeration. "We have the possibility of paying clients already. They can afford to pay a little extra."

Amelia couldn't help a wan smile. She laid a shilling on the table. "At least let me pay for my tea."

"If you insist." Prudence laid their own share on the table beside Amelia's. Her sisters' reckless generosity was all very well, but a shilling was a shilling.

"I see you're a member of the WSPU." Amelia gestured to the badge Constance wore on her lapel.

"Yes, but I don't make it public." Constance unpinned the badge. "Because of *The Mayfair Lady*. I write a lot of political articles and we're lobbying for women's suffrage. I don't want people to guess that I might have anything to do with the newspaper. I wore the badge this afternoon to reassure you, since I'm guessing you sympathize with the Union."

"It did reassure me," Amelia declared, getting to her feet. "I have to keep my affiliation a secret too. I can rarely get to meetings."

"That will change," Constance stated. "One of these days that will change."

"Yes, Con's working on a Member of Parliament," Chastity said mischievously. "We have high hopes that the Right Honorable—" She broke off in confusion as Prudence trod hard on her foot and she realized what she had been about to reveal.

Fortunately, Amelia was too anxious to be on her way to pay much attention. She scribbled the address she had for Henry Franklin in the margin of *The Mayfair Lady* and Constance promised that they would pay their visit to Kent at the beginning of the following week.

"Meet us here next Thursday afternoon at the same time," Prudence said, giving Amelia her hand. "We'll have some news for you then."

Amelia nodded, seemed about to say something, then shook her head in a brief hurried gesture and left the Corner House.

"I'm sorry." Chastity said as soon as the door had shut with a definitive ring of its bell on the departing client. "I can't think what made me forget she would know Max Ensor. She lives under the same roof as the man, for heaven's sake." She shook her head in self-disgust.

"Have another cake," Prudence said. "There was no harm done."

Chastity gave Constance a contrite smile. "Forgive me?"

"Sweetheart, there's nothing to forgive." Constance returned the smile. "Besides, it's true. You know I intend to work on him."

"I shouldn't have gabbed about your personal life," Chastity said.

"Forget it, Chas. My personal life in this instance is entirely bound up with my political life, and as such is hardly personal at all."

Prudence gathered up her belongings. "Either way, it should enliven the weekend somewhat. More than tennis anyway."

Constance was more than happy to take her sister's cue and let the subject drop. "I'm not sure I'm going to approve of this Henry Franklin," she said as they went out. She clapped her hand to her hat as a particularly energetic gust of wind whistled around the corner of Marylebone Street.

"We don't have to approve of him," Prudence pointed out. "Just bring him up to the mark. Shall we take a cab?"

"Only if we can afford it, Prue dear," Constance teased.

"Well, I'm not sure that we can," Prudence retorted. "With you and Chas insisting on forgoing our fees. How are we to make ends meet when we don't charge the clients?"

"We have to haul in the rich ones," Constance said. "I couldn't bring myself to take that poor woman's money, and neither could you."

"No," Prudence agreed. "We'll call the experience payment enough."

"A happy solution." Constance hailed a hackney. "I have a feeling we're going to need all the experience we can get to make Go-Between a success. How on earth are we to compile a list of eligible bachelors? And we have to find a suitable country mouse for Anonymous. At least he's prepared to pay."

"Oh, that's simple." Chas climbed into the hackney. "Just take a look around at our next At Home. We'll find eligible bachelors and eligible maidens aplenty."

"And we compile our own registry," Constance said. "So simple, and yet so brilliant." She applauded her sister.

"I can think of a country mouse or two already. How about Millicent Hardcastle? I know she's no spring chicken but she's definitely on the market and she hates London, she always says so." Prudence leaned out of the window. "Ten Manchester Square, cabby."

Max Ensor stood beneath the clock in the center of Waterloo Station, a calm of presence amid the chattering, rushing throng beneath the cavernous vaulted roof of the concourse. On the platforms behind him trains puffed and blew shrill steam. Max stepped aside as a sweating porter raced past him pushing a trolley laden with baggage. A woman on very high heels that threatened to trip her at any moment clung to the arm of a red-faced man as they half ran behind the porter.

It was eleven-thirty on Friday morning and Max assumed the Duncan party would arrive with time to spare. He couldn't imagine any of the sisters in panicked haste. His valet had taken his valise and tennis rackets to the platform and was already stationed at the point where the first-class compartments would stop when the train came in.

He saw the sisters arriving through the central doors—as he expected, strolling in leisurely fashion, two porters carrying their bags. Lord Duncan was not with them, which surprised Max. It had seemed clear that the sisters were expecting their father to join them for the house party.

Constance greeted him with a wave and extended her hand as she came up with him. "Ah, Max, you're here nice and early."

He took the hand and lightly kissed her cheek as if they were old friends, before turning to shake hands with Chastity and Prudence.

"Where's your bag, Mr. Ensor . . . oh, no, that's ridiculous. If Con calls you Max, we can hardly persist in this formality. Max it shall be. Where's your bag, Max?" Chastity asked from beneath the floppy brim of a most fetching bonnet with tulle ribbons. Little did Max suspect that the bonnet was in its fourth reincarnation.

"Marcel has it on the platform. I hope it's all right if my manservant accompanies me. I can perfectly well do without him, if space is a problem."

"Oh, no, it's perfectly all right. David Lucan never goes anywhere without his valet. He's his mother's spy, you see. Poor David can't take a step without him," Chastity told him with her sweet smile.

"Platform Twelve, madam," one of the porters stated pointedly, shifting the weight of the bags from one hand to another. "Train'll be in by now."

"Oh, yes, of course. Let's go." Constance followed the porters across the concourse, her stride long and easy. Max kept pace beside her.

"Your father's not accompanying you?"

"Oh, yes . . . no . . . it's so vexing," she said. "I'll tell you when we're installed. And you have every right to be annoyed."

He looked askance but said nothing until the four of them were ensconced in a first-class carriage, their luggage safely stowed, the porters tipped, and Marcel sent off to his seat in third class.

"It's all the earl of Barclay's fault," Chastity said, unpinning her bonnet. She stood up to set it on the luggage rack. "He's an old friend of Father's and he's just acquired a motor. And, of course, he had to offer to drive Father down to Romsey in it."

"And, of course, Father had to accept," Constance said. "It puts me in such an awkward position, Max. You were so understanding about our little problem and it was all for naught."

"Oh, quite the opposite," he said with a gallant bow. "Now I have the company of all three Duncan sisters."

"Instead of just me," Constance said with a mock sigh. "I'm sure I would have been sad company."

She was poking fun at him, at the suave and automatic little compliment he'd paid them, just as she had accused him of being insincere during their dinner the previous evening. It exasperated him that she would object to a formal courtesy, even if it was an empty compliment.

"Yes," he agreed. "People who don't know how to accept a compliment with grace do tend to be poor company."

Constance's eyes widened. She had not expected a comeback and she had never been accused of gracelessness before. For the moment she was silenced.

She inclined her head in acknowledgment and offered a half smile that held a hint of rueful apology. Her mother had often warned her about the dangers of her too-smart tongue, of how it could come back to bite her. And she remembered how Douglas too in his quiet way would offer a smiling reproach when she hadn't been able to resist the pointed witticism that had a sting in its tail. He had told her that she shouldn't make a habit of employing her wit to put others at a disadvantage. Not a very attractive quality, he had said once. She could hear his voice now, so gently and earnestly reproachful, and suddenly bit her lip, turning to gaze out of the window at the passing countryside until the lump in her throat had dissolved. Maybe she would have been a much nicer person if Douglas had lived. But he hadn't. So she would just have to watch herself and her tongue a little more carefully. And certainly with Max Ensor. She was developing a healthy respect for him as an opponent.

Max rose to pull down the window. He looked along the platform. "Are you expecting any of your other guests on this train?"

It was Prudence who responded. "I hope not. We usually take the early one so that we're there ahead of people. Most people take the two o'clock and arrive in time for tea."

The compartment door opened and a gentleman in the frock-coated uniform of a headwaiter bowed to them. "Will you be taking luncheon with us today, ladies . . . sir?"

"Oh, yes," Constance said, recovering her poise.

"The dining car will open at twelve-thirty. Will it be a table for four?"

"Certainly," Max said.

The dining-car attendant bowed and withdrew, drawing the compartment door closed behind him, and Constance turned back to the carriage.

"A train journey wouldn't be the same without brown Windsor soup in one's lap," Prudence observed, unfolding a copy of the *Times* and adjusting her spectacles.

"Oh, I love eating on the train," Chastity declared. "Particularly tea. Those delicious scones and clotted cream, and those lovely little chocolate sponge cakes. Although," she added, "breakfast runs it a close second. Kippers and brown bread and butter."

"Pork sausages," Constance said. "Sausages and tomatoes."

"I get the impression you ladies are hungry," Max observed with amusement.

"Well, we were up very early and it's been a long time since breakfast," Prudence said. None of them mentioned that since Lord Duncan had not graced the breakfast table the usual delicacies had not appeared. The sisters made do with toast and marmalade.

"Do you do crosswords, Mr. . . . uh . . . Max?" Prudence took a sharpened pencil from her handbag.

"Not habitually, but I'm willing to help." He rested his head against the starched white antimacassar and prepared to relax.

Constance was sitting opposite him and he was enjoying the view. She had unfastened the top buttons of her blue linen jacket, which nipped her waist in the most satisfactory fashion. He could see the pulse at the base of her throat, the slender rise of her neck, the slight glisten of moisture on her skin in the stuffy warmth of the compartment. Her legs were crossed at the ankles, very slender ankles, he noticed, and very long and slender feet encased in navy blue kid shoes. He wondered lazily about the rest of her leg, the calves and knees and thighs running up beneath the thin material of her skirt. Her legs were long, that fact required little detective work. And they would be as slender as the rest of her. Her wrists were slim, her fingers long, but her hands nevertheless had a strength to them. They were competent hands. Miss Duncan was a competent woman. Combative, however. But he'd always liked a challenge and this one promised to be more than ordinarily enticing.

She was leaning now to look at the newspaper her sister held, a frown on her brow as she puzzled over a clue. He could see the faint blue veins in her temple. Suddenly she raised her eyes and looked at him. Her eyes were dark green, the green of moss beneath the trunk of an ancient oak. They held a question, a hint of speculation, and he knew she had been aware of his observation. He had a feeling she was sizing him up in her turn.

Max smiled and she dropped her eyes to the crossword again, but not before he'd seen the tiny twitch of her mouth. The weekend, he reflected, could take some interesting turns.

Chapter 8

W here are you going to put him?" Prudence asked in a low voice as they stood on the platform of Romsey station. Max was out of earshot, supervising the unloading of their bags.

"The South Turret," Constance replied in the same conspiratorial undertone.

Chastity chuckled, adjusting the wide brim on her beribboned straw boater. The South Turret had one rather special attribute. "Just what do you have in mind, Con?"

A speculative glint sparked in her sister's eyes. "I'm thinking I'd like to show Mr. Ensor what can happen when a woman takes the initiative. I don't actually think he believes that women *can* take the initiative. I'm certain he believes they *shouldn't*," she added. "It might open his eyes a little to the idea of women playing on an even field. What do you think?"

"Not to pour cold water or anything, Con, but you might be a little overconfident," Prudence observed with a frown. "I don't think the Right Honorable Gentleman is that easy a target. He certainly gave you your own on the train." She took off her glasses and blinked myopically at her sister in the bright sunshine.

Constance grimaced. Practical Prudence, as usual, had put her finger on the flaw in her plan. "I hate to admit it but he had a point," she said ruefully. "But that just makes it more of a challenge." She thought about Max's speculative and almost hungry scrutiny in the railway carriage. If she could exploit that, it would be a weapon in her arsenal more than powerful enough to meet the challenge.

"So you're going to try to seduce him?" Chastity asked, with a hint of alarm. Her hazel eyes beneath the brim of her hat were filled with doubt.

"Not entirely," Constance denied. "Just play with him a little, make him feel a little less sure of himself. He'll be more fertile soil for planting if he loses some of that utterly masculine conviction of superiority."

"I hope you know what you're doing," Chastity said.

"I'm not sure that I do," her sister confessed. "But the idea's appealing. I'll just see where it leads."

A man in the leather waistcoat, apron, and britches of a groom emerged from the tiny station house. "Bags are all loaded, Miss Con. The gentleman's waiting with the trap."

"Thank you, George." The sisters followed him through the station, calling a greeting to the stationmaster, who touched his forelock in salute. The Duncan family had owned Romsey village and most of the outlying countryside since feudal times. In these more enlightened days the tenant farmers and villagers worked independently of the Manor House, but social tradition died hard.

Outside, on a sunny square of daisy-studded grass, a dun-colored pony in the harness of a trap nibbled the grass. Max stood at its head, idly scratching between the animal's pointed ears. Marcel was adjusting the straps that held the bags securely on a shelf at the rear of the trap.

"Is it far to walk to the house?" Max asked as the sisters came over.

"About a mile. Why? Who wants to walk?" Prudence asked.

Max gestured to the trap. "I doubt there's room for us all in the trap. I'm happy to walk; I could do with stretching my legs after the train."

"Oh, two of us can stay here and George will come back," Chastity said. "It'll only take half an hour."

"Actually, I wouldn't mind the walk myself," Constance said casually.

"Then that's settled." Max waved a hand towards the lane in invitation. " 'Lead on, Macduff.' "

"It's actually 'Lay on, Macduff,' " Constance corrected him. "People always get it wrong." She declaimed with a theatrical air, " 'Lay on, Macduff; and damned be him that first cries.' " She paused and her sisters joined in with a rousing chorus, " 'Hold, enough!' "

"I can see I'll have to be a little more careful with my quotations," Max observed wryly.

"Oh, yes, around us you will," Prudence agreed, climbing into the trap. "We are the daughters of Emily Duncan, whose knowledge of Shakespeare was quite awe-inspiring. She could pluck a quote out of midair to suit any occasion."

"How intimidating," Max murmured.

"It was, rather," Chastity agreed, settling on the bench beside her sister. "And it wasn't only Shakespeare Mother had at her fingertips. She could quote freely from all of the major poets and most of the minor. We'll see you back at the house." She waved gaily as George cracked his whip in a halfhearted fashion and the pony with an equal lack of enthusiasm raised its head from the grass and sauntered off down the lane.

"Your mother was a scholar, it seems," Max observed as he and Constance followed the trap.

"She was very erudite," Constance agreed. "Let's go over the stile; we don't want to swallow their dust, and anyway, it's prettier across the fields." She gathered up her skirt and waded through knee-high yarrow and ragged robin to a crooked and very rickety stile half buried in the overgrown hedge.

Max surveyed the stile doubtfully. "That doesn't look very safe."

"Oh, it's perfectly safe. I just have to be careful not to tear my skirt on a loose nail." She examined the obstacle in her turn. "Actually, I'll have to hitch my skirt up fairly high."

"I'll close my eyes," he offered.

"That's very gallant but quite unnecessary," she said. "I won't show you my knickers." With which she raised her skirts above her knees and hopped with agility if without elegance over the stile, giving Max all the empirical evidence he needed to confirm his guess about the length and shapeliness of her legs.

"There." She shook down her skirt and gave him a grin that was pure seductive mischief and completely took his breath away. "Now you. Watch out for the nail on the top bar. It's right where you have to swing your leg over." She pointed helpfully to the sharp piece of rusty nail. "It could catch you in the most awkward spot."

Max pulled on his right earlobe. It was an automatic gesture going back to his childhood whenever he was at a loss for words or confused by a situation. At present he was suffering from both conditions. Either this woman was teasing him shamelessly or she was issuing an equally shameless invitation. There were two questions: Which was it? And what in either case should he do about it?

Constance stood with her head to one side, watching him. "If you're afraid you'll tear your clothes I'll come back over and we'll go on the lane."

He made no answer, merely stepped onto the crosspiece, swung his leg over the top bar, and jumped down into the clover-strewn field beside her. She nodded her approval and turned to head across the field.

Max decided that whatever the answer to the first question, he knew what he was going to do about it. "Just a minute," he said. He caught her arm and swung her back towards him, turning her into his body. Her look of surprise was very gratifying. "I think I can take a hint," he said, clasping her face between both hands.

It was a hard kiss, nothing exploratory about it, and Constance, after a startled instant, let it happen. Her head fell back and she opened her mouth beneath the insistent pressure of his lips and tongue. He moved a hand behind her head and held her firmly for the utter possession of his mouth and tongue. He drove deep within the moist softness of her mouth, his tongue probing every corner of her cheeks, the roof of her mouth, the even lines of her teeth; their tongues joined in a dancing duel until Constance was breathless, her head held so firmly she couldn't move it aside if she wanted to.

She could feel his body hardening against her, the insistent nudge of his penis into her lower belly, and her loins tightened, then seemed to swell and open in response. She caught herself thinking that this was not the way she had intended to play this, but nevertheless she was clasping his buttocks, pressing her fingers deeply into the rock-hard muscles, squeezing and kneading, holding him tightly against her so that he could feel the knobbly bones of her hips beneath the fine linen of her skirt.

And then he let his hand fall from her head and lifted his mouth from hers. He stepped back from her, drawing a ragged breath. She saw the rigid bulge in his trousers and could guess at his discomfort. Her own disjointed sense of interruption, of abrupt deprivation, so disoriented her for a moment that she could only stand there, taking quick shallow breaths through her mouth.

Finally she closed her mouth, put her hands to her face, feeling its heat. She touched her lips; they felt twice their normal size. "Yes," she said. "You could say that."

"Say what?"

"That you can take a hint." Her eyes involuntarily darted down his body again. He was still hard.

He followed her eyes and gave a rueful sigh. "An inevitable consequence."

"Yes, I realize. If it's any consolation, I'm not exactly comfortable myself."

"One should not begin something one's not prepared to finish," Max said dryly. "But you were extremely provoking."

And she had been right that he needed to have the upper hand, Constance reflected. It was a pity she'd been so sure of herself she hadn't anticipated such a response to provocation. She began to wonder if Prue was right and perhaps she had bitten off more than she could chew. Seduction was a dangerous game if it got out of hand, and she'd certainly lost the initiative in this round.

Max seemed unaware of her cogitation. He was much more interested in the field around them. "We appear to have entertained the cows at least."

Constance saw that they were surrounded by a circle of interested bovines, placidly chewing the cud and gazing at them with soulful brown eyes. She advanced a few steps, stamped her foot, and clapped her hands. They ignored her.

"I actually don't like cows," Max confided, regarding their audience dubiously. "I'm not a country boy, I'm afraid."

"They won't hurt us. We'll just walk through them." Constance stepped forward with a purposeful air, still clapping her hands. To Max's relief the cows turned aside as if the curtain had come down on a theatrical performance.

They continued their walk in a reflective silence. Uneasily, Constance tried to sort out what had just happened. It was clearly the opening volley in a game, one she had started, but now she wasn't so sure that she wanted to continue it. It was one thing to control the moves, quite another to have them controlled. Maybe seduction was not the way to go about converting Max to her cause. He had proved himself a dominating man—not domineering necessarily, but definitely dominating. She had thought she could handle him, manipulate him to her own ends, but she had not reckoned with her own responses. That kiss had shaken her out of her complacency. It had happened so quickly, taken her off guard, but whatever excuses she made she could not deny that it had rocked her to her core. She had kissed many men with varying degrees of enthusiasm. Only Douglas had aroused her deepest responses. The last few minutes had opened something inside she had almost forgotten. A very dangerous hunger. But was it a danger to be avoided or to be embraced?

Max walked just ahead of her, swishing at the overgrown hedgerows with a stick he'd snapped from the hedge. The repetitive motion quietened the turmoil in his head. He was startled at the ease with which Constance had returned his kiss. Did she habitually yield to casual sexual encounters? In general he avoided them himself but he was deeply disconcerted by the power of his own suddenly revealed lust for the woman walking nonchalantly behind him across the field. He hadn't expected it at all. He had known, or thought he had, exactly where he was going with this lightly flirtatious pursuit. He merely wanted to get some insight from this exasperating woman into the workings of the WSPU.

And then she'd provoked a response and he'd intended to teach her a little lesson by giving her more than she'd bargained for. Instead of which, the shoe had been on the other foot. So much for the best-laid plans of mice and men.

Romsey Manor was at its core a lime-washed, half-timbered Tudor house that had been added to by successive generations of Duncans, so that it now had a mix-and-match style of architecture that gave it a charmingly untidy and informal air. They walked up from the river that ran at the bottom of a sweep of lawn leading to a long terrace at the side of the house.

Prudence and Chastity were standing on the terrace, leaning over the low parapet as Max and Constance came up. "We guessed you'd come across the fields," Chastity said.

"It's quicker," Constance responded, hoping that all signs of that lust-filled embrace had diminished. "I'll show Max to his room."

"Jenkins is organizing tea, and George has gone back to the station to meet the next train. William's gone with him in the gig, so they should be able to bring most people back in one trip."

"Is Father here yet?"

"Not yet."

"Let's hope they haven't overturned in a ditch," Prudence said. "I don't trust Lord Barclay any farther than I can throw him. He's probably pickled in brandy by this time in the afternoon and won't be able to see straight."

Constance grimaced. "In that case Father will be driving, and that's not going to advance our cause. You know what he's like once he gets the bit between his teeth." She shrugged. "Come, Max, I'll show you upstairs. I expect your valet will be waiting for you."

Max had the sense that the Duncan sisters found their father, as affable as he seemed to be, something of a trial. He followed Constance into the cool house. The smell of last winter's wood smoke from the fireplace, potpourri, and beeswax mingled pleasantly in the air. A bevy of young girls, brought in from the village to help for the weekend, he guessed, were setting out tea in the long, beamed-ceiling drawing room under the watchful eye of Jenkins, who had presumably come down from London on an earlier train.

"Is Mr. Ensor's valet in his room, Jenkins?"

"Yes, Miss Con. Miss Prue said the South Turret, so I sent him there with the bags."

Constance nodded and led Max across a dark hall, with the same Tudor beams and a massive fireplace and inglenook at one end, and up a curved Elizabethan staircase. "The South Turret is in the Queen Anne part of the house," she said, turning aside down a long corridor. At the end there was a narrow flight of stairs spiraling upwards and around a corner.

He followed her up. At the very top was a thick oak door. Constance opened it and entered the round chamber lit by four round mullioned windows. Marcel was hanging evening clothes in a Jacobean armoire.

"It has its own bathroom." Constance gestured to a door in the far wall. "Small but adequate. The water's heated with a gas geyser and it takes ages to run a bath."

"I'm duly warned." He looked around the room. It was immediately obvious that it was totally private. Anything could go on up here and no one in the rest of the house would be any the wiser. He glanced speculatively at Constance. She smiled blandly.

What was she up to now? Before the encounter in the field among the cows he would have assumed it meant nothing. Someone had to have this bedroom. And it was a very pleasant room. But now he wasn't so sure. He returned the bland smile without comment.

"It's one of my favorite rooms in the house," Constance said. "I usually give it to first-time guests." She turned back to the door. "Well, I'll leave you to refresh yourself and see you downstairs for tea."

The door closed behind her. Max, whistling softly to himself, went to one of the open windows and looked out over the surrounding Hampshire countryside. From his aerie the gorse and bracken-covered heaths and hillocks of the New Forest stretched in a golden sea to a line of wind-battered pine trees on the horizon. Beyond them would lie the sea itself. He could smell the salt in the air. It was as powerful as the rich scents of lust.

He wondered what the next steps in this dance would be, as he turned back to the bedroom, to what could so easily become a cozy little love nest, to respond to Marcel's inquiry about his dress for the evening.

"I've had an idea," Constance said, swinging her croquet mallet as she watched the play on the green. It was early evening and the sinking sun slanted through the summer dry leaves of the copper beech tree that shaded the croquet lawn. Max was in the process of knocking Lord Duncan's ball out of play.

"You're full of them," Prudence said. "Oh, well played." She applauded as Max's ball cracked neatly against his opponent's, sending it shooting to the far side of the lawn. "That's going to give Father a challenge."

"He'll enjoy it," Constance said. "Anyway, I think we have to find David Lucan a wife."

"That won't be easy. He only wants Chas," Prudence pointed out.

"Well, he can't have me," Chastity stated. "And I have to admit, I'm beginning to get just a little fed up with the doe eyes that follow me everywhere. I might even have to be rude."

"All the more reason for us to find him another goddess." Constance shielded her eyes against the sun and looked across to where Lord Lucan stood with a group of nonplayers holding cocktail glasses as they watched the game.

"But what about Mama-darling?" Prudence asked. "I don't think she wants him to be independent."

"True enough. We have to find a wife for him who will be the perfectly submissive daughter-in-law so that she can bully both of them in her benevolent fashion and cluck over their children and tell them exactly how to bring them up. And," Constance added on a note of triumph, "I have just the lady in mind."

"Sounds like a pretty grim fate," Prudence pointed out. "Are you sure you want to condemn some poor innocent maiden to such a life?"

"It won't be so bad if the poor innocent maiden is unenlightened," Constance said. "We can't expect to liberate the entire female sex from ordinary domestic oppression in one fell swoop. We have to recognize that there are some who genuinely don't want freedom. Even Mother said that."

"So which innocent maiden did you have in mind?" Chastity inquired, leaning her mallet against a wrought-iron bench.

"Hester Winthrop."

"Hester?" Both sisters stared at her, then looked across the croquet lawn to the very young lady, dressed in a modestly styled evening dress of a pastel pink and standing demurely beside her mother.

"She's very pretty. She's very docile. She comes from an excellent family and there's no shortage of money there. How could the dowager Lady Lucan object to such a match?"

"But she's so shy. She'd never put herself forward to attract his attention," Prudence objected.

"Isn't that a task for the Go-Between?"

"Girls . . . girls . . . surely you should be mingling with our guests."

The sisters sighed in unison and turned with almost identical polite smiles to greet their aunt, Lord Duncan's sister, who assumed the role of official hostess at her brother's social events since it was considered an unsuitable function for a young unmarried daughter. And the Duncan sisters had not yet reached the age where the sobriquet of spinster would be automatically attached to them. The boring organizational details of social events their aunt cheerfully ceded to her nieces, but the social obligations she performed with the utmost aplomb.

"I didn't know you'd arrived, Aunt Edith." Constance bent to kiss her. "We were just waiting our turn."

"Well, mingle with the guests." Edith shooed at them even as she accepted dutiful kisses from Prudence and Chastity. "What will people think to see you standing like wallflowers talking among yourselves?"

"We *are* playing croquet, Aunt," Constance pointed out. "We're just waiting our turn."

"Go and talk to that nice Lord Lucan, Chastity. And Prudence, Lady Anne needs someone to talk to."

Rescue came as Lord Duncan, finally in possession of the ball, missed his next shot and it was Constance's turn to play for the Duncans against the so far invincible team headed by Max Ensor.

"You'll have to excuse us, Aunt," she said with a smile. "It's time for us to play. Chas, I'm going to take your ball right the way round." She pointed to the hoops. "You'll come in for the final shot against the marker."

"You think you can?"

"What do you think?"

"Go to it." Chastity waved her on. She was a fairly weak player and Constance was as competitive a player as her father, and now had the edge that age had taken from him.

Lord Duncan came forward as his oldest daughter stepped onto the immaculate lawn. "Now, Constance, you have to get my ball back in play."

"Yes, Father," she said. "But I have something else to do first." She gave Max a sweet smile as he stood to one side with his mallet resting lightly on the grass. "A little revenge."

"Don't waste your shots," Lord Duncan boomed irritably. "Just keep your ball in play and get mine close to the sixth hoop."

"Good advice," Max said as she took up her position, legs apart, mallet held with both hands between her feet, ready for her swing. "Why go after me? I'm not presenting any threat to you lying over there."

"Oh, yes, you are," she said, clipping her bottom lip between her teeth. "Believe it or not, Mr. Ensor, I can play this game rather well. And I have my own strategy."

"I'm certain you do," he murmured. "I've noticed how skillfully you play your games, Miss Duncan."

She paused, her mallet halfway in position for the swing. It was pure gamesmanship, of course, but it seemed a trifle underhanded to confuse croquet with the other game they were playing. But then, in croquet all was fair. It was a no-holds-barred competition and she was as cunning and ruthless as anyone when it came to trickery. She swung the mallet back between her feet and tapped the ball through the first hoop.

She walked to her ball, took up her position, and once again tapped it with just sufficient force to touch Chastity's ball, which lay in a direct line with the second hoop. She lined them up and this time hit hers smartly so that it pushed Chastity's ball through the hoop and rolled merrily after it.

Max leaned against the beech tree and watched with both amusement and admiration as Constance took her own and her sister's ball through every hoop, tapped the finish post with her own ball, and handed the mallet to her sister so she could perform the final service with her own ball.

"Oh, well played, Chastity. Well played." David Lucan applauded loudly.

"David, I didn't do anything, except for the last shot," Chastity protested, setting aside her mallet. "Constance played my ball as well as her own. Didn't you see?"

The young man looked discomfited, and Chastity immediately smiled and went over to him. "Doesn't she play well?"

"Oh, yes," he said, "but not as well as you."

Chastity decided that it was time Hester Winthrop entered the scene.

"Now, do you have the seating plan, Prudence?" Edith asked, fussing with her fan. "Where have you put Mr. Ensor? He should be at your father's end of the table, I believe. He and Lord Barclay. They can talk politics."

"It's possible they don't want to, Aunt," Prudence said. "They have enough of politics in London. We put him between Constance and Lady Winthrop." She understood now why Constance had put Hester and Lord Lucan together, as far from Lady Winthrop as it was possible to get.

"Oh, well, if you think that will please everyone, dear, I'll leave it to you." Edith smiled vaguely and went off to chat with her own cronies.

Prudence, waiting for her turn, thought about Hester Winthrop and David Lucan. It was an inspired match. But how on earth were they to levy some kind of fee when they set up the happy couple if the happy couple didn't know they'd been set up? It was all very well Constance having these inspired matchmaking ideas, but how were they to make any money out of them?

She picked up her mallet and went onto the lawn as her father knocked the finish post with his ball.

"Such delightful young women . . . such a pity they can't find husbands," Lady Winthrop confided to her bridge table after dinner. "I wonder why Chastity doesn't take Lucan?" She raised her pince-nez and looked across the drawing room to where the subject in question was talking with Hester. David Lucan stood behind the sofa gazing at Chastity like an anxious puppy.

"He would be a good catch . . . four spades," her partner said. "But Emily brought them up with some strange ideas . . . most unsuitable. Of course, poor dear Constance would have been married years ago if—" She placed a finger over her lips as Edith Duncan approached the table.

On the other side of the room Chastity smiled over her shoulder at David Lucan and said, "Do sit here and keep Hester company, David. I have to make sure everyone has what they need."

She patted the sofa invitingly as she rose to her feet. "Don't look alarmed, Hester. David doesn't bite. Besides, you two have something in common. You both love dogs."

Of course, Hester loved King Charles spaniels, and David bred Staffordshire bull terriers, but that was a mere detail, she thought as she went off, leaving them sitting awkwardly beside each other on the sofa. A few moments later she was gratified to see that they were at least talking.

"See," she said to Prudence. "I think Con has the right idea. We go out and find our clients."

"Yes, and just how do we tell them that although they didn't know it, an organization called the Go-Between set them up together and now it wants to charge them a fee?" Prudence demanded.

"Awkward," agreed Chastity. "But we can't talk about it now. Aunt Edith is convinced we're not doing our hostly duty. Every time she sees us talking together she does that wave of hers."

"We'll discuss it tonight. But what do you think's going on with Con?" She looked across the drawing room to where her elder sister was playing at a second bridge table, partnered by Max Ensor.

Chastity followed her gaze. "I don't know, but something. Whatever it is between them you can almost feel it from here. They're radiating some kind of electricity."

Prudence nodded. "I've never seen Con lose her detachment with a man before . . . at least not since Douglas died. I just wonder if she knows she has."

"Perhaps she hasn't," Chastity said. "She's always the one in charge, and we know she's playing her own game with Max."

"Somehow I don't think she's playing anything but bridge right now," Prudence said.

"No," Chastity agreed thoughtfully. "Do you think she's forgotten how much he annoyed her at the beginning? Surely he hasn't changed over night. A person doesn't just lose those opinions at will."

"Maybe he hasn't lost them," her sister said. "Maybe he's just playing them down because he knows they annoy her, and he doesn't want her annoyed . . . at least not until he's had his wicked way with her," she added with a grin.

She expected her sister to laugh but Chastity's expression remained solemn. "If he has an ulterior motive in pursuing Con, I hope it's not one that's going to hurt her."

"Oh, Lord!" Prudence sighed. "What should we do?"

"I don't think we can do anything. You know how Con is. Once she's decided upon something, nothing will distract her."

"What do you think of Max Ensor? Do you like him?"

Chastity shrugged. "I don't know. Sometimes I do, and sometimes I have a feeling that he's a bit too glib for comfort. He's ambitious, that's for sure."

"Mmm," murmured Prudence, reflecting that in her own way so was Constance.

Chapter 9

Constance would not have been surprised at her sisters' observations. They knew her almost as well as she knew herself. As the evening had progressed she had had to force herself to concentrate on her cards. Once or twice she had been in danger of unforgivably trumping her partner's ace when she lost track of trumps. Her gaze kept drifting disconcertingly to her partner's hands, which were constantly in play as he shuffled cards, riffled through his hand, made his discard. While she'd admired them before, she hadn't noticed how strong and flexible his fingers seemed to be . . . and in the next moment she caught herself thinking of those hands on her body, the fingers playing upon her skin.

This was not going according to plan. Goose bumps prickled on her bare arms and her stomach kept doing a nosedive. One minute she was cold, drawing her richly hued shawl of Indian silk up over her shoulders, and the next plying her fan vigorously. She could only hope that her distraction was not obvious to her fellow players, though Max Ensor seemed aware of it. Although he played with steady concentration, once or twice he raised his eyes from the cards and glanced at her across the table. It was a glance that contained the speculative hunger she had noticed on the train and that had emboldened her to play her little game at the stile.

They were fighting some battle here, fighting for control of whatever was to happen next. Lascivious anticipation flooded her, ran swift and hot in her veins. She wanted his body, wanted to touch every inch of him, bury her mouth and nose in his skin, taste him from the pulse in his throat to his big toes. She wanted to look at his sex, hold it, stroke it, lick it. She wondered if he had hair on his back and if it ran down his spine to his backside. Were his thighs hairy? His toes even? And what of his chest? Were his nipples small and almost invisible, or would they be prominent and dark, and harden quickly beneath the flick of her tongue?

Dear God, she thought in sudden desperation, aware of the moistening in her loins, the sudden pulsing of her sex. She had never been able to do that to herself just by thinking. Her only hope lay in the possibility that Max was suffering the same agonies of frustrated lust. But when she looked at him she saw nothing but the calm, neutral expression of a skillful bridge player.

"Constance, it's your bid." Her father's impatient voice crashed into her lubricious reverie with the icy force of an avalanche.

"Oh, yes, I'm sorry. What's the bidding? I didn't hear."

"I bid one heart, your father bid two spades, and Lord Barclay passed." Max regarded her with a curious little smile and she had the uncomfortable impression that he'd been listening in on her thoughts. Which of course was absurd, when she couldn't read his at all.

"We need forty points for the rubber," Max reminded her.

Constance couldn't imagine how they'd found themselves in a winning position with the way she'd been playing. Max was obviously skilled enough to compensate for her own absentmindedness.

She looked again at her cards. "Three no trumps."

"What?" Max stared at her in disbelief. For forty points that was sheer overkill and Constance would have to play it. He didn't have much faith in her play this evening.

Constance shrugged her shoulders but said nothing. She had a three no trump hand and if Max had enough points to bid a heart, so long as she kept her wits about her and counted carefully, they would make it. It went against the grain to play for less than they could get. Adrenaline surged through her as her competitive spirit finally vanquished all distraction. She no longer needed to force herself to concentrate, and steadily gathered tricks with her high cards. At the end, she looked up triumphantly. "There," she said, laying down her last card. "We made it."

"So I should hope," her father said. "With a hand like that, how could you lose?"

"I have a feeling Max thought I could lose very easily," she said, looking at him across the table.

He raised his hands palms up in disclaimer. "Not at all. I had every faith."

"Oh, yes?" She gathered up the cards. "I think that's as much as I can play tonight. Shall I find someone to make a fourth?"

"No, I too have played enough," Max said, rising from the table. "Gentlemen, I thank you." He smiled amiably at their opponents.

Lord Duncan set two guineas on the table and the earl of Barclay did the same. The baron pushed them across the table. "Your winnings, Ensor. I'll leave it to you to divvy it up with my daughter." He got to his feet. "Let's find that single malt I've been keeping, Barclay. You care to join us, Ensor?"

Max shook his head. "No, thank you, sir. I'd like to take a stroll in the garden with my partner, if you would permit it?"

Lord Duncan gave a low rumble of laughter. "You jest, sir. My daughters have all been beyond my control since they gained their majority . . . and probably before it," he added. "Come, Barclay." He flung an arm around his crony's shoulders and ushered him off.

"Does the lady permit it?" Max inquired, handing Constance her share of the night's winnings. Her green eyes had an unusual glitter in them as she took the money.

She tucked the winnings into her evening bag. "I think there must be a full moon. Perhaps that explains why I was so absentminded during the rubber."

"You gained it back for the last hand," he observed.

"Perhaps the clouds obscured the moon."

"Perhaps." He gave her his arm and she laid her hand on the silky black sleeve. A little current ran through her hand and up her arm. She tried to ignore it.

They walked out onto the terrace and Constance was relieved to find that they were not alone. It was a warm night and indeed a full moon and most of the house party had come outside. She couldn't see her sisters anywhere, but she did spy David Lucan and Hester Winthrop standing in awkward silence against the parapet. Maybe easing that match along a little would help her to ignore these ridiculous twitches.

"I just want to talk to Lord Lucan," she said. "He looks as if he needs a helping hand with Hester."

Max regarded the couple. "He looks old enough to conduct a conversation with a young woman without guidance," he objected.

"Yes, but Hester is so very shy and David's not very forthcoming at the best of times. I'll just go over and smooth the path for them." She took her hand from his arm. "You really don't have to come."

"I do if I want your company," he stated.

Prudence came out of the house at this juncture and Constance beckoned her over. "Prue, I thought we might encourage David and Hester a little."

Prudence looked in their direction. "They need more than a little."

"Are you matchmaking?" Max demanded.

"No . . . of course not," Constance denied. "But we do have a responsibility to ensure that our guests are enjoying themselves in congenial company."

"And you've decided that those two are congenial company for each other? Sounds like matchmaking to me . . . arrant interference." He shook his head. "Typical female nonsense. I shall go and join your father and Lord Barclay over the single malt."

Constance watched him return to the house with his long rangy stride. "Typical female nonsense, indeed!" she said indignantly.

"The leopard doesn't appear to have changed his spots." Prudence gave her a sister a shrewd look. "Or do you think he has?"

Constance shook her head. "Oh, no. Not in the least."

"So you're still intent on taking him down a peg or two?"

Constance glanced at the moon, then confessed, "Yes, absolutely. The problem, Prue, is that my body's not as much in my control as my mind. For some reason lust is on a rampage. I've never felt anything like it before. It's so perverse. I'm determined to use him; I dislike everything he stands for; but my body doesn't seem to give a damn." She shook her head. "It must be the moon."

"What are you going to do about it?" Prudence regarded her sister with fascination and a degree of alarm.

"I have no idea." Constance opened her hands in a gesture of hapless resignation. "Part of me says, sit back and enjoy the ride, but the rational side of me says, run like hell. Oh, well . . ." She shook her head again, reached into her handbag, and took out her bridge winnings. "By the way, this was my share of the game against Father and Lord Barclay, might as well put it back into the family coffers."

Prudence took it. "Circulation," she said. "Now, that's an idea. Maybe if you could keep winning against Father we could keep his money circulating within the family and out of the clutches of the outside world."

"Nice idea," her sister responded with a sardonic smile. "If you ask me, I think we'd do better to wean him off Lord Barclay. The man gives me the shivers. I know he and Father have been friends for years, but it seems to me he's always got some scheme that he wants Father to get involved in. Either that or he's gambling and carousing with him."

Prudence nodded. "I feel the same way. Mother didn't like him either. On a more hopeful note . . . what shall we do with those two would-be lovebirds?"

"Tennis," her sister said. "Tomorrow afternoon. We'll partner them together and Hester will see how masterful he is on the court, and David will be able to protect her and make her plays for her."

Prudence laughed, although she couldn't fault her sister's reasoning. They crossed the terrace to where the pair stood half facing each other, half facing away, their awkward uncertainty palpable.

"David, Hester, isn't it a beautiful night?" Constance said cheerfully. "Have you looked at the moon?"

"It's lovely, Miss Duncan," Hester responded in subdued tones.

"Hester, do call me Constance. 'Miss Duncan' makes me feel so old."

Hester blushed and stammered that she'd had no intention of imply-ing any such thing.

Constance merely laughed. "David, I think you should take Hester across the lawn to the ha-ha and look at the moon on the river. It's al-ways spectacular on the night of the full moon."

Lord Lucan was too well-bred to voice the objections that sprang to mind. His mother would not approve of his walking in the moonlight in such a secluded spot with a young lady, and besides, he didn't know what to say to her.

Hester murmured that she should ask her mama but Constance said bracingly, "I'll tell your mama if she asks for you. But she's playing cards and I'm sure she won't notice your absence for at least ten min-utes. Do go and look at the moon on the water."

Lord Lucan offered his arm and Hester took it with proper maidenly hesitation and they walked off across the lawn.

"There," Constance said, dusting off her hands. "That's done. And I'll lay any odds that Lady Winthrop won't object to the match."

"There's still the dowager to consider."

"Oh, she'll be easier than you think. We'll visit her when we're back in town and sing Hester's praises discreetly. We can hint that David seemed to find her congenial and then we can take Hester to visit her ourselves. She'll charm the old biddy with that sweet shyness. And the two mamas will get on perfectly well and have a wonderful time plan-ning the wedding and arguing and competing over the arrangements. The lovebirds won't need to worry about a thing."

"How are we going to profit from this particular piece of Go-Between business?" asked Prudence. "Even assuming we pull it off."

"Well, I was thinking . . . if the mothers did decide that it was a good match, they might be grateful enough to make a contribution to a char-ity we support, one that helps indigent gentlewomen . . . poor spinster ladies down on their luck?" She raised her eyebrows at her sister.

Prudence stared at her in astonishment. "Con! That is so . . . so *devi-ous*!"

Constance shrugged. "Needs must, Prue. And I don't really see that it matters in what guise we get paid. We'll still have performed the serv-ice."

"You're shameless," her sister declared.

"You may well be right," Constance said, glancing once more up at the moon. "I have a feeling the rational side of me is going to yield the fight tonight. What have I got to lose, Prue?"

"Your objectivity," her sister responded promptly. "If you fall for him he'll be of no use to you. You won't even want to influence him."

"I'm not going to fall for him," Constance declared. "I'm just going to get lust out of my system. I couldn't fall for someone who believes women should be kept pregnant, barefoot, and in the kitchen."

"He's not quite that bad," Prudence remonstrated.

"Perhaps not," Constance conceded. "He believes we should devote ourselves to the nursery and the household and in exchange be kept plied with chocolates on silken sofas with pleasant little amusements like shopping and gossip." She smiled. "What do you think it's going to do to his preconceptions when I grab the tiger by the tail?"

"God knows!" Prudence threw up her hands.

"I'm going to have a bath," Constance said. "I'll tell Aunt Edith on my way upstairs."

"Since you can't be good, be careful," Prue advised.

Constance laughed, kissed her sister's cheek, and went back into the house. In the bathroom she shared with her sister she ran a bath and undressed as the water ran. She took out the pins from the chignon at the nape of her neck and removed the pads that had supported the mass of her hair piled elaborately on top of her head. She brushed it to loosen the tightness of the back-combing and then twisted it into a simple knot on top of her head and pinned it securely.

She sprinkled lavender-scented bath salts into the hot water. The geyser labored and wheezed and complained but the hot water came out nevertheless. The soft glow of the gas lamp threw shadows across the vast space that was a converted bedroom. In winter the wind found its way under the door, through every chink in the window frames, and seemed to search out cracks in the plaster ceiling to chill every inch of a bather's skin exposed above the water, but on a warm summer night the bathroom with its huge wide-edged claw-footed tub was inviting.

She stepped into the gently steaming water and with a sigh of pleasure lay back, resting her neck on the edge of the bath. The full moon was a great golden round filling the open window that faced the bath. She could hear the soft murmur of voices from the terrace below as the late-retiring guests continued to chat, and the sweet strains of a piano drifted upwards. Chastity was playing; she recognized her touch with the Mozart sonata. When would Max decide to retire, she wondered, closing her eyes.

She reviewed the contents of her wardrobe, considering what to wear when she climbed the stairs to the South Turret. There was a robe of Chinese silk that had belonged to her mother. It was a wonderful emerald green that did very nice things to her eyes. A fiery orange dragon twisted and twined down the back, and it had lovely wide mandarin sleeves. But then there was the filmy muslin negligée over the white silk shift. Did she want demure or sexy; bold or artlessly seductive?

There was a discreet knock at the door and she turned her head lazily against the rim of the bath. Prue or Chas would have an answer. "Come in."

The door opened and Max Ensor stepped into the soft glow of the bathroom.

Constance was too surprised to move. She simply stared at him.

He closed the door and turned the heavy key that the sisters always ignored. The bathroom was their private domain and no one but themselves would enter it except a maid in the morning to clean it.

"Your sister told me I would find you here." He leaned his back against the door and surveyed her through hooded eyes.

That would be Prudence, Constance thought. It would never have occurred to her that Max would act on that information in such a breathtakingly brazen fashion. It hadn't occurred to Constance either. But once again he had whipped the initiative out of her hands.

She didn't move as she considered what to do, aware that every moment she kept silent would make dismissing him that much harder. Pride warred with desire. She felt her nipples peaking below the level of the water as his gaze roamed over her. Her body beneath the lavender-scented water was clearly visible. Still she said nothing.

Max pushed himself away from the door and slowly took off his coat. He hung it over the top rung of the towel rail and unfastened his diamond cuff links. He placed them on the top of the wooden chest, where they glinted in the glow of the gas lamp on the wall above.

Deliberately he rolled up his sleeves. Constance watched him, mesmerized by the slow neat movements of his long fingers. His forearms were dusted with curly dark hair. He came over to the bath and sat on the edge, a half smile playing over his mouth as he looked down at her. He dipped a forefinger in the water then reached forward and touched her forehead where her hair grew back in a widow's peak. He drew the finger down over the bridge of her nose, over her lips, beneath her chin to the rapidly beating pulse in her throat.

Ah well, Constance thought, closing her eyes. So much for pride. She waited, barely breathing. The finger continued its progress down between her breasts, dipped into her navel, slipped over her belly, to come to rest at the line of curly water-dark hair at the apex of her thighs.

His hand slid beneath the water to cup the soft mound of her sex without pressure or demand, and he leaned forward, bracing himself with his free hand on the edge of the bath, to kiss her. A light, brushing kiss this time, his tongue sliding over her lips, not demanding entrance, dipping into the corners of her mouth. Then he straightened, kissed the tip of her nose, and withdrew his hand from between her thighs, but she could still feel the warmth of his palm, the light touch of his fingers.

He reached for the large round sponge on the edge of the bath and soaped it. He didn't take his eyes off her and the golden silence enwrapped them. He drew the soapy sponge over her neck, then held one breast clear of the water and soaped it, watching the nipple stand up from the white bubbles, hard and pink against the dark brown circle of the areola. Her breast was firm and round in his hand, neither large nor small. He paid the same attention to its fellow, then dipped the sponge in the water, rinsed it, and reapplied the soap.

"Shall I do your back?" The sound of his voice, soft though it was, was startling in the suspended silence of the bathroom.

Constance sat up and leaned forward. Max moved behind her. She had an elegant back, long, narrow, curving gently at her waist and then flaring at the hip. Tendrils of damp hair escaping from the knot wisped on the back of her neck. He soaped her pointed shoulder blades and down her backbone to the base of her spine, where the cleft of her buttocks began. His breath caught in his throat and the deliberate composure that had accompanied him into the bathroom abruptly left him. He dropped the sponge into the water and stood up.

"Don't be long," he said, taking a towel from the rail and dropping it onto the stool by the bath where she could reach it easily. He picked up his coat and cuff links and left the bathroom, closing the door softly behind him.

Constance exhaled slowly. Every inch of her body was sensitized from the tips of her toes to her prickling scalp. She traced the path of his finger down her body and between her legs. The slight brush of her fingertip against her sex sent a rush of sensation that almost engulfed her. She stood up in a shower of drops and reached for the towel, stepping carefully onto the thick, fluffy bath mat. She looked at herself in the mirror on the wooden chest and saw that her cheeks were flushed, loose tendrils of hair clinging to her damp forehead. Her eyes glowed with expectation.

"God in heaven!" she muttered, leaning over to pull the plug from the bath. She was way out of her depth here. She had had the advantage of surprise for the briefest of time at the very beginning of this embryonic relationship, but now she was the one with the ground cut from beneath her feet. It didn't seem to matter what she wore up the stairs to the South Turret. Any message she might have intended to give had already been read and answered.

She wrapped herself in a fresh towel and went into her bedroom next door. She smoothed a body oil scented with sandalwood into her skin, took the pins from her hair, and brushed it again until it fell in a gleaming russet cascade down her back. It occurred to her that she was preparing herself like some seraglio inhabitant for a night with the pasha. The thought brought her a flash of much-needed amusement and perspective.

She chose the Chinese robe anyway. It had little mother-of-pearl buttons all the way down the front, but she stopped fastening them when they reached her knees. It would take far too long to undo them all. She turned the gas down low and left her room.

The stairs to the South Turret were in shadow, the only illumination moonlight pouring through a window at the top, sending a narrow silver path down the middle of the stairs. Constance didn't knock on the door but lifted the latch and pushed it open.

The round chamber was flooded with moonlight. The gas lamps had not been lit. Max lay in a dressing gown on the bed, propped against the carved headboard, his hands linked behind his head.

"Welcome," he said, swinging off the bed. He came towards her, hands outstretched. She put her hands in his and he drew her against him. "You smell delicious."

"Rather like a love slave in a harem, I was thinking."

He laughed against her mouth. "You do realize that laughter is the antithesis of an aphrodisiac."

She drew her head back and looked into his eyes. "Is it?"

For answer, he unfastened the top six buttons of the robe. With remarkable dexterity, Constance thought. He slid his hands beneath to cup her shoulders, then brought his hands to her breasts, holding them as he had done in the bath. He flicked the nipples with his fingertips until once again they were hard and erect.

"I don't know how slowly I can do this," he murmured, lifting her breasts free of the robe that was now slipping off her shoulders. He bent his head to her breasts and she shrugged her shoulders slightly so that the partially unbuttoned robe fell down her arms to slide from her body in a silky rush.

She stood naked in the warm light of the summer's full moon. And now it became imperative that Max too should show himself. She unfastened the girdle of his robe and without finesse pushed it off his shoulders. Then they stood face-to-face, her breasts touching his chest, the slight roundness of her stomach curving into the hollow of his. Her arms were around his waist, her hands on his backside. His penis flickered against her belly. She stepped closer and stood on his bare feet with her own. Now they were so close their thighs were pressed together, their faces barely an inch apart.

"We'll go slowly another time," Constance said, flattening her palms on his backside and pressing him hard against her loins.

He could feel the heat of her body like a forest fire. The scent of her arousal mingled with the scent of sandalwood. He put his hands to her waist and lifted her off his feet. She was no featherweight and he dismissed quickly any romantic notions of carrying her to the bed. He set her down and it was she who led him to the high poster bed.

He fell down onto the bed and pulled her on top of him, having a vague notion that this might prolong matters a little. But he was mistaken. Constance swung astride him, and the minute the heated core of her body touched his belly, she bit her lip hard. She rose up on her knees, took his penis between her hands, and guided him in.

For a moment they lay still, conjoined, neither daring to breathe as they learned the feel of each other. He was so big inside her, he seemed to fill her. He moved once, just the slightest lift of his hips, and the rush of the orgasm that had been waiting to explode for hours ripped through Constance, and as she felt the deep pulsing throb of his flesh within her it happened again. Another wave of intense orgasmic delight, smaller this time but just as blissful, brought a cry of pleasure to her lips and she fell forward, burying her face in his chest as his hand weakly stroked her hair.

After a long and insensible time Max lifted her off him. She rolled to her side as they disengaged and lay inert, watching as he slid the protective shield from his now flaccid flesh.

"I didn't think of that," she said almost apologetically. She had been aware of the sheath when she'd held him but in the heat of the moment it had barely registered.

He shrugged. "It only takes one of us."

"I suppose it does." The image of Amelia Westcott swam across her internal vision. Henry Franklin hadn't thought of precautions, and if Amelia had had an experience that in any way resembled Constance's in the last minutes, she couldn't blame Amelia for not having the foresight. It was a humbling reflection.

"Thank you for thinking of it. I'm embarrassed I didn't." She touched his cheek as he lay down beside her, then closed her eyes. "I think I have to sleep a little."

He slipped an arm beneath her, rolling her into his embrace.

They awoke together an hour later. The moon had dropped below the level of the window and the round chamber was now in darkness. The utter stillness of a sleeping house lay below them. Constance rolled onto her back, shivering in the cold night air.

She nudged Max, who was stirring beside her. "It's cold, Max. Can you move for a minute so that I can pull the covers over us?"

He muttered sleepily, then sat up and swung his legs over the bed, struggling into a sitting position. He stood up and stretched, then lit the gas lamp on the bedside table. "Someone thoughtfully provided a decanter of cognac. Would you like a glass?"

"Not a whole one. I'll have a sip of yours." She pulled back the sheet and coverlet and plumped up the squashed pillows, setting them against the headboard. "I'm not at all sleepy now."

He filled a glass from the decanter on the dresser and came back to the bed, climbing under the covers beside her. He handed her the glass and she took a sip. He turned his head to look at her as she lay back on the propped pillows. "Somehow I get the impression that wasn't your first time."

Constance shot him a puzzled and wary look. "Does that shock you?"

"I'll admit to surprise," he said, taking a sip of brandy. "This afternoon in the field, I was surprised. But not since."

"And not shocked?" she pressed.

"It's unusual."

"For unmarried women not to be virgins," she stated flatly.

"Yes," he agreed. "Would you deny it?"

"I wouldn't know," Constance said. "It's not a question I go around asking the unmarried women of my acquaintance."

He laughed and held the brandy goblet to her lips. "Come, don't get on your high horse, Constance. I'm not criticizing, how could I possibly after such a night? I was merely stating a fact."

"Are you sure you're not going to say that you couldn't respect a woman of easy virtue?" Constance took the glass from him and drank.

"I've told you before not to put words into my mouth." He swung off the bed and filled another glass, since it seemed he'd lost possession of the first one. "You were engaged, were you not?"

Constance stiffened. "What's that got to do with it?"

He shrugged and turned back to the bed. "Obvious, I would have thought. Did you anticipate the wedding night?"

Constance closed her eyes for minute, thinking about Douglas. "No," she said flatly. "Douglas had a finely honed sense of right and wrong, honor and dishonor." She smiled slightly. "It could be quite exasperating sometimes."

"Did you love him?" He watched her closely, seeing how her mouth had softened.

"Oh, yes," she said quietly. "He was my life. I was twenty-two when he was killed, and I thought my life was over. I knew absolutely that no other man could ever match up to Douglas." She opened her eyes. "And I was right."

He winced slightly, although he knew he had no reason to feel insulted. One brief and passionate tumble didn't entitle him to compliments, let alone favorable comparisons with a dead fiancé. They didn't even know each other in any real sense.

"And yet you've spent time with other men," he said neutrally. "You'll forgive me if I say you seem to enjoy the pleasures of sex."

"I do," she said. "When it suits me. After Mother died the three of us decided that virginity was a burden we'd rather lose. Marriage isn't exactly a top priority for any of us, but we didn't want to die wondering, if you see what I mean."

Max looked at her with fascination. He'd never met any woman whose ideas remotely resembled those of Constance and her sisters. He wasn't sure whether their attitudes repelled him or attracted him.

Constance took another sip of cognac and continued, "So we gave ourselves a year, and by the following New Year's Eve we were all three no longer in possession of our virginities."

"Did you choose your . . . your . . ." Max gave up and waved a hand helplessly.

"Our deflowerers?" Constance said. "Oh, yes, of course we did. They were all decent men for whom we felt both attraction and liking. And they had to be willing and in our confidence. It was all very straightforward and pleasant and we all still like each other very much."

"Do I know any of them?"

"I don't think you'd want to know names," Constance responded, turning her head on the pillow. "Why on earth would you?" She made a move to get up.

"Don't go," he said softly. "It doesn't seem right to end the evening on this fractured note. If I've offended you, I apologize. We don't really know each other very well yet."

Constance hesitated. He was right. It seemed both ungracious and silly to spoil what had been a glorious few moments. She flipped aside the covers in invitation and he set down his glass and slid in beside her again.

"Shall we take our time this time," he murmured, kissing her ear.

For answer, her fingers tiptoed delicately down his body.

Chapter 10

"Lord Lucan is a wonderful partner for Hester," Chastity observed to Lady Winthrop as they sat beneath an umbrella outside the tennis court watching the game of mixed doubles in progress. "He seems to be able to anticipate her every move across the court."

"Hester is not in general overly fond of any kind of sporting activity," Lady Winthrop declared. "Indeed, I advised her most strongly not to take part this afternoon. It's far too hot to be running around like that. If she's not careful she'll start to perspire, and that's so unattractive in a woman."

"I think David is doing most of the running around, Lady Winthrop," Prudence pointed out, refilling glasses from the tall jug of lemonade. "That's why he makes such a perfect partner."

"He's a very personable young man," Lady Winthrop conceded, taking a delicate sip from her glass. "I'm slightly acquainted with his mother, although she doesn't go about much. Rather frail, I understand."

There was very little that was frail about the Dowager Lady Lucan, Prudence reflected even as she murmured agreement. "David is a wonderful son," she said. "So caring and supportive of his mother."

"Excellent qualities in a son," Lady Winthrop muttered, fanning herself vigorously. "And a goodly fortune, I understand." This was a mere reflective murmur, to which her companions made no response.

"Con seems to be doing her best to give Hester and David a win," Chastity said quietly to her sister as they moved away from the group under the umbrella. "But I get the impression Max is not too happy about it."

Prudence chuckled. "He looks mad as fire. He's playing his heart out and every time the serve comes to Con she just pats it across the net to fall at Hester's feet so that she can't possibly miss it."

"And dear sweet David can't see what she's doing and just assumes that Hester's playing like a goddess," Chastity said on a bubble of laughter. "Con's so devious."

"I told you about her plan to collect donations from the satisfied mamas for a charity for indigent spinsters," Prudence reminded her. "She's utterly shameless. I don't know where she gets it from."

"Mother was not exactly straightforward in all her dealings," Chastity replied. "Look how she pulled the wool over Father's eyes."

"I don't think Con's pulling the wool over Max Ensor's eyes," Prudence observed, shading her eyes against the afternoon sun as she watched the court. "He looks ready to whack her with his tennis racket."

"They certainly don't look like lovers who spent a night of unbridled passion," Chastity agreed. "Has she said anything to you about it?"

"Not a word. But there hasn't been much opportunity today for a sisterly tête-à-tête." They fell silent, listening to the summery twang of tennis balls on rackets, the rhythmic thud as the ball hit the well-manicured grass.

On the court, Constance served to Hester. Her ball hit the net and Max muttered savagely from his position close to the net. He picked up the ball and slammed it back at her. She caught it on her racket, smiled sweetly at him, and delivered her second serve. It rolled across the net to land at Hester's feet. Hester hit it with the air of surprise she'd been wearing since the game started and laughed delightedly when it went over the net. Max returned it easily but he was so out of temper that he sent it over the back line.

"Game, David and Hester!" Constance called cheerfully. "Change ends."

"What the hell are you playing at?" Max demanded in a fierce undertone as they walked to the other end of the court.

"Tennis," she said with the same sweet smile. "Of course, my arm is nowhere near as powerful as yours. I am a mere woman, after all. But I'm doing my best."

"Don't give me that!" he exclaimed. "You're playing pat ball to Hester."

"Oh, but look how happy it's making her . . . and see how David is glowing with pride in her. He's looking at her in just the way he looks at Chastity . . . or, I hope, *did* look at Chastity."

He spoke through thinned lips. "I tell you straight, Constance, you had better play this next game competitively or I shall walk off the court."

"Oh, how unsportsmanlike," she protested. "There's more to a game than just winning."

"Not in my book," he retorted, moving to the back of the court to accept David's serve. "And mark me well, I mean what I say."

Constance pursed her lips. She hadn't expected him to like what she was doing, but she hadn't expected quite such a furious reaction. He obviously had a very finely honed competitive streak. She understood it, since she was fiercely competitive herself, except in certain circumstances, like the present. However, she decided she'd better give this game her best shot in the interests of keeping the peace.

Max nodded grimly when she began to play with more verve and the game picked up speed. They were still a set down but at least Constance was finally giving their opponents a game, and if she played properly they might win this one and have a chance for the match. It didn't take him long, however, to see that every time they pulled ahead she would subtly drop a point. It annoyed him so much, it put his own game off and they lost the set and the match by an infuriatingly narrow margin. He controlled his irritation sufficiently to congratulate the winners, shaking hands warmly with the beaming David and the rosily delighted Hester, but then he stalked off the court without a word to Constance and headed for the house.

Constance swung her racket thoughtfully, then she hurried after him, catching up with him as he reached the terrace. "Max?"

He stopped without turning around. "Well?"

She put a hand on his arm, laughing up at him. "Oh, don't be cross. It was all for a good cause."

"I don't consider arrant meddling in other people's affairs a good cause," he declared, glowering at her. "It's just blatant matchmaking."

"But it's not doing any harm." Constance wiped her damp brow with the back of her hand.

Max's annoyance vanished into the humid air. There was something overpoweringly sensual about her flushed cheeks and the beads of perspiration gathered on her brow and in the hollow of her neck just above the open collar of her white silk blouse. He pictured her breasts as he'd seen them that morning when she'd finally left his bed, and he imagined the little trickle of sweat that would be gathering in the deep cleft between them.

"Just leave me out of such nonsense in future," he demanded, taking her elbow and moving decisively with her behind a screen of box trees planted in big tubs along one side of the terrace.

Constance offered no objection to their abrupt seclusion in the narrow space. She rested her hands on the parapet behind her and leaned back, tilting her head to look up at him with an inquiring air.

"Suddenly I find myself with an overpowering need to kiss you," he said, running a finger over her slightly parted lips. "There's something incredibly sensual about a woman all flushed and bedewed with exertion, although, given the way you were playing, I'm astonished you managed to break a sweat at all."

"Not in the last game," she protested, as her heartbeat quickened and a thrill of anticipatory desire prickled over her scalp and down her spine, setting her nerve endings on edge.

"Yes," he conceded, "you worked very hard at losing that one." He laid a fingertip on the moist skin of her throat, feeling the pulse run swift beneath his touch. Her tongue touched her lips, and her eyes in the greenish shade of the trees glowed deepest emerald. Little sparks of light flickered in their depths as she tilted her head farther back, offering her throat for his mouth.

His lips followed the fingertip and he pressed his mouth into the hollow, licking the sweat from her skin, up beneath her chin, as if it were an ice cream. She laughed softly, running her hands over his back, feeling the heat of his skin beneath the thin fabric of his white linen shirt.

He moved his mouth to hers, lightly brushing at first, then with more force, pressing her lips open even as she pretended to resist. His tongue played with hers, touching the tip, curling around, stroking the underside. Desire shimmered, flashed between them.

His hands were on the buttons of her blouse, flipping them open with deft haste. He unbuttoned the camisole she wore beneath and she felt the air on her bare skin. He took his mouth from hers and bent to kiss her breasts, running his tongue up the cleft between them to her throat, savoring the salty sweetness of her skin. He held her waist between his hands as he devoured the creamy blue-veined roundness of her breasts, the erect rose-pink nipples, his breath a warm, swift rustle across her sensitized flesh. She bit her lip to keep from crying out as desire grew, spreading a honeyed warmth through her loins and belly. She caught his head between her hands, curling her fingers into the luxuriantly thick silver of his hair, tracing the shape of his ears, pinching his earlobes in an effort to contain the surging power of her need.

They didn't speak. Their breathing fast, they fumbled with her white linen skirt and lacy knickers, with the buttons on his trousers. He lifted her against him and she clung to his neck as he slid within her. She kissed him, sucking on his mouth, his tongue, nipping at his lips, holding herself still as he thrust deep to her core. She threw back her head as he drove once more hard and fierce inside her and left her body the instant the wave broke over them.

Only as the violent beating of her pulse slowed in her ears did Constance hear the voices on the terrace beyond the screen of box trees. She put her hand over her mouth, laughing silently. Max shook his head at her and hastily rearranged his clothes before tucking her breasts back into her camisole and rapidly rebuttoning her blouse while she pulled up her knickers and dropped her skirt over the general muddle beneath.

"How shocking of us," she whispered in a voice that didn't sound as if she was in the least shocked. "What are we going to do? They're all having tea. We can't just walk out of here as if it's the most normal thing in the world for a couple to skulk behind a hedge."

The level of voices beyond the trees rose slightly and under cover of the buzz Max hissed, "Over the parapet." He swung himself onto the ledge and then dropped to the flower bed beneath behind the shelter of a luxuriant buddleia bush. "Come on." He held up his hands.

Constance grinned and sat on the edge, swinging her legs over. She dropped to the ground beside him, pressing backwards against the wall. She whispered, "You go first. I'll have to go upstairs before I can show myself in public."

He nodded, turned to go, then turned back and kissed her with something akin to savagery. "You are a very wicked woman," he murmured, sounding almost angry, then he sauntered away, hands in his pockets, around the side of the house.

Constance waited a few minutes, then keeping close to the wall, hidden by the bushes in the flower bed, hastened away to the back of the house. In the bathroom she stripped to her skin, tossed her tennis clothes into the hamper, and sponged herself down. In her bedroom she changed into an afternoon dress of dark green muslin and tidied the tangled mess of her hair. Laughter bubbled continuously inside her like a mountain spring. She would never have expected such a flagrant indiscretion from Max Ensor. Perhaps the man was not completely beyond redemption after all. If he could forget his principles and hidebound attitudes in such spectacular fashion, surely he could be persuaded to broaden his mind in other areas too.

Humming to herself she returned to the terrace, immaculately tidy, only the darting sparkle in her eyes an indication that anything out of the ordinary had happened.

Prudence shot her a speculative glance and Constance gave her a sunny smile. Prudence abandoned her teapot and the platter of sandwiches she was offering and came over to her sister. "You look very smug," she accused.

"Well, with reason. Look how David and Hester are getting along. My little tennis ploy seems to have worked a treat."

"I notice your partner didn't think much of it. Where is he?" She looked around the terrace. "I haven't seen him since he left the court looking like thunder."

Constance shrugged. "Probably licking his wounds in private. Have you been working on Lady Winthrop?"

"Chastity and I have dropped a few well-placed comments, which she seemed to take to heart."

"Good. Then we'll go to work on Lady Lucan as soon as we're back in town."

"Don't forget we have to see Anonymous on Wednesday morning and we need to go in search of Henry Franklin on Tuesday, before we meet again with Amelia on Thursday. When are we going to have time to visit Lady Lucan?"

Constance gave a wry smile. "The Go-Between seems to be up and running. And we have to put together the next issue of *The Mayfair Lady* too. An edition every two weeks is a lot of pressure."

"No peace for the wicked," Prudence said with a shrug. "Where are you intending to spend tonight?"

"Why?"

"Well, we could work on the paper if you didn't have other plans."

"I think I will have," Constance said. "But we could do some work first."

"You can't do without sleep altogether," her sister protested.

"Oh, for the moment I can," Constance said. "Just for two more nights. Once we're back in town it'll be different. Look, there's Father in that wretched motorcar of Barclay's." She gestured to the driveway, where a motorcar was chugging up to the house, Lord Duncan in driving goggles behind the wheel.

"We're never going to keep him from buying one of those," Prudence said with a sigh.

"He can't buy it if there's no money," Chastity pointed out. Her sisters hadn't heard her soft-footed approach.

"He'll borrow it at some outrageous rate of interest," Prudence stated, her mouth tight.

"Perhaps we can pawn the silver," Constance suggested. "And Mother's diamonds. They must be worth the price of a motor."

"You're not serious!" Her sisters stared at her.

She shrugged. "I can see it coming to that. Either that or we prepare to have a major confrontation and force him to acknowledge the truth."

Her sisters gazed out over the garden in bleak-faced silence. Constance was right. They could manage the ordinary expenses of daily life and some of the luxuries their father considered necessaries, but any expense as extreme as a motorcar was beyond their ingenuity.

"Perhaps we could put him off the idea," Chastity said thoughtfully. "Supposing he had a miserable experience with one. You know how he can make up his mind one minute and change it the next without so much as a blink of an eye. Maybe we could just put him off the whole idea."

"Chas, you are very clever," Constance said, patting her sister's shoulder. "I'm sure we can come up with a plan."

"Oh, yes, easy," Prudence scoffed. "In our copious free time."

"Don't be gloomy, Prue." Constance leaned over and kissed her sister. "We haven't been defeated yet."

"Satisfied passion seems to have made you overly optimistic," Prudence declared.

Constance smiled.

"Oh, I think I'm too scared, Lord Lucan. The lake's so deep and cold." Hester stood on the little jetty at the side of the ornamental lake clutching her parasol. "What if the boat overturns? I can't swim." She gazed up at him, her eyes round and large as platters beneath an enchanting straw bonnet festooned with flowers.

"There's nothing to be afraid of," he said, patting her shoulder. "I'll row you safely across to the island, I promise you." He offered her a smile that managed to be both protective and slightly patronizing as he held the little rowboat against the side of the jetty. "It's very pretty over there," he added in a cajoling tone.

Hester looked doubtfully across the expanse of smooth green water to the little island adorned with a Grecian temple. Two other rowboats with a full complement of passengers were already approaching the island, and no one so far had managed to get their feet wet.

"Come, Hester, David will take care of you," Chastity said from her position in the rowboat. "He's a very good oarsman, I can vouch for it, and we'll have the most beautiful view of the sunset from the temple."

"Oh, I do so wish to see it, but . . . oh, dear." Hester bit her lip and fixed her eyes once more upon Lord Lucan, who unconsciously straightened his shoulders.

"I rowed for Harrow, Hester," he offered, and it seemed to Chastity that his voice had somehow become deeper as his posture became more commanding. Her lips twitched. Little Hester certainly seemed to arouse the man in David Lucan.

Chastity exchanged a glance with Constance, whose own eyes were alight with amusement as she stood on the jetty with Max, who was tapping his foot with ill-concealed impatience at this shilly-shallying.

Max stepped around Constance and twitched the painter out of David's hand, murmuring into his ear, "For God's sake, man. Just pick her up and put her in the boat while I hold it steady."

The tips of David's ears burned crimson. He stared at Max, then cleared his throat, and without further ado took the advice. Hester gave a little scream as he lifted her off the jetty and deposited her rather unceremoniously into the rowboat. She sat on the thwart with a gasp, clutching her parasol, and gazed at David in awe as he jumped down into the boat beside her.

He was still blushing as he stammered, "F-forgive me, Hester. I thought it best to help you make up your mind."

"Oh, yes, David," she breathed, her eyes shining. "I won't be at all frightened now. I know it's quite safe."

Max tossed the painter down to David. "Give me strength!" he muttered to Constance. "How the hell deep is this damn lake?"

"No more than three feet," Constance returned with a chuckle. "Don't be such a curmudgeon. It's young love we're promoting here."

He gave her a look to curdle milk and declared, "We'll take that other boat." He gestured to a skiff, the last remaining craft at the jetty.

"There's room for us all in David's boat," Constance murmured.

"We'll take the other one," Max repeated. "My patience won't stand another second of that simpering."

"Oh, you are so unromantic," Constance declared. She called out to her sister, "Max wants to take the skiff, so we'll see you over there."

"You want me to be romantic?" Max demanded in clear surprise as the rowboat pulled away. "That's rich, coming from someone who doesn't have a romantic bone in her body."

Constance laughed. "Unfair and ungallant." She untied the skiff's painter. "Are you rowing or am I?"

"I am." He rolled up the sleeves of his shirt and Constance caught herself watching his hands again, the deft movements of his long fingers. She had noticed already that his forearms and angular wrists were very strong, and she wondered not for the first time what he'd done with his life before he'd gone into politics. There was something very physical about him. Not the kind of man to have spent time in dusty offices or the halls of academe. How strange that she'd had no real interest in his past. It had seemed sufficient to know that he was Letitia's brother and an MP who could be put to good use. Now, however, she wasn't so sure. She still didn't even know his age, let alone whether he'd ever been married.

She jumped unaided into the skiff. "How old are you, Max?"

He gave her a quizzical look as he stepped in beside her. "That's rather sudden."

"Not really. I've just never thought to ask before. I'm twenty-eight, if you want an exchange of information."

He shook his head as he sat down on the mid thwart. "It never occurred to me to wonder." He took up the oars. "I'll be forty in two months' time."

"Ah." She nodded. "I guessed around there."

He laughed and pulled away from the jetty. "Any other questions?"

She let her hand dangle in the cool water as he rowed. "Ever been married?"

"No."

It was her turn to look quizzical now. "Ever been in love?"

"That's a different matter."

"What happened?"

He shipped his oars and the little skiff bobbed gently as two stately swans glided by. "I met her in India. She was the wife of the commander of the garrison at Jodhpur. She was lonely, bored, rather older than I was." He shrugged. "To cut a long story short, we had a very passionate liaison. She was going to leave her husband, ask him for a divorce, and we were going to come back to England and live, social outcasts of course, but happily ever after."

His mouth twisted in an expression of self-mockery and his blue eyes had an ironic gleam in them that Constance didn't like very much. "But you didn't," she said.

"No, we didn't. She decided she couldn't bear the disgrace, that it would damage her family's reputation. There was a child, a son, and she was afraid that her husband wouldn't permit her to see the child if she left him."

He took up his oars again and resumed course towards the island. Constance felt that she should be satisfied with his answers, but she knew he'd left a lot unsaid. She took her hand from the water and shook silvery drops from her fingers, watching as they caught the light from the sinking sun that was turning the surface of the lake a soft pink.

"What were you doing in India?"

"After Oxford I joined the East India Company's cavalry." He gave a short laugh. "I didn't get on with my father and putting an ocean between us seemed like a good idea. I resigned my commission when . . ." He shrugged and let the sentence hang. "So there you have my history, Miss Duncan."

"And now you're a politician." She dipped her fingers in the water again, making little circles on the smooth surface.

"It seemed a suitable career for a man of my age and gravitas." He glanced at her and she saw he was smiling now, the laugh lines creasing around his brilliant blue eyes as he squinted against the sun.

"And what political issues interest you the most?" she inquired, drying her fingers on her handkerchief.

"That's far too big a question to answer now." He pulled strongly on the oars and the skiff darted up to the jetty on the island, where the guests were beginning to climb the hill to the temple.

"Jenkins is opening the champagne on the terrace," Prudence said, giving her sister a hand out of the skiff. "If we don't hurry, though, we'll miss the sunset. You took ages getting across."

"Ah, well, Max is not too expert with a pair of oars," Constance said with a devilish smile. "He caught at least three crabs."

"Calumny!" he exclaimed.

She laughed and began to stride up the little hill in the wake of their guests, who were already crowding onto the paved terrace outside the little white structure. Jenkins and a manservant moved among them with trays of champagne flutes.

"You seem to be getting along remarkably well with our Right Honorable Gentleman," Prudence said in an undertone, taking a glass from the tray. "Are you sure you haven't lost your objectivity, Con?"

Constance hesitated. She glanced to where Max stood at the edge of the terrace, glass in hand. She always thought he looked very striking in ordinary formal dress, but he was undeniably attractive with his tall lean frame clad in white flannels and open-collared shirt, the sleeves rolled up to his elbows, revealing bronzed forearms. His hair glistened in the sun. "Just to look at him makes my knees go weak," she said. "Whether that's the same as losing my objectivity, I don't know. Don't you think he's the most handsome man?"

Prudence laughed. "He's good-looking, I'll give you that. You don't think he's pompous and arrogant anymore?"

"Oh, yes, he's both of those things," Constance declared. "It's just that there are some physical compensations that at the moment seem to outweigh the disadvantages."

"That won't last," Prudence said. "Lust has a time limit."

"Then my objectivity, if it is temporarily lost, will soon return," her sister responded.

Prudence raised an eyebrow but made no comment.

Chapter 11

Max was striding up the steps of the house in Manchester Square early on Tuesday morning when the door opened before he could reach it and the three sisters emerged, dressed for the street.

"We'll be back late this afternoon, Jenkins," Constance was saying over her shoulder as she stepped out, drawing on her gloves. "Oh, Max. What are you doing here?"

It was a less than ecstatic welcome, he thought. "I should have thought that was obvious," he said with a wry smile. "I was coming to call upon you. What are you doing out so early? It's barely nine o'clock."

"I'm afraid that we have to go out."

"Anywhere special?"

"We're taking a train," Chastity said.

"Yes, an early train and we must hurry, or we'll miss it," Constance said. "I'm so sorry, Max. Can you call another time?"

"Where are you going by train?" he inquired, intrigued but also a little put out by her casual demeanor. They had parted company at Waterloo the previous day on their return from Romsey. It had been a decorous farewell, taking place as it did in public, but he had rather expected a hint of special warmth in her manner towards him when they met next. He had actually tried to resist the urge to rush around to Manchester Square at the earliest possible opportunity, but the impulse had been irresistible. Now he was beginning to regret it.

"Oh, just an errand we have to run in the country," she said with a vague gesture, starting down the steps. "But you could call tomorrow. We'll be out in the morning, but tomorrow afternoon we have our At Home."

"Unfortunately I must be in the House of Commons tomorrow afternoon for Prime Minister's Question Time," he said a little stiffly. "I was hoping to invite you for lunch today. I was going to leave an invitation with Jenkins since I assumed you would not yet be up and about."

"I'm so sorry." Constance had already begun to walk quickly along the pavement. "That would have been lovely, but we have this other engagement, you see. Prudence, can you hail that cab coming around the corner?"

"Well, I won't keep you." He bowed and waited as the three sisters climbed into the hackney. Constance waved to him as the hackney moved off, and he could read only distraction in her gaze, not a hint of intimacy or even regret at her abrupt departure.

He frowned. He was far too experienced to be put out by a woman's seeming indifference, let alone to suffer from piqued pride. It was an old feminine trick to blow hot and cold. For some reason women thought it made a man more eager. But he'd learned to ignore it before he was out of adolescence. It was strange, though. Constance was the last person he would have expected to employ such a hackneyed girlish trick.

Constance sat back in the corner of the cab, hanging on to the leather strap as the hackney swung around the corner into Marble Arch. "Well, that was a little awkward."

"You were a little brusque," Prudence observed.

"It's just that I know where we're going," Constance said. "We're in cahoots with his sister's governess, on an underhanded mission to liberate her from Letitia's tyranny. I couldn't think what to say to him."

"You could have invited him for dinner this evening. Or even suggested he take you out," Chastity pointed out. "He did look rather hurt," she added sympathetically.

"I suppose so." Constance fixed her gaze on the street beyond the window. Chastity's sensitivity was having its usual chastening effect. She said slowly, "But in truth I don't want things to move too fast. It was one thing while we were at Romsey, but back in London it seems, well, too precipitate."

"You certainly didn't hesitate about jumping into his bed," Prudence observed in a rather dry tone. "I would call that more than a little precipitate."

"Maybe I got a little more than I bargained for," Constance said frankly. "I seem to be paying for it with doubts now." She turned back from the window and gave her sisters a rather helpless little smile. "Some kind of lover's remorse."

"So, you did lose your objectivity." Prudence looked at her sharply.

"I must have done." Constance shrugged. "But it's coming back now. I have to take control of things again. And the only way to do that is to go slowly."

Her sisters merely nodded. They didn't disagree with her, but they had watched her spectacular loss of control with some trepidation and both rather doubted her ability to get it back again as easily as she seemed to think.

"So, how are we going to proceed with Henry Franklin?" Prudence asked.

"First we have to find him. Then we have to get him alone," Constance said, happy to have the subject changed. "We'll try his father's office first."

"Are we going to cajole him or bully him?" Chastity asked.

Constance considered. "Maybe both," she said. "Of course, it depends what he's like. How resistant he is. But maybe you should be nice and I should be nasty. Then when he doesn't know which way is up, Prue can chip in with some practical suggestions."

"That might work," Prudence agreed. "But if he's really weak and already bullied by his father, we're going to have to give him courage . . . build him up, not knock him down."

"Let's decide when we meet him."

The hackney drew up outside Waterloo station and they hurried onto the concourse. The train for Ashford was already steaming at the platform. "We'll buy tickets on the train," Constance said. "There's no time to stand at the ticket window."

They settled into a compartment, bought their tickets from an elderly and avuncular ticket collector, and Constance unscrewed the lid of the thermos flask she carried in a capacious straw handbag. She filled three dainty cups and passed them around as the train's whistle blew and the train jerked forward.

"Did you bring sandwiches?" Chastity leaned forward to peer in the basket.

"Cheese scones and cold sausages," her sister told her. "But we should save them until later. I've no idea whether we'll get any lunch."

"Oh, but there's Bakewell tart too," Chastity declared happily, ignoring her sister's suggestion and taking a slice of the almond and jam tart. "Mrs. Hudson's specialty. We can have that now. It goes so well with coffee."

The journey took an hour and a half and the train chugged into Ashford station just before noon. The sisters descended to the platform and looked around for a pony and trap to hire to take them into the town.

"Franklin Construction," Prudence said, reading off the paper that Amelia Westcott had given them. "West Street."

"Let's ask the stationmaster."

Constance went into the small station house. A grizzled man gave her a nod and told her that while there were no traps for hire she could walk into the center of town in fifteen minutes and would find West Street running off the market square. Franklin Construction was the gray building halfway down on the left.

Constance thanked him and returned to her sisters. "Looks like it's shank's pony."

Prudence glanced up at the overcast sky. "Let's hope it doesn't rain."

Franklin Construction turned out to be a substantial building occupying the center block of West Street. Constance looked up at the sign over the door. "I get the impression that Franklin Senior has a thriving concern here."

"More than enough to support a musically talented son," Chastity agreed.

"Mmm." Prudence nodded thoughtfully. "Well, let's see what we can discover." She walked boldly to the door and turned the knob. A bell jangled as it opened onto a neat office, with three desks and a wall of filing cabinets.

A man with a drooping moustache and pale sad eyes behind wire-rimmed spectacles looked up from a stack of inventories as they entered. He offered a hesitant and somewhat puzzled smile and rose to his feet. "What can I do for you, ladies?"

"We're looking for Henry Franklin," Constance said, deciding that the direct approach was the best. "Do you happen to know where we could find him?"

"Well, right here, madam. I am Henry Franklin." He gazed at them in frank bewilderment. There were ink stains on the white cuffs of his shirt showing beneath the slightly short sleeves of his coat. His appearance was untidy, careless, as if it mattered not a whit to him, and his hair was too long. But his hands were long and white, the nails meticulously manicured. A pianist's hands, Constance thought. It was hard to guess at his age but he looked so worn and dispirited that she thought he was probably younger than he appeared.

"What can I do for you?" he asked again.

Constance looked around the office. She could hear voices from behind a door in the far wall. "Are you in a position to leave here for a few minutes and talk privately with us?"

"But what is it about?" He glanced nervously to the door as the voices rose; one in particular was loud and peremptory.

Papa Franklin. The sisters exchanged a quick glance.

"Amelia." Chastity spoke in a soft and gentle whisper, coming over to him, regarding him intently from beneath the upturned brim of her crushed-velvet hat as she laid a hand on his arm. "Where can we go to talk?"

He looked at her like a panic-stricken deer. "Has something happened to her? Is she all right?"

Constance glanced at Prudence and received a faint nod of agreement. "Yes to the first, and no to the second," Constance stated, her voice as low as Chastity's but nowhere near as sympathetic. "You need to talk with us, Mr. Franklin." She glanced to the door behind him. "We would not wish to involve anyone else."

His complexion was now ashen. "In the Copper Kettle, on Market Street. I sometimes take my lunch there. I will meet you in fifteen minutes."

"Then we will see you in fifteen minutes," Chastity said in the same gentle tones. "Please don't worry, Mr. Franklin. We mean you no harm." She followed her sisters outside, casting him a further encouraging glance as she went through the door. He did not look encouraged.

"Will he come, d'you think?" Prudence asked.

"Oh, yes," Constance declared. "He'll come. Out of fear. He probably thinks we're going to blackmail him."

"Well, we are, after a fashion," Prudence said.

Constance regarded her in surprise for a second and then laughed. "If it comes down to it, Prue, of course we are. We're discovering any number of dubious talents that we never knew we possessed."

The Copper Kettle was a small chintzy tea shop. The sisters examined the menu.

"The Welsh rarebit is very good, madam," the waitress told them, pointing with her pen to the item. "We gets lots of compliments on the rarebit."

"What about the veal and ham pie?" Prudence asked.

The woman shook her head. "Wouldn't go for it myself, madam. That jelly stuff's not so fresh . . . Cod 'n' chips is good, though."

Prudence grimaced. "I have enough cod in my life. What do you think, Con?"

"Welsh rarebit," Constance replied. "And a pot of tea." She added sotto voce to Prudence, "I don't trust the coffee here."

"Three rarebits it is, then, and a pot of tea for three." The woman scribbled on her pad.

"We are expecting someone else to join us," Chastity said. "Mr. Henry Franklin."

"Oh, Mr. Henry always has sardines on toast," the waitress said cheerfully. "Every day . . . rain or shine, it's sardines on toast." She gave them a curious look. "New to town, aren't you? Friends of Mr. Henry, are you?"

"Yes," Prudence agreed with a smile.

The waitress hesitated, her expression hungry for more information, but something about the calmly smiling impassivity of the three women before her shut off her curiosity like a closed tap. "Well, I'll put in Mr. Henry's sardines on toast, then, and bring another cup." She took her pad and went off.

Henry Franklin came into the café a few minutes later. He looked around with an air of anxious suspicion, then approached the table, unwinding his muffler. An unnecessary garment given the humidity of the overcast day, the sisters reflected as they smiled and gestured to the fourth chair at the table. But perhaps he had a throat condition.

"The waitress says you always eat sardines on toast, so we ordered them for you," Chastity said with a reassuring smile. "We're all having the Welsh rarebit."

"I hear it's excellent." He sat down, his eyes darting from side to side. "I only have half an hour. Please tell me what you want." He took off his glasses and polished them on a less than pristine handkerchief. His eyes without their protection were weak and watery.

"We don't want anything," Chastity said, leaning across the table towards him. "We're here for Amelia because she cannot be here for herself."

"I don't understand. She . . . Amelia and I . . . we agreed not to see each other again. It's impossible." He returned his glasses to his nose. "My father would never permit such a match. What has *happened* to Amelia?"

"What often happens when two people make love," Constance said calmly, pitching her voice low so that no one but her immediate audience could hear her.

Henry sagged in his chair. He wrung his hands convulsively and gazed helplessly at them. "I d-don't understand."

"What don't you understand?" It was Prudence's turn now. She sat next to him, turning sideways to face him. "It's a simple fact of life, Henry. These things happen. But when they do, then decisions have to be made."

"You would not expect Amelia to carry this burden alone." Chastity rested a hand on his. "You are far too good a man to do that, Henry. I know you are."

The waitress appeared behind them with a laden tray, and Constance said, "It's so nice to see you again, Mr. Franklin. We were passing through Ashford on our way to Dover and thought how delightful it would be to catch up with you. We had such a delightful time at the musicale in Dover. Do you still play?"

Henry mumbled something. His grayish pallor was waxen and beads of perspiration stood out on his brow. He stared down at the table until the waitress had set down their plates and left, her backward glance brimming with speculation.

"Why didn't she write and tell me?" he said, poking at his sardines with his fork. "I don't understand why she didn't write to me."

"But she did," Prudence said. "She told us she had written several times, although she didn't mention her present situation. But you never wrote back."

"I didn't receive her letters. We'd agreed not to see each other again, so I just assumed that she was holding to that."

"Well, what could have happened to her letters?" Constance asked, taking her fork to the crisp bubbly cheese topping of her rarebit.

Henry looked up and stated bitterly, "My father sees all the post that comes into the house before anyone else does. He distributes it at the breakfast table."

"And he knew about your understanding with Amelia?" Constance took a mouthful of her lunch. It was surprisingly good, with just the right mustardy bite to the cheese.

"Someone told him they'd seen us out walking in the evenings. He was very unpleasant about it." He shuddered at the memory. "I couldn't bear to listen to him . . . to the things he said about Amelia. He said she wasn't good enough for a Franklin, that she was a woman of loose morals . . . oh, dreadful things."

"Why didn't you stand up to him?" Prudence asked, pouring tea from the big brown pot.

"That's easy for you to say," he responded as bitterly as before, cutting his sardines into minute fussy little pieces. "You don't stand up to my father. No one does. He threatened to throw me out on the street if I ever saw or spoke with her again. It was no idle threat, I can promise you."

"Then what are you going to do?" Chastity's voice was still soft and sympathetic.

He made a helpless gesture with his hands. "What *can* I do? He'll throw me out without a penny and I can't support a wife and child without money."

"You could always earn it," Prudence pointed out dryly.

"Doing what?" he exclaimed in an undertone. "I'm good for nothing but playing the piano."

"You work as a clerk in your father's office," Constance pointed out. "You could find such a job elsewhere."

"It's killing my soul," he said with a mournful sigh, echoing Amelia's observation.

"And what do you think carrying an illegitimate child is doing to Amelia's soul?" Constance demanded, her patience all but exhausted.

Henry looked as if he was about to cry. He covered his face with his hands.

"Do you love Amelia?" Chastity asked.

"We can't live on love!" He looked up and the hopelessness in his eyes stirred even the impatient Constance to sympathy. She glanced at Prudence.

Prudence took off her glasses and then replaced them, pushing them up the bridge of her nose with a firm, decisive forefinger. "This is what you must do."

Henry gazed at her with the soulful hopeful eyes of a dog unsure whether he was about to receive a stroke or a kick.

"You have to declare your independence from your father before you do anything else. You will come to London, where you will marry Amelia in a civil ceremony at the registrar's office in the borough where Amelia lives. You will find a job as a clerk. We shall help you do that—in fact, we shall hold your hand throughout. Once you've sorted that out, then you will take Amelia to visit your father. It will be a fait accompli and I'm willing to bet that the prospect of a grandchild will soften him. You will present him with your own plan. Amelia is a clever woman, good with figures, with writing letters . . . she has any number of the skills essential for running an office. She'll take over the office instead of you, and you will start building a private practice teaching piano. If he refuses to be reconciled, and he won't, then you simply return to your job in London. If he knows that he can't bully you, he'll think twice. I promise you."

"Oh, masterly, Prue," Constance said. "So what do you say, Henry?"

He looked winded. He could no more imagine withstanding the incredible force of this trio of women than he would an avalanche. "How will I get his permission to go to London? He'll never give me the time off."

"You weren't listening, Henry." Constance leaned across the table towards him. "Prue said that you have first to declare your independence from your father. You won't ask his permission. You will simply leave here and commit yourself to a new life. If you can't face him in person, then write him a letter. Take the night train if it'll be easier. You can stay with us for a few days until you can find somewhere for both of you to live. I would think Amelia could hide her marriage and go on working at the Grahams for another month or so, if necessary. It would give you more time to get established. But first you *must* get married."

He rubbed his eyes with the heel of his palms. "But a registry-office wedding. Surely Amelia would not want that. She'll want a proper wedding."

"Amelia wants a wedding . . . *any* wedding . . . just as long as it comes with a marriage certificate and a ring on her finger," Constance declared. "Now, if you write her a letter telling her what you've decided we'll take it to her when we see her on Thursday."

"I have pencil and paper." Prudence rummaged in her handbag and produced a small notebook and a pencil. "There."

Henry took them. He looked down at his now cold sardines, then back at the three women who were regarding him steadily. They were an irresistible force, and perhaps, just perhaps, they were a match for his father. He felt a faint stirring of energy. With them at his back, there was no telling what he could do. "When shall I come to London?" he asked.

They all smiled at him and he felt their approval like a warm bath.

"The sooner the better," Prudence said. "This coming weekend, if you like. We'll expect you on Sunday."

He took a deep breath, then said in a rush, "Yes . . . all right. On Sunday."

"We'll arrange with Amelia for the marriage license, and next Thursday, on her afternoon off, you can be married."

"Oh, dear," he said, shaking his head. "It's . . . it's quite overwhelming." He began to write in the notebook. The sisters returned to their cooling lunch.

Half an hour later they were on their way back to the station, Henry's letter to Amelia tucked into Constance's bag.

"Do you think he'll come?" Prudence asked with a slightly worried frown.

"Yes. I don't think he'll let Amelia down once he's made a promise," Chastity responded. "Besides, he's not going to risk our coming back here and talking to his father. Con implied, in no uncertain terms, that we would if he didn't show up on Sunday."

"It was a bit heavy-handed," Constance admitted of her parting shot as they had left the café. "But I thought fear might give him more backbone." She added with a rueful grimace, "I just hope we're doing the right thing for Amelia by forcing this. Henry's such a broken reed."

"I don't think you need worry about that," Prudence said stoutly. "Amelia's strong enough for both of them. It isn't as if she doesn't know his weaknesses. She'll run their marriage and he'll do as he's told. If she can manage the kind of brat that young Pamela Graham seems to be, I'm sure managing Henry will be a walk in the park."

Constance nodded with a chuckle. "I'm sure you're right. I wonder if Max has a secretary."

"Why?"

"Well, if he doesn't, I'm sure he needs one. I would have said we have the perfect candidate in Henry Franklin."

"Is there no limit to your deviousness, Con?" Prudence demanded as they reached the station.

"I don't know. I haven't found one yet," her sister responded with a grin. "I'll just have to see if I can persuade him."

"So the husband works for Max, and the wife for his sister, and neither of their employers knows they're married?" Chastity shook her head.

"It'll only be like that until Amelia has to leave the Grahams because of her pregnancy," Constance said piously. "It's hardly a deception at all."

"Tell that to the marines!" scoffed Prudence.

Constance laughed. "Well, I can talk to him anyway."

They sat down on the station platform to wait for the train and Chastity sighed. "It's very tiring work, this Go-Between business. And tomorrow we have to take care of Anonymous and his requirements."

"No peace for the wicked," Constance agreed.

"No peace for those in straitened circumstances," Prudence amended.

"We'll wait behind the curtain at the back of the shop, Chas," Prudence said the following morning, glancing quickly behind the counter. "Mrs. Beedle says we'll hear everything that goes on from there if you and Anonymous conduct your business over by the biscuits." She gestured to a dusty corner where packets of biscuits lined the shelves amid jars of liquorice sticks and farthing candies.

"You've time for a nice cuppa, Miss Con. If the gentleman's not coming until eleven o'clock." A round woman with her white hair in a neat bun, her starched apron rustling with her step, emerged from behind the curtain of heavy drugget, the brass rings rattling on the rod as she pulled it aside. "I always have a cuppa about now. And a nice bite of lardy cake, just made this morning. We'll hear the bell if anyone comes in." She gestured to the bell over the shop door.

"Oh, I love lardy cake," Chastity said. "It'll give me heart for my lonely task."

"Chas, I'll do it if you're really uncomfortable," Prudence said quickly.

"No, of course I'm not. I was only joking." Chastity followed her sisters behind the counter and through the curtain into a small neat kitchen where a kettle whistled merrily on the range.

"Sit you down now." Mrs. Beedle gestured to the round table on which reposed a very sticky currant-studded sugary concoction. She set out cups, warmed the teapot, measured tea, and filled the pot. "There now." She set it on the table with a milk jug and sugar bowl. "You'll have a piece of lardy cake, Miss Con."

Constance hated lardy cake. It was far too greasy for her taste, but she asked for a tiny slice for politeness' sake. She could always slip it onto Chastity's plate when their hostess wasn't looking.

The bell rang in the shop and Mrs. Beedle twitched aside the curtains. "Oh, it's just Mr. Holbrook, come for his newspaper and his cigarettes." She bustled out, greeting the customer cheerily.

Chastity took a large bite of her cake and licked her fingers. "This is so sinful."

"It's terrible," Constance said, pouring tea. "I don't know how you can eat it."

"It's a very fine lardy cake," Prudence declared, licking her own fingers.

"Have mine." Constance put her slice on Chastity's plate and glanced at the clock. "It's nearly eleven. I wonder if he'll be early."

The doorbell jangled again. They all looked towards the curtain. A man's voice, lowered to a bare murmur, reached them from the shop. "It's him." Chastity wiped her fingers on her napkin, took a quick gulp of tea, and stood up, adjusting her thick black veil. "Can you see my face?"

"Barely."

"I'll try my French accent."

Mrs. Beedle emerged from the shop. "Gentleman's here for you, miss."

"Thank you." Chastity nodded at her sisters, braced her shoulders, and went into the shop. Her sisters moved as one away from the table to the curtain. Constance tweaked it aside a fraction so that the corner of the shop where the biscuits were arrayed was visible.

"You are looking for me, m'sieur." Chastity's exaggerated French accent caused her sisters momentary disarray as they struggled with involuntary laughter. She sounded like a French maid in a Feydeau farce, Constance thought.

"You are the Go-Between from *The Mayfair Lady*?" The man was in morning dress, carrying a top hat and a silver-knobbed cane. His hair was gray and rather sparse on top and he wore pince-nez perched on the end of a long, thin nose. A neat little moustache graced his upper lip. He looked undistinguished but perfectly respectable.

"I am its representative," Chastity said.

He took off his gloves and offered his hand with a bow. She gave him her own gloved hand and gestured to the corner of the shop. "Let us talk there, if you please. We will be quite private."

He looked around. "I had expected an office."

"We have our own reasons for wishing to remain anonymous also, m'sieur."

The sisters behind the curtain exchanged approving nods.

"But you can help me?"

"I will know that better, m'sieur, when you have answered some questions." They moved into full view of the watchers behind the curtain. "You must understand that the ladies who are interested in our service request only the most impeccable referrals."

"Yes . . . yes . . . of course. I would not expect otherwise," he said hastily. "Please do not misunderstand me, madam. I meant to cast no aspersions—"

Chastity held up a hand, cutting him off. "That is all right, m'sieur. We understand each other. Let us review your circumstances and the qualities you desire in a wife. You say that you prefer to live in the country?"

"Yes . . . yes. I have a small estate in Lincolnshire. Not a grand mansion, you understand, but more than comfortable. I am possessed of a comfortable fortune." The words seemed to be tumbling over themselves in his haste to get them out. Constance and Prudence knew what was happening. Chastity frequently had this effect on people. Her very posture and the softness of her voice, even in its present disguise, always implied sympathy and an empathetic ear.

"And you are looking for a wife." Chastity nodded her veiled head. "Someone with quiet tastes, no doubt."

"There is little excitement in our village, madam. Of course, my . . ." He coughed behind his hand. "My wife would entertain the vicar and his wife, the squire and his lady from the next village. We have little card parties, and occasional musical evenings. But in general we lead a quiet life."

"And as I understand it, you require neither beauty nor fortune?" Chastity managed to sound slightly incredulous.

"I require a companion, madam. From what I have read, beauty makes a poor companion. It is too much interested in itself. I abhor vanity in a woman."

"And just what have you been reading, my friend?" Constance inquired sotto voce behind the curtain. Prudence kicked her ankle.

"That does not concern the Go-Between, m'sieur," Chastity said with a neutrality that neither of her sisters could have managed. "We are only in the business of making introductions. It is for our clients to decide if they will suit."

"Quite so . . . quite so." He coughed again. "As for fortune, I believe I have more than sufficient to support a wife." He turned his hat around between his hands, brushing nervously at the brim. "I would not care for an extravagant wife, madam. My fortune is sufficient for a quiet and comfortable life, but we do not indulge in excessive luxury in Lincolnshire."

Chastity nodded, her expression hidden behind the muslin folds of her veil. "And do you have any other requirements, m'sieur?"

"I must have a wife of good family . . . who can hold her head up in our little society." He reddened, then continued hesitantly, "A lady not beyond the age of . . ." He cleared his throat. ". . . of child bearing would be an advantage. An heir, you understand?" He gave an embarrassed smile.

"I understand perfectly," Chastity said. "And it is possible that I have a recommendation for you, m'sieur. I can effect an introduction if you so desire."

"I would be most grateful, madam." He clasped his hands together in a fervent gesture.

"Next Wednesday you should come to the address on this card at three o'clock." Chastity handed him a visiting card. "It will be a simple At Home. The lady I would recommend to you will be wearing a white rose in her buttonhole. You will ask your hostess to make the introduction if you decide you wish to meet the lady."

He looked down at the engraved card and said doubtfully, "Manchester Square. This is Mayfair. Would a lady of retiring tastes frequent such an elegant address?"

"M'sieur, you want a lady of impeccable lineage. Where else would you expect to find such a one? Everyone's tastes vary, regardless of their position in society."

"Oh, bravo, Chas!" Prudence applauded silently.

"Of course . . . of course." Anonymous nodded vigorously, still examining the visiting card. "The ladies at this address . . . the Honorable Misses Duncan . . . they will know why I'm there? How should I introduce myself?"

"With your name, m'sieur. I assume if you decide to pursue this further you would see no difficulty in making your identity known at that point."

"No," he agreed. "No, it would not serve a useful purpose to remain anonymous if I'm to court a lady. But what of my hostesses? Are they associated with the Go-Between?"

"The Go-Between has nothing whatsoever to do with Ten Manchester Square," Chastity lied smoothly. "The At Home is merely a convenient way for you to meet a possible wife in secure and respectable circumstances. You will present your card to the butler in the usual way and when you are announced to your hostesses, you'll simply say that you are an acquaintance of Lord Jersey's who happened to mention that he would be at Manchester Square that afternoon and you wish to talk with him. Needless to say, he will not be there, so there will be no awkwardness, and since many people attend the ladies' weekly gatherings, no one will think anything of your dropping by. How you choose to pursue the introduction once it's made is no concern of the Go-Between."

"I see. It seems very complicated."

"It is simply in the interests of discretion, m'sieur. For both you and the lady." Chastity managed to sound rather stern.

He nodded hastily. "Yes . . . yes, of course. Most necessary." He turned the card over in his hands. "Is there a fee for this consultation, madam?"

"You have paid the fee for this morning's consultation, m'sieur," Chastity said. "However, if you wish to take up the recommendation and present yourself at Manchester Square, then there is an additional five guineas owing now. If you choose not to, then, of course, we have no outstanding charges."

"May I know something more of the lady before I decide?" He asked the question with all the hesitation of a schoolboy afraid of making a fool of himself.

It seemed to Chastity that for the extra five guineas he was entitled to some more information. "She is a lady of good family . . . her father is a clergyman. I believe her to be this side of thirty-five. Of pleasant appearance and demeanor but no fortune, and she has a devout temperament. I would imagine she would enjoy the company of the wives of squires and vicars."

"It seems you have understood my needs very well, madam. I assume that the lady is interested in acquiring a husband."

"I believe so. But the Go-Between can make no guarantees as to her response."

"I understand." He extracted five guineas from his coat pocket. "I will attend the At Home at Manchester Square on Wednesday, precisely at three o'clock."

"Perhaps you should make it closer to half past," Chastity said, tucking the note into her handbag. "People don't always arrive on the dot of three."

"Oh, no. Quite . . . quite. Ladies are often unpunctual." He stroked his neat, waxed moustache, an enthusiastic gleam now in his eye.

Chastity said, "I trust you will find that this recommendation suits your requirements, m'sieur." She extended her hand. "I bid you good morning."

He shook it eagerly. "Good morning, madam." He bowed and left the shop, something of the cock in his walk.

Chastity threw back her veil and breathed deeply, fanning her hot face with her hand.

"You were amazing, Chas." Prudence pulled back the curtain with a clanking of the brass rings.

"That accent is straight out of Feydeau," Constance said. "I can't think Anonymous believed in it for a minute."

"I don't think he cared," Chastity said. "Anyway, all we have to do now is ensure Millicent Hardcastle comes on Wednesday, and we have to contrive to put a white rose in her buttonhole. But I don't think I should be there, just in case he recognizes me."

"No," Prudence agreed. "Even without the veil and the phony French accent his suspicions might be aroused if he talks to you."

"I'll make myself scarce. But now I need more lardy cake."

"As much as you want, duckie." Constance held the curtain aside for her. "That was an astonishing performance. I don't know any Lord Jersey. Is there one?"

Chastity grinned and sat down at the kitchen table. "Not to my knowledge. That's why he won't be there on Wednesday. I was quite proud of myself. And actually I think Anonymous will really suit Millicent." She bit into the cake. "Mrs. Beedle, this is the best I've ever had."

Jenkins's sister beamed. "Eat it up, m'dear. Eat it up. It doesn't keep. I'll be back to minding the shop now. Take your time." She headed for the curtain, then said, "Oh, quite slipped my mind. There's another letter for you. I put it up behind the tea caddy." She pointed to the shelf and the brightly painted tin tea caddy.

Constance took down the letter. "Aunt Mabel or the Go-Between . . . any guesses?"

Her sisters shook their heads and waited expectantly. Constance slit the envelope and opened it. She read in silence, her expression rapt.

"Well?" Prudence demanded finally.

"It's a letter from a reader in Hampstead asking if we would publish the schedule of meetings for the WSPU," Constance said slowly. "She writes that it would be a great service for people who can't attend regularly or declare their affiliation openly." She looked up, eyes shining. "We're getting through! Finally we're reaching these women."

Her sisters rose and hugged her. It was Constance's triumph but it was also their mother's, and as such belonged to them all. They stood close together for a minute, silent with their own memories. Such moments still happened often between them and they had learned to live with the knowledge of loss and take comfort from the shared memories.

When they moved apart, Chastity dashed a hand across her eyes and asked, "So, what now? These five guineas are burning a hole in my pocket. How about we treat ourselves to lunch?"

"Something modest," Prudence said. "If we spend it as soon as we get it we're never going to be solvent."

"Modest, it is," declared Constance. "And afterwards we'll have time before the At Home to scoop up little Hester and take her to visit her future mother-in-law, then bring her to the At Home, where David is bound to be in attendance. That should be good eventually for a substantial donation to the fund for indigent spinsters."

Chapter 12

A secretary could only add to your consequence," Constance said from her supine position on a blanket on the lush green riverbank just below Windsor Castle.

"And why would my consequence need such an addition?" Max inquired, looking down at her with a quizzical gleam in his eye. "I'm quite satisfied with it as it is."

"Oh, but you're bound to be a Cabinet Minister soon," she said. "And there must be so many details of your life that need to be arranged. Appointments, topics for speeches. Why, you might even want someone to write speeches for you. And I'm sure you could use the help of someone to look things up for you . . . references, legal and parliamentary precedents. Those sorts of things."

"What are you up to?" he demanded, reaching to refill their glasses from the champagne bottle on the grass beside him.

"Why would you think I was up to anything?"

"Oh, Constance! Don't treat me like an idiot."

She sat up. One really couldn't play games with Max Ensor. She said with an air of open frankness, "There's a man I'd like to help. He wants to marry an acquaintance of mine but he needs to get regular employment if he's to support a wife and family. He's very able at office work, although his passion is music. He's a very talented pianist but he can't make enough teaching piano. So I thought perhaps you might try him out."

"Very well. Send him to see me."

"You'll see him . . . just like that?" She couldn't help her astonishment.

"Why not? Isn't that what you wanted?"

"Well, yes, but I thought I'd have to work on you a lot harder."

"Oh, so that's what lies behind the charming, compliant, sweet-tempered façade I've been treated to all morning," he declared. "I should have known. You were just buttering me up. I would never have expected it of you . . . you of all women!"

Constance felt her cheeks warm at this well-justified accusation. "I have to use what tactics are available to me," she said defensively. "I wasn't to know you would be so compliant yourself. You haven't exactly demonstrated that tendency in the past."

"Neither, my dear, have you."

The arid observation brought a rueful smile to her lips. "True enough. We're not the most peaceable pair, are we? I admit I had a reason for trying to make sure we didn't have any differences of opinion to spoil the mood. But it was a lovely picnic lunch and I enjoyed both it and your company regardless of ulterior motive."

He was silent for a minute, then said, "You didn't seem too pleased to see me the other morning."

"You took me by surprise," she said. "I had things on my mind and you took me by surprise."

"I'll know better another time," he said as dryly as before. He was quite certain that there was more to it.

She hesitated, wondering if this was the right moment to move things onto a more confiding level. If she was to influence his opinions they needed to be a lot more intimate and trusting with each other. Lust alone wouldn't do it. She had no idea whether they could move their affair into something meaningful, let alone what would happen if they did, but the possibility intrigued her. Of course, if he had no intention of taking things to a deeper level, and he had given no indication that he did, then if she pushed now it might drive him away.

The silence had gone on too long and she made up her mind. Do or die. "I was . . . am . . . afraid that things are moving too fast. I know I was responsible for what happened at Romsey Manor, but when we got back to London I started to think that we don't really know each other at all. I enjoy your company." She gave a tiny little laugh that almost sounded embarrassed. "I'm in lust with you. But in the cold light of day that's not enough."

Max was taken aback. He had not expected such a frank invitation, or was it a challenge, to explore the possibilities of a deeper relationship. At least not so soon. In truth, he hadn't thought her interested in anything more than a passionate, lighthearted affair, and it hadn't occurred to him to consider whether he was interested in more than that either. Was she saying now that if he turned down this invitation—or challenge—then their present involvement was at an end? He certainly wasn't ready for that to happen.

"Then perhaps we should start to get to know each other," he said in a considering tone. "Perhaps we have been putting the cart before the horse." He turned sideways on the grass to look at her, his blue eyes resting intently on her face. "Tell me about the most important thing in your life. Apart from your family, I mean. What stirs you, Constance? What makes your blood run hot?"

She gave another little laugh. "You mean apart from having sex with you?"

"Be serious," he chided. "You were the one who started this conversation."

"Women's suffrage," she said, her fingers tightening around the stem of her glass at the familiar surge of energetic fervor the topic always brought her. "I am passionate about women's suffrage. About equal rights for women. It is the driving force of my existence."

"I knew your views on the subject," he said. "You don't hide them. But is it really *that* important to you? The driving force of your existence?"

"Absolutely," she said, returning his intent gaze. "Without exaggeration."

He was once more taken aback. How could anyone describe a single political issue as the driving force of her existence? It was the description of a fanatic. "Then you're a member of the WSPU?"

"Of course," she said. "But I don't broadcast it. It would upset my father. The time will come to be open about my affiliation, but not yet."

"I see."

She continued to look at him with the same intensity, as if she would read behind the seemingly placid façade of his countenance. "You think a member of the Union makes an uncomfortable bedfellow, Max?" There was a hint of mockery in her voice. "Better to know that now rather than later."

"You are always putting words into my mouth, Constance," he snapped. "Give me a chance to respond in my own way."

"I'm sorry," she said swiftly. "It's a terrible habit I have, I know."

He almost laughed. "Do you really know it?"

"Yes. I jump too quickly. I've been told it many times."

"By whom?" He watched her now, his gaze slightly softened as he saw the flash of distress cross her eyes.

"My mother . . . Douglas . . . my sisters. All people I love . . . loved." She shrugged. "I don't seem to have learned the lesson, though."

"No," he agreed. "But I think that's enough self-flagellation for one day. And to answer your question, if that's what it was, I don't see the point of women's suffrage, as I've said before. But I'm perfectly happy to tolerate an opposing viewpoint."

"Tolerate!" Constance exclaimed. "That is so patronizing, Max."

He thought for a minute, then said, "My turn to apologize."

Constance accepted this in silence. Then she said, "If you would come to a meeting, you might see the point. You could meet Emmeline Pankhurst. At least open your mind."

It would also give him the opportunity to see the organization from the inside, he reflected. The closer he got to its inner workings, the more he would discover.

"You could also tell us what the government is doing, or thinking," she continued into his silence. "You wouldn't be betraying any secrets. You told me that they were at least looking into the issue of whether women tax and ratepayers should qualify. I don't suppose that's a government secret."

What a conniving creature she is, he thought with a flicker of amusement. She had every intention of milking him for useful information. Which put them both squarely on the court on opposing sides of the net. One of them was going to be useful to the other. It would be interesting to see which one served first.

"I can tell you nothing that the newspapers don't report every day," he said with an easy shrug. "But I will come to a meeting with you."

"There's a meeting at Kensington Town Hall at seven o'clock the day after tomorrow. Could you make that?"

"Possibly." He cast her another sidelong glance. "Are there any demonstrations planned?"

Constance shook her head. "It's just a meeting," she said. "I'll meet you on the steps, if you like."

"I assume I'll need someone to vouch for me."

"Not necessarily, but we do keep an eye on who attends. We can't be too careful, there's so much hostility to the cause."

"Ah." He nodded, and she frowned slightly, wondering why she felt a sudden stir of unease, as if something wasn't quite right. She looked over at him, but he seemed his usual perfectly relaxed self.

"And after the meeting you may dine with me," he said.

It was a statement, not an invitation. "If that's the bargain," she responded without expression.

"Oh, dear." He shook his head. "Let me try that again. Miss Duncan, porcupine though you are, will you do me the honor of dining with me after the meeting?"

"I should be delighted, Mr. Ensor, thank you. It will give us the opportunity to discuss your reactions and deepen your understanding of the issues." She offered him a bland smile, but beneath he could detect a hint of triumph. She was convinced she had had the last word. And she was right, he concluded. For the moment anyway.

"The pleasure will be all mine, ma'am."

Time to back off, Constance decided. She was sufficiently wary of Max's ability to bite back not to belabor the victory. "I should get back," she said, stretching languidly. "That was such a clever picnic. Those lobster sandwiches were wonderful. And those baby veal and ham pies . . . I adore them. Did Letitia's cook prepare it for you?"

"Actually, the dining room at the House of Commons," he said, tipping the remains of the champagne into their glasses. "The chef is very good. I hope you'll dine there with me one evening."

"I should love to," Constance said with a gracious smile. She drained her champagne and gave him her glass as he packed the remains of their picnic away in the hamper.

She got to her feet and shook out her cream muslin skirt. "I shouldn't have worn this, it's so pale it shows every stain." She peered over her shoulder to check the back. "Are there any grass stains?"

Max examined her back view with considerable interest. He smoothed out the folds, patted them back into place. "Not that I can see."

"And you certainly took a good look."

"What did you expect?"

She made no reply, concentrating instead on tying the wide green ribbons of her straw boater in a bow beneath her chin.

Max hoisted the picnic basket over one arm and gave her his other and they walked up the bank to where his motorcar was parked on the narrow lane.

"What kind of motorcar is this?" Constance asked as she walked around the shiny dark green vehicle while Max stowed the wicker hamper in the space beneath the front passenger seat.

"A Darracq. They make them in Paris."

"Is it very expensive?" She ran a hand over the gleaming bulbs of the two massive headlights. It looked enormously expensive.

"Yes," he said succinctly.

"How reliable are they in general?" She continued her tactile exploration of the vehicle. It was a beautiful thing.

"Not very," he said, struggling to fit the hamper in the tiny space. "But it's the price you pay. It adds to the excitement."

"So they often break down in inconvenient places?"

"Oh, they always choose the most inconvenient places to break down." He straightened and brushed off his hands. "As I say, it's the price you pay for vanity."

"For showing off," she accused with a grin.

"If you insist."

"Actually, I can't say I blame you. It's very beautiful." Constance stepped onto the running board and looked at the chrome-and-brass interior, inhaling the rich smell of leather. "So, what makes them break down? That lever over there?" She pointed to the gear shift.

"No, the gears are generally reliable enough, so long as you treat them properly. It's the engine and the fuel feed usually. Are you getting in?"

"Oh, yes, of course. Sorry." She jumped off the running board so that he could open the door for her. "I could have climbed over that. It's barely a door at all."

"True enough." He closed the door after her and went around the front to crank the engine. It fired on the third turn, he stowed the crank and then swung a long leg over the door on the driver's side and slid into his seat behind the wheel.

"So, what could cause a problem in the engine or the fuel feed?" Constance asked as the car jumped forward on the dirt lane.

"The wrong fuel mixture. A loose wire. Any number of things." He turned the car in the narrow lane.

"Could one make that happen?" she inquired.

Max finally realized that there was some significance to this apparently artless interest in the workings of the motorcar. He looked over at her. "Be more specific."

"Well, if for instance one wanted a car to break down at a certain point a long way from convenient assistance, is there any way to do that?"

"Am I being involved in some nefarious scheme here?"

"It's my father. He tells us he's taking delivery of a new Cadillac tomorrow afternoon. But we can't let him keep it," she said simply. "He has very little patience and if it causes him the slightest inconvenience he'll give up on it in disgust. We have to find a way to fix the engine so that happens."

"Dear God!" he exclaimed, hooting his horn at a cow that was wandering slowly across his path. The animal kicked up its heels at the strident sound and ran for the open field across the lane. "You and your sisters are planning to sabotage your father's new car?"

"In the interest of his safety, yes," Constance said with a sweetly innocent smile. "Better a damaged car and a live parent than the reverse."

"And you want me to help you?" He was incredulous, and yet it seemed entirely in keeping with what he had learned about the Honorable Misses Duncan since they'd first swum into his ken.

"If you wouldn't mind. It is in a very good cause. Life and death, really. We'd do it ourselves but we don't know much about engines. As yet," she added.

"As yet," he muttered. "Perhaps you'd like to drive us home."

"Oh, I'd love to. May I?" Constance turned sideways in her seat, her eyes shining. "I've been watching you, and it doesn't look that difficult."

It wasn't once you'd mastered the gears, Max admitted to himself. But he wasn't about to admit that to Constance. "I don't think it's something that would come easily to women," he stated. "They're not mechanically minded and the gear changes are quite complex."

Constance gave a crow of laughter. "Why did I expect you to say anything different? Just wait and see, Mr. Ensor. Women will be driving these things before you know it."

"And in the meantime, on your own admission, you don't know much about engines," he reminded her. He wasn't prepared to contest her statement, since he was beginning to get the suspicion that if society was peopled by women like Constance Duncan and her sisters, there would be women behind every steering wheel in the country.

"No," she agreed. "Which is why I am so humbly asking for your help."

"And how am I supposed to help?" He kicked himself for asking the question. It was only going to lead him into trouble.

"We thought that after Father takes delivery and after his first run, then when he stables it, or whatever it is you do with motorcars in the mews, we could fiddle with it so that when he next took it out it would be unreliable."

"And when is this operation to take place?"

"Tomorrow night." She looked across at him. "Are you free tomorrow night?"

"For sabotage?"

"That's harsh."

"But true."

"Yes," she agreed. "He'll be so thrilled with the motor after his first run that he'll want to take it out the next day, and we'd like it to break down on him just far enough from the city for it to be incredibly inconvenient. He won't want to drive it after dark the first day, so once he's stabled it tomorrow evening we could do what's necessary. In fact," she added with growing enthusiasm, "you don't need to do anything yourself. Just tell us what to do. You won't be involved in any way."

"No, just an accessory after the fact."

"Don't worry, we won't hand you over to the authorities."

"And I won't worry about tarnishing my spotless reputation as a

Member of Parliament." He raised his eyebrows in sardonic punctuation.

"Will you help?" Her voice was suddenly serious. "Just tell us what to do."

"For God's sake, Constance, isn't there a simpler way to achieve your object?" he demanded, fighting the unnerving sensation of slipping fast down an icy slope. "Why do you have to come up with such a devious scheme?"

"Believe it or not, it is the simplest way," she said. "Father has to decide for himself to give up the idea, he won't listen to anyone else." She turned sideways on her seat and laid a hand on his arm. "We really need you to help. There's no one else we can ask."

"Oh, God help me," he muttered. "All right, I'll come round and I'll tell you what to do." Even as the words emerged, Max couldn't believe what he was saying. How could he possibly be agreeing to help in such an addled scheme? He should surely be showing male solidarity with Lord Duncan rather than with the man's eccentric daughters. He looked at Constance in exasperation and found something in the glow of her dark green eyes that answered his question. When she wanted to be, Constance Duncan was irresistibly bewitching. No man stood a chance.

"Thank you," she said with a radiant smile. "Will you come round at about ten o'clock tomorrow night, then? Father will be at his club."

"I can't promise a time," he said. "It depends how late the House sits."

"Yes, of course," she said amenably. "Whenever it's convenient . . . we'll just wait up for you." She busied herself retying the ribbons of her hat more securely against the rush of wind as Max increased his speed.

"By the way, what's the name of this potential secretary you're sending me?"

"Henry Franklin. Should he come to the House of Commons next Monday morning?"

He adroitly swung the wheel to avoid a stray dog that had run barking into the road at the sight of the motorcar, and then said, "It would be simpler to send him to my house. I meant to tell you . . . I've found a suitable house in Westminster. I signed the lease yesterday."

"Oh, that's splendid. Does that mean we might—" She bit off the rest of the sentence in some confusion. Here she'd been telling herself to pedal slowly and now suddenly she was back in the Tour de France.

"It certainly means we could," he said solemnly. "Should you decide to speed things up a little again."

Constance bit her lip. "I haven't. It just slipped out. I told you I'm in lust with you. But I'm serious about learning things about each other."

Max took his eyes from the road for a minute to look at her. There was nothing playful about her at the moment; in fact, he thought she looked somewhat confused. "Let me return the compliment," he said, and she gave him a quick and rather grateful smile.

"I don't see why we can't gratify lust and a thirst for knowledge at the same time," he suggested. His wind-tossed hair shone in the sun, and the blue of his eyes seemed even more intense than usual as they rested on her countenance. The sight of him made her knees go weak again.

She cleared her throat. "About this house . . . ?"

"It's furnished. I have the key." He patted his breast pocket.

"That's convenient. I should be interested in looking at it."

"That could be arranged."

* * *

"Where were you all day?" Prudence asked as Constance came into her bedroom dressed for dinner.

"Having a picnic along the river at Windsor," her sister replied. "I came to borrow your topaz earrings. They go so well with this dress."

"In the box." Prudence gestured to the jewel box on her dresser. "What about the rest of the day?"

"Max has taken a lease on a house in Westminster."

"Oh. Objectivity went by the board again, did it?"

"Maybe." Constance sifted through the box and selected the earrings. "Honestly, I don't know, Prue. I don't know whether I'm on my head or my heels. I've never felt like this before."

"Not even with Douglas?" Prue turned on the dresser stool to give her sister her full attention. It was unlike Constance to express this kind of confusion.

Constance shook her head, tossing the earrings from hand to hand. "No, it was very straightforward with Douglas. I knew I loved him and he loved me. There was nothing . . . nothing oppositional about our relationship. I didn't feel the need to best him all the time. And yet with Max it's as if there's an edge to almost everything we say. I feel I can't let myself be vulnerable . . . let my guard down. And yet he's never done anything to justify that feeling. Only his Neanderthal attitudes about women."

She shrugged, and fastened the topaz earrings. "Normally I just despise men who hold those views, but it's not possible to despise Max."

"No," agreed Prudence with conviction. "One could loathe him, but one certainly couldn't despise him."

"And I don't loathe him," Constance said with a resigned smile. "Quite the opposite. It's very confusing, Prue."

"I can believe it."

"But on a more positive note," Constance continued, "I did get Max to agree to see Henry. On Monday at his house."

"Oh, wonderful." Prudence turned back to the mirror and took up her comb again. "Amelia sent a note to say that she's arranged for the license, and the wedding is scheduled for next Thursday afternoon at four o'clock at the registry office in Caxton Hall. We're to be witnesses."

"Always assuming Henry plucks up the courage to get himself here," Constance said a touch gloomily. "The farther I'm away from him, the more pessimistic I get."

"Don't be. Chas is confident he'll come. She's never wrong."

"You have a point. Where is she tonight?"

"Dining with David and Hester at Lady Winthrop's."

"Ah." Constance raised an eyebrow. "Matters move along, then."

"So it would seem," her sister agreed.

"I also persuaded Max to help us with the motor business," Constance said, a gleam now in her eye. "Tomorrow night."

"I don't believe it," her sister declared. "He's so straitlaced, how did you ever persuade him to lend himself to such a trick?"

"It was surprisingly easy, actually. He tried to resist, but somehow . . ." She gave a blasé shrug. "He just couldn't."

"You are so wicked!"

"I'm in good company, sister dear. As I recall, this was Chas's idea."

Prudence acknowledged this with a resigned chuckle and rose from the dresser stool. "Are you ready to go down? Lord Barclay is dining with us."

"Oh, God help us!" Constance exclaimed. "And I was having such a satisfactory day."

Chapter 13

"Is that the doorbell?" Chastity sprang to her feet the following evening and ran to the parlor door.

Constance glanced at the clock. It was just ten-thirty. "It must be Max." She followed her sister out onto the landing, Prudence at her heels. "Jenkins, is it Mr. Ensor?"

"It is indeed." Max appeared in the dim light of the hall and put one foot on the bottom stair, looking up at them as they clustered at the top of the stairs. "Did I keep you up?"

"No, no, of course not," Constance said. "Come upstairs to the parlor. Jenkins will bring you a whisky if you'd like. Otherwise we have cognac up here."

"Or hot chocolate," Chastity called cheerfully.

"Whisky, thank you, Jenkins," Max said, and came up the stairs. "Your father's out of the way?"

"Yes. He's been gone all evening. Jenkins has the keys to the motorcar."

Max's eyebrows lifted. "Your butler knows about this?"

"Oh, yes, Jenkins knows everything about this family. Every dirty little secret we have," Prudence declared. "He would help us himself but he doesn't know anything about motors."

Max's eyebrows remained uplifted.

"You look very clandestine," Constance said approvingly. "Very secretive with that long black cloak. You'll just blend into the shadows."

"I thought I had better dress the part." He assumed she had no secrets from her sisters and gave her an unceremonious kiss. Their lovemaking the previous afternoon had been of a rough-and-ready nature, a wild tumble in the deserted house, and he was somehow still in the same frame of mind. She was dressed simply but with customary elegance, in an evening gown of lavender crepe, and he had an urge to rumple her, to pull the pins from her hair, to roll her on the carpet and kiss her senseless. It was not his usual style at all and he found this strange aberration amusing, although puzzling. He put it down to the disreputable if not downright illegal character of the evening's activity.

After an instant of surprise at the salute, Constance offered no resistance to the kiss, and a gleam showed in her eyes, as if she could read his mind and was indulging her own memories.

Her sisters exchanged a glance and moved farther into the room, turning their backs to the doorway. Jenkins came up the stairs with a tray bearing the decanter of whisky and a glass. Without haste, Max raised his head and straightened, moving away from Constance into the parlor. The smile lingered on his mouth and in his eyes, however.

"Did you bring anything to do this with?" Chastity asked, noting his empty hands and clearly empty pockets.

"I don't need anything. Constance said the motor was a Cadillac . . . Oh, thank you, Jenkins." He took the proffered glass.

"It is, but what's the significance of that?" Constance asked.

"I'll show you when we look at the motor. You need to understand that while I hate to disappoint you, I have no intention of doing damage to that motorcar. It's far too valuable a machine."

"I quite agree with you, sir." Jenkins paused on his way to the door.

"Oh, Jenkins, how could you?" Prudence said. "You know how things stand."

"Yes, I do, Miss Prue, but if there's a way to persuade his lordship to give up the motor without vandalizing the vehicle, then I think we should consider it."

"Well, of course we don't want to do wanton damage," Constance said. "What *are* we going to do, then, Max?"

"A little trick with the fuel tank," he said, taking a sip of whisky and nodding his appreciation. "Lord Duncan knows his single malts."

"Our father's tastes are as perfect as they are expensive," Prudence declared. "Only the best of anything comes into this house."

Max wondered at the caustic undertone to the comment, but he didn't pursue it. He'd already noticed that something was amiss between Lord Duncan and his daughters, but he didn't feel inclined to pry. Maybe as he got to know them better it would come out. Not that he wasn't already well on the way to getting to know them all far too closely for comfort, he reflected dryly. Engaging with them in an act of sabotage at dead of night was as intimate a deed of friendship as he could imagine. It was certainly as close as he wanted to get to the nefarious heart of the Duncan trio. He had the feeling there was very little they wouldn't do if they saw a need, and he doubted they'd have any scruples as to the tools they used to go about it. He had certainly been shamelessly co-opted.

He glanced across the room to where Constance sat perched on the wide arm of a sofa, so casual, so elegant, yet so wonderfully, wildly sensual when the mood took her, and he understood with absolute clarity why he had allowed himself to be so co-opted.

He set down his empty glass. "This is a rather messy operation, and since I have no intention of dirtying my own hands, I'm wondering if you three shouldn't change into something a little less delicate."

"Oh, we can do that." Chastity was already heading for the door. "We'll only be a few minutes."

"How messy?" asked Constance warily. She had the feeling that Max was rather relishing the prospect of standing aside in pristine elegance while they got themselves covered in whatever grease and mess went into a motorcar's engine.

"Very," he said with a glimmer in his eye that told her she had been right. "And smelly too." And now he couldn't help a grin of satisfaction.

Reprisal time, Constance thought with reluctant acceptance. She followed her sisters to the door. "We'll be back in a minute."

Max poured himself another drink and idly glanced around the room. It was a pleasant, informal parlor, with an endearing shabbiness. He wandered over to the secretaire and his eye fell on a copy of *The Mayfair Lady*. It was hardly surprising to find the broadsheet here since he knew they read it. He turned aside, and then spun back. Something had caught his eye. Something very odd. He picked up the sheet and stared at the date. *Monday, July 31st.* But that was two weeks hence. What were they doing with an advance edition?

But of course it was obvious. They were responsible for it. His earlier hunch had been right.

He heard voices in the corridor and dropped the sheet on the desk and walked swiftly to the window. When the door opened he was innocently looking down onto the dark garden, his recharged glass in his hand.

Constance immediately sensed something different about him. A sudden tension between his shoulders, the set of his head. He turned from the window and said, "What a pleasant room this is."

"Yes, it was our mother's favorite room, very much her own. We haven't changed anything since her death." Constance's eyes darted around the room, fell upon the secretaire and the broadsheet lying in full view. How could they have been so damnably careless? *Had he seen it? Should she ask him, mention it casually, and see how he responded?*

It was a ridiculous dilemma. She didn't want to draw his attention to something he might not have remarked. Even if he had seen it he might not have noticed the significance of the date. Current issues were to be found everywhere, so finding one here was not remarkable. But if he had seen it and noticed that it was not the current issue, then their secret could be broadcast throughout Mayfair by tomorrow evening if he chose to betray it. He wouldn't do that, of course. At least not without talking to her first. She was sure of it. *Wasn't she?*

She walked casually to the secretaire and as casually tidied up the papers on the top. Her gaze flicked across to him but he didn't seem to be aware of what she was doing. Inconclusive, she decided, but there was no time to worry about it at the moment.

"So, are we suitably protected for this dirty work?" Chastity asked cheerfully. "We're wearing our oldest clothes."

Max regarded them with his head cocked as he considered this. They were swathed so completely in heavy cotton aprons that he couldn't see what they wore beneath.

"We have gloves too." Prudence showed him the thick cotton gloves. "They're what the housemaid uses to clean the grates."

"You'll do," he said. "Let's get on with it."

Constance led the way downstairs. They took another flight of stairs down into the vast basement kitchen. Three oil lamps stood on the massive deal table.

"There's no gas light in the mews, so we'll have to take oil lamps. Jenkins filled them and trimmed the wicks for us," Constance explained. She asked doubtfully, "Are you sure we don't need anything? A knife or something?"

"I already told you, you're not going to do any damage . . . not so much as a scratch on the paintwork," he said, following them out into the small courtyard behind the kitchen. He thought it was like following a trio of Florence Nightingales as they rustled along in their aprons, holding their lamps high. Three very subversive ladies with lamps. How had he possibly found himself in this absurd position?

They crossed the courtyard and went through a gate into the mews. It was in darkness, no lights showing from the coachman's accommodation above the stable block. The smell of hay, horseflesh, and manure was strong in the air and a horse whinnied from the stable as they crossed the cobbles.

"It's in here," Prudence whispered, turning a key in a double door in the building next to the stable. The doors creaked open and they went in, holding their lamps high. The light fell on a gleaming vehicle, all chrome and brass, and the smell of new leather was stronger even than the stable smell.

"Beautiful," Max said involuntarily. He ran a hand over the motor's shining hood. "These Cadillacs are magnificent . . . an ideal model for our purposes," he added.

"Give me a horse anyday," Chastity declared, setting her lamp on an upturned barrel. "Do we need the keys? Con has them."

Max shook his head. "We don't need to start it." He walked around to the back of the car and bent to look underneath. "Good, just as I thought. Cadillacs usually have a tap, so we don't need to siphon." He stood up. "Now, one of you find a bucket. Constance, feel under here." Constance knelt on the stone floor and reached a hand under the car. "Just to your left, there's a tap. Can you find it?"

"Yes, it's here." Her fingers closed over the tap.

"All right. Keep your hand there. Prudence, bring the bucket and position it beneath the tap. That's right. Now, Constance, open the tap. Let the spirit trickle out slowly . . . very slowly, so you can control the flow. No . . . that's too fast. Close it off again."

"It would be so much easier if you would do this," she said, gritting her teeth with concentration. Her voice was muffled, her fingers cramping from the strain, her shoulders tight with the awkward position. "You know what you're doing."

"Oh, no. This is your show. My hands are going to stay clean." As if in emphasis, he drove them into his coat pockets. "Chastity, you'll need several more buckets."

"I'll get them from the tack room."

"What is this stuff, anyway?" Prudence asked, wrinkling her nose as she straightened. She took off her glasses, which had misted over, and peered at him myopically in the shadowed garage.

"Fuel. Motors have to run on something, or didn't you know that?"

"There's no need to sound so patronizing," Prudence said, replacing her glasses. "As it happens, I'm with Chastity when it comes to a preferred method of travel." She bent again to the bucket. "Can you manage, Con?"

"I think so. I think I've mastered the flow now . . . if I keep the tap at half cock."

"All right, that's enough. You don't want to drain it," Max instructed.

Constance swiftly closed the tap. She stood up, wiping her reeking hands on her apron with a grimace of distaste. "I think I get the point of all this. How much have we left in?"

"Enough for about two miles, I would guess. A motorcar as big and heavy as this won't do more than ten miles to the gallon. But there'll be spare cans stowed at the back for refueling. Probably in a little compartment behind the jump seat."

Constance found the compartment. "There are three in here."

"Take 'em out."

She lifted them out with a grunt of effort. They seemed to weigh a ton. She shot Max a resentful glare, which he either didn't notice or chose to ignore.

"Now pour about half of each one into the spare buckets. But be very careful. It's dangerous stuff, very volatile . . . it doesn't take much to ignite it."

"How comforting," Constance murmured. "I suppose you wouldn't consider lifting this damned can yourself?" She heaved the first one up onto her hip.

"Absolutely not. Aren't women supposed to be a match for men in everything?"

"There are some physical facts you can't get around," she said with a distinct snap. "And being sardonic isn't helping matters."

"My apologies." He tried to hide a grin but failed.

"Let me help." Prudence came to her sister's aid, supporting the can as Constance tilted it into the bucket.

"Chastity, can you find some lamp oil from somewhere?" Max inquired.

"How much?"

"As much as you can."

"I'll look in the scullery. I believe there's a barrel of it stored there." Chastity started for the door, then paused, her hand on the latch. "I'm sure I can manage to roll it across the kitchen courtyard without assistance."

There was an instant's expectant pause but Max remained silent, nonchalantly leaning against the stone wall, hands still firmly inactive in his pockets.

"I'll help you, Chas." Prudence released her supporting hand on the fuel can as Constance took its now reduced weight, and went off with her sister.

Constance set down the half-empty can, unscrewed the top on the second one, and hefted it onto her hip. She didn't look at Max.

He couldn't maintain the charade as he watched her struggles in the flickering lamplight. "Here, let me do it."

"I can manage, thank you," she said with icy dignity. "You wouldn't want to spoil your clothes. Or dirty those so-perfect hands. Why, you might even break a fingernail."

"Give that to me." He stepped forward and laid hold of the can. For a moment she resisted, then realized that they were both going to end up drenched in this foul-smelling spirit if they wrestled over its possession.

She relinquished it, controlling a sigh of relief, and stepped back, wiping her hands again on her apron.

"So, the idea is for my father to run out of fuel so that the car will strand him somewhere?"

"That is the idea." He set down the half-emptied can and unscrewed the top on the third one.

"But won't he notice that these are only half-empty?" Constance was fascinated now.

"They won't be. We're going to mix the spirit with lamp oil." He set down the third can and casually wiped his hands on Constance's apron. "Is there a tap in the yard?"

"By the horse trough."

She followed him out into the moonlit yard and stood back while he rinsed his hands at the tap and dried them on his handkerchief. She followed suit at the tap. "What will happen then?"

"You have to get the mix of spirit and lamp oil exactly right for the engine to run smoothly. We're not going to worry about the correct proportions, so the motor will run for a little once the tank's been replenished from the spare cans and then sputter and die. It won't come to any harm, but it will be very inconvenient for the driver."

"You mean that every time he thinks he's got it going again, it'll stop?" she said with an awed nod. "Oh, that is very clever. It will drive him mad. I think I may have underestimated you, Mr. Ensor."

"Now, that would be unwise." He looked at her as she stood in the shadowy silver light of the moon, apron-wrapped, disheveled, her hair coming loose from its pins, a streak of dirt smeared across her cheek, a film of sweat on her forehead. "I ceased to underestimate *you*, Miss Duncan, somewhere around the time you were climbing over stiles."

She smiled slowly, brushing a loose strand of hair from her forehead with the back of a damp hand. "And has anything else occurred to confirm that opinion, Max?"

Would he say anything about The Mayfair Lady? *Drop just a hint that would tell her whether he'd seen the edition in the parlor?*

The sound of a barrel rolling across the cobbles stilled any response he might have made. Chastity and Prudence rolled the wooden barrel of lamp oil towards the open garage doors. Max licked the corner of his handkerchief and wiped the smear of dirt from Constance's cheek before following her sisters into the garage.

Thoughtfully, Constance followed. Tomorrow there was the WSPU meeting, and afterwards they were to have dinner. There would be opportunities to probe a little then. But she decided she wouldn't mention the matter to her sisters, not until she had some idea of whether they had cause for concern.

"I hope we didn't go too far," Chastity said in Fortnum and Mason the following afternoon. "He went out in that motor at eleven o'clock this morning and he wasn't home when we left." She took a forkful of the meringue on her plate, neatly scooping up escaping crème chantilly as she bore the morsel to her lips.

"In the company of the earl of Barclay," Prudence reminded her, re-filling her teacup. "I'd worry more if he was alone."

"I think the company of Barclay is worse than no company at all," Constance stated, setting down her pen and raising her head from the sheet of paper on the table in front of her. "I was having a rather inter-esting conversation with Dolly Hennesy this morning. I bumped into her at the hairdresser's."

"Gossip, Con?" Prudence took an almond slice from the plate on the table. She raised her eyebrows, her light green eyes teasing. "I thought you didn't have time for it."

"I don't," her sister replied, sipping her tea, unperturbed by the teas-ing. "But this is germane gossip. Barclay, it seems, is suspected of philan-dering."

Prudence no longer looked amused. "That's hardly unusual," she said grimly, driving her fork into the cake. "Father's not exactly pure as the driven snow."

"But I don't believe our father goes around fathering offspring on women in his employ."

Prudence set down her fork and pursed her mouth in a silent whistle. "No," she agreed. "That he would not do. What are you saying?"

"That the earl of Barclay is well known for dabbling in such brooks," Constance declared. "At least two women, from what I heard." She leaned forward, her voice dropping. "I also hear that he has something of a reputation in his clubs for not being . . . how shall I put it? Not be-ing exactly prompt about settling his gambling debts."

"I know he's loathsome," Chastity said, her own eyes wide at this rev-elation. "But surely not even Barclay would do something so . . . so un-gentlemanly," she finished for want of a better description. A failure to settle gambling debts in a timely fashion was probably the most heinous social crime.

"If it's true why hasn't he been blackballed?" Prudence asked, going straight to the heart of the matter.

Constance shrugged. "It seems that no one is prepared to come out and accuse him to his face."

"But why ever not?" Chastity picked up a neglected hazelnut with delicate fingers. She gazed intently at Constance as she popped the nut between her lips.

"I was thinking a discreetly anonymous hint at the possibility of a scandal in the pages of *The Mayfair Lady* might elicit an answer," Constance said with a distinctly evil smile. "I don't really care a fig about the gambling debts but I cannot abide men who won't honor their responsibilities to women. We brought Henry Franklin up to the mark, why not Barclay? Mother would approve."

Prudence nodded with a degree of satisfaction. "That is certainly true." She wiped her mouth on her napkin and frowned for a moment in thought. "And he couldn't possibly get back at us," she said slowly. "We're anonymous. It's just an anonymous broadsheet."

Constance hesitated, wondering whether perhaps she should confide her anxieties about what Max might have seen the previous evening.

"Something bothering you, Con?" Chastity, as usual, caught the flicker of uncertainty on her sister's face.

"No," Constance said definitely. "I'm trying to think how to write an obliquely accusatory piece. Have another meringue . . . those coffee ones look delicious."

"Not that you would sully your delicate taste buds to try one," Chastity observed, helping herself to the pale golden meringue.

"My pleasure is of the vicarious variety." Constance glanced at the clock at the end of the tearoom. "I have to get to Kensington Town Hall by six o'clock, to meet with Emmeline before the meeting itself starts."

"And you have to dress for dinner with Max afterwards," Prudence said. "We should get going."

"Well, take a look at this." Constance passed across the paper she'd been writing on. "I was roughing out the piece on Barclay. It's crude at the moment, but we have time to refine it." She gestured to the waitress for the bill.

Prudence glanced at the sheet, shook her head doubtfully, and passed it to Chastity. "However you refine it, Con, it's incendiary."

Constance shrugged. "Men who do what he does have to bear the consequences."

"I hope to God he never discovers who wrote it."

"Father will be mad as fire if his friend's attacked like this," Chastity observed, rather anxiously, as she perused the paper. "You know how devoted he is to Barclay. And he always stands by his friends regardless of the rights and wrongs of an issue."

"We won't publish it yet. I need to check some of the facts and gather more ammunition. It may take a couple of months to get it all together." Constance took back the paper. "Dolly had the name of one of the women. She's in some Home for Fallen Women in Battersea. I'll go and talk to her first."

"How does Dolly know these things?" Chastity asked.

"Her housekeeper happens to be the cousin of Barclay's housekeeper." Constance folded the paper and slipped it into her handbag. "Dolly has tentacles that reach everywhere when it comes to gossip."

"I hope they *don't* reach everywhere," Prudence said with feeling. "At least not as far as Ten Manchester Square." She gathered up her gloves and bag. "Let's go. Maybe Father will have made it home by now."

They caught an omnibus outside Fortnum and Mason and arrived home to find Lord Duncan, red-faced and bursting with frustration and fury, pacing around the hall.

"Damned machine!" he exploded as they walked through the door. "Had to leave it in Hampstead. Right in the middle of the heath!"

"Why, what happened?" Constance asked, drawing off her gloves, her expression all sympathetic interest.

"Broke down! Not once but four times, would you believe! Damnable things, they are. Horses don't break down on a man." His lordship wiped his sweating brow with the jaunty checkered cravat he'd worn for his drive.

"Oh, dear," said Chastity, laying a soothing hand on his arm. "How disappointing for you. Jenkins, bring his lordship a whisky." She kissed her father's cheek. "Tell us exactly what happened."

"No, don't," Prudence murmured sotto voce to Constance, as Chastity urged her father into the calming atmosphere of the drawing room. "I don't think we need to know."

Constance shot her a warning look and followed her sister and parent, unwinding her chiffon scarf as she did so.

"Wouldn't have been so bad if Barclay hadn't been there," her father declared, his voice still brimming with fury. "There I was, boasting of this damned Cadillac, supposed to be more reliable than that Panhard of Barclay's, and what does it do but strand us in the middle of the heath. First hill we come to, it gives up, rolls back to the bottom." He took the full glass of whisky offered to him by a studiously impassive Jenkins.

" 'Run out of fuel,' Barclay says, 'must have used more than you thought yesterday,' so we refill it and it starts . . ." He paused to drain the glass. Jenkins, at his elbow, took it from him without instruction. "Starts up sweet as a nut. We get to the top of the hill, go a quarter of a mile, and it stops again. Just stops dead." He took the refilled glass. "Three times . . . we refilled it three times, would you believe?"

Oh, yes, we would. Constance carefully avoided her sisters' eyes.

"Drained all three damned cans, then we had to walk all the way to the Bull and Bush. Just leave the bally motor right in the middle of the heath and walk. Miles, it was. Hot as hell. If it hadn't been for that Ensor fellow, it would still be sitting in the middle of the heath and we'd be twiddlin' our thumbs in the pub."

"Max Ensor?" Constance stared at her father. "How did he come into this?"

"Turned up at the Bull and Bush in a Darracq. Damned fine-looking motor. Drove us back to the Cadillac and towed the damned car back to the mews. And that's where it's going to stay until they come and take it away. Give me a damned horse anyday." He drained the second glass.

"How convenient that he appeared so fortuitously," Constance said. "As it happens, I'm having dinner with him tonight." She kissed her father. "I'm glad you're back safely. It must have been very frustrating, but Cobham won't be sorry to see the back of the motor."

Her father gave a reluctant crack of laughter. "No, damn his eyes. If his legs weren't so stiff he'd have danced a jig when he saw it towed in . . . well, I approve of Ensor. You have my blessing. Not that that would make any difference to you one way or the other," he added gruffly.

"Yes, it would," Constance said. "I wouldn't want to disoblige you, Father, in anything. None of us would."

He regarded her closely, then smiled. He seemed to have recovered his equilibrium. "No, I don't believe you would. Just like your mother . . . all of you. But you'd oblige me by getting a husband or two. Take a closer look at this Ensor, Constance. I like the fellow."

"Oh, I think I'll wait to be asked before I start planning my wedding," Constance said lightly. "Now, I must go and dress."

Chapter 14

Kensington Town Hall was deserted at six o'clock when Constance arrived. She hurried across the foyer and into a small cramped office at the rear. Emmeline Pankhurst and her daughter Christobel were talking in low tones with several other women.

"Constance, there you are," Emmeline greeted her with a warm smile. "There's coffee, if you'd like." She gestured to the coffeepot, but Constance, who knew how thin and ungrateful a beverage it contained, declined.

"We were just talking about a petition," Emmeline said. "One we would present at Westminster. If we could get together a large group of women prepared to march together to present it, we might get some favorable publicity. We thought we'd bring it up at the meeting tonight."

"We'd certainly get publicity," Constance said. "I wouldn't want to bet on whether it would be favorable."

"Well, it doesn't matter. Publicity is what we want if we're to raise the consciousness of women," Christobel declared with a militant air. Her mother, who took a rather more patient, long-term view of their movement, frowned a little, but knew better than to antagonize her daughter.

"I've invited a guest tonight," Constance said, brushing crumbs off the corner of the metal table before perching on it. "A Member of Parliament."

"A supporter?" Emmeline leaned forward with interest.

"Not yet. In fact, he says he doesn't see the point of women's suffrage, but he goes so far as to say that he's willing to tolerate an opposing point of view." She couldn't help a slightly ironic lift of her eyebrows.

"Pompous ass!" declared Christobel.

"He can be," Constance conceded, wondering why her hackles prickled at Christobel's declaration when she'd almost invited it. It was one she had been known to make herself. "However, isn't part of our mission to educate?"

"Is he educable?" demanded the younger Pankhurst with the same scorn.

"He's not a simple primate, Christobel," Constance said sharply. The other woman flushed slightly and fell silent.

"We might learn something from him ourselves," Constance continued in a milder tone. "He already mentioned that the government was considering the issue of women taxpayers. Maybe he can tell us more."

"Who is he?"

"Max Ensor. His constituency is Southwold. He won a fairly recent by-election, but from what I can gather he has the ear of the Prime Minister."

"Well, let's meet him this evening. Any interest shown in the movement by an MP is promising, even if he's not yet a supporter." Emmeline gathered up a sheaf of leaflets from the table. "Will you hand these out at the door, Constance? It's just a notice about the petition."

Constance took them. "Who's taking names tonight?"

"Geraldine, would you?" Emmeline turned to a thin, tall, elegantly dressed lady standing by the window.

"Yes, of course," she said in a soft voice.

"Then I think we're ready for the fray. Christobel is going to speak tonight and we'll invite questions from the floor." Emmeline rose from her chair. "Let's open the doors."

Constance took up her post at the door, handing out her leaflets to the women who hurried up the steps. They were women from every social stratum, some well dressed, some shabbily, some worn down with manual labor, some with hands that had never touched a washing-up bowl. But they all bore a similar expression, eyes bright with excitement and hope, energy and commitment radiating from them. They took the leaflets, some greeting Constance by name. She kept her eyes on the steps, watching for Max. There were a few men present, some alone, some with women. Constance was relieved to see that it was going to be a sizable crowd. It would have been embarrassing, not to mention unhelpful to the cause, for Max to have witnessed a sparsely attended meeting.

As it happened, she was in deep discussion with a woman she knew very well and missed his arrival.

"Do I get one of those?"

She jumped at the sound of the rich voice behind her and spun around. "Oh, I was looking out for you and then I got distracted." She held out a leaflet. "If you want one, then of course you may have one."

"Thank you." He took it, glancing at it as he did so. "A march on Westminster?"

"The presentation of a petition," she said. "You'll hear more if you come in. We're about ready to start."

He nodded and followed her into the hall. Constance stopped at a small table where her colleague sat with the sign-in book. "Geraldine, this is the Right Honorable Max Ensor. Max, may I introduce the Honorable Mrs. George Brand."

Geraldine offered her hand. "Good evening, Mr. Ensor. Welcome."

"Will you sign your name, or would you prefer not to make your attendance a matter of record?" Constance asked, trying not to make a challenge of the question. "We don't insist."

"I have no objection," he said, and signed his name in the book. "Why should I?"

"No reason that I can see," Constance said. "I'll sit with you. Normally I sit on the platform, but I won't this evening."

He smiled. "I am honored, ma'am."

"Don't be," she responded. "I merely intend to ensure that you sit it out to the end."

He shook his head in mock admonition and followed her to the front of the hall.

It was a lively meeting. Christobel had the ability to fire an audience in a way that her mother lacked. She spoke with a militant fervor that had the audience cheering, and questions came thick and fast when her speech was over. Constance contributed nothing, but sat quietly, vibrantly aware of Max beside her. He said nothing either, but he had evinced no restlessness, no impatience, no hostility to the speech. She cast him several sideways glances but could read nothing from his expression. The meeting ended promptly at eight-fifteen; there were many women in the audience who had to be back under their employers' roofs when the two hours between tea and supper that constituted their evening out were over.

As Constance rose to her feet she glanced behind her and saw Amelia standing at the rear of the hall. She must have arrived late. She had said how rarely she could make a meeting. Max had stood up now and he seemed to Constance suddenly to stand out like a sore thumb, head and shoulders above everyone else in the hall, exuding male power and privilege. She pushed past him with unseemly haste and as she reached the aisle managed to catch Amelia's eye. But Amelia had already seen her employer's brother. For a second she shot a startled, questioning glance at Constance, then she turned and hurried from the hall into the gathering dusk on the street.

One other complication that would have to be explained, Constance thought. They had decided not to tell Amelia in advance that they had designated Max as Henry's prospective employer. It had seemed a bridge best crossed if the plan worked out.

"Why the hurry?" Max asked when he'd finally managed to ease his way out of the row and into the aisle.

"Sorry, I didn't mean to push past you, but I thought I saw someone I wanted to speak to. I wanted to catch her before she left, but it wasn't her." She smiled up at him. "What did you think?"

"I don't know," he said. "I need time to digest."

"Would you like to meet Emmeline and Christobel? I told them you would be here."

"In what capacity?"

"A neutral observer," she replied.

"That seems accurate enough. 'Lay on, Macduff.' "

"A most educable primate," Constance murmured.

"I beg your pardon?"

"Oh, nothing . . . nothing at all." She gave him her radiant smile and took his arm. "Come, let's meet the Pankhursts."

They went up to the platform where the speaker and the women who'd accompanied her on the dais were surrounded by a group of voluble questioners.

"Constance, this must be Mr. Ensor." Emmeline, with impeccable courtesy, moved through the throng as soon as she saw them. A curious silence suddenly fell as they all realized there was a man among them.

Max felt like a circus animal. He smiled with what he hoped was a pacifying benignity and shook Mrs. Pankhurst's hand. "Thank you for allowing me to listen in, ma'am," he said. "A most interesting meeting."

"Interesting or merely amusing, sir?" The sharp question came from Christobel before her mother had had a chance to respond. She stepped forward, regarding him with sardonic hostility.

"I do not find this issue amusing, madam," Max said in a voice that would cut steel. His eyes, as cold and blue as glacier ice, stared at her with undisguised contempt. "You would do well to consider that if you wish to make friends of those in a position to help you, it's sensible not to make enemies of them first."

Constance drew in a sharp breath. She knew he could bite, but she hadn't realized quite how hard. She was torn between loyalty to Christobel and the reluctant acceptance that the woman had been unpardonably rude without provocation.

"We're all a little wary, Max," she said. "We've made friends with influence before and they've let us down. You have to understand that we don't trust easily." Her voice was quiet and reasonable.

Christobel's angry flush died down and she extended her hand to

Max. "Constance is right, Mr. Ensor. It's a case of once bitten twice shy. But I apologize if my comment was gratuitous."

He smiled without resentment and took the proffered hand. "I understand, Miss Pankhurst."

"I hope you'll come to another meeting," Emmeline said. "We're quite shameless in our desire to recruit supporters in the government."

Max tapped the leaflet he held in the palm of his other hand. "You're planning a march on Westminster."

"It would help us greatly if a Member of Parliament would be willing to accept the petition," Emmeline said.

Constance felt Max stiffen and stepped in quickly. "Let's not make assumptions, Emmeline. We're not the press gang. This is not conscription."

Emmeline nodded. "You're right. Your mother would have cautioned in exactly the same way." She smiled at Max. "You never met Lady Duncan. She was a remarkable woman."

"I can imagine. I've met her daughters," he replied.

Constance decided she'd had enough of this. "You'll have to excuse us, Emmeline . . . Christobel. Max has another engagement."

They made their farewells, and once out on the street, where a few gas lamps now glimmered, Constance exhaled in a soft whistle.

"Awkward," Max agreed. "I hadn't expected to be ambushed."

"No," she agreed. "But desperation can cause generally intelligent people to sabotage their own interests." She tucked her hand into his arm as they began to walk down Kensington Church Street. "On the subject of sabotage, how did it happen that you turned up in the right place at exactly the right time in order to rescue my father?" She looked up at him, raising a quizzical eyebrow.

"Mere coincidence," he said.

"Liar. There was nothing coincidental about your arrival at the Bull and Bush on Hampstead Heath at the same time as my furious parent."

"He was certainly not a happy man," Max said. "I rather got the impression that your little device had succeeded. He was swearing he'd never touch a motorcar again."

"Yes, it succeeded, all right. But I still want to know how you happened to be there at the same time."

"I didn't see any virtue in making him any more uncomfortable than was necessary to achieve your object," he said. "So I followed them out of London. You have no objections, I trust."

"No . . . no, of course not. The poor darling was at the end of his tether by the time he got home as it was."

Max puzzled over the warm, affectionate tone she had used. It didn't seem to jibe with the exasperation he had noticed usually accompanied references to Lord Duncan. "Is your father a difficult parent?" he asked, stopping under a street lamp outside a small restaurant. He hadn't meant to probe this subject but somehow couldn't help himself.

Constance laughed, but it was a slightly self-conscious laugh, he thought. "No, he's incredibly indulgent. He never interferes with us at all."

"Then why does he annoy you?"

"Annoy me?" she exclaimed. "How could you say such a thing?"

"Give me some credit, Constance. I'd have to be blind and deaf not to notice how exasperated you and your sisters often seem when his name's mentioned."

Constance sighed. She could see no alternative to offering him a partial truth. "He's very stubborn," she said. "He gets ideas in his head that he won't let go. And they're not always very good or sensible ideas. Our mother managed him very well, so well that he never noticed he was being managed. When she died there was no one to put the brakes on. He lost a lot of money at one point on a foolish venture and we decided we'd have to learn to do what our mother did if we weren't going to end up in the poor house. We don't succeed all the time, and we do get frustrated."

"I see. I didn't mean to pry. Shall we go in . . ." He gestured to the restaurant behind them. "I made a reservation here. It's pleasant and very quiet. Unless, of course, you'd rather go somewhere more distinguished."

"No, this will be lovely." She was surprised at his choice of such an unpretentious, out-of-the-way spot, but also charmed by it. It was very small, the six tables basking in the soft glow of candles. They were shown to a table in the window by a cheerful woman, who greeted Max by name and shook his hand warmly.

"I've a wonderful pot-au-feu tonight, Mr. Ensor. I know how much you like that."

"We're in your hands, Mrs. Baker," Max said, holding Constance's chair out for her. "Or at least," he added, taking the seat opposite her, "I am, as always. I'm not sure about Miss Duncan, she likes to make up her own mind." His tone was teasing.

Constance unfolded her napkin and accepted the gibe with good grace. "Tonight I'll follow your lead, Max." She smiled up at Mrs. Baker. "I too am in your hands."

"Very good, madam." The woman returned the smile and hurried away. Within a couple of minutes a waiter appeared with a bottle of claret, which he opened, tasted himself, and poured for them.

Max nodded his thanks. He said to Constance, "The Bakers used to work for my family. Mr. Baker was my father's steward and his wife was our housekeeper. They came into a little money and decided they wanted to run their own business." He gestured to the small room. "This is the result. They're doing very well, and I come as often as I can."

"It's charming," she said. She took up her glass and surveyed him thoughtfully over the lip. She'd said they needed to learn more about each other, to deepen their relationship beyond its undeniably wonderful sexual component, and there was something about the intimacy of their surroundings that seemed to encourage confidences. She wondered if he'd chosen it for that very reason.

"So, when is this march to Westminster supposed to take place?" he asked. "It doesn't say on the leaflet and I didn't hear a date mentioned at the meeting."

"I don't think it's fixed yet," she said. "Why? Are you thinking of joining us?"

"I hardly think so." He sat back as the waiter set bowls of onion soup in front of them, with a basket of crusty bread. Max took up his spoon and inhaled the aroma hungrily. "This is wonderful stuff. It cures whatever ails you."

Constance dipped her spoon into the rich brown liquid. Cheese bubbled in its depths. "If I eat this I'll never eat anything else."

"Oh, yes, you will," he said with confidence. "You won't be able to resist the pot-au-feu."

"It's very wintery food," she observed, twisting strands of cheese around her spoon. She took a mouthful. "Oh, but it is *very* good. Doesn't make for elegant eating, though," she mumbled through strands of cheese.

He laughed and leaned over to break the recalcitrant tangle with his fork as it dripped from her mouth. It was an intimate gesture, yet so natural that she barely noticed it.

She sipped her wine and wondered where this amazing ease had come from so suddenly. Exactly what kind of man was he? He was an expert and considerate lover; in bed he could be tender one minute and powerfully dominating the next. It made for wonderfully exciting love play. And in everyday life it was the same thing. He could be considerate, charming, entertaining one minute, and then arrogant, sarcastic, even pompous the next. She supposed that everyone had contradictions in their personalities, but Max's seemed more extreme than most.

"Why don't you just ask it?" he said into the silence that had gone on longer than she'd realized.

"Ask what?" She dipped her spoon in the soup again.

"Whatever question is burning on your lips," he said. "I can see you're dying to ask me something. So go ahead. I won't snap your head off."

"I was just wondering why, after your affair in India, you never found another woman. It's unusual for a man to be approaching forty wifeless."

"Perhaps I just never found a woman I wanted to marry," he said. He set his spoon down and refilled their wineglasses. "Perhaps I feel that women aren't really to be trusted."

"That's a bit sweeping," Constance said. "Just because one woman broke a promise doesn't mean they all do."

"No, intellectually I know that. Let's just leave it that after the debacle in India I've never found another woman I wanted to get really close to."

"And you're not lonely?"

He shook his head. "Far from it. I don't have any difficulty finding congenial companions, my dear."

"Like me?" She could have bitten her tongue on the question but it came out anyway.

"Now, how am I supposed to answer that?" he demanded. "Either answer would be an insult."

"Answer it anyway." In for a penny, in for a pound, she thought.

He regarded her thoughtfully. "All right, I will. As it happens, you don't fall into the category of congenial companion. Partly because much of the time you're not in the least congenial, you're argumentative, and challenging, and very opinionated."

"Oh!" Constance gave a crow of laughter. "You only like women who agree with you and hang on to your every word, is that it?"

"No, it's not." He was smiling himself now. "This is an absurd conversation, Constance. But now I've started, I might as well finish. Those characteristics aside, I also find you exciting, somewhat puzzling a lot of the time, and when you choose to be, utterly captivating. There. Satisfied?"

She found she was blushing slightly. "I'm sorry I asked."

"Answer a question of mine now."

She nodded. It was only fair, although she was a little nervous as to what he would ask.

"You're a very passionate woman, both physically and intellectually. Don't *you* get lonely sometimes?"

Constance traced a pattern on the tablecloth with the tines of her fork. "I have my sisters. I'm not lonely in that respect at all."

"And in others?"

She looked up then and said frankly, "I never give it much thought, or at least, I didn't, until I met you."

"Should I take that as a compliment?"

"It's a fact. One I hadn't acknowledged until just now."

They fell silent as the waiter took away their soup bowls. Max wondered if the moment was ripe to ask her point-blank about *The Mayfair Lady*. But then he decided he would rather she told him herself. At some point he would try to tease a confession out of her, but he didn't want to spoil the present atmosphere.

The pot-au-feu was as delicious as Max had said it would be and Constance had no difficulty at all in finishing the plate. They followed it with a richly aromatic cheese from the Pyrenees, and Max ate a large slice of apple pie, which Constance regretfully declined.

He took a forkful of the flaky pastry with the thick slices of golden apple and plump raisins and held it to her lips. "You have at least to try it. Mrs. Baker makes the lightest, fluffiest pastry. Open up."

Constance opened her mouth and closed her eyes. It was divine. She took up her own fork and helped herself to another mouthful from Max's plate.

"Are you sure you wouldn't like a slice of your own?" he inquired.

"Oh, no," she said. "I couldn't possibly eat another morsel." She reached across and dug in again.

"I give up." He pushed the plate across to her. "Eat that and I'll get another for myself."

"But I don't want any more," she protested. "I don't have a sweet tooth . . . except," she added with a rueful grin, "that this isn't at all sweet. It's just heavenly."

It was past midnight when they left the restaurant and walked into the warm darkness. Constance felt strangely light-headed, the wine perhaps, but it might be due more, she thought, to the sensation that she had never passed a more delightful and companionable evening. And she hadn't even missed their usual sparring. It had been remarkably relaxing and peaceable.

"Home?" he asked, hailing a hackney carriage that was clopping slowly towards them.

"Yours or mine?" She climbed in.

"That's a question whose answer I'm inclined to leave to the lady," he said, still standing on the pavement, waiting to tell the cabby where to go.

"Yours, then," Constance said, still feeling slightly and delightfully dizzy. "You can drive me home later."

"At your service, ma'am. Canon Row, cabbie."

"Right y'are, guv." The horse clopped on.

Constance turned her head lazily on the cracked leather squabs and watched Max's face in the alternating light and shadow as the carriage passed beneath street lamps. He reached out and touched her cheek, caressing the curve in the palm of his hand. The air was suddenly charged. Constance caught her breath as almost without warning lust engulfed her. She turned into his body, pressing her mouth to his. Her mouth opened beneath his, eager for the deep penetration of his tongue. She moved a hand to the bulge of his penis, pressing and rubbing the hard shaft through the fine material of his trousers. He groaned against her mouth. Heat swept up her body, setting her skin afire.

Max reached a hand beneath her skirt, sliding up the silk-clad length of her leg. His fingers insinuated themselves into the wide lace-edged legs of her drawers, crept upwards as she squirmed on the seat, found what they were looking for. She gasped, her thighs falling open in wanton abandon to give him easier access. Her belly clenched, her loins tightened, then she bit her lip hard to keep silent as the wave of pleasure peaked and receded.

"Dear God," she whispered. "We're in a hackney cab."

He laughed softly, although his breathing was ragged and his own eyes glowed, luminous with his own urgent desire. "I wasn't expecting that," he said, withdrawing his hand slowly. The scent of her was on his fingertips. "Of all the incontinent urges." He laughed softly again.

Constance straightened her skirts, smoothing them over her knees with fussy little pats that occupied her until her heart had slowed, although the languid afterglow of that brief but intense climax still infused her. "I feel guilty," she said. "We didn't share it."

"Oh, yes, we did," he murmured, his eyes still glowing as they held her gaze. "Touching you drives me wild. You feel so lush and open, so hot and eager. I want to bury my mouth in you, lick every drop of your arousal, drive my tongue to your core. And I shall."

He smiled a smile of pure sensual promise. "Just as soon as we get behind a closed door. I shall take every one of those elegant garments from you, one by one, and when you're naked I shall possess every inch of your body with my mouth and my hands. I intend to make you sob with pleasure, Constance. I intend to take you to heights you've never reached before. And when I'm finished, I promise you you will not be able to move a muscle."

Constance swallowed, the sound loud in the darkness. Her body was once again surging, her belly in a tumult. She shifted on the seat, trying to quiet the lusting clamor of her loins that were filled with liquid fire. "No more," she begged. "Don't say anything else until we get there. I can't bear it."

His smile now was both satisfied and wicked. "I love watching you like this," he murmured. "I love the idea that I can bring you almost to orgasm just by talking."

"It's sadistic," she said. "Pure sadism."

"Oh, come now. I'm only bringing you pleasure."

"Some pleasure is very close to pain," she said. The conversation was giving her much-needed distraction, enough at least to enable her to get out of the cab with some composure.

"And by the same token, some pain is very close to pleasure," he observed. "As the marquis describes so eloquently."

"You've read de Sade?" This was much better, she told herself desperately. Concentrate on a topic that, if not exactly far removed from sex, did at least have an intellectual component. "He's banned, isn't he?"

"One can buy underground copies in Paris. Would you like to borrow *Justine*? It's probably the best."

"Cannon Row, guvnor." The cabbie called from the box as the carriage came to a halt.

"We'll finish this fascinating discussion some other time," Max said, with that same wicked smile. "I have other things on my mind at present." He swung open the door and jumped down, giving Constance his hand to alight.

She stood on the pavement looking up at the tall terraced house while Max paid the driver. The house was in darkness, Max had hired no domestic staff as yet except for a daily cleaner. Marcel, his valet, had the night off and would not make an appearance until early morning.

"Would you really lend me *Justine*?" she asked as he inserted his key in the lock. "I would have thought you'd consider it unsuitable material for a woman."

"Don't try to distract me, sweetheart." The door swung open.

"I'm trying to distract myself," she said, stepping into the dark hall. She turned into his arms. It was a kiss that would devour her, an embrace that would swallow her whole like Jonah in the whale. She reached against him, standing on tiptoe to match her length with his. His hands spanned her narrow back, gripped her bottom fiercely, pressing her loins against his so that she could feel the pulse of his constricted penis. Her breasts were crushed against the starched white of his shirtfront. She wanted her clothes off, to feel the air on her skin, her body bared for his touch as he had promised.

As if he had divined her need, he stepped back, pausing to draw breath. It was dark in the hall, only a dim illumination from the lamp outside the door. He took her hand and pulled her behind him into the drawing room. The curtains were drawn back and again the street lamp offered a faint glow.

"I need to see you," he said softly. He struck a match and lit the candles on the console table against the wall. The light was gentle and softening.

"We should draw the curtains," she said.

"No one can see in." He came up to her, took her hands, drew her over to the fireplace. He undressed her as he had promised, garment by garment, without haste, lingering over buttons and hooks, touching her skin as he revealed it inch by inch, kissing her shoulders, the pulse in her throat, the cleft between her breasts. Then she was naked and he was no longer leisurely. She writhed in his hands and beneath the mouth that explored and possessed her, opened her and probed her, branding her with a piercing pleasure that left her trembling, insensate, in thrall to the magic of this possession.

When he could bear his own need no longer Max pulled off his own clothes, maintaining contact with her body even as he did so, a stroking finger, a brush of his lips, the quick dart of his tongue while she stood as if robbed of all will. Then when he too was naked, she slid down his body, her hands running down his length, and took his penis in her mouth, giving back the pleasure he had given her and taking her own in the giving.

Finally he came down to the floor with her, kneeling in front of her, kissing her mouth, where he could taste his own arousal that mingled on his lips with the taste of Constance. He eased her to the floor, their mouths still joined, then he drew her beneath him, her thighs opening for him, the tender, now acutely sensitive entrance to her body closing around him as he thrust within. He pressed deep inside her. She held her breath as the spiral of pleasure tightened and she could sense the moment of explosive joy coming closer and closer. She tightened her inner muscles around him the instant before the coil flew apart and she screamed in the deserted house as the climactic finale ripped through her so that for a moment the only reality was sensation. She felt his body jarring, shuddering, the clenched, corded muscles in his upper arms as he held himself above her, then he too shouted out with the same wild abandon and then collapsed on her.

They lay together, breathing fast, their sweat-slick skin sticking together, until at last some sense of time and place returned to them. Constance weakly stroked his back and shifted her body in mute appeal. He rolled off her and lay on his back, his hand resting on her stomach.

"God's good grace," he said.

"God's good grace," she said. This was a man who knew how to keep his promises.

Chapter 15

The doorbell rang early on Sunday evening. The sisters were gathered in the drawing room, where they'd been all afternoon, trying to distract themselves from the agony of expectation. There was no guarantee that he would come, indeed even Chastity had begun to be plagued by doubts.

At the sound of the bell they looked at one another in silence. Chastity put her steepled hands to her mouth and they waited. Jenkins opened the door. "Mr. Henry Franklin, ladies."

Henry stepped hesitantly into the room. He carried a small valise and looked as harried and worn as he had done in the Copper Kettle. He set down his valise by the door and solemnly shook their hands.

"Jenkins, could you bring the sherry?" Constance asked. "I think Mr. Franklin looks as if he could do with something heartening."

"Certainly, Miss Con." Jenkins left the drawing room.

"I just walked away," Henry said, sounding bemused. "I wrote a letter and left it on the mantelpiece and I walked away. I caught the afternoon train." He shook his head in some kind of wonder. "He'll never forgive me."

"Don't be too sure of that," Prudence said, drawing him to the sofa. "We'll follow through with our plan and I'm sure he'll come round in the end."

Henry sat on the sofa, turning his hat between his hands. "How is Amelia?"

"Desperate to see you," Constance said. "Oh, thank you, Jenkins. I'll pour." She nodded to the butler as he set the tray with decanter and glasses on a side table. "Lord Duncan isn't dining in tonight, is he?"

"No, Miss Con. He's dining with Lord Barclay as I understand it."

"Then we'll dine with Mr. Franklin at eight as usual."

"Very well, miss. I'll take the gentleman's valise to the blue room."

Constance poured sherry and gave Henry a glass. He sipped it cautiously then with an air of sudden abandon gulped it down. Constance refilled his glass.

"Dutch courage," he said with an embarrassed smile.

"You don't need it now," Chastity said warmly. "You're here and it's done. Tomorrow afternoon I'll walk with you in the park when Amelia is walking her charge. We've arranged to meet, accidentally of course, in the rose garden. The child won't think anything of it if you and Amelia talk for a few minutes while I walk a little way with Pamela."

"And you have an interview with the Right Honorable Max Ensor tomorrow morning," Constance told him. "He's looking for a secretary. I told him you would make an excellent one. The work might even interest you. It's got to be more challenging than slaving in the office of a construction company."

Henry downed his second sherry. "I can't take it all in," he said.

"You don't have to all at once," Chastity told him. "The wedding is arranged for Thursday afternoon at Caxton Hall. It'll be a very simple ceremony and you and Amelia can have an hour to yourselves afterwards before she has to return to the Grahams."

"And as soon as you have employment and can find suitable lodgings, then Amelia can leave her employers and you'll set up house together," Prudence stated.

Henry looked dazed. "I don't know anything about London. I've never been here before. It's so noisy, even on a Sunday. I think I feel a headache coming on."

"I'll show you to your room and you can rest a little." Chastity rose from her chair. "Poor Henry," she said sympathetically. "We must seem such a managing group of females."

"You are," he said frankly.

"We only manage people for their own good," Chastity reassured him, taking his hand in a warm clasp. "We won't do you any harm, I promise."

He shook his head. "No," he said. "No, I don't suppose you would. Not intentionally." He allowed himself to be led from the drawing room.

"Oh, dear," Constance said when the door had closed behind them. "Do you really think he's what Amelia wants?"

"She said so," Prudence stated, pouring more sherry. "I don't think it's our place to veto her choice."

"No," Constance agreed. "But I foresee a very tedious evening."

"Do you think Max will try him out?"

Constance smiled involuntarily, reflecting that every time she thought of Max these days this fatuous smile came to her lips. She just couldn't help it. "I think he'll do his best to see promise in him," she said.

Prudence was very aware of her sister's recurring smile. "I think you're in love," she stated.

Constance shook her head vigorously. "No, of course I'm not. I'm just in lust."

Prudence shook her own head as vigorously. "Don't fool yourself, Con. You certainly can't fool Chas and me. We've never seen you like this. Not even with Douglas."

"It'll pass," Constance declared.

"Do you want it to?"

Constance blew out her breath in a sound of pure frustration. "I don't know, Prue. I don't want to be in love with someone who's not in love with me."

"And he's not?"

"I don't think so."

"And would you know?" Prudence asked shrewdly.

"I would think so," Constance said. "Wouldn't you?"

"I don't know. Sometimes the last person to know something is the person closest to it." They turned as one to the door as Chastity returned.

"Is he all right?"

"He's just so befuddled, poor soul. I don't think he can believe what he's done." She looked closely at her sisters. "What were you two talking about?"

"Max," Prudence said. "Whether he's in love with Con. What do you think, Chas?"

"I think it's quite likely, but it's possible he doesn't know it," Chastity said after a moment's consideration. "Just think how he's changed since he met you. And he helped with the motorcar. He would never have done anything so unconventional before."

"And he went to a WSPU meeting with you," Prudence reminded Constance.

As if she needed reminding, Constance thought. That evening was indelibly etched in her memory. "I'll agree he's more open-minded than I had originally thought," she said cautiously. Then she shrugged. "Let's get back to Henry. If Max does employ him, then he'll need somewhere to live. I don't see him doing that alone, do you?"

"Maybe we should start up a housing rental agency," Prudence suggested. "In addition to the Go-Between, Mabel, and the Agony Aunt and all the rest of it."

"I trust you jest, sister," Constance said. "Our plates are so full we can barely keep the balls we have in the air. Did anyone invite Millicent to the At Home yet?"

"Yes, I did. I called round yesterday, just for an informal visit. I pressed her a little and she said she would definitely be here." Chastity took up her sherry glass again. "How are we going to put a white rose in her buttonhole?"

"We have to give different colored ones to every woman," Prudence said. "It doesn't matter how many reds and pinks and yellows we have, we just make sure there's only one white. And white will go with whatever color she's wearing."

"That'll serve," Constance agreed. "I should take Henry to visit Max, don't you think? He might never get there on his own."

"We should probably warn him to keep the name of his intended to himself," Prudence pointed out. "Just in case it comes up in conversation and he lets it slip to Max."

"Oh, what a tangled web we weave," Constance muttered. "I shall be so glad when we've got these two lovebirds safely joined in legal matrimony."

Henry was a quiet dinner companion, eating steadily, drinking very moderately, but he seemed to be a little less dazed by his present circumstances, and when the sisters rose from the table, suggesting he'd like to enjoy a glass of port, he said he never partook of anything stronger than wine or sherry and would accompany them to the drawing room, where, if they would like it, he would be delighted to play for them. He had noticed a particularly fine pianoforte in the room.

"How lovely," Constance said. "Thank you."

He smiled then and it was a very sweet smile and the sisters began to get some inkling as to what had appealed to Amelia. They understood completely when Henry began to play. It was as if he was transformed. The shy, weak bumbler was gone; in its place a man supremely confident in his talent. And it was a considerable talent. His execution was flawless, his interpretation both creative and sensitive.

They sat transfixed for close to two hours as he played tirelessly, and frequently from memory. Once or twice he paused between pieces to flex his long fingers, but they had the feeling that he wasn't really in the room with them. His expression was transfixed, abstracted. He was lost in the world of his music.

When at last he stopped, after a spirited rendition of a group of Chopin waltzes, the sisters applauded spontaneously. "That was wonderful, Henry," Chastity said. "No wonder you hate clerical work. If I had such a gift I wouldn't want to do anything else with my life."

He beamed, flushing with pleasure. "That's so kind of you."

"No," Constance said. "Not kind, just utterly truthful. We'll have to find a way for you to use your gift, but I think we have to stick with the original plan for the moment."

"As long as I have access to a piano I'm willing to do other work. Now, if you'll excuse me, I've had a very long day." He offered a jerky little bow and left them.

"That was something of a revelation, although I don't suppose it should have been," Prudence observed through a yawn. "But I feel happier about Amelia's choice now."

Henry was visibly relieved to have an escort to Westminster. He nodded when Constance said he should not mention Amelia's name in the upcoming interview. "I wouldn't see the need," he said. "My private life is no business of a prospective employer."

They took the omnibus to Westminster and Constance rang the bell of the house on Canon Row. Max himself opened the door. "Good morning, Constance. I didn't expect to see you." He shook her hand with solemn formality.

"Mr. Franklin is new to London and I thought it would be nice if I made the introduction personally," Constance said. "Mr. Henry Franklin, the Right Honorable Max Ensor."

The two men shook hands, Henry regarding the taller man rather warily. He exuded London sophistication in a morning coat that bore all the marks of impeccable and expensive tailoring. Henry felt distinctly provincial in his Ashford tailored frock coat.

"I'll leave you to it, then," Constance said. "You can find your own way back, Henry?"

"I hardly think Mr. Ensor would consider employing me if I was that incompetent," Henry said with a surprising touch of acerbity.

"No," Constance responded swiftly. "I was just being a mother hen. Forgive me."

Max's eyebrows crawled into his scalp at this description. He stared at her in open amusement. "Mother hen?"

"Good morning, Mr. Ensor," Constance said, and turned away, hiding her own laughter.

She walked over Westminster Bridge then hailed a hackney to take her to Battersea. The driver gave her a curious look when she alighted outside the drab building that housed the Battersea Home for Fallen Women. "I think you'd better wait for me," she said, looking around the mean streets. "There don't seem to be too many hackneys plying their trade around here."

"Not much trade to be 'ad, miss," he observed, unwinding his muffler. " 'Ow long you'll be, then?"

"Not above a half hour," she said. "I'll pay for the wait."

He nodded, took out his newspaper, and began to study the racing pages.

Constance rang the bell of a door scarred and scuffed with peeling paint. It was opened by a rather fierce-looking woman in black with a stiffly starched apron. She looked like some kind of warder, Constance thought. Either that or a matron. And she was scrutinizing Constance in a less-than-friendly fashion.

"I wonder if I might talk to Gertrude Collins." Constance tried to strike a happy medium between haughtiness and supplication, although she deeply resented the harsh stare.

"Why would you want to do that?"

"I might have some helpful information for her." Somewhere in the cabbage- and disinfectant-smelling depths of the house came the wail of a baby. "I mean her no harm, I assure you." She hesitated for a second then said boldly, "I am no friend to Lord Barclay."

The woman stared at her even more closely but now Constance could detect a slight crack in the harsh demeanor. "Are you a relative?" the woman demanded.

"No. Just someone who wishes her well."

"There's few enough of those around," the woman said. She opened the door a little wider. "She's maybe no better than she ought to be, but to be taken advantage of when she had little enough choice in the matter and then abandoned is sheer cruelty. I'd shoot 'em all."

Constance believed her. She accepted the implicit invitation to enter the house and followed a gesturing hand into a dank little sitting room with hard-backed chairs ranged along the walls and black and white oilcloth on the floor. A minute or so later a woman entered carrying a baby on her hip.

"What do you want with me?"

Constance left the dreary house half an hour later fired with righteous indignation and a soaring triumph. She had enough facts to make her story credible. The gutter press would pick it up with relish and Gertrude would reap the financial rewards while Lord Barclay was crucified on the cross of society's opinion. Such opinion would turn a blind eye to discreet peccadilloes with members of the underclasses, but it wouldn't turn a blind eye to scandal. And Constance in the pages of *The*

Mayfair Lady was going to make a stink that would reek to the heavens. Barclay wouldn't be able to show his face in Town.

She arrived home in the middle of lunch, to be told that Henry had returned from his interview flush with success. He had liked Max Ensor and the feeling had apparently been mutual. He was prepared to start work the following Monday. He'd eaten some bread and cheese and gone out to buy an engagement ring for his beloved.

"It's astonishing how he's blossomed," Prudence said. "He even walks differently."

"We'd better find him another roof soon, though," Chastity put in, pouring lemonade into her glass. "Father's bound to terrify him at dinner. So, where have you been, Con?"

She told them as she helped herself to a dish of cauliflower cheese. When her recital was finished, Prudence said thoughtfully, "I just hope this crusading zeal isn't going to cause trouble, Con. It's not that I don't agree with you. The man's despicable. But we're playing with fire."

"How could he possibly associate the piece with the Duncan sisters, Prue?"

Prudence shrugged. "I don't know. But it makes me uneasy."

"Well, I'm going to meet Henry in the park for our stroll to the rose garden." Chastity rose from the table. "I can't wait to see them meet. It's so romantic."

"Henry . . ." Prudence exclaimed.

"Romantic," Constance exclaimed.

"Well, the idea is," Chastity said. "And I'm going to wear my best bonnet in honor of the occasion."

She dressed with great care as she'd promised and set out for the park twirling a sunshade. Henry was waiting for her as instructed just inside the Stanhope Gate. "Do you think she will like this?" he blurted as Chastity came up to him. He held out the small box. "It's an engagement ring. I know she can't wear it, but I felt it was the right thing to do."

"It's lovely," Chastity said, taking the ring and holding it to the sun. "Any woman would love it. It's so delicate."

"It's all I could afford."

"It's lovely," she reiterated firmly. "The rose garden is this way."

In the quiet fragrance of the garden they sat on a bench in the sun to wait. Henry kept getting up and pacing the narrow gravel paths between the vibrant rose beds. Every so often he seemed inclined to chew his fingernails but resolutely thrust his hands into his pockets.

Chastity heard the shrill tones of Pamela Graham from quite some distance away. She stood up, nodding to Henry. "Take my arm, Henry, and we'll stroll towards the gate over there. Try to act as if it's just a pleasant surprise to meet Amelia and her charge here."

"I'll try," he whispered.

Amelia opened the little iron gate, ignoring the protestations of her charge.

"I don't want to go in there, Miss Westcott. I don't like flowers. You promised we would find the swings."

"And so we will, Pammy," Amelia said calmly. "But I want to show you the birdbath in the middle of the garden. It's a dolphin." Her quick glance darted towards the two approaching her and her color ebbed for a second, her step faltered. Then she picked up her pace again.

"Miss Westcott, how nice to meet you here. Isn't it a beautiful afternoon." Chastity smiled and extended her hand. "May I introduce Mr. Franklin?"

"Mr. Franklin and I are already acquainted," Amelia said softly, offering her hand to Chastity and then to Henry.

"He used to teach me the piano," Pamela pronounced. "Why are you in London, Mr. Franklin? You're not going to teach me piano again, are you?" She sounded horrified at the prospect.

"No, I don't believe so, Pamela," he said, his nervousness dissipating at the child's artless question. He realized he was still holding Amelia's hand and dropped it rather hastily.

Chastity bent down to the child. "Pamela, you probably don't remember me. I'm a friend of your mother's. And your uncle's," she added calmly.

"Uncle Max?"

"Yes, he comes to our house sometimes."

"I thought I saw Mr. Ensor with Miss Duncan the other day," Amelia said, her voice amazingly steady.

"Yes, they're old acquaintances," Chastity said. Chastity's romantic inclinations had been immediately satisfied by the look that had passed between the two as their hands had touched.

"I want to go to the pond," Pammy stated, dancing agitatedly on the path.

"I'll come with you," Chastity said. "I love to sail twigs on the pond. We'll play a game." She took the child's hand and led her off, studiously avoiding a backward glance at the reunited lovers.

After a decent interval that would not seem remarkable to Pamela they returned to the rose garden. Amelia was there alone. "I was about to come in search of you," she said. Her cheeks were slightly flushed, her eyes very bright with what Chastity was sure were tears. "Such a charming gentleman, Mr. Franklin."

"Yes, how curious that we should both know him," Chastity said. "Pamela, do you see that beautiful butterfly over there. On the yellow rose." She pointed towards a Red Admiral butterfly resting on the flower some ten paces away. Pamela ran over. Chastity turned back to Amelia. "Is everything all right?"

"Oh, yes. Wonderful. But . . . but, Chastity, I own I'm uncomfortable with the involvement of Mr. Ensor."

"Don't be. Constance has him well in hand," Chastity said, aware that she was probably promising a great deal more than the truth. "He doesn't know anything about you and Henry, and once you're married it's none of his business anyway."

"I suppose that's so," Amelia said with a little sigh. Then her expression brightened. "He gave me a ring, Chastity. Such a pretty engagement ring."

"And on Thursday you'll have the gold band to go with it," Chastity said, giving her a quick hug. "We just have to find Henry a place to live."

"I think," Amelia said quietly, "that Henry can do that for himself. You and your sisters have done enough."

"If you think so," Chastity said. "We don't wish to interfere."

Amelia laid a hand on her arm. "Once we're married, Henry will take on the responsibilities of a husband. I assure you."

"Oh, I believe you," Chastity returned. "He played for us last evening. It was sublime."

Amelia smiled. "Yes," she said. "Sublime." She stood in reflective silence for a minute, then called, "Come, Pammy, it's time to go."

On Wednesday afternoon, a large display of cut roses stood on the hall table, their thorns clipped, the stems neatly wrapped in tissue paper. Chastity fussed over them, rearranging them in order of color, then mixing them up again. "It's a very eccentric thing to do," she said, setting the single white rose just a little apart. "To give out roses."

"It's a charming gesture," Prudence said stoutly. "People will be enchanted. My only worry is that Millicent will fail us. We know Anonymous will come because he paid to do so, but supposing Millicent changed her mind, or had a headache or a more pressing engagement?"

"Let's cross that bridge when we come to it," Constance said in a somewhat distracted tone. She was reading a letter that had just been delivered. "Max makes his apologies, he can't call this afternoon, but he's inviting me to dine with him in the House of Commons this evening."

"Will you go?"

Constance gave her sister a look that declared an answer was hardly necessary.

"Wear the green and black silk," Prudence said with a laugh. "It's so striking."

"And Mother's diamonds," Chastity said. "With that gorgeous emerald green shawl."

"Whatever you say," Constance agreed. "I wouldn't argue with either of you." She moved towards the drawing room as the doorbell rang. "Don't forget, Jenkins. The white rose for Miss Hardcastle."

"I have not forgotten, Miss Con," the long-suffering butler declared as he crossed to the front door.

The sisters exchanged a quick grin. "I'll make myself scarce," Chastity said. "Good luck." She crossed her fingers and went upstairs to await the outcome. Her sisters hastened to position themselves in the drawing room to receive their guests.

Anonymous arrived punctually at half past three. He handed his card to Jenkins, offered his excuse for being there, and was ushered into the drawing room. A buzz of conversation rose and fell from the small group gathered there. The women all wore roses pinned to their corsages, but a quick glance revealed no white rose.

Jenkins announced him: "Arthur Melvin, Esquire."

Constance came forward, just the right questioning note in her voice as she said, "I don't believe we've had the pleasure, Mr. Melvin. I'm Constance Duncan."

"Forgive the intrusion," he said. "I was given to understand Lord Jersey would be calling upon you this afternoon, and I have an urgent need to meet with him."

Constance made a show of looking around the drawing room. "I'm so sorry, he hasn't appeared as yet. Perhaps later. Do come and meet my sister, and you'll take tea, I hope."

She exchanged a speaking glance with Prudence as she introduced him. There was still no sign of Millicent. The no-longer-anonymous client was looking around rather restlessly, but he managed to comport himself graciously when introduced to the other guests.

"Miss Hardcastle, Miss Duncan," Jenkins intoned from the doorway, and Millicent, sporting the white rose, came in.

"Constance, Prudence, I'm sorry to be so late," she said, coming towards them, hands outstretched. "One of our housemaids had the most dreadful toothache and I had to take her to have it pulled. She was too terrified to go alone."

Millicent was neither plain nor attractive, but she had a certain sweetness of countenance that bespoke her nature. She was approaching her mid-thirties and beginning to accept society's opinion that she would never catch a husband. Or at least she gave the impression of such acceptance for the sake of dignity, nothing was worse than being pitied, but in private she yearned for a home of her own away from the constant attendance upon her invalid mother, who was a past mistress at the art of manipulating her ailments to control her daughter. Millicent dreamed sometimes of a child, a house in the country, and a quiet, undemanding husband. But she kept her dreams to herself.

The sisters greeted her warmly and she turned from them to acknowledge other acquaintances. Arthur Melvin was balancing his teacup in one hand and a plate of cake in the other. He stood on the outskirts of the group as Millicent chatted, inquiring about health and families with an air of genuine concern.

Arthur noted her costume: a neat and very plain coat and skirt of brown serge, with a matching hat adorned with a pheasant's feather. It was serviceable rather than elegant. He liked the softness of her voice and her general demeanor that bespoke a rather retiring nature. All in all, he thought, on first acquaintance Miss Hardcastle exactly matched his specifications. He moved around the group to where Miss Duncan stood by the piano talking to a very young girl.

"Ah, Mr. Melvin." Constance smiled at him as he approached. "May I get you more tea?"

"No, I thank you." He set his cup and saucer and plate on the top of the piano. "I was wondering if I might have an introduction to Miss Hardcastle."

"Why, certainly," Constance said. "She's such a charming woman." She led him across to Millicent and performed her first true client introduction, then she stepped back and left them to it.

"How do you think it's going?" Prudence murmured half an hour later.

"I don't know. But they're still talking," Constance murmured back. "I think we've earned our fee."

Chapter 16

Constance draped the emerald green silk shawl over her bare shoulders and fingered the diamond necklace nestled around her throat. "You don't think the diamonds are a little too much?"

"Absolutely not," Prudence declared. "But the tiara might be since it's only dinner."

"That's a relief," her sister said. "I was afraid you were going to insist on it."

"If you were going to a ball, I would." Prudence clasped a diamond bracelet high up on her sister's forearm where it wouldn't be hidden by her long gloves. "Let Chas put the finishing touches to your hair."

Constance sat down in front of the mirror watching critically as Chastity tied a black velvet ribbon around the elaborate braided chignon at the nape of her neck. "This style suits you so well," Chastity said, teasing a few strands onto Constance's forehead to soften the line. "And the simplicity sets off the gown and the diamonds."

Constance rose from the stool and examined her reflection in the long mirror. Her gown was of pale green silk interwoven with a delicate black filigree pattern. Black silk gloves, an ivory fan, and a tiny diamond-studded evening purse completed the ensemble. "I think I look rather untouchable," she said.

"Tantalizingly so," Prudence said with a laugh. "What more could a man want?"

"In the august halls of the Houses of Parliament a man's mind should be on serious matters," Constance said with a righteous air. "I wouldn't wish to distract him."

"Well, if you're to arrive punctually you should go now." Chastity went to the bedroom door. "Cobham will be waiting for you."

Constance followed her, as Prudence adjusted the set of the shawl. "I hope this evening goes all right. I feel bad about abandoning you to Henry and Father."

"Oh, it'll be fine, don't give it a second thought," Prudence said, giving her a little push through the door. "Father's never discourteous with strangers even if they annoy him. And once Henry starts to play after dinner, you can lay odds he'll be heading for his club."

Constance couldn't argue with this, and wasn't inclined to. Her sisters accompanied her to the street, where Cobham waited with the carriage. "If you decide on another night on the tiles," Prudence said with a knowing smile, "make sure you're back in plenty of time for the wedding tomorrow."

Constance didn't deign to reply. She climbed into the carriage and sat back in the dim interior as the carriage moved at Cobham's stately pace along Whitehall to the Houses of Parliament. She alighted at St. Stephen's Gate and the police inspector who had charge of the gate came forward to greet her.

"Miss Duncan, Mr. Ensor told us to expect you. He's awaiting you on the terrace. One of my men will escort you."

A policeman offered a deferential bow and she followed him through the long stone corridors and out onto the terrace that overlooked the Thames.

Max was standing with a group of people beside the balustrade, his eyes on the doors. As soon as he saw her, he came across with swift step. "Constance." He took her hand and raised it to his lips. An unusual salute but one that seemed in keeping with their setting and the exquisite formality of her costume.

"You take my breath away," he murmured into her ear as he tucked her gloved hand into the crook of his arm. "We aren't dining alone since unchaperoned ladies are rather frowned upon here, but I trust you'll find our companions congenial."

Constance had expected this. It was one thing to dine alone with a man who was neither relative nor fiancé in the Café Royal or an out-of-the-way restaurant on Kensington Church Street, quite another in this bastion of male power and privilege.

She was, however, surprised to find herself dining with the Prime Minister and three of the most influential members of his Cabinet, all accompanied by their wives. The startling thought occurred to her that she was being vetted as a suitable wife for an up-and-coming politician. In these circles, a man's wife was a vital asset. She could make or break a parliamentary career.

She gave Max a speculative glance as they were seated at a prominent, large round table in the Members' dining room. He gave her a bland smile and turned to address a remark to the lady on his right. Constance picked up her own conversational ball with the ease of habit and training, ensuring that nothing revealing, nothing of any importance was said by herself or either of her table neighbors.

Her fork faltered when the Chancellor's wife declared in a voice that carried into one of those moments of silence that sometimes fall on a group, "As Asquith always says, man is man, and woman is woman. Parliament cannot make them the same." She plied her fan, a tiny pink patch of indignation blooming on her cheeks.

Constance caught a sudden warning in Max's eyes. She picked up her fork again and poked at her roast beef. So she was to be muzzled. Her opinions would embarrass him. Well, so be it. This dinner table was hardly the forum for an impassioned diatribe on the manifest injustice of the disenfranchisement of women. It would win neither her nor her cause any friends.

But Max's warning rankled. He'd accompanied her to a WSPU meeting. He'd met the Pankhursts. He knew how passionately she felt about this. Surely if he had any respect for her views he wouldn't prevent her from presenting them for informed and respectful discussion.

The ladies rose when the Prime Minister's wife gave the signal, and repaired to the retiring room, leaving the gentlemen to enjoy port and cigars, while the women gossiped companionably, made what repairs were necessary to appearances, and sipped coffee in the adjoining lounge.

Constance was prepared for the inquisition. "How long have you known Mr. Ensor, Miss Duncan?" Lady Campbell-Bannerman inquired, settling back on the sofa with her coffee.

"A few weeks," Constance responded. "I know his sister, Lady Graham."

"Oh, yes, of course. A charming woman. Her husband takes his seat regularly in the Lords, I understand."

"So I believe." Constance sipped her coffee. She appeared perfectly relaxed, no hint of the coiled spring of tension as she waited for the test that was bound to come.

"Lord Duncan too, I understand, is most assiduous in his parliamentary duties."

"My father takes his seat regularly," she said. "He always has done."

"And you, Miss Duncan? Are you interested in politics?"

"Very." She smiled the smile of the tiger.

"It's a little unseemly for a woman to be interested in politics. Even those of us whose domestic lives are governed by our husbands' political work," Lady Asquith said. "Our role is to provide him with the atmosphere in which to do that work . . . nothing contentious, perfect harmony at home."

"Oh, yes, we must make certain that he's never aware of the little domestic trials and tribulations that beset us," one of the other women confided, leaning across to Constance, patting her hand. "Our men do the vital work of the country. We're so privileged to assist them."

Constance smiled faintly.

"It's the least we can do, after all, when we're so fortunate to have such men to decide all these matters for us, to come to decisions for our own good. Don't you think, Miss Duncan?"

"No," Constance said, setting down her coffee. "No, ma'am, I don't think so at all. I find nothing fortunate or privileged about having decisions made for me by men, who make them simply by virtue of being men. I consider myself perfectly capable of making decisions for my own good."

There was a shocked silence. Only Constance, it seemed, was unmoved by her speech. She waited a few moments, then, when it seemed no response was to be forthcoming, rose with a murmured excuse and made her way out to the terrace again.

She heard Max's voice as she passed an anteroom to the dining room. She paused, unwilling to enter in case it was one of the areas restricted to women. It was a fair assumption that it was, since women were allowed in very few areas of the Houses of Parliament. And not even Constance would break such a rule.

He was speaking clearly, as were his companions, the Prime Minister and Asquith. And she listened unabashed once she heard the first sentence.

"There's to be a deputation to the House with a petition," Max said. "I don't know when, the date hasn't been decided as yet."

"We must refuse it," Asquith said. "If we accept a petition we're giving legitimacy to the question."

"That's certainly a point," Max replied. "But it will also enrage them." He gave a short laugh. "I've seen these women in action, Prime Minister, and they're very passionate about their cause. I see our best course of action as appeasement. We take the petition, we just don't act on it."

I've seen these women in action. Constance could barely swallow her rage. Her nails bit into her gloved palms as she held herself still and quiet. How could he sound so dismissive? How *dare* he make light of the confession she had made to him of her own driving commitment? She had been trying to change his mind about women's suffrage, but she had also been willing to share confidences with him because she thought something good for both of them might come of it. And what did he do with those confidences? Make light of them, and use them to work against the Union.

"I have an ear to the ground," Max was saying. "I can probably get details of their next move before it goes public. It'll give us time to plan a strategy."

"Good man. Forewarned, as they say."

Constance left her post. She wanted to leave the House altogether but caution held her back. Until she had decided what to do, she didn't want Max to know what she'd overheard. The cold voice of reason told her that acting in haste and fury was always unwise. This betrayal required an altogether subtler response. For the moment her anger masked her hurt, and for the moment she welcomed that distance. When it came it was going to be wretched. She had allowed herself to get close to him, to conjure with the idea of love, and therefore of a future. Instead she had invited betrayal.

The cooler air of the terrace fanned her cheeks, cleared her head a little, and when Max came up behind her she was able to turn and greet him with a smile.

"I didn't realize you were out here alone," he said, leaning beside her on the parapet, resting his arms along the ledge. Below them the tide was high and the river was still busy with laden barges heading for the docks despite the late hour.

"I found my companions' conversation rather irritating," she said flatly.

"Oh." He shook his head. "I was afraid of that."

"Then why did you invite me? Weren't you also afraid I might embarrass you?"

"No," he said, sounding surprised. "Far from it. Why would you think such a thing?"

She shrugged. "I don't know. I'm tired, Max. I've had a rather busy day."

"Then I'll take you home." He gave her a searching look. Constance was rarely tired. She always seemed to have boundless energy. And yet she certainly seemed to be drooping a little tonight. He thought perhaps it had something to do with her woman's cycle. He had noticed often enough how at certain times of the month perfectly rational, even-tempered females became emotional and distracted.

Constance wondered how he could stand there, talking to her, behaving exactly as usual when he had just come from a conversation where he had talked so matter-of-factly of deceiving her, as if it was the only course of action, the obvious course of action. It was almost impossible to believe. But she had heard what she had heard. Her first impression of

Max Ensor had been the correct one, and she had allowed her emotions, her self-indulgent impulses, to rule her. Typical female, she thought in disgust.

She couldn't bear his company another minute and said abruptly, "Would you make my excuses. I don't feel at all well. I'll take a cab home."

"No, I'll take you home. Did you have a cloak?"

"No." She drew the shawl tighter around her. There was no graceful way to refuse his escort home, and she was not ready to confront him yet.

Max made no attempt at conversation. He put an arm around her in the cab but when she twitched aside he let his arm drop immediately. He couldn't imagine what could be wrong between them, therefore there wasn't anything wrong. She was tired. It was the wrong time of the month. It could be no more than that.

He walked her to her door and bent to kiss her. She turned her face aside so his lips made contact with her cheek not her lips. "I expect you have a headache," he said sympathetically. "I understand about these things."

Constance stared at him. *Understand?* Understood what things? How could he possibly understand? And then it dawned on her as she looked at him, saw the warmly concerned but nevertheless slightly patronizing smile in his eyes. Of all the typical male conclusions to draw. He could think of only one explanation for why she suddenly seemed less accessible to him.

Max hesitated, wondering whether to say something else in the sudden silence, then while he was still wondering, she had bidden him good night and disappeared inside, using her own key in the door.

Max stood on the pavement, frowning. Then he shook his head and walked away, unaware of Constance at the landing window watching him go.

Constance went into the parlor where, as she'd known, her sisters were waiting up for her.

"What in the devil's name has happened?" Prudence demanded the instant Constance walked in.

"Con, you look as if you've seen a ghost," Chastity said in concern. "Are you ill, love?"

"Sick at heart," Constance said with a bitter smile. "I am so stupid! Here am I priding myself on how clever I am and how I can outwit anyone, particularly any man, and I fall for the oldest trick in the book. What a dupe!" She poured herself a glass of cognac and stood by the empty grate, one elegantly shod foot on the fender.

"I think you'd better tell us the whole," Prudence said. "I'm assuming this has to do with Max?"

"Everything to do with Max."

She told them and they listened in stunned silence. "And do you know what?" Constance asked with a short laugh as she finished her recital. "He decided that my sudden reticence was because I have the curse. Of all the insulting . . ." She gave another bitter laugh and drank her cognac.

"What are you going to do?" asked Prudence, deciding to leave the sympathy to Chastity, who, tearful herself, was already hugging her sister. Constance needed practical help as well as sympathy.

Constance disengaged from Chastity's embrace and dug into her purse for her handkerchief. She wiped her damp eyes with a decisive movement, as if putting all pointless emotion behind her. "I am going on the attack," she declared. "In the pages of *The Mayfair Lady*. If we get it to the printer in the morning, will it make Saturday's edition, Chas?"

"I would think so," her sister replied. "Sam's usually pretty flexible. If necessary he can just add another page."

"Good," Constance stated. "Max Ensor isn't going to know what hit him."

"It seems appropriate," Prudence agreed. "But shouldn't you talk to him first about what you heard?"

"No." Constance shook her head firmly. "I shall avoid him, or perhaps *evade* is the better word, until after the article is published. If I have to meet him, he'll have nothing but smiles. I want him to be completely off his guard, and then ambushed. Totally blindsided." Her mouth was set in a grim smile. "For the next day or two I can be in seclusion with my *womanly troubles*."

The grim smile took a suddenly wicked turn. "You two can have some fun with that. If he comes a-calling, you can offer some delicate little evasions and hints. It'll feed right into his insulting assumptions. I might even hide behind the curtains while you do it."

"You won't, not if you expect us to be convincing," Prudence declared, but she too had a wicked gleam in her eye. "But I own it might be amusing. Don't you, Chas?"

Chastity looked less entertained by the prospect than her sisters. She wore a preoccupied frown. "Will you name him in the article, Con?"

"Oh, no, Chas." The smile grew grimmer. "I'll just make sure that there are enough details to identify a certain Right Honorable Gentleman . . . *right honorable, indeed!*" She shook her head again in disgust and refilled her glass. "You two go on to bed. I'm too worked up to sleep, so I'll get started on my article." She moved energetically to the secretaire, glass in hand.

"If you're sure," Chastity said doubtfully.

"Quite sure. I'll not be good company right now. I need to do this if it's to get to the printer's in time for next week's edition." She sat down and drew a pad of paper towards her. "Oh, by the way, how was Henry?"

"Nervous as a stray kitten," Prudence said. "He barely managed a word at dinner despite Father's best efforts to draw him out, and then he played the piano for over an hour afterwards. Father listened politely for about half an hour, then beat a retreat to his club. We sent Henry to bed at eleven. Chas would have tucked him in if I'd let her."

Constance smiled, but it was a distracted one. "We'll get him to Caxton Hall tomorrow, then?"

"Oh, yes, no doubt," Prudence stated. "And Amelia will manage him from then on." She paused, her hand on the door. "Quite sure you're all right, Con?"

"Quite sure." Constance had already begun to write.

Her sisters exchanged a glance and then with a murmured good night left her to it.

It was close to three o'clock before Constance finally set down her pen, satisfied at last with what she'd written. If Max Ensor's ears weren't on fire at this minute they certainly should be. A wave of tiredness washed over her. She stood up, yawning. She felt purged of her hurt, or was it only masked by her anger? By the satisfaction of venting that anger?

In her heart she knew she hadn't begun to touch the wound. It was easier for the moment to blame herself for failing to trust her instincts and to rage at Max for his treachery. The pain would come later. She went up to bed, and to her surprise slept like a log until mid-morning.

She was awoken by Chastity, who came in softly carrying a tea tray. She set the tray on the dresser and drew back the curtains at the long windows. Gray light entered the room. "Oh, dear," Constance said. "Not a pretty day for a wedding."

"No, but it's not raining." Chastity poured tea and brought it over to the bed. "You slept late."

"I worked late." Constance sat up and took the tea with a grateful smile. "Just what I need, Chas."

Chastity sat on the edge of the bed with her own cup. "Prue's taken your article to the printer, then she's going to the florist to choose the flowers. We thought a red rose for Henry's buttonhole and we'll all wear white ones. Then we thought a small bouquet of pink roses and maybe lilies of the valley for Amelia. Whatever looks fresh and pretty. Prue is good at flowers."

"Do we know what Amelia's wearing?"

"It has to be black."

"Black?" Constance raised her eyebrows. "Why, pray tell?"

Chastity grinned. "Amelia wrote to say that she'd managed to get an extra hour off this evening . . . nice of Letitia, wasn't it?"

"Charming," Constance agreed. "What convinced her to be so generous? A dying mother?"

"Almost," Chastity said. "The funeral of a dearly beloved aunt."

"Hence the black." Constance laughed but without much humor. "At least any color flower will go with that." She held out her cup for a refill. "The ceremony's at four?"

"Four-thirty, to give Amelia time to get there, since she can't leave the Grahams until four. Prue and I will bring Henry. We thought you should escort Amelia, since you're sisters under the suffrage flag." Chastity's smile was a little teasing. "You'd be the most suitable maid of honor. We'll play groomsmen."

Constance frowned slightly. "I feel bad that you're doing all the heavy lifting with Henry."

"Oh, don't give it a second thought." Chastity stood up. "Prue and I have Henry down to a fine art. You'll wait for Amelia outside the Grahams' when she gets off at four and escort her to Caxton Hall. Then we'll go to Claridges for a celebration tea afterwards. We booked a private room, so there'll be no danger of running into anyone. It would be a little awkward if we bumped into Letitia, or Max, wouldn't it?"

"Extremely," Constance agreed dryly.

Chastity continued, "After that they'll have a couple of hours to . . . to . . ."

"Consummate their union," Constance finished for her. "Where are they going to do that?"

"Henry found a little residential hotel on the Bayswater Road. Quite cheap, but he says it's clean and respectable. He's going to move there until he can find lodgings. Apparently Max gave him an advance on his salary to help him get set up."

At the mention of Max's name Constance's expression grew somber. "Well, at least he can be generous," she conceded.

Chastity said only, "I'll leave you to get up, then."

Constance tossed aside the covers. "I'll be down in half an hour." Chastity nodded and left with the tea tray.

Constance examined the contents of her wardrobe, her expression abstracted. She needed something suitable for a registry-office wedding and a subdued celebration. Finally she chose a suit of pale gray shantung with a deep green silk blouse. She plaited her hair and looped it into a chignon at the nape of her neck, then went downstairs. She was midway down the stairs when she heard Max's voice coming from the open doors of the drawing room.

She stopped dead, her hand on the banister, one foot raised for the next step down. Prue was saying in conspiratorial tones, "Oh, I'm so sorry, Max, but Con's not feeling too well this morning. A touch of stomach ache, you know."

"Yes, and a headache," Chastity chimed in. "It's so trying," she added with a heavy sigh. "And poor Con seems to suffer more than any of us."

"I see." He coughed and Constance grinned to herself. He sounded distinctly discomfited at this confidence.

"She was not too well last night," he continued with another little cough. "I thought perhaps it was . . . well . . . I do understand." Despite her delight in his obvious embarrassment, his voice, rich and mellow, sent the usual prickles up her spine. Lust, it seemed, was invincible, resistant even to treachery.

"Do give her my best regards," Max said, his voice coming closer as he moved to the door. Constance hastily stepped up the stairs, out of sight of the hall. "I'll call tomorrow, when I hope she'll be feeling better."

"Oh, I would leave it for several days," Chastity advised. "At these times, Con's often not comfortable leaving the house for a while."

Constance choked on her laughter. Chastity was rarely outrageous but when she chose to be, no one could better her. She could almost feel sorry for Max, whose footsteps receded rapidly across the hall and out of the door opened by an impassive Jenkins.

"Chas!" Constance exclaimed, hurrying down the stairs. "That was not in the least subtle."

"It wasn't intended to be," her sister said with a touch of defiance. "He deserved it."

"At least it ensured he won't be ringing the doorbell for a couple of days," Prudence said. "Are you going to have a late breakfast, or wait for an early lunch?"

"Oh, I'll wait. I'm not particularly hungry. I want to show you my article and we'll decide where to run it. It'll mean rearranging the layout since it's rather a long piece."

"In that case, I'll bring coffee to the parlor, Miss Con," Jenkins announced from the middle of the hall, where he'd been listening and drawing his own conclusions.

"Oh, yes, please, Jenkins. And if Mrs. Hudson has made some of those little coconut cakes, could we have some of those too?" Chastity said over her shoulder as she ran up the stairs.

"I'll see what there is, Miss Chas." Jenkins hesitated, then said, "Am I to assume that Mr. Ensor is no longer welcome, Miss Con?"

Constance paused, then said, "No, Jenkins, for the moment he's perfectly welcome. In a few days I guarantee he won't darken our doors again."

Jenkins allowed himself the merest lift of an eyebrow. "I see." He went off into the back regions of the house.

At three-thirty Constance left the house and took the omnibus to Park Lane. She walked to the Grahams' house on Albermarle Street and strolled casually along the opposite side of the street, hoping that Amelia would emerge before someone in a neighboring house noticed the lady carrying a bridal bouquet who seemed to have nothing better to do on an overcast afternoon than walk up and down the street.

Punctually at four o'clock Amelia, clad in black and heavily veiled, appeared from the side entrance to the house. She paused for a moment, looked up and down the street, saw Constance, and without acknowledgment hurried towards Park Lane. Constance followed.

On the relative anonymity of Park Lane, Amelia stopped and Constance came up beside her. Again they didn't acknowledge each other. Constance hailed a hackney. "Caxton Hall," she said as she climbed in. Amelia followed her.

Once in the seclusion of the cab's dim interior Amelia put back her veil. "My heart's fluttering like a bird's," she said. "I can't quite believe it's really going to happen."

"Believe it." Constance took her hand and squeezed tightly. "Henry will not fail and neither will my sisters."

At that, Amelia gave a weak smile. "Poor Henry. Subject to this monstrous regimen of women."

"Better that than his tyrannical father."

"True enough." Amelia leaned back against the squabs. "I never imagined going to my wedding in funereal black . . . but then," she added with a tiny laugh, "I never imagined going to my wedding at all."

Constance handed her the bouquet. "Maybe this will put you in a bridal frame of mind."

Amelia took the flowers and inhaled their delicate scent. "You and your sisters seem to think of everything. I can't tell you how grateful I am."

"There's no need for gratitude," Constance said easily. "Just think that in an hour you will be a married woman." She smiled encouragingly at Amelia, who was very pale. "And in about seven months you'll give birth to a perfectly legitimate seven-month child. Henry will be a successful private secretary to a Member of Parliament, and you'll take the babe to visit his grandfather, and Justice Franklin will embrace his grandchild and accept his daughter-in-law and take his son back into the fold."

Amelia turned her head against the squabs to look at Constance. "Are you the optimist you make yourself out to be?"

"Where men are concerned?" Constance asked after an instant's deliberation. "No, Amelia."

"That's rather what I thought," Amelia said. "Neither am I."

"But this will turn out all right," Constance stated.

Amelia smiled again. "Yes," she said. "I know it will. I don't place much faith in Henry's father, but Henry will stand true."

"With you behind him."

"Yes," she said with a laugh. "With me behind him."

The hackney drew up outside the imposing edifice of Caxton Hall. Constance paid the hackney and took Amelia's arm. "Ready?"

Amelia nodded and dropped her veil. "I suppose they're used to this hole-in-the-corner business in a registry office."

"Don't think like that," Constance chided. "This is perfectly legal and it doesn't matter what anyone thinks. Let's go inside." She strode towards the double doors, her arm firmly tucked into the bride's.

Henry was waiting in the foyer with Prudence and Chastity. If anything, he looked paler than Amelia. He kept one hand in his breast pocket, clasping both the marriage license and the wedding ring. His free hand he gave to his bride as she reached him.

"Is all well, dearest?" he asked in a low voice in which a distinct tremor could be heard.

"Yes, perfectly well." Amelia put back her veil and smiled at him. "You're very brave, Henry."

He shook his head vigorously. "No, dearest, you are the brave one."

"I think you're both very brave," Prudence declared before this exchange of denials could continue into the evening. "Now that we're all here we can go into the anteroom." She led the way across the galleried foyer, towards a door at the rear. Henry and Amelia followed, with Chastity and Constance close behind.

The registrar's clerk greeted their arrival with a pointed look at the clock. It said four twenty-five. He made elaborate play of looking into an appointment book. "Mr. Franklin and Miss Westcott?"

"Yes," Henry said. He cleared his throat. "I am Mr. Franklin and this is my . . . my . . . Miss Westcott." He stepped forward, holding Amelia's hand tightly in his.

The clerk looked askance at Amelia's funereal garb then looked again at the clock. He neither spoke nor moved until the hands touched the half hour, then he rose, gathered up a file folder, and disappeared through another door.

"Friendly fellow," Prudence observed.

"He just likes the power," Constance responded acidly. "Petty bureaucrats are all the same."

"Both sexes," Prudence said with a half smile.

Constance shrugged. "Probably, but there aren't that many women in positions of power, however petty."

"Yes, Con," Chastity agreed with an exaggerated sigh that made them all laugh. Henry and Amelia hadn't taken their eyes off the door through which the clerk had disappeared, and when he returned still clutching his book they simultaneously straightened their shoulders.

"The registrar is ready for you," the clerk intoned. "If you would give me the license." He held out his hand.

Henry relinquished the paper and they followed the clerk into a pleasant paneled room that was nowhere near as institutional as Constance and her sisters had feared it would be. There was even a vase of daisies on the marble mantlepiece. The registrar nodded at the little party and took the license from his clerk. He showed little expression in either voice or countenance as he went through the simple businesslike ceremony.

Henry and Amelia made their responses with conviction; indeed, it seemed to Constance that Henry grew taller and more assured with each declaration. When he slipped the ring on Amelia's finger his hands were perfectly steady; the bride's trembled. The registrar stamped the document with his official seal and Mr. and Mrs. Franklin exchanged a kiss.

"Congratulations." The registrar shook both their hands and smiled a courteous dismissal. The Duncan sisters exchanged smiles of relief.

"And now," Chastity said when they were all once more in the street, "we eat cake. I ordered a beautiful gâteau at Claridges."

"And champagne," Constance said. "Tea seems a little pedestrian for a wedding feast."

The newlyweds didn't appear to be taking much in. They both seemed stunned as they stood hand in hand on the pavement.

"Two cabs, I think," Prudence said with a significant glance at her sisters. Constance nodded and stepped to the curb. She put two fingers to her mouth and produced a most unladylike whistle that had instant success. They urged Amelia and Henry into one cab and Constance told the cabby to deposit them at Claridges. She closed the door on them and brushed off her hands with a gesture of satisfaction. "That'll give them ten minutes of privacy."

It was a privacy they clearly put to good use. Amelia emerged from the seclusion of the cab looking rather flushed and rumpled, her hair escaping its pins. Henry had an air of complacent satisfaction and he kept a possessive arm around Amelia's shoulders.

Prudence slipped into the hotel ahead of the rest of the party, and when they joined her in the foyer, a footman stood ready to escort them to a small private room.

"You're such a sentimental Scrooge, sister dearest," Constance murmured affectionately, taking in the table set with cake and champagne. "I wish I'd thought of this."

"It only takes one of us to do this," Prudence said in the same low tone. "You've fixed up Henry with a job. They can take it from here."

Constance nodded, reflecting that that minor deception would have meant very little if she and Max still had the possibility of remaining friends. It felt rather different now.

Chapter 17

Henry was sorting the mail when Max entered his office at home early one morning several days later. "Anything of interest, Henry?" He tossed his newspaper onto the windowsill.

"Mostly bills, sir. A couple of letters from constituents." Henry indicated the neat pile of opened mail on the desk.

"You're here bright and early," Max remarked, standing at the window looking out onto the street, where a few pedestrians battled heads-down against a strong gusty wind that was sending hats tumbling into the road.

"I was wondering, sir, if I could start an hour early every morning and leave at half-past three on Thursdays," Henry asked timidly, a flush blooming on his cheeks.

Max turned from the window. "Do you have something special to do on Thursday afternoons?" he inquired in a friendly fashion.

"Well, yes, sir, as it happens."

Max smiled. "Why do I think it must have something to do with a young lady?"

Henry's blush deepened. "As it happens, sir . . ."

Max laughed. "I see no difficulties, Henry."

"Thank you, Mr. Ensor." Henry went back to work with his paper knife.

Max picked up the already opened mail and flicked through it. He was feeling restless, dissatisfied in some way, although he couldn't put his finger on the cause. Unless, of course, it was because he hadn't seen hide nor hair of Constance for days.

"You did make sure those flowers were delivered to Miss Duncan at Manchester Square yesterday?" he asked.

"Yes, of course, Mr. Ensor. The florist promised they would be delivered by four o'clock. In fact, I believe this is a letter from Miss Duncan."

Henry proffered a slim white envelope emblazoned with the Duncan crest.

Max took it, trying not to betray his eagerness. He recognized her writing, a bold but elegant flowing script that matched the writer. He slit the envelope and unfolded the thick sheet of vellum. The message was disappointingly short.

Dear Max,

What lovely flowers. Thank you so much for the kind thought. I had wanted to thank you in person for such a lovely evening at the House of Commons but I was a little under the weather when you called the next morning. Please forgive my negligence and accept my thanks now.

In haste,

> *Constance.*

Max read and reread the short note. It had no perceptible warmth in it and contained not even a hint of a future meeting. It didn't make any sense. And why the haste? He crumpled the vellum and tossed it into the wastepaper basket. Of course, it was always possible she was rather busy. Putting out that broadsheet every fortnight must take up a lot of her time. He frowned in thought, trying to remember the date on the mockup that he'd seen in the parlor. He couldn't remember it exactly but it had to be around now. Maybe the Duncan sisters had been taken up with their editorial activities.

"Henry, I'd like you to go in search of the latest edition of a publication called *The Mayfair Lady*."

"I don't believe I've heard of it, sir." Henry raised inquiring eyebrows.

"No, it has a relatively small circulation, I believe. You might have to try several newsagents. I would think you might find a copy around Parliament Square somewhere. It has a certain political thrust to it and I would imagine its editors would try to place it prominently with Westminster vendors."

"Very well, sir. I'll go right away." Henry took up his hat.

Max sat down at his desk to begin tackling his constituency mail but after a minute his hands fell idle and he stared frowning at the window. A light scatter of raindrops hit the glass. Perhaps he should simply pay a morning call at Manchester Square. He realized that a few days ago he wouldn't have thought twice about such a visit. It was perfectly natural, a perfectly acceptable thing to do on a Saturday morning. She would either be there or she wouldn't. And yet something indefinable held him back. Unease, a nameless unidentifiable sense of trouble, kept him sitting at his desk staring out at the stormy morning.

What could possibly be wrong? Had something happened to her? Some family trouble? With her father perhaps? Or one of her sisters? If so, then he must go to her. But she hadn't asked for his help, or his comfort, or anything else that he might usefully have to offer if something was wrong. And surely they were close enough for her to turn to him. When it came to making mischief with her father's car she hadn't hesitated to co-opt him. Perhaps, he thought, she was so taken up with the WSPU at the moment that she had no time for anything else. That would not be surprising. She had described her involvement there as the driving force of her existence.

He stood up abruptly. It was a ridiculous business. She had to be exaggerating the passion of her involvement. She was an intelligent, reasonable woman, not some wild fanatic. Somehow he would have to get her to see reason, to step back from the whole enterprise. She was entitled to her opinions, he would never dispute that, but he couldn't possibly have a wife who was an active suffragist. God knows what it would do to his career.

Max dropped his pen to the desk and ink spattered across the blotter. He had just silently given words to something he hadn't realized he had been contemplating. But, of course, in the deepest recesses of his mind it had been there for weeks now. She had fascinated him from the very first moment he had met her. And little by little that fascination had become the all-powerful need to have and to hold her, to claim her for his own, now and forever.

He was not given to fanciful turns of phrase and he found himself absurdly trying to hide an embarrassed smile from the deserted room. He told himself that she would make him the most unrestful wife. But then there was the reverse side of the coin. Excitement. She exhilarated him and excited him, even as she challenged him. But she was an impossible wife for a career politician.

Which left him precisely where?

He heard the front door close, the sound of Henry shaking an umbrella in the hall, his quick step. "Just started raining cats and dogs, Mr. Ensor," Henry observed as he came in. "But I found the paper. Yesterday's date, so it's the latest edition." He took the folded broadsheet from inside his coat. "I don't think it's wet." He handed it to his employer. "The newsagent said it was selling like hotcakes."

Max nodded absently as he scanned the headlines. He noticed that the list of contents now included information on upcoming WSPU meetings, to be found on the back page. There was the usual black box: **Will the government give votes to women taxpayers?** Then his gaze was riveted by the headline to the article immediately underneath.

The Government resorts to spying

Shame on Sir Henry Campbell-Bannerman and his Cabinet. It has come to our notice that a certain Right Honorable Gentleman has undertaken to supply the government with information about the plans of the WSPU by posing as a friend to the Union. A secret informer. Is the Union so threatening to the entrenched ranks of our government that they must resort to such underhanded trickery to get the better of it? Are women so threatening? Can they not be faced in the open? What does this say about the moral courage of our government? Must we conclude that women frighten them so much they can't possibly face giving them even the simple power of the vote? The Right Honorable Gentleman, who, one has to say hardly deserves the title, has weaseled his way into the confidence of members of the Union with false statements of interest and friendship, only to betray them. One wonders how his constituency, the urban center of S——wold, will view such behavior in the man they have so recently elected to represent their interests in Parliament. It is hardly the behavior of an honorable man. Or an honest man. Or a courageous man. The Right Honorable Gentleman, eagerly embracing the dishonorable trade of a spy, is no more than the Prime Minister's cat's paw.

There was more of the same but Max barely took it in, although his eyes followed the print. His anger surged in a great crimson wave and he was unaware that he had lost all color, his complexion ghastly, a gray shade around his mouth that had thinned so as to be almost invisible.

"Is everything all right, Mr. Ensor?" Henry stared at him, unable to conceal his shock at this abrupt transformation. "You don't look well."

Max looked up from the paper. His blue eyes pierced Henry like sharpened icicles and the secretary took an involuntary step back. "I am quite well, thank you, Henry." Max folded the broadsheet and tucked it in the inside pocket of his waistcoat. His voice sounded unfamiliar to Henry. It was curiously clipped and had quite lost its mellow tones. "I am going out. I don't know when I shall be back. I would be glad if you would answer this correspondence for me. I'm sure you'll know exactly what to write. Leave the letters on the desk for my signature."

"Certainly, sir," Henry said to Max's fast-disappearing back. The door closed with a soft click that was somehow more menacing than a slam. Henry scratched his head, wondering what it was in *The Mayfair Lady* that had so incensed his employer.

Max went upstairs for his waterproof driving coat, his vizored cap, and goggles. He moved like an automaton along the current of his fury. It was all clear to him now. Her sudden withdrawal that evening, her avoidance of him since. Constance must have overheard his conversation with the Prime Minister in the House of Commons after dinner last Wednesday. He couldn't recollect the exact words that had been spoken but he could imagine how the gist would have sounded to that particular eavesdropper. And she'd been preparing her revenge ever since.

Below the level of his rage ran the acknowledgment that she was entitled to her own anger at what she would have perceived as deception. But why didn't she simply come out with it, confront him? Any man would have done so. Instead she chose to attack him in such a fashion . . . to hold him up to the scorn and mockery of his friends and colleagues. Such an embarrassment could ruin him. It was unendurable. *And by God, she was going to pay for it.*

He was halfway down the stairs, buttoning his coat, when the doorbell pealed. The male half of the couple he'd recently employed to run the house for him emerged from the back regions and went to the door.

"Is Mr. Ensor in?"

It was Asquith's voice. Max felt his jaw clench, his nostrils flare. So it had begun already. He stepped into the hall. "Thank you, Billings, I'll look after Mr. Asquith."

The manservant moved away from the door. "Very well, sir."

The Chancellor entered the hall, shaking rain off his tall beaver hat. "Ah, Ensor, do you have a minute?"

Max nodded and gestured to the morning room. "You've seen *The Mayfair Lady*, I assume?"

"It arrived with my breakfast. My secretary found it in the newsagent's on his way in. What's to be done about it? Scurrilous rag!" Asquith declared as he entered the room. "Who's responsible, that's what I'd like to know. I'll have 'em jailed for libel."

"Except that it's not," Max observed dryly. "Coffee, or something stronger?"

"Nothing, thank you. What d'you mean it's not libel?" Asquith brushed the brim of his hat with a rough sweep, sending raindrops flying across the room.

"I certainly had the intention of using any inside knowledge I gained to keep the government informed." Distantly Max wondered whether he was losing his mind. He was going to wring her neck . . . tear her limb from limb . . . boil her in oil. And yet it sounded as if he was defending her.

"But this!" Asquith pulled the broadsheet from his pocket and waved it disgustedly at Max. "What kind of cowardly attack is this?"

Max merely raised an eyebrow. He forced himself to put his anger aside for the moment. He would only survive Society's malicious gossip and the inevitable—if veiled—pleasure his peers would naturally take in his discomfiture by appearing detached and relatively indifferent. He had to treat the matter in public as one not deserving of attention or even a hint of annoyance.

In private it would be a different matter. "It'll blow over," he said.

Asquith gave him a shrewd look. "It implicates the government in something shady. The Prime Minister's not too happy."

"No, I don't suppose he is." Max perched on the arm of the sofa. He shrugged. "It's a scurrilous piece with no proof offered. No one really takes any notice of these termagants. They just don't realize it yet." Even as he said this he felt a pang of conscience. Constance and her friends were too intelligent, too passionate, too committed to a basically selfless cause to be dismissed with such contempt. But she deserved it, he told himself. She had thrown down the gauntlet and had no right to object to the manner in which he chose to pick it up. He would meet public mockery with its like.

Asquith was still regarding him closely. "I suppose you have no idea who's behind it? Seems likely it's someone who knows you."

"Someone with a grudge," Max said. "Politics is a world that harbors grudges, Asquith. And whoever's responsible for this broadsheet clearly enjoys exploiting them."

"I suppose so." Asquith looked at the broadsheet in his hand with a puzzled frown. "Not the first time you've been mentioned in it."

"No," Max agreed without expansion.

Asquith gave him another look. "Not a case of hell hath no fury, is it?"

Max gave a short laugh. "No," he declared with finality. Constance could not complain of being scorned by her lover. The deception that had produced such a savage attack had had nothing to do with the glories of their shared lust . . . their deepening emotional intimacy. It wasn't directed at Constance personally . . . unlike the fiercely personal nature of her revenge.

His mouth tightened again. He stood up abruptly. "If you'll excuse me I've some business to attend to. I'll wait upon the Prime Minister this afternoon if he wishes it. But there's little I can offer in the way of explanation." *Or excuse.* But he kept the addendum to himself.

"Of course . . . of course. I'm sure the Prime Minister will understand. Such things happen in public life. We all know it." Asquith nodded with a vigor that was not quite convincing. "Best let it just blow over, as you say."

Max nodded and accompanied his visitor outside onto the wet street. "I'm going to the mews for my motor. Can I drop you somewhere?"

"No, thank you, I'll take a cab to Downing Street. It's no distance." Asquith extended his hand. "We have to deny this rumor, of course."

It seemed that the Chancellor had finally come to the point, Max reflected as they shook hands. He had been sent with the message that it was Max's responsibility to ensure that the rumor caused Downing Street no embarrassment.

"Of course," he said. "But I wonder whether by denying it we give it credence?"

The Chancellor coughed into the gloved hand now returned to him. "The PM thought that perhaps you could discredit it. Imply a personal grudge . . . that kind of thing, don't you know?"

Max felt his anger return in full flood. She had put him in the most impossible position. To attack the anonymous editors of *The Mayfair Lady* would make him look a fool, tilting at windmills. To expose Constance and her sisters as the editors, to so much as hint at his relationship with Constance, was out of the question. Unimaginable.

But the Honorable Misses Duncan were going to bear the full brunt of his outrage. And Constance was going to write a retraction.

"Assure the Prime Minister, if you will, that I have the situation in hand."

"Of course." Asquith was all acquiescent courtesy. A gentleman's word was his bond and a gentleman didn't question its ramifications.

They nodded, exchanged smiles, and parted company. Max strode to the mews, where his Darracq was garaged. He put up the canvas roof, reflecting that its open sides would give him little protection from the rain, but it was better than nothing. Within ten minutes he was driving to Manchester Square, swiping the rain off his goggles every few seconds.

He parked the car in the square and mounted the steps to the front door of the Duncan mansion, his urgency belied by his measured pace. He pressed the bell, resisting the impulse to keep his finger on it. It was opened in Jenkins's customarily stately fashion.

"Mr. Ensor, how nice to see you," the butler declared without cracking a smile. "Miss Duncan is not at home, I fear."

"I see." Max put a foot in the door. "Miss Prudence, or Miss Chastity, perhaps?"

"They are at home, sir. But I don't know if they're receiving visitors."

Max reflected. He didn't want a showdown with Constance's sisters. It would be a pointless waste of energy. "Do you happen to know where I might find Miss Duncan, Jenkins?" he inquired mildly.

"Not offhand, sir. I expect she will be home this afternoon."

Max felt the crackle of the broadsheet inside his waistcoat. It was Saturday. There was bound to be a meeting of the WSPU at lunchtime when shop workers would be beginning the half holiday that started the weekend. Constance was probably in attendance. What better place to confront her?

"Thank you, Jenkins. I'll call again later." He smiled a benign smile and ran lightly down the steps to his car as if he had not a care in the world. He cranked the engine, getting soaked in the process, and then under the inadequate shelter of the car's canopy he examined the back page of the broadsheet. There was a meeting at noon in a church hall on Brompton Road. He put the car in gear and headed for Knightsbridge.

Jenkins waited until the visitor had driven off before he closed the door. The sisters had not confided in him, which was in itself unusual, but he knew that something was amiss, and that it had everything to do with Miss Con and Mr. Ensor. He went upstairs to the parlor.

"Mr. Ensor was here inquiring after Miss Con," he declared from the doorway.

Prudence looked up from the ledgers she was balancing. "Did he say why, Jenkins?"

"No, Miss Prue."

"Did you tell him where she was?" Chastity asked from the depths of a sewing basket where she was selecting stockings that needed darning.

"No, Miss Chas."

"Well, that's all right, then." Chastity smiled at him.

"May I inquire as to the problem?" Jenkins asked.

Chastity wrinkled her brow. "I think Con had better tell you. It's not really our business."

Jenkins bowed. "I understand, Miss Chas." He left them to their darning and their bookkeeping, understanding perfectly.

"Are you sure you're ready to do this, Constance?" Emmeline asked as they stacked papers on the table beside the door to the church hall.

"Yes, it's time I was blooded," Constance said with a grim, tight smile. She was going to make her maiden speech at today's meeting.

"This resolution has nothing I suppose to do with that extraordinary revelation in *The Mayfair Lady*?" Emmeline inquired with a shrewd look. "I assume you've seen it. Everyone else seems to have done."

"I saw it," Constance said shortly. "And I blame myself. I introduced the man, after all. I don't know how I was so blind."

"But who *did* know what he was up to?" Emmeline wondered. "It's intriguing you must admit."

"Very," Constance agreed.

"We're blithely assuming it's true," the other woman mused. "There was no hard evidence presented, though."

Constance glanced at her. "I don't doubt it."

"No, well, you know him better than I do."

"I thought I did."

Emmeline nodded and left it at that. "There might be press here this morning to hear your speech," she warned. "Are you ready for the publicity?"

"I'm ready to stand up and be counted," Constance responded. "My father will be quite apoplectic, but he'll get over it."

"And your friends?"

"If they're my friends they'll stand by me. If they're not it's no loss." She sounded much more nonchalant than she felt. Her anxiety stemmed not from the prospect of speaking in public and making her affiliation known to the world, but at the possibility that someone might link her with *The Mayfair Lady*. But her sisters were resigned to that chance, accepting that it was time for Constance to declare herself. If there were rumors and whispers, then they would face them down with placid denial.

Constance went up to the platform to check her notes. People were beginning to trickle into the hall, shaking umbrellas, discarding wet hats and coats. The smell of damp wool was in the air. She wondered if the rain would keep people away. She wondered if Max had yet seen *The Mayfair Lady*. Apprehension niggled. What would he do? He would have to do something. Another man maybe would let it go, but not Max. And mingling with apprehension was the uncomfortable thought that perhaps she had gone too far. It was such a personal attack. Her sisters had said nothing about the piece, although she assumed they had read it before Prue took it to the printer. Their silence she felt was eloquent.

In all honesty Constance admitted to herself that the virulently personal tone of her revenge stemmed from her own hurt and sense of betrayal. It was not a well-thought out response. There was nothing balanced about it. And even though she felt it was justified, she couldn't control her uneasy anticipation of his response. Or the recognition that he was entitled to come at her with the same teeth she had used on him.

She looked up from the notes in her hand as the other leaders joined her on the platform. The hall was two-thirds full, expectant faces raised to the dais. The doorkeeper was just closing the door when Max Ensor walked in.

Constance froze.

Max looked straight at her as she stood behind the table on the dais. For a moment she was aware only of his eyes. They were like twinned blue sheets of fire and she had to resist the instinct to draw back from the scorching heat of his anger, the blistering power of his determination.

Clearly he *had* read the new edition of *The Mayfair Lady*. And clearly, as she had suspected, he had seen the mock-up of the broadsheet that evening of sabotage and put two and two together.

But then her own anger returned fresh and raw to banish the tremor of alarm at the sight of him. *How dare he come here now? What was he intending to learn this morning? Did he really imagine he would be permitted to stay now that his deceit had been exposed?*

She glanced down at her hands. To her surprise they were quite steady. She spoke, her voice carrying across the heads in the body of the hall, and the slight buzz of conversation died.

"This is a meeting for supporters of the WSPU, Mr. Ensor. We do not welcome spies. I must ask you to leave."

Max had not expected this. The sheer brazen effrontery of her head-on attack took his breath away. He took a step towards the dais.

"I should warn you, sir, that if you do not leave of your own free will then there are plenty of people here to help you on your way. What as women we may lack in physical prowess we make up for in numbers." Stinging irony edged her voice. "I can imagine the national press would find it a most interesting story."

There was dead silence in the hall. No one seemed to breathe for a minute. All eyes swiveled to the man standing at the back of the hall, gloves in hand, driving goggles pushed up on top of his rain-soaked cap.

Max could barely credit what he was hearing, but he wasn't going to put her sincerity to the test. He had no choice but to accept an ignominious defeat and retreat.

"We will have an accounting, Miss Duncan. Make no mistake." He didn't raise his voice but every word was as clear as if he'd used a megaphone. He turned on his heel and walked from the hall, letting the door slam behind him.

And now Constance's hands shook so hard that the notes she was holding fell to the table. She concentrated on putting the scattered sheets together, keeping her eyes down, aware that she was the focus of everyone's attention both in the hall and on the dais.

"You didn't expect that, I gather," Emmeline murmured, helping to scoop up the papers as Christobel broke the momentary hush by reading the minutes of the last meeting.

"I didn't expect him to come here," Constance returned in a low voice. "He must have suspected that a lot of the people who would come to a WSPU meeting would have read the article. *The Mayfair Lady* is known as a pro-suffragist publication."

"Perhaps he wanted to defend himself," the other woman observed.

"This is not the forum for it," Constance said with a snap. She knew she had overreacted and her anger now was directed only at herself. "You wouldn't have tolerated his presence, surely?" She heard the defensive thrust to the question.

Emmeline shook her head. "I don't know." She hesitated, then said, "It doesn't do our cause much good to make enemies in high places, Constance."

"He was an enemy already," Constance said. She felt a flash of empathy for Christobel's impatience with her mother's softly-softly approach. She glanced at Christobel who raised her eyebrows interrogatively. Constance nodded. She was as ready as she would ever be. Christobel took her seat as Constance moved to the podium.

Chapter 18

Max sat behind the wheel of his motor as the rain drummed on the canvas roof. It took five minutes to clear his head. Of all the lunatic impulses! To put his head in the lion's mouth like that. It would simply feed straight into the rumor mill and add yet more titillating detail to the article in *The Mayfair Lady,* which would be on every tongue by the end of the day. It was bound to reach Fleet Street by some route or another, and if there had been any members of the press in the hall they were going to have a field day. He had been blinded by his own fury, his desire to exact vengeance on that arrogant, insulting, impossible woman. How had he ever thought he could make her his wife? Madness . . . sheer madness.

But he had to concentrate on damage control. Raging at Constance wasn't going to help at the moment. When he got his hands on her, then he would have an accounting, but for the moment he had to think clearly.

He cranked up the engine, climbed in, and drove back to Manchester Square, where he parked on the far side of the square garden from the Duncan house. A massive oak tree in full leaf offered sufficient cover if anyone cast a casual glance around the square, but he was perfectly positioned to observe any comings and goings at No. 10.

He saw Lord Duncan leave in the family carriage soon after one o'clock and it was close to two o'clock before a hackney cab delivered Constance to her door. By that time his already vile temper was incendiary. It had stopped raining finally but his waterproof driving coat was still soaked through, and rain dripped from the sodden canvas hood above his head, unerringly finding a path inside his collar and down his back.

He got out and walked across the garden, heedless of the effect of puddles and wet grass on his once-shiny shoes. He mounted the steps to the front door and pressed the bell, this time keeping his finger on it until the door was opened.

"Mr. Ensor." Jenkins looked at him askance, at the finger still resting on the bell.

"I saw Miss Duncan come in a few minutes ago," Max said brusquely, pushing past the butler into the hall. "Where is she?"

"She's at luncheon, sir." Jenkins's eyes darted involuntarily towards the door to the small family dining room, where the ladies ate when they were alone.

"Then she won't mind being disturbed." Max gave him a nod and strode to the door. Jenkins, for once disconcerted, scurried behind him murmuring protestations.

Max flung open the door and stood there in the doorway. The three sisters stared at him, for the moment too taken aback by the abrupt nature of his arrival to react. "Constance, I want to talk to you," he stated. "You two, leave us alone, if you please."

"We're having luncheon," Prudence protested. "You can't throw us out of our own dining room."

"Actually, Prudence, I both can and will. Now, you and Chastity, *out*, please." The " 'please' " did nothing to soften the command.

Constance stood up. "There's no need to disturb my sisters. We'll go into the drawing room. There's no one there." She swept past him without an upward glance. It seemed to her that he was radiating so much heat, he was too hot to touch. Her heart pounded uncomfortably and her palms were suddenly clammy. She didn't look at her sisters either, knowing that if they guessed at her sick turmoil they would insist on standing behind her.

Max followed her, leaving Jenkins to close the dining room door.

"Blood is going to flow." Prudence half rose from her chair and then sat down again. "But I think we'll be surplus to requirements."

"We'll mop up later," Chastity said with what her sister considered remarkable composure. She smiled at Prudence. "Don't worry, Prue. This has to happen if Max and Con are ever going to accept that they love each other."

"Last week I might have agreed with you," Prudence said. "But I can't help thinking things have gone too far. Con actually threatened to throw him physically out of a meeting. In *public*. It's all totally out of hand now."

"Oh, I wouldn't be so pessimistic." Chastity sliced lemon meringue pie. "They're both extreme, passionate people, they're going to loathe each other as much as they love each other. It'll always be like that. Let's just hope they don't break too many plates, at least not of the heirloom variety."

"You are so sanguine." Prudence shook her head and helped herself to pie.

There was silence in the drawing room as the two faced each other. Constance had walked swiftly and without thought to the spot where she felt most comfortable, with her back to the fireplace. Max remained by the door for the moment, his back against it, as if to hold it against intruders.

"If you'd like to start with an apology, I'm listening," he said after a minute, amazed at the mildness of his tone. It bore no relation to the state of his temper.

"Oh, live your fantasy," Constance exclaimed. "You want *me* to apologize. What for? I merely exposed you for what you are. A trickster, a spy, a dishonest—"

"Enough," he declared, his voice rising a notch as he came across the room towards her. "I have had enough of your insults, Miss Duncan. One more and I won't answer for the consequences."

"Oh, typical male response," Constance scoffed. "Threats of violence are always the answer." She sounded braver than she felt. He seemed to have grown somehow taller and broader in the last few minutes.

Max inhaled sharply. He was not going to play that game, but he was prepared to match her when it came to wrestling in the mud. He turned aside and sat down on the arm of the sofa, idly slapping his gloves into the palm of one hand. "You will apologize, Constance, and you will write a retraction for the next edition of that broadsheet," he stated. "If you do not, somehow it will become common knowledge that you and your sisters are behind *The Mayfair Lady*."

"You would *do* that?" She stared at him.

"If you make it necessary. Just bear in mind that you fired the first salvo."

"Because you *used* me," she said, soft and fierce. "You pretended to like me . . . to share things with me, and all along you were merely interested in using me as a way into the secrets and plans of the Union. I *heard* you. I heard what you said to the Prime Minister. 'I've seen these women in action. I have an ear to the ground.' "

Max winced, remembering. But he wasn't going to allow her the high ground. "Just one minute, I did not pretend—"

"No, *you* wait just one minute," she interrupted. "Deny it if you can. Deny that you said those things."

"You're taking them out of context."

Constance laughed. "Oh, a typical politician's defense. Whenever you're caught, the old excuse is trotted out: *taken out of context*." She mimicked his tone. "What was the context, Max? A quiet collegiate postprandial conversation in the bastion of male power. I heard what I heard."

Her voice rose as she saw that she had him on the run. "You deceived me, pretending to . . . Oh, I can't talk to you. I can't bear to be in the same room with you." She made a brusque, dismissive gesture, turning her head aside as she tried to control the choke in her voice, to force back the tears that were both angry and hurt. She would not show him any weakness.

But he heard it anyway and came back at her. "And weren't you intending to use me in the same way? To get me to use my political influence to advance your cause. Wasn't that behind your initial interest in me?"

"That's not the same thing at all."

"Isn't it? You mean I'm fair game and you are not?" He was incredulous. "Come on, Constance. You insist women are men's equals, so why do you demand special treatment?"

"I'm not," she declared. "That's a thoroughly spurious argument and you know it. I didn't attack you personally, manipulate you, pretend to feel something . . . anything . . . just to gain information that I could use against you."

"And what do you consider this?" He pulled the sodden paper that had once been the broadsheet from inside his coat. "This is the most blatant, underhanded, utterly personal attack . . . far far worse than anything I intended. It's designed to ruin my career. Can you live with that, Constance, while you prate your high principles and moral convictions?" He threw the paper to the carpet at his feet.

"How *dare* you deny what you intended? How *could* you lie? I heard you . . . I heard what you said to your Cabinet friends. You were going to use our . . ." She waved an all-encompassing hand. "Whatever you want to call what I stupidly thought was between us, simply to advance your career. You can't deny that."

"I can deny that I meant you any—" The rest of his sentence was drowned in a cascade of water as Constance, enraged beyond thought or reason, took advantage of his seated position, picked up a round bowl of sweet peas, and tipped it over his head. Water and fragrant, vividly colored flowers dripped from his head, clung to his shoulders, fell into his lap.

He jumped up with a violent execration, scattering sweet peas left, right, and center. Constance stared at him aghast, her fingers pressed to her lips. Laughter suddenly bubbled in her eyes, inappropriate but helpless laughter.

"What the *hell*!" He dashed at the water. "What the *hell* was that?"

"I'm so sorry," she said through the bubbling laughter. "But you provoked me to such an extent that I couldn't help it. Here, let me." She approached with her handkerchief and dabbed ineffectually at his shoulder. A flower was caught in his hair, another one behind his ear. Solicitously she reached up to dislodge them. He slapped her hand away.

"I'm so sorry," she said again. "But you were already very wet anyway. In fact," she added with her head on one side, "I think the floral touch is something of an improvement. I'll get a towel." She moved to the door but he caught her arm, swinging her back towards him.

"Oh, no, you don't. Not until I've wrung your neck. You *vixen*, Constance." Laughter still mingled with anger glittered now in his eyes and was matched with hers. His hands encircled her neck, the fingers pushing up her chin. "*Shrew*," he said.

"I think at this point in the play you're supposed to say, 'Come on and kiss me, Kate,' " she murmured.

"Will you ever stop putting words into my mouth?"

"I doubt it."

"Then, 'Come, kiss me, Kate, we will be married o' Sunday.' "

"Oh, nicely capped," she whispered. "Very nice, Mr. Ensor."

"Be quiet!" His mouth enforced the command. The passionate force of his kiss had little of the lover about it. He held her head in a vise; the pressure of his lips on hers was so fierce it was as if he would brand her with the imprint of his mouth. Constance couldn't resist even had she wanted to, and indeed matched force for force, as if the kiss was some kind of exorcism that finally blunted the blade of their mutual anger.

"I told you everything would work out," Chastity said from the doorway, surveying the couple, who seemed to be locked in some elemental struggle.

Constance drew away from Max and looked over his shoulder at her sisters. She touched her swollen lips with her fingertips and caught her breath. "You're not supposed to creep up on people."

"Well, we got worried when the shouting stopped," Prudence said, coming fully into the room with Chastity. "So we thought we'd better make sure you weren't both bleeding on the floor. Whatever happened to Max? He's growing sweet peas."

Max ran his hands through his hair, dislodging a bloom. Water dripped from his hair. "I trust Constance is the only virago in the family." He shrugged out of his driving coat and went to the door. "Jenkins?"

"Right here, sir." Jenkins stepped instantly out of the shadows beneath the staircase.

"Take this and see what you can do with it, please. And bring me a towel."

Jenkins took the coat, holding it at arm's length. "May I suggest your morning coat also, Mr. Ensor. A warm iron will have it good as new. And perhaps I could offer one of Lord Duncan's shirts."

"Just take care of these two." Max handed him his black coat. "I don't imagine the ladies will object to my shirtsleeves."

"Not in the least," Chastity said, ignoring the ironical note to his statement.

"Are you sure you wouldn't like a dry shirt?" Constance asked.

"Quite sure, thank you. Your solicitude overwhelms me. Bring me a large whisky, will you, Jenkins?"

"Very good, sir." Jenkins bore his sodden burden towards the kitchen.

"So you've patched things up," Prudence said, surveying the flower-littered carpet.

"Far from it," Max replied. "Matters couldn't be further from patched."

"Oh," Chastity said in surprise. "We rather thought, seeing you—"

"Never jump to conclusions," Max said. "Your sister and I still have a great deal to discuss . . . a small matter of reparations, for instance."

All eyes turned to Constance who was now standing with her back to the room, seemingly oblivious of her companions, gazing out at the dripping trees.

"Reparations, Con?" Prudence queried.

"Max and I do perhaps have things to discuss," Constance said without turning back to the room.

"Then we'll leave you to it." Chastity tapped Prudence's arm imperatively. "I think we're once again surplus to requirements, Prue."

"Oh . . . yes . . . yes, I suppose we are." Prudence followed her sister somewhat reluctantly to the door just as Jenkins entered with a tray and a large towel draped over one arm.

"I took the liberty of bringing you a glass of sherry, Miss Con, since you don't care for whisky." He set the tray on a console table and handed Max the towel. He cast an impassive glance around the room, his gaze coming to rest on the flower-strewn wet carpet. "Should I clear this up, Miss Con?"

"Not just for the minute, Jenkins. The carpet's seen worse."

Jenkins offered a half bow in acknowledgment and left the drawing room. In the hall he encountered Prudence and Chastity, who were hovering a few feet from the door. He coughed pointedly before making his stately progress to the kitchen regions.

"He's right, we shouldn't listen," Prudence said. "Con will tell us everything later."

"I read somewhere about a trick with a glass," Chastity said rather wistfully. "If you put it upside down against an adjoining wall you can hear what's going on on the other side."

"No," Prudence declared. "We're going upstairs to the parlor." She took her sister's arm and bore her off.

In the drawing room there was silence while Max rubbed his hair dry with the towel and blotted as much water as he could from his trousers. He rolled his sleeves up to his elbows, combed his now unruly hair with his fingers, and then filled a glass from the whisky decanter.

"Would you like sherry, Constance?"

"Yes, please." She turned finally from the window and drew in a quick breath.

"What is it?" The question was sharp.

She shook her head. "It's nothing . . . just that when you look like that . . . all disordered and casual and careless . . ." She stopped. She wanted to say, *as you look when you've been making love*, but now didn't seem quite the moment to invoke such an image.

He waited, eyebrows raised, but she shook her head again. She wasn't going to tell him she found him irresistible, that he turned her knees to butter, and her loins to molten lava. He handed her a glass of sherry and she took it with a murmur of thanks.

The doorbell rang and they both paused, listening, both assuming it would be Lord Duncan. Jenkins's step crossed the hall, there was a soft murmur of voices, feet moving to the stairs. Constance breathed again. Her father would not be a welcome intrusion at this point.

"So, how are you going to put this right, Constance?" He gave the broadsheet at his feet a disdainful nudge with the toe of his shoe.

"If it's untrue, why don't you write a denial? We'll publish it in the next edition."

"No, I'm not going to dignify the accusation with a denial. I intend to ignore it. You will retract it."

Constance set down her sherry glass. She folded her arms and surveyed him. "I am willing to apologize to you for the personal nature of the attack, but I will not retract the statement that you intended to spy on us. I was not mistaken. I heard what I heard."

"Those meetings are public. Anyone, supporter or opponent, can gain entrance."

"But not anyone can listen to the private deliberations of the leaders of the Union. That was what you intended doing, and you intended to prepare the government for any action we decided to take."

Max sighed. "Maybe I did. But I never pretended to you that I was a supporter of your cause. Quite the opposite. I said I was willing to listen to your point of view, that was all. You had absolutely no excuse to go off the deep end like that." He held up a hand as her mouth opened in protest. "No, just hear me out. I did not lie to you about any of my feelings. I did not use you, or trick you, or pretend to feel something for you that I did . . . *do* . . . not. Is that clear?"

Constance still stood with her arms folded, frowning at him. "What did . . . *do* . . . you feel for me?" she asked slowly.

He tossed back the contents of his glass before speaking. Then he said, sounding more exasperated than anything, "Let me put it this way. I was perfectly serious about the statement when I capped your Shakespearean quote a few minutes ago."

"You mean *The Taming of the Shrew*?"

"Precisely."

"*Come, kiss me, Kate,*" she murmured, then her eyes opened wide as she recalled how the quote had finished.

"Married?" she demanded in utter bewilderment. "You want me to marry you?"

A look almost of pain crossed his face. "God knows why. I must have done something unspeakable in a past life to be condemned to such a fate in this one."

Constance did not take the declaration amiss in the least. Her heart seemed to be turning somersaults. "I won't stop putting words into your mouth," she said, wondering at the absurdity of such a response at such a moment.

"I don't doubt it. However, I have discovered a full-proof way of silencing you." A smile lingered now in the depths of his eyes, tugged at the corners of his mouth. "So, Miss Duncan, will you marry me?"

"I wonder what *I* did in a past life," she mused, tapping her mouth with her fingertips.

"Is that my answer?"

She nodded. There was no other response possible. They were made for each other, on the battlefield or in the bedroom. She loved him, even when she was cursing at him for an arrogant, opinionated louse. And how perverse was that? But she knew it was the same for Max. That edge they shared was what made them perfect partners. She could never consider marrying anyone else. No one else could come close to Max. The younger Constance would have lived in loving harmony with Douglas, she knew that. But she also knew that the person who had been forged by his death and her mother's would not have suited the gentle Douglas at all. What strange twists fate took. Constance had known without articulating it to herself for weeks now that she could never be happy with anyone but Max. She hadn't believed it could happen, because the one issue on which they could not agree was totally divisive. There was no room for compromise.

She said with some difficulty, feeling as if she was killing a fledgling that had not felt its wings, "What about your career? I can't compromise my work with the suffragists."

"Can't or won't?" He watched her closely over his shoulder as he took his glass to the decanter on the console table.

"Both," she said simply. "You can't marry me, Max. It'll ruin you."

He had thought that himself once. Now it seemed merely something that had to be worked around. He filled his glass and turned back to her. "We'll just have to find a way to accommodate the driving force of your existence and the driving force of mine. In fact at this juncture marriage will repair what damage you've managed to do to my reputation in the pages of that paper of yours. It seems like a very elegant solution to me."

Puzzled, she frowned at him. "I don't understand how . . . Oh, yes I do." She laughed, shaking her head. "Of all the devious tricks, Max. Is that the only reason you want to marry me?"

"Absolutely," he said blithely. "I make it a habit to use you, if you recall, to manipulate you for my own ends."

The laughter died in her eyes. "I'm willing to bury that if you are."

He set down his glass again and opened his arms. "Come here, you."

She crossed the carpet and reached her own arms up to encircle his neck. Her head fell back, exposing the column of her throat as she looked into his eyes. She read there love, desire, hungry need, and she felt the surge of all three flowing swiftly in her blood.

"I love you," he said, holding her waist between his hands. "And I will stand by you always. Even when I don't agree with you in private I will support you in public. You will never have cause to doubt my loyalty to you . . . my wife. That is a promise I make to you now, every bit as binding and solemn as the promises I will make at the altar."

"I love you," Constance said. "And I will support you in public. You will always know what I am doing or am about to do if it will have an impact on your career. That is the promise I make to you now, as binding and solemn as the promises I will make at the altar."

He kissed her then, still holding her lightly, his lips tender this time, gently exploring the corners of her mouth, the tip of her nose, the edge of her chin in a playful caress. He kissed the fast-beating pulse in her throat, and Constance pressed herself against him, feeling light as air, thistledown in the wind, as if some massive burden had been lifted.

"So," he said softly, palming the curve of her cheek, "we have dealt with that little matter once and for all."

"Once and for all. And once the engagement is made public—Max Ensor to wed an outspoken suffragist—no one would dare give credence to that article."

"I'll get Henry to send the notice of the engagement to the *Times* for tomorrow's edition," he said. "The sooner it's public, the sooner this will die down." Then he frowned. "Of course, I must talk to your father first."

"Oh, there's no need for that. I'll tell him myself when he comes in," Constance said airily. "He already told me he'd find you a perfectly acceptable son-in-law, so he won't make any objections."

"You've had this conversation?"

"No, it wasn't a conversation," Constance corrected. "It was one of Father's little declarations that follow his laments. He makes them at frequent intervals in the hopes that one of us will make it to the altar."

Max decided not to pursue that line of discourse. "Be that as it may, I should talk to Lord Duncan."

"You're not marrying into a conventional family, Max."

He scratched his head and yielded the issue. "I suppose I knew that." He bent and picked up the discarded copy of *The Mayfair Lady*. "I imagine you'll be continuing with this." He sounded resigned.

"I must. It's our only means of support."

"What?" He stared at her. "I don't find that amusing."

"No," she agreed. "Neither do we. But it's the plain truth nevertheless. And now you're going to be one of us, I suppose we should let you into all our shady secrets."

Dear God! Max thought. *Now he was going to be one of them.* Somehow her calmly matter-of-fact statement brought it home to him with vivid reality. He was marrying Constance, but she came in a trio. Take one, take all, when it came to the Duncan sisters. He would never have a minute's peace again.

Constance read his thoughts with remarkable accuracy, but then, they were fairly transparent. "It's not as bad as you think," she said, laying a comforting hand on his arm. "We're really quite harmless."

"You are not in the least harmless," he stated with some vehemence.

Constance laughed. "Come upstairs with me now. We have to tell Chas and Prue and then we'll try to put you in the picture about our finances. You ought to know I come with no fortune, merely a load of debt. But it won't concern you in the least. The three of us are working it off nicely now and I'm quite self-supporting." She took his hand and led him to the door. "Come and be welcomed to the family."

Max went willy-nilly, still trying to comprehend what she had said about being self-supporting. A man took a wife, he supported her. That was the way it was. The way it *had* to be. *Didn't it?* He decided not to pursue that line of discourse either for the moment.

As they entered the hall, voices came from beyond the curve of the staircase. Prudence, Chastity, and Amelia came into view, talking intently as they descended. Prudence saw Max and Constance first. Her step faltered as she wondered whether to bundle Amelia back upstairs before she encountered Max, but Amelia took the decision out of her hands. She came down to the hall.

"Constance, I was talking with your sisters," she said with a fair assumption of ease. "Good afternoon, Mr. Ensor."

Max was wondering what on earth his sister's governess was doing paying an afternoon call in Manchester Square when she was supposed to be in charge of his niece.

"Miss Westcott," he said politely, managing just a hint of question in the greeting.

"Not Miss Westcott," Constance said, wishing that this revelation could have come at a more suitable moment. There'd been all too many revelations thus far today. "This is Mrs. Henry Franklin, Max."

Max looked at her. He looked at her blandly smiling sisters. He looked at the serious yet determined countenance of Amelia Westcott. "Henry?" he inquired on a note of incredulity. "My secretary, Henry Franklin?"

"Well, yes, as it happens," Constance said, regarding him rather warily. "Secretaries are permitted to marry, I believe."

"It's hardly my business," he said, raising his hands in disclaimer. "My sister, however . . ."

"I have left Lady Graham's employ, Mr. Ensor," Amelia informed him. She was rather pale, but utterly determined.

"I see. Is this recent?"

"As of one hour ago," Prudence said. "Your sister, Max, saw fit to accuse Amelia of neglecting her duties by attending WSPU meetings during her hours of liberty."

"Which were few and far between," Chastity put in.

Amelia broke in softly, "Lady Graham leveled her accusations when I happened to discover her going through my private correspondence. I felt I had no choice but to resign immediately."

"And how long have you and Mr. Franklin been married?"

"Just over a week, sir."

Constance had persuaded him to employ Henry. He had seen no need for a secretary, but she had said she wanted to do a favor for an acquaintance who wanted to get married and needed a situation so that he could support a wife. No wonder Henry wanted to take off early on Thursdays, Max reflected somewhat dourly. As he recalled that was the governess's afternoon off.

Max looked at the three sisters, who returned his look with a mixture of defiance, bravado, and confidence. He turned a somewhat sardonic gaze on his bride-to-be. "More matchmaking, Constance?"

"It *is* part of our business," she said with a tiny shrug. "I explained that we need to support ourselves."

"Yes," he said faintly. "Yes, so you did." He turned back to Amelia. "Pray accept my congratulations, Mrs. Franklin."

"Thank you, Mr. Ensor." Amelia hesitated, then said, "I hope this won't jeopardize my husband's—"

Max interrupted swiftly. "Hardly, ma'am. Your husband and I deal very well together. I wish you all the best in your future life. If I can do anything to ease matters between you and my sister over your resignation, then please don't hesitate to tell me."

"Well, actually you could," Chastity said before Amelia could refuse an offer that from experience she accepted as merely form kindness. "Letitia is refusing to allow Amelia to fetch her clothes or any of her belongings."

"I'll take care of that," Max responded. "Give me the address, Mrs. Franklin, and I will see that your possessions are delivered there in the morning."

"You are too kind, Mr. Ensor."

He bowed. "It's the least I can do, ma'am. My sister is frequently overhasty when matters don't go her way, but she is quickly brought to reason again."

The Duncan sisters exchanged glances at this nice brotherly apology. Amelia took her farewell and Chastity went to Max and kissed him soundly on both cheeks. "So, have you set the date?"

Max didn't trouble to question how or why Constance's sisters had come to that conclusion. He said merely, "I'm assuming your sister will do that."

"But we have to put you in the picture first," Prudence said. "It's not quite as simple as you might think around here, Max."

He raised his hands again in disclaimer. "Oh, no, Prudence, make no mistake. I am under no illusions. If you think it will do me good, then by all means put me in the picture. But if you think it wouldn't hurt to spare me the details, then I don't insist on full disclosure."

"In for a penny, in for a pound," Constance said, taking his hand once more and leading him to the stairs, following her sisters.

"Love one, love all," he murmured.

"Only up to a point," Constance whispered. She raised her voice. "Prue, we'll talk about this later."

Prudence glanced back. "Of course." She winked and followed Chastity into the parlor.

"We go this way." Constance turned down a side corridor and opened the door to her bedroom. "I think you need to get out of those wet clothes." Her fingers moved over the buttons on his shirt. "Shall I draw you a bath?" She touched her tongue to his nipples, smiling as they hardened beneath the caress. Her hand slid into the waistband of his trousers, slithering flat-palmed over his belly. Her fingers reached down. "A bath now or after?"

For answer he pulled the pins from her hair, untangling the russet cascade with his fingers. He unbuttoned her blouse, his fingers deft despite his haste. He pushed the thin white lawn from her shoulders and unbuttoned her chemise. He took her breasts in his hands and kissed the nipples, as she had done for him. His hands spanned her rib cage, then lifted her bodily and tumbled her onto the bed at her back.

"I—" she began.

"No words." He kissed her into silence. "Words only get us into trouble."

Constance smiled, a lazy languid smile of agreement, as she helped him push aside her skirt and petticoat and drawers. With fingers as deft and as urgent as his she unbuttoned his trousers, helping him to push them down his ankles. She took his penis between her hands, held it between her breasts, took it in her mouth. She inhaled the essence of this man who was to be her husband. She tasted his sea-salt taste. She gloried in her possession of him. Her fingernails raked his buttocks as she drew him deep into her mouth, watched with open eyes his face as he reared above her, his eyes glowing with passion, his wonderful mouth parted on an ecstatic breath.

Then slowly, infinitesimally, he withdrew from her mouth. He moved down her body, laid his head on her belly, and smiled up at her. "Even stevens, sweetheart. Between the sheets or on the dueling field."

"Oh, yes," she breathed, as his mouth found her core. "Oh, yes."

Chapter 19

"More wedding presents, Con." Chastity staggered into the parlor under a pile of packages, kicking the door shut with her foot. "And Aunt Edith is arriving this evening." She set her burdens down on the floor.

"Dear Aunt Edith," Prudence said with a note of resignation. "Why does she think we need a mother figure for this wedding? She's a sweetheart but she'll only interfere with all the arrangements and then we'll have to rearrange them again."

"You know how she's always tried to take Mother's place," Constance said somewhat absently without raising her head from her writing. "She thinks it's the thing to do. We can live with it."

Prudence laughed. "You're becoming so mellow these days. Has Max told you yet where you're going to honeymoon?"

Constance set down her pen and turned to face the room. "No," she said, not sounding in the least mellow. "I can't get anything out of him. He says it's traditional for the groom to keep the bride in the dark about the honeymoon. I mean, really! Who gives a damn about tradition?"

"Max, clearly," Chastity said, sitting on the floor beside the newly arrived packages and attacking the bindings with a small knife. "But he's only teasing you."

"I am aware of that," Constance said. "And it doesn't make it any easier. How do I know what to pack in my so-called trousseau if I don't know what we're going to be doing? For all I know we could be climbing the Pyramids or rowing a boat down the Amazon."

"That doesn't sound like Max's kind of thing at all," Prudence observed, kneeling beside Chastity to help with the unpacking.

"I'm not sure *what* his kind of thing is," Constance said in some disgust.

"Well, come and help us unpack this stuff. Maybe it's a second set of cutlery."

"I just want to finish this." Constance turned back to the secretaire. "I want it ready for the next edition."

"That'll come out when you're on honeymoon," Chastity said. "You'll miss the fireworks . . . Oh, no it's not cutlery, it's silver candlesticks." She held them up. "They're lovely. From the Armitages. You can say what you like about Elizabeth, but she has impeccable taste."

Constance set down her pen again. "Let me see. Oh, yes, they are gorgeous." She shook her head slightly. "People are so amazingly generous. I can't help feeling rather guilty. I'm sure I don't deserve any of it."

"It's a wedding, Con. Everyone loves a wedding, particularly this one. Your maiden speech for the WSPU is splashed all over the newspapers, and then in the same breath in the same papers your engagement is announced to a politician who's been excoriated in that dreadful rag *The Mayfair Lady* for spying on the Union. It's the most delicious topic of gossip the town has had in many months."

Constance couldn't help a rueful laugh. "At least the engagement mollified Father. I really thought he was going to have an apoplexy when he discovered about me and the Union."

"Well, since Max can do no wrong in his eyes you're basking in vicarious approval now," Prudence commented.

"Long may it last." Constance took up her pen again. "He's not going to like this, though. I'm actually quite glad I won't be here when it comes out. I know it's cowardly of me, and he won't know I wrote it, but I'm still glad I'll be well away."

"You're really laying into Barclay?" Chastity stood up and came to read over her sister's shoulder. Her eyes widened. "I'm not sure I want to be around either."

"I have no choice," Constance said. "The deeper I dug the more dirt I came up with. The man's in league with the devil. Once this hits the streets, all the national press are going to take it up. I've identified three women he's basically raped, made pregnant, and then abandoned. They'll all get paid to give their stories, which is some consolation for them, and then I've—"

A brisk knock at the door gave her pause. Max entered on the knock. "Good afternoon," he said cheerfully. "Oh, those are lovely." He picked up one of the candlesticks. "Don't we have half a dozen of these already?"

"No," Constance said. "That's cake forks."

"Oh." He came over and kissed the back of her neck. "So diligent . . . what are you doing, writing thank you letters?"

Constance hesitated. "Uh . . . yes," she said.

"*What* are you doing?" he demanded, not fooled for a moment.

"Oh, just something for the next edition of *The Mayfair Lady*," she said vaguely, blotting the paper and managing to leave the blotting paper covering the sheet. "Tell me where we're going, Max."

It was a safe distraction. He shook his head, laughing at her. "Wait and see. This time tomorrow you will know."

"Well, will it involve a boat journey?"

He laughed again.

"A train? . . . Your motor car?"

"I told you, wait and see. I am really relishing imposing good old-fashioned tradition on you for once, my dear, and I'm not about to give up the pleasure too soon."

"There are times," Constance declared, "when I can't imagine why I'm marrying you."

"Would you like a reminder?" His eyes narrowed.

"I think this is our cue to find something else to do," Chastity said, heading for the door. "When you're finished reminding and remembering we'll be in the drawing room waiting for Aunt Edith."

"Perhaps we should take these with us," Prudence said, swiftly removing the papers from the secretaire. "Wouldn't like the wind to blow them away." She whisked out of the parlor with the incriminating sheets. Max was still something of a tender flower growing in the soil of the Duncan sisters' activities and mustn't be given too many shocks at once.

"So?" Max said thoughtfully. "What should I remind you of first?"

"Better start at the beginning," Constance said, slowly rising to her feet. "I seem to be suffering from total amnesia."

The
Bride
Hunt

Chapter 1

"Here you are, Miss Prue." Mrs. Beedle took a pile of envelopes from a top shelf in her kitchen. "Quite a few of them today. This one looks very serious." She selected a long thick vellum envelope from the sheaf and peered quite unselfconsciously at the printed heading.

Prudence sipped her tea and made no attempt to hurry her hostess. Mrs. Beedle moved at her own pace and had her own way of doing things . . . very much like her brother, Jenkins—a man who combined his duties as butler with those of friend, assistant, and sometimes partner in crime to the three Duncan sisters in the house on Manchester Square.

"Any news of Miss Con?" Mrs. Beedle inquired, finally setting the envelopes on the well-scrubbed pine table and reaching for the teapot.

"Oh, we had a wire yesterday. They're in Egypt at the moment." Prudence pushed her cup across to be refilled. "But they've visited Rome and Paris on the way. It seems like a wonderful trip."

She sounded slightly wistful, and, indeed, the six weeks of her elder sister's honeymoon had passed very slowly for Prudence and her younger sister, Chastity, left behind in London. The sheer effort of keeping their household running smoothly, eking out their meager finances, all the while ensuring that their father's willful ignorance of the family's financial situation remained undisturbed, took a much greater toll when there were only two of them to manage it. On occasion in the last weeks, Prudence and Chastity had both had to fight the temptation to force their father to acknowledge reality, a reality that he had caused by a more than foolish investment just after their mother's death. But the memory of their mother had kept them silent. Lady Duncan would have protected her husband's peace of mind at all costs, so her daughters must do the same.

When they added to that struggle the burden of putting out the broadsheet, *The Mayfair Lady*, every two weeks, without Constance's editorial expertise, and trying to stay on top of the Go-Between, their matchmaking agency, it was no wonder she and Chastity fell exhausted into a dreamless sleep every night, Prudence reflected.

The doorbell from the shop at the front of the house chimed as a customer entered and Mrs. Beedle hurried away to attend to the counter, smoothing her pristine apron as she did so. Prudence drank deeply from her refilled cup and helped herself to a second piece of gingerbread. It was warm and tranquil in the kitchen behind the shop. She could hear Mrs. Beedle's chattily cheerful voice interspersed with that of another woman, rather shrill and high-pitched, complaining about the poor quality of the butcher's lamb chops.

Prudence stretched her legs towards the range and sighed, grateful for the brief respite from the workaday concerns, and idly riffled through the envelopes addressed to *The Mayfair Lady* that were sent poste restante to Mrs. Beedle's corner shop in Kensington. The editors of *The Mayfair Lady* had to preserve their anonymity at all costs.

The thick vellum envelope had a distinctly official feel to it. The printed address in the top left-hand corner read *Falstaff, Harley & Greenwold*. Prudence felt a chill of apprehension. It sounded like a firm of lawyers. She reached for the butter knife, intending to slit the envelope, and then put it down again with a quick, unconscious shake of her head. The sisters had an unspoken convention that they opened correspondence relating to their shared endeavors together. And if this one brought bad news, and Prudence found herself fancying a miasmic vapor oozing from the vellum, it was most definitely not to be opened alone.

She thrust all the letters into her capacious handbag and drained her teacup. Mrs. Beedle was still engaged with her customer when Prudence went out through the shop, drawing on her gloves.

"Thank you for the tea, Mrs. Beedle."

"Oh, it's always nice to see you, Miss Prue." The shopkeeper beamed at her. "And Miss Chas, of course. Bring her with you next week. I'll make some of my lardy cake, I know how she likes that."

"She'll be sorry she missed the gingerbread, but she had to visit an old friend this afternoon," Prudence said with a smile, nodding politely to the customer, who was regarding her curiously. A lady with a Mayfair accent wearing a rather elegant afternoon gown was something of a novelty in a corner shop in Kensington, particularly when she appeared from the owner's quarters in the back.

Prudence picked up a copy of *The Mayfair Lady* in the magazine rack at the back of the shop. "If you're looking for something to read, ma'am, you might enjoy this publication." She held it out to the woman, who was so surprised, she took it.

"Well, I don't know," she said. "Mayfair Lady . . . sounds a bit hoity-toity for the likes of me."

"Oh, it's not at all," Prudence reassured warmly. "Mrs. Beedle reads it, I know."

"Aye, that I do, once in a while," the shopkeeper said. "You try it, Mrs. Warner. Just the ticket on a cold afternoon when you're knitting by the fire."

"I don't have much call for reading," the customer said doubtfully. "How much is it?" She turned the broadsheet around in her hands, as if unsure what to do with it.

"Just twopence," Prudence said. "You'd be surprised how much of interest there is inside."

"Well, I don't know, but I suppose . . ." The customer's voice trailed off as she opened her purse for two pennies that she laid on the counter. "I'll try it."

"You do that," Mrs. Beedle said. "And I tell you what, if you don't like it, you just bring it back and I'll refund the twopence."

Mrs. Warner brightened visibly. "Well, you can't say fairer than that, Mrs. Beedle."

Prudence raised a mental eyebrow. How were they supposed to make money out of the broadsheet when people read it "on approval"? But she couldn't say that to Mrs. Beedle, who only meant well, so with a cheerful farewell she left the shop, going out into a chilly afternoon that was already drawing in even though it was barely four-thirty. Autumn seemed to have come earlier than usual this year, she thought, but perhaps it was only in contrast to the long and unusually hot summer that had preceded it.

She hurried towards an omnibus stop, thinking again of Constance in the desert heat of Egypt. It was all right for some, she concluded as the motorized omnibus belching steam came to a halt at the stop. She climbed on, paid her penny fare, and took a seat by the window, watching the streets of London crawl by as the bus stopped and started at the behest of passengers.

She wondered how Chastity's afternoon had progressed. Despite what Prudence had told Mrs. Beedle, her sister hadn't been visiting an old friend. Chastity, in her role as Aunt Mabel, was in fact writing her responses to a trio of problem letters from beleaguered readers, for publication in the next edition of the broadsheet. Prudence had left her chewing the top of her pen, bewailing crossed nibs that splattered ink all over everywhere, and trying to think of a diplomatic way to shoot down *Desperate in Chelsea,* who seemed to think that her elderly parents had no right to spend any of their capital on frivolous pursuits while their daughter was waiting for her inheritance.

She hopped off the bus at Oxford Street and walked up Baker Street towards Portman Square. She turned onto Manchester Square, her cheeks pinkened by the freshening breeze, and ran up the steps to No. 10. Jenkins opened the door for her just as she put her key in the lock.

"Thought that was you, Miss Prue, when I heard the key."

"I was visiting your sister," she said, stepping into the hall. "She sent her greetings."

"Hope she's in good health."

"She certainly seemed to be. Is Chas upstairs?"

"She hasn't put her head out of the parlor all afternoon."

"Oh, poor love," Prudence said. "Did she have tea?"

At that Jenkins smiled. Chastity's sweet tooth was a family joke. "Mrs. Hudson made a chocolate sponge this afternoon. Miss Chas had three slices. It bucked her up a little, if I might say so. She was looking a little peaky before."

"Inky probably," Prudence said with a laugh as she hurried to the staircase. She paused halfway and asked over her shoulder, "Is Lord Duncan dining in tonight, do you know, Jenkins?"

"I don't believe so, Miss Prue. Mrs. Hudson's made a nice shepherd's pie for you and Miss Chas with the cold lamb from Sunday's roast."

If one had to eat leftovers, mutton was infinitely more palatable than fish, Prudence reflected. She opened the door to the parlor that she and her sisters had shared since their mother's death just four years previously. It was a pleasant, lived-in room, somewhat shabby and faded, and rather cluttered. Even more so this afternoon. Chastity sat at the secretaire, knee deep in scrunched-up balls of paper, evidence of frustrating literary effort. She turned as her sister came in.

"Oh, I'm glad you're back, now I can stop this." She ran her hands through her curly red hair that had escaped its ribbons during the throes of composition and now fell loose to her shoulders. She stretched and rolled her shoulders. "I never thought I'd lose sympathy for these tormented souls but some of them are so childish and spoiled . . . Oh, wait. I have something to show you. Jenkins brought it up half an hour ago."

Her tone had completely changed and she jumped up, walking energetically to the sideboard. "See here." She flourished a newspaper. "The *Pall Mall Gazette.* Con said it would happen!"

"What would happen?" Prudence ran her eye over the paper and saw the answer. She whistled soundlessly at the headline. PEER OF THE REALM

IN VICE SCANDAL. She began to read the text. " 'The earl of Barclay has been accused in the pages of the anonymous broadsheet The Mayfair Lady of violating his youthful maidservants and abandoning them pregnant and poverty-stricken on the streets.' "

Her voice faded as she continued reading under her breath, aware that Chastity probably knew the article by heart by now. When she reached the end she looked up at her sister, who was regarding her expectantly. Chastity said, "They actually interviewed the women Con used in the article."

"And they offer their own condemnation of the licentious peer, in their own inimitable style," Prudence observed. "Full of almost religious fervor, trumpeting condemnation for such lewd behavior while titillating their readers with scandalous details."

"It's exactly what we all hoped would happen," Chastity said. "Just four weeks after the original Mayfair Lady article. That only produced a few behind-the-hand whispers and the occasional glare for Barclay from straitlaced Society matrons. His own cronies didn't turn a hair and he seemed to ignore it totally. I thought it had all blown over now. But when this hits the streets and the clubs and the drawing rooms, he'll be pilloried."

"Yes," Prudence agreed, but she sounded uneasy. She opened her handbag and took out the official-looking envelope. "This was in the mail."

"What is it?"

"It looks like it's from a firm of solicitors."

"Oh," Chastity took the envelope and turned it over as if she could intuit its contents. "I suppose we'd better open it." Prudence handed her a paper knife and she slit the envelope, withdrawing a densely covered sheet of vellum. She began to read, Prudence at her shoulder.

"Oh, hell!" Prudence said when she'd reached the end. Even through the dreadful, obfuscating legalese the message was clear as a bell.

"Why's Barclay suing us for libel—or rather, The Mayfair Lady—and not the Pall Mall Gazette?" wondered Chastity. "It has much more clout than we do."

"The Gazette only came out today," Prudence said glumly. "We came out guns blazing a whole month ago. He's had four weeks to put this together. And if he wins this case he can go after the Gazette."

"So, what do we do?" Chastity nibbled her bottom lip as she reread the letter. "It says they will be seeking punitive damages of the highest degree possible on behalf of their client. What does that mean?"

"I have no idea . . . nothing good, you can be sure of that." Prudence flung herself into the depths of the chesterfield, kicking off her shoes. "We need advice."

"We need Con." Her sister perched on the arm of a chair and crossed her legs, swinging one ankle restlessly against the corner of the sofa table.

"What in God's name is Max going to think of this?"

"It won't do his career much good if it comes out that his wife wrote the original," Chastity said gloomily.

"We're going to have to make sure it doesn't come out, for the sake of all our enterprises, but I don't see how we can keep it from Max." Prudence picked up the letter from the table where Chastity had let it fall. "Oh, I didn't see this, right at the bottom here . . . 'In addition to damages for the libel concerning our client's relationships with his employees we will be seeking substantial damages for innuendo and inference regarding our client's financial practices.' "

"Did the *Pall Mall Gazette* pick up those hints we dropped?" Chastity reached over for the discarded paper. "I didn't see anything."

"No, they probably had the sense to leave it alone. There's no evidence for it, or at least none that we offered. I'm sure there's some somewhere, but we were all so fired up about nailing Barclay, we just threw everything in." Prudence sighed. "What naive idiots we are."

"No," Chastity said. "Were. We were, but I don't think we are anymore."

"A case of shutting the stable door after the horse has bolted," Prudence pointed out with a dour smile. She turned towards the door at a discreet knock.

"Would you like the sherry decanter in here, Miss Prue? Or will you be using the drawing room this evening?" Jenkins inquired.

"No, I don't think we're in the mood for the drawing room tonight," Prudence said. "We'll take sherry in here, and we'll eat shepherd's pie in the little dining parlor."

"Yes, I rather thought that would be your decision." Jenkins entered the room and set down the tray he was carrying. "What time shall I tell Mrs. Hudson you'd like dinner?" He poured two glasses and carried them over on a silver salver.

"Eight, I should think?" Prudence looked a question at her sister, who nodded her agreement. "And I don't think we shall dress, Jenkins. We'll serve ourselves, if you like. I'm sure you've got things you'd rather do this evening."

"When I've served you, Miss Prue, I shall go off duty," Jenkins stated with a note of reproach. He bowed and left them.

"He's only going to the pub for his pint of mild-and-bitter," Chastity said, taking a sip of sherry. "It doesn't warm up there until around nine o'clock."

"All the same, elaborate service for shepherd's pie seems a little unnecessary," Prudence observed. "Why don't we eat up here on trays beside the fire?"

"Because Jenkins and Mrs. Hudson would be horrified," Chastity said, laughing slightly. She set down her glass and went to throw another shovel of coal on the fire. *"There's no call for a lowering of standards, Miss Prue, just because times is hard."* It was a perfect imitation of the housekeeper, Mrs. Hudson, and Prudence laughed and applauded.

The moment of levity, however, died a swift death. "How do we find a barrister?" Chastity asked.

"I think we're supposed to find a solicitor who will then instruct a barrister on our behalf. I'm sure that's the way it works," Prudence replied.

"You know more than I do." Chastity took up her glass. "Father would know someone, of course. Could we sound him out, d'you think?"

"You mean ask a couple of casual questions?" Prudence leaned forward, her light green eyes sharp.

"He's not going to put two and two together," Chastity pointed out.

"No." Prudence pursed her lips. "I just wonder if he'll know the kind of lawyer we're looking for."

"Someone inexpensive," Chastity stated the obvious.

Prudence shook her head. "This kind of barrister comes expensive. However we can but try. There might be some way around it."

The sound of impatient footsteps in the corridor outside reached them just before the door was flung open after the most perfunctory knock. Lord Arthur Duncan stood on the threshold, his whiskers awry, his cheeks rather redder than usual, his bowler hat clutched to his striped waistcoat. "I have never heard the like," he declared. "Bounders, absolute bounders. Should be hanged from the nearest lamppost. Oh, I see you've seen it." He gestured to the *Pall Mall Gazette*. "Disgraceful, disgusting calumny. It was one thing for that effeminate gossip rag to point the finger . . . no self-respecting red-blooded man gives a tinker's damn what a group of airheaded cowards have to say . . . but when that sanctimonious, tub-thumping twit in the *Gazette* starts pointing the finger, there's no knowing where it will lead."

He sat down heavily in a wing chair beside the fire. "If that's sherry, I'll have a glass, Prudence."

"It is, and certainly, Father." She poured and brought him the glass. "Is Lord Barclay very upset?"

"Upset?" his lordship boomed. "He's beside himself." He drained his small glass in one sip, and glared at it. "Not enough to slake the thirst of a butterfly."

"Would you like Jenkins to bring you whisky?" Chastity asked with customary solicitude.

"No . . . no need to bother him." He wiped his moustache with his handkerchief. "Just fill it again for me." He gave her the glass.

"What is Lord Barclay going to do about it?" inquired Prudence, leaning over to stir the coals with the poker. "He must have some redress, surely."

"Well, he's suing that *Mayfair Lady* disgrace, for a start. That'll fold once Barclay and his lawyers have finished with it. Won't have a penny to its name and its editors will be lucky to escape gaol."

"I imagine he must be using the best lawyers in the business," Chastity said, bringing a recharged glass over to the earl.

"Oh, yes, you mark my words . . . best money can buy."

"Are there many good libel lawyers in London?" Prudence asked. "We never meet any."

"Hardly surprising, m'dear." He regarded his middle daughter with a benign smile. "Not saying that you and your sisters couldn't compete with the brightest brain, but these men don't frequent the kind of circles you girls like. You'll find 'em in clubs, not drawing rooms."

Prudence looked askance. "I wonder if that's true. Give us some names of the really good barristers and Chas and I will see if they ring any kind of a bell."

"Party games," he scoffed, but he seemed to have calmed down somewhat in the soothing companionship of his daughters and under the equally soothing influence of the sherry. His cheeks had taken on a less rubicund hue.

"Well, now, let me see. Barclay's solicitors, Falstaff, Harley, and Greenwold, have briefed Samuel Richardson, KC. Any name there ring a bell?" He gave his daughters a smug smile. "I'll wager not."

"We don't expect to know the solicitors," Prudence told him. "But Samuel Richardson . . ." She shook her head. "No, you win that one. Give us another."

Lord Duncan frowned, thinking. "Malvern," he said finally. "Sir Gideon Malvern, KC. Youngest KC in a decade, knighted for his services to the bar." He chuckled suddenly. "I believe it was for services to the king . . . one of His Majesty's friends found himself in a spot of bother, you know the kind." He tapped the side of his nose significantly.

"Malvern defended him . . . man came out smelling like a rose garden. But I'll wager you haven't heard of him either, for all the royal connections. They say he's the brightest candle in the Inns of Court sconce these days. Man's far too busy to mingle."

He set down his glass and rose rather heavily to his feet. "Well, I have to dress, I'm dining with Barclay in Rules. Must show solidarity, you know. Can't let this kind of . . ." He waved a disdainful hand at the *Gazette*. "Spiteful rubbish . . . that's all it is. Can't let that rubbish win the day over honest men." He dropped a paternal kiss on each forehead and left them.

"Honest men," Prudence said with heavy scorn, taking her glass to the decanter for a refill. "It's not as if Father's either blind or stupid. What is it about Barclay that so captivates him?"

"Oh, I think it has something to do with the fact that the earl was there when Mother died," Chastity said quietly, gazing into the fire. "Father was distraught, and so were we. Distraught and exhausted after nursing her those last few months."

Prudence nodded, crossing her arms over her chest in an involuntary hug. Their mother's final days had been excruciatingly painful, and all the laudanum available to them hadn't been sufficient to ease her suffering. Lord Duncan hadn't been able to bear his wife's pain and had retreated to his library, where Lord Barclay had kept him company while Lord Duncan's daughters had shared vigils at their mother's bedside. They had had no energy to spare for their father's grief—not until many months later, by which time Lord Barclay had become Lord Duncan's most intimate confidant.

Prudence let her arms drop and raised her head. "Well, there's nothing we can do to change that now. Let's see what we can discover about this Sir Gideon Malvern."

"If he's made King's Council, he has to be at the top of the tree," Chastity said. "I wonder what it means to be the youngest KC in a decade."

"We need a recent copy of *Who's Who,*" Prudence said. "At least that'll tell us which of the Inns of Court he's affiliated with. The volume in our library is decades old; it probably predates his law degree. We'll go to Hatchards in the morning and take a quick look under the M's."

"*Who's Who* won't give us an address, though."

"No, but once we know which of the Inns he belongs to, we can go there and find his chambers. I'm sure if he's that important and well-known he'll have chambers somewhere around the Temple."

"But we can't just beard him in his chambers," Chastity pointed out. "I thought we had to go through the proper channels, get solicitors to brief him."

Prudence shook her head. "I think if we have any chance at all of getting his help we're going to have to jump him . . . surprise him. If we give him time to think for one instant, he'll laugh us into the street."

" 'Be bloody, bold, and resolute,' " Chastity quoted with an upraised fist.

" 'Laugh to scorn the power of man,' " her sister continued.

"If only," Chastity said, getting to her feet. "We'll go to Hatchards first thing in the morning." She stretched tiredly. "I'm hungry and it's nearly eight. Shall we go and eat shepherd's pie?"

"I wonder what Con's eating for dinner," Prudence mused as she accompanied her sister downstairs.

"Goats' eyeballs," Chastity said promptly. "I read that's what the Bedouin nomads eat in the Sahara."

"Oh, I can imagine Max's reaction faced with a goat's eyeball. Can't you, Jenkins?" Prudence took her seat in the small dining parlor they used when they were alone.

"As I understand it, Miss Prue, the eyeballs of sheep are a delicacy. I believe that the goats are roasted whole and the meat is considered most succulent." Jenkins held the steaming dish of shepherd's pie at her elbow.

"I'm not sure goat or sheep make much difference to the concept," Prudence said, helping herself. "This smells delicious . . . thank you, Jenkins."

He moved around the table to Chastity. "Mrs. Hudson used grated cheese on the potato. I think you'll find it nice and crispy."

Chastity cut through the crisp crust, and the butler presented a dish of buttered cabbage before filling their wineglasses and quietly removing himself.

"It is actually very good," Prudence said after a forkful.

"Mrs. Hudson does remarkably well with what little she has to work with much of the time," Chastity said. "Did we manage to pay her this month?"

"Oh, yes. I had to pawn those little pearl earrings of Mother's, but we'll redeem them as soon as we get the *charitable donations* from Lady Lucan and Lady Winthrop."

"That's such an outrageous idea of Con's," Chastity said. "To ask them to donate to a charity for indigent spinsters as a means of collecting our Go-Between fee."

"Well, they have no idea that they—or rather, their progeny—received the services of the Go-Between," Prudence reminded her, helping herself to more cabbage. "It's going to be a most useful way of collecting payment . . . should we find ourselves setting up other couples for their own good."

Chastity couldn't help a grin. "For their own good. How altruistic that sounds, when all we want is their money." She took a sip of wine and pulled a face. "This is a thin and ungrateful beverage."

"I know," Prudence agreed with a rueful headshake. "Jenkins found some bottles of a burgundy at the back of the cellar that are clearly over the hill. We thought we ought to drink them up, those that Mrs. Hudson isn't using for cooking."

"Don't let Father get a sniff of them."

Prudence shook her head again and took a sip from her own glass. "It's not too bad with food, but you couldn't possibly drink it alone."

"So, when are we going to receive these charitable donations from *La Lucan* and *La Winthrop*?"

"They promised to bring checks to the next At Home. I suggested around fifty guineas apiece would be suitable," Prudence told her blithely.

Chastity choked on a forkful of potato. "Fifty guineas apiece! That's outrageous, Prue."

"Con thought it was a little much too, but I thought it was worth a try. It isn't as if they can't afford it," her sister declared. "The wedding is to take place in December, and it'll be the biggest, most lavish Society affair of the year. Hester and David are so absorbed in each other it's nauseating. And their mothers are pleased as punch. We did them all a great service. Not to mention you," she added with a grin. "Anything to give David an alternative love interest."

"The adoration *was* getting a little tedious," Chastity admitted. "By the way, were there any other letters for *The Mayfair Lady*? Besides the legal one."

"Several. They're still in my bag. We'll look at them after dinner."

"I wonder what's for pudding?" Chastity mused.

"Apple crumble and custard, Miss Chas." Jenkins answered the question as he reentered the parlor on cue. "Mrs. Hudson was wondering if you'd like her to make some scones for the At Home?" He gathered up their plates.

"Oh, yes, please," Prudence said. "We're collecting money at the next one, so the sweeter the tea, the better."

"Yes, Miss Prue. I'll explain to Mrs. Hudson. I imagine she'll make another chocolate sponge." Jenkins was quite matter-of-fact as he bore away their discarded plates. The dubious moneymaking activities of Lord Duncan's daughters met only with his approval.

Chapter 2

The sisters entered the bow-windowed bookshop on Piccadilly within minutes of its opening. They headed straight for the reference section at the rear of the shop and found what they were looking for. "We probably ought to use the lending library for research," Chastity said in an undertone. "It seems like cheating to use a bookstore. I'm sure they'd rather we bought the up-to-date *Who's Who*."

"I'm sure they would," Prudence agreed. "But it's five guineas that we don't have, and we only need one entry." She leafed carefully through the pages. "Ah, here we are, the M's." Her finger ran down the entries. "Maburn . . . Maddingly . . . *Malvern*. This is it. 'Sir Gideon Malvern, KC; Member of the Inns of Court, Middle Temple; Appointed to the bar, 1894; Appointed King's Council, 1902; Education: Winchester, New College, Oxford . . .' Predictable enough." She raised her head. "Well, that gives us what we need."

"Isn't there anything else, anything personal?" Chastity inquired, peering over her sister's shoulder. "Oh, look at this. It says he's divorced. 'Married Harriet Greenwood, daughter of Lord Charles and Lady Greenwood, 1896; Divorced, 1900. One daughter, Sarah, born 1897.' "

She looked up with a frown. "Divorced . . . that's unusual."

"Very," Prudence agreed. "But it's not going to affect us. We know where to find him, or at least his chambers. Let's go to Middle Temple Lane and look at some nameplates." She closed the tome gently and replaced it on the shelf. Outside, they jostled with the shoppers crowding Piccadilly until they found an empty hackney cab.

"Victoria Embankment, please," Prudence called as she climbed in, Chastity on her heels. "The issue now," Prudence said, her brow furrowed, "is how to approach this famous man. D'you have any ideas, Chas?"

"Nothing specific," her sister said, adjusting the brim of her straw hat. "We need to make an appointment first. Isn't he likely to be in court . . . the Old Bailey or somewhere? The Bailey is open for business now, isn't it?"

"Early this year, I believe," Prudence said vaguely. "Even if he's not practicing there, he's most likely to be in some criminal court this morning. We probably won't get further than his law clerk today, always assuming, of course, that we don't get thrown out onto the street before we can open our mouths."

"Well, we look respectable enough," Chastity said.

That was certainly true, Prudence reflected. Her own neutral tweed jacket and skirt with a plain black straw hat was understated, unfrivolous, respectable, and unremarkable. Chastity's day dress of dark brown silk was a little more adorned, but still could not be called frivolous. She had debated their both dressing to the nines in an attempt to overwhelm the barrister with their elegance and femininity but had decided in favor of a more moderate approach. Once she had some idea of the kind of man they were dealing with, they could adapt accordingly.

Divorced was interesting, though. It was very unusual in their circles, and carried considerable stigma. But, of course, more for the woman than the man, she thought acidly, hearing in her head Constance, the suffragist, railing against the injustice of society's laws when it came to women, both openly in the courts and in covert daily convention. Who had been the guilty party in this case? Sir Gideon, or his wife? If they could discover that, it might give them some clues as to how to deal with the barrister.

The hackney stopped on Victoria Embankment and they got out, pausing for a moment to look across the gray sweep of the Thames to the South Bank. The sun was struggling to emerge through an overcast sky and a few faint rays lit the dull, rolling surface of the water. A brisk gust of wind sent colored leaves tumbling from the oak trees in the Temple Gardens behind them.

"It's too cold to stand around," Prudence said. "Let's walk up Middle Temple Lane. You take one side and I'll take the other."

Every door on either side of the lane bore copper nameplates listing the occupants of each tall, narrow building. Each name was followed by the insignia *Barrister At Law*. Sir Gideon Malvern's name was found midway up the lane.

Prudence waved at Chastity, who crossed over towards her. "This one." Prudence indicated the nameplate.

Chastity tried the shiny brass doorknob and the door swung open into a gloomy interior that could barely qualify as a foyer. A set of wooden stairs rose directly in front of them. The sun had gone in again and there was little enough natural light at the best of times from the narrow window at the corner of the stairs, but someone had thoughtfully lit the gas lamp at the top, so a little illumination showed the way up the ancient, rickety staircase.

The sisters exchanged a glance. The shiny nameplate and doorknob facing the street belied the shabby interior, but Prudence knew enough about the practice of law to realize that she should not judge the barrister by the air of dilapidation in his chambers. Rooms in the ancient Inns of Court were highly prized and available only to the select few. It was a matter of pride and tradition that no modern conveniences should invade the hallowed chambers.

"I'm surprised there's a gas lamp," she murmured. "I thought they hadn't progressed beyond oil lanterns and candles."

"Shall we go up?" Chastity asked in a similar undertone.

"That's what we came for." Prudence sounded more confident than she felt. She set foot on the stair, Chastity behind her. It was too narrow for two to climb abreast.

The door at the head of the stairs stood slightly ajar. Prudence knocked, thought it had been too timid a knock, and rapped rather more smartly. A creaky voice bade her enter. Presumably it did not belong to Sir Gideon Malvern, KC, she reflected. Her father had described him as the youngest barrister to achieve that accolade in a decade and she remembered from the entry in *Who's Who* that he'd been appointed to the bar twelve years ago. He couldn't be more than forty, she calculated. She went in, leaving the door ajar, and failed to notice that Chastity didn't follow her.

"Madam?" An elderly man in a threadbare frock coat and frayed collar looked at her in surprise from behind an overloaded desk. He glanced up at the clock, which chimed eleven o'clock as he did so. "Can I help you, madam?" He rose from a tall stool and peered at her in the gaslight.

"I would like to see Sir Gideon Malvern," Prudence stated, glancing around her with interest. The walls were invisible behind bookshelves groaning beneath the weight of thick leather-bound volumes. A telephone hung on the wall behind the clerk's desk, an expensive piece of modernity that surprised her even more than the gaslight. It stood out like a sore thumb. On a coat rack beside the door hung the barrister's working garb, a black gown and an elaborate white curled wig.

The clerk opened a ledger on his desk, slowly turned the pages, and then peered through pince-nez at the entries. He looked up after what seemed an interminable length of time. "Sir Gideon has no appointment for this time, madam."

"That's because I haven't made one," Prudence said, an impatient edge to her voice now. She took off her gloves, aware that the gesture felt almost symbolic. The man was playing games with her. "As I'm sure you are well aware. I would, however, like to make one."

"You are a solicitor, madam?" He stared at her, and she saw that his eyes were a great deal sharper than his rather bumbling manner might indicate.

"Hardly," she said. "But, nevertheless, I wish to brief Sir Gideon on a libel case. One I think he will find both interesting and profitable." The last lie slid off her tongue as smoothly as water off oiled leather.

The clerk pinched his chin, regarding her in silence for again an unnerving length of time. "This is most unorthodox, but if you have the documents pertaining to the case, I will look them over and consider whether Sir Gideon might be interested," he said finally, holding out his hand.

"Do you make up Sir Gideon's mind for him?" Prudence inquired, the same acerbic edge to her voice. "I would have thought such a distinguished barrister would be capable of making up his own mind."

"All briefs to be considered by Sir Gideon are presented through me," the clerk stated.

They seemed to have reached an impasse. Prudence knew that if she turned and left she would never be able to return, but if she meekly handed over the papers she had in her handbag she had no guarantee that they wouldn't go straight into the already overflowing wastepaper basket beside the clerk's desk. So she simply stood her ground.

Sir Gideon's clerk continued to regard her with that same shrewdness from behind his pince-nez. He was thinking that his principal had a rather eccentric attitude to some of the cases he took. Sir Gideon frequently took on a brief that Thadeus considered a complete waste of time, quite unworthy of his principal's attention. When he expressed his reservations they were always met with a careless shrug and the comment that a man's brain needed something out of the ordinary now and again to keep it alive and well.

Thadeus was wondering what Sir Gideon would think of his present visitor. A lady of undeniable quality, and some considerable strength of will, he decided. She wouldn't stand out in a crowd—but then, Sir Gideon didn't care for the flamboyant, except when it came to the exotic dancers he seemed to prefer as mistresses.

Prudence glanced at the closed inner door, and then at the barrister's court dress on the coat rack. If it was there, then the barrister was presumably not in court. "Is Sir Gideon in chambers?" she asked.

"No, madam, not as yet."

"When do you expect him?"

"Sir Gideon's personal arrangements are no concern of mine, madam."

"Ah." So, whatever had taken him from his office this morning was not related to the law, she inferred.

"Leave me the brief, madam, and I assure you that Sir Gideon will see it," the clerk stated. "Otherwise, I must ask you to excuse me. I have work to do."

There seemed nothing for it. Prudence opened her bag and took out the copy of *The Mayfair Lady,* with the article marked, and the solicitor's letter. "The suit concerns this broadsheet," she said. "You will see that I have marked the relevant piece."

The clerk took the thin sheaf of papers. "This is the brief?" he asked, raising incredulous eyebrows.

"No, I wouldn't call it that," Prudence said. "I'm not a solicitor, as we've just established. But everything Sir Gideon will need to understand the situation is there."

"With the exception of your name, madam."

"This libel suit is filed against *The Mayfair Lady,* that's all the name Sir Gideon needs."

Thadeus looked at her and the semblance of a smile touched his thin mouth. "You do not know my principal, madam. I do assure you he will need a great deal more than that."

"Well, if he decides to take the case, he shall have more than that," Prudence declared brusquely. "In the meantime, a message sent to this address will reach me." She handed him a folded paper.

Thadeus unfolded the sheet. "Mrs. Henry Franklin, Flat A, Palace Court, Bayswater," he read aloud. He looked again at her, his gaze drifting to her ringless fingers. This was not a lady with a Bayswater aura. She exuded Mayfair, for all the simplicity of her dress.

"A message to this address will reach you?"

"That is what I said, I believe." Prudence put on her gloves, her movements crisp. "I will expect to hear from Sir Gideon by the end of the week. It shouldn't take him very long to make up his mind. The issue is very straightforward."

"Libel is rarely straightforward, madam," the clerk responded. He offered her a small bow. "I bid you good morning."

"Good morning." Prudence turned back to the door, only then realizing that Chastity was not immediately behind her. She went out onto the landing, pulling the door closed behind her, revealing her sister, who had been standing in the shadows behind the door. "Chas, why didn't you come in?" she whispered.

"It was so cramped in there," Chastity explained. "It seemed better to stay outside. Did you mind?"

"No. To tell you the truth, I didn't realize you weren't in the room," Prudence said, still keeping her voice low as she descended the stairs. "Didn't you think he was an obstreperous man?"

"Yes, but you stood up to him beautifully. He obviously sees himself as Cerberus, guarding the gates to *his principal.*"

Prudence chuckled, then shook her head. "I only hope he shows the papers to that *principal.*" She laid a hand on the handle of the street door, talking over her shoulder as she did so. The door opened abruptly, nearly knocking her sideways, and she reeled back, still clutching the knob.

"Oh, I beg your pardon, I didn't realize anyone was on the other side." A male voice that was both well modulated and unusually quiet spoke above her.

She looked up at the owner of the voice, too startled for a minute to respond. It was hard to get much of an impression in the dim light of the narrow hallway, but she thought his eyes were gray. "Sir Gideon Malvern?" she asked directly.

"At your service, madam." There was a questioning note to the courteous response. The gray eyes moved beyond her to Chastity, who still stood on the bottom step.

"*The Mayfair Lady,*" Prudence said, holding out her hand. "Your clerk will explain the situation."

"Indeed." He took her hand, his clasp firm enough to be called a grip. "How intriguing." He dropped her hand and consulted the fob watch that hung from his waistcoat pocket. "I would ask you to explain it yourself, but unfortunately I have to be in court in half an hour."

"Your clerk knows how to reach us," Prudence said, smiling faintly. "Good morning, Sir Gideon."

"Good morning, madam." He bowed and stepped aside so that she could pass into the street. He smiled at Chastity with the same inquiring air as she stepped down from the stair. "Two Mayfair ladies?"

Chastity merely inclined her head, murmured, "Good morning," and followed her sister into the street. The door closed behind them.

"At least that will ensure that the obstreperous clerk won't withhold the papers," Prudence said, looking at the closed door, tapping her lips with a gloved forefinger. "Sir Gideon said he was intrigued, so he's bound to ask what we were doing. His clerk can't deny we were here."

"No," agreed Chastity. "That was a good morning's work. I don't see what else we can do until we hear from him."

"I think we've earned coffee at Fortnum's," her sister declared.

"It was an inspiration to use Amelia and Henry's address," Chastity said as they walked towards Chancery Lane. "No one will connect the Franklins with the Duncans of Manchester Square."

"Unless the barrister hires a private detective. He could discover the connection between Henry and Max in the blink of an eye. Politicians' secretaries are not hard to trace." Amelia Westcott and Henry Franklin had been the Go-Between's first official clients. Now happily married and expecting their first child, they had kept close connections with the Duncan sisters, and Henry worked as secretary for Constance's husband in the House of Commons.

"He's hardly going to go to those lengths," Chastity protested. "If he wants to take the case, he'll get everything he needs from us. If he doesn't, why would he go to the trouble and expense of investigating us?"

"There's truth in that," Prudence agreed. But she felt vaguely uneasy. Although it had only been a momentary encounter, and a perfectly pleasant one, something about those gray eyes had disturbed her; but she couldn't put her finger on it.

Sir Gideon Malvern entered his chambers and greeted his clerk in his usual fashion. "Coffee, Thadeus, as strong as you can make it."

"The water's already heating, Sir Gideon. I trust your meeting at Miss Sarah's school was satisfactory." The clerk had risen from behind his desk to attend to the water on the spirit stove.

"Yes, Sarah's headmistress had only good things to say," Gideon said.

"Not surprising, sir. Miss Sarah is as bright as a button."

"And as sharp as a needle." Gideon's laugh was both proud and affectionate as he capped the cliché. He took off his gloves and bowler hat, laying them on the bench by the door. "So, tell me about our visitors."

Thadeus poured boiling water onto the coffee in a copper jug before he spoke, then he straightened slowly, the jug in his hand. "Visitors, sir? I only saw one."

"Oh, there were two, all right." Gideon went into the inner office. "Mayfair ladies, they called themselves. In other circumstances with such a name I would have thought they were a pair of madams seeking business." He went behind the massive oak table that served as his desk but didn't take a seat.

Thadeus permitted himself a frown of disapproval as he set the coffee and a cup on the table. "The only one I met, sir, was very respectable."

"How dull." Gideon poured coffee, inhaling the aroma with a sigh of pleasure. "I couldn't see them clearly in the gloom downstairs. I wonder if we should install another gas lamp in the hall."

"We have sufficient gas lamps, sir," the other announced repressively. "But I would consider an additional oil lantern on the hook beside the door."

"No . . . no, leave it as it is." The barrister waved a dismissive hand. "So, enlighten me."

Thadeus went into the outer office and returned with the papers Prudence had left him. "A libel case, sir. But the lady wishes to act as her own solicitor. She wishes to brief you herself."

"Oh, now, that's novel. Not in the least dull; just goes to show how appearances can be deceiving." Gideon drank his coffee and glanced at the copy of *The Mayfair Lady*. He nodded his comprehension. "We have an explanation for our Mayfair ladies, it seems."

"I have not, as yet, had the opportunity to read the details of the suit," Thadeus said, as if conscious of some dereliction of duty.

"How could you have done? They've only just left you." Gideon set down his drained coffee cup in the saucer and gathered up the papers. "I'll read these while the jury's out at the Old Bailey. It's an open-and-shut case. I'm hoping they won't be out more than an hour, so it won't be worth going back to chambers while they're discussing a verdict. I may as well use my time profitably." He strode energetically into the outer office, swinging his black gown off the coat rack.

"There's an address in Bayswater, Sir Gideon. The lady said we should contact her there."

"*Bayswater?*" Gideon turned in surprise, his wig in his hands. "Neither of those ladies carried the mark of Bayswater."

"No, I didn't think so either. I'm assuming the address is purely in the nature of a poste restante, to preserve anonymity."

"Now, why do they want to preserve their anonymity?" Gideon crammed the wig on his head and took a cursory glance in the mirror to check its position. "Every brief I've had in the last six months has been utterly tedious. I'm in need of a change and a challenge, Thadeus. Maybe this will furnish both."

He turned the wig a fraction so it no longer sat askew over his left ear, and mused, "Of course, what I'd really like is a nice juicy murder, but our two ladies didn't look like murderers. However, as I just said, appearances can be deceiving. We must live in hope." He raised a hand in farewell, and left in a whirlwind of energy that Thadeus regarded with approval and a faint sigh of vicarious exhaustion.

* * *

"I could wish we didn't have to deal with an At Home this afternoon," Chastity said as the sisters returned home. "It's so much more tedious without Constance."

"Don't forget, this is a fee-collecting occasion," Prudence reminded her. "We're working." She put her key in the door. "Just imagine a hundred guineas in the bank account."

"Oh, that'll keep me at the grindstone," Chastity said. "Hello, Jenkins," she greeted the butler cheerfully as he came into the hall from the library.

"Miss Chas, Miss Prue." The butler had a smile on his face.

"What is it, Jenkins?" Chastity demanded. "You have a secret. Don't deny it."

His smile broadened. "A telegram, Miss Chas."

"From Con?" the sisters asked in unison.

"So I believe." He walked with stately tread to the table that held the mail. "Postmarked Calais, unless I'm mistaken."

"*Calais?* They must be on their way home." Prudence took the wire. "When did it arrive?"

"About an hour ago. I've laid a cold luncheon in the small dining parlor for you. Lord Duncan is lunching at his club."

"Thank you." Prudence tore open the wire.

"So, when are they arriving?" Chastity tried not to hop with impatience.

"She doesn't say exactly . . . the boat is . . . was . . . supposed to leave yesterday morning, but the sea was rough, so they decided to wait . . . except she can't wait. Oh, here, you read it." Prudence thrust the wire at her sister, her eyes dancing with delight. "Any day now, I think."

"The sooner the better," Chastity said jubilantly as they went into the dining parlor for luncheon.

"We have to give them a day to get settled in," Prudence said, surveying the table's offering. Cold ham, a beetroot salad, bread, and cheese.

"You know Con won't wait a moment before she comes over," Chastity said, slicing bread thickly and passing a hunk to her sister on the tip of the knife.

"She might regret being in a hurry when she hears what we have to tell her," Prudence observed, buttering her bread and taking several slices of ham from the platter. "I wonder how soon we shall hear from Sir Gideon. It can't take him too long to read the article and get the picture."

"It might take him longer to make up his mind." Chastity speared beetroot. "Shall I pour coffee?"

Prudence nodded her thanks through a mouthful of bread and ham.

Her mind turned now to the afternoon ahead. There was nothing that could be done to hurry the barrister's decision, but the two hours a week when the Honorable Misses Duncan were At Home had proved fruitful ground for acquiring clients for the Go-Between. They were gathering quite a register now of eligible men and women, who were, of course, sublimely unaware that they had been chosen as possible partners for some future unknowns should the opportunity present itself.

"I wonder if Susanna Deerfold will come this afternoon," Chastity said, tuning in to her sister's thoughts. "I thought she was getting along rather well with William Sharpe last week."

"We sowed a few seeds," Prudence agreed. "If they do come, I thought I'd suggest they visit the Elgin Marbles together. Susanna was extolling the virtues of Greek sculpture the other night, and I'm sure I heard William lecturing someone on the glories of the Parthenon."

"And once we've set them on the merry course to matrimony, do we demand a charitable donation?" Chastity inquired with a grin.

"Oh, definitely, but maybe not for indigent spinsters, maybe some fund to help preserve the treasures of Greece," Prudence said airily.

"Isn't this illegal . . . something akin to fraud? Raising money under false pretenses?" Chastity asked.

"I'm sure it is. But what's a working woman to do?" Prudence tossed her napkin on the table and pushed back her chair. "I'll go and change, then check the flowers in the drawing room."

"I'll join you."

By half past three the sisters surveyed a pleasantly humming drawing room. "No sign of Lady Lucan or Lady Winthrop," Chastity murmured as she passed her sister carrying a platter of scones.

Prudence offered a minute shrug in response and turned as Jenkins announced Lady Letitia Graham and Miss Pamela Graham. "Letitia, how lovely to see you." She went forward to greet Constance's sister-in-law with a brushing kiss, then bent to the small girl who stood beside her mother. "Good afternoon, Pamela." She shook the girl's hand and refrained from commenting that children of Pamela's age were better employed, not to mention more amused, in the schoolroom on an autumn afternoon. A drawing room full of adult gossip was a tedious place for a six-year-old.

"Oh, the governess left," Letitia said with a sigh and an outflung hand. "No notice, would you believe? She just packed and left straight after breakfast. And this is Nanny's afternoon out and the nursemaid has the toothache . . . so inconsiderate. So, here we are, aren't we, Pammy?" She gave the child a brittle smile that the child received in stolid silence.

"Oh, how tiresome for you, my dear." Lady Bainbridge beckoned imperiously from her armchair. "You seem to have so much trouble with governesses, dear. Perhaps you need to try another agency. Do come and sit by me . . . I'm sure I can remember the agency who sent me the treasure who took care of Martha and Mary . . . what was her name?" She swung her rather large head towards her daughters, who sat primly side by side on the sofa opposite.

"Miss Grayson, Mama," supplied Martha.

"She was with us for more than ten years, Mama," reminded Mary.

Chastity noted the faintest hint of sarcasm in the daughters' responses, not enough for their mother to notice. Lady Bainbridge was deaf to all such nuances, but it was quite heartening to hear from a pair of downtrodden sisters who hadn't managed to look their mother in the eye from the moment of their births.

"Lady Lucan and Lady Winthrop," Jenkins announced as the two dowagers sailed into the drawing room.

Chastity set down her plate of scones and went over to where Pamela, now abandoned by her mother, stood beside Prudence. "Would you like to help me pass around the cream for the scones, Pamela?" She took the child's hand and led her off to the sideboard, freeing her sister to greet the donators to the charity for indigent spinsters.

"Lady Lucan . . . Lady Winthrop . . ." Prudence smiled her best smile. "How delightful to see you. How are the wedding plans progressing?"

"Oh, very well," said the Dowager Lady Lucan.

"Quite splendidly," said the Dowager Lady Winthrop. "Hester is an angel in her wedding gown. The train is nearly ten feet long." She took a tiny scrap of lace from her sleeve and dabbed her eyes. "Winthrop would have been so proud . . . to have walked her down the aisle. Such a loss for a poor girl on her wedding day."

"But her brother, Lord Winthrop, will support her admirably, I'm sure," Prudence said. "And of course she will have David waiting for her at the altar." She smiled at Lady Lucan. "It must gladden your heart, Lady Lucan, to see your only son so happy."

"I won't say that it doesn't," the dowager countess allowed herself to say. "And Hester's a good girl."

How to prod these two dowagers for the promised fifty guineas apiece?

"Let me get you some tea," Prudence said with a nod at Jenkins, who was circulating with the silver teapot. She steered the dowagers to an empty sofa beside the French windows opening onto the terrace and sat down on a lower chair beside them. When they had teacups and cucumber sandwiches, she said, "I had a wire from my sister Mrs. Ensor. She's having her honeymoon in Egypt—"

"Egypt!" Lady Bainbridge exclaimed. "What a strange place for a honeymoon . . . all that sand and dust."

"Yes, quite ruinous for the complexion," put in Letitia. "And dear Constance has always had such a lovely skin."

"I doubt it's suffered, Letitia," Chastity said, guiding Pamela's rather wavering hand wielding clotted cream. "But we shall discover soon enough. They're on their way home."

"Oh, how delightful it will be to see dear Constance again, and Pammy misses her uncle most dreadfully, don't you, Pammy dear?" The mother smiled fondly at the child, who rather firmly shook her head and licked the remnants of clotted cream from the serving spoon.

"Constance has always been so devoted to the charity she supports." Prudence doggedly turned the conversation in a more useful direction. "She said in her wire that she has been gathering support from diplomatic circles in Paris and Rome, and, of course, in Cairo."

"Oh, yes . . . yes . . . of course. The charity." The Dowager Lady Winthrop opened her tiny silk reticule. "I was forgetting, dear. I had promised a donation . . . such a worthy cause. Fifty guineas, wasn't it?"

"Thank you," Prudence said in an undertone, taking the bank draft. "I cannot tell you what a difference this will make to the lives of these poor gentlewomen. They are destitute through no fault of their own. Without what little we can give them they would be obliged to sell themselves on the street."

Lady Lucan put up her not inconsiderable chins and opened her own reticule. "Well, I had thought fifty guineas at first, but in the circumstances, I decided seventy would be more appropriate."

Lady Winthrop stared into space as her neighbor with an air of quiet triumph handed a bank draft to Prudence.

"You are both so kind and generous," Prudence said, rising gracefully, both drafts tucked into her palm. "I can't thank you enough . . . and these poor women will be eternally grateful." Smiling, she moved away to the sideboard, where surreptitiously she opened the linen drawer and dropped the two drafts softly among the tea napkins.

"Outrageous," whispered Chastity at her ear.

"The devil drives, sister dear."

Chapter 3

Gideon laid aside the copy of *The Mayfair Lady* with a frown. He reread the solicitor's letter and glanced again at the broadsheet before reaching for a silver cigarette box. He took a cigarette, lit it, and pushed back his chair, going over to the narrow window that looked on the street. He smoked thoughtfully, gazing down at the few pedestrians still about at this hour of early evening. Law clerks for the most part, hurrying home to lonely garrets or wives and children in humble terraced houses on the outskirts of London. It was not a profession that paid well.

As if prodded by the reflection, he left the window and went into the outer office, where Thadeus was sifting through a pile of paper on a small table. "Do I have an opening for an appointment with this Mayfair Lady?"

Thadeus abandoned one pile of paper in favor of another and unearthed the appointment book. "The case interests you, Sir Gideon?"

"Not so much interests as irritates me," the barrister said, throwing his cigarette into the fire. He tossed the broadsheet on the table. "I've seen this publication lying around, of course, but never bothered to look at it. I assumed it was full of female gossip and clothes talk."

"And is it, Sir Gideon?"

"It has its share of that," Gideon said. "But it also seems to be some suffragist tract as well."

The clerk's upper lip curled in an involuntary gesture of disdain. "What would women do with the vote, Sir Gideon?"

The barrister shrugged slightly. "As far as I'm concerned, Thadeus, the jury's still out on that question. But this article . . ." He tapped the paper with a forefinger. "It seems to me Barclay's well within his rights to sue. This is a piece of unadulterated malice."

"But what if it's true, Sir Gideon?" The clerk tilted his head to one side like an inquiring hedge sparrow.

The barrister waved a dismissive hand. "Maybe there's no smoke without fire, but this kind of sensationalist trash is worse than the sins it's intending to expose. I am going to tell whoever wrote this piece of scandalmongering libel exactly what I think of this *Mayfair Lady*. The very idea that they would approach *me* to defend such a disgraceful malignant torrent of slanderous rubbish is insulting. Who the hell do they think I am? Some half-trained lawyer grubbing for clients in the gutter?"

Sir Gideon had quite a head of steam up, Thadeus reflected as he consulted the ledger. He was beginning to feel sorry for the woman who was going to walk unknowingly into that wall of fire. "Next Thursday afternoon, Sir Gideon. You have an opening at four o'clock."

"Then send a message to that Bayswater address requesting the presence of the Mayfair Lady in my chambers at that time."

"As you say, Sir Gideon. I'll send it by messenger right away."

Gideon reached for his greatcoat and muffler on the coat rack. "Oh, and make sure they're aware that my fee for an initial consultation with no guarantees is fifty guineas."

"I would have done so anyway, Sir Gideon." Thadeus sounded faintly reproving.

"Yes, of course you would," his employer said, heading for the door. "I'm on my way home now, Thadeus. Sarah invited some school friends for supper and I have strict instructions to be home in time to be introduced. I gather their parents need to know that even though Sarah has no mother, her father is perfectly respectable. Don't stay overlong yourself." He raised a hand in farewell and hurried out into the dusk.

The shiny green motor drove around Manchester Square and drew to a halt outside No. 10. Max Ensor turned to his wife with a slightly quizzical smile.

"Don't forget you don't live here anymore, Constance."

She laughed and shook her head. "As if I would."

"Oh, I wouldn't be so sure," he said, still smiling. "You haven't seen your sisters for six weeks. I'll lay odds that the minute you're in their midst you'll forget everything that's happened since you saw them last."

Constance shook her head again and laid a gloved hand on his as it rested on the steering wheel. "That I could never do, Max." Her dark green eyes were serious now, although they held a sparkle in their depths. "Every moment of the last six weeks is indelibly printed on my memory . . . and not just my memory," she added with a quick and slightly mischievous grin. "My body bears its fair share of imprints."

Max laughed and got out of the motor to come around and open the passenger door for her. "You're not alone in that, my love. There's something of the female leopard about you on occasion."

"The female leopard?" she inquired with raised eyebrows. "Now, why would that be?"

"I read once a very vivid description of the mating habits of the leopard," her husband informed her solemnly as she stepped to the pavement. "It seems to be a very violent coition, in which the female spends most of her time growling and scratching her mate, finally flinging him off her back with an open-clawed wallop."

"Did I do that?" Constance said in mock awe. "I have no recollection. It doesn't sound at all like me. I have such a mild temperament."

"Now, that, my dear wife, reveals a staggering level of self-deception," he scoffed. He lifted her chin with his forefinger and looked down at her, not so very far since she was almost as tall as he. "I'll come back for you in two hours."

"Don't be ridiculous, Max. I'll take a hackney home."

"No, I'll come and fetch you. I don't trust you in your sisters' company. Besides," he added, silencing her incipient protest with a finger on her lips, "I've missed them too, and I should certainly pay my respects to your father."

Constance considered this, then shook her head in resignation. "Very well, but there's no need to hurry your business at Downing Street."

"I won't. I merely intend to bring myself back into the Prime Minister's sights, just in case I slipped his mind during the summer recess."

"I doubt you did that," Constance declared. "Once met, Max, you could never slip anyone's mind."

"You flatter me," he returned with a dry smile. He kissed her mouth, his lips lingering for a moment despite the fact that they were standing on the open street. Then reluctantly he raised his head. "I'll be back in two hours."

Constance turned to the steps leading up to the house. "Don't hurry," she said, blowing him a kiss over her shoulder as she walked quickly to the door.

He watched as she used her own key to let herself in, and when the door had closed on her he returned to the motor and drove off towards Westminster and the Prime Minister's residence at 10 Downing Street.

Constance had barely closed the door before Jenkins appeared from the shadows of the staircase. "Why, Miss Con . . ." He coughed. "Mrs. Ensor, I should say."

"No, no, Jenkins, I couldn't get used to anything but Con," she said, coming towards him with swift step and kissing his cheek. "How have you been? It seems I've been away an eternity. Is Mrs. Hudson well?"

"Everyone is well, Miss Con," the butler stated, his delighted smile belying the formal tone. "Miss Chas and Miss Prue are in the parlor upstairs."

"No, we're here," Chastity's light and cheerful tones chimed. "Con, we didn't dare to expect you so soon." She came flying down the stairs, followed with as much haste by Prudence.

Constance disappeared into their embrace and Jenkins nodded his satisfaction as he watched the three heads of various shades of red bob and blend in the way he knew so well. "I'll bring coffee to the parlor," he announced.

"Oh, and some of those almond slices that Mrs. Hudson made yesterday," Chastity emerged from the tight circle to call after him as he walked back to the kitchen.

Constance hugged her. "I didn't expect you to have lost your sweet tooth in six weeks, Chas."

Her youngest sister gave an exaggerated sigh. "No, I'm a lost cause. And I seem to be getting rounder." She pulled a comical face as she traced the swell of her breasts beneath her muslin blouse and plucked at her hips that curved voluptuously beneath the wide belt of her striped grosgrain skirt.

"Sometimes, sister dear, I think you suffer from the besetting sin of vanity," Prudence stated, even though she was laughing. "You know perfectly well it suits you."

"For the moment," sighed Chastity. "But soon it will turn to fat, and then, alas, what shall I do?"

"Give up cakes," Constance said, linking arms with her sisters. She looked closely at Prudence and saw that she had a drawn look about her eyes. She looked again at Chastity, and realized that the light banter had merely masked a similar unquiet air.

"Let's go upstairs," she said. "I want to hear everything that's happened since I left."

"First we want to hear everything about your honeymoon," Prudence said as they went upstairs. "Your telegrams were so brief. Did Max really take you to the pyramids?"

"Yes, but we visited them on horseback, not by camel. Could you imagine Max on a camel? And we went down the Nile on the most luxurious riverboat all the way to Alexandria." Constance opened the door to the parlor and gave an involuntary smile at the welcome familiarity of the room. "Oh, I've missed home," she said.

"We've missed you," Prudence said, hugging her. "But I have to say, Con, that there is nothing Egyptian about that dress." She regarded her sister's outfit with a knowing eye.

"Well, we did go to Cairo via Paris and Rome," Constance reminded her.

"That would explain the unmistakable mark of a Parisian modiste." Prudence closed the door behind them. "I saw in one of the fashion magazines that those straight skirts are becoming all the rage on the Continent. Do you have trunksful?"

"Not quite." Constance drew off her gloves and tossed them onto a console table. "But I do have several for you both. The trunk's following me here in a hackney. There wasn't room in the motor." She examined her sisters. "I don't think they'll need altering, although Chas might have grown a little rounder since I last saw her."

"Calumny!" Chastity exclaimed, laughing. "But I can't wait to see them. And that hat, Con! Is it a hat?"

Constance unpinned the small pillow of mink that sat atop her head. "They call it a hat on the Rue de Rivoli, but I think it looks more like a rabbit's scut. Max liked it, though."

"How *is* Max?" Prudence asked, trying not to put too much emphasis on the question as she geared herself for the revelations to come.

Constance smiled and tossed the fur pillow to join her gloves on the table. She perched on the wide arm of the chesterfield, smoothing out the creases in the tawny silk skirt that stretched tight across her thighs, and unbuttoned her wasp-waisted black jacket to reveal a lace-trimmed blouse of ivory silk. "I believe him to be in fine health."

Chastity threw a cushion at her. She ducked, caught it, and threw it back. "We had a wonderful time."

"So, we can assume he's in a relaxed frame of mind," Prudence said.

Constance swung her gaze sharply towards her sister. "What is it? I knew something was wrong the minute I walked in."

She paused as a knock at the door heralded Jenkins's entrance with a tray of coffee. "How's Mrs. Beedle, Jenkins?" she asked as she rose to clear space for the tray on the paper-littered table.

"Very well, I thank you, Miss Con." Jenkins poured coffee into three cups and judiciously added sugar to the one that he handed to Chastity.

"I hope she's received lots of letters for *The Mayfair Lady.*"

"Prue collected the last delivery a couple of days ago." Chastity selected an almond slice from the plate as the door closed behind the butler. They couldn't wait forever before putting Constance in the picture.

"Yes," Prudence said. "Some quite interesting correspondence."

Constance's expression was serious. "What is it?" she asked again.

Prudence went to the secretaire, where a mountain of paper threatened to tumble to the carpet. "You remember the piece you wrote about the earl of Barclay?" She removed a sheet from the pile.

Constance rose to her feet too. "Yes. How could I forget?" Her tone was hesitant. "I knew it would cause a stir . . . we all knew that it would."

"He's suing us—or rather, *The Mayfair Lady*—for libel," Chastity told her, getting to her own feet.

"But he can't. It was all true and well documented," Constance said.

"Here's a copy of the solicitor's letter." Prudence handed her the document that she had painstakingly copied before leaving the original with Sir Gideon's clerk.

"He doesn't have a leg to stand on," Constance said. "I had the names of three women whom he'd seduced and abandoned."

"And the *Pall Mall Gazette* picked up on it as we'd hoped," Prudence said. "But their article has only just come out. It's going to put Barclay in the pillory." She leaned over her sister's shoulder and jabbed with a forefinger at the paragraph at the bottom of the letter. "I think that's where the real trouble lies."

Constance read it. "Oh, God," she murmured. "The financial stuff. I should have left that out. I didn't have any hard evidence, and yet I know it's true." She steepled her fingers at her mouth as she looked at her sisters. "I'm so sorry."

"It's not your fault," Prudence said, removing her glasses and wiping at a smudge with her handkerchief. "Chas and I stand behind what you wrote. We know he reneged on gambling debts and we know some of his financial dealings have been suspect." She replaced her glasses.

"But we had no evidence," Constance said. "I got carried away by the excitement of exposing his philandering and I thought I could throw in the dishonesty and no one would question it because the rest was incontrovertible."

"Well, he questioned it," Prudence said flatly. She pushed her glasses up the bridge of her nose with a jab of her forefinger. "Obviously he thinks that if he can sue us successfully for libel on this, then he'll be vindicated on the other accusations as well. And then he can go after the *Pall Mall Gazette*. After a court triumph, no one will dare to whisper about his sexual peccadilloes."

Constance tossed the document back onto the secretaire with an air of disgust. "Any ideas?"

"Well, we've got the ball rolling," Prudence said, and explained about Sir Gideon Malvern. "Amelia Franklin came around this morning with a message that he'll see us next Thursday at four o'clock," she finished. "Obviously, I didn't want to give him this address, at least not at this stage, so I gave him Amelia and Henry's as a contact."

Constance nodded. "I'm sure they didn't mind."

"No, quite the opposite. Amelia's always offering to help with *The Mayfair Lady*."

Constance nodded again. "Then there's not much we can do until we see him. I wonder if Max knows him. He's bound to be expensive if he's a KC."

"We'd come to that conclusion ourselves," Prudence said gloomily. "He's already said that his initial fee will be fifty guineas. But apart from that, how do we keep our own names out of this? Barclay can sue *The Mayfair Lady*, but someone's going to want to know whose hand actually penned the so-called libel."

Her sisters made no immediate response to that truth.

The heavy slam of the front door downstairs broke their silence. "Father," said Chastity. "He'll be so pleased to see you, Con." Her tone was a trifle lackluster.

"I imagine he's totally taken Barclay's part in this," Constance stated without question or surprise. She walked to the door. "I'll run down and see him." She reached the top of the stairs just as Lord Duncan began to ascend them.

"Constance, my dear," he said, hurrying up towards her, a smile splitting his face. "Your sisters weren't sure when you'd be here. Your wire said something about the boat being delayed by the weather."

"Oh, it cleared up and we sailed on yesterday morning's tide. We got back to London late last night, but I couldn't wait another minute to see you all," she said, opening her arms to him. She hugged him as he kissed her soundly. "Are you well?"

"Oh, yes . . . yes, indeed." He stood back, holding her shoulders as he examined her. "Marriage suits you, my dear. You have quite a glow about you."

She laughed. "I believe it does. Max will be coming round in an hour or so to pay his respects."

"I look forward to seeing him. I'd welcome his opinion on a bad business." He shook his head. "A very bad business."

"Prue and Chas were saying something about—" Constance began, but Lord Duncan swept on.

"That disgraceful rag . . . *Mayfair Lady* . . . libeled Barclay, would you believe? The brass nerve of it." Lord Duncan's already ruddy complexion took on a deeper hue. "Absolutely outrageous. And now this wretched *Pall Mall Gazette* has taken it up."

"Yes, we told Con all about it, Father," Chastity said in soothing tones from behind her sister.

"It's a disgrace. That an honest man can be pilloried by some scandalmongering underground broadsheet . . . Anonymous writers, don't even have the courage to declare themselves honestly to stand by their lies. I don't know what the civilized world is coming to."

He shook his head again and made a visible effort to compose himself. "But we don't need to spoil your homecoming, my dear. I'm sure you have much to tell your sisters, but when you're ready to come down to the drawing room, we'll open a bottle of the vintage Veuve Clicquot in celebration. There are a few bottles left, I believe. I shall tell Jenkins to put one on ice." He patted his eldest daughter's cheek, nodded benignly at her sisters, and returned to the hall.

"*Do* we have any of the vintage 'widow' left?" Constance inquired.

"No, but there are a couple of bottles of Taittinger that Jenkins put away. He'll produce those instead," Prudence said. She found their father's refusal to believe, let alone accept, the general depletion of his wine cellars a particular source of anxiety among her many financial worries. She danced a constant ballet of the bottles with the able assistance of Jenkins, who knew the contents of the cellar down to the last label and exactly what substitutes Lord Duncan would accept.

Constance picked up her coffee cup again. "Let's talk about something more cheerful. Give me an update on the magazine. Have we any more paying clients for the Go-Between?"

"Speaking of paying," Chastity said, "you should have seen the way Prue squeezed fifty guineas out of *La Winthrop,* and then, would you believe, not to be outdone, *La Lucan* chipped in seventy. Prue was masterly."

Constance laughed. "I wouldn't have expected anything less. Have Hester and Lucan set a date yet?"

"Christmas Eve," Prudence told her. "Have you decided on an afternoon for your At Homes?"

Constance shook her head with a grimace. "There's no need just yet. Everyone's going to be making bride visits. As soon as it's known that I'm back in town, Society will be beating its curious and gossipy path to my door. You know what it's like, they'll be scrutinizing the furniture and the general decor of the house and asking me pointed little questions while they try to decide whether I'm content with my lot." Her tone dripped sarcasm.

"Or in the process of giving your husband an heir," added Prudence, regarding her sister with a lifted eyebrow.

"The only babies I'm going to be producing are in print," Constance declared. "At least until *The Mayfair Lady* and the Go-Between are truly solvent."

"Which won't happen at all if we can't beat this libel suit," Prudence said, her expression once more grave. "I'm just praying that this

Malvern isn't going to be prejudiced against three women operating a *scandalmongering, underground rag*." Her tone was a fair imitation of her father's.

They were silent for a minute, then Constance said, "We'll ask Max if he knows him. Maybe he could put in a good word for us. You look doubtful. Why?"

"Oh, I'm just wondering whether you want Max to read the piece in question," Prudence said, with a hesitant little shrug. "You know him best, of course, but . . ."

Constance grimaced. "You have a point. But I can't see any way of keeping it from him."

"His wife as defendant in a libel suit isn't going to advance his career any," Prudence commented.

"Which is one of the major reasons why it *can't* come out."

Another silence fell, then Constance said with effort, "Let's not think about it anymore, just for the moment. You still haven't told me if we have any new Go-Between clients."

"Two possibles." Chastity followed her sister's cue and went to the secretaire. She came back with two letters. "This one from a girl, at least she sounds more like a girl than a woman, who says she's desperate for a husband as a means of escaping a tyrannical stepmother who's determined to marry her off to someone old enough to be her grandfather. She wants to elope. I suspect she's been reading too many romances."

Constance took the letter and read the somewhat passionately incoherent screed, the writing liberally splattered with stains that one had to assume were tears.

"The poor child does seem to fancy herself between the pages of some melodramatic romance, doesn't she?" Prudence remarked, watching her sister's slightly derisive expression. "I doubt she's even of age. In my opinion we should just write her a sensible response saying we only accept clients who are over twenty-one."

"Except that's not strictly true. We found Hester Winthrop a husband," Constance pointed out.

"Yes, but that was to give Lucan a love interest other than Chas, and we knew it was a perfect match for both of them. We wouldn't have promoted it if we'd had any doubts. I don't want to meddle in the affairs of someone this young, about whom we know nothing. This so-called stepmother could be the most devoted and considerate woman, whose motives have been totally misunderstood by a spoilt gaby."

"Yes, you have a point." Constance folded the sheet and tapped it thoughtfully into the palm of her hand.

"Apart from anything else," Prudence continued resolutely, "we don't have the resources to offer a youth-counseling service. We'll be wasting an entire afternoon, not to mention the train fares to Wimbledon, if we agree to see her." The glance she shot at Chastity told Constance that her sisters had been around this maypole several times already. It was hardly surprising. Chastity's soft heart and truly empathetic nature frequently clashed with her sister's pragmatic nature and unsentimental opinions. Constance, as the eldest, was often required to cast the deciding vote.

"I'm with Prue," she said. "Sorry, Chas, but we have to be practical."

Chastity merely nodded. Despite her gentle inclinations, she knew when to fight a battle and when to yield. In this instance, the damsel from Wimbledon would have to find her own salvation.

"So, that's settled." Constance set the letter on the table. Prudence looked relieved—she hated being at odds with either of her sisters. She offered Chastity a rueful smile that her youngest sister returned with a tiny shrug of resignation.

"What about the second letter?" asked Constance.

"Rather more promising, I think." Chastity handed her the second letter. "Prue and I think we know who it's from, although she's using a pseudonym." She pointed to the signature at the bottom of the neatly penned letter. "She can't really be called Iphigenia."

"Unlikely," Constance agreed. "Wasn't Iphigenia sacrificed by Agamemnon to get a fair wind to sail to Troy?" She read the letter. "Oh, I see. You think it's written by Lady Northrop," she said when she'd finished. "She's always peppering her conversations with totally inapposite classical allusions."

"Doesn't it sound like her? Widowed, if not sacrificed, four years ago, in her prime . . . not yet ready to settle for a loveless future—"

"By which, of course, she means sexless," Prudence interrupted Chastity. "And look how she describes herself. Wealthy, brunette, brown eyes, well-endowed figure, impeccable dress sense, attractive to men. Isn't that Dottie Northrop to a tee? Apart from the dress sense," she added with the authority of one who knew her own was beyond reproach. "That I'd quibble with."

"She's certainly not one to hide her charms," Constance agreed. "And she's certainly well endowed."

"She's also the most notorious flirt," Chastity added.

"So, why does she think she needs help finding a suitable husband? She's a veritable mantrap already." Constance rose to refill her coffee cup from the tray on the sideboard.

"The men she attracts are not of the marrying kind," Prudence pointed out.

"But whom do *we* know that she doesn't that we could put in her way?"

"We'll have to think about it. If we can come up with a few possibilities, we can get them together at an At Home, as we did with Millicent and Anonymous."

"We could always suggest she moderate her necklines and be a little less flamboyant with the perfume and the diamonds," Chastity suggested. "We could make it sound as if it were the sort of general advice we give all our clients."

"We'll leave that to you, Chas. Tactful advice is right up your street. One thing we do know: Dotty can afford the finder's fee." Prudence turned at a knock on the door. "Come in."

Jenkins opened the door. "Mr. Ensor is with Lord Duncan, ladies. They would like you to join them in the drawing room for champagne."

"Thank you. We'll be down straightaway." Constance examined her reflection in the mirror above the mantelpiece, tucking a loose strand into her elaborately piled mass of rich russet hair.

"It's not like you to check your appearance, Con," Prudence said with a mischievous grin. "Marriage has certainly worked some changes."

"There's quite a wind blowing," Constance declared with an air of mock dignity. "It was gusting as I left the motor."

Laughing, they went downstairs. Lord Duncan's raised voice reached them as they crossed the hall to the drawing room. They exchanged comprehending glances. His lordship was expounding with great fervor his indignation at the libel of his friend. Judging by the speed of the monologue, his son-in-law was making no attempt to respond.

"Oh, hell," muttered Constance. "He's bound to have shown Max the article and I haven't even had a chance to prepare him." She swallowed slightly, stiffened her shoulders, and opened the drawing room door. "You're early, Max. You said two hours. Did you see the Prime Minister?" Her eyes darted to the table that stood between the two men. Both the *Pall Mall Gazette* and *The Mayfair Lady* lay there, their pages turned to the incriminating articles.

Max followed her gaze, then regarded her with a less than loverlike air. "I saw him," he said shortly. He greeted his sisters-in-law with rather more warmth, although there was a certain hint of reserve that was not normally present in his dealings with them.

"I've just been telling Ensor about this disgrace," Lord Duncan thundered, gesturing to the papers on the table. "If I ever discover who wrote that first piece of trash, I'll take a horsewhip to him. Thrash him to within an inch of his life."

"I can't say I'd blame you, sir," Max said aridly, casting another glance at his wife. Constance met his gaze.

"Well, enough of that for the moment. Ah, Jenkins, you've brought the champagne. Why the Taittinger? I specifically asked for the vintage Veuve Clicquot." His lordship frowned fiercely at the bottle's label as if it offended him.

"There is no more of the Clicquot, your lordship," Jenkins said placidly. "Harpers are unable to lay in any more supplies of that vintage."

Lord Duncan harrumphed. "Seems they're always running short of supplies these days. I shall complain to Harper himself."

"Yes, sir." Jenkins eased off the cork and poured the straw-colored liquid into five crystal glasses. He handed them around, and if he was aware of the tension that connected the sisters like a taut rope, he gave no sign. He bowed and left the drawing room.

The next half hour was for the sisters excruciating, for their father a pleasantry, and for Max Ensor a period of tightly reined annoyance. At last, after the minute details of the Nile river trip had been discussed with Lord Duncan, Max set down his glass.

"Constance, we should not neglect to visit my sister," he said. "She would feel slighted if we failed her on our first day home."

"Of course," Constance said readily. "Father, I hope you'll dine with us soon."

He received her kiss with a smile. "Yes, delightful, my dear. I look forward to seeing you in your new home. Perhaps you could invite Barclay."

Constance's smile was as flat as the Dead Sea. "Yes, of course. And maybe some of your bridge cronies. We could arrange a rubber after dinner."

"Lovely, my dear." He patted her shoulder and turned to his son-in-law. "So good to have you back in town, Ensor. I look forward to discussing the new Parliament with you."

"It will be my pleasure, Lord Duncan," Max said smoothly, allowing himself to be swept on the tide of his wife and her sisters out into the hall.

Once there, he said with a peremptory nod at the stairs, "That parlor of yours, I believe."

"Now is as good a time as any," Constance agreed, moving ahead to the stairs. "We need some information, Max."

"I doubt that's all you need," he muttered, standing aside to allow Prudence and Chastity to precede him.

Chapter 4

Constance felt her husband's hand on the small of her back as she followed her sisters up the stairs. It could have been a gently proprietorial gesture, but she was not fool enough to misinterpret the pressure of the touch. Max was not best pleased.

Max closed the parlor door behind them. He glanced around and then strode to the secretaire, where lay a copy of the broadsheet. A tense silence hung over the room while he reread the article. "I had the idiotic hope that this was some deranged figment of my imagination," he muttered when he'd finished reading.

He rolled the paper tightly and stood flicking it against his thigh as he looked at Constance. "Of course you wrote this."

She nodded. "Weeks ago, before we were married."

His exasperation got the better of his composure. "For God's sake, woman, are you completely out of your mind?"

Constance lost her apologetic demeanor. "Don't use that tone with me, Max. And I won't be called *woman* in that patronizing manner."

Prudence and Chastity exchanged a glance, then sat side by side on the sofa and regarded the bristling couple with unabashed interest.

"What do you expect me to say?" Max demanded. "Couldn't you have warned me you were going after Barclay? This is the most vitriolic attack on a respected—"

"Wait a minute—" Constance interrupted even as both her sisters jumped to their feet.

"There's nothing respected or respectable about Barclay," Prudence stated, her usually pale complexion flushed, her light green eyes alive with conviction. "Constance interviewed all three women mentioned in the article—"

"*And* I saw their children and the miserable conditions in which they were living," Constance declared. "They weren't lying, Max."

"Can you imagine what it would be like to be raped by your employer, then thrown into the street pregnant without a character reference . . . no money, no home?" Chastity weighed in with her twopence worth and Max almost physically backed away from the sisters, who were facing him like lion tamers.

"I'm not excusing him," he said. "But this is too much." He waved the rolled-up broadsheet again. "It's such a personal attack. A complete character assassination."

"It's his character we were attacking," Constance stated aridly. "The man's a philanderer, a rapist, a cheat, an embezzler—"

"Where's the evidence for that?" Max asked, a forefinger jabbing the air in front of him.

Prudence grimaced. "Rumor is all we have."

Max spun around to stare at her. "That's going to be your defense? Rumor? I'd credited *you* with more sense, Prudence." Constance stared at the carpet, hearing the inference in the emphasis. It was true she was not always as circumspect as her younger sister.

Prudence, for her part, flushed, but said stolidly, "We agree we'll have to do better than that. Once we've found a lawyer to defend *The Mayfair Lady*."

"We think we've found one," Chastity said.

"Yes, Sir Gideon Malvern," Prudence put in. "He's seeing us next Thursday. We were wondering if you knew him, Max."

Instead of answering her, Max demanded, "How are you going to keep your identities secret in a court of law?"

"We don't know yet," Constance said. "We were rather hoping that this Sir Gideon might have some idea."

"Yes. *Do* you know him, Max?" Prudence pressed. "He's a member of the Middle Temple and—"

"Yes, I know that," her brother-in-law snapped.

Prudence glanced at her elder sister, who shrugged with a gesture of resignation. They would get nowhere by resenting Max's tone at this point. They needed what enlightenment he could offer them.

"Would you like a whisky, Max?" Chastity invited with a conciliatory smile.

He regarded her with narrowed eyes, then let his gaze drift to her sisters, who were clearly struggling with the need to placate him while surging with indignation at his high-handed approach to their problem. He grinned suddenly. It was a moment to be savored. One rarely got the better of the Duncan sisters.

"What's funny?" Constance demanded, all suspicion. "You look like you did in the mews with Father's Cadillac."

"The only other occasion when I felt that I had the upper hand with the three of you," he said, his grin broadening.

"All right," Constance said. "You've had your fun at our expense. Now tell us what you know of this barrister."

"Do you have any idea how much a barrister like Malvern is going to cost you?" he asked with mild curiosity.

"We're not without resources," Prudence said tightly, her myopic gaze fierce behind her spectacles. "We have emergency funds, Max. Not that it's any business of yours," she added, and immediately regretted the addition. "I'm sorry." She pinched the bridge of her nose. "I didn't mean to be ungracious. I'm just feeling a little overwhelmed."

"You're not dealing with this alone, Prue," Constance said swiftly. "I know you bear the lion's share of the business management, but we're all in this one together."

Prudence managed a faint smile. "I *know* that. I just can't imagine what will happen if we lose."

"Well, Gideon Malvern can go a long way to ensuring that you don't," Max said, offering the brisk reassurance that he knew the sisters would appreciate more than sympathy. "He has the reputation of being the most innovative and able KC in the Inns of Court. He rarely loses a case."

That was all very well, Prudence reflected. Exactly what they wanted. But how the hell were they going to pay for what they wanted? For all her bravado, she could see no possible way of managing a top barrister's fee. The initial fifty guineas was going to be hard enough to find. If it weren't for the indigent spinsters' charity, she'd be wracking her brains for something to pawn.

Her sisters knew this intellectually, but sometimes she felt they didn't grasp the realities as clearly as she did. The management of the family finances was her responsibility. Naturally enough, since she was the bookkeeper, the mathematician, the obviously practical one of the sisters. She didn't resent the responsibility but sometimes she felt she carried it alone.

"He might suit you, because he likes challenges," Max continued. "He picks and chooses his cases; he can afford to do so," he added, watching them, not at all fooled by Prudence's defensive statements about hidden resources. "He has been known to take a case pro bono if it really appeals to him." He saw three pairs of green eyes sharpen with interest. "Or he's been known to come to a contingency agreement whereby if he wins he takes a share of the damages awarded to his client."

"Seems fair," Prudence said, frowning. "He gets paid to win."

"You'll have to persuade him that there's sufficient interest and challenge in the case to make it worth his while."

"Well, I don't think that's going to be difficult," Constance said with a short laugh. "There's got to be a more than ordinary challenge in taking on as clients three subversive women who insist on remaining anonymous."

"That problem I leave in your more than capable hands, ladies." He gave them a small bow.

"Was Sir Gideon knighted for services to the bar, or did he inherit the title?" Prudence asked quickly as Max reached to open the door.

"He was knighted after he defended a particularly difficult case that involved one of the king's rather more dubious friends," Max said, turning the knob. "Are you coming, Constance? We really should visit Letitia."

"Yes," she said reluctantly. "I suppose we should. Let's all meet at Fortnum's for tea this afternoon, Prue. We can talk strategy then."

Prudence nodded. "Max, does this Sir Gideon always defend? Or does he prosecute too?"

"He specializes in defense."

"Well, that's something," Chastity declared. "We just have to convince him that it would be a travesty of justice to find *The Mayfair Lady* guilty of libel."

"One of you," Max said. "I would most earnestly suggest that only one of you keeps the appointment."

"Why?" Constance had gathered up her gloves and now stood before the mirror above the mantel inserting pins in the mink pillow atop her russet head.

Max hesitated, searching for the most diplomatic answer. "He's a formidable man but you wouldn't want him to feel ambushed," he said finally. "I don't know how he views women in general, but I'd lay odds he's never come across any quite like you three."

"And we might put him off?" Constance asked with a sweet smile, turning from the mirror. "A trio of viragos, perhaps?"

"We are not going to have this conversation, Constance," Max said firmly, opening the door for her. "I merely gave my opinion. You may take it or leave it as you wish."

"We'll probably take it," Prudence said. "Oh, and be warned, Con. Letitia is firmly convinced that you've been camping in the desert and have a skin pitted with sand and hair matted with dust."

"Well, I daresay I shall be able to put her right on both those scores," Constance said.

"Oh, did you eat sheeps' eyes?" Chastity said, accompanying them to the stairs. "We were wondering."

"Good God! Whatever gave you that idea?" Max exclaimed, revolted.

"We thought that was a chief delicacy among the nomads of the Sahara," Chastity informed him.

"I don't think we ate any," Constance said, appearing to consider the question with appropriate solemnity. "Max actually refused to eat anything he couldn't identify."

"How unadventurous of you, Max," Prudence said reproachfully. "I would have thought when you go to somewhere as exciting as Egypt you would want to experience the culture at its richest. Mother would certainly have encouraged it."

Max knew from experience that the only way to put a stop to what could turn into a very convoluted discussion at his expense was to abandon it. "Come, Constance." He took her hand and hastened down the stairs, Constance blowing a farewell kiss to her sisters over her shoulder.

"Con, we'll see you at Fortnum's at four," Chastity called after them, laughter alight in her voice. It died fairly rapidly, however, when she saw Prue's expression. She put a hand on her arm. "We'll get out of this, Prue. We have to."

Prudence sighed. "I know. But if Max, who's formidable enough in his own right, considers Malvern to be intimidating, how on earth are *we* going to deal with him?"

"We're considered quite formidable ourselves," Chastity said. "Even Max said as much. You'll be a match for him."

"*Me?*" Prudence took off her glasses and peered at her sister. "Since when did I draw the short straw?"

"It just seems obvious to me," Chastity said. "I didn't give it a second thought." She frowned, wondering why that was the case. "We'll see what Con thinks this afternoon. Maybe she's expecting to do it."

"She did write the piece," Prudence said, turning back to the parlor. But she knew from the sinking feeling in the pit of her stomach that the task of convincing Sir Gideon Malvern had her name on it. Once again she pictured him as she'd seen him in the dim light of the hall. She'd had the sense of a presence rather than any specific details about height or form or coloring. But his eyes had most definitely been gray. Gray with a certain piercing quality to them . . . a light that had fixed upon her like a torch beam. And his voice . . . now, she had liked his voice.

She was feeling in a rather more positive frame of mind that afternoon as she walked along Piccadilly to meet her sisters. Chastity had written her

letter to the melodramatic miss from Wimbledon and had left early to
stop at the post office to send it on its way, so Prudence was enjoying a
solitary walk. It was a lovely crisp autumn afternoon, when London
showed itself at its best. The trees were turning deep red and burnt orange and there was the faint scent of roasting chestnuts on the air. She
passed a vendor at his brazier and hesitated, tempted by the aroma, but
she was within a few yards of Fortnum's and she couldn't really walk
into the tearoom with a newspaper cone of chestnuts.

How difficult could it be to persuade a barrister of the legitimacy of a
case that shrieked legitimacy? So, maybe they didn't have much . . . no,
any . . . evidence for the fraud accusations, but maybe, just maybe there
was an obvious place to start looking. The idea so startled her that she
stopped dead on the pavement. A man behind her dodged sideways to
prevent a collision and passed her with a quick sidestep, staring at her.

Prudence offered a smile of apology and began walking slowly again.
Why had they not thought of it before? It seemed obvious now. But perhaps they'd been blinded by their father's loyalty and dependence on
his friend. She caught herself humming and relished a lighthearted feeling that had become a stranger just recently. She smiled at the doorman
who held open the glass doors for her and entered the wide marble expanse of the tearoom. The usual string quartet was playing on the dais,
and swallowtail-coated waiters, and waitresses in frilly white caps,
moved between the crowded tables with trolleys laden with rich cakes
and silver-domed serving platters.

"Mrs. Ensor and the Honorable Miss Prudence Duncan are seated in
the far alcove, Miss Duncan." The maître d'hôtel bowed. "If you'd like to
follow me."

"Thank you, Walter." Prudence followed him, aware of the eyes on
her. Every new arrival was scrutinized in this fashion, chattering tea
drinkers hoping for some intimation of scandal. Constance would have
been the object of every gossiping tongue in the room since it was her
first public outing since her marriage. Her clothes and general appearance would have been taken apart to the last stitch. Prudence smiled
and nodded at acquaintances but didn't stop to greet anyone.

Her sisters were seated at a round table in a relatively secluded alcove
behind a pillar. They waved as she came up. "There you are, Prue. We
thought it better not to sit in plain sight today. To save Con some gaw-
ping and congratulating," Chastity explained.

"Oh, I think I'm already the subject of conversation at most tables,"
Constance said as Prudence took the chair Walter pulled out for her.

"Your dress must be," Prudence declared with approval. "It's gorgeous. I love those black and white stripes and those sleeves . . . the

way they puff at the top and then are tight and buttoned to your wrists. Are those mother-of-pearl buttons?"

"Yes, aren't they pretty? What do you think of the hat?" Constance lifted the black spotted veil that covered her eyes.

"Stunning," Prudence said. "So different from that little mink thing you were wearing this morning. I love those orange plumes against the black velvet."

"I must say, I'm enjoying my new wardrobe," Constance confessed almost guiltily, drawing off her gloves. "Max is the driving force. He has the most avant-garde taste. Quite surprising, really, for someone who's always seemed so conventional."

"He married you, didn't he?" Prudence remarked. "Not the mark of a conventional man."

"Perhaps not." Constance was as unaware of the little smile playing over her lips as she was of the glow on her cheeks, and the luminous sparkle in her eyes.

"Nice afternoon?" Chastity inquired blandly as she poured tea for her sister.

Constance gave her a sharp look and then laughed a little self-consciously. "Is it that obvious?"

"It's fairly obvious you didn't spend the entire afternoon with Letitia."

Constance changed the subject. She glanced up at the waitress who was hovering at the table. "Anchovy toast," she said. "I would like two pieces, please. What?" She looked at her sisters, who were regarding her with amusement.

"You don't usually eat tea," Chastity observed.

"I seem to be hungry this afternoon," Constance declared repressively. "And you're a fine one to talk. Look at that decadent concoction on your plate."

"Oh, it's delicious, you should try one." Chastity dipped her finger into the raspberry cream and licked it slowly. "Heavenly. Raspberry and chocolate. I can never decide whether chocolate and orange is a better combination. It all depends on which one I'm eating at the time."

"I'd like a marron glacé," Prudence said, looking the cake trolley over somewhat absently. "Thank you." She smiled at the waitress who poured her tea.

"What's the matter, Prue?" Constance inquired after a few seconds. "You've been looking at that marron glacé as if you've never seen anything like it before."

"I had a revelation on the way here," Prudence said.

"About the case?" Chastity leaned forward eagerly.

Prudence nodded. "Just a thought about this fraud business."

"Go on," Constance invited, sniffing hungrily at the fragrant plate of anchovy toast that had been placed in front of her.

"All right." Prudence took off her glasses and rubbed the bridge of her nose with a finger. "When Father threw his fortune behind that lunatic scheme to run a railway across the Sahara—"

"And lost every penny he possessed," Chastity stated.

"Precisely. Well, he didn't consult us, did he? And if he'd consulted Mother she would have put a stop to it with one soft word, but, of course, she wasn't there."

"True," Constance said, watching her sister closely.

"But who was there?" Prudence replaced her glasses. "The one person whose voice Father listened to, whose influence he bowed to."

"Barclay," her sisters said in unison.

"Yes, Barclay. The man who never left his side, who comforted him and stood his friend throughout his grief. But what if . . ." Prudence lowered her voice, leaning across the table, and her sisters automatically brought their heads closer to hers. "What if Barclay was preying on a man unbalanced by grief? What if he put Father up to that scheme for his own ends?"

"Father said only that it was some investment company that was behind the project," Chastity said, frowning.

"Yes," Prudence agreed. "And he said he expected the shares to quadruple in price in the first year."

"But the company went bankrupt," Constance said slowly.

"If there ever *was* a company." Prudence sat back and surveyed her sisters. "It's not difficult to counterfeit documents. Barclay could have invented the company out of whole cloth and convinced Father of its credentials. I'll bet there's some documentation somewhere among Father's papers. If we can link Barclay to the scheme, then we're home and dry. Not even the kindest interpretation could call selling shares in a trans-Sahara railway less than fraudulent."

"Oh, clever, Prue," Constance said quietly. "Not just a pretty face, are you?"

Prudence's smile was smug. "I don't know why we didn't think of it before."

"We've been too busy trying to deal with the aftermath," Constance pointed out. "The train wreck called family finances."

"The only problem is that Father's going to look an absolute fool," Chastity said. "If we have to expose his—What would you call it? Arrant stupidity? Lunacy?—in court, he'll be a laughingstock. We know it was an aberration when he was out of his mind with grief, but who else is going to take that into account?"

"Maybe we can manage to leave him out of it," Prudence suggested. "If we can marshal evidence to expose the scheme, we don't have to say who fell victim to it."

"Unless the barrister insists," Chastity said.

"You'll have to bring it up when you meet him," Constance said. "Chas and I were saying before you arrived that it has to be you. You know more about the finances than we do. And there's no way that this Sir Gideon will fail to take you seriously. People always take you seriously, even when you're not being serious."

"Yes," agreed Chastity. "Everything about you exudes gravitas and rationality, Prue."

"That sounds very boring," Prudence grumbled. "Like some kind of Miss Prim. I'm sure it's only because of the glasses." She pushed the spectacles farther up her nose with a gesture of faint disgust.

"It's not just that," Constance said. "It's your character. Mother always said you could grasp a situation instantly and see all its ramifications long before the rest of us. There's no way this Sir Gideon is going to dismiss you as a Society fribble, an ignoramus with nothing in her head but fashion and gossip."

"I doubt he'd dismiss you on such counts either," Prudence stated.

"But he might dismiss *me* on those grounds," Chastity observed without rancor. "He might well decide I'm some flighty flirt of very little brain."

"Chas!" her sisters exclaimed. "Don't be absurd."

"It's true," Chastity said. "That's often the first impression I make. Oh, I grant you, it doesn't last. But first impressions in this instance are going to be all we've got. I agree with Con. It's up to you, Prue."

"So, I'm it," Prudence said, and finally ate her marron glacé. A waitress appeared immediately with the trolley and Prudence examined the contents. "One of those, I believe." She indicated a strawberry tart.

"I'll have a piece of that chocolate sponge," Chastity said. "What about you, Con?"

Constance shook her head. "I'm happy with my toast. Although," she added on impulse, "perhaps I'll have a scone with clotted cream and strawberry jam."

"There's Dottie Northrop," Chastity said suddenly. "On the dance floor with old Sir Gerald."

"That old roué. She won't find a match there." Constance turned in her chair to look at the dance floor. Dottie Northrop was a woman in her early forties, but dressed as if she were at least ten years younger in a tea gown of cream muslin liberally adorned with lacy frills. The neckline was daringly low for the afternoon and her face, beneath a pale pink straw hat, was a mask, thick with powder and rouge. "If she smiles, her face will crack open." It was a statement of fact made quite without malice.

"If we're going to find her a respectable husband we're going to have to transform her," Prudence said. "But how do we do that tactfully?"

"Tact is Chas's speciality," Constance said. "Together with giving advice to the lovelorn."

"You know, the ideal man would be someone like Lord Alfred Roberts," Prudence said thoughtfully. "I know he's rather older, but he seems virile enough, and he looks so sad and lonely most of the time. Dottie might enliven his life nicely."

"That's a thought," Constance agreed. "I wonder—"

"I thought you'd still be here." Max's smooth voice interrupted her from beyond the pillar and the three women looked up in some surprise.

"Max, what are you doing here?" Constance asked.

"I was hoping to have tea." He nodded his thanks to the waiter who had discreetly provided another chair. "Is that anchovy toast you're eating?" He gestured to his wife's plate.

"Yes, it's very good," she responded, spooning clotted cream onto her scone.

"Then I'll finish it for you since you seem to have abandoned it." He smiled at the hovering waitress, who had set down a fresh pot of tea and another cup. He took a piece of toast from his wife's plate while Prudence poured tea for him. "I was making some inquiries about Malvern at my club. What his courtroom style is like, that kind of thing."

"And?" Prudence prompted warily.

"He's known for his confrontational techniques," Max said. "From what I could gather, he goes for the jugular."

"I don't like the sound of that," Prudence said.

"I think you're going to have to try to get him off guard," Max said. "Surprise him somehow, so he doesn't have time to react against you."

"Ye gods!" Prudence muttered. "You really think he's going to start off prejudiced against me?"

Max bit into his toast with evident enjoyment. "I think it's possible," he said when he'd finished his mouthful. "I certainly would be straight off the bat." He glanced across at Prudence, who was looking far from reassured by this brutal candor. "You're going in as the advance guard?"

"We thought she'd be the best one of us," Chastity told him. "I don't look serious enough."

"And I'd rather not have to introduce myself as your wife," Constance pointed out.

"I appreciate your concern," Max said dryly. "But Malvern is going to know soon enough what my connection is."

"It won't hurt to delay that revelation," Constance said. "Prue's the natural choice because she manages the finances to a large extent. She'll sound very knowledgeable and serious."

"And I'll wear my thickest glasses," Prudence said, trying to sound lighthearted. "And my most earnest air."

"Dear God, what an image. I could almost find it in my heart to feel sorry for Malvern," Max declared.

"Oh, yes, Prue at her most grave and solemn is a force to be reckoned with," Chastity said.

Prudence's responding smile lacked conviction, but it went unnoticed amid her sisters' amusement.

Chapter 5

"Well, what do you think?" Prudence stood in front of her sisters on the appointed Thursday afternoon and awaited their judgment.

"You look like a cross between a nun and a schoolteacher," Constance observed.

"No, more like a librarian than a nun," Chastity said. "You have a very earnest and learned look about you."

"That was the effect I was hoping to achieve," Prudence said with her head on one side as she critically surveyed her appearance in the mirror. "I particularly like the felt hat." She lifted the navy blue veil that fell discreetly to just below her nose. The hat itself was of dark gray felt with a demurely turned-up brim.

"It goes with the suit. Dark gray serge . . . you could almost be in mourning," Constance said.

"Do you have the fifty guineas?" Chastity asked, brushing a piece of lint off Prudence's shoulder.

"Surely he'll send a bill," Prudence said, looking at Constance for confirmation. "He's not selling cabbages off a stall."

"I'm sure he will. But I should take it anyway. If he's horribly insulting and dismissive, at least you'll have the satisfaction of giving him his pound of flesh as your own parting shot."

Prudence grimaced. "I know Max meant well but I wish he hadn't found out what he did about Malvern. Just imagining his confrontational manner makes me so nervous I'm sure I'll be completely tongue-tied."

"No, you won't," Chastity said firmly. "You wouldn't let his clerk intimidate you the other day, and you won't let the barrister."

"I hope not. If he's the best there is, I can't afford to," Prudence said with a rather brave smile. "We have to net him."

Constance nodded. "By the way, you might want to pretend that we have no money worries. Once he's caught, then we can negotiate."

"It seems a bit underhanded, but I agree." Prudence pulled on navy blue gloves and picked up a capacious handbag. "I have a complete set of copies of everything I left with his clerk the other day. Just in case they were misplaced in the clerk's office," she added with an ironical shrug. "I only wish I had something concrete to back up the accusations of embezzling and cheating."

"But you can tell him we know how to go about getting such evidence," Constance reminded her.

"We *think* we do," Chastity emphasized.

"I don't intend to allow a hint of doubt," Prudence declared, and dropped the veil. "I'd better make tracks. It's nearly three-thirty."

Her sisters accompanied her in a hackney as far as the Temple Gardens. "We'll wait for you here," Constance said, kissing her.

"No, wait for me at Fortnum's," Prudence said, opening the carriage door. "It looks like rain and I don't want to be worrying about you getting wet. I've no idea how long this is going to take."

"The longer it takes, the more hopeful the outcome," Chastity said. "We'll go to Fortnum's for tea, then, but I shan't be able to eat a thing until you get there."

Prudence laughed at that. "It would be a momentous event indeed that would keep you from your cake, Chas." She climbed out of the hackney, waved once to her sisters, who were hanging out of the window, and then strode resolutely up Middle Temple Lane.

Outside the door to Sir Gideon Malvern's chambers, she paused, preparing herself. Then resolutely she turned the knob and marched up the narrow staircase to the door at its head. She knocked once and entered without waiting for an invitation. The same clerk sat behind his desk. "I have an appointment with Sir Gideon," she told him firmly, keeping her veil in place.

The clerk consulted his ledger as if to confirm this, then he looked up and peered at her. "The Mayfair Lady?" he asked.

"As you are aware," Prudence said, wondering why he always had to play games. "I believe I am exactly on time." She glanced pointedly at the clock.

"I will tell Sir Gideon that you are here." The clerk sidled from behind his desk and opened the door in the far wall a veritable crack, through which he insinuated himself with a rustle of his coattails.

Prudence waited. The door to the inner chamber opened fully and the man she had bumped into on her last visit stood in the doorway. "So, we meet again, Madam Mayfair Lady," he said in the voice she remembered, and disconcertingly the tiny hairs on the nape of her neck prickled. "Won't you come in?"

He held the door, and Prudence with a murmur of thanks entered the sanctum. The clerk gave her another appraising look, then removed himself with the slither that seemed his preferred motion.

Sir Gideon moved a chair forward for his visitor. "Pray sit down, Miss . . . Mrs. . . . ? Forgive me, I am at something of a loss."

Prudence put up her veil. "I assume everything that is said in this room is confidential, Sir Gideon? Even if you decide not to take the case."

"Whatever is said between a barrister and a client, prospective or not, is privileged communication, madam."

Prudence nodded. She had known that, of course, but she had needed it stated. "I am the Honorable Prudence Duncan," she said. "One of the editors of *The Mayfair Lady*." She gestured to the copy that lay open on the massive oak table that appeared to serve as his desk.

He moved back behind the table as she sat down, and stood for a minute, his hand playing over the broadsheet as he regarded her with a close and unblinking scrutiny. "I seem to recall that there were two of you before."

"In fact, there are three of us."

Sir Gideon was rarely taken aback, a career in the law courts inured a man against surprise, but he was puzzled. The lady in his office bore little resemblance to the image he had taken away from their brief meeting in the hallway. Of course, it had been hard to see clearly in the gloom. The woman sitting in front of him struck him as a rather dull, plain-looking mouse of a creature. He couldn't really see her eyes, hidden as they were behind a pair of hideous, thick tortoiseshell spectacles. Her clothes were uniformly gray, unenlivened by the touch of navy blue, and he thought she looked prim and uninteresting. Which didn't sit quite right with the image of a woman who could write some of the racy and undeniably witty articles in the broadsheet.

Prudence returned the scrutiny with equal interest. She was pleased to recognize his initial surprise, but there was something in his eyes, a certain flicker, that caused her hackles to rise. He was weighing her, and unless she was mistaken, mentally dismissing her.

He was probably around Max's age, as she had calculated. Forty or so. Unlike Max, he had no gray hairs. His hair was a thick, well-coiffed dark brown mane sweeping off a broad forehead. Deep frown lines creased between his rather sculpted eyebrows, but she couldn't decide whether they were the result of a disagreeable nature or were merely indicative of hours of deep thought. He had a calm mouth beneath a long thin nose that dominated his countenance. His gray eyes were sharp and filled with intelligence, but they definitely held no friendliness in their depths. Was it her or her cause that he was dismissing? Or was that simply his habitual expression?

"And who are the other two editors?" he asked after the silence seemed to have elongated. He still did not sit down, which Prudence found even more disconcerting.

"My sisters," she said.

"Ah." He smoothed the broadsheet and she noticed that his hands were very long and white, the filbert nails well manicured. More like a pianist's hands than a lawyer's. He wore an emerald signet ring and the diamond studs in his shirt cuffs glittered, as did the pin in his lapel. Nothing ostentatious, simply an elegant, understated indication of wealth and position. Everything about his presence confirmed the impression. This was a man supremely confident in himself, and his position in the world. He was also intimidating. But Prudence had no intention of letting him know that.

She folded her gloved hands in her lap. "I left all the details relevant to the situation with your clerk, and I see that you have a copy of the article in question, so I assume you're up-to-date with the facts, Sir Gideon."

"Such as they are," he said. "Am I correct in believing that the Honorable Constance Duncan recently married Mr. Ensor, the politician?"

"You are. But that is not germane, and should not influence you in any way."

A sparkle of definitely derisive amusement showed for a second in his eyes. "I do assure you, my dear madam, that nothing influences me but my own assessment of a situation and my own inclination."

Prudence controlled her rising anger at his condescending tone. She said neutrally, "I'm glad to hear it, Sir Gideon. One would not wish to be represented in court by a lawyer who could be swayed from the truth by some personal whim."

His eyes were suddenly hooded, his countenance completely without expression, and she had no idea whether she had stung him or not. Was this his courtroom face? Giving nothing away? If so, it was a very effective weapon. She found herself resisting the urge to break the silence with some irrelevant babble.

She rose to her feet. "Forgive me, but if you choose not to sit down, Sir Gideon, I would prefer to stand too for the extent of this consultation."

His expression remained the same, his eyes still hidden under half-lowered lids. However, he gestured to the chair again, said, "Please," and sat down himself behind the table. He lightly tapped the article in the open broadsheet in front of him.

"Did you write this, Miss Duncan, or one of your sisters?"

"My elder sister, as it happens. But its authorship is not germane either. We're all in this together."

He smiled. "All for one and one for all. The three musketeers alive and well in the streets of London."

Prudence curled her gloved fingers into her palms, glad that there was nothing conveniently at hand to throw at him. She said nothing, keeping her face expressionless, aware that thanks to her convenient glasses he couldn't see the anger and chagrin she knew her eyes would reveal.

"What is it you and your sisters want me to do for you, Miss Duncan?" His voice was still quiet, but it was crisp, and now there was no mistaking the acerbity in the well-modulated tones.

"We would like you to defend *The Mayfair Lady* against Lord Barclay's libel suit." Prudence, for all her annoyed discomfiture, was aware of relief that at last the ball was in play. Maybe he had a problem doing business with women, but when they got down to brass tacks and she could steer him towards the evidence, which he must have read, he would lose his prejudices.

He said nothing for a minute, looking down at the broadsheet in front of him. Then he looked up, clasping his hands on top of the paper. "You see, Miss Duncan, I would find that very hard to do. Reading this, I am in complete sympathy with the earl. It is an outrageous, malicious piece of scandalmongering, and its authors deserve the full penalty of the law. If I were prosecuting, I would demand the maximum in punitive damages, and I would not rest until this . . ." He swept a dismissive hand across the paper. ". . . this gossip-feeding rag was put out of business."

He stood up again. "Forgive my bluntness, Miss Duncan, but there are realities that you and your sisters don't seem to have grasped. Women are not equipped to enter these kinds of battles. This is an emotional, unthought-out attack on a peer of the realm, designed to cause him maximum embarrassment, which I can see it has. He is entitled to financial redress for pain and suffering caused by this piece of rumor-mongering. May I suggest that in future you and your sisters confine your gossip to your social circles and keep well away from pen and ink."

He moved out from behind the desk as Prudence remained sitting, for the moment utterly stunned.

"If you'll excuse me, Miss Duncan, I have briefs to prepare." He went to the door, opening it. "Thadeus, escort the Honorable Miss Duncan to the street."

Numb, Prudence rose and allowed herself to be swept from the inner chamber, her hand given a perfunctory shake, and within two minutes she was standing in the drizzling rain outside the closed door to Sir Gideon's chambers.

She looked at her fob watch. It was barely four-twenty. In less than thirty minutes she had been roundly scolded and dismissed like a rather dim schoolgirl. Max had warned her to seize the initiative and she had let it slip. She heard the barrister's voice, that so quiet yet so clear voice, delivering the insulting, patronizing speech. No one had ever dared talk to her in that manner.

She spun on her heel to face the door again and threw it open. Not even Sir Gideon Malvern, KC, was going to get away with that.

In the gently humming tearoom at Fortnum's, Chastity and Constance sipped tea, watching through the long windows as pedestrians dodged from doorway to doorway along Piccadilly while the steady drizzle intensified to a solid rain.

"I wonder how she's getting on?" Chastity murmured for the sixth time. "I can't even eat this macaroon, and I *love* macaroons."

"Depriving yourself won't help Prue or alter the outcome of the interview," Constance pointed out, taking a cucumber sandwich from the plate on the table. "Let's think about finding a husband for Dottie Northrop instead. Have you thought any more about how to advise her tactfully on her appearance?"

Chastity welcomed the diversion. She rummaged through her handbag and produced a sheet of paper. "I thought it best just to drop a few hints in the letter." She handed the paper across the table. "I've suggested that she attend the At Home at Ten Manchester Square next Wednesday afternoon, when she should ask for an introduction to Lord Alfred Roberts, whom she might find an eligible party."

"How are we going to get Lord Alfred there?" Constance inquired. "He's a club man like Father. I can't see him holding a teacup and conducting small talk with the likes of Lady Winthrop or Mary and Martha Bainbridge."

"Father will bring him," Chastity declared with satisfied finality. "I've already asked him. I said we needed some more interesting society on Wednesday afternoons and that since Lord Alfred was a particular friend of Mother's and we think he's rather lonely, we'd like to include him."

Constance laughed. "What did Father say?"

"He hummed and hawed a little, but then said that now he thought about it, Alfred was a little less than chipper these days, and maybe he did need to be taken out of himself a little. So he's promised to bring him. As long as we have more than tea to offer them," she added, spooning sugar into her own cup.

"That's easily done. So, now we need a tactful hint about Dottie's necklines and the amount of face powder she uses."

"Oh, I've covered that. In the last paragraph." Chastity mumbled inelegantly through a mouthful of macaroon. She waved a finger at the paper her sister held.

Constance read the relevant passage and broke into a peal of laughter. "Oh, you're so good at this, Chas. It's priceless. 'The gentleman in question is rather old-fashioned, of a somewhat shy disposition, and a little alarmed by the ladies so *The Mayfair Lady* would recommend only the most decorous afternoon dress for the first introduction. The editorial staff at *The Mayfair Lady* are convinced that Lord Alfred Roberts will, with the right kind of gentle understanding and encouragement, soon lose his reticence and show himself to be a wonderful companion who enjoys all that life and Society have to offer.' "

"I thought it was quite good," Chastity said complacently. "And the more I think about it, the more I think it would be a perfect match. They can fill each other's gaps, if you see what I mean. Oh, do stop laughing, Con." She dissolved into laughter herself, choking on a cake crumb.

Constance leaned sideways and patted her on the back. "Prue will love this letter." As one, they turned to look out of the window again, hoping to see a hackney cab disgorging their sister at the curb.

Gideon almost jumped to his feet, so startled was he at the precipitate return of his visitor. But this was not the same woman who had been ushered firmly from his chambers a mere three or four minutes previously. The appearance was essentially the same but the aura was quite different. This woman crackled like a newly kindled fire. He still couldn't see her eyes behind the thick lenses but he could almost feel their heat.

"I do not understand what makes you think you have the right to treat me, or indeed any client, with such contempt and condescension," Prudence declared, setting her capacious handbag down on the barrister's table. "Since you had already prejudged the issue, I cannot understand why you would have agreed to a consultation. Unless, of course, you wished merely to amuse yourself. Women are perhaps playthings for you?"

She drew off her gloves finger by finger, each movement punctuating her words. "You did not do me the courtesy of even the pretence at a proper hearing. Did you imagine that I would come to a business meeting unprepared to discuss the evidence I left with your clerk?" She tapped the papers on the table. "We have more than enough evidence to prove our accusations against Lord Barclay. As I understand the law, if there is proof there can be no libel. I am perhaps mistaken?" She raised her eyebrows in ironic inquiry.

Gideon found a moment to catch his breath. He cleared his throat, and his visitor removed her glasses for long enough to polish them on her handkerchief. Her eyes were a revelation. A clear, lustrous light green, lively with anger and intelligence. And they were fixed upon him even as she rubbed smudges from the lenses with a derision that the lauded barrister of the King's Council had dished out often enough but never before received.

"Am I mistaken, Sir Gideon?" she repeated, setting her glasses back on her nose, resituating them with a vigorous forefinger.

"Ordinarily, no, Miss Duncan." He stood up as he found his voice. "But the anonymous nature of the accusations makes them appear less than credible and I doubt that a jury will look with sympathy on what seems . . ." He cleared his throat again. "On what could seem a cowardly stab in the back." He gestured to the chair. "Won't you be seated?"

"I don't think so," Prudence said. "Thank you. I can see that anonymity could pose difficulties, but we really have no choice in the matter. We couldn't produce the broadsheet if our identities were known, as you would have realized if you'd given it a moment's intelligent thought. You will have to find a defense that takes that into account."

He opened his mouth but she swept past his first syllables. "I assume you took the trouble to read my sister's notes taken during her interviews with the women in question. Perhaps you'd like to look at them again and refresh your memory. Of course . . ." She removed her glasses again and directed a challenging look in his direction. It was a look to make the bravest man wilt.

"Of course, if you continue to prejudge this issue then I will pay you your consultation fee, fifty guineas, I believe, although I would hesitate to call this little interview a consultation, and leave you to your prejudices." She took a wad of banknotes from the depths of the bag and laid them on the table with a careless flick of her hand. Her companion would never guess what the gesture cost her.

Gideon ignored the banknotes. "Do sit down, Miss Duncan, this could take a few minutes. Would you like tea?" He laid a hand on a silver handbell on his table.

"No, I thank you." Prudence did, however, sit down. High dudgeon had carried her this far, but its aftermath had left her a little shakier than she was prepared to admit.

"Oh, but I insist," he said, and rang the bell. Thadeus appeared instantly in a sliver of doorway. "Bring us some tea, Thadeus, and toast a couple of crumpets, if you would."

The man silently withdrew and Prudence declared, "I am not in the least hungry, Sir Gideon. This is not a social call."

"No, but it is teatime," he pointed out mildly. "And I'm certainly ready for mine." He selected a file from the pile in front of him, opened it, and began to read.

Prudence said nothing, merely watched him closely. She recognized the copies of her sister's notes and felt a fresh surge of annoyance at the implication that he really hadn't bothered to read them earlier. Thadeus arrived with a tea tray, and the enticing fragrance of the crumpets swimming in butter made Prudence regret her lofty refusal.

"Shall I pour, sir?" Thadeus intoned.

"Unless Miss Duncan would do the honors." Sir Gideon looked up and gave her a smile that made her feel she was in the presence of a quite different man. The smile crinkled the skin around his eyes in a most attractive fashion, and gave to the clear gray gaze an appealing gleam.

She shook her head in brief negative and the clerk poured tea into two delicate cups that Prudence would have sworn were Sèvres china. She took the one handed to her because to refuse now would be simply churlish, but she shook her head again when she was offered a crumpet. Dealing with all that melted butter while perched on a chair in her coat and hat would detract from the dignified air of hauteur she was trying to maintain. Sir Gideon seemed to have no such reticence and ate both crumpets with relish even while he continued to read, pausing now and again to make a notation on the pad at his elbow.

At last he looked up, after dabbing the last morsel of crumpet into the remaining butter on his plate and conveying the whole to his mouth without a single drip or smear of grease.

"Very well, I admit that I saw no point in reading the background material once I had read the article. Maybe I acted in haste, but that said, I see nothing here to substantiate the accusation of financial misconduct." His voice now was as cool as it had been earlier, the smile gone from his expression, his eyes sharp and assessing.

"There is a certain lack, we all agree," Prudence said calmly. "However, we're convinced of the truth of the charge."

"Your being convinced is hardly the same as a jury's conviction," he pointed out, the tinge of acid once more in his voice.

"We have a fairly good idea where to look for evidence to substantiate the accusation," Prudence told him, setting her empty cup on the table.

He regarded her rather quizzically. "Would you care to explain, Miss Duncan?"

"Not at present," she said, thinking it might be wise to keep a few cards up her sleeve until he'd committed himself to the cause. If she told him about her father's dealings with Barclay and he still refused to represent them, then she would have exposed her father unnecessarily. It didn't matter that it would be confidential, she just didn't like the idea of this supercilious bastard looking down on her father . . . not unless the revelation would serve a purpose. "But I can assure you we know exactly how to go about it."

He merely raised his eyebrows and said, "You said your sister wrote the article in question, as I recall."

"Yes, Constance."

He nodded. "Is she responsible for the lion's share of the writing?"

"When it comes to political issues, particularly those relating to women's suffrage, yes."

He acknowledged this with another slight nod. "And what is your role in the production of this . . ." He gestured to the paper on the table. "This publication?"

Prudence detected the trace of derision again in his tone and her anger rose anew. She got to her feet as she spoke. "I take care of the business end, Sir Gideon. The finances and matters of that nature. Now, if you will excuse me, it's clear that we have nothing further to discuss, so I'll not take up any more of your valuable time. Thank you for the tea." She swooped onto the pages that contained Constance's notes and swept them into her bag in one movement, conspicuously leaving the banknotes where they were.

Gideon stood up abruptly. "It's not at all clear to me that we have nothing further to discuss."

Prudence paused as she was putting on her gloves. "You have made no attempt to disguise your contempt for *The Mayfair Lady*. I'm sure it strikes you as the work of rank amateurs. What you perhaps don't understand—"

"Don't put words into my mouth, Miss Duncan," he interrupted. "Or thoughts in my head."

"Do you deny it?" she demanded.

"I won't deny that I'm doubtful about the merits of this case," he said. "But I'm willing to keep an open mind while you attempt to prove to me that I might find it an interesting exercise." He smiled again and

Prudence steeled herself against the charm. It was, she was convinced, entirely artificial, turned on as and when it suited the barrister.

"Have dinner with me tonight," he said, the smile deepening. "And do your worst." He spread his arms wide. "I swear I will come undefended, unprejudiced, open to all and any argument. What could be fairer than that?"

Prudence was so taken aback, she was momentarily without words. He had moved the interview from a business footing to a social one, and more than that, there was something undeniably seductive in his manner. He knew the power of his smile, the deeper resonance of his voice. But why bother to turn it on her? Did he want something from her?

There was only one way to find out.

"I won't turn down the opportunity to persuade you, Sir Gideon," she said, hoping she sounded cool and collected rather than astonished and disturbed.

"Then you accept my invitation?" He looked a little peeved, she thought, at her halfhearted response, and it gave her more confidence.

"Certainly. Although I fail to grasp what a conversation at the dinner table could achieve that couldn't be achieved in your chambers."

"Then you'll have to wait and see," he responded, immediately putting her back up again. "I might surprise you. If you'll give me the address, I'll send a motor for you at eight o'clock."

It would have been more courteous of him to have offered to come for her himself, Prudence thought. She was annoyed, very much so, but common sense dictated that she swallow her annoyance in the interests of another chance to win his support. Also, he intrigued her, reluctant though she was to admit it. He was on the one hand ungracious to the point of rudeness, arrogant, high-handed, and contemptuous, yet on the other he was charming, smiled readily, judging by the crow's feet around his eyes, and was undeniably attractive when he chose. He must also have a formidable mind, a rare quality that she had always found irresistible in a man. But why was he bothering to charm a woman who had gone out of her way to present herself as a spinsterly dowd?

"Ten Manchester Square." She walked to the door, making no attempt to soften the curtness of her response with a smile of farewell, but he slid out from behind the table and reached the door ahead of her.

He took her hand and bowed over it. "I look forward to the evening, Miss Duncan. I'll show you out." He picked up a large umbrella from the stand by the door and escorted her down to the street. The rain was coming down hard and he said, "Wait here. I'll fetch a cab." Before she could protest, he had left the shelter of the doorway and was dodging puddles under the protection of the umbrella.

Prudence was yet more puzzled. From what she'd seen of his manners so far, she would have expected him to send his clerk on the errand, if he hadn't simply left her to go off on her own in the rain. A man of curious paradoxes, and he had warned her not to rush to judgment. On such slight acquaintance it was probably a warning best heeded.

A hackney cab swung around the street corner and drew up at the doorway. Sir Gideon jumped down and held the umbrella over Prudence until she was safely ensconced. "Where shall I tell the cabbie?"

"Fortnum's," she said. "I'm having a second tea."

He laughed, a soft, rich sound that she hadn't heard before. "No wonder you scorned my crumpets. Until this evening, madam." He waved a hand and Prudence lifted hers in involuntary response, aware that she was smiling.

Gideon, a thoughtful frown now creasing his brow, returned to his chambers. He stood just inside the door to his inner sanctum, tapping his lips with a forefinger. What on earth did he think he was doing? The case was impossible, he'd known that from the first line of the article. He had no sympathy with the editors of *The Mayfair Lady*. The article in question was a piece of malicious gossip in a publication devoted to a morass of half-baked political opinions and self-righteous declarations about the unfair treatment of women. There was absolutely no way that that dowdy brown mouse, lively green eyes and termagant's temper notwithstanding, could persuade him to view the case in any other way. So, why in heaven's name had he invited her to try . . . condemned himself to an evening of crushing boredom with an inevitably unpleasant conclusion when he told her, as he fully intended to do, that he had not and never had had any intention of taking the brief?

He wondered for a second if there was any way he could rescind the invitation. He could send a note to Manchester Square, say something unexpected had come up, express his regrets, and never lay eyes on her again. His eye fell on the wad of banknotes on the table. Her voice rang again in his head, filled with angry contempt. He saw again the careless flick of her hand as she'd almost thrown the money down in front of him. Unless he was much mistaken, the Honorable Miss Duncan was not entirely what she seemed. Maybe the evening wouldn't be quite such a waste of time after all. Pursing his lips thoughtfully, he locked the banknotes in a drawer beneath the tabletop.

The cab deposited Prudence at the door of Fortnum's and she entered the now almost-deserted tearoom. Chastity waved at her from the table by the window and Prudence hurried to join them.

"Well?" they both said in unison.

"I'll tell you," Prudence said. "No, thank you." She waved the cake trolley away. "I'll have a cup of tea, though." She set her bag and gloves on the floor. "He gave me about fifteen minutes of his time, during which he subjected me to the most insulting, arrogant, patronizing speech I've ever heard. Not once did he indicate that he'd even looked at our evidence, and before I knew it I was outside in the street, staring at a closed door."

Constance whistled silently. "You went back in." It was a statement, not a question.

Prudence nodded. "I don't remember ever being so angry."

Chastity poured tea for her sister and pushed the cup across the table, reflecting that Prue rarely lost her temper, but when she did, it was a fairly spectacular tempest. "He listened to you this time?"

"Oh, yes," Prudence said, sipping her tea. "He even took the time to read the material I'd left with his clerk two days ago."

When she said nothing else for a moment, Constance prompted, "And is he going to take the case?"

"I don't know." Prudence set down her cup carefully in the saucer. "He invited me for dinner tonight." She regarded her sisters, who were now staring at her wide-eyed. "He kindly invited me to try to persuade him over dinner."

"What?" Constance's jaw dropped. "What kind of business practice is that?"

"I don't know." Prudence shrugged. "But I couldn't turn down the opportunity, could I?"

"Did you remember he's divorced?" Chastity asked. "Maybe he's not very punctilious in his personal life?"

It was Prudence who stared now. "To tell you the truth, I forgot about that."

"Divorced?" Constance said. It was the first she had heard of this interesting tidbit.

"Yes, we looked him up in *Who's Who*." Chastity said. "He's been divorced for about six years. There's a daughter too."

"Well, I don't suppose he sees much of her," Constance said scornfully. "Legally she belongs to him, so he probably makes all the decisions concerning her life but leaves her care to her mother. It's the usual way."

"Probably," Prudence agreed. She took a cucumber sandwich and then stared at it as if wondering how it had arrived in her hand.

"What?" Constance asked.

Prudence put the sandwich down. "You know, there were times when it was almost as if he was flirting with me. Every so often he'd lose that dismissive arrogance and have an almost complete personality change. It was very strange."

"It's not unheard of for a divorced man to flirt," Constance observed. "Quite the opposite. Although I'd say it's unprofessional for a barrister to flirt with a potential client."

"Unless he has no intention of taking us on as clients. If he's a licentious libertine he could be leading Prue on." Chastity had abandoned her half-eaten macaroon. She opened her hazel eyes very wide and dropped her voice to a whisper. "To have his wicked way with her."

"Oh, Chas!" Her sisters laughed, as they were intended to, but the amusement didn't last very long.

"Now, why would a licentious libertine have any interest in me in my present guise?" Prudence demanded. "I look like a prim, dowdy, spinster governess."

"I imagine that image slipped somewhat when you got angry," Constance said with a dry smile. "Did you take your glasses off?"

"I don't know, I . . . Oh, for heaven's sake, Con. What if I did?"

Her sisters said nothing, merely regarded her with quizzically raised eyebrows. "Oh, give me strength." Prudence took the sandwich again and devoured it with two vigorous bites.

"So, you accepted this invitation," Chastity said.

"Yes, I told you," Prudence said. "I couldn't turn down the opportunity to try again to get him to take the case."

"Is he attractive?"

Prudence considered this. "Not to me," she said definitely. "But I can see how some women might find him so. I just don't fall for the superior male type."

Her sisters nodded.

"Of course, he does have a rather nice voice," Prudence said with scrupulous fairness. "And when his smile's genuine some women might think it's attractive."

"But you were never taken in by the display of charm," Constance said, taking up her teacup.

"No," her sister stated. "Not for one minute."

"Well, it'll be interesting to see what the evening brings," Chastity said neutrally.

Prudence took another cucumber sandwich.

Chapter 6

"Going out, my dear?" Lord Duncan paused in the hall as his middle daughter came down the stairs that evening, her coat over her arm.

"Yes, a dinner party," Prudence said as she took the last step. She was aware of her father's rather surprised look as he took in her appearance. His daughter did not ordinarily attend dinner parties dressed for a funeral. There was something distinctly unmodish about her untrimmed gown of brown tabby. In fact, he couldn't remember ever having seen it before.

Prudence had no intention of inviting a comment on her dress and said swiftly, "Good evening, Lord Barclay." A thin layer of ice coated the polite greeting, but neither the earl nor his host heard it.

"Evenin', Prudence," the earl declared. He gave her a facetious smile. "Some eligible young man, is it?" He reached out to pat her cheek but she drew back in the nick of time.

The earl chuckled. "No need to be coy with me, Miss Prudence." He tapped the side of his nose. "A word to the wise, miss. It's all right for a debutante to be coy, but it don't sit pretty on a woman past her first few seasons."

Prudence glanced at her father and saw that he was looking with marked disfavor at his friend. It surprised her, since Lord Duncan was in general blindly loyal, but it also gave her heart. Perhaps he wasn't completely convinced of the earl's innocence, although he was loud in his denunciation of his friend's accusers. Either way, there was something acutely distasteful in the earl's veiled references to Prudence's age and unmarried situation, and Lord Duncan was both fastidious in his manners and a most loving father.

Prudence offered a chilly smile and said, "How is your libel suit progressing, my lord?"

The question had the desired effect. His lordship's complexion turned a rather unattractive shade of purple. "Damned cowards haven't responded yet . . . not a peep out of 'em, my solicitors say. Slippery as eels, they are. But if they think they can play mum and get away with it, they can think again."

"They're hardly going to hide forever, Barclay," Lord Duncan pointed out.

"Oh, no, we'll get 'em, and when we do I'll string 'em up, every one of 'em," he declared savagely. "I'll flay 'em alive and take 'em for every penny they've got."

"Somehow I doubt even the full penalty of the law will allow you to do all three," Prudence observed mildly. "How many defendants do you think there are, sir? You seem confident it's more than one."

"Of course there's more than one . . . a whole team of sissies, backstabbing men masquerading as women, up to all sorts of perversions, you mark my words." He glared at Prudence and wagged a finger very close to her nose. "You mark my words, miss, we'll have every copy of that filthy rag confiscated and burned in the streets. I'll ruin 'em and see 'em rot in jail, every damn one of 'em."

"You don't think it's possible that these writers are *actually* women, Lord Barclay?"

He stared at her as if she'd grown two heads. "Nonsense . . . nonsense. Women, indeed!" He laughed uproariously, clapping Lord Duncan on the shoulder. "*Women*. Women writing that kind of filth, digging up those lies, going into those places . . . what d'you think of that idea, eh, Duncan?"

Lord Duncan frowned. He was thinking of his late wife. "Unlikely," he agreed. "But not impossible."

"Oh, your brain's addled, my friend," the earl declared. "No respectable woman would have anything to do with it."

"Respectable women seem to read it, though," Prudence pointed out. "My own mother, as I recall, used to find the broadsheet's articles stimulating."

This comment effectively silenced Lord Barclay, since he could hardly pour scorn on his friend's dead wife.

Prudence gave him a minute to find a suitable response, and when it seemed he would be grasping for words for rather a long time said, "Are you dining in, Father?"

Lord Duncan was visibly relieved at the change of subject. "Yes, I thought we would. Jenkins and Mrs. Hudson could rustle something up for us."

Prudence reflected that the butler and housekeeper would have appreciated some notice, particularly since the household income didn't allow for a pantry stocked with delicacies just on the off chance that their employer would decide to dine in and invite a few friends. But she and her sisters had long given up expecting their father to acknowledge the household's straitened finances.

She glanced at the grandfather clock. It was nearly eight. Chastity was dining with Constance and Max this evening, so there was no one but herself to steer Mrs. Hudson through her initial dismay when it was made clear to her she would have to produce a passable dinner in the next hour.

"I'll go and talk to Mrs. Hudson," she said. "There's a fire in the library. I'll send Jenkins with whisky." She draped her coat over the newel post and hurried into the kitchen, the skirts of her gown rustling stiffly around her.

"Is that his lordship, Miss Prue?" Mrs. Hudson had been sitting in her rocking chair beside the range in anticipation of a quiet evening with no dinner to prepare, but she got to her feet as Prudence entered the kitchen.

"Yes, I'm sorry, Mrs. Hudson. His lordship and Lord Barclay would like dinner. Do we have anything in the pantry?" Prudence opened the pantry door even as she asked the question.

"Oh, dearie me!" the cook muttered. "And I gave young Ellen the evenin' off. Mr. Jenkins will have to help me."

"I'd help you myself, but a motor is coming for me at eight." The chime of the front door rang from the row of bells above the kitchen door. "Oh, that must be it now. There are some venison chops in here, could you roast them?"

"I was a bit doubtful about those," Mrs. Hudson said, pushing past Prudence into the pantry. "I had my doubts about whether the venison had hung long enough." She picked up the chops and sniffed them critically. "Have to do, I suppose. With a few potatoes, and I've some brussels sprouts here somewhere . . ." Her voice faded as she moved farther into the pantry, poking along the shelves. "A drop o' red currant jelly and a glass of Madeira in the gravy, maybe . . ."

"And a Queen of Puddings for after," Prudence suggested.

"Oh, aye, that I can do. And there's some of that Stilton left that his lordship's so fond of." Mrs. Hudson backed out, dangling two thick venison chops from her fingers. "I'll just throw these in the roasting pan. Don't know what to do for a first course, though."

"The motor is here for you, Miss Prue," Jenkins announced from the door. "I understand his lordship and Lord Barclay will be dining in tonight."

"Yes, and Mrs. Hudson has come up trumps as usual," Prudence said.

"And Father would like you to take whisky to the library. I'm sorry I can't stay to help but—"

"Just you run along and enjoy yourself, Miss Prue," Mrs. Hudson said. "Mr. Jenkins and me, we'll manage. They can have sardines on toast to start. A few springs of parsley and a little chopped egg'll dress it up nicely."

Prudence smiled. "You're a wonder. Don't wait up for me, Jenkins. I have my key."

"The chauffeur said he'd been sent by a Sir Gideon Malvern," Jenkins mentioned casually as he preceded her into the hall. He took her coat from the newel post and held it out for her. "An elderly gentleman, is he, Miss Prue?" The puzzled glance he cast over her dowdy dress was covert and yet its meaning was quite clear to Prudence. Jenkins was not accustomed to seeing any of the ladies of the house venturing outside in anything but the most stylish and elegant of dress. And Miss Prue was exceptionally meticulous in all matters sartorial.

"I wouldn't have said so," she replied, buttoning her coat.

"I heard there was a barrister of that name, Miss Prue. Quite a famous one."

"Yes, Jenkins," she agreed as he opened the door for her. "And we need him rather desperately, so wish me luck. I need to be especially persuasive tonight. I'm hoping I look very serious and businesslike, ready for an evening of grave discussion, not idle pleasure." She raised an eyebrow, inviting his opinion.

"That's certainly the impression I have, Miss Prue," he said tactfully, escorting her down the steps to where a liveried chauffeur stood beside the open door of a black Rover. "I'm sure your business will prosper."

"You have more faith in my powers than I do, Jenkins." Prudence stepped into the back seat of the car with a smile at the chauffeur and a wave for Jenkins. The chauffeur began to close the door. "Where are we going?" she inquired.

"Long Acre, madam." He closed the door and went around to the driver's side.

Prudence sat back. The car had a top but the sides were open and she was glad the rain had stopped and it was a mild and windless evening. Nevertheless, she tied the scarf she wore to protect her hair more tightly beneath her chin and turned up the collar of her coat. Covent Garden was a strange choice of venue in the circumstances, she thought a little uneasily. The restaurants around the Opera House and the theaters of Drury Lane would be very public, and there were bound to be people she knew. If she was seen with Sir Gideon, there would inevitably be talk, and maybe later, when the trial started, someone would remember seeing them together and start to wonder. It was a little too risky for comfort. It seemed stupid now that she hadn't asked where he was taking her, and yet at the time the question hadn't occurred to her. When a man asked you for dinner you either accepted or didn't. You didn't base your response on the kind of entertainment he was offering.

The chauffeur drove slowly and considerately through the puddle-strewn streets. The ripe stench of horse manure was thick in the air, stirred up by the afternoon's rain, but the rain had also settled the dust. When they turned into the thronged narrow streets around Covent Garden, Prudence drew farther back into the vehicle's interior and wished she'd thought to bring a veil.

The car drew up outside a discreet-looking house with shuttered windows and a door that opened directly onto the street. The chauffeur helped Prudence to the street and escorted her to the door. She glanced up at the house. It bore none of the telltale signs of a restaurant. In fact, she thought, it had the air of a private home.

The door opened a minute after the chauffeur had rung the bell. A gentleman in austere evening dress bowed a greeting. "Madam, Sir Gideon is awaiting you in the red room."

Red room? Prudence glanced at the chauffeur as if for enlightenment but he had already stepped back to the street. She found herself in an elegant hall with a black and white marble floor and elaborately molded ceilings. A flight of stairs with gilded banisters rose from the rear.

"This way, madam." The man preceded her up the stairs and along a wide corridor. Voices, both male and female, came from behind closed doors, together with the chink of china and glass. Prudence was as intrigued as she was puzzled.

Her escort stopped outside a pair of double doors in the middle of the corridor, knocked once, then with an almost theatrical flourish opened both doors wide. "Your guest, Sir Gideon."

Prudence stepped into a large, square room, furnished as a drawing room except for a candlelit dining table set for two in a deep bow window overlooking a garden. It was immediately obvious why it was known as the red room. The curtains were red velvet, the furniture upholstered in red damask.

Gideon Malvern was standing beside the fireplace, where a small fire burned. He set down the whisky glass he held and came across the room. "Good evening, Miss Duncan. Let me take your coat."

His evening dress was impeccable, tiny diamond studs in his white waistcoat. Prudence, as she removed her head scarf, had a flash of regret at her own carefully chosen costume. In the interests of making absolutely certain the barrister understood this meeting was not a social occasion, she had decided to preserve the image of the dowdy spinster that she'd created in his chambers that afternoon. In fact, without exaggeration, she looked a fright in a hideous brown dress she'd unearthed from a cedar closet that hadn't been opened in ten years. She had no idea where the dress came from. It certainly wasn't something her mother would ever have worn. She unbuttoned her coat with some reluctance and allowed him to take it from her. He handed it to the man who had ushered her upstairs. The man bowed and withdrew, closing the doors gently behind him.

Gideon surveyed his guest, one eyebrow lifting a fraction. He was trying to imagine how any woman, let alone one as relatively young as this one, could deliberately choose to dress with such abominable lack of taste. One had to assume she had *chosen* the gown she was wearing, just as she had chosen her costume that afternoon. Perhaps, he thought, she was color-blind as well as shortsighted, or whatever problem she had with her eyesight that obliged her to wear those thick horn-rimmed spectacles. She was certainly fashion-blind. His nose twitched. Could that possibly be a whiff of mothballs emanating from the folds of that dreadful evening dress?

"Sherry," he said. "May I offer you a glass before dinner?"

"Thank you," Prudence responded, well aware of his reaction to her appearance. It was exactly what she had intended, but it still left her chagrined. She was far more used to admiring glances than the barrister's mingled pity and disdain.

"Please sit down." He gestured to one of the sofas and went to the sideboard, where decanters of sherry and whisky stood. He poured sherry and brought the glass over to her.

"Thank you," she said again, with a prim little smile that she thought would be appropriate to her appearance. "What is this house?"

"A private supper club," he said, taking a seat on the sofa opposite her. "I thought a restaurant might be a little too public." He sipped his whisky.

"It wouldn't do for us to be seen together," she agreed, smoothing down her skirts with a fussy little pat of her hand.

Gideon could only agree wholeheartedly. He wasn't sure his social reputation would survive being seen in public with such a wretchedly drab companion. He watched her covertly for a moment. She wore her hair twisted tightly onto her nape in an old-fashioned bun stuck with wooden pins. But the stuffy style couldn't do much to disguise the lustrous richness of the color. Somewhere between cinnamon and russet, he thought. No, something wasn't quite right. He couldn't put his finger on it, but there was something out of kilter about the Honorable Miss Prudence Duncan. He remembered that moment in his chambers when she'd taken off her glasses as she launched her attack. The image of that woman with the one in front of him somehow didn't gel. And after his late afternoon's reading he was not about to jump to conclusions about any of the Duncan sisters.

"As I recall, Miss Duncan, you said you took care of the business side of the publication. I assume you're something of a mathematician."

"I wouldn't say that precisely," Prudence stated. "I would describe myself as a bookkeeper."

At that he laughed. "Oh, no, Miss Duncan, I am convinced that you are no more a bookkeeper than your sister is the writer of Penny Dreadfuls."

Prudence looked startled. "Have you been reading copies of *The Mayfair Lady* since this afternoon?"

"I discovered an unexpected source of back issues," he said dryly. "Curiously enough, under my own roof. My daughter and her governess appear to be avid readers."

"Ah," she said. "Your daughter. Yes."

"That appears to come as no particular surprise to you," he observed.

"Who's Who," she said. "We looked you up."

He raised an eyebrow. "So you know more about me than I do about you, Miss Duncan."

Prudence felt herself flush as if he was accusing her of prying. *"Who's Who* is a matter of public record," she stated. "Besides, if we hadn't looked you up we wouldn't have been able to find you."

"Ah," he said. "Sensible research, of course."

"Does your daughter live with you?" She couldn't hide her surprise.

"As it happens," he responded shortly. "She attends North London Collegiate for her formal schooling. Her governess takes care of the wider aspects of her education. It seems that women's suffrage is of particular interest to Miss Winston, hence her familiarity with your publication." He rose to take his glass to the sideboard to refill it, after casting a glance towards Prudence's barely touched sherry glass.

This was a man of surprises, Prudence reflected, unable to deny that her interest was piqued. North London Collegiate School for Ladies, founded in 1850 by the redoubtable Frances Buss, one of Prudence's mother's female icons, was the first day school to offer a rigorous education to young women. Miss Buss, like the late Lady Duncan, had been a fervent supporter of women's rights as well as education.

Prudence took a healthy sip of her sherry. "You believe in women's education, then?"

"Of course." He sat down again, regarding her a little quizzically. "I imagine that surprises you."

"After your diatribe this afternoon about how women are not equipped . . . I believe I have that right . . . not *equipped* to enter the battleground of lawsuits and suchlike, I find it incredible. I think you advised me and my sisters to confine ourselves to the gossip of our own social circles and keep away from pen and ink." She smiled. "Do I have *that* right, Sir Gideon?" She leaned over to put her now empty glass on the sofa table.

"Yes, you do." He seemed completely untroubled by the apparent contradiction. "The fact that I support the education of women does not deny my assertion that the majority of women are uneducated and ill equipped to deal in my world. More sherry?"

He reached for her glass when she nodded and went back to the sideboard. "Were that not the case, there would be little need for my support for the cause." He refilled her glass from the decanter and brought it back to her. He stood looking down at her with that same quizzical, appraising air. Prudence was distinctly uneasy. It felt as if he were looking right through her, through the facade she was presenting, to the real Prudence underneath.

"Your daughter . . ." she began, trying to divert his attention.

"My daughter is hardly relevant here," he responded. "Suffice it to say that under the guidance of Miss Winston she's a passionate supporter of women's suffrage."

"And are you?" The question was quick and sharp. Without thinking, she took off her glasses as she often did in moments of intensity, rubbing them on her sleeve as she looked up at him.

Gideon took a slow breath. Wonderful eyes. They did not belong to this spinsterly dowd. So, just what game was Miss Duncan playing here? He had every intention of discovering before the evening was done.

"I haven't made up my mind on that issue," he answered finally. "Perhaps you should try to convince me of its merits while you attempt to persuade me to take on your defense." A smile touched the corners of his mouth and his gray eyes were suddenly luminous as they locked with hers.

Prudence hastily returned her glasses to her nose. That gaze was too hot to hold. And there was a note in his voice that made her scalp prickle. Every instinct shrieked a warning; but a warning about what? Rationally, he couldn't possibly be attracted to her, and yet his eyes and voice and smile said he was. Was he playing some cat-and-mouse game? Trying to fool her into a false position? She forced herself to concentrate. She had a job to do. She had to persuade him that he would find their case interesting and . . .

Her mind froze. Was this part of what would make it interesting for him? An elaborate, cruel game of mock seduction? Was there some kind of quid pro quo here to which she was not as yet a party?

Prudence thought of *The Mayfair Lady,* she thought of the mountain of debt that they were only just beginning to topple. She thought of her father, who so far had been protected from the truth, as their mother would have striven to protect him. With those stakes, she could play Gideon Malvern at his own game, and enjoy the sport.

She gave her skirts another fussy pat and said with a schoolmistressy hint of severity, "On the subject of our defense: As we see it, Sir Gideon, our weakness lies in the fact that we do not as yet have concrete evidence of Lord Barclay's financial misdoing. However, we know how to find that. For the moment, we have ample evidence to bolster our accusation of his moral failures."

"Let's sit down to dinner," he said. "I'd rather not discuss this on an empty stomach."

Prudence stood up. "I'm impressed by your diligence, Sir Gideon. I'm sure you had a full day in your chambers and in court, and now you're prepared to work over dinner."

"No, Miss Duncan, you are going to be doing the work," he observed, moving to the table. "I am going to enjoy my dinner while you try to convince me of the merits of your case." He held out a chair for her.

Prudence closed her lips tightly. This was the man she had met that afternoon. Arrogant, self-possessed, completely in control. And much easier to deal with than the glimpses she'd had of the other side of his character. She sat down and shook out her napkin.

Her host rang a small bell beside his own place setting before sitting down. "The club has a considerable reputation for its kitchen," he said. "I chose the menu carefully. I hope it will meet with your approval."

"Since you've just told me I'm not going to have the opportunity to enjoy it, your solicitude seems somewhat hypocritical," Prudence said. "I would have been content with a boiled egg."

He ignored the comment and she was obliged to admit that he was entitled to do so. She took a roll from the basket he offered while two waiters moved discreetly around them, filling wineglasses and ladling delicate pale green soup into deep white bowls.

"Lettuce and lovage," Gideon said when she inhaled the aroma. "Exquisite, I think you'll find." He broke into a roll and spread butter lavishly. "Tell me something about your sisters. Let's start with Mrs. Ensor."

"Constance."

"Constance," he repeated. "And your younger sister is called . . . ?"

"Chastity."

He sipped his wine and seemed to savor this information. There was a distinct gleam in his gray eyes. "Constance, Prudence, and Chastity. Someone had a sense of humor. I'm guessing it was your mother."

Prudence managed not to laugh. She declared, "We are the perfect exemplifiers of our names, I should tell you, Sir Gideon."

"Are you indeed?" He reached to refill her wineglass and once again shot her that quizzical look. "Prudence by name and prudent by nature?" He shook his head. "If they match their names as appropriately as I believe you match yours, Miss Prudence Duncan, I cannot wait to meet your sisters."

Prudence ate her soup. She wasn't going to step into that quicksand. If he was beginning to see through her pretense, she wasn't going to help him out.

"This soup is certainly exquisite," she said with one of her prim smiles.

He nodded. "It's one of my favorite combinations."

She looked at him, curiosity piqued once more despite her intentions to stick with business. "I get the impression you're something of a gourmand, Sir Gideon."

He put down his soup spoon. "We have to eat and drink. I see no reason to do either in a mediocre fashion."

"No," Prudence responded. "My father would agree with you."

"And you too, I suspect." He twirled the stem of his wineglass between his fingers. Her appreciation of the white burgundy in her glass had not gone unnoticed.

Prudence realized that her facade had slipped. She said with a careless shrug, "No, in general I'm indifferent to such things. We live very simply, my sisters and I."

"Really," he said, his voice flat as a river plain.

"Really," she said firmly, starting to reach for her glass, then instead putting her hand back into her lap.

The waiters returned, removed soup plates, set down the fish course, and left.

"Plaice," the barrister said, taking up his fish knife and fork. "A seriously underappreciated fish. Simply grilled with a touch of parsley butter, it's more delicate than the freshest Dover sole."

"In your opinion," Prudence murmured, slicing into the slightly browned flesh. The addendum passed unnoticed by her companion, who was savoring his first mouthful. She took her own and was forced to admit that he had a point.

"There is no way to fight Barclay's libel action without you and your sisters divulging your identities."

It was such a stunning change of subject, Prudence was for a moment confused. It was an attack rather than a continuation of their conversation. She blinked, swiftly marshaled her thoughts, and entered the fray. "We can't."

"I cannot put a newspaper on the stand." His voice had lost all trace of conversational intimacy. He pushed aside his plate. "I spent the better part of two hours reading back issues of your broadsheet, Miss Duncan, and I do not believe that you and your sisters lack the intelligence to imagine for one minute that you could escape the stand."

Prudence wondered if this was an ambush. Part of the cat-and-mouse game. "We cannot take the witness stand, Sir Gideon. Our anonymity is essential to *The Mayfair Lady*."

"Why?" He took up his wine goblet and regarded her over the lip.

"I do not believe *you* lack the intelligence to answer that question yourself, Sir Gideon. My sisters and I cannot divulge our identities, because we propound theories and opinions that because we're women would be automatically discounted if our readership knew who was responsible for them. The success of the broadsheet depends upon the mystery of its authorship, and its inside knowledge."

"Ah, yes, inside knowledge," he said. "I can quite understand that no one would speak freely to you if they knew they could be opening themselves to the ironical, if not malicious, pen of *The Mayfair Lady*."

"I would dispute *malicious*," Prudence said, a slight flush warming her cheeks. "Ironical, yes, and we don't suffer fools gladly, but I don't consider we're ever spiteful."

"There's a difference between malice and spite," he said.

"It's a little too subtle for me," she responded frostily.

He shrugged, raised his eyebrows, but made no attempt to amend his statement.

Prudence took a minute to recover her composure. She knew that she and Constance had a tendency to indulge their own sharp and sardonic wit, but it was a private pleasure. Chastity was usually their only audience and even she, the gentler-natured sister, could be roused to blistering irony in the face of social pretension or arrant stupidity, particularly when someone was hurt by it. In the broadsheet they certainly made fun of such failings, but they never named names.

He spoke again while she was still collecting her thoughts. "Miss Duncan, if you cannot defeat this libel, your broadsheet will cease to exist. If, as I understand you to say, your identities are forced into the open, then your broadsheet will also cease to exist." He set down his glass. "So, now, tell me what legal help I can offer you."

So that was it. In his judgment they had no possibility of winning. Never had had. So it *was* cat and mouse. But why? Why this elaborate dinner just to watch her squirm like a butterfly on the end of a pin? Well, whatever the reasons, she was not about to accept his assessment meekly and go on her not-so-merry way.

Once again she took off her glasses and rubbed the lenses with her napkin. "Maybe, Sir Gideon, we're asking the impossible, but I was given to understand that you specialized in impossibilities. We are not prepared to lose *The Mayfair Lady*. It provides us with a necessary livelihood, both the broadsheet and the Go-Between. We would never get clients for that service from among our own social circle if they knew whom they were dealing with. That must be obvious to you."

"The Go-Between . . . that's some kind of matchmaking service that you advertise. I didn't realize you ran it yourselves." He sounded both amused and faintly incredulous.

Prudence said as coldly as before, "Believe it or not, Sir Gideon, we're doing rather well with it. You'd be surprised at the unlikely matches we've managed to make." She said nothing further as the pair of waiters returned, did what they had to, and left them with veal scaloppini on their plates and a very fine claret in their glasses.

Gideon sampled both wine and veal before he said with a slight shake of his head, "You and your sisters are certainly an enterprising trio."

Prudence, still holding her glasses in her lap, directed her myopic gaze at him. Immediately she remembered that this was a mistake. Whenever she took off her glasses his expression changed unnervingly. She put them back on and now fixed him with a deep frown between her brows and a hard glare behind her lenses. Everything in her expression indicated conviction and the absolute determination to deal with the impossible. "Enterprising or not, we have to win this case. It's as simple as that."

"Simple as that," Gideon said, nodding slowly. "I am to put a sheet of newspaper on the witness stand. Just supposing we set that difficulty aside, there is another one. Would you mind telling me exactly how you propose defending the publication's accusations of fraud and cheating?"

"I told you earlier, Sir Gideon, that we have a fairly good idea where to find the evidence."

He touched a finger to his lips. "Forgive me, Miss Duncan, but I'm not sure that that assertion is sufficient."

"You will have to find it so. I cannot at this point be more specific." She sipped from her wineglass, clasped her hands on the table, and leaned towards him. "We need a barrister of your standing. Sir Gideon. We're offering a case that you should find challenging. My sisters and I are not hapless defendants. We're more than capable of acting vigorously in our defense."

"And are you capable of paying my fee, Miss Duncan?" He regarded her now with unmistakable amusement, his eyebrows lifted a fraction.

Prudence hadn't expected the question but she didn't hesitate. "No," she said.

He nodded. "As I thought."

Her frown deepened. "How could you have known?"

He shrugged. "It's part of my business sense, Miss Duncan. I'm assuming that your brother-in-law, Max Ensor, is not offering to support you."

Prudence felt the heat again rise to her cheeks. "Constance . . . we . . . would never ask him to do so. And he would not expect it. This is our enterprise. Constance is financially independent of her husband."

His eyebrows lifted another notch. "Unusual."

"We are not usual women, Sir Gideon. Which is why we're offering you the case," Prudence declared with sublime indifference to the realities. "If we win—and we *will* win, because our cause is just—then we'll happily divide the damages at whatever proportion you dictate. But we cannot broach our anonymity."

"You think you will win because your cause is just?" He laughed, and it was the derisive laugh she detested. "Just what makes you think the justice of your cause guarantees justice in the courts? Don't be naive, Miss Duncan."

Prudence smiled at him without warmth. "That, Sir Gideon, KC, is precisely why you will take our case. You like to fight, and the best fights are those that are hardest to win. Our backs are against the wall, and if we lose, we lose our livelihood. Our father loses his illusions and we will have failed our mother."

She spread her hands in a gesture of offering. "Can you resist a battle with such stakes?"

He looked at her. "Were you designated spokeswoman because of your persuasive tongue, Prudence, or was there another reason?"

"We divide our duties according to circumstance," she responded tartly, noticing only belatedly that he had used her first name for the first time. "Either of my sisters would have willingly tackled you, but they had other things to do."

"Tackled me?" He laughed, and this time it was with pure enjoyment. "I have to tell you, Prudence, that you'd have done a better job of tackling me without the . . ." He waved an expressive hand. "Without the playacting . . . that prim smile and that ghastly dress." He shook his head. "I have to tell you, my dear, that it's simply not convincing. Either you improve your acting skills or you give up the pretense. I know perfectly well that you're a sophisticated woman. I also know that you're educated and you don't suffer fools gladly. So I would ask that you stop treating me like one."

Prudence sighed. "It was not my intention to do so. I wanted to be certain you took me seriously. I didn't want to come across as some flighty Society flibbertigibbet."

"Oh, believe me, Miss Duncan, that you could never do." The disconcerting smile was in his eyes again, and she hadn't even taken off her glasses.

Prudence took the plunge. She had to at some point and it would at least banish that smile. "Very well," she said. "Will you take the case?"

Chapter 7

There was a moment of silence, broken by the return of the waiters. Prudence sat quietly until they had left. She was aware of a sinking feeling in her stomach, a slight quiver in her hands that were now clasped in her lap. She had hazarded everything on that one throw of the dice. If he said no, it was over. She had no other arguments, no further powers of persuasion.

The waiters left a cheese board, a bowl of grapes, a basket of nuts and fresh figs. They set a port decanter on the table at Gideon's right hand, then melted away.

Gideon offered her port, and when she declined with a quick shake of her head, filled his own glass. He gestured to the offerings on the table, and again she declined, watching as he helped himself to Stilton and snipped a small bunch of grapes from the branch with the tiny scissors.

"So," she prompted, when she could bear the silence no longer. "Will you defend us?"

"What a terrier you are," he observed, taking a sip of port.

"Will you?"

Gideon opened his mouth to give her the answer he had always intended to give, but his tongue seemed to have a life of its own. To his astonishment, he heard himself say, "Yes."

Prudence felt quite weak with relief. "I thought you were going to refuse," she said.

"So did I," he agreed aridly. "I had no intention of saying yes."

"But you can't change your mind now," she said swiftly. "You said yes. You can't renege."

"No, I don't suppose I can." He returned to his cheese and grapes with a little shrug of resignation. He was not an impulsive man. Lawyers, by definition, were never swayed by such an unreliable force. So, if his agreement was not impulsive, what was it? An interesting question to be explored at leisure.

Prudence drank the last of her claret. He didn't sound exactly enthu-siastic about the prospect of the case. Did that mean he wouldn't take too much trouble over it? Would the fact that they couldn't pay him limit the amount of time he would spend?

She took a deep breath. "If you don't think you can give the case all your attention, I think it would be best if you *did* decline after all."

He looked at her, his eyes suddenly sharp, his mouth hard. "What are you implying?"

Prudence began to regret she'd brought up the subject. But since she had, she could see little choice but to continue. "You seem ambivalent," she said. "And since we can't pay you, I thought—"

He interrupted her, one hand raised in emphasis. "You thought that I would take on a case and fail to give it my full professional attention. Is that what you thought, Miss Duncan?" His tone was harsh, his voice, while still soft and well modulated, was incredulous. "What kind of bar-rister do you think I am?"

"An expensive one," she said, refusing to be cowed. "I wondered if you had a sliding scale of fees appropriate to the amount of effort you expended. I wouldn't call that unethical. In most circumstances one pays for the service one gets."

"I have never, *ever* taken on a case to which I did not devote every ounce of my legal knowledge, intellect, and energy," he declared, qui-etly enunciating every single word. "I give you fair warning, Miss Dun-can. Do not *ever* impugn my professional integrity again." He flung down his table napkin and rang the little bell with considerable vigor.

Prudence could think of nothing to say. She was taken aback by the force of his reaction but supposed she had unwittingly trampled on his pride. Something to be careful of in the future. She made a mental note.

"Let's move back to the fire for coffee," he suggested as the waiters reappeared with a tray of coffee. His voice was once again pleasantly neutral. He rose from the table and drew back her chair for her.

Prudence stood up and picked up her handbag. "Would you excuse me for a minute?" She looked expectantly towards the door.

"This way, madam." One of the waiters moved to the door instantly and she followed him. He showed her to a small water closet just down the corridor, well equipped with basin and mirror, soap and towels. Again more suited to a private residence than a restaurant. She took a few minutes to compose herself, dabbing cool water on her wrists. She ought to feel jubilant at her victory. But instead she felt uneasy, even slightly deflated. This partnership was not going to be easy to manage. Gideon Malvern was not going to be easy to manage. And somehow they had to find a way to pay him for his services. The Duncan pride was a pretty fierce variety too. An idea nibbled at the corners of her mind. She found herself smiling. It was such a perfect solution. But would the barrister find it so?

She went back to the drawing room and took her seat on the sofa once more, accepting a cup of coffee from her host. She cleared her throat. "I would like to discuss the question of your fee, Sir Gideon."

"Certainly," he said promptly. "If Barclay fails to prove his case, he'll be required to pay all the legal costs, yours as well as his own. And in addition I'll be asking the court to award damages to *The Mayfair Lady*, whose reputation was damaged by his frivolous suit. If, therefore, Miss Duncan, we should win—and mind you, it's a big if—then my share over and above my fee, which will be paid by the other side, will be eighty percent of the damages awarded."

Prudence absorbed this, keeping her expression neutral. Then she said coolly, "I understand you're divorced, Sir Gideon."

He drew his head back like a startled cat. "What has that to do with anything?"

"It must be difficult to bring up a child, particularly a daughter, without a wife." She stirred her coffee.

"I don't find it so," he said, watching her with a frown in his eyes. "And I fail to see what this has to do with my terms. You accept them or you don't."

She took a sip of her coffee and set the tiny cup back into the saucer. "Well, you see, I have a rather more equitable suggestion."

"Oh?" He raised his eyebrows. Against his will he was intrigued. He had expected some shock, if not downright outrage at his proposed split. Certainly not this cool, considered reaction. "How so?"

"An old-fashioned barter, Sir Gideon. An exchange of services." She leaned forward to put her cup and saucer on the table. "In exchange for your legal services the Go-Between will undertake to find you a wife and a stepmother for your daughter."

"*What?*" He stared at her, incapable of coherent thought for a minute.

"It's simple enough, surely. Of course, if we fail to find you the right partner, then the eighty-twenty split will stand." She smiled placidly. "And even if we lose our case, we will still hold true to our side of the bargain. We will find you a wife." She opened her hands again. "How can you lose?"

"How, indeed?" he murmured with a soundless whistle at this mixture of effrontery and ingenuity. "But as it happens, Miss Duncan, I am not in the market for a wife."

"You may not be looking actively, but if the right prospect dropped into your lap, surely you would not be averse. A life's companion, a mother for your daughter. It's very hard for a daughter to grow up without a mother's influence."

"Believe it or not, one divorce is plenty," he said, his lips suddenly thinned. He moved a hand in a dismissive gesture. "Plenty for me, and I'm sure more than enough for any child. But you wouldn't know, would you, Miss Duncan? Husbands have not come your way."

Prudence was unperturbed by this cutting statement. Gideon Malvern was not to know that her unmarried status was a matter of sublime indifference to her. She ignored the snub, and considered. She wanted to ask him who had been responsible for the divorce, but couldn't get her tongue around the words. It seemed far too intrusive a question under the circumstances.

"Yes," she said. "I can see that. Once bitten, twice shy. But a second failed marriage doesn't necessarily follow from a first." She steepled her hands, touching them to her mouth. "You don't have to agree to anything except to let us suggest some possibilities. As we work together and get to know you better, we'll have a much clearer idea of the kind of woman who might suit you."

Gideon was not accustomed to delivering a coup de grâce and having it ignored. He looked at her with renewed interest as he said brusquely, "It's a ridiculous idea. I have no time for romantic fantasies."

"Ah, but what I'm suggesting is the antithesis of romantic fantasy," Prudence pressed. "I'm merely suggesting that we come up with some possible candidates, you look them over. If there are any that interest you, we'll arrange a meeting. No strings. As I said before, how can you lose?"

He had a sense that Miss Duncan wasn't going to give up easily. His interest grew, although it had nothing to do with her proposition. More to do with the set of her head and that aura of firmly competent determination, he decided. So ludicrously at odds with her prim and dowdy exterior.

He supposed it could do no harm to agree to this absurd bargain. It might be amusing to play along for a while—and even useful to discover how the Duncan sisters worked. He shrugged and said, "I won't stop you trying, but I should warn you, I'm a very hard man to please. I think I'll rely on the eighty-twenty split."

"Assuming we win."

"I don't often lose," he said.

"And we don't often fail," she returned in much the same calmly superior tone. "So, we have a bargain?" She held out her hand.

"If you insist." He took the hand.

"Oh, you may think you're humoring me, Sir Gideon, but you'll be surprised," Prudence said with rather more confidence than she felt.

He inclined his head in half-laughing acknowledgment. "You'll have to forgive me if I'm skeptical. But as you say, I can't lose."

"Then I think we have brought this evening to a satisfactory conclusion," Prudence stated.

"Must we conclude?" he asked. "I hate to close a social evening on a business note." His gray eyes had gone dark as coal and Prudence found her own eyes focused on his mouth. A very sensual mouth, she realized, with a long upper lip and a deep cleft in his chin.

"It was a business evening, Sir Gideon," she declared, rising to her feet.

"Do you wear your glasses all the time?"

"If I want to see," she said with asperity. "And as it happens, I'm more interested in good eyesight than my appearance."

"That I doubt," he said. "I hope to see you in your true colors next time we meet."

"The appearance I choose to present depends upon the impression I choose to make," she responded stiffly. "Could you ring for my coat, please?"

He stepped over to the table and rang the handbell, then turned back to her, a slightly quizzical smile touching his mouth. "Is there a man in your life, Prudence?"

The direct question astounded her, and to her annoyance she found herself answering it as directly. "No, not at present."

His smile deepened. "Has there ever been?"

Her eyes flashed. "I fail to see what business that is of yours, Sir Gideon. I am your client, my personal life does not enter into our business relationship."

"I was merely interested in discovering whether you used your own services," he said. "It would be something of a recommendation, don't you think?"

There was no possible answer to that. Fortunately, the reappearance of the waiter in response to the summons made her silence unremarkable. Gideon asked for their coats and gave orders for his motor to be brought round from the mews. Then he turned back to Prudence. The smile had gone.

"So," he said, "to avoid any further misconceptions, let me make one thing clear: your personal business is about to become mine. Yours and your sisters'. No area of your lives will be immune from my questions."

Prudence stared at him. It was the most inflammatory statement, made all the more so by his manner, so relaxed, so cool, and so infuriatingly confident. "What are you talking about?"

"It's quite simple. I am now your barrister. And in that capacity I'm afraid I'm going to have to ask you and your sisters some very personal questions. I have to know everything about you. I can't risk any surprises in court."

"How could there be surprises in court when no one will know who we are?"

"I win cases by leaving nothing to chance," he responded. "And if you and your sisters can't guarantee me your complete cooperation, then I'm afraid our bargain is null and void."

Prudence frowned. She could see his point, but deeply resented his tone. "You may find it a case of the biter bit, Sir Gideon," she said. "In order to find a suitable match for you, we too will have to ask some very personal questions."

"There is one difference. I may choose not to answer yours since I'm less interested in finding a suitable mate than you're interested in preserving your livelihood. Your stakes are much greater than mine, Prudence, as I'm sure you'll agree."

Prudence recognized that that was game, set, and match. "I think we have nothing further to discuss this evening."

"Perhaps not," he agreed amiably. He took her coat from the waiter, who had returned, and helped her into it. He put on his own heavy overcoat and driving gloves as she tied her scarf around her head.

"The night's quite chilly," he commented as pleasantly as if that acerbic exchange had not taken place. "There's a lap rug in the motor." He escorted her down the stairs to the hall, one guiding hand lightly clasping her elbow.

The vehicle stood, engine already running, at the curb. He tucked the rug over her knees when she was seated and took his own place behind the wheel.

"I'll see you and your sisters in my chambers at eight-thirty tomorrow morning," he stated, guiding the motor expertly through the crowded streets. The Opera House was disgorging its clientele and hackney cabs jostled for space with private vehicles awaiting their owners.

"Eight-thirty!" Prudence exclaimed. "That's the crack of dawn."

"I have to be in court at ten," he said. He glanced across at her. "Believe it or not, Prudence, I do have other clients, all of whom at present are neither pro bono nor contingency cases . . . not to mention barter arrangements," he added with a touch of acid.

He was such an arrogant bastard! He was treating her offer as if it was no more than a joke . . . and a feeble one, at that. Prudence stared rigidly ahead, wishing she could tell him to jump in the Thames and take his conceited smugness with him. But then he'd have to take his legal expertise as well, so of course she couldn't.

"When you come tomorrow, I'll need you to explain to me how you're going to back up your accusations of Barclay's financial improprieties. I can't prepare a case until I have that evidence in my hands."

"I won't have the evidence tomorrow," Prudence said. "But we have a lead. I can explain that tomorrow."

"Then I suppose I must be thankful for small mercies," he said, drawing the car to a smooth stop at the curb outside 10 Manchester Square. He turned sideways on the seat, and before she could respond he had taken her face between his hands and brought his mouth to hers. Prudence tried to pull back but he was holding her too firmly and he was kissing her with far too much authority for resistance.

He moved one hand behind her head, displacing the scarf as he held her head in his palm, his fingers working through the tight bun at her nape. She tried to put her hands on his shoulders to push him away, but he was holding her too closely to give her the freedom of movement. She pushed her head back against his palm, trying to turn her mouth aside, but his lips merely moved to the corner of her mouth, his tongue lightly stroking her lips. She was breathless when finally he raised his head and smiled down at her. Her face was hot, flushed with anger, and for a moment she was speechless. Not so Gideon. "Well, that satisfies my curiosity," he said. "I've been wanting to do that ever since you stormed back into my chambers this afternoon."

"How *dare* you?" she demanded, outrage throbbing in her voice as she tried to tidy her disordered hair, pushing loosened pins back into the russet bun. "Without even *asking*? What gave you the right to assume that *I* wanted it?" She glared at him, and even through the thick lenses he could almost feel the sparks of rage in her eyes. He could certainly imagine them.

"What did you think you were doing?" she continued with the same fury. "Taking payment for your services?"

"Oh, you are so sharp, you could cut," he said with a soft laugh, pulling her back into his embrace. He kissed her again, his closed mouth hard against her lips, then released her as abruptly. She caught her breath on a gasp and was momentarily silenced.

"Actually," he said gravely, although his dancing eyes belied his tone, "I thought it might help you to know what kind of woman just *might* suit me when you commence your search. And it might be helpful for any prospective candidates to have some idea of the kind of lover I might make. You could probably make a more informed assessment of both issues now." He got out of the motor and came around to open her door, offering his hand to help her out.

She remained seated and said with icy deliberation, "You are a cad, Sir Gideon. We do not accept as clients men who ride roughshod over women. Men who assume that they can sweep a woman off her feet with some absurd attempt at mastery are of no interest to me . . . I mean us," she amended hastily. Ignoring the hand, she stepped down to the curb.

"There's a time and a place for every approach," he said without the blink of an eye. "And sometimes surprise is the essence of a successful campaign. Good night, Prudence." He raised her hand to his lips in a courtly gesture that shocked her almost as much as the kiss. "Don't forget. Tomorrow at eight-thirty sharp in my chambers."

She took back her hand with a jerk and without a word of farewell turned to the steps, infuriatingly aware of his soft laugh at her back.

He stood on the bottom step until she had let herself into the house, then returned to the motor. As he drove home, he began to wonder just what in hell he thought he was doing. He was *not* a man of impulse. Never had been. He'd agreed against every judicial instinct to work with the woman. Then on a pure impulse he found himself kissing her. What in hell's teeth did he think he was doing? He was beginning to have the unnerving sensation of loosing his moorings, casting himself adrift on a sea of blind compulsion.

Prudence had barely closed the door behind her when her sisters came running down the stairs to greet her.

"Con, what are *you* doing here?" she asked in surprise.

"Oh, Max had a division bell just as we were finishing dinner and had to go to the House of Commons for a vote. He might be there most of the night, so I decided to come back with Chas and hear what happened." Constance regarded her sister closely. "You look a little disheveled, love."

"In the circumstance, that's not surprising," Prudence answered somewhat sharply as she took off her coat. "Let's go up to the parlor and I'll tell you all about it." She became aware of her sisters' incredulous stares. "Why . . . What's the matter?"

"That dress is frightful," Constance said. "Where did it come from?"

"The old cedar chest. It was supposed to keep the barrister's mind on business," she added somewhat bitterly.

"And it didn't?" Chastity asked. "This is very intriguing, Prue." She followed her sister to the stairs. "But can you at least put us out of our misery and tell us if he agreed to take the case?"

"Yes, he did, finally," Prudence answered, opening the door into their parlor, where a fire burned brightly in the grate. "But I'm beginning to think it's a very bad idea to get mixed up with Sir Gideon Malvern, KC."

"Couldn't you handle him?"

"No," Prudence said frankly. "I thought I could, but I can't . . . at least not alone."

Constance closed the door and stood leaning against it, her gaze rather anxious as it rested on her sister. "You're all right, Prue?"

"Yes, just about." She touched her lips, which still seemed to be tingling. "As well as can be expected after an assault."

"*What?*" Both sisters stared at her.

"What do you mean, Prue?" Chastity put a hand on her arm. "Who assaulted you?"

"Oh, that's a bit melodramatic," Prudence said with a sigh. "It wasn't an assault, it was just a kiss. But it was unexpected and he didn't ask permission and I don't like being grabbed as if I have no say in the matter."

Her sisters untangled this and came to the correct picture. "He's the masterful type, then?" Constance said with some scorn.

"He certainly likes to think so." She changed the subject abruptly. "Are you spending the night, Con?"

"Yes, in my old room," her sister replied, leaving the door to take up the goblet of cognac she had abandoned when they'd heard Prudence's return.

"Doesn't Max mind? It's a bit soon after your wedding to abandon the marital bed, isn't it?" Prudence tossed her head scarf onto the sofa, following it with her discarded coat, aware that the teasing note she had been aiming for was somehow missing. Her voice sounded rather raw.

Constance sipped her cognac, still keeping her eyes on her sister. It was generally better with Prue to let her tell her story at her own pace, so she answered easily, "To tell you the truth, I didn't actually ask him if he minded. I just left him a note. But he won't be back until close to dawn, I imagine, so I'm sure he won't mind at all."

"Well, it's a good thing you are going to be here first thing in the morning," Prudence said, examining her disordered appearance in the mirror above the mantel. "Since we have to be at the barrister's chambers at eight-thirty tomorrow."

Her sisters exchanged a quick glance. The hostility in Prue's voice was unmistakable. "So, you said he's agreed to take the case," Chastity prompted, wondering which avenue would lead to more discussion about the unwanted kiss. Her sister was clearly disturbed, and the subject couldn't simply be abandoned.

"Yes." Prudence sat down and kicked off her shoes. She pressed her fingertips to her temples. "I have had too much wine."

"Where did you go for dinner?"

"Some supper club in Covent Garden. In the interests of privacy," she added. "Oh, and by the way, you were wrong, Con. His daughter apparently lives with him, not her mother."

"Oh," Constance said, sipping her cognac. "Well, he obviously has custody. He probably prevents the mother seeing her."

Prudence shook her head. "No, much as I'd like to agree with you, I don't think you can go off on one of your antipaternalistic diatribes in this instance. I don't know what caused the divorce, but he seems a rather enlightened parent. He sends her to North London Collegiate and allows her to read *The Mayfair Lady* with her governess and makes no objections to the governess's teaching the girl about women's suffrage."

Constance raised her eyebrows. "Well, that's novel. But to get back to the case. He's agreed to take it, so how do we pay him?"

"His suggestion is an eighty-twenty split of any damages *The Mayfair Lady* might be awarded if Barclay's case is thrown out as frivolous. Sir Gideon will ask for recompense for damage done to the broadsheet's reputation, in addition, of course, to all our legal costs, which would include his fee. Of course, we have to win for all that to happen."

"Oh, that seems a very reasonable split," Chastity said.

"Eighty for Sir Gideon, Chas. We get the twenty."

Constance grimaced, but shrugged. "We don't have any choice but to accept his terms."

"I suggested a different arrangement," Prudence said, and explained.

"That's a brilliant idea, Prue!" Chastity exclaimed. "What kind of person would suit him?"

Her sister gave a short laugh. "More to the point, what kind of woman would put up with him? You won't like him, I'll tell you that much. He's arrogant, conceited, imperious, rude." She shrugged. "You name it, he's it."

"And he has a habit of grabbing women and kissing them against their will," Constance prodded.

"He didn't hurt you, though, Prue, did he?" Chastity asked anxiously.

Her sister shook her head and tried for a reassuring smile. "Only my pride. I don't like being manhandled. I wish I'd slapped him, only he took me so much by surprise I could only gape at him like a gaffed fish."

"Is he really all bad?" Chastity pressed. "Is he attractive, at least? Or even interesting in some way?"

Prudence frowned. "Don't take this the wrong way, Con, but he reminds me of the way Max was at the beginning. You thought he was the most arrogant, supercilious bastard ever to walk the streets of London."

"I still do think that sometimes," her sister responded. "But the good qualities far and away outweigh the bad. Besides," she added with brutal candor, "I'm no angel myself. I can be every bit as obnoxious in the right circumstances. It makes us rather a good match." She laughed slightly. "Surely this Sir Gideon must have *some* good qualities."

"So far I haven't seen any," Prudence declared. "I find him detestable. But I believe he's a brilliant lawyer, and that's all that concerns us. I'll just have to try to keep my antipathy from being too obvious."

Chastity cast her sister a shrewdly speculative glance. Was there a hint of overprotest in Prue's voice? She asked, "Does he think we have a chance in court?"

"At first he said absolutely not. Because we won't take the stand."

A short silence fell as they contemplated the ramifications of this. "It is difficult, I can see that," Constance said after a minute. "Is there a way around it?"

"He must have some ideas or he wouldn't bother with us," Chastity pointed out.

Constance regarded Prudence with raised eyebrows. "You said *at first*. Something made him change his mind? Do you know what it was?"

"Not really," her sister said. "Perhaps persistence paid off. Perhaps I wore him down." She shrugged. "Whatever the reason, he agreed. We got what we wanted." She wondered why he had not been in the least perturbed by her angry response to his kiss. Quite the opposite, he had actually laughed at her indignant rejection. *Odious creature.*

She leaned her head against the back of the sofa and yawned. "I'm exhausted and we have to have our wits about us first thing in the morning." She stood up with a groan. "And I warn you, we'll need all the wits we possess. Our barrister doesn't miss a trick, and he's already warned me that he's going to be asking some very personal questions."

"I don't suppose you warned him that we have a tendency to bite if someone crosses our boundaries," Constance said, rising to her feet with her sister.

"I thought we'd let him find that out for himself," Prudence returned, managing a smile. "Breakfast at seven? I'll leave a note for Jenkins." She went to the overburdened secretaire and scribbled a few words, setting the paper beneath her sister's empty cognac goblet, where the butler would find it first thing in the morning.

"Into the breach once more." Constance linked arms with her sisters until they separated at their own doors.

Chapter 8

Constance awoke a very few hours later in the gray light of dawn. She wasn't sure what had woken her until she heard the door click shut. She peered blearily into the dimness and smiled, brushing hair out of her eyes as she struggled up against the pillows.

"Good morning, Max. I assume it is morning. Why aren't you fast asleep in your own bed?"

"That was rather the question I was going to ask you," her husband said somewhat aridly as he set a tea tray on the dresser. "I get home to find a cold and empty bed and a scribbled note from my wife telling me she's returned to the bosom of her family."

"Only for tonight . . . I mean last night," Constance protested. "I didn't think you'd mind, as you'd be working most of the night."

"Well, as it happens, I think I do mind," he declared, pouring tea. He brought two cups over to the bed and sat on the edge, handing her one.

"Oh, come on," she said. "You know you don't really." She sipped gratefully of the steaming brew. "Did you make this yourself, or is Mrs. Hudson up and about already?"

"Jenkins made it. He said you'd left a note saying you wanted breakfast at the crack of dawn, so I thought I'd wake you myself."

"That was very thoughtful of you," Constance said. "But I'd have liked a good-morning kiss before the tea."

He took the cup from her and set it, with his, on the bedside table, then leaned over and kissed her, murmuring against her mouth, "Not that you deserve it, deserting me like that."

"Good morning, Con—oh, Max, are you here too?" Chastity spoke even as she opened the door and came in, followed by Prudence, carrying a tea tray.

"Since the mountain wouldn't come to Mohammed, Mohammed had no choice but to come to the mountain," Max observed, straightening slowly, turning to look at his sisters-in-law.

"I told Con you wouldn't like it," Prudence said. "We brought tea, but I see you have some already."

She poured for herself and Chastity and the two of them sat companionably in their night robes on the bed beside Max, who seemed as unconcerned as they about their dishabille.

"Actually, it's very convenient that Con's here," Prudence said, "because we have an appointment with Gideon Malvern in his chambers at half past eight."

"Did he agree to take the case?" Max took up his teacup again.

"Prue persuaded him," Chastity said. "I think he fancies her, but Prue's not saying."

"*Chas,*" Prudence protested.

"It's only Max, and he's family," her sister said. "And I didn't say anything about your fancying the barrister."

"I told you perfectly clearly what I thought of him," her sister stated.

"And what's that?" inquired Max.

"Eminently dislikable," Prudence said crisply.

"Just the reaction Con had to—" Chastity stopped, coughing violently, the cup rattling in her saucer.

"You are so indiscreet, Chas," Prudence accused.

Max raised his eyebrows. He was far too used to the sisters to be in the least surprised or put out by anything they could say or do. He glanced at his wife for enlightenment.

"Don't give it another thought, Max," Constance instructed. "We were just being silly, as is our wont."

"I don't believe I've ever seen any of you being in the least silly," he commented. "So I'll take that as a roundabout way of telling me to mind my own business." He stood up. "I'll leave you to get dressed and keep your appointment." He put his cup on the dresser. "You will be back for luncheon, Constance." It was statement rather than question.

"Yes, of course." She gave him a placatory smile. "We'll probably have coffee at Fortnum's to fortify ourselves after our ordeal in chambers, but I'll come straight home afterwards."

He nodded, kissed her again, kissed her sisters on the cheek, and left the bedroom.

"Sorry, Con," Chastity said. "It's too early in the morning for me to think clearly."

"Oh, it doesn't matter in the least," her sister reassured. "Max knows perfectly well what I thought of him when I first met him. I still throw it in his face when we fight."

"I remember when you threw a vase of daisies in his face," Chastity said with a laugh.

Constance shook her head. "I do rather regret that," she said ruefully.

"Well, that's water under the bridge," Prudence stated, sliding off the bed. Ordinarily she would have been happy to reminisce with her sisters, but she was filled with a restless impatience this morning. "We need to turn our attention to Gideon Malvern. Did you bring a day dress, Con? Or do you want to borrow something?"

"No, I packed a skirt and jacket." Constance threw aside the covers. "It's not quite as smart as I would have brought if I'd known I wouldn't be going straight home this morning, but it'll do. I don't have a hat, though. Should I borrow one? Is he a great stickler for the niceties?"

Prudence gave a short laugh. "Not when it comes to taking liberties."

Constance pursed her lips. "He's not going to be doing that when we're all together."

"He's not going to be doing it ever again," Prudence declared, going to the door. "I'm going to keep a hat pin up my sleeve. Come on, Chas. We'll see you in the breakfast room in half an hour, Con."

In her own bedroom Prudence reviewed the contents of her wardrobe. It was time to abandon the ill-fated attempt at old-maid dowdiness. But she must still avoid all hint of frivolity. She wanted something that said . . . said what? She chewed her lip, riffling through the silks, tweeds, wools, velvets. Cotton or muslin would be too thin for a crispish autumn morning. What image did she want to project to Gideon this morning?

Definitely businesslike. Nothing too dressy that would look as if she had made a particular effort . . . but nothing too understated either. Something suitable for an everyday business appointment, but with a little extra flair to it. Much as she hated to admit it, her pride had suffered sorely under her previous disguise.

Prudence, her sisters would agree, had an infallible dress sense. She always knew what would suit a particular occasion and her sisters happily bowed to her judgment. She pulled out a rather smart black woolen suit that had belonged to her mother and had gone through several reincarnations to reach its present form. Lady Duncan, her daughter remembered, had worn it when she was in a confrontational mood. And Prudence was in a confrontational frame of mind.

She laid it on the bed and tried pairing it with a severe white silk shirt, high-buttoned at the neck, and stood back to examine the effect. No, she decided instantly. Much too funereal. She turned back to the wardrobe, and found what she sought.

The dark red silk blouse with a floppy cravatlike tie at the neck was exactly right. It lightened and softened the black suit but it was also very elegant and the color was almost indistinguishable from her hair. So, no hat; definitely no hat.

When she came downstairs to the breakfast room as the grandfather clock in the hall struck seven, her sisters were already there. "Oh, bravo, Prue," Chastity applauded.

"Yes, exactly right," Constance agreed, buttering a piece of toast. "No hat, though."

Prudence laughed and shook her head. "The pompadour is good enough, I think." She touched her hair that was piled and pinned on top of her head over pads, forming an elaborate coiffure.

"Perfect," Constance said, reaching for the coffeepot to fill her sister's cup. "Chas and I are dressed to fade into the background so that you can take center stage."

Prudence merely grinned. Constance was wearing a gray-and-white-striped skirt, tightly belted at her narrow waist, with a dark gray fitted jacket and neat buttoned boots. Chastity wore a dark green dress with a bolero jacket and full sleeves that buttoned tightly at her wrists. There was no possibility of either of them fading into the background when it came to fashion, even though both outfits, like Prudence's, had been through several makeovers.

"I would have thought you'd have abandoned your pre-Max wardrobe by now," Prudence remarked, cracking the top of a boiled egg.

"Somehow it goes against the grain to throw away perfectly good clothes," Constance said seriously.

"You could give them to charity," Chastity suggested, dipping a finger of toast into her own boiled egg.

"I haven't had a chance to go through them yet," Constance pointed out. "Anyway, this was one of Mother's favorites. Now, Prue, prepare us a little for this morning. We need to come up with a concerted attack . . . or defense. I don't know which we're talking about."

"Probably both," her sister said.

Gideon had reached his chambers soon after six o'clock that morning. The janitor had lit the fires in both chambers but the coals were still showing little life. His clerk had not yet arrived, so he lit the spirit stove, set water to boil for the strong coffee that would compensate for too little sleep, and hauled selected tomes off the bookshelves. Once settled at his desk, still wearing muffler and gloves because the night's chill took a while to disperse through the ancient stone walls despite the fires, he looked for precedents on a libel suit when the defendants were anonymous. By the time Thadeus had arrived an hour later, the barrister had found none.

Thadeus flourished his toasting fork and offered toast and marmalade.

"Yes, thank you," his employer grunted in response to the offer, heaving open another volume.

"Trouble, Sir Gideon?" Thadeus hovered in the doorway.

"Anonymous clients, Thadeus." Gideon looked up, two fingers pressed to his eyes.

"There was a libel case, sir, in 1762 I believe, when the defendants were shielded from the court by a curtain." Thadeus disappeared into the outer chamber, returning almost immediately with a plate of hot buttered toast. "More coffee, Sir Gideon?"

"Yes . . . and the precedent." Gideon bit into the toast.

"Right away, Sir Gideon." And it was right away. Within a minute, Thadeus set down the relevant volume, opened at the correct page. A nicotine-stained finger underlined the passage in question.

"You are without price, Thadeus," Gideon said without looking up.

"Thank you, sir." Thadeus was well pleased. "I'll show the ladies in when they arrive."

Gideon looked up. He examined his office and found it wanting. "Oh, yes, and see if you can find another two chairs. I can't have two sisters standing."

"I have already done so, Sir Gideon. Sir Thomas Wellbeck's clerk has lent us two extra chairs."

"Again, Thadeus, you are without price." This time Gideon smiled. His clerk returned the smile.

"At your service, sir. Always at your service." He backed out.

Gideon finished the last piece of toast as he read, then he wiped his fingers on the napkin thoughtfully provided by his clerk and drained his coffee cup. He had the beginnings of a strategy now. He heard the door to his outer office open at precisely half past eight and rose to his feet behind the table to greet the three sisters as Thadeus showed them in.

His greeting smile was bland and courteous, no indication of his swift assessment of the sisters. He had been very curious to meet the other two and was not disappointed. They were as striking a trio of women as a man could hope to meet. And Prudence, now sporting what were clearly her true colors, had an even more powerful presence than he had expected. He was hard-pressed not to laugh at the memory of her previous incarnations when compared with this elegant, impeccably dressed woman. Her fashionably elaborate hairstyle showed off the rich, lustrous color of her hair, complemented so beautifully by the red blouse. Gone too were the thick horn-rimmed glasses. In their place a delicate pair of gold-rimmed spectacles that perched on the bridge of her nose and offered no impediment to the view of the light and vivid green eyes beneath. She was a sight for the sorest of eyes.

His swift assessment led him to conclude that there was something almost formidable about the front they presented. Despite their very obvious individuality in both appearance and manner, they seemed to share an aura of combative intelligence. The same kind of sharp intellect that informed the content and writing of *The Mayfair Lady*. The barrister in him noted this with satisfaction. They would make excellent witnesses. Except, of course, that they were insisting he couldn't put them on the stand.

But he would meet that difficulty head-on. He became aware that he was the subject of silent scrutiny and assessment by Constance and Chastity and he couldn't help wondering what Prudence had told them about the previous evening. Prudence herself was giving nothing away. Her expression was composed and unsmiling.

"Good morning, Sir Gideon," she said formally. "May I introduce my sisters."

"Let me guess." He came out from behind the table, hand extended towards Constance. "Mrs. Ensor. I'm delighted to meet you."

Constance took the hand, her own grip as firm as his. "I won't ask how you guessed."

He merely smiled and turned to Chastity. "Miss Chastity Duncan."

"That's me," Chastity said, her handshake every bit as decisive as her eldest sister's. "Do I look two years younger than Constance?"

"Somehow, I don't think I want to step into that particular quicksand," he said, waving a hand to the three chairs. "Please . . . sit down."

They sat in a semicircle facing him, all three coolly composed, hands resting in their laps. All three of them had green eyes, he noticed somewhat distractedly. Prudence's were lighter than her elder sister's, and Chastity's had hazel lights in their depths. The same with their hair, three different shades of red.

Dear God! What an impression they would make on the witness stand.

He cleared his throat. "Mrs. Ensor, I understand you were the author of the offending article."

"The article in question," she stated. "I did not, and indeed *do* not, consider it to be offensive."

"Nevertheless, it certainly offended Lord Barclay."

"Some people are offended by the truth."

"Yes, quite inexplicable," he observed, taking up the relevant issue of

The Mayfair Lady. "Hard to imagine why a man would be offended at being accused in a public forum of being a rapist, a despoiler of young girls, a cheat, a thief, an embezzler." He set aside the sheet and regarded the sisters, who met his ironic gaze with unwavering sangfroid.

"I thought we'd covered this ground yesterday," Prudence said. "And we also dealt with the issue that no *one* of us is responsible for this libel suit. We are all involved to exactly the same extent. *The Mayfair Lady* is the defendant. And that publication is a composite of the Duncan sisters."

"You're not making my task any easier."

"We don't intend to make it any more difficult than it has to be," Prudence said tightly. "Our views on Lord Barclay are clearly stated in the article. If we hadn't believed in the truth of the accusations we would not have made them." She glanced at her sisters and saw that they were willing to let her lead the advance. She could also see that behind the shared calm exterior they were aware that the rude and imperious side of Sir Gideon Malvern was definitely coming to the fore.

Gideon glanced down at the paper again. "Yes, it's clear that you are all champions of the downtrodden female. I assume you are also suffragists."

"What have our political opinions to do with this?" demanded Prudence.

He looked over at her. "A jury may not find them sympathetic."

"And we need a sympathetic jury," Constance put in.

"Quite frankly, I think that's going to be very hard to find."

Chastity leaned forward in her chair. "Sir Gideon, are you so desperate that just the faintest chance of coming away with eighty percent of possible damages is sufficient motivation for you to take on a case that you clearly don't believe in?"

On the rare occasions when Chastity was roused to anger she could outdo both her sisters. Prudence and Constance exchanged a quick look but said nothing.

Gideon's nostrils flared for an instant, then he said, "I thought your matrimonial agency was going to find me a suitable wife as payment for my services." There was no mistaking the disdainful note in his voice.

"You might need to cultivate a more pleasant manner," Prudence stated. "We can't work miracles."

"Neither can I, Miss Duncan." In leisurely fashion he reached for a silver cigarette box on the table beside him. He flipped the lid. Hesitated. Some women did smoke these days, but only in private. In general it wouldn't occur to him to offer the box to a woman, but with these three . . . ? He gave a mental shrug and leaned over the desk, proffering the box first to Prudence.

"No, thank you, it's one means of shocking the world we haven't embraced," she said, her voice chilly enough to give a polar bear shivers.

"Then I hope you don't mind if I do," he responded, ignoring the chill. "I find it helps me to think." He lit a cigarette and smoked in silence for a couple of minutes, staring at a point on the wall somewhere above his visitors' heads.

"I have the unmistakable feeling that we're wasting your time," Prudence said at last.

He waved her into silence with a gesture that infuriated all three of them, and continued with his cigarette. Only when he'd thrown the stub into the fire did he speak again. "This broadsheet of yours is inflammatory even when it's not directly and personally attacking a member of Society. I am merely pointing out that an all-male jury, twelve good men and true, are unlikely to find against one of their own in favor of a group of subversive women."

"Not necessarily," Prudence said. "It's not inevitable that every man on that jury will be of the same social standing as the earl. It's possible that they might have some sympathy for the women Barclay has ruined."

"Yes," Chastity put in. "There may even be one or two who for whatever reason—envy, personal discontent—would enjoy seeing someone like Barclay get his comeuppance."

"Ignoble motives, but certainly to be considered," Gideon said. "However, I can't put together a case for the defense if I don't have some basis for a defense." He tapped the sheet and the pile of notes Prudence had left him with a flick of his fingertips. "Now, Prudence, is the moment to give me what you have to support these accusations of fraud, theft, and cheating."

Prudence took a deep breath. "At present, nothing. But we suspect that Barclay was responsible for inveigling our father into a fraudulent scheme that resulted in the loss of his entire fortune."

"And Prue is convinced she'll find evidence in support of that among our father's financial papers," Constance said.

Gideon frowned. "This smacks of a personal vendetta. That won't sit well with a jury."

"Since no one will know our identities, no one will make the connection," Prudence pointed out.

Gideon shook his head and leaned forward. "Now, listen to me." He pointed an imperative finger. "Do you really think for one minute that Barclay's legal team will allow you to remain anonymous? They will turn heaven and earth upside down to discover who you are. And when they do, they will crucify you."

"There's no need to sound so patronizing," Prudence snapped. "We're not blind to the realities."

"Forgive me," he said in much the same tone as before. "But I think you are."

He sat back in his chair for a moment, then suddenly glared at Prudence, his gray eyes hard and cold as a gravestone. "Madam, do you have any personal reasons for this vendetta against his lordship? Has he perhaps made an unwelcome advance to you?"

"No," Prudence said, sounding shocked. "No, not at all."

"Are you asking the jury to believe that this crusade against a respected member of Society was entirely motivated by a desire for the public good?" He raised his eyebrows in sardonic disbelief.

"No . . . I mean yes," Prudence said, aware that she was stumbling now, her cheeks suddenly warm. "There's nothing personal about it. Lord Barclay ruined—"

He silenced her with a raised hand. "We don't need to hear your scurrilous accusations repeated, madam. The jury should note that they are the accusations of a few servants, young girls, easily manipulated, probably more than willing to gain their employer's favor in return for favors of their own. It's a common enough situation."

Prudence jumped to her feet an instant before her sisters. "How dare you!" She jabbed a finger at him across the table. "What kind of bullying monster do you think you are? We have no need to listen to another word." She spun around to the door, but Gideon moved quickly, leaning across the table to grasp her wrist.

"Sit down again, Prudence. I want to hear you answer me." His tone was peremptory and she tried to jerk her wrist free of his grasp. His fingers tightened. "Sit down. All of you, sit down."

"You were wrong, Prue," Chastity declared. "He's a lot worse than Max ever was."

Gideon was for a moment bewildered by this remark, which seemed to have no bearing on anything. He looked from one to the other of them, and his clasp of Prudence's wrist loosened. She liberated her wrist and deliberately rubbed it, taking advantage of the barrister's momentary disadvantage.

"I'm sorry," he said in evident chagrin. "Did I hurt you?"

Prudence made him wait. Then she said frigidly, "I thought I had made clear last night that I do not tolerate being touched without my permission. If you cannot keep your hands to yourself, Sir Gideon, this arrangement is at an end."

Gideon looked so shocked, so utterly taken aback, that Prudence could almost have laughed. Finally she had the satisfaction of besting him, of making him uncomfortable.

After a minute he said in a more moderate tone, "Forgive me. I was only trying to make a point. Please sit down. All of you."

They took their seats again and Prudence, whose anger had faded under a few minutes' calm reflection, said, "I suppose you were giving us a taste of what it might be like with a hostile prosecution in court."

"I was."

"But we've already explained that we can't appear as witnesses," she said, sounding impatient again. "We're going around in circles on this one, Gideon."

"Not quite. I think I see a way to break the circle. One of you will have to appear on the witness stand." He looked at them each in turn. "I'm sure you can lay hands on a really heavy veil, one that will totally conceal features."

"I suppose we could," Prudence said, glancing at her sisters. "Would it work, d'you think?"

"You'd have to disguise your voice," Constance pointed out. "But we could practice that."

"And if Con and I wear veils too, we could sit in the courtroom," Chastity observed, frowning in thought. "At least we'll be there for moral support."

"Why me?" Prudence asked.

No one answered and she gave an accepting shrug. She had been the main player from the start, it was logical she should continue. "It's risky," she said.

"Everything about this case is risky, Prudence," Gideon declared.

"You're being patronizing again," Prudence exclaimed. "Do try not to keep telling us what we know already and to our cost."

Gideon Malvern was one of the top barristers in the country and he was most definitely not accustomed to being taken to task for his professional manner by anyone, let alone by an indigent client. However, he resisted the impulse to put her in her place. He had the absolute conviction that an attempt to set one sister straight would bring down the wrath of the other two and he wasn't sure he could handle them in concert. One at a time . . . *maybe* . . . but definitely not all at once.

He chose the dignified course and ignored her remark, instead saying, "How would you answer the question in court, Prudence?"

She frowned. "As I recall, it was not so much a question as a repellent inference designed to appeal to a male jury."

"It was also designed to fluster you."

"As it did."

"So, give me your response." He sat back in his carved chair and folded his arms.

"I would probably say that—"

"No," he interrupted. "I want a spontaneous answer."

"We gathered sufficient evidence from the young women who had been violated and abandoned by the earl of Barclay, and from those who had assisted them, to substantiate their claims beyond any doubt. The press took up—"

"The gutter press, madam. The *Pall Mall Gazette,* which thrives on sensationalism. Did it appear in the *Times,* in the *Telegraph,* the *Morning Post*? No, it did not." Gideon leaned forward, pointing a finger at her. "No respectable person gives any credence to yellow journalism. If that's your only evidence, Madam Mayfair Lady, I can see no possible justification for the jury to find in your favor."

"Oh, I like that," Constance said. "Madam Mayfair Lady."

"Yes, a splendid alias," Chastity said.

"Just a minute, Gideon, are you saying that despite all our evidence we're not on solid ground with those accusations?" Prudence asked.

"His lawyers will certainly try to discredit your evidence." Gideon took up the legal document that Prudence had brought him the previous afternoon. "I was trying to point out how shaky the ground is even when you have fairly strong support for the accusations. Where you don't have . . ." He shrugged as he perused the document.

"I told you, we will get what's needed," Prudence declared.

"Yes, so you've said. I'll reserve judgment until I see it." He didn't raise his eyes from his reading.

Prudence closed her mouth firmly and gazed at the ceiling. He looked up then and the corners of his eyes crinkled. He seemed to have won that point. It was curiously satisfying, almost childishly so, he thought. He said, flourishing the document, "Falstaff, Harley, and Greenwold are as good as solicitors get when it comes to libel. And they've briefed Sam Richardson, KC, as counsel. Which was inevitable. They always work together."

"And he's good."

"Yes, Prudence, the very best."

"I thought you were."

"In some areas I am. But I've had less experience than Richardson in libel cases," he returned matter-of-factly.

"This case will, however, add to your stock," Prudence said. "A potent motive for taking it on."

"It was one of several," he responded without a flicker. He laid the solicitor's letter on the table again. "So, ladies, we go on the attack. I'll draft the letter and get it to the solicitors by this afternoon. Then we sit back and wait for a trial date. Or at least," he added, "I get on with my other cases, while you try to get me some evidence for an adequate defense." He stood up. "If you'll excuse me. I have to be at the Old Bailey by ten."

It was a firm but perfectly courteous dismissal and Prudence gathered up her gloves and handbag, her sisters following suit. In the outer chamber Gideon donned his black gown and white curly wig. "I'm lunching with Sir Donald at the noon recess. I'll be back this afternoon, Thadeus."

"I'll work on the brief for the Carter case this morning," the clerk said, handing him a thick folder of papers. "The witness statements are all there."

Gideon riffled through the folder and nodded. "If I need anything extra, I'll send a runner." He turned to his visitors. "Let me escort you downstairs."

He followed them downstairs, his gown swishing around the striped trousers of his morning dress. In the street, Prudence said, "You'll keep us informed?"

"Oh, yes, on a daily basis," he said, putting a hand to his wig as a gust of wind whistled around the corner of the building. "We have much to do to prepare you to take the stand, so you may rest assured that you will hear from me again very soon." He gave her a little nod and then turned and strode off towards the Old Bailey.

"And that last, Prue, was entirely for you," Constance observed when he'd disappeared from view. "For all his arrogance, our barrister friend is nowhere near as hostile as he makes out. I would say he's definitely interested in you."

"He has a strange way of showing it," Prudence returned rather dourly.

"Oh, but I think Con's right," Chastity said. "Even after that set down you gave him." She shook her head in awe. "I'm amazed he was able to recover from it."

"The man has the skin of a rhinoceros," her sister stated. "But if he dares put a hand on me again for *any* reason, I shall stick him with my hairpin."

"I would be a little careful I didn't get stuck back," Constance said with a laugh. "I wouldn't want to push our barrister friend too far."

Chastity chuckled. "No, indeed," she agreed. "There's something a little dangerous about him." She glanced sideways at Prudence, adding slyly, "Of course, some women might find it attractive. Some women like playing with fire."

Prudence felt an unusual flash of irritation at her sisters' levity. For some reason she couldn't find anything amusing in the situation. Ordinarily she wouldn't mind being the object of her sisters' teasing, but she didn't feel like being teased about Gideon Malvern. She said nothing.

If her sisters noticed her lack of response, they let it go. Chastity said cheerfully, "Actually, Con, he *is* worse than Max."

"Oh, they're all the same, these successful professional men," Constance said airily. "They're so sure of themselves, so ready to mow down all opposition, but to tell you the truth, I'd rather have that breed of arrogance than the aristocratic kind that's based solely on inherited wealth and doesn't need a brain to back it up. Don't you agree?" She glanced at Prudence for confirmation, then said quickly, "Something wrong, Prue?"

"No, not at all." Prudence shook her head and forced herself to join their mood. "And you're certainly right," she agreed. "I can hear Mother saying the same thing."

Chastity gave her a searching look, hearing the slight hesitation in her sister's voice. Prudence smiled and said, "It's nearly ten o'clock. Fortnum's will open in half an hour. Let's go and have coffee and cakes, and plan this campaign of investigation."

Chastity was not convinced that Prudence was her usual self, but now didn't seem a suitable moment to pry. "Good idea," she said with an easy smile. "I have a craving for a slice of Battenburg cake."

"And this afternoon we can sit down and draw up a list of suitable marriage prospects for Sir Gideon," Constance said. "Or at least decide what kind of woman we think might suit him. Now that we've all met him, we ought to have some ideas." She waved at a passing hackney, saying as she climbed in, "You'd better come to my house. I probably ought to stay in for bride visits this afternoon."

Chapter 9

"Have you had any bride visits yet, Con?" Chastity asked as she walked into her sister's drawing room that afternoon.

"Oh, this is such a pleasant room," Prudence said, following on her sister's heels. "I do like that Chinese wallpaper."

"Lady Bainbridge turned up her nose," Constance said. "She was here half an hour ago. Very supercilious she was on the subject of these newfangled tastes." She plumped up a silk cushion embroidered with peacocks. "She examined me very carefully, clearly looking for an expanding waistline."

"It would be too soon for that, even if you were thinking about it," Prudence pointed out, casting a glance at her elder sister's slender figure. "Who else has been?"

"Letitia . . . oh, and Aunt Agnes. She was very complimentary about the Oriental theme."

"She would be. Agnes has never said a critical word about anyone," Chastity said fondly of their father's sister, their favorite aunt.

"Let me get some tea," Constance said, "and then we can talk about lists." She pulled the fringed bell rope beside the fireplace. "I've been wracking my brains trying to think of eligible women for the barrister—" She broke off as a maid appeared in answer to the bell. "Could you bring us some tea, Brenda? Thank you."

"What kind of woman would suit him?" Chastity asked, settling into a corner of the sofa.

"I haven't the faintest idea," Prudence said, depositing herself into a deep armchair.

"That's not very helpful," Constance chided. "This was your idea, remember."

"I remember." Prudence sighed. "And it seemed like a good one at the time. Before I realized that I wouldn't wish him on my worst enemy."

"Don't exaggerate," Constance said, bending to clear a marquetry table to receive the tea tray brought in by the maid.

Prudence grinned reluctantly and leaned over to take a cucumber sandwich from the plate. The maid poured tea and left.

"Well, who's going to start the ball rolling?" Constance sat down on the end of the sofa opposite Chastity.

Chastity frowned and instead of answering that question posed one of her own. "Did it occur to you that it might be very difficult to find a woman willing to marry a divorced man?"

"He's rich and successful," Prudence pointed out. "He's well connected. There's nothing particularly unfavourable in his appearance."

"Talk about damning with faint praise," Constance said with a crow of laughter. "I think he's rather distinguished-looking."

"He has good eyes," Prudence conceded. "And a good head of hair."

Chastity chuckled and spread honey on a buttered crumpet. "Nice voice too."

Constance declared with a touch of acid, "Divorce isn't the same handicap for men as it is for women."

"No," Chastity agreed.

"But we don't know who was the injured party," Prudence pointed out.

"Even if it was his wife, I'm sure he did the decent thing," Chastity said. "It would be unthinkable otherwise."

"Allowing her to divorce him?" Prudence frowned. "With most men I would agree with you, but in my experience, Gideon doesn't play by all the rules."

"He only kissed you, Prue," Chastity said.

"Without my permission!" her sister fired back. "How would you like it, Chas?"

Chastity shrugged. "It often happens to me. I just pat their cheeks and explain that I'm not interested."

Prudence surveyed her with slight exasperation. "But I'm not you, Chas. I don't flirt, and I don't shrug these things off. I expect men to leave me alone unless I invite them closer."

"This isn't getting us anywhere," Constance said. "Let's look at what qualities we think Gideon would insist upon in a second wife."

"Faithfulness," Prudence said with a short laugh.

"That goes without saying."

"A submissive type, probably," Prudence added. "One who doesn't mind being grabbed at will."

"Prue, you are not helping," Constance rebuked.

Prudence nodded. "All right," she said. "Since he believes in women's education, I'm sure he'd prefer a woman with an educated mind." She drank her tea.

"And of course someone who could hold her own in the kinds of social gatherings he frequents." Chastity rummaged in her bag for a notebook and pencil. "Let's make a list of what we see as necessary qualities and then you can show it to him, Prue. See if he has any others to add."

"We have to consider the daughter's feelings too," Constance said. "I wonder how much it would matter to him that the child should like a potential candidate."

"I think it would have to be someone who liked children, who got along well with them," Prudence said definitely. "In all conscience, we couldn't possibly promote a marriage in this case where we knew the potential bride had an antipathy for children."

"Prue's absolutely right," Chastity said, and Constance nodded her agreement.

"I would think a potential candidate's level of education would be important too," Constance put in. "If he's sending his daughter to North London Collegiate, he must be intending her for Girton, wouldn't you think? He'd want another woman in the house to be able to keep up with the girl's education."

Prudence considered. Girton, the women's college at Cambridge University, now allowed women to sit public examinations. They still weren't allowed to take a degree, but the cachet was enormous. "Then he'd be expecting her to pursue some kind of career," she mused. "Teaching, I suppose."

"Who do we know who's qualified to teach? Not a governess, of course, but at undergraduate level, or at least in one of the good girls' schools. That would cover the necessity for getting along with children too."

"Astrid Bellamy," Chastity suggested. "She's passionate about women's education. She went to Lady Margaret Hall at Oxford."

"She's too old," Prudence stated instantly. "She must be nearly forty."

"But we don't know that age would matter to him," Cosntance pointed out. "Unless he wants more children, of course."

"He'd have been looking more actively for himself if that was the case," Prudence pointed out. "He must be forty himself."

Constance frowned. "Maybe so. But once we get him interested in this process it might become a factor."

"I suppose so," Prudence said, sounding doubtful.

"Well, we could ask him." Constance regarded her sister with the same frown.

"We could," Prudence agreed.

"You seem less than enthusiastic about this, Prue," Constance observed.

Prudence shook her head. "No, I'm not. Not in the least. Of course I'm not."

"Ah," Constance said. "My mistake."

Chastity cast a quick glance between her sisters, then returned to her note-taking. "What about looks?" she asked. "Do you think those are important to him? Must it be a beautiful woman?"

Prudence thought about this. "I would say looks were less important than brains and personality, but . . ." She shrugged. "What do I know?"

"More than we do," Chastity said, chewing the tip of her pencil. "You spent an evening with him."

"I can't see around his domineering, overbearing personality," Prudence stated. "What woman of strong character with a mind of her own would give him the time of day?"

"I seem to remember some comparison with Max," Constance murmured from the depths of her sofa. "But then, perhaps I'm not a woman of strong character with a mind of my own."

Prudence threw one of the fringed peacock cushions at her. "Max has redeeming features."

"We might find some in Gideon Malvern if we look hard enough," Chastity said. "What do you think about Agnes Hargate? She's fairly young, fairly attractive, well read, although she didn't go to university."

"She's a widow with a five-year-old son," Prudence said.

"So we know she likes children," Constance said.

"We don't know he wants a ready-made family," Prudence objected.

"Again, we could ask him," Chastity said. "I'm sure Agnes would be interested. I know she's lonely."

"Did he say anything to you, Prue, anything at all after you proposed this bargain?" Constance asked, leaning forward slightly.

"Yes," Chastity said. "Did he give any hint of the kind of woman who might appeal?"

Prudence hesitated. What had he said after he'd taken that kiss? Something about how having kissed him she would now know what kind of woman would suit him. How she would now know what kind of lover he would make. Somehow she didn't feel like sharing that with her sisters.

"No," she said. "He said only that he wasn't in the market for a wife and he was very hard to please."

"Well, that's encouraging," Constance observed aridly. "More tea?"

Prudence passed her cup. Constance was right, of course. She wasn't entering into the spirit of this exercise with genuine enthusiasm, but why not? It had been her idea to find the barrister a bride. It was a brilliant solution to the generally intractable problem of finances. But every woman who came to mind as possible struck her as impossible. She was just depressed, she decided. Depressed and oppressed. The more she dwelt on the libel suit, the more impossible it seemed to defeat it.

Constance glanced at her and then looked across at Chastity, who made a comprehending face. Something was wrong with their generally imperturbable sister. Prudence was always on an even keel, the reins of business firmly in her hands. Her sisters could take off on emotional flights of fancy on occasion, but never Prudence. She was too sensible, her concentration on the subject at hand unwavering. But not this afternoon, for some reason.

"Excuse me, madam." The maid appeared in the doorway. "Fred just delivered this for Miss Prue." She extended a letter. "It went to Manchester Square and Mr. Jenkins thought it might be important, so he sent it straight round."

"Thank you, Brenda." Constance took the letter and glanced at the envelope. "From the chambers of Sir Gideon Malvern, KC." She handed it to Prudence. "He didn't waste any time, did he?"

Prudence slit the envelope and unfolded the paper. "He says that he's received immediate acknowledgment from Barclay's solicitors that he's the barrister of record in the matter of *Barclay v.* The Mayfair Lady." She looked up. "Gideon said he'd send them a letter this afternoon. I wonder if it's a bad sign that they responded so quickly." A worried frown creased her brow.

"It'll be a relief to get it over with," Constance said.

"What else does it say?" Chastity leaned forward.

"He says they are requesting an early trial date, and he's not going to contest that. He wants to see me this evening to start preparing for the case." She handed the letter to Chastity. "You'd think that he would try to postpone as long as possible, wouldn't you? We don't have the evidence for the fraud accusations as yet."

"We haven't had a chance to search Father's papers," Chastity said, laying a soothing hand over her sister's that was twitching on the arm of the chair. "We'll do it at the first opportunity."

Prudence nodded. "I know. It's just happening too fast."

"Well, we must have at least a month to put it all together," Constance said bracingly. "Cases don't come to trial overnight."

"No, true enough." Prudence managed a smile. "So, I suppose I'd better send a message back to say I'll be there . . . which is where?" She took back the letter and read it again. "Oh, Pall Mall Place. Number Seven." She looked up with a shrug. "I'd have expected his chambers."

"Perhaps he has another office," Chastity suggested.

Prudence shrugged. "I'll find out at seven o'clock."

"He doesn't say anything about dinner," Constance observed.

"Which, I trust, means that this is a purely business meeting," Prudence declared crisply. "He's not sending his chauffeur for me either."

"So, with any luck you won't have to be fending off unwelcome advances," Chastity murmured.

Her sister ignored this. She said coolly, "If Father's not using the carriage this evening, I'll get Cobham to drive me in the barouche. And I'll tell him to come back for me at eight o'clock so I'll be home in time for dinner. An hour should be sufficient for the barrister. It'll certainly be enough for me," she added.

"Are you going to take this list?" Chastity indicated her notebook. "Or at least ask him whether he has any particular preferences?"

"I won't take the list, but I will ask him about preferences," her sister said, rising to her feet. "We should go home, Chas. It's nearly five o'clock. Are you dining in tonight, Con?"

"No, at Number Ten," her elder sister said, referring to the Prime Minister's official residence with an exaggerated sigh.

"Oh, that's an honor," Prudence said, regarding her sister with narrowed eyes. "Something in the wind?"

Constance smiled. "I don't know, Max won't say anything. But I have a feeling . . . just a feeling."

"A Cabinet post?" Prudence asked quickly.

"As I said, Max is mum."

"Well, he deserves it," Chastity said, hugging her sister.

"Let's hope it's one that doesn't clash too much with a vocal suffragist wife," Prudence said, voicing an awkward truth in customary practical fashion.

Constance grimaced slightly. "We'll cross that bridge when we come to it."

"Yes, of course you will." Prudence kissed her. "We'll talk tomorrow . . . exchange accounts of our evenings."

Constance laughed and showed them out. Max was just drawing up to the curb outside the house as they said their farewells on the top step. He ran up the stairs. "Are you two leaving?"

"We just came for tea," Prudence said.

"Well, hold on a minute and I'll get Frank to drive you home before he puts the motor away." He kissed his wife and hurried into the house, calling for his manservant.

* * *

Just before seven o'clock Prudence stepped up into the barouche, greeting the elderly driver with a warm smile. "How are the horses, Cobham?"

"Oh, well enough, Miss Prue," he said. "Getting ready to be put out to pasture. Just like me." He cracked his whip and the two glossy chestnuts picked up their hooves and started off at a smart trot around the square.

"They don't seem ready to be put to grass," Prudence observed. "Any more than you do. You're looking very sprightly, Cobham."

"Well, that's right kind of you, Miss Prue. But I'll be seventy next birthday. Time for a nice little cottage in the country."

Prudence realized that she was being given a serious message. If Cobham was ready to retire, then he had every right to do so. And every right to the pension that would enable him to live as he chose in the little cottage in the country. But there was no provision for pensions in the budget. Her mind worked fast, adding and subtracting expenses. Adding and subtracting necessities. She scraped for Cobham's wages every week, even though in this day of motorized omnibuses and frequent hackney cabs they really could manage without a coachman, let alone the horses that cost a fortune to feed and house in London. But it wasn't remotely conceivable to turn the old man off.

However, if the horses went to pasture at the country house at Romsey, they would be much cheaper to keep. Then she could rent out the mews at Manchester Square. Mews courts were being turned into garages for the new motor vehicles all over fashionable London; it would be an income, of sorts, that would contribute to Cobham's pension. And if he took one of the cottages rent-free on the estate at Romsey, then he could live comfortably on half his London wage, which would probably be the equivalent of the rent on the mews. He could have a very comfortable retirement and the family finances would benefit.

"Had you thought where you would go, Cobham?" she asked.

"The wife's a hankering for the old village," he said, slowing the horses across a slippery patch of cobbles. "Spent enough time in London. Misses her sister."

Prudence nodded. Cobham's wife came from Romsey. It was how Cobham, a Londoner to his bootstraps, had come to work for the Duncan family at the Manor.

"There's a vacant tenant cottage on the road to Lyndhurst, if you'd be interested. Of course there'd be no rent to pay. It would be part of your pension, if that was agreeable."

There was silence while the coachman ruminated into his whiskers. After a minute he said, "Reckon so, Miss Prue. I'll talk to the wife."

"Good. Let me know what you decide and we'll settle the details." Prudence sat back with the sense of a job well done.

The barouche turned off the wide thoroughfare of Pall Mall and onto a quiet cul-de-sac of tall, narrow houses.

"Number Seven, Miss Prue." Cobham reined in his horses and looked back at his passenger.

"So it would seem," Prudence said, examining the Georgian house with its telltale fanlight above a shiny black front door, its black railings and white steps, the double frontage with the two bow windows. This was no private supper club. This, unless she was much mistaken, was the residence of Sir Gideon Malvern, KC. And once again he'd sprung a surprise that threw her off balance.

Cobham let down the step and opened the door for her. "Thank you, Cobham. Would you come back for me at eight, please?"

"Of course, Miss Prue." He closed the carriage door and put up the step again. "Since it's only an hour, I'll have a tankard in the Black Dog, just over on Jermyn Street, if that's all right with you."

"Of course," she said, heading to the front door. "In an hour." She took up the shiny door knocker in the shape of a lion's head and rapped it smartly.

It was opened immediately by the barrister, still in morning dress, as if he'd just this minute returned from his chambers. Prudence was glad that she too was wearing what she had worn for their meeting that morning.

"A carriage," he said with a smile, watching Cobham drive away. "Expensive to keep horses in London." He stepped back, holding the door for her.

"Yes," she agreed, moving past him. "But nothing compared to a motorcar. Believe me, I looked into it. My father was very keen of having one, until he realized how unreliable they were." She drew off her gloves as she took a quick survey of her surroundings. Subdued elegance, she decided.

"They can be unpredictable," he agreed with an affable smile. "May I take your coat?"

"Thank you." She thrust her gloves into her pockets and shrugged out of her coat. "Do you ordinarily conduct business in your own house, Sir Gideon?"

"Only when my business has to be conducted after-hours," he said, gesturing towards a door that stood open at the rear of the hall. "When I'm short of time, Miss Duncan, I have to sacrifice some of my leisure, and it's more comfortable to do it here."

Prudence followed the gesture and found herself in a pleasant library with a very masculine air. There was a lingering smell of cigar smoke, leather and oak furniture, an Aubusson rug on the highly polished oak floor, dark velvet curtains at the long windows, not yet drawn against the encroaching shadows of night. There was not an inch of space visible in the bookcases that lined three out of the four walls.

"Drink?" Gideon asked, closing the door behind them.

"No, thank you," she said. "I'm here to talk about the case."

"I often discuss cases over a drink," he said casually, pouring himself a whisky. "Please . . . sit down." He indicated a comfortable armchair in front of a cherry wood table on which reposed a small pile of neatly arranged papers and nothing else.

Prudence sat down. "Why did the earl's counsel respond so quickly to your letter. Is it a good sign?"

Gideon considered. "Neither good nor bad," he said, sipping his drink. "They may think their case is foolproof and just want to get on with it, or they may have doubts and want us to show our hand."

"As soon as we can look at my father's papers we'll have all the evidence we need," Prudence stated.

He leaned his forearms on the table and his eyes were now sharp, his voice clipped. "Well, as I said this morning, I'll wait until I see it before I'm convinced. Let's deal now with what we have."

He was all business, Prudence reflected. Not a hint of personal connection in his demeanor. She should find it reassuring, except that it put her back up. She shook her head in an unconscious gesture designed to banish her own inconvenient personal reactions. "Very well," she said briskly, and folded her hands in her lap. "You have questions for me."

He drew a sheet of paper towards him and took up a pen. "I need some hard and fast facts. When did the publication first come out?"

Prudence considered. "I'm not positive. My mother started it. We began to help her when Con was fifteen, I think. So I would have been fourteen."

"I don't think we want to bring your mother into this," he said, frowning. "It'll complicate matters too much. When did you and your sisters take over the sole running of the publication?"

"Four years ago, on our mother's death."

"All right. And have you been sued before?"

"No, of course not."

"There's no *of course* about it. How many adverse reactions have you had? Complaints from readers, for instance?"

"Not many."

"How many? More than ten, less than five?"

"Probably more than ten."

"So, you would agree that this is a controversial publication?" He was writing as he spoke, not looking at her as he fired the questions.

"Yes."

"Do you set out to be offensive?"

"*No*. What kind of questions are these?"

"The kind you're going to be asked in court. And if you give way to a show of petulance or indignation, you're going to lose the jury and give the prosecution ammunition. If you lose your composure, you're lost." He picked up his glass and went back to the pier table where the decanters stood. "Are you sure you won't have a sherry?"

"No, thank you. I need to keep my wits about me if I'm going to survive this ordeal."

"I don't mean to make it one." He refilled his glass.

"Yes, you do," she contradicted.

"Only for your own good." He sat down again.

"This hurts me more than it hurts you?" she scoffed.

He shook his head with a gesture of exasperation. "No." He reached for a cigarette in the silver box on the table.

" 'A cigarette is the perfect type of a perfect pleasure. It is exquisite, and it leaves one unsatisfied,' " Prudence quoted.

"That sounds like Oscar Wilde," he said.

"Yes, *The Picture of Dorian Gray*."

He smiled a little. "I only smoke when I'm working. Now, can we get on with it?"

Prudence nodded with a sigh. "By all means, carry on. I have to leave at eight o'clock."

He looked momentarily taken aback and then as quickly his expression resumed its calm neutrality. "Do you and your sisters ordinarily consort with—" He was interrupted by a knock at the door. "Yes?" His voice was not inviting.

The door opened and a girl's head appeared. "I didn't mean to disturb you, Daddy, but Mary is out for the evening and I have all these literature quotes to identify and I just can't get them all." Gray eyes, her father's eyes, darted around the room, fixing on Prudence, who now leaned back in her armchair and prepared to discover what she could about the barrister and his daughter.

"Why don't you bring the rest of you in here," Gideon said. "I don't care to converse with disembodied heads."

"Like the Cheshire cat's smile," the girl said with a sunny smile of her own as she inserted herself fully into the room, although she stayed by the door. "It's just two references that I can't identify, Daddy. Please, can you help?" Her tone was pleading and made Prudence smile. This was one child who knew how to manipulate a compliant parent.

"I'm with a client, Sarah," her father said. "And judging by the monthly accounts from Hatchards and Blackwell, you have a substantial library of reference books. I must ask Mary why a *Dictionary of Quotations* is somehow missing from the schoolroom shelves."

Sarah looked a little self-conscious. "I'm sure we have one, I just couldn't find it, and I have so much other preparation to do for tomorrow, Latin and French, that I thought maybe . . ." She cast him a quick mood-assessing glance, and then before he could respond, said, " 'Beauty is truth . . .' "

" 'Truth beauty. That is all ye know on earth and all ye need to know,' " Prudence said. "Keats, 'Ode on a Grecian Urn,' 1820."

"Oh, thank you," Sarah Malvern said. "And there's one other: 'Love built on . . .' "

" 'Love built on beauty, soon as beauty dies,' " Prudence said. "John Donne. The elegies, I think." She frowned in thought. "Fifteen ninety-five, I *think*."

Sarah beamed. "Thank you so much, Miss . . ."

"Duncan," Prudence said, rising and holding out her hand. "I'm a client of your father's."

The girl shook it with considerable warmth. "I didn't mean to disturb your meeting."

"No, of course you didn't," her father murmured from the far side of the table. "If your curiosity has been satisfied, Sarah . . . ?"

"It wasn't curiosity," the girl denied. "It was genuine research."

Gideon nodded. "Oh, yes, of course. Research." A smile quirked the corners of his mouth.

"Thank you for your help, Miss Duncan," Sarah said politely. She backed out of the door, asking just before she closed it, "Are you dining out, Daddy?"

His eyes glanced off Prudence, who had returned to her seat and was gazing studiously out into the now complete darkness beyond the window. "Apparently not," he said. "I'll come up and say good night in an hour."

Sarah bobbed a curtsy. "Good night, Miss Duncan. Thank you again for your help."

Prudence smiled. "I enjoyed the exercise. Good night, Sarah."

After the door had closed on the girl, Gideon observed, "So, you're something of an expert on English literature."

"We all are," Prudence said. "It was one of our mother's passions. We imbibed it at the breast."

He nodded, rising to draw the heavy velvet curtains, shutting out the night. "Sarah has a particular affinity for mathematics. She also plays the flute."

"Music and mathematics tend to be complementary talents," Prudence observed. "She seems to be an avid student. Which reminds me of some questions I need to ask you." She opened her handbag and took out her own notebook. "We were beginning to put together a list of possible brides this afternoon and there are one or two issues we'd like to clarify."

Gideon returned to his seat. He leaned back and folded his arms, then raised his eyebrows, his mouth set in an expression that was not encouraging. "I should warn you that I have very little time to spend on this brief, Miss Duncan. If you want to take some of that valuable time away from your own affairs, that is of course your business."

"It seems to me we have to work in tandem," Prudence said. "You have your job to do and I have mine, but they are intimately connected. Now, we're assuming you would only consider prospective brides who would be sympathetic to Sarah. Someone whom she would be able to confide in, to feel comfortable with."

"If you're asking me whether I would consider marrying again just to provide Sarah with a mother, the answer is no." He shook his head vigorously. "That seems to me to be the worst possible reason for tying oneself to someone, and I can't imagine any woman worth her salt settling for such a bargain. No, if I ever married again it would be because I met a woman who suited *me*. I would like to think that Sarah would find such a woman both likable and sympathetic."

He unfolded his arms and leaned his elbows on the table. "Now, if that answers your question, perhaps I could return to mine."

"Well, you obviously couldn't consider someone who disliked children," Prudence pressed on. "There's one possibility who might suit you. A widow called Agnes Hargate. A charming woman, very attractive. She has a five-year-old son. Would that be a disadvantage?" She looked up from her notebook and raised one hand to adjust the set of her glasses as she examined his expression.

"The prospect leaves me less than joyful," he stated. "Now, are you and your sisters in the habit of consorting with fallen women?"

"*No,*" she said. "At least, I don't know what you mean by *fallen* women. I'm sure there are plenty of women of our acquaintance, not to mention of Lord Barclay's, who've indulged in a little extracurricular activity. And that's another question for you. Are you only interested in prospective brides who have an unblemished reputation?"

He sighed. "I'm trying to get across to you, Prudence, that I am not at present in the least interested in any prospective brides." He glanced impatiently at the clock, and his voice was irritable as he said, "We haven't covered as much ground as I wanted to this evening. I was hoping we could have a working dinner, something simple, but since you have to leave . . ."

"Your message—or summons, rather—made no mention of dinner," she said. "But I would have had to decline, anyway," she fibbed blithely. "I have another engagement."

"It wasn't a summons," he said. "It was a request."

"It read like a summons."

"Then you must forgive me." But he didn't sound in the least apologetic. He got briskly to his feet and suddenly pointed a finger at her. "Are you and your sisters in the habit of consorting with women of the street, Madam Mayfair Lady?"

Prudence opened her mouth to answer a resounding and indignant negative and then realized what he'd said. "They won't know there's more than one of us," she protested. "We've agreed. It's just one representative. The Mayfair Lady. They couldn't ask that question because they won't know anything about us."

He shook his head. "Don't be so certain. They're going to move heaven and earth to track you down. It wouldn't surprise me if they employed a detective agency. I assure you, they're going to be no happier than I am at putting a sheet of newspaper on the stand." He moved out from behind his desk as the grandfather clock in the corner of the library struck a sonorous eight bells.

"Detectives?" Prudence said, sounding shocked. "Surely not." She thrust her arms into the sleeves of her coat that he was holding for her.

"Just be on your guard," he said, going to open the door for her.

Prudence went past him. "How long do we have, do you think, before the trial date?"

He shrugged. "Three, maybe four weeks. Sam Richardson has some influence on the bench and his clerks are extraordinarily efficient. They'll discover who's presiding, and Sam, I'm sure, will have a pleasant chat over a more-than-satisfactory dinner in his club, and the case will come up when he wants it to."

Prudence frowned. "But don't you have influence like that?"

"Certainly I do, but I don't intend to use it."

"But we still don't have our case put together."

"Bring me the evidence, Miss Duncan, and I believe you said that we'll have all the case we need." He opened the front door. The street lamps were now lit and Cobham sat smoking his pipe on the driver's seat of the barouche, the horses shifting their hooves impatiently as the autumnal night air grew chilly.

Gideon walked her down the steps and saw her into the carriage. "But do *you* believe that?" she asked, stung by the tinge of sarcasm in his tone.

At that he laughed, but it wasn't a particularly pleasant laugh in Prudence's estimation. "I have no choice but to do so, my dear. Confidence is half the battle. I can't go into court expecting to lose."

"But do you expect to?" She took off her glasses and fixed him with an anxious gaze, the light of the streetlamp giving her eyes a golden hue, tingeing the russet hair with touches of gold.

For an instant an arrested gleam appeared in his gray gaze; he half opened his mouth, as if about to say something, then shook his head with another slight laugh, stepped back, and waved her away.

Chapter 10

"Another letter for you, Miss Prue. From Sir Gideon." Jenkins put the long envelope beside her plate at breakfast the next morning. "If I may say so, the barrister seems an assiduous correspondent."

"I trust it means he's equally assiduous in his efforts on our behalf," Prudence said tartly. She slit the envelope with her butter knife and perused the contents.

"You have no reason to believe otherwise, Prue," Chastity protested mildly, looking over the top of the *Times*.

"No, I don't suppose I do," Prudence agreed with a little sigh. "It's just that he made me feel last night that it was a wasted effort and we had no chance of winning and basically he resented the time he was spending." She crumpled the letter and tossed it into the fireplace.

"Maybe he just wasn't in the mood to talk about brides," Chastity suggested. "You'd just met his daughter, after all. That must have been awkward for him."

"No, it wasn't," her sister stated. "He was not in the least put out. The girl was being curious and he had no real problem with it at all. It amused him. I just don't think he's serious . . . ever has been . . . about this bargain. He's going to insist on his eighty-twenty split." She shrugged and refilled her coffee cup.

"Well, we can but persevere," Chastity said with customary optimism. "I was wondering about Lavender Riley, or even Priscilla Heyworth." She regarded her sister with a raised eyebrow, waiting for the objections she instinctively expected.

Instead, Prudence shrugged again and said, "They're possibilities, I suppose."

"So, what was in the letter?" Chastity gestured with a piece of toast to the crumpled sheet that had not yet caught flame.

"A surprisingly polite request that I make myself available all day tomorrow for a more intensive preparation session."

"In his chambers?"

"No, he says he will collect me here at the house at eight-thirty in the morning."

"He does like to make an early start, even on a Sunday," Chastity commented. She folded the newspaper carefully along the crease. Lord Duncan had not yet come down to breakfast, and he abhorred an obviously previously read newspaper.

"Well, he made it clear last night he has to work on this brief in his leisure. I can hardly insist on mine, even though tomorrow *is* Sunday." She took up her coffee cup again.

"Good morning, my dears." Lord Duncan entered the breakfast parlor, his complexion ruddy from his morning ablutions, his white hair impeccably coiffed. "Jenkins has promised me kippers," he said, rubbing his hands. "A morning that starts with kippers can only lead to good things."

"You're very cheerful this morning, Father," Chastity observed, placing the newspaper at his plate. "Considering that it's pouring with rain." She gestured towards the long windows, where rain slanted against the panes.

"Oh, what's a little rain?" his lordship said. "I'm going with Barclay to meet with his solicitors and the barrister. They want me to take the stand as a character witness."

Prudence took an overly large gulp of hot coffee and choked, tears filling her eyes as she buried her face in her napkin.

"Really," Chastity said rather weakly. "How good of you."

"Good God, it's hardly good to stand by a friend in need. Oh, delicious, Jenkins, thank Mrs. Hudson for me." Lord Duncan sniffed hungrily at the aroma rising from the plate of steaming kippers placed before him. "And brown bread and butter, of course." He patted his embonpoint, where his silver watch and chain rested in state.

Prudence poured coffee for him and passed the cup. "Will it be a long meeting?"

"Oh, no idea," her father said. "Judging by the exorbitant fees these fellows charge, it ought to last all day." He attacked a kipper, scraping aside the larger bones before taking a forkful that he consumed with an air of bliss. "Manna," he murmured. "Sheer manna. Can't think why you girls don't eat them."

"Too many bones," Chastity said. "By the time I've fiddled with them, the kipper's stone cold and I've lost my appetite."

"Oh, you just chew 'em up," Lord Duncan said, suiting action to advice. "The little ones don't do you any harm." He opened the newspaper with a flick and perused the headlines.

"Will you be in for luncheon?" Prudence inquired, spreading marmalade on her toast.

"Shouldn't think so, m'dear. If we're done with these lawyer fellows in time, Barclay and I'll lunch at the club. What's today?" He glanced at the date on the newspaper. "Oh, Saturday. Odd that they work on a weekend." He shrugged. "Not to worry. It's steak and oyster pie today. We'll definitely be lunching at the club."

"You haven't forgotten we're having dinner with Constance and Max this evening?"

"Oh, no. Pity Barclay couldn't accept the invitation. Some relative or other come to town."

"I think Con's invited the Wesleys though," Prudence said. "You know how much you like to play bridge with them. Con will partner you."

"Oh, yes, it'll be a capital evening, I'm sure. Capital." He returned to his paper.

Prudence glanced at Chastity and folded her napkin. "If you don't mind, Father, we'll leave you to your breakfast. Chas and I have a few errands to run this morning." She pushed back her chair and dropped a kiss on her father's cheek as she headed for the door, Chastity at her heels.

In the hall, she paused, tapping the folded thumb of her fist against her chin. "We have to do it this morning, Chas."

"Go through the papers?"

"Yes. There's no knowing when we can be sure Father will be out of the house again for a decent stretch of time."

Chastity nodded. "Should we send a message to Con?"

"Yes, get Fred to run around to Westminster. With three of us looking, if there's anything to find we'll find it."

Chastity hurried off to the kitchen. Fred, the errand boy and general handyman, was polishing shoes by the range and chatting amiably with Mrs. Hudson. "Lord Duncan's delighted with his kippers, Mrs. Hudson," Chastity said.

"Oh, I thought he'd find 'em tasty," the housekeeper said. " 'Tisn't often the fishmonger has 'em on his cart when he comes of a Thursday, but this week he did. And they weren't too expensive neither. Twopence halfpenny apiece."

"Well, they gave his lordship more than fivepence worth of pleasure," Chastity told her. "Fred, when you've finished with the shoes, could you run around to Mrs. Ensor and ask her if she could visit this morning? As soon as she can."

Fred spat on one of Lord Duncan's evening shoes. "I'll be done here in ten minutes, Miss Chastity." He polished vigorously, working the spittle into the leather.

"Miss Con will be here for lunch, then, Miss Chas?" Mrs. Hudson inquired.

"Yes, but bread and cheese will do fine."

"Oh, I might turn my hand to a bit of pastry," the housekeeper said. "Seeing as there's no dinner to cook this evening. There's a nice piece of ham in the pantry and I think I could lay my hands on a bit of stewing veal. How would you fancy a veal and ham pie?"

"Very much," Chastity said.

"And a jam roly-poly for pudding."

"You spoil us, Mrs. Hudson . . . even on our budget."

"Oh, 'tis not difficult, Miss Chas, if you've an eye for a bargain," the woman said with a pleased smile. With an answering smile, Chastity left the kitchen, reflecting that they should all count their blessings when it came to Jenkins and Mrs. Hudson. But, of course, they did, every waking minute.

She had stopped smiling when she reached the upstairs parlor. "We have to stop Father from taking the stand," she stated as she entered. "What if he recognizes your voice, Prue. Even if you disguise it, you're his *daughter*."

"I know," her sister said. She was standing at the window watching the drumming rain and the sodden trees in the square garden. "And Gideon will be cross-examining him. It'll be hideous, Chas." She crossed her arms over her breasts.

"Everything we tell Gideon about Father will be armor for his cross-examination." Chastity shook her head. "I don't see how we can do it, Prue."

"We have to," her sister said simply. "We have to find a way. We can't lose, Chas, you know that. If we do, Father will be devastated . . . broken."

"Then you're going to have to act as you've never acted before," Chastity said, now briskly accepting the reality. "You need a voice, one that won't slip under pressure, and won't bear any resemblance to your own."

"The one thing we have in our favor is that it would never occur to Father in his wildest nightmares that we would have anything to do with the case," Prudence said, turning away from the window. "Even if he had an inkling that there was something familiar about the veiled witness for the defense, he would never associate her with one of us."

"I only hope you're right." Chastity came over to the window to stand beside her sister, and they stood looking down onto the street until a hackney disgorged Constance, under a big umbrella.

Constance didn't pause on the pavement to look up at the parlor window as she might have done on another day, but scurried up the steps to the house. The door opened as she reached the top, and she nearly ran into her father, similarly equipped with a big, black umbrella.

"Good morning, my dear," he said hastily while waving his umbrella at the cab that had just delivered his daughter. "Can't stop. I'll take your cab."

"I'll see you this evening, Father," Constance said to his retreating back. She turned to the door, shaking the rain off her umbrella.

"I'll take that, Miss Con." Jenkins deftly removed it. "It'll dry in the back scullery. Weather's not fit for ducks."

"That it's not," Constance agreed, taking off her hat in the hall. "Are my sisters upstairs?"

"Waiting for you, Miss Con."

Constance nodded, and ran up the stairs. "So, what's happening?" she asked as she opened the door. "That was a rather urgent message to someone who's giving an important dinner party this evening." She was laughing as she spoke, but her laughter died when she saw her sisters' expressions. "Trouble?"

"Of a kind. But we also need your help this morning." Prudence explained the situation.

"Damn and blast," Constance said. "He would, wouldn't he?"

"Yes, he would," Prudence agreed with a resigned shrug. "Loyalty to his friend."

"And we're going to blow that loyalty to smithereens," Chastity stated.

They were silent for a minute, then Prudence said heavily, "Well, let's go and find the evidence to do that. I asked Jenkins to light a fire in the library." She went over to the secretaire and opened one of the small drawers. "I have a key to the safe."

"When did you get that?"

"Months ago. Jenkins had it copied for me. I can't keep control of the finances if I don't know what Father is spending. All his bills are in the safe, so I see them before they come due. That way I can make sure there's enough in his bank account to cover them . . . or at least make sure that he's not too overdrawn."

Constance put a hand on her sister's shoulder. "Prue, why didn't you tell us?"

"This is my job. I didn't see any reason to burden you both with the more dubious aspects of its operation. I don't like the idea of snooping and prying into Father's personal affairs, but since he won't give me any information freely I had to find a way to get it without his knowledge." She tossed the tiny key from hand to hand, her expression hard to read.

"Prue, love, this isn't a burden you carry alone," Chastity said. "We would have supported you in this if you'd told us. You don't need to feel guilty."

"Maybe not. But I do. Let's go and dig ourselves deeper into this slough of deceit." She strode to the door.

"So, how was your evening, Prue?" Constance asked as they entered the library. "Does our barrister seem to have a handle on the case?"

Prudence closed the door behind them, and then after an instant's hesitation, locked it. "He's very aggressive with his questions but I'm sure he's right that opposing counsel will be and I need to be fore-armed." She leaned against the door for a moment. "He also says that we can expect them to put detectives onto finding our identities."

Her sisters turned to stare at her. "Detectives?" Chastity repeated.

Prudence nodded. "I suppose, if you think about it, it's almost inevitable."

"Where would they start?" Constance wondered. "Oh, *The Mayfair Lady,* of course."

"Yes," Prudence agreed. "That was what I was thinking. They could start asking questions at all the places that stock it. No one knows us, of course. When we go to collect our money, we're always heavily veiled, but . . ." She shook her head. "It's still alarming. Maybe on Monday we can go to some of the outlets we use—Helene's Milliners, Robert's of Piccadilly, a few of the others—just to see if there's been any unusual interest or inquiries."

"We'll do the rounds," Constance said.

"That might put our minds at rest. Help me with the Stubbs." Prudence went to the far wall and moved aside a large George Stubbs painting of a racehorse. Constance held it to one side while her sister unlocked the wall safe behind and took out its contents, passing them to Chastity.

"There's so much stuff in here . . . I'm sure a lot of it's out-of-date." She reached into the depths of the safe for the last few pieces of paper, then closed the safe door. Constance let the painting swing back into place.

Chastity put the pile of papers on the cherry wood desk that stood in the bay window looking out onto the walled back garden. "Shall you go through these, Prue, while Con and I go through the desk drawers?"

"Yes. We're looking for anything that resembles a legal contract. Any piece of paper that has a law-firm heading . . . or something that sounds like one."

"Jaggers, Tulkinghorn, and Chaffanbrass," Constance said, sitting at the desk and opening the top drawer.

"You're mixing your authors," Prudence observed, gathering up the pile of papers liberated from the safe and crossing to the sofa in front of the fire. "Chaffanbrass was Trollope, not Dickens."

"I know," Constance said. "They just had a nice ring to them." She drew out a folder from the drawer. "So when are you seeing our barrister again?"

"Tomorrow." Prudence leafed through her pile. "At some godawful hour. I'd like to have something concrete to show him."

"I wonder why he's not meeting you in his chambers," Chastity said, on her knees in front of the cupboard in the side of desk. "If he's preparing you for the witness stand, why's he coming to fetch you in his motor?"

"I have no idea," her sister said. "The man's a mystery to me."

"Of course it is Sunday," Constance pointed out.

She looked up, aware that Prudence wasn't listening. "What is it? Have you found something?"

"I don't know," Prudence said slowly. "There's a note here, signed 'Barclay.' No date." She turned it over. "It refers to *our agreement.* " She frowned. " 'As per our agreement of last week, the payment schedule should be advanced to take advantage of the present favorable market. I am advised by the principals that interest rates will rise in the next month to our disadvantage.' "

"But it doesn't say what the agreement is?"

"No, Chas. Nothing specific. But it seems that he's asking for money. I wish there was a date on it."

"Let me see." Constance came over to the sofa. Prudence handed her the note. "Well, it's not recent," Constance said. "The paper's got an old stain on it . . . here, at the bottom." She indicated a brown smudge. "See how it's faded?"

"The paper's a bit yellowed too," Chastity observed, peering over her sister's shoulder. "And the ink's faded."

"We'd make very good detectives," Prudence said. "So, let's assume that this is about three years old, about the time of Father's investment in the Trans-Saharan Railway. We're talking interest rates, payment schedules . . ."

"But no indication of what for," Constance said.

"Perhaps they had a verbal agreement," Chastity suggested. "If Barclay was up to something fraudulent, maybe he didn't want anything on paper."

"Surely Father wouldn't agree to something so huge without something in writing?" Constance said.

"Wouldn't he?" Prudence responded glumly. "A man who'd believe in a chimera in the Saharan desert?"

No one could find an argument for that. "Let's just go through everything thoroughly, just to make sure we don't miss anything," Prudence said, folding the note carefully. "I'll give this to Gideon tomorrow. Maybe he can see a way to use it."

At the end of another hour, she looked at the piles of paper with something like despair. "That's it," she said. "We've gone through everything with a fine-tooth comb."

"There must be something else we can do." Chastity threw another shovel of coal on the fire.

"The bank," Prudence said suddenly. "We have to get access to his bank records."

Constance said from her perch on the arm of the sofa, "The bank manager must know you because you do all the dealings with the household accounts, maybe he'd be willing to let you look at Father's personal records."

Prudence shook her head. "Not Mr. Fitchley. He's a real stickler for the rules, and I'm sure he'd think an unauthorized examination of a personal account would be unethical." She paced restlessly to the window and stood looking out on the rain-drenched garden, drumming her fingers on the sill. "But maybe there's a way to get Father to sign an authorization for me," she said slowly.

"How so?" Chastity asked.

Prudence turned from the window and stood resting her palms on the sill behind her. "He signs things I put in front of him," she said, sounding so reluctant, it was almost as if the words were being dragged from her. "Bills, orders for the household, those kinds of things. Usually he doesn't bother to look at them." She watched her sisters as comprehension dawned.

"It's so deceitful," Chastity said with a tiny sigh. "I really hate the idea."

"We all do, love," Prudence said. "But I don't see any other way. I'll write an authorization and slip it into the middle of a pile of other papers and catch him this evening before we go to Con's. He'll have had a good lunch with Barclay, and by then he'll probably have had a whisky while he was dressing for dinner. He won't give anything a second glance."

"It is horrid," Constance said, "but I don't see we have any choice. Once you get the authorization you can go to the bank on Monday morning."

"I'll write it now." Prudence went to the secretaire and selected a sheet of paper headed with her father's crest. She took her pen and inscribed, "To Whom It May Concern."

Her sisters sat in silence until she had finished and blotted the ink. "Tell me if that seems official enough." She held it out to them.

"It might be even more convincing if we could get Father's seal for the envelope," Constance said, going over to the desk. "He keeps it in this drawer, I think." She opened the top drawer. "Yes, here it is. He doesn't usually lock it away, does he?"

Prudence shook her head. "Not as far as I know. Why would he? He's not expecting it to be misappropriated." There was a touch of irony in her otherwise dull tone. Then she shook her head again, as if dismissing her bleak thoughts. "We're doing it for his benefit, after all."

"That's exactly right," Chastity affirmed. "This is a case where the end definitely justifies the means."

Prudence took the paper back. "I'll put together some other papers, then, and get it over with this evening."

"I'd better go home," Constance said, rising to her feet. "Since this is my first official dinner party as Mrs. Ensor."

"Oh, what happened last night, at Downing Street?" Prudence asked, suddenly remembering. She'd been so taken up with their own concerns she'd forgotten to ask if anything significant had come out of the Ensors' dinner with the Prime Minister.

Constance smiled. "This whole business put it right out of my head. After the ladies had withdrawn, leaving the gentlemen to their port and cigars, the Prime Minister offered Max the Ministry of Transport."

"That's wonderful," her sisters said in unison. "He must be delighted."

"I think he'd have preferred the Foreign Office or the Home Office," Constance said with a grin. "Maybe even the Exchequer, but you have to start somewhere."

"I think it's amazing to get a Cabinet post after only one year on the back benches," Prudence said.

"Yes, so do I. And he really does seem quite pleased with himself. He was still smiling when he woke up this morning."

"Well, we can celebrate this evening," Chastity said, accompanying her sister to the door. "Eight o'clock?"

"Thereabouts," Constance said, kissing her sisters before hurrying down the stairs.

* * *

Prudence dressed for dinner early and then waited in the parlor until she heard her father's tread on the stair. She popped her head out. "Are you going to dress, Father?"

Lord Duncan paused on his way to his dressing room. "Yes. I won't be very long. What time are we expected?"

"Eight. Cobham will bring the barouche at quarter to," she said. "When you're ready, I'd like you to sign a few orders and bills for me. There are some papers to do with the estate at Romsey, a couple of tenant roofs that need to be replaced. I'd like to get them in the post on Monday."

Lord Duncan nodded agreeably. "I'll be down in the library in half an hour."

Prudence returned to the parlor and picked up the pile of papers she had assembled. For the tenth time, she riffled through them. And as before, the one she wanted hidden seemed to stick out like the proverbial sore thumb. But that was only because she knew it was there, she told herself.

Chastity came into the parlor, also dressed for the evening. "We'll do this together," she said, seeing her sister's strained expression. "Let's go down to the library and wait for him. Jenkins will bring us sherry, you look as if you could do with some Dutch courage."

Prudence nodded. "I need something, Chas." They went downstairs arm in arm. Jenkins was arranging some late chrysanthemums in a copper vase on the hall table. He turned to greet the sisters. "Where would you like sherry, Miss Prue?"

"In the library," Chastity answered. "Lord Duncan will be joining us there in a few minutes."

"I'll bring the whisky too, then," he said, standing back to survey his flower arrangement with a critical air. "I don't know why it is, but I don't seem to have your touch, Miss Chas."

"You don't need a touch, Jenkins," Chastity said with a smile, coming over to the table. "With chrysanths, all you need to do is pick them up, like so . . ." She lifted the flowers out of the vase. "And then drop them back and let them find their own arrangement. See?" She suited action to words and the big-headed blooms fell into a natural composition.

Jenkins shook his head. "I'll fetch the sherry."

Chastity laughed and followed her sister into the library. Prudence laid the papers on the table and stood back, looking at them. Then she approached them again, squared them off, and patted the top sheet. "It doesn't look natural," she said. "Perhaps I should just give them to him, put them in front of him when he sits down. What do you think?"

"I think that if you don't relax, Prue, you're going to make him suspect something the minute he walks in." Chastity leaned over the desk and spread the papers out a little as if they'd just been dumped there. "Where's his pen? Oh, here it is. I'll put it beside them. Now we'll both sit down, and when he comes in you can gesture to them very casually and ask him to sign them."

"Why are you so calm?" her sister asked, sitting on the sofa.

"Because you aren't," Chastity replied. "Only one of us at a time can panic."

That produced a smile from her sister just as Jenkins came in with a tray. Lord Duncan followed him. "Ah, good, Jenkins, whisky. You read my mind."

"Father you always have a whisky at this time of the evening," Prudence said lightly. "Jenkins doesn't have to be a mind reader." She rose from the sofa with a casual air. "The papers I need you to sign are on your desk. There's a pen there, I think. Oh, thank you, Jenkins." She took the sherry glass from the tray and was relieved to note that her hands were quite steady. She resumed her seat on the sofa.

Lord Duncan took a deep draught of his whisky and moved behind the desk. He didn't bother to sit down, merely picked up the pen and began to sign the papers. "Did you know that Max has been offered Secretary of Transport in the Cabinet?" Prudence asked swiftly as he set aside one signed order form and his eye ran down the paper beneath.

"Is this the farrier's bill?" he asked, picking it up and holding it close. "Don't recognize the name."

"No, he's new. He took over from Beddings," Prudence said. "Did you hear what I said about Max?"

Lord Duncan scrawled his signature on the paper and set it aside. His daughter's letter of authorization was now uppermost. It seemed to Prudence that it glared up at her father, trying to attract his attention. "Max," she said. "They were dining at Downing Street last night and the PM offered him a Cabinet post."

Her father looked up. "Well, how splendid," he declared. "Always knew he was going far. Constance did very well there. Transport, did you say?" As he spoke he scribbled his signature on Prudence's sheet.

"Yes," Chastity said, moving to the table. She leaned over and scooped the signed papers to one side, sliding the letter of authorization under the pile. "Constance joked that he'd have preferred the Exchequer or the Home Office, but of course he's very pleased." She straightened the remaining papers for him. "Just a couple more."

"Oh, yes." He resumed his task. "Better take something to celebrate this evening. How about a bottle of that Coburn's, the '20 vintage, Prudence? Ask Jenkins to bring one up."

"Yes, Father." Prudence went to the door, aware that her legs were like jelly and her palms wet. "I think there's only one bottle left."

Her father gave an exaggerated sigh. "Always the way these days. Whenever I ask for something special, there's only one bottle left . . . if we're lucky enough to have any, that is. Never mind. Bring it up anyway. It's not every day a man's son-in-law is given a Cabinet post."

Prudence left the library and stood for a minute in the hall, leaning against the closed door while she waited for her heart to settle down. She'd been frozen in her seat the minute the incriminating paper had been revealed. But it was done . . . over. Thank God for Chastity's quick thinking. Now all she had to do was visit Mr. Fitchley at Hoare's Bank on Piccadilly. There must be something there. There *had* to be.

Chapter 11

"There." Prudence pressed her father's seal into the melted wax on the envelope that contained the bank authorization. She glanced out of the library window. It was barely dawn and only she and Chastity were up in the silent house. Lord Duncan was snoring sonorously after a late night of bridge and substantial quantities of Coburn's 1820 vintage.

"Let's go back to bed," Chastity suggested, hugging her dressing gown closely around her.

"You go, I'm wide awake now," her sister said, returning the seal to its drawer. "I'll make some tea and read a little. I have to be ready to leave at eight-thirty anyway."

"It's barely six now," her sister pointed out, yawning. "I'll see you at breakfast."

"Eight o'clock," Prudence said, closing the drawer gently. She glanced around to make sure everything was in its place, then extinguished the gas lamp and followed Chastity from the room.

In the house on Pall Mall Place Gideon too was up and about at the crack of dawn. He rarely slept more than a few hours a night and he found himself even more wakeful than usual. Prudence Duncan wouldn't leave his mind. He felt challenged by her, as if she herself was a case he had to win. He had not seen her the previous day, but he had not stopped thinking about her . . . or rather, he corrected himself swiftly, about the case and her role in it. Part of his job as a barrister was to coach witnesses. And since Prudence Duncan was the only witness he was going to have, he couldn't afford any mistakes.

He ran hot water into the basin in the bathroom and began to shave. Lathering his face with slow circular movements, he contemplated the day he had planned. He had decided that their next meeting should be in different surroundings, somewhere removed from the official background of chambers and law books. Even his library in his own house was more like an office. He wanted to see what she was like when she was relaxed, in a more social frame of mind.

He drew his razor through the lather, frowning at his reflection in the mirror. He wanted to catch her off guard. Would she make a better witness if she was not on the defensive, not combative, not challenging? He had provoked this response from her, and he was obliged to admit it had not always been intentional. There was something about the way they reacted to each other, the proverbial oil and water, which he didn't quite understand because he couldn't control it. However, he had certainly intended to see how she would respond under pressure. He knew now from his own bristling reaction that a judge and jury were not going to sympathize with her in that guise.

He washed off the lather, burying his face in a steaming washcloth with a little sigh of pleasure. He peered closely in the mirror to make sure he hadn't missed a spot, before stepping into his bath. He slipped down beneath the surface of the water, wondering if the day he had planned for them would achieve his goal.

He wanted, no, needed, to soften her reactions, persuade her that she would have to appeal to the male responses in the courtroom, appeal to masculine sympathy. Convincing her of that necessity would not be an easy task, he was under no illusions on that score. She would initially see it as weakness, as evidence that her case was not just if she had to resort to acting. But if he could get her in the right frame of mind, one where she quite naturally lost her combative edge, then perhaps he'd have a better chance. So long as he didn't inadvertently put her back up. She was as prickly as a blackberry bush.

Nevertheless, he was feeling in a relatively optimistic frame of mind when he went down to the breakfast parlor. Sarah, in riding dress, was consuming a mound of scrambled eggs. She greeted him with a sunny smile. "Milton said he was bringing the motor around. Are you going somewhere, Daddy?"

"For a drive in the country," he said, bending to kiss the top of her head.

"There's deviled kidneys for you." The girl gestured to the covered dishes on the sideboard. "Are you going for a drive on your own?"

Gideon helped himself to kidneys. "No," he said. "With a client." He sat down and took up the newspaper.

"With Miss Duncan?"

Now, how had she guessed that? He gave his daughter a rather exasperated glance over the top of the *Times*. "As it happens."

"But you don't usually see clients on a Sunday. And you don't go for drives with them." She drank from a cup of milky coffee and took a piece of toast from the rack.

"There's a first time for everything."

Sarah spread butter and then marmalade on her toast. "Do you like Miss Duncan?"

There was something deceptively casual about her tone. Her father shrugged and turned to the editorial page with a decisive crackle of paper. "That's hardly to the point. She's my client."

"Do you think she's pretty?" The question was muffled by a mouthful of toast and marmalade.

"Don't talk with your mouth full."

She swallowed, dabbed her mouth with her napkin. "But do you?"

Gideon folded the paper beneath the leader. "No," he said definitely, without taking his eyes off the printed page. "That is not a word I would use to describe Miss Duncan."

Sarah looked disappointed. "I think she is."

"Well, you are entitled to your opinion." He set down the paper and looked across at her, his tone softening. "What are your plans for the day?"

"Oh, I'm going riding in the park with Isabelle this morning. Then she's coming back here and Mrs. Keith is making us Sunday lunch of roast chicken with blancmange for pudding. Yesterday we went to Madame Tussaud's exhibition." Her eyes gleamed. "There's a real chamber of horrors there, with an actual French guillotine. Well, it's wax, of course, but they say you can't tell the difference."

Gideon grimaced slightly. "I expect you could if you were about to lose your head to it."

Sarah laughed. "You're so silly, Daddy. Of course you could tell. The wax one would bend."

He laughed with her. "Did Mary take you?"

"No, Isabelle's governess. Mary's gone to visit her sister for the weekend. Did you forget?"

"I suppose I must have done. Hadn't you better get ready?"

Sarah pushed back her chair and came round to him. He put an arm around her waist and hugged her to him. "Don't fall off your horse, will you?"

She laughed again at the absurdity of such an idea, and kissed his cheek. "What time will you be back?"

"I'm not sure exactly. It's quite a long drive, so probably after you're in bed." She nodded cheerfully and danced her way from the room. Gideon, still smiling, returned to his kidneys and newspaper in peace.

* * *

The black Rover drew up at the curb punctually at eight-thirty that morning. "He's here," Chastity said from the parlor window where she'd been watching the Square. "Driving himself, no chauffeur. He looks very dapper this morning. You get your things and I'll run down and tell him you're on your way." She whisked out of the parlor.

Prudence went to her own bedroom, where she studied her reflection for a moment in the cheval glass. She smoothed the long jacket of her mulberry-colored wool suit over her hips and shook out the pleats of the long skirt, which was edged with darker red braid. She was aware of a certain nervousness, a slightly swifter heartbeat than usual, and her pale complexion was tinged with rose. Why she should feel so unsettled, she couldn't imagine. Gideon Malvern didn't alarm her.

Did he? Ridiculous idea. She'd handled him perfectly well from their first meeting, and while their preparation session today might be a little unpleasant, she knew that it was only intended to armor her against the much greater unpleasantness she could face in court. But she couldn't help wishing her sisters were coming along for the ride. There was strength in numbers. But what on earth did she need strength for, she demanded crossly of herself. He was just a man. A perfectly ordinary man. She'd been alone with men often enough. And she'd never felt this anxiety on those occasions.

She shook her head as if to dismiss the buzzing of her thoughts, and slipped on the fawn silk-and-alpaca dust coat that would protect her dress from the dust of the road, and tied a heavy silk veil over her felt hat. She could drop the veil over her face if the dust was really bad. But where were they going? Why had he come for her in the motor? Perhaps they were just going to his house again and he was being overly polite by coming to escort her in broad daylight. No, she decided. That was not Gideon's way.

She pulled on her leather gloves, picked up her purse, handkerchief, notebook, and pencil, and Lord Barclay's note, and dropped them all into the deep pockets of the dust coat, then went downstairs.

Gideon and Chastity were talking in the hall, the front door ajar behind them. He was wearing a wolfskin coat and a flat woolen motoring cap with a visor. He was definitely dressed for something more than a short drive through the London streets.

He turned and smiled at her as she came down the stairs, then the smile vanished. "No," he said decisively, "that won't do at all."

"What won't?" she demanded, taken aback.

"What you're wearing. You'll freeze to death. It's sunny but it's cold."

"But we won't be in the motor for long?" she protested.

He ignored the hanging question, merely repeating, "You'll freeze to death. You must have something warmer."

"The fur, Prue?" Chastity suggested with a tiny shrug.

"It seems so unnecessary. It's only October and the sun's shining."

"If you have fur, I'd really suggest you go and put it on," he said, making a big effort to sound conciliatory. "Trust me, you'll need it."

Prudence hesitated. For a minute she almost laughed, because the effort he was making to subdue his customary imperiousness was so obvious. She was tempted to question it but then decided to honor the attempt. She turned back to the stairs.

The sisters had inherited a silver fox coat, hood, and muff from their mother, as well as three strands of matchless pearls. They shared both jewelry and furs according to whose need was greatest. Prudence took them out of the cedar chest in the linen room, where they had resided throughout the summer, and held up the coat. It smelled faintly of cedar, but unlike the dress she'd worn the other evening, not of moth-balls.

She tossed aside the dust coat and slipped the fur on. Immediately she felt invested with an aura of luxury and elegance. It was a wonderfully extravagant garment with a high collar that caressed her neck. The hood fitted closely over her head, hugging her ears, but revealing the carefully arranged russet curls on her forehead. She buried her gloved hands in the muff and decided with a grin that even if she was roasting it was well worth it for the effect. She didn't need a mirror to tell her she looked stunning. She took a second to transfer the contents of the dust coat's pockets into the muff and went back downstairs.

Chastity was still in the hall, but there was no sign of Gideon. "You look fabulous, Prue."

"I know," Prudence said. "This coat always has that effect, whoever wears it. Where is he?"

"He'd left the motor running and he didn't want to leave it unattended."

"Did he say where we were going?"

Chastity shook her head. "I tried to ask but he just said you might be late this evening and we weren't to worry, you were in safe hands."

"Ye gods, he's *impossible*," Prudence exclaimed. "Does he think women like to be pushed around like that?"

"I don't think he can help it," Chastity said, laughing slightly.

The blast of a horn from outside made them both jump. Prudence threw up her hands and Jenkins moved smoothly across the hall to open the door. "I believe Sir Gideon is waiting, Miss Prue."

"I wonder how you guessed," she said. She gave Chastity a quick kiss. "I'll see you later."

"Good luck."

Prudence hesitated. "Why would I need good luck, Chas?"

Chastity shrugged. "I don't know, it just seems that you might."

Another imperative blast of the horn sounded and Prudence raised her eyes heavenward and hurried outside.

Gideon stood beside the car, one foot on the running board, one hand resting on the horn mounted on the dashboard. His eyes widened as Prudence came running down the steps. "I should really have a horse-drawn sledge and a frozen Russian lake for you," he observed.

"The horses would have run off by now with that blasted horn," Prudence said with asperity. "There was no need for that."

"I know, I'm sorry," he said. "I do try for moderation, but I am a little short on patience, I'm afraid." He opened the door for her, spoiling the apologetic effect with the unwise addition, "But you'll get used to me."

"I'm not sure that's an overriding goal," Prudence murmured, stepping into the motor.

"I beg your pardon?" He stood holding the door.

"Nothing," she said with a sweet smile. "I have a habit of talking to myself. You'll get used to me." She tucked her legs neatly under the dashboard.

He raised his eyebrows, closed the door on her, and went around to take his own seat. "Oh, you'd better put these on." He reached into the back and felt around. "Here." He handed her a pair of tinted goggles in wide metal-and-leather frames. "They should fit over your glasses."

He put on a pair himself as Prudence examined the ones he'd given her. "Why would I need these?"

"To protect your eyes, of course. The wind can be fierce when you're driving." He put the motor in gear and the car moved smoothly forward.

"You must need very little sleep if you always start your day this early," Prudence observed, still turning the goggles around in her hands. "It is a weekend, after all."

"Forgive me if I stole your beauty sleep," he said cheerfully. "But even driving at twenty miles an hour, it'll take us nearly three hours to get where we're going."

"Three hours!" Prudence turned sideways to stare at him. "Where in the devil's name are we going?"

"It's a surprise," he said. "I told you, I think, that surprise is frequently the essence of a successful campaign."

"In the law courts," she said.

"Oh, certainly there," he agreed with a laugh. "But, as you so rightly say, today is Sunday, so we won't talk about the law."

"But I thought we were going to prepare for the trial."

"Well, we are, in a way, but not as we have been doing. We don't want to waste a beautiful day with too much stress and strain on the nerves. Besides, in general I like to keep my weekends free from excessive work. It ensures my mind stays fresh."

Prudence could think of nothing to say immediately. She was sitting in this motor going God only knew where, for reasons not vouchsafed, with a man she disliked more by the minute. "So you lied," she said finally. "Just to inveigle me into spending the day with you."

"That's a little harsh," he protested, smiling slightly. "I have told you once before that getting to know you is a very important part of my preparation."

There was really very little objection she could raise to what was a perfectly logical aim. "I would have thought you'd spend your Sundays at least with your daughter," she said.

"Oh, Sarah has better things to do this Sunday," he responded. "Her day is packed to the minute, she has no time to spare for her father."

"I see." Their speed had picked up and she was conscious now of the wind making her eyes water. Resigned, she put on the goggles and turned to look at her companion.

For some reason he was smiling, and even though she couldn't see his eyes behind the goggles, she knew the skin around them would be crinkling and there would be little dancing lights in their gray depths. His mouth had not become less sensual since she'd last seen him and the cleft in his chin seemed even more pronounced. She dragged her gaze away and stared out at the road ahead, tucking her hands deeper into her muff. "So, where are we going, Gideon?"

"Oxford," he said. "We should be there just in time for luncheon at the Randolph. Then, if it's not too cold, I thought we could take a punt along the river. But you're so well wrapped that it wouldn't matter much if it was snowing."

"We're driving fifty miles there and fifty miles back in *one* day?"

"I love to drive," he said with a complacent smile. "And I love this motor. It'll do twenty miles an hour without a problem. It's a beautiful day, if a bit nippy. Do you have any objections?"

"It didn't occur to you that I might have plans for this afternoon?" she said tightly.

"It did, but I assumed you would have sent me a message if my invitation wasn't convenient." He glanced sideways at her and his smile deepened. "I did try very hard to make it sound like an invitation and not a summons. I hope I succeeded."

Prudence was obliged to concede this point. "It was a rather more politely couched summons than your usual," she said.

"Oh, that is so ungenerous," he exclaimed. "I'm trying to reform my manner and you won't give me the least credit."

"I have no interest in your manner of conducting yourself," she stated. "I am interested only in how you conduct yourself in court. And, on that subject, I have some information that might interest you."

Miss Duncan was as tough a nut to crack as he'd expected, he reflected ruefully. Women usually responded when he took the trouble to turn on his charm. He took one hand off the wheel and held it up. "Let me enjoy my Sunday a little first, Prudence. Get the cobwebs out of my head. There'll be time enough for work later."

And there really wasn't anything she could say to that. The man was entitled to a little rest and relaxation now and again. Her fingers closed over the notebook in her muff. Ah, now, there was a topic to be explored.

"Well, maybe we could work on something else, then," she said, taking out the notebook. "Since we're going to be sitting side by side for the next three hours, we might as well do something productive." She opened the notebook and sucked thoughtfully on the end of the pencil.

Gideon looked a little alarmed. "What are you talking about?"

"Have you forgotten that we're charged with finding a suitable candidate for you to marry?" Prudence inquired in mock surprise.

He sighed. "Not that again. I'm not in the mood, Prudence."

"I'm sorry," she said. "But you agreed to consider our suggestions. If we can find you a bride it will make the difference between twenty percent and a hundred percent of our damages. And that's deadly serious business to us."

He shook his head. "You really *are* a terrier. All right, if you want to play this game, then let's play it."

"It's not a game," Prudence said. "And I insist that you treat it seriously. We've drawn up a list of qualities that we think will be important to you. If you would just assign a number, on a scale of one to five, to each one as I go through them, that would be a great help."

"Fire away," he invited, assembling his features into a suitably earnest expression.

Prudence shot him a suspicious look. She couldn't see his eyes behind his goggles but there was a telltale twitch to the corner of his mouth. "First, age," she said. "Do you have a preference?"

He pursed his mouth. "I don't think so."

"Oh, you must have some idea," Prudence exclaimed. "Does the idea of a young woman in her first season appeal, or would you rather meet someone of more mature years?"

He seemed to give the matter some thought as he swung the motorcar around a stolidly plodding horse and cart. The driver cursed and waved his whip at them as the horse shied, and the motor sped ahead in a cloud of dust.

"One of these days people are not going to turn a hair when they see a motor," Gideon observed. "They'll be the only way to get around."

"Something will have to be done about the roads, in that case," Prudence said as the vehicle bumped violently into a muddy rut. "They're not designed for something traveling at this speed."

"The Royal Automobile Club is lobbying Parliament for better roads. Are you getting dreadfully bounced around?"

"I'm not wonderfully comfortable," she said. "But please don't let the prospect of my discomfort for the next three hours affect your plans in any way."

"It's not that bad," he said. "And we'll stop for coffee in Henley. I'll need to refill the fuel tank then anyway, and you can stretch your legs."

"How nice to have something to look forward to." She returned to her notebook. "You haven't answered my question. What age would you like your wife to be? Within about five years."

"Extreme youth is very tedious for a man my age. Inexperience is equally so. I have no interest in educating a virgin in the ways of the bedroom."

This, Prudence reflected, was rather more information than her question had sought. However, the more information they had, the better able they would be to find a suitable match, so she merely nodded in a matter-of-fact way. "So, a mature woman would suit you."

"Mature . . . now, I'm not so sure about that," he responded. "It's a word that conjures up images of desperate spinsters or languishing widows. I don't think either category would suit me. Of course," he added, "you have taken into account the difficulties inherent in matching a forty-year-old divorced father of a ten-year-old daughter with an eligible woman."

"We decided that those difficulties were more relevant for a woman than a man," Prudence said. "You have much to recommend you."

"How kind. I'm flattered."

"Don't be. I merely meant that your profession and your financial situation will probably compensate for your disadvantages with all but the most rigid adherents to the social code."

"Oh, I see. I am suitably put in my place."

Prudence was aware of a most inconvenient urge to laugh. She suppressed it sternly and said, "So, we're looking for someone in her early thirties perhaps? Not over thirty-five. I know you didn't like the sound of Agnes Hargate with her son, but are you averse to widows in general?"

"No. So long as she be not languishing in her maturity. Neither would I object to a spinster, as long as she be not desperate in hers." He glanced sideways at her. "But I think thirty-five is a little too old for what I had in mind. Maybe you could look for someone in her late twenties." He nodded. "Yes, the more I think about it, the more I realize that late twenties would be the perfect age."

"All right," Prudence said, making a note in her book. "That gives us somewhere to start." She knew perfectly well what he was doing and she was not going to allow him to do it. He would not discompose her. She took a breath and asked casually, "Now, must she be beautiful?"

"Beauty is in the eye of the beholder."

"Don't be glib. Do a woman's looks matter to you?"

"Let's leave that question. I don't know the answer," he said, sounding serious for the first time.

Prudence shrugged. "Education, then? How important is that on a scale of one to five?"

"Well, until a week or so ago I would have said about two and a half. Now it's definitely a five."

Prudence wrote it down. He looked at her again. "Aren't you going to ask what changed my mind?"

"No," she said firmly. "It's not relevant. What kind of personality do you like?"

"Oh, meek and mild," he said definitely. "A woman who knows her place, who knows when to hold her tongue, who knows that I know best."

That was too much. Prudence snapped the notebook shut and thrust it back into her muff. "All right, if you won't take this seriously—"

"But I answered your question," he protested. "Wouldn't you assume that someone as arrogant and combative and self-opinionated as myself would want a helpmeet who would revel in those qualities—"

"Qualities," Prudence interrupted. "They're not qualities, they're vices."

"Ah. I stand corrected." He turned the motor into a narrow lane at a signpost that said HENLEY, 2 MILES.

Prudence fell silent, watching the passing autumnal countryside through her tinted goggles as the wind whipped past her fur-encased ears. The fields were brown stubble, the hedgerows rich with luscious blackberries and crimson holly berries.

"And they're vices you agree I have?" Gideon's question in his quiet voice startled her out of a moment's unquiet reverie.

"I told you earlier, I'm not interested in anything about you except what relates to your ability to win this case," she stated.

"Then let's talk about you," he said. "Has marriage ever tempted you, Prudence?"

"How is that question related to our suit?"

He seemed to consider this before saying, "I would prefer it in court that you didn't come across as an ill-tempered, man-hating, embittered spinster."

Prudence inhaled sharply, but he was continuing calmly, "As I've said before, you can be certain that Barclay's barrister will do everything he can to put you in an unfavorable light. I would like to give them a warmhearted, crusading female who is out to protect the most vulnerable of her own sex from hurt and exploitation. A woman gentle of tongue but resolute. A woman who has only the softest feelings towards the male of the species, except those who are patently not deserving of softness."

Prudence shifted slightly in her seat, suddenly feeling unsure of herself. "Do I really come across in an unfavorable light?"

Again he considered before saying mildly, "On occasion. When your hackles are raised. I'd like you to be able to control that response."

"Because they will try to provoke it in court."

"I think you should be prepared for it."

Prudence was silent. He had every right to point that out, and she couldn't help but recognize its truth. But it was a wretchedly uncomfortable recognition nevertheless.

Chapter 12

They were driving down the high street in Henley-on-Thames now. The pavements were crowded with Sunday-morning strollers, the green lawns edging the river dotted with pedestrians enjoying the sunshine. A few rowboats were on the river and Prudence realized that the air was a lot warmer now. But that, of course, could have something to do with the fact that their speed had slowed to a crawl and in her fur casing she was beginning to feel like a hibernating bear.

Gideon spun the wheel and turned under an archway into the cobbled back court of an Elizabethan timbered inn. He turned off the engine and jumped down. Prudence was too eager to make her own descent to await his help and stepped down, resisting the inelegant urge to rub her backside that seemed rather numb after the jolting drive.

"Go in and order coffee," he said. "I'll join you in about five minutes when I've put more fuel in the engine." He hauled out a can labeled PRATTS MOTOR SPIRIT from the enclosed compartment at the rear of the motor.

Prudence stretched and rolled her shoulders, then took off her hood and the fur coat. "It's far too hot for these." She laid them on the passenger seat of the car. "I'll see you inside."

The Dog and Partridge had a comfortable parlor just off the saloon bar. A cheerful maid promised coffee and currant buns and directed Prudence to the ladies' lounge. When she emerged, refreshed, her hair tidied, she found Gideon already sitting in the bow window, pouring coffee. "I'd suggest we take a walk along the river but I want to be in Oxford for luncheon," he said as she sat down.

"Why do we have to go all that way? Why don't we stop here?" Prudence selected a sugar-sprinkled currant bun from the plate.

Gideon frowned, as if puzzled by the question. "I intended to drive to Oxford," he said.

"But you could change your mind," Prudence said, regarding him quizzically. It occurred to her that perhaps he couldn't.

As if in confirmation, he said, "When I've made a plan, I like to stick to it."

"Like to, or need to?"

He added sugar to his coffee with careful deliberation. It was not a question he'd ever asked himself, but the answer was immediate. "Need," he said. He looked across at her with a rather rueful smile. "Does that make me very rigid and pedantic?"

She nodded, and drank some coffee. "I would say so. I'll need to bear that in mind when I'm looking at candidates. Some women find that quite comforting . . . knowing that someone isn't going to change his mind."

"Somehow I think that you are not one of them," he observed, taking a bite of currant bun.

"Spot on," she said with a cool smile, breaking a tiny piece off her bun.

"We seem to be concentrating on my character flaws this morning," Gideon observed. "I *had* been hoping for a pleasant day of getting to know one another."

"Isn't that what we're doing? Flaws and all?" she inquired. "And on that subject, if Barclay's barrister is going to attack me, wouldn't it be better if you asked me first the hostile questions he might ask . . . spike his guns, as it were. Then I might be able to respond with proper composure."

"That was one of the tactics I was considering," he conceded. "But whenever I start to ask them, you attack with all the ferocity of a swarm of hornets."

"Ah, but that was because I hadn't realized it was a tactic. Now I know that it's just preparation and you're not expressing your own views, I'll practice moderating my responses." She took off her glasses and rubbed them on a napkin, unaware that it was a reflex action whenever she felt on her mettle. "Am I right to assume that you *aren't* expressing your own views?"

"It wouldn't matter if I were. My views are not at issue here." He pushed aside his coffee cup and sat back in the deep leather armchair. The light was dim in the low-ceilinged parlor, and the diamond-paned windows let in little sunshine. In the gloom he noticed how her hair glowed a rich copper and how her eyes were a brilliant glinting green in the smooth cream oval of her face.

"To answer an earlier question," he said, "I have decided that a woman's personal appearance is very important to me."

Prudence set down her coffee cup. "She must be beautiful?"

He shook his head. "No, not at all. Interesting . . . unconventional. Those are the adjectives I would choose."

"I see."

"Aren't you going to write that down?"

"My notebook is in the motor." She wanted to glare at him; she wanted to smile at him. But instinct told her she could do neither. Not unless she was prepared to let down her guard. He was trying to draw her into playing this game of allurement. It wasn't naked seduction, it wasn't as banal as flirtation, it was just a beguiling invitation to join the dance. And a little voice that she tried to ignore was questioning: *Why not join the dance?*

The answer, however, was as clear as day. She . . . her sisters . . . they all needed this man's complete professional attention. *She* needed his single-minded professional attention on the issue, or she'd lose her own. There was no room for anything but a purely business relationship with the barrister. And besides, she reminded herself, she disliked him excessively.

When it was clear that he was not going to get a more interesting reaction, he said neutrally, "Ready to continue?" He stood up, shoveling a handful of coins from his pocket onto the table.

"Since Oxford needs to be the destination," she said, rising in her turn.

"You will enjoy it," he promised, moving ahead of her to open the door to the bright, sunlit outdoors. "And I own, I'm curious to see how well I remember punting. It's been nigh on twenty years." He gave an exaggerated sigh. Prudence closed her lips firmly. She was not going to give him the compliment he was fishing for. She was not going to join this dance.

"I don't think I need this fur," she commented when they returned to the motor. She folded it carefully over the back of her seat.

"You'll need the hood and the goggles," Gideon said, putting on his own goggles. "And I think you'll find in a few minutes that you need the coat. Once we're on the open road." He put on his own coat then turned his attention to the crank that would start the engine. It sprang to life after a couple of turns and he stowed the crank and climbed behind the wheel, saying as cheerfully as if he was not beginning to feel disheartened, "Ever upwards and onwards."

"How far is it from here?"

"About twenty miles. We should do it in an hour, or just over. The road's quite good. I'll be able to open her up."

Prudence fastened the hood beneath her chin, reflecting that his clear enthusiasm at the prospect of bouncing along rutted roads at top speed was not something she could share. She pulled the fur coat up over her shoulders as the rushing air chilled her anew and rather gloomily contemplated the prospect of the three-hour return journey. By the time they left Oxford, the sun would be going down and the air would be even colder. Her companion, who was humming contentedly to himself, obviously had no such qualms.

"Are you ever free in the afternoons?" she asked.

Gideon stopped humming. "Unless I'm actually in court, or have a business meeting, I can be," he said. "Why?"

"We usually use our At Homes to introduce likely couples. I was thinking that you could vet some of the possibilities one afternoon."

A terrier with a bone, no other description would do. He sighed and accepted the inevitable. "And do you have any possibilities in mind? Apart from this Agnes Whatever-Her-Name-Is."

"Hargate," she said. "And I really think you're doing yourself a disservice by not at least meeting her. You would like her very much. You haven't even listened to a description."

"I had an instinctive reaction," he stated. "The minute you mentioned her, I knew we would not get on at all."

Prudence surveyed him with growing irritation. "I don't know how you can be so certain."

"Well, I am."

Prudence opened her notebook again. She looked at the few names that she and her sisters had come up with. "All right, let's try again. You might get on well with Lavender Riley. I'm sure I could get her to come to an At Home if you were available on a Wednesday."

"No," he said firmly.

"No, you wouldn't be available on a Wednesday?"

"No, I would not be interested in Lavender Riley."

"How could you possibly know that? I haven't told you anything about her." Exasperation rang in her voice.

"You told me her name. I forgot to mention that names are very important to me. Perhaps you should write that in your little book. I could not possibly live with someone called Lavender."

"That is so ridiculous. You could give her another name . . . a pet name."

"I find the whole concept of pet names quite revolting," he said. "Besides, everyone else would be calling her Lavender. I'd never get away from it."

"If you're just going to make frivolous objections—" She stopped abruptly. She was just laying herself open to mockery by persisting, and she wasn't going to encourage him any further.

However, it seemed he didn't need any encouragement. He continued blithely into her frozen silence, "Now, the names of the virtues I find most appealing. Hope——"

"Hope is not a virtue," Prudence snapped.

"Oh, I think a hopeful character is a virtuous one," he demurred. "But Charity is an appealing name; Patience, I like. Oh, and Prudence, of course. Now, that's a very attractive name, if a rather stolid virtue."

Prudence clasped her hands inside her muff and refused to smile.

He glanced at her and grinned. "Come on," he said. "I can see you want to laugh. Your eyes are shining."

"You can't possibly see what my eyes are doing behind these goggles."

"I can imagine them very easily. Your mouth is quivering just the tiniest fraction, and when it does that your eyes sparkle. I've noticed often."

"Considering what little reason I've had to smile in your company since we first met, I find that an unlikely observation."

"It was intended as a compliment," he said rather plaintively.

"An empty one, in that case." She shrank deeper into her coat as the motor's speed increased and the wind whistled by.

"You are a very stubborn woman," Gideon said. "I had planned a delightful day out and you're doing your level best to spoil it."

Prudence turned sideways in her seat to face him. "*You* had planned a delightful day out. Without one word of consultation with me. Without a moment's consideration of my own possible plans, or indeed of my wishes. And now you're accusing *me,* who was dragged along willy-nilly, of spoiling *your* plans. You said we were going to work on the case."

"Well, we are, but unfortunately it's not going as well as I had hoped," he said. "I wanted to see how you are when you're relaxed, comfortable, not on the offensive . . . or defensive. I had thought that if I provided the right situation and surroundings, you would show me that side of yourself. If such a side exists," he added a shade dryly. "If it doesn't, this is indeed a wasted day."

Prudence was silent for a minute. Then she said, "It does, actually. Why do you need to see it?"

"Because that's the side that's going to win this case for us," he said simply. "I want the warm, intelligent, compassionate Prudence Duncan on the witness stand. Can you give her to me?"

There was silence then between them. Prudence was absorbed in her own reflections and assumed her companion was in his. It was such a simple, reasonable explanation, and she was beginning to wonder why she had resisted the appeal of this outing, fighting his efforts to charm her, disarm her, amuse her, with such dogged persistence. There was surely no need to do so, not when his objective was so directly related to their libel suit.

Gideon broke the silence finally. "It's a lovely day, we have a delicious lunch waiting for us, followed by a quiet trip on the river. We'll stop for dinner in Henley on the way back, and then you can sleep the rest of the way home curled up in your furs. How could you possibly resist such a prospect?"

"It is irresistible," she responded, feeling the tension suddenly leave her shoulders. She hadn't even realized how tightly clenched her muscles had been, as if she had been arming herself against something. "If you promise not to annoy me, I will show you my other side."

"I can't promise," he said, turning to smile at her. "Sometimes it's inadvertent. I'll ask that you give me the benefit of the doubt if something slips."

"All right," she agreed. "Just for today. But in return I ask that you listen to two things about the case that I have to tell you. We don't need to discuss them, but you need to hear them so that you can think about what we should do."

"Fire away."

"First, my father is going to take the stand as a character witness for Barclay." She watched for his reaction but there was none. He merely nodded.

"Don't you see how awkward . . . in fact, terrible . . . that is?"

"Not really."

"But you'll have to attack Father."

"I will attempt to shake his faith in his friend's probity, certainly."

"But you won't be unpleasant to Father?"

"Not unless he makes it necessary."

Prudence absorbed this. He sounded so matter-of-fact and unperturbed by what for her was a hideous prospect. "I'm afraid he might recognize me . . . or my voice, rather," she said after a minute. "I don't know if I can disguise my voice well enough to fool him."

"What did you have in mind?" he asked curiously.

Prudence chuckled. They had decided she should adopt the accent Chastity had used when meeting their first paying client, Anonymous, at the very beginning of the Go-Between venture.

"Oh, but I am from Paris, *moi*. *En France* we do not ask ze ladies such questions. *Non, non, c'est pas comme il faut*, you comprend? Ze Mayfair

Lady, she is most *respectable*. *Vraiment respectable*. Respectable, that is what you say over 'ere, *n'est ce pas?*"

"Can you keep it up?" Gideon demanded through his laughter.

"I don't see why not," Prudence said airily. "My French is good enough to combine the language enough to add a little confusion to the mix, while still not making myself completely incomprehensible. I thought that would be a good idea."

"A mysterious, veiled French lady," Gideon mused. "It'll certainly be intriguing. It might also make you seem more sympathetic. Your regular Englishman is fascinated by the somewhat—how shall I put it?—somewhat *uninhibited* reputation of the French female. They might be rather less hostile to the views expressed in *The Mayfair Lady* if they believe they're perpetrated by a woman not of their own kind. A woman who might be expected to be a little outrageous."

"So, it's a good strategy all around," Prudence declared.

"It'll serve if you can hold it together in the face of some fairly relentless interrogation."

"I'll practice with my sisters," she promised.

"It will also depend upon your identity remaining hidden at the time of the trial," he reminded her. "As I said before, I can promise you that the prosecution will do everything they can to discover your identity. They're probably setting a search in motion already."

"We're going to discover next week if there have been any strange inquiries at the various places that distribute *The Mayfair Lady*."

"Sensible," he said. "So, what's the second thing?"

Prudence reached into her muff for the earl of Barclay's note, and read it to him. "It's not dated, but it's certainly not recent."

"It's not good enough," he stated. "Find this schedule of payments, find me dates, find out what your father was buying. I'm not opening this can of worms without unshakable evidence."

"You could surely question the earl about it," she said, bristling at his brusque dismissal despite their earlier compact. "Maybe rattle him a little."

He shook his head. "No, it's not sufficient even to bring the subject up. You'll have to dig deeper."

"Well, as it happens, I have authorization to examine his bank records. I'll go to Hoare's tomorrow."

"How did you get that?" His surprise was evident.

Prudence huddled deeper into the coat, turning the collar up. "It was a trick. Not one I'm proud of, so can we leave it at that?"

"Of course," he said instantly. "Are you cold?" His quiet voice was now concerned and sympathetic.

"A little," she admitted, although it was not really a bodily cold, more an internal chill.

"We'll be there in less than half an hour. See the spires?" He gestured with one hand towards a faint outline on the horizon. Oxford's gleaming spires in the valley below them.

"It's strange, but I've never been to Oxford," Prudence said, resolutely putting aside her depressing thoughts. "Cambridge, yes. But never Oxford."

"I prefer Oxford, but then I'm prejudiced."

"You were at New College?"

He nodded, then placed a hand on her knee. It was a fleeting touch but it felt oddly significant to Prudence. In fact, she realized this whole journey had taken on a significance that she couldn't identify. But it was more than the sum of its parts. A lot more.

They drove up in front of the Randolph Hotel on Beaumont Street just as the city's clocks chimed noon. Prudence stepped down and stretched her shoulders again. The sun was very warm, more like early summer than autumn, and once again she discarded her furs.

Gideon scooped them off the seat. "We'll take them inside. They'll be safer than lying on the seat in the open."

A doorman hurried to escort them into the lofty hall of the hotel. An elegant sweep of staircase led to the upper floors. "The ladies' lounge is upstairs," Gideon said. "I'll wait for you at the table." He strode off to the restaurant.

When Prudence joined him, he was perusing the wine list. A glass of champagne sat by her place.

"I took the liberty of ordering you an aperitif," he said. "If you'd rather have something else . . ."

"No," she said, "this is lovely." She sat down and took a sip from the glass. "It does seem to cheer one up."

"And I get the impression you need cheering up," he said. "Let me try for the rest of the day to do just that." He leaned over and placed a hand over hers on the tablecloth. "Will you?"

Oh, yes, Prudence thought, this day was very much more than the sum of its parts. She slid her hand out from under his quite gently and opened her menu. "What do you recommend? I assume you know the dining room."

"I know it well," he said, accepting her change of subject. If she wouldn't give him a spontaneous answer, then he wasn't going to press for one. He had his pride, and he was not accustomed to rejection, but he allowed none of his pique to show, saying coolly, "The kitchen is very good. How hungry are you?"

"Starving."

He examined his own menu. "Saddle of lamb," he suggested. "Unless you'd prefer the Dover sole."

"Lamb sounds good," she said. "I'm not feeling fishy. What should I have to start?"

"The smoked mackerel pâte is delicious, but if you're not in a fishy mood . . ." He frowned at the menu. "Vichyssoise, perhaps?"

"Yes, perfect." Prudence closed her menu, took off her glasses to rub them on her napkin, and gave him a smile. Gideon was not prepared for the effect of a smile that he had seen all too rarely. When combined with the luster it gave to her lively green eyes, it was quite stunning. It was something of a consolation prize, he decided, but it was not one to be sneezed at.

"Burgundy or claret?" he asked, picking up the wine list again.

"I'm more in a claret mood."

"Then, a *bon Bordeaux* it shall be."

Prudence sipped her champagne and leaned back in her chair, looking out of the long windows at the Martyrs' Memorial in the little square opposite, and the bicycling undergraduates, their black gowns flapping as they pedaled vigorously along St. Giles. Her mood had changed. She was feeling suddenly relaxed, contented, looking forward to her luncheon. Her companion's attention was entirely on the wine list and she had the opportunity for a leisurely if covert examination of his features.

The thick hair was swept back off a broad, rather knobby forehead, and she thought his hairline was probably receding slightly. In another five years that broad forehead would be even broader. Her gaze tracked down over the aquiline and very dominating nose, the mouth that she found disturbingly attractive, and the deep cleft in his chin that she found even more so. His hands with their filbert nails were delicate for a man—long-fingered, like a pianist's. She remembered that had been one of her first observations.

It had been a long time since she had consciously found a man attractive, even longer since she had found one sexually inviting. She had lost her virginity the year after her mother had died. She and her sisters had made a pact that while none of them were set on marriage, they *were* determined not to die wondering about sex. So they'd given themselves a year. At the end of that year they were none of them virgins.

Prudence's experience had been, she supposed, pleasant enough. Or at least, not unpleasant. But she had certainly felt that something had been missing. Some transport of delight or similar sensation that their reading of Victorian pornography had given the sisters cause to expect.

Perhaps *The Pearl* and other books of its ilk had magnified the transcendent delights of orgasmic *spending*. But Prudence had definitely been left wondering.

Now, however, she caught herself imagining those hands on her body. Her mouth already knew about Gideon's kisses. But the deep-seated thrill of excitement in her belly was not a familiar sensation. It was a shock to admit it, but it seemed that she was attracted to Gideon Malvern.

How was it possible to be attracted to a man one disliked? Well, at least there would be no temptation to do anything about it. She needed the man's mind, not his body, and had no intention of confusing the two.

"Penny for them?" he said, looking up from the wine list.

Prudence blushed. And the more she blushed, the more embarrassed she felt, and the more she blushed. He was looking at her, his gray eyes searching as if he would read her mind. Her face was as hot as hell's fire, and, she was sure, as red as a beetroot.

Then he turned his gaze away to address the sommelier, who had appeared opportunely. Prudence breathed slowly and felt the heat in her face subside. She took up her water glass and surreptitiously pressed it to the pulse below her ear. It had an immediate cooling effect, and by the time Gideon had finished his consultation with the sommelier, she was her usual self, cool and composed, her complexion its customary pale cream.

"A St. Estèphe," he said. "I hope you'll approve."

"I'm sure I shall. I never presume to question the choice of an expert," she said lightly, breaking a bread roll and spearing an artful coil of butter from the glass dish.

"That's a sage and intelligent attitude," he observed. "You'd be surprised how many people lack the sense or are too inflicted with vanity to bow to the voice of experience."

Prudence shook her head at him. "Gideon, you may be right, but your manner of being so is sometimes insufferable."

"What did I say?" He looked genuinely surprised.

She shook her head again. "If you don't know, there's no virtue in my pointing it out."

The waiter appeared and Gideon gave their order before saying, "Point it out, Prudence. How will I ever learn otherwise?"

And that made her laugh. "You missed the irony in my statement, and you missed it because it didn't occur to you that I might be something of an expert with a wine list myself."

"Are you?"

"You'd be surprised," she said, thinking of how much she had learned about the wine trade while manipulating the contents of her father's cellars with Jenkins.

Gideon considered her with a half smile as he sipped his champagne. "You know, I don't think there's much about you that would surprise me, Prudence. Tell me how you became an expert."

Prudence frowned. She and her sisters were intensely private about their household matters and the shifts they were obliged to make to keep their heads above water. No one in their society must know that the Duncan family for close to three years had dodged bankruptcy on a near daily basis. The Go-Between and *The Mayfair Lady* were beginning to bring in an income, but they were still far from out of the woods. But then, she reflected, they had no secrets from the barrister, they couldn't have. He already knew they were in financial difficulties, and why. He just didn't know that Lord Duncan was kept blissfully unaware of the true situation.

She waited until they had been served their first course, then as she slowly stirred her soup she explained the situation in all its detail. Gideon, spreading mackerel pâté onto toast, listened without comment until she had fallen silent and had turned her attention to her soup.

"Are you really doing your father any favors by keeping him in ignorance?" he asked then.

Prudence felt a familiar prickle of annoyance. There was an unmistakable note of criticism in his tone. "We believe so," she responded tautly.

"Oh, it's none of my business, I realize that," he said. "But sometimes an outside perspective is helpful. You and your sisters are so close to the situation, maybe you're missing something."

"We don't think so," she said in the same tone, aware that she was sounding defensive, which somehow gave credence to his criticism, and yet unable to help herself. "We happen to know our father very well. And we also know what our mother would have wanted."

Gideon said calmly, "How's the soup?"

"Very good."

"And the wine. I trust it meets with your expert approval."

She looked at him sharply and saw that he was smiling in an appeasing fashion. She let her annoyance fade and said, "It's a fine claret."

After luncheon they strolled through the city and down to Folly Bridge, where Gideon rented a punt.

Prudence surveyed the long flat boat and the unwieldy length of the pole with some trepidation. "Are you sure you know how to do this?"

"Well, I used to. I assume it's like riding a bicycle," he said, stepping onto the flat stern and holding out a hand. "Step in the middle so it doesn't rock."

She took the proffered hand and stepped gingerly into the punt, which, despite her caution, rocked alarmingly under her unbalanced weight.

"Sit down," he instructed swiftly, and she dropped immediately onto a pile of cushions in the prow. They were surprisingly soft.

"I feel like a concubine in a seraglio," she said, stretching out in leisurely fashion.

"I'm not sure the clothes are quite right," Gideon observed, taking the monstrously long pole from the boathouse attendant.

A punt with a trio of laughing undergraduates was approaching as Gideon pushed off from the bank. The punter dug his pole energetically into the mud, failed to pull it up in time, and the punt slid gracefully out from under him, leaving him hanging on to the pole in the middle of the river. There was riotous applause from the spectators on the bank, and Prudence watched with some sympathy as the luckless punter did the only thing he could—dropped into the water while his punt came to a stranded stop a few yards distant.

"Are you sure you can do this?" she asked Gideon again.

"Oh, ye of little faith," he scolded. "I'm not some callow undergrad, I'll have you know."

"No," she agreed. "That you're not." She regarded him with slightly narrowed eyes. "I wonder if you ever were."

He didn't answer, merely pushed the pole into the riverbed, let it slide back up in his hands with an instant and to-the-manor-born rhythm. Prudence lay back on the cushions, replete with lunch and wine, her eyelids drooping as the afternoon sun warmed them, creating a soft amber glow behind. Idly she trailed a hand in the cold river water and listened to the sounds of the world around her, laughter and voices, birdsong, the steady rhythmic plash and suck of the pole. London seemed many miles away, and the brisk chill of that morning's drive a mere memory.

Gradually she became aware that the sounds of other punters had vanished and now there were only the river sounds, the quack of a mallard, the trill of a thrush. She opened her eyes slowly. Gideon was watching her, his gaze intense and intent. Automatically she took off her glasses to wipe them on her handkerchief.

"Is something the matter? Do I have a smudge on my nose? Spinach in my teeth?"

He shook his head. "Nothing's the matter. Quite the opposite."

Prudence sat up straighter on the cushions. There was something lurking in the depths of those piercing gray eyes that sent a shiver of suspense up her spine and made her scalp prickle. She had a sense of imminent danger. But paradoxically, no sense of threat. Her own eyes seemed locked on his and she couldn't avert her gaze.

Dear God, what was she getting herself into?

With a supreme effort of will she broke the locked gaze and forced herself to cast an apparently casual glance at the scenery as she replaced her glasses. They had reached a point where the river branched around a small islet.

Gideon took the left-hand fork and the punt slid past a lush grassy bank with sides that sloped with gentle invitation down to the river. A small hut was set back a little on the bank. "I think it's safe enough to take this side at this time of year," he said as lightly as if that intense but silent exchange had never taken place.

"Why wouldn't it be safe?" She looked around with sharpened curiosity.

"Over there lies Parsons' Pleasure," he said with an airy gesture of his free hand towards the grassy bank and the little hut. "Had the water not been too cold for swimming, we would have been obliged to take the other side, which is not nearly so pretty."

Prudence regarded him warily. There was a distinct note of mischief in his voice, a hint of laughter in its quiet depths. "What's swimming got to do with it?" she asked, knowing she was supposed to. She felt like a sidekick in a comic routine at the Music Hall.

"Parsons' Pleasure is the private bathing spot for male members of the university. Since it's exclusively for men, bathing suits are considered unnecessary," he informed her with some solemnity. "So women are forbidden to punt on this stretch of the Cherwell."

"Yet another example of male privilege," Prudence observed. "But I fail to see how women can be *forbidden* on this piece of the river. It's a free country, no one owns the water."

"I rather guessed that would be your reaction," he said. "And you're by no means the first. I'll tell you a story, if you like."

"I like," she said, once again lying back on the cushions. The danger seemed to have passed for the moment, although she was not blind or fool enough to imagine it would not again rear its head.

"Well, on one glorious, hot summer day, while the parsons were taking their uninhibited pleasure on that bank, an enterprising group of women decided to protest this bastion of male privilege, as you put it."

Prudence grinned. "You mean they punted past?"

"Precisely. Although I believe they were rowing. Anyway, as the story goes, all the gentlemen leaped to their feet, covering their private parts with towels, all except for one notable scholar, who shall remain nameless, who reacted by wrapping his head in a towel."

Prudence struggled to keep a straight face. This was not a tale a respectable gentleman should tell any respectable gentlewoman. The image, however, was deliciously absurd.

Gideon's expression remained solemn, his voice grave as he continued, "When questioned by his colleagues as to this peculiar reaction, the scholar is said to have replied: *'In Oxford, I am known by my face.'*"

Prudence tried; she tried as hard as she could to stare at him with unmoving disapproval. "That is a most improper story," she declared, a quaver in her voice. "It's certainly not for a lady's ears."

"Maybe not," he agreed amiably. "But I doubt the Mayfair Lady would consider it anything other than delightfully amusing." His eyes were laughing at her. "In truth, I believe there is nothing ladylike about the Mayfair Lady. You can't fool me, Miss Prudence Duncan. You don't have a prim and prudish bone in your body. And neither do your sisters."

Prudence gave up the struggle and began to laugh. Gideon began to laugh too. In his distraction, the punt pole slipped through his hands, and instead of making contact with the river bottom slid away from him. His laughter died on the instant. Swearing vigorously, he grabbed for it, swaying precariously on the stern of the punt as he tried to get control of the unwieldy pole. Water splashed over the stern, soaking his feet. Prudence was now laughing so hard, she couldn't speak. What price the elegant, self-assured barrister now?

Finally Gideon wrestled the pole into submission and resumed his firm but now rather damp stance on the stern. "That was no laughing matter," he said rather stiffly. He was clearly put out at having been made to look like a clumsy amateur.

Prudence took off her glasses again to wipe her eyes as tears of laughter streamed down her cheeks. "I'm sorry," she said. "I didn't mean to laugh at you. But you looked as if you were wrestling a sea serpent. A truly modern Laocoön."

Gideon didn't deign to reply. She took her trailing hand from the water, aware that her fingers were growing numb with the cold, and said solicitously, "Your feet are so wet. Do you have any dry socks?"

"Why would I?" he asked somewhat sourly.

"Perhaps we could buy some on our way back to the hotel. You can't squelch your way back to London. You'll catch your death. Perhaps we could get you a mustard bath at the Randolph before we start driving home. They say it can ward off a chill. You wouldn't want— Oh!" Her sweet-voiced speech was abruptly cut off by a shower of water as

Gideon pulled the pole from the river with sufficient vigor to send a significant quantity of the Cherwell spraying across the punt.

"You did that deliberately," Prudence accused, brushing at the drops scattered across her dress, shaking out her booted feet.

"Not a bit of it," he said innocently. "It was purely accidental."

"Liar. I was only thinking of your well-being."

"Liar," he fired back. "You were making mock."

"Well, it was rather funny," she said. "On top of the story." Her laughter, her pure enjoyment of the last few minutes, had brought a soft glow to her cheeks, and once again, with her glasses now in her lap, the lustrous sparkle of her eyes was revealed. Gideon began to think that his momentary discomfort had probably been worth it just to produce that effect.

"Well, since we're both somewhat damp, I think it's time to turn around," he said, glancing up at the sky through the yellowing tendrils of the weeping willows that lined the bank. "It's going to get really chilly once the sun goes down."

"It's going to be a very cold drive home," Prudence observed. She replaced her glasses, well aware of his thoughtful scrutiny of a minute earlier. Thoughtful and definitely appreciative. The air between them was taut and singing with tension.

"You have your furs," he reminded her. "And we'll break the journey in Henley for dinner."

They handed in the punt and began to walk back briskly towards St. Giles. "Gideon, I can hear you squelching," Prudence said as they passed a men's outfitters. "Go in there and buy yourself some socks."

"I'm not going to admit to some shopkeeper that I got wet in a punt," Gideon stated.

"Then I'll buy them." Before he could argue, Prudence had disappeared into the shop, setting the bell ringing. She emerged within five minutes with a paper bag. "There." She presented it to him. "One pair of black socks. Large. I guessed the size, but I don't think you have particularly small feet."

He took the bag, peered inside. "They have a pattern on them."

"It's just the ribbing on the silk," she said. "It's not really a pattern at all. You should be grateful I didn't buy you plaid."

Chapter 13

They stopped at the same hostelry in Henley where they'd stopped for coffee that morning. It was dark by then and Prudence hurried into the warm, softly lit lounge, already glad of her furs. She wondered for a fleeting instant if Gideon had reserved a table for dinner, but it was only a fleeting instant. He was not a man to leave anything to chance. They were greeted as expected guests, ushered into a cozy private room, where a fireplace gave out comforting warmth. Sherry and whisky decanters stood on the sideboard, and as Prudence shed her outer garments, Gideon poured drinks.

"They seem to know you here," she observed, taking her glass and sitting down in a deep chintz-covered armchair beside the fire.

"It's been a favorite spot of mine since my undergraduate days." He took the opposite armchair. "I took the liberty of ordering dinner beforehand."

"On the telephone?"

"How else?" He sipped his whisky. "The Dog and Partridge is renowned for its local Aylesbury duckling. Plain roasted with a touch of orange sauce, it's hard to fault, so I hope you like duck."

Prudence thought he sounded a little anxious and found it both refreshing and surprisingly endearing that over some things he was not surging with confidence in his own supremacy. "I love duck," she said.

He smiled and rose from his chair, uncoiling his long, lean body with a slow deliberation that reminded Prudence of an indolent lion preparing itself for a night's hunting. The atmosphere in the room changed abruptly, no longer relaxed, but singing with that same dangerous tension of before. He leaned against the mantel, glass in hand, one foot resting on the fender, and looked at her.

"Prudence." He spoke her name softly, thoughtfully, rolling the syllables around his tongue. His gray gaze was once again intent and intense. She resisted the urge to take off her glasses, knowing from experience that that gaze was too hot to hold without the defense of her lenses. She began to feel rather strange, light-headed almost. Her stomach felt as if it was floating. Whatever this was, it was not supposed to be happening.

She was impaled in her chair, her body pressed back against the over-stuffed cushions by some invisible weight. Gideon moved away from the mantel. He took the few steps necessary to reach her. And yet still she sat unmoving, waiting. He leaned over, his hands braced on the arms of her chair. His face was very close to hers. She could feel the warmth of his breath on her cheek, and could almost imagine that she felt the sparks that lit the gray eyes now fused with hers. She let her head fall back against the cushions behind her, exposing the column of her throat in a movement that expressed both abandonment and submission. A tiny sigh escaped her.

He kissed her. A very different kiss from the one he had first given her. The one he had first *taken* from her. The pressure of his mouth on hers was light, almost exploratory, and if she had wanted to turn her head aside, to push him away, she could have. But she didn't. His tongue stroked across her lips, and then gently but with absolute deliberation pushed into the warm velvet of her mouth. His breath mingled with hers as his tongue slid delicately over her teeth, touched the inside of her cheeks, danced with her own. Her eyes were closed, her lips parted, and she tasted hungrily of his tongue, drawing him farther within. Her body was in control now, her mind for once subservient to this unfamiliar but imperative need. She moved her hands up to clasp his head, and her tongue darted with swift serpentine movements between his lips, exploring his mouth as he'd explored hers.

It was only breathlessness that forced them apart, and Prudence finally let her hands fall into her lap, reluctant to lose the heady scent of his skin, the warm taste of his mouth. He smiled down at her, still keeping his hands braced on the arms of her chair.

"This is ridiculous," she said. "I dislike you intensely."

"All the time or some of the time?" His face was still so close to hers, his breath rustled warm across her cheek.

"Some of the time . . . it would seem," she added, sounding both puzzled and slightly indignant.

"Does it help if I tell you that the feeling is entirely mutual?" he asked, still smiling. "There are times when I dislike you every bit as intensely."

"Then this isn't supposed to happen."

"The world is full of surprises. It would be a very boring place if it weren't." He moved closer and suddenly kissed the tip of her nose. "Don't you agree?"

"I suppose I must," she murmured. "But there are surprises and sur-prises, and this kind has no right to happen."

"That bad, huh?" He kissed the corner of her mouth, a light butterfly touch of his lips. Both eyes and voice were now amused.

Prudence made a movement to straighten in the chair and instantly he stepped back, but without taking his eyes off her. She took off her glasses and blinked. "I don't want things to become confused," she said. "And it seems to me that this can only lead to a morass of confusion."

He continued to look down at her, then he leaned forward and took the glasses from her hand. He said, "It doesn't have to. I don't see why lovers can't also work together."

Prudence blinked myopically at his now blurred expression. Without her glasses, matters looked rather different. The brisk, businesslike, highly focused, prudent Prudence Duncan existed behind those gold-rimmed lenses. Without them the world moved into softer focus and the hard realities of every day receded into a rather convenient mist.

When he reached down a hand to pull her to her feet, she offered no resistance. He put his hands on her shoulders and lightly kissed her eye-lids. "Should we have dinner first?"

There was no mistaking his meaning and Prudence was not one to play coy games. She touched her tingling mouth with her fingertips. It happened sometimes, when the sensible, logical side of her nature was somehow driven out by rash instinct, and it was definitely happening now.

Slowly she took her glasses from him and returned them to her nose, testing. If when she could see straight her prudent nature once more gained the ascendancy, she would know this was all some kind of bad joke. But all that happened was that she could now see Gideon's face clearly and it made not the slightest difference to what she wanted.

"Will the duck keep?" she asked.

Gideon nodded, his smile deepening. "Wait here," he said, and left her in solitude.

Prudence took up her sherry glass and drank down the contents as she stood by the fire, gazing into the flames. Whatever this madness was, she had neither the will nor the inclination to stop it, and to hell with the consequences. But she jumped nevertheless at the sound of the door opening, even though she was expecting it. Her heart banged against her ribs as she turned away from the fire.

Gideon stood in the doorway, a small valise in one hand. His other he extended in invitation. She stepped across the room and took his hand. His fingers closed tight and warm over hers. "We'll be more comfortable upstairs," he said.

Prudence inclined her head in brief acknowledgment. She was no longer in control of anything, and for once in her life had no desire to be so. They walked up a shallow flight of stairs to a narrow, carpeted corridor. Gideon, still holding her hand, opened the first door they came to. It led into a bedroom, complete with four-poster bed, low beamed ceiling, and uneven oak floors. There was a fire in the grate and chintz curtains drawn across two small windows.

"How cozy," Prudence murmured.

He looked sharply at her as if he suspected a sardonic edge to the description, but there was nothing in her expression to confirm the suspicion. He was beginning to feel uncharacteristically nervous. He'd made love to a goodly number of women, and never—apart from the first few times in his youth—felt any qualms as to his ability to please.

He realized he didn't even know if Prudence was a virgin. Ordinarily he would assume that an unmarried woman of her birth and social position would have to be. But he was learning not to expect the ordinary when it came to the Honorable Prudence Duncan. He wondered whether to ask, and then decided he couldn't manage the question with any aplomb at the moment, which in itself was an unusual problem. Asking difficult questions was his stock-in-trade, after all.

"No," she said with a sudden smile. "I'm not. I'm not particularly experienced either, but I do have a pretty good idea of what's what."

He looked a little chagrined. "How did you guess?"

"It seemed an obvious thought you would have, and you were looking rather indecisive and uncomfortable." She found that instant of vulnerability she had glimpsed on his face reassuring, drawing her closer to him. He was perhaps as uncertain, as unsure of himself and his instincts at this moment as she was. And she could only like him the better for it.

She walked to the fire and bent to warm her hands, although they weren't in the least cold. The strange light-headed sensation grew ever more powerful and she began to wonder if perhaps she was dreaming and none of this was really happening. And then she felt his arms around her, his body hard against her back, and she knew it was no dream.

He pressed his lips to the nape of her neck, his hands tracing the swell of her breasts beneath her jacket. She leaned her head back against his shoulder, so that her breasts filled his palms.

"You have too many clothes on," he murmured, moving his mouth to her ear as his fingers deftly unbuttoned her jacket, and as neatly drew it backwards off her shoulders. His fingers slid between the buttons of her cream silk blouse and explored the warm swell of her breasts through the thin chemise. He could feel her nipples hardening against the material. His tongue darted into the tight shell of her ear, and she squirmed with a tiny squeal. He laughed softly, his breath tickling her ear anew.

He unbuttoned her blouse, the tiny pearl fastenings flying apart, and he was no longer nervous, unsure of himself, and he could sense her own rising urgency for the touch of skin upon skin. The blouse fell to the floor with the jacket and he slipped his hands into the low neck of the chemise and held her breasts in his palms, surprised at how full they were. Her frame, elegant though she always looked, was thin and angular rather than shapely, but her breasts in his palms were round and smooth.

Prudence touched her tongue to her lips as her nipples grew harder and more erect under his circling thumbs. She was aware now of a clutch in her belly, a fullness in her loins, and with sudden urgency she placed her hands over his, pressing them against her breasts.

He turned her to face him with the same urgency and she began to fumble with the buttons at the waist of her long, pleated skirt. Impatiently he pushed aside her hands and did the job himself. She stepped out of the skirt and stood in her one undergarment, a combination of chemise and drawers of lacy, beribboned silk taffeta, gartered silk stockings, and buttoned kid shoes.

He put his hands at her waist, bunching the chemise, feeling her skin warm beneath the silk. It delighted him that she was wearing no corset of any kind. It made her body accessible in the most alluring fashion. There would be no ridges of whalebone etched onto her skin, and the body he felt was the same as the one he would feel when she was naked. He drew a deep, shuddering breath and removed her glasses, laying them carefully on the mantel. "You don't mind?"

She shook her head; the mist softening her vision at the moment had nothing to do with myopia. Her own hands went to the buttons of his coat. "Hurry," she whispered, her voice quivering with a surge of passionate need. "I have to see you . . . touch you."

He helped her, shrugging out of the coat, pulling off his tie, the starched wing collar of his shirt, discarding his waistcoat and the shirt. She touched his nipples and caught her bottom lip between her teeth when they hardened instantly. "I didn't know men's did that."

"We aim to please, madam," he said, a husky note now in his quiet voice. He reached for the buttons of the chemise, opening it before drawing her against him so that their bare skin touched. It was Prudence's turn to inhale with a little shudder of excitement as her sensitized breasts pressed against his chest. Her hands caressed his back, running down the clear line of his spine to the waist of his trousers.

He took the cue and stepped back an instant to unfasten his waistband and fly and push the striped trousers off his legs. "Oh, damn," he muttered as they met the obstacle of his shoes. He fell back on the bed and Prudence, with a gurgle of laughter, unfastened his shiny black shoes and pulled off his socks with his trousers. The prosaic moment interrupted the intensity, and the brief instant when passion yielded to the mundane only intensified her anticipation.

He stayed stretched on the bed, wearing only a pair of long woolen drawers, and she gazed down at him, at the hard swell of his penis. She reached down and touched it. It jumped against her hand and she closed her fingers over the jutting bulge, feeling the throb of the veins through the wool.

"Take it out," he whispered, his eyes now closed, his breath ragged.

Prudence sat on the bed and undid the buttons. She slid her hand into the opening and drew out his penis. It sprang up against her hand. With a little frown of concentration she explored the feel of it, reaching beneath to find his balls. She had never explored a man's body in any detail before, outside the anatomical pictures in the pages of a medical encyclopedia or Greek statues in the British Museum. Her only previous experience of sex had been too quick for such intimacies. She enclosed his penis in her hand, experimented with tightening and loosening her grip. She heard Gideon groan and then he reached down, took her wrist, and removed her hand.

He took a deep breath, murmured, "Let's take this slowly, sweetheart." He sat up, still holding her hand.

"I was enjoying myself," she said.

"So was I. But I'd like to share this first time." He stood up and pushed the undergarment off his hips and kicked his feet free. "Your turn now."

Prudence gazed at the long, lean length of him. For a man who spent his days studying law books and pontificating in a courtroom, he had a remarkably athletic body—muscled thighs, a flat belly, hard biceps. She put her hands on his narrow hips, running her thumbs over the sharp pelvic bones. A glow of excitement and pleasure spread through her. She slid her hands around to his backside, her fingers pressing hard into the taut flesh. "You have a beautiful body," she murmured, lightly touching her tongue to his nipples. "You could have modeled for Michelangelo."

Gideon looked startled. "I'm not sure that's a compliment."

"I think it is," she said, grazing his nipples with the tips of her front teeth.

"Then I'm suitably complimented . . . I think." He began to unpin her hair as her head remained bent against his chest. He tossed the pins in the direction of the dresser, heedless of those that missed and fell to the floor. He combed his fingers through the wavy russet mass as it fell to her shoulders and down her back. Then he cupped her face in his hands and tilted it up. He bent and kissed her eyes and said softly, "I need to see you now."

She nodded and slid the opened chemise off her shoulders. It fell to her hips, and Gideon dropped to one knee, hooking his fingers into the tops of her drawers. He pulled them down slowly, inch by inch, his lips trailing kisses over her belly, over the creamy flesh of her thighs thus revealed. She stepped out of the puddle of taffeta and lace and lifted her feet as he removed her shoes, then unfastened her garters and peeled off her stockings.

Still kneeling, he ran his hands up the backs of her legs to clasp the soft cheeks of her bottom. "That feels good," he murmured with a smile of satisfaction, kneading the silky roundness. He kissed the base of her belly, then slid his hands around to press apart her thighs.

Prudence quivered at the intimate exploration, the deep recesses of her body moistening, opening. She felt laid bare, more naked than she was, and she reveled in the feeling, her feet shifting on the wooden floor as she parted her thighs yet farther in mute encouragement as passion surged. She clasped his head, pressing it against her belly, her fingers raking through his hair. A wave of delight was building deep in her loins, swelling into a racing breaker. She bit down on her bottom lip, her fingers curling tightly in his hair as the wave crested and broke. She heard herself cry out. Her knees shook uncontrollably. Gideon stood up, holding her against him until she'd regained her balance.

"Oh," was all she could manage to say. "Oh."

He smiled down at her and kissed her damp forehead. "So passionate," he said softly, turning her towards the bed, taking the opportunity to run his eyes hungrily down her back, narrow and elegant, the nip of her waist, the flare of her hips, the curve of her backside, the long, clean sweep of her thighs.

Prudence fell on the bed, rolling onto her back, opening her arms to him. She was filled with an urgent need to share this pleasure with him. He knelt above her and she raised her legs, curling them around to press her heels into his buttocks. "Come," she demanded. *"Now."*

"At your service, madam," he said. "In just one second." She watched as he slipped a rubber sheath over his penis. Vaguely she wondered if he always carried them with him, but it seemed an irrelevant thought as he slid within her still-pulsating body and she tightened her inner muscles around him, glorying in the feeling as he filled her, pressing deep within her.

He looked down at her and she smiled up at him, her light green eyes alive with pleasure. "Don't move, sweet," he said. "I want to make this last, but I'm so close to the brink."

"You call the tune," she replied, stretching her arms way above her head in a gesture of abandonment that was so sensual, he inhaled sharply, clinging desperately to the last threads of self-control. He withdrew slowly, then as slowly sheathed himself within her again. She gasped, her eyes closing, her belly tightening as the wave began to build once more.

He withdrew again, closing his own eyes, holding himself on the very edge of her body, then with a soft cry he drove hard and deep to the very edge of her womb, and her body convulsed around him as his penis throbbed and pulsed within her.

He fell upon her with a groan, crushing her breasts so that she could feel the rapid beating of his heart, so close to her own. She clasped his sweat-slick back, lay still until her breathing slowed and her heartbeat returned to normal.

Gideon stirred and rolled off her. He lay on his back, one hand resting on her belly, the other flung above his head. "Jesus, Mary, and Joseph," he murmured. "You are miraculous, Miss Duncan."

"You're not so bad yourself, Sir Gideon," she returned with an effort. "Now I really won't die wondering."

He turned his head slowly to look at her. "What does that mean?"

She merely smiled and closed her eyes. She certainly knew now what had been missing in the past. And although she would never have admitted it to herself before, she had been just a little envious of Constance, who obviously found nothing missing in the realms of passion with Max. The smile was still on her face when she plunged into a deep and dreamless sleep.

She awoke an hour later to the sound of soft voices coming from the doorway. Lazily she propped herself on one elbow and looked towards the door. Gideon, in a dressing gown, was talking to someone in the corridor outside. She flopped back on the pillows, realizing that without disturbing her sleep Gideon had managed to pull back the covers and somehow insert her between the sheets.

The voices ceased and the door closed. Prudence struggled up against the pillows, holding the sheet up to her neck. "Where did the dressing gown come from?" It was a particularly elegant garment of brocaded silk and didn't look as if it formed part of the guest supplies of this hostelry.

"I brought it with me." He picked up the small valise that she now remembered noticing earlier.

"You mean you planned for this?" she demanded, not at all sure that she liked the idea that he had set out that morning completely prepared for seduction. Condom and all.

He shook his head. "You're so suspicious, my sweet. No, I did not plan for *this*. I've spent most of the day trying to overcome our mutual dislike. But I am a motoring enthusiast, as you probably realized."

"More of a fanatic, I would have said."

"Yes, well we won't quibble about the degree of my enthusiasm." He was opening the valise as he spoke. "However, as an experienced motorist, I know that even the most reliable vehicle can strand one in the most inconvenient circumstances on a long drive, so I'm always prepared." He took out a silk garment and shook out the folds. "This is for you."

He laid the garment on the bed. It was a dressing gown of emerald green Chinese silk, beautifully embroidered with deep blue peacocks.

Prudence fingered it. "It's lovely, but we have to go home straightaway."

"No," he said. "We have to have dinner straightaway. Roast duck, if you remember."

She pushed aside the covers, casting an agitated glance at the clock on the mantel. It was close to nine-thirty. "Gideon, I have to get back. My family will be worried out of their minds."

"No, they won't," he said with that calm assertive confidence that so often put her back up. Not this evening, though. "Milton knows the uncertainties of motoring, so he was not surprised to be told that if we had not returned by ten o'clock he should drive to Manchester Square and explain that we had been benighted and would return in the morning."

She stared at him, still with some degree of incomprehension. "But what about the morning? It's Monday, don't you have to go to work?"

"My first appointment is at noon. We'll leave early and we'll be back in plenty of time."

Prudence lay back again and pulled the covers up. "Is there any detail you've missed?"

"I don't believe so," he returned rather smugly. "I have hairbrush, toothbrush, tooth powder, and a nightgown for you. Although," he added, regarding her consideringly, "I doubt you'll need the latter."

"Perhaps not," she agreed. "If we're going to eat roast duck, shouldn't we dress and go downstairs?"

"No, we're going to eat in here. It seems like too much effort to go downstairs, and they want to close the dining room soon anyway."

"Ah." She fingered the dressing gown again. "Then I suppose I'll get up and put this on."

"That might be a good idea," he agreed. "The bathroom is right opposite. I don't think anyone else is staying on this corridor, so we don't have to share it."

Prudence put on the robe, tying the girdle at her waist tightly. "Did you say something about a hairbrush?"

"I did, but I'd like to do that myself. There's something about your hair that drives me wild." He came up to her, tilting her chin on his forefinger and kissing the corner of her mouth.

She merely smiled and padded barefoot to the door. The bathroom was small but contained the necessities: a claw-footed tub, a basin, and a water closet. Prudence began to draw a bath and while the water was running twisted her hair into a knot on top of her head and returned to the bedroom. "What happened to the hairpins?"

Gideon took a handful off the dresser and stuck them judiciously into the piled mass. "Would you like company in the bath?"

"It's very small," she said doubtfully.

"We could wash each other's back."

"Irresistible." She reached up and caressed his cheek, observing with a smile, "You're stubbly."

"Five o'clock shadow," he said. "I usually shave in the evening as well as the morning."

"I rather like it," she said. "It adds a certain something . . . a *je ne sais quoi*. It gives you a more rugged look."

He bent and rubbed his cheek gently against hers. "You prefer rugged to smooth, then?"

"Depends," she said. "On circumstances. I must get the bath before it overflows."

He followed her into the bathroom, watching her cast aside the dressing gown, stand for a minute naked, aware of his gaze, offering herself to it, before she stepped into the bath.

"There really isn't enough room for two."

"Nonsense," he said, throwing off his own dressing gown and stepping into the bath at the opposite end. Water slurped over the edge as he struggled to sit down, drawing his knees up to his chin to fit.

Prudence pushed her feet under his backside and wriggled her toes. He grabbed her ankles and water cascaded over the edge of the bath onto the wooden floor.

"Stop that," he said, squeezing her ankles. "It'll leak through the floor to the ceiling below in a minute."

"I told you it was too small for two." She leaned against the back of the tub, still idly wriggling her toes against his nether parts.

Gideon heaved himself to his feet, sending a further wave of water onto the floor, and stepped out. He grabbed a towel from the rail and threw it into the puddle to soak up the mess. "I'll shave instead," he said, returning to the bedroom for his razor and strop.

Prudence soaped herself lazily, enjoying the intimacy of their shared ablutions. It had a wonderfully sensual undercurrent, one that built on the glory of their earlier lovemaking, somehow solidified it, while creating a delicious surge of anticipation. Her toes curled and she moved the soapy washcloth to her thighs . . . and between them, idly visiting the sites of her earlier pleasure.

"Would you like some help there?"

The quiet voice made her jump, and her eyes, that she hadn't realized were closed, flew open. Gideon stood at the side of the bath, his own eyes darkened to a charcoal gray as they watched her.

"No, thank you," Prudence said with as much dignity as she could muster. "We've already proved the bath is no place for games."

He laughed and reached for a dry towel. He unfolded it and held it invitingly. "Out. Otherwise I'll begin to feel superfluous."

She stood up in a shower of drops and stepped out, trying to think of a snappy response to the statement and failing utterly. He wrapped the towel around her and then stepped into the bathwater.

Prudence dried herself vigorously, shrugged into the Chinese silk robe, and left him in the bath. In the bedroom she saw that a table had been set in front of the fire, with an already opened bottle of Pouilly-Fuissé, a basket of hot rolls, a dish of butter. She poured the wine into the two glasses and sat at the table, breaking open a roll, spreading butter thickly. Sex seemed to stimulate the appetite.

Gideon came back as she took the first sip of the wine. "Is it good?"

"Delicious. Haven't you tasted it?"

"No, but the landlord has made sure it's not corked." He took the seat opposite her. His hair was wet and Prudence noticed with some amusement that when wet it had a springly curl to it. It was rather frivolous, not at all suited to the fearsomely intimidating barrister she had first met.

A knock at the door heralded two waiters, who placed a three-tiered stand piled high with shellfish on the table. "Oysters, Sir Gideon, clams, cockles, shrimp, lobster claws, winkles, and smoked mussels," one of the waiters intoned, pointing with a fastidious forefinger as he listed the offerings.

"Thank you." Gideon nodded and the waiters faded from the room. He took a small pointed stick and selected a tiny shellfish. "These are quite delicious." He picked the minute winkle from its shell and passed Prudence the stick.

She popped the winkle into her mouth. Ordinarily she considered these tiny shellfish barely worth the trouble to extract, but now she realized what she had been missing. She nodded and took one for herself. She was beginning to learn that Gideon treated the business of food with utter seriousness. They ate their way through the tiers of shellfish with a dedicated concentration, punctuated by the occasional appreciative murmur and the odd remark, and when a waiter returned to clear their plates and the stripped-bare stand, they merely sat back, sipped wine, and nodded with satisfaction.

"I would never have put you down as such a thoroughgoing hedonist," Prudence said into the satisfied silence. "It doesn't go with being a barrister."

"Oh, now, there you're wrong, sweetheart," he said. "Barristers live as indulgently as the members of any other profession . . . and more than some. We have our own clubs, our own pubs, our own restaurants. We don't have much conversation, I'll grant you that. Mostly law talk, case discussions, but we do ease business along with the good things in life."

Prudence nodded, reflecting how easily the endearments slipped off his tongue. She liked them, they made her feel special and enhanced the sensuality of this interlude, but she was not used to them. Her father had never been one for demonstrative speech, and even her mother had used endearments sparingly. She didn't feel comfortable using them herself and wondered if Gideon would notice that she only used his name. But perhaps he would notice the different tone she had now when she spoke his name. Her tongue rolled the syllables around as she took the last sip of her wine.

Roast duck appeared, with orange sauce, succulent green beans, crispy roasted potatoes. A bottle of Nuits-St. Georges was opened, the waiters faded away once more. Gideon took the tip of his knife and slid it beneath the crispy skin of the bird. He sliced upwards and then took his fork to spear the golden brown paper-thin skin.

He leaned over, holding the fork to her lips. "Greater dedication hath no barrister than to give the best morsel of a roast Aylesbury duckling to his client."

Chapter 14

Gideon was awakened in the morning by the slither of a soft body across his recumbent form, by lips pressed into the hollow of his throat. He didn't open his eyes and he didn't move as Prudence covered his face with tiny butterfly kisses, his eyelids, his nose, his cheekbones, the corners of his mouth, the cleft of his chin.

"Don't pretend you're asleep," she murmured between darting flicks of her tongue into that fascinating cleft. "I can feel that the most important part of you is wide awake." She moved her lower body over his in emphasis.

Gideon stroked down the length of her back as she lay long upon him, languidly caressed her bottom. "My mind, like the notable Oxford scholar's, is generally considered to be the most important part of me," he murmured into the fragrant mass of russet hair.

Prudence chuckled. "That depends on the circumstances. Right now, I have to tell you that your mind is of not the slightest interest to me. This is." She moved a hand down, slipping it beneath her to grasp the jutting evidence of his wakefulness. "I'm wondering if it's possible to do it like this."

"Certainly it is." The languid note in his voice was fading fast. "Move back and raise yourself just a little."

"Like this?"

"Just like that." With a leisurely twist of his hips he entered her as she hung above him.

"Oh, this is quite different," Prudence said, sounding rather surprised.

"There are an infinite number of ways to enjoy each other," he said. "Don't tell me you haven't read the Kama Sutra, because I wouldn't believe it."

"We have read it, of course, but some of those positions looked completely impossible, not to mention tortuously uncomfortable." She pushed back onto her knees, circling her hips slowly around his penis buried deep within her. "Have you tried them all?"

"No. I've never found a partner willing to entertain the idea." He clasped her hips, pressing his thumbs into the pointy hipbones. "Lean forward just a tiny bit . . . ah, that's good." He smiled, lifting his hips rhythmically as she pressed the cleft of her body against his belly, rising and falling with him.

He watched her face; her eyes were closed, and he said softly, "Open your eyes. I want to see where you are."

She opened her eyes, fixing her gaze on his. He watched for the deepening glow in the light green depths, the spark of excitement as her pleasure grew closer to its climax, and when he saw it he touched her sex lightly with his fingertips. Her eyes widened and he thrust upwards, holding her bottom with his free hand, pressing her down hard upon him. Then, with a swift, deft movement just as she cried out in delight, he rolled her sideways to the bed, disengaging the instant before he allowed his own climax to rip through him.

Prudence felt the orgasmic shudders quiver through her body for several minutes. Her body was a weightless mass of delicious, languorous sensation, her muscles utterly powerless, her loins drained. She turned on her side, resting her head in the damp hollow of his shoulder as he lay on his back. With an effort, he reached a hand to brush strands of damp hair that were stuck to her cheek. Then his hand fell limply to her flank.

"I wonder if one could ever have too much of this good thing," Prudence murmured when she could speak. She calculated that since eight o'clock last evening they had made love four times, and judging by the light in the window, it was only just past dawn.

"Not I," he said.

"Nor I," she agreed with a complacent chuckle.

"Unfortunately, or perhaps fortunately, daily life makes other demands," Gideon said, sitting up with a groan of exertion. "We have to get on the road and get you home before your family calls out the police."

"You said they would have a message." Prudence forced her own muscles into action, struggling up against the pillows.

"They will have, but they're still going to want to see you alive and well before the morning's too much advanced," he pointed out, swinging his legs to the floor. "Shall I run your bath?"

"Please." She leaned back, exhausted by the simple effort of getting herself semiupright, and closed her eyes again. Soon she heard the sound of water running and her mind woke up to full consciousness. *Where were they to go from here?* It had been the most wonderful night, full of transcendent delights. But now what?

Almost as if he read her thoughts, Gideon reappeared. "Prudence, your bath is drawn. Get up now. We have to get moving."

Her eyes shot open and she looked at him, startled by the imperative tone. During the long hours of their loving she had forgotten that he had that tone—assertive, authoritative, impatient. Now she caught herself wondering if perhaps this manifestation was his normal self and the soft, tender lover who issued only endearments in the exciting, sensual richness of the words of loveplay was an occasional visitor.

"I'm up," she said, getting off the bed and reaching for the dressing gown. She brushed past him in the doorway and went into the bathroom. She wondered fleetingly if he would follow her, but was not surprised that he didn't. The idyll was definitely over, and reality had once more reared its demanding head.

She performed her morning ablutions quickly and returned to the bedroom. Gideon was dressed once more, and even though he was wearing the casual morning dress suitable for weekend, it was clear he had reverted to his former physical self. The charming disorder of his curly hair had been tamed, he was clean-shaven, even his posture had somehow straightened, become more rigid. He was the barrister again, utterly in control, utterly sure of himself and his superiority.

Prudence went to the dresser and grimaced at the state of her hair. It was a wild tangle that she knew would take ages to return to order. She sat down on the small stool and picked up the hairbrush, dragging it through knotted strands.

"Let me." He stood behind her, reaching over her shoulder for the brush.

She relinquished it, observing, "Since you're responsible for this mess."

The gray eyes gleamed and she caught a glimpse of the lover. "Not entirely responsible," he demurred, putting his hand on the top of her head and pulling the brush down with resolute strength. "Sorry," he offered at her wince of pain. "Is there a gentler way of doing this?"

"No. Just do your worst." She squeezed her watering eyes tightly shut, bent her head, and let him get on with it.

He laid the brush down after five minutes of tugging and pulling. "There. I think that's the best I can do."

Prudence opened her eyes and combed her fingers through the now relatively straight mane. "I'll manage from here."

"Right." He went to the door. "I'll order breakfast in the coffee room. Can you be ready in ten minutes?"

"In a pinch," she said dryly.

"Put the robe and everything else in the valise when you've finished with them. I'll send a boy up to take it to the motor."

Prudence, coiling and pinning her hair, nodded, and he went out, his step energetic, and she could fancy there was an almost military click to his heels. She dressed quickly—trying not to think of those moments when she had undressed—and packed the valise, reflecting as she closed it and snapped the locks that there was something symbolic about this putting away and closing up. It was a neat tidying up of a delightfully untidy idyll. She glanced once around the room before leaving it. Nothing was out of place, apart from the wildly tumbled bed, where the sheets and coverlets straggled to the floor. Her eye caught a couple of hairpins on the floor and she remembered how Gideon had drawn them out. With a quick shake of her head, she left and hurried downstairs.

Gideon was reading the newspaper when she came into the coffee room. He rose politely as she sat down. "Newspaper? I ordered two." He handed her a neatly folded copy of the *Times*.

Prudence couldn't help a smile. This was a man who did not like breakfast conversation. She poured tea, buttered a piece of toast, and opened her own newspaper, offering her companion no distraction from his paper or plate of kidneys and bacon.

Then they were once more in the motor, driving through the quiet early morning streets of Henley. A few shopkeepers were opening up, but there were few customers as yet. Prudence had again donned her furs and tucked her hands into her muff. Conversationally, she opened a subject that had aroused her curiosity. "Gideon, this morning we didn't use a condom, but you withdrew at the last minute. Is that uncomfortable for you?"

He shrugged. "Neither method is ideal from a man's point of view, but the possible consequences of ignoring precautions don't bear thinking of."

"Ah." Prudence absorbed this. Her fingers closed over her little notebook. He'd given her entrée into another issue. "Would you want more children . . . in the right circumstances, I mean?"

"Do you want children, Prudence?" he asked, casting her a quick glance, but she couldn't really see his expression behind the visor and goggles.

"I asked *you*. If you were going to get married again, I mean."

He gave her a look of pure disbelief. "You've put your hands on that notebook again, haven't you?"

She felt herself flush slightly. "I just thought I'd ask since the subject had come up."

"We have just spent a night of fairly ecstatic lovemaking and you've now turned your attention to finding me a bride?" he demanded. "I don't believe this, Prudence. It's so utterly inappropriate."

"No, it isn't," she said firmly. "You said last night that there would be no confusion. We are each other's client. I expect you to do your best for me, and I will do my best for you. We agreed you would like a bride young enough to give you another child, but we didn't actually talk about whether you would want one. Obviously, if you don't I can't introduce you to a woman who's desperate to have children." She turned to look at him. "Be reasonable, Gideon, you can see that."

He stared straight ahead at the winding road and declared through thinned lips, "I don't want to have this conversation."

"You have your head in the sand," she said, throwing up her hands. "How can I do my job when you won't respond?"

Gideon only shook his head.

"All right," Prudence said, "we'll stop talking about possible brides for the moment. But surely you don't mind thinking about some factors. Would Sarah like a ready-made sibling, do you think?"

"I thought we'd put Agnes Hargate to rest."

Prudence ignored the acid tone. "I'm not talking specifics here. I'm trying to establish some parameters. You must have an opinion, surely."

Gideon, against his will, found himself considering the question. He realized he had no idea what Sarah would think about a stepmother, let alone a half sibling. Let alone a stepsibling. "I don't know," he said finally. "I'd have to ask her."

With what she recognized was now personal curiosity, Prudence asked, "How would you feel if a potential bride had, say, an illegitimate child?"

That piqued his interest. "Do you know anyone in that situation?"

She didn't, of course. Women in the circles they would be considering did not have, or at least own to having, illegitimate children. "None that would acknowledge it."

"Then why ask?"

She'd asked because she wanted to know which was the real Gideon Malvern. He cultivated the appearance of conventionality, lack of flexibility, lack of sympathy for those who didn't quite meet his standards, and yet she had seen beneath that surface, seen that he could be quite the opposite, embracing the unorthodox, open to change. But was that the right way round? Maybe the open, unorthodox side of him was an appearance to create a certain response, and the real Gideon was the rigid and aggressive barrister, with no time or sympathy for anyone who didn't play by his rules. Her own peace of mind seemed to rest on the answer to the conundrum.

"Well," she said thoughtfully, resorting once more to the lighthearted tenor of their earlier conversations, "we do know that you would like to meet a future partner who's willing to explore the delights of the Kama Sutra."

"I'm certainly willing to give some of the less extreme positions a try," he said, turning to look at her fully. And now he was smiling. "What's the point of all this, Prudence?"

"I am trying to find you a suitable wife."

"Maybe that's something I would prefer to do for myself."

"You agreed to the terms."

"I agreed to let you try."

"And I am trying. By the way, you're about to run over a farm cart," she observed. "I'm sure you're supposed to keep your eyes on the road when driving."

Gideon swore as he wrenched the wheel to the side just in time to avoid a stolid horse pulling a cart piled with manure, driven by an old man smoking a pungent pipe that was nevertheless insufficient to combat the powerful odor from the cart.

"That would have been a messy experience," Prudence said when they were clear.

"Why don't you just enjoy the scenery and let me concentrate?" He sounded as annoyed as he looked. Prudence thought of his wet socks and bit back a smile. Gideon was not a man who liked to make mistakes.

"Very well," she agreed amiably. "I'm a little short of sleep, as it happens." She huddled into her coat, drawing up the collar, and closed her eyes behind the goggles.

She had not expected to sleep but she came to with a groggy start when the engine stopped, and saw that they were outside the house on Manchester Square. "I slept all that way."

"You did," he agreed, coming around to open the door for her. "Snoring peacefully."

"I do not snore." She stepped onto the curb.

"How would you know?"

"I'll tell you something, Gideon, this habit you have of conversing in combative questions grows irksome," she declared. "It might serve you well in a courtroom, but it's annoying and uncomfortable in a social conversation." She removed her goggles and tossed them onto the seat she had vacated.

He pushed his goggles up over his visor. "Does it occur to you that I might find your way of conversing in distinctly personal questions just a little irksome?"

"I was only doing my job," Prudence declared. Then she shook her head in a little gesture of resignation. "I think we're disliking each other again."

"So it would seem," he agreed. "I imagine it will go in cycles." He put a finger on the tip of her nose, raising his eyebrows.

"Maybe so," she said, aware of a softness in her voice that she hadn't intended, but he was disarming her now, showing her the other side of Gideon Malvern. "Maybe so," she said again, "but you provoke those reactions, Gideon. I'm generally a peaceable, easygoing person. Ask my sisters."

"I don't think I'll bother. I'm sure they'll back you to the hilt. Instead, I'll concentrate on the memory of the wildly passionate lover whenever you become quarrelsome, and then I won't be tempted to respond in like fashion." He bent and kissed the tip of her nose and then the corner of her mouth. "Find me some accurate records of Lord Duncan's dealings with Barclay, Prudence. I can't do anything without them. And come to my chambers tomorrow afternoon, after five. We'll talk about how to present you in court and what impressions you have to avoid giving." He gave her a wave before she could respond, and turned back to the motor.

Prudence hesitated, words tumbling in her head, but none of them seemed adequate. One minute he was kissing her and calling her sweetheart, the next issuing brusque instructions. She waited until he had disappeared around the corner of the square and then went up the stairs to the front door.

Jenkins opened the door as she inserted her key in the lock. "Miss Prue, what happened?" He couldn't hide his concern.

"Prue, is that you?" Chastity appeared at the head of the stairs. "Did you have an accident. Are you all right?"

"No, no accident, and yes, I'm all right, love." Prudence swiftly climbed the stairs. "Motors have a habit of breaking down. We spent the night at an inn in Henley." She gave her sister a quick kiss as she hurried past her. "I have to change my clothes, Chas. They're the same ones I wore all day yesterday."

"Yes," Chastity agreed. "Did you sleep in them?"

There was something in the question that caused Prudence to stop on her way to her room. She turned slowly. Chastity was regarding her with her head tilted to the side, a slight smile on her lips.

"No," Prudence said. "I didn't."

"So, what did you sleep in?"

"If I told you the inn had spare nightgowns for benighted guests, would you believe me?" Prudence was aware now that her own lips were curving.

"Not a bit of it," Chastity said. "Are you going to spill the beans?"

"Of course." Prudence laughed. "Come and help me wash my hair. It's a mess."

She had told Chastity the whole and was sitting by the parlor fire drying her hair in a towel when Constance came in. "You're back. Thank goodness. I was quite worried when I got Chas's message last night. What happened?"

"Oh, Prue had an impulse to which she yielded, and it seems to have led to a night of unbridled passion in Henley-on-Thames," Chastity said with an airy wave.

Prudence emerged from the tent of the towel. "In a nutshell."

"That's quite a nutshell." Constance perched on the arm of the sofa. "Is he a good lover?"

Prudence felt herself blush. "I didn't have much to compare him with," she said. "But I can't imagine how the night could have been better."

Constance grinned. "That sounds fairly definitive," she said. "The question, though, is how does this—"

"Affect our business dealings with the barrister?" Prudence interrupted. "I know, Con. And don't think I haven't considered it. But I really don't believe it will make one iota of difference. Sir Gideon Malvern, KC, is not the same person I spent such a wonderfully crazy night with. He reverts with surprising ease." She picked up her hairbrush and began to brush her still-damp hair with vigorous strokes.

"That's good, isn't it?" Chastity asked doubtfully.

"Of course it is," Prudence declared, smothering her own doubts. "And on the subject of business, he's adamant that that note from Barclay isn't sufficient for him to base a case on." She sighed a little. "So, it seems there's nothing for it. I'll have to go to Hoare's first thing tomorrow morning. It's too late today."

"I thought we'd already agreed on that plan," Chastity said, throwing another shovel of coal on the fire.

"I know, but I had a smidgeon of hope that we could avoid it."

Constance shook her head. "We're in too deep for regrets now, Prue. Did Chas tell you what I've been doing this morning?"

"No, I haven't had a chance," Chastity said. "I had to stay here for you, Prue, so Con went out alone to see if she could discover whether anyone had been snooping around." She looked worriedly at her eldest sister. "Was there anything, Con?"

The sisters' lightheartedness of a moment earlier was now quite dissipated. "Tell us," Prudence said. She knew instinctively that they were going to hear nothing good.

Constance paced to the window and back again. "As we agreed, I went to some of the main outlets we use, Helene's Milliners, Robert's of Piccadilly, a few others. I tried to make it seem we were doing the usual rounds to see how many copies they had sold of last week's issue."

She paused, and her sisters waited. "Every one of them said other people had been asking questions about how the broadsheet was delivered to them, who checked on supplies, took orders, collected the money."

"Detectives," Prudence said flatly. "Employed by Barclay's solicitors. Gideon was right."

Constance nodded. "Of course, no one knows who we are, we're simply representatives of *The Mayfair Lady*. We're always veiled, and nothing can be traced to this address. But I'm thinking we should hold next week's issue."

"Not publish?" It was a concept so foreign to the sisters that Chastity's exclamation came as no surprise to the other two.

"Maybe we should cease to publish until after the court case," Constance said reluctantly.

"But that's giving in to them," Chastity said, her mouth set with unusual firmness. "I think it should be a last resort."

"What about Mrs. Beedle? They're bound to have followed up on the poste restante address," Prudence said with a worried frown. "She wouldn't betray us, but we can't have her harried."

"One of us should go there tomorrow and talk to her," Constance said.

"I can't." Prudence stood up, shaking out her hair. "I have to go to the bank. One of you will have to go."

"I will," Chastity volunteered.

"I don't suppose during your night of unbridled passion you had a chance to advance our search for a bride for the barrister?" Constance regarded her middle sister with the hint of a raised eyebrow.

"I did try," Prudence said. "He won't have anything to do with Agnes or Lavender. Quite adamant he was on that score."

"But he hasn't even met them," Chastity protested.

"I don't think that matters a whit to him. To be brutally frank, I don't think his heart is in this bargain."

"Then why did he agree to it?" Constance demanded.

Prudence shrugged. "I think he thought it was a joke, something he didn't have to take seriously."

Her sisters looked at her thoughtfully. "Of course, matters might be a little more complicated now," Constance observed. "One lover finding the ideal bride for the other. A situation almost perverse, one might say."

"One might," Prudence said aridly.

"In fact," her elder sister continued with a speculative air, "one might wonder if *your* heart is still in the search."

"I assure you that my heart is as much in it as it ever was," Prudence declared with asperity. "A brief fling with a client does not have to affect one's objectivity."

"No," Constance agreed. "Of course it doesn't. A brief fling, that is."

Chapter 15

Prudence stood outside the narrow entrance to Hoare's Bank in a steady drizzle. She was nerving herself to go in when the glass door opened and the liveried doorman emerged, holding up a big umbrella. He bowed and came towards her. "Are you coming into the bank, madam?"

"Yes," she said. "I'd like a word with Mr. Fitchley if he's in today."

"He certainly is, madam." The doorman held the umbrella high as she took down her own, shaking the drops off. He escorted her into the hushed interior of the bank, where everyone for some reason that Prudence had never been able to fathom spoke in undertones.

"The lady is for Mr. Fitchley," the doorman said almost behind his hand to an elderly, hovering clerk.

The clerk recognized the visitor without difficulty. It was sufficiently unusual for women to transact financial business for themselves to make Miss Duncan a distinctive client. "Good morning, Miss Duncan. I'll tell Mr. Fitchley you're here." Prudence smiled her thanks. She sat down on a straight-backed velvet-cushioned chair, holding her handbag in her lap, and hoped she didn't look too self-conscious. The silently busy clerks and cashiers in their cubbyholes cast her barely a glance, but she could feel her guilt radiating from every pore.

Mr. Fitchley himself came out of his office to greet her. "Miss Duncan, good morning. This is a pleasure. Do come in, come in." He waved expansively towards his office.

"Good morning, Mr. Fitchley. A rather wet one, I'm afraid." She offered another smile as she went past him into the sanctum. It was a small, dark room with a smoldering coal fire in the grate.

"Pray have a seat." The bank manager gestured to a chair in front of the desk, where not a scrap of paper was to be seen. He folded his hands on the immaculate surface and said with a smile, "What can we do for you this morning, Miss Duncan?"

Prudence opened her handbag and took out the envelope containing the letter of authorization. Her fingers were not quite steady as she turned it over so that the earl's official seal was immediately visible. "I need to examine Lord Duncan's bank records, Mr. Fitchley. I realize it's unusual, but my father has some concerns about some past transactions. He would like me to look into them." She leaned forward and laid the envelope in front of the banker.

Mr. Fitchley put on a pince-nez and lifted the envelope. He turned it over in his hands several times. "I trust Lord Duncan's concerns have nothing to do with the service Hoare's Bank has provided. The earl's family has banked with us for four generations."

Prudence made haste to reassure him. "No, of course not. It's just that he wants to refresh his memory on some transactions that took place about four or five years ago." She offered a self-deprecating smile. "As you know, Mr. Fitchley, I tend to manage the financial affairs of the household. My father has little time to spare for such chores."

The bank manager nodded. "Yes, your late mother, dear Lady Duncan, used to tell me the same thing." He took up a paper knife and slit the envelope, unfolding the crisp, headed vellum. He read it very carefully—almost, Prudence thought, as if he would memorize every duplicitous word. Then he laid it down on the desk, smoothing it with the palm of one soft, white hand.

"Well, that seems to be in order, Miss Duncan. If you'd like to follow me . . . we have a private office where clients may examine their effects without disturbance." He rose from his desk and led the way into the main room. Prudence followed him across the marble-tiled expanse, past the cubbyholes where diligent workers kept their eyes on their desks as the manager walked by. He opened a door and stood aside for Prudence to enter a rather cell-like room, furnished with a table and chair. Gray light came from a small window.

"A little chilly, I'm afraid," he said. "We don't keep a fire in here unless a client has made a previous arrangement to come in."

"I'm sorry . . . I should have done, of course. But this came up rather suddenly," Prudence said.

"That's quite all right, Miss Duncan. If you'd like to make yourself comfortable, I'll have a clerk bring you the ledgers. Will you be wanting the safe-deposit box as well?"

"Yes, please."

The bank manager bowed himself out, closing the door behind him. Prudence shivered in the damp chill and paced the small space from wall to wall. Within ten minutes the door opened again and a clerk came in with an armful of ledgers, followed by another with a locked box.

They set these on the table. "Should I light the gas, madam?" the first clerk asked.

"Yes, please." Prudence took the key that lay on top of the box and slipped it into the lock. The gas flared, casting at least the illusion of a warm and cheerful glow over the cheerless room.

"Would you care for coffee, madam?"

"Yes, that would be lovely, thank you."

They left the cell and she sat down at the table, lifting the lid of the box. She had the feeling that if her father had anything he wanted kept secret he would put it under lock and key, not leave it in an open ledger. The box contained only a sheaf of papers. She took them out just as the clerk returned with a tray of coffee and some rather stale-looking digestive biscuits, which he set down beside her. She smiled her thanks and waited until he'd retired, closing the door once more, then she spread the papers on the desk.

Her parents' marriage certificate; the sisters' birth certificates; her mother's death certificate; her mother's will; her father's will. None of these interested her. She knew that her mother's small estate had all been spent on *The Mayfair Lady*. It hadn't occurred to Lady Duncan to charge for the publication, so her own money had kept it afloat. Lord Duncan's will was straightforward . . . everything to be divided equally among his three daughters. Not that there was anything, really, other than debt, to pass along, she reflected, without rancor. Maintaining the country house in Hampshire, with its tenants' cottages and dependencies, together with the house and staff in London, would take up whatever small revenues the country estate brought in. But that was the way it was now, so they were quite used to that. She returned the papers to the box as she looked them over and then she came to the last one.

She stared at it, feeling suddenly queasy, for a moment unable to believe what she was reading. It was a legal document. A lien on the house on Manchester Square. The house that had been owned by the Duncan family since the time of Queen Anne. She looked at the document blankly. Took a sip of coffee. Looked at it again. It was dated April 7, 1903. And the lien was held by a company called Barclay Earl and Associates.

It didn't take a brilliant mind to make the connection. The earl of Barclay held a lien on 10 Manchester Square. A house that had never in all its history had so much as a mortgage against it, at least to Prudence's knowledge. A slow burn of anger grew in her throat. *Why?* What on earth could have possessed her father to hand over the house that was his inheritance, his pride, his family's pride?

Desperation.

There was no other explanation. There could not be another explanation.

Prudence dropped the document into the box as if it was something vile. She found the ledger for 1903. The payments started in January . . . payments to Barclay Earl and Associates. Every month the sum of one thousand pounds. And then in April they stopped. But in April Lord Duncan had given Barclay a lien on his London house. No longer able to make the payments that he had presumably contracted to make, he had done the only possible thing.

She took up the ledger for the previous year. The payments started in October. But there was nothing to say what they were for. Was her father being blackmailed by Barclay? No, that was too absurd. The two men were fast friends, or at least Lord Duncan certainly seemed to think they were.

She reached into her handbag for the note from Barclay that they had found among the papers in the library. Payments . . . schedules . . . interest. She went back to the safe-deposit box, and there she found it, tucked into a slit that formed a pocket in the lining. October 5, 1902, a few weeks before his wife's death, while she lay in the agony he could not endure to see, Lord Arthur Duncan had agreed to finance a project to build a trans-Saharan railroad. He would make payments of one thousand pounds a month to Barclay Earl and Associates, who would manage the project.

And when he could no longer make those payments, he had accepted a lien on his house. She slid her hand into the pocket again. There was another sheet of paper. Half a sheet, rolled thin as a cigarette, as if the recipient hadn't been able to bear reading it. When she unrolled it, Prudence understood why.

> *My dear Duncan,*
> *So sorry to bring bad news. But it's a bad business. Trouble with the Mahdi again, and people still remember the spot of bother with Gordon in Khartoum. Unfortunately, no one seems too keen on our little project at present. The rolling stock is in place, our people are set to start work. But the backers have decided to renege on our agreement. Political concerns, don't you know. We're all in the hole to the tune of a hundred thousand pounds. Just to reassure you, we won't be taking up the lien unless matters become desperate.*
>
> *Barclay*

Presumably, they had not yet become desperate, Prudence reflected. There was no way her father could have resumed making thousand-pound payments out of the household budget without her knowing. So the lien hung there, the veritable sword of Damocles. Her father must be in torment. And yet he was prepared to stand up in court as a character witness for this thief, this charlatan, this out-and-out villain?

It was beyond her imagining. She could understand how a man unhinged by grief could make unbalanced decisions, but her mother had been dead for almost four years. Surely their father had regained sufficient control of his senses to see what had been done to him.

Prudence sat back in her hard chair, drumming the tip of her pencil on the table. Pride would keep Arthur Duncan from admitting his mistakes or confronting the man who had fooled him. Pride would keep his head firmly buried in a dune in the Sahara.

She sat up straight again. Whatever their father's present state of mind, they did now have something to bolster their accusations of financial shenanigans. They needed to investigate the credentials of Barclay Earl and Associates. Did it exist as a legitimate entity? Had it ever? The whole idea of a railway across the Sahara had always been absurd. At least to people not crazed by grief, she amended. But to make their case, they would have to prove that it had been fraudulent from the start. That Lord Duncan had been inveigled into investing in a fraud. Investing so deeply that he handed over the family property when he couldn't meet his payments.

Prudence, no longer in the least guilty, calmly removed all the relevant papers from the box and the relevant pages from the ledger and put them in her handbag. Gideon would know whom they could use to look into the credentials of Barclay Earl and Associates. There must be a registry of companies somewhere. She swallowed the last of her coffee, relocked the safe-deposit box, tidied the ledgers, and left the cell. A clerk escorted her to the door and she went out into the rain, putting up her umbrella with a satisfying snap.

Chastity stood at the corner of the small street outside an ironmonger's and looked across at Mrs. Beedle's shop. It had been ten minutes since the man in the homburg and rather shabby mackintosh had set the doorbell tinkling on his way inside.

It was drizzling and she was both well protected and relatively invisible in a Burberry raincoat, a waterproof hat with a half veil, and a large umbrella. She had strolled down the street once since he'd gone in, but hadn't been able to see into the shop from the opposite pavement and was reluctant to cross over and risk drawing attention to herself.

The door of the corner shop opened and Chastity turned to look in the window of the ironmonger's, feigning interest in the display of cast-iron kettles. She glanced over her shoulder and saw the man in the homburg stroll down the street in the direction of the bus stop. Mrs. Beedle's shop was visible from the bus stop, and Chastity decided she couldn't risk going in to the shop until the man had boarded his bus . . . but since she couldn't stand in the open street for any length of time either without causing remark, she went into the ironmonger's, shaking out her umbrella.

A man in a baize apron emerged from the back at the sound of the bell over the door. "Mornin', madam. What can I do you for?" He surveyed her with an acquisitive gleam in his eye. Run-of-the-mill customers in this part of Kensington could not in general afford Burberry raincoats. His mind ran over the more expensive range of goods he could show her.

Chastity thought rapidly. "A flatiron," she said. "I need a flatiron."

"I've got just the thing for you, madam. Cast iron; nice, even surface. Heats up in a jiffy. Your laundry maid will love it." He hurried into the back, and Chastity stood at the window, craning her neck to see if the man wearing the homburg had left the bus stop as yet. She had no desire to burden herself with a heavy piece of totally unnecessary and probably expensive cast iron, but she couldn't leave if he was still there.

She couldn't see the bus stop, so she opened the door and peered into the street. At the sound of the bell, the ironmonger came rushing out from the back, afraid he'd lost his customer. Chastity saw the horse-drawn omnibus round the far corner of the street, and the man climbed aboard.

"Here's the iron, madam," the ironmonger said behind her. "Just the thing."

"Oh, yes." Chastity turned. "Actually, I think I'll send the laundry maid instead. Since she'll be using it, she might as well choose what she'd like. Expect to see her this afternoon." With a smile from beneath her veil, she whisked out of the shop, leaving the disconsolate ironmonger holding the flatiron.

The bus passed her as she waited to cross the street, and once it had lumbered around the corner, she darted across to Mrs. Beedle's shop.

"Why, is that you, Miss Chas?" Mrs. Beedle looked up from the counter, where she was refilling a large glass jar with peppermint humbugs. "You just missed a man asking after you. Second time he's been."

Chastity propped her umbrella against the door and put up her veil. "Did he say who he was? What did he want?"

Mrs. Beedle knitted her brow. "Wouldn't really say who he was, just that he was interested in talking to someone from *The Mayfair Lady,* and did I know where to find you. He said something about having some good news for you." She shook her head and resumed her task. "Didn't like the look of him . . . something didn't smell right."

"So, you didn't tell him anything?"

The woman looked up. "Now, Miss Chas, you know better than that. I told him I don't know nothing. I just receive the letters that come in the post."

"But he must have asked who picked them up?" Chastity was still anxious, even though she knew that by pressing she could offend Mrs. Beedle.

"Aye, he did. And I told him a boy comes every Sunday. Don't know his name, don't know nothing about him. None of my business. That's what I said, both times." She screwed the lid firmly back on the jar and wiped her hands on her apron. "You look as if you could do with a nice cup of tea, Miss Chas. Come on in the back." She lifted a hinged piece of countertop so her visitor could get behind.

"Thank you," Chastity said, dropping the top in place before following her hostess through a curtain into the cheerful kitchen beyond. "I didn't mean to imply anything, Mrs. Beedle, it's just that we're very anxious at the moment."

"Aye, m'dear, I'm sure you must be." She poured boiling water into the teapot. "We'll let that mash for a minute or two." She opened a cake tin and placed bath buns on a flowered plate that she set on the table, where Chastity had taken a seat. "Have one of those, Miss Chas. Made fresh this morning."

Chastity took one with unfeigned enthusiasm. "We think they hired detectives," she said. "They're snooping everywhere and our barrister says they'll be very determined to discover who we are, so they'll just keep coming back."

"Well, they won't hear nothing different from me," Mrs. Beedle declared, pouring tea. "Drink that down now. It'll keep out the damp." She set the cup of strong brew in front of Chastity. "Strange weather we're having. Yesterday it was almost like spring. And now look at it."

Chastity agreed, sipped her tea, nibbled her bun. "Is there any post for *The Mayfair Lady* today?"

"Just a couple." Mrs. Beedle reached up to a shelf and took down two envelopes. She handed them to her visitor, who after a cursory glance tucked them into her handbag.

"Now, don't you be worrying about these detective folk, Miss Chas. They'll not discover nothing from me, and no one else knows about you.

Apart from our Jenkins, of course." Mrs. Beedle always referred to her brother by his working title.

"And Mrs. Hudson," Chastity said. "But you're right, Mrs. Beedle. We know our secret's as safe as the grave with all of you. And we're so grateful to you."

"Nonsense, m'dear. We'd have done the same for your sainted mother, God rest her soul."

Chastity smiled, and drank her tea. The shop bell rang and Mrs. Beedle hastened through the curtain to greet her customer. Idly, Chastity listened to the conversation as she took another bath bun. A pleasant male voice with the hint of an accent that she thought was Scottish greeted Mrs. Beedle by name.

"Good morning, Dr. Farrell," the shopkeeper replied with a genuine note of welcome in her voice. "And what a wet one it is."

"Indeed it is, Mrs. Beedle. I'll take a pound of humbugs, and another of licorice sticks, if you please."

"Right you are, Doctor," Mrs. Beedle said. Chastity heard her opening jars, shaking sweets into the scales. Who would buy a pound of humbugs and a pound of licorice? Curious, she set down her teacup and walked softly to the curtain. She twitched aside a corner and peered behind. A tall man was leaning against the counter. His shoulders were as broad as a wrestler's, she thought. He had a rather rugged countenance, with the skewed nose that indicated it had once been broken. Oddly, rather than marring his face it seemed to enhance it, Chastity thought with a somewhat detached interest in her own observations. He was hatless and his wet hair clung to his scalp in a springy mass of black curls. He wore a mackintosh that had clearly seen better days, but he had the most delightful smile.

He turned from the counter as Mrs. Beedle weighed the sweets, and strolled to the magazine rack. He was a very big man, Chastity noted. Not fat at all, but all brawn. He made her feel quite small and delicate. As she watched, he picked up a copy of *The Mayfair Lady* and flicked through its pages. Something made him stop to read more closely.

"All ready, Dr. Farrell. That'll be sixpence for the humbugs and fourpence for the licorice."

"Oh, and I'll take this too, Mrs. Beedle." He laid the copy of *The Mayfair Lady* on the counter and counted out change from his pocket.

Chastity waited until he had left, setting the bell ringing vigorously, his vital step seeming to exude energy. She returned quickly to the kitchen table.

Mrs. Beedle bustled back behind the curtain. "Such a nice man, that Dr. Farrell. Hasn't been in the neighborhood long."

"Does he have a surgery around here?" Chastity inquired casually, setting down her teacup and preparing to take her leave.

"Just off St. Mary Abbot's," Mrs. Beedle said. "Bit of a rough part of town for a gentleman like Dr. Farrell to be practicing, if you ask me." She began to clear the table as she talked. "But our Dr. Farrell can take of himself, I reckon. Told me once he used to wrestle for the university. Oh, and box too." She shook her head, clucking admiringly as she put the cups in the sink.

Now why would such a man be interested in reading The Mayfair Lady? Chastity took her leave, pondering the question.

She walked to Kensington High Street and hailed a hackney, unwilling to face the damp crowds and steamed-up windows of the omnibus. She hadn't needed reassurance that Mrs. Beedle would keep their secret if she could, but the persistence of the earl's solicitors didn't bode well. They were clever; there was no knowing what devious tricks they would use to trap the unwary. Mrs. Beedle was a good, honest woman, but she would be no match for the conniving of an unscrupulous and sophisticated detective agency.

Chastity reached home just as a rain-soaked gust of wind blew across the square, almost turning her umbrella inside out. "Miserable day," she said to Jenkins as she entered the hall. "Is Prue back yet?"

"Not as yet, Miss Chas." He took the umbrella from her.

Chastity unpinned her hat, shaking out the veil. "Mrs. Beedle sends her best regards, Jenkins." She took off her mackintosh, handing it to the butler. "I'll be in the parlor when Prue gets home."

Jenkins bowed and went to dispose of the rain-drenched garments. He heard Prudence let herself into the house a few minutes later and with stately gait retraced his steps to the hall.

Prudence greeted him rather distractedly. The documents in her handbag seemed to have acquired some kind of physical weight on her journey home. All the familiarity of the hall in which she stood gently dripping seemed to waver, to take on some strange patina. Because, of course, this hall no longer legally belonged to the Duncan family unless her father could discharge his debt. *Or prove that debt fraudulent.*

"You look a little pale, Miss Prue. Is everything all right?"

Jenkins's disturbed tone brought her out of her reverie. "Yes," she said. "Quite all right. Just wet." She managed an effortful smile as she relinquished her outer garments. "Any messages?"

"A telephone call from Sir Gideon, Miss Prue."

Prudence was aware of a surge of adrenaline, a rush of pure physical excitement that, however momentarily, chased all else from her mind.

"What was the message?" she managed to ask, busily unpinning her hat.

"He said that since the weather was so miserable, you shouldn't go to his chambers this afternoon. He'll send his chauffeur to fetch you at six o'clock."

"How considerate of him," Prudence murmured. "Thank you, Jenkins. Could you send a message to Con. Ask her to come around at her earliest convenience?" She hurried upstairs to the parlor. Chastity had just sat down to begin answering letters to the Aunt Mabel column of *The Mayfair Lady* when Prudence entered the parlor. She turned in her chair at the secretaire.

"Anything? I have." Her expression was anxious.

Prudence nodded. "You first," she said.

Chastity described the events of the morning. "I'm just worried they'll dig something up, however closed-mouthed everyone is. Maybe we *should* cease publication. Go to ground."

"Like the hunted fox." Prudence bent to warm her chilled hands at the fire, then straightened, a gleam in her eye that gave Chastity some heart.

"What did you discover?"

Prudence opened her handbag. Silently, she handed the documents to her sister. Chastity would need no elaboration to grasp the implications. She read in silence, laying the sheets on the secretaire as she read them. Then she looked up. "Con needs to see these."

"I asked Jenkins to send for her."

Chastity shook her head in disbelief. "Barclay basically owns our house."

Prudence opened her hands in a wordless gesture of agreement.

"There's more at stake than *The Mayfair Lady*, then."

Prudence nodded. "A stake through the heart comes to mind."

"Well, we'd better wait for Con before we talk about murder," Chastity said. "Mrs. Beedle was holding a couple of letters. Shall we look at them while we're waiting?" She reached for her handbag and took out the envelopes. "I'm almost afraid to open them."

She slit them with an onyx paper knife. "This one seems quite straightforward. It's a request for an introduction to people who have a passion for poetry. Not exactly a matchmaking request, the writer wants to set up a poetry circle." She looked up and shrugged. "What do you think? Shall we come up with a list?"

"I don't see why not," her sister said. "We do put people in contact with like-minded souls. It seems harmless enough."

Chastity nodded and tossed the letter onto the desk. She turned her attention to the other one. Silently she handed it to Prudence.

> *To whom it may concern:*
> *An interested party has some information of considerable benefit to the owners and editors of The Mayfair Lady regarding the present libel suit. Evidence has come to light that will be of service to them in their defense. A private meeting is requested at a location of the editors' own choosing. The information we have is of the greatest importance and must be delivered in a timely fashion. Please respond to the above address without delay. And please believe us to be the most sincere admirers and supporters of The Mayfair Lady.*

Prudence looked up. "It's a trap."

"But what if it isn't?"

"It has to be." She nibbled a fingernail. "It's anonymous."

"As are we," Chastity pointed out. "If it's a friend of Barclay's, or maybe an ex-friend, he might not want to be known. Supposing he has evidence of Barclay's fraud, maybe he was a victim, like Father. Can we afford to discount it?"

Prudence tore off the piece of nail she had loosened with her teeth and threw into the fire. "I don't know, Chas."

"You could show it to Gideon."

Prudence nodded. "I'm seeing him this evening. I'll show it to him then." She folded the letter and slipped it back into its envelope.

"Oh, there's Con," Chastity said at the sound of their sister's unmistakable footstep on the stairs.

Constance entered the parlor, took one look at her sisters, and said, "We need to go out for luncheon."

"That's the best idea I've heard all day," Prudence said. "But read these first. I have to change my shoes, they're soaked." She gestured to the documents on the secretaire. "Oh, and the letter. Give it to her, Chas."

Chastity handed it over. "Where are we going for luncheon?"

"Swan and Edgar's?" Constance suggested, her eye already scanning the papers in her hands.

"Perfect," Prudence approved on her way to the door. "They do a nice luncheon and I want to buy a paisley scarf to go with my sage evening dress."

Constance looked up for an instant. "Are you seeing the barrister tonight, then?"

"As it happens. But if you finish reading you'll see that a business meeting is somewhat urgent," her sister declared. "I'll tell Jenkins we won't be in for luncheon."

"Business?" Constance murmured with a raised eyebrow as the door closed behind Prudence.

"I doubt Prue has either the time for or the interest in anything else right now," Chastity declared with unusual acerbity. "If you'd read what's in your hand, you'd realize that."

Constance's eyebrows reached her scalp but she said nothing. Her baby sister would have a reason for snapping. When she'd finished reading she understood.

"Barclay has a lien," she said in an incredulous whisper.

Chastity nodded.

Chapter 16

Prudence stepped into the motor when it arrived punctually at six o'clock that evening and gratefully accepted the mackintosh lap rug that the chauffeur provided. She was just as grateful for the leather curtains that he had rolled down over the open sides. When they reached the house on Pall Mall Place, the front door opened the minute they attained the top step, under the shelter of the chauffeur's umbrella.

"Oh, you were exactly right about the time, Milton," a childish treble declared. "You've been gone exactly three quarters of an hour."

"Unless there are unexpected delays, I am in general correct about such things, Miss Sarah," the driver said with an indulgent smile.

"Good evening, Miss Duncan," Sarah Malvern said.

Prudence smiled down at the rather untidy schoolgirl and took the small hand extended in greeting. "Good evening, Sarah." She had time for a closer examination of the girl than had been afforded by their previous unexpected meeting. Sarah's countenance was more freckled than Prudence had noticed, and she was rather skinny, dressed this evening in a conventional school tunic of blue serge with a white blouse, somewhat ink-stained on the sleeves. Two thick ropes of fair hair hung down her back, a straight fringe brushing her forehead.

"Won't you come in?" Sarah said, pulling the door wide. "I'm to entertain you while Daddy's finishing the truffled eggs. If you'd like to come in here, you could take off your coat and scarf." She led and Prudence followed into a small bedchamber leading off the hall. A dresser, a mirror, a jug and ewer of hot water, a towel, brush, and comb all lay ready for any guest in need.

"There's a water closet through that door," the girl said matter-of-factly, gesturing to a door at the rear of the room. "I found some camellias in the garden." She perched on the end of the single bed. "I thought you might like them."

Prudence noted the little vase of heavy-headed red camellias still speckled with raindrops. "They're very pretty," she said. "Thank you," she added, taking off her coat.

"Oh, it was no trouble," the child said with a sunny smile. "And I put out hot water in case you were dusty. What an elegant dress."

Prudence didn't need to look in the mirror to know that this was true. It was one of the Parisian creations that Constance had brought back from her honeymoon for her sisters, and it perfectly suited her coloring and her figure, making the most of her less-than-imposing bosom. She had decided on this occasion to dress as if she'd received an invitation for dinner, since—to put it euphemistically—experience had taught her that the barrister was sometimes a little forgetful about declaring his intentions.

Truffled eggs, though?

"It came from Paris," she said, and unpinned her scarf. She had chosen to wear her hair in a thick, braided chignon, tied with a velvet ribbon at her neck. It was a style that softened her rather angular features and made the most of the deep copper of her hair.

"If you're ready, we'll go into the drawing room," the girl said. "I'm glad you didn't get wet on the drive."

"Milton was very solicitous," Prudence said, following her diminutive hostess across the black-and-white marble-paved floor and into a long, narrow drawing room that stretched the length of the house. It was a pleasant room of soft shades of cream and gold, welcoming sofas, and floor-to-ceiling bookshelves. Unlike the library, the only other room she had seen, it didn't strike her as having anything masculine about it at all. Did it date from Sarah's mother's day, a reflection of her taste? Or some other woman's? Had there been another woman in Gideon's life since his wife?

Prudence was realizing how little she still knew about this man who had become her lover. There was the little matter of his failed marriage, for instance. That was a history she needed eventually to unravel.

An open exercise book lay on a sofa table, with pen and inkwell beside it. "I have the most pesky algebra problem," Sarah Malvern declared. "Daddy said you might be able to help me with it."

Oh, did he, indeed? Prudence merely smiled. "I wonder what gave him that idea. Let me have a look."

The girl gave her the exercise book, then flitted across to a sideboard. "May I pour you a glass of sherry?"

"Yes, thank you." Prudence sat down on the sofa with the exercise book. It took her a few seconds to figure out the answer to the problem. She took the glass of sherry Sarah had carried carefully across the

Aubusson carpet. "Do you want me to help you figure this out or just do it for you?"

"That would be cheating," Sarah said, taking the exercise book from her guest.

"Well, yes, I suppose it would." Prudence couldn't help smiling as she sipped her sherry. The girl was clearly struggling with her conscience. "But then again," she said, "if I showed you how to do it and you followed along, you would learn for the next time, so it would be a lesson rather than a cheat."

Sarah considered this, her head on one side, a frown on her freckled face, then she grinned. "I don't think even Daddy would argue with that. And he argues with most things. He says it's a good mental exercise."

"What's he doing with truffled eggs?" Prudence inquired casually as she took up the pen.

"Making them," Sarah replied matter-of-factly. "They're one of his specialities. You're having quails stuffed with grapes too. They're tricky to cook because they have so many bones and Daddy has to take them all out when the birds are raw. It always makes him swear." She glanced up at Prudence as she sat on the sofa beside her. There was a rather mischievous, if speculative, gleam in her gray eyes. "He doesn't cook them very often," she said. "Only for special occasions."

Prudence ignored the significant tone and the speculative gleam and took back the exercise book. She felt on much firmer ground with algebra. "All right, here is how we do this." She began to explain the solution to the problem, Sarah leaning close to her, listening intently.

"Now see if you can do it." Prudence handed her the pen at the end of her explanation.

"Oh, it's easy now," Sarah said confidently. "Two to the power of three . . ." She worked quickly and neatly, impressing Prudence considerably. It was a far from simple problem for one so young. But then, she was the daughter of Sir Gideon Malvern, the youngest-ever KC. And she attended North London Collegiate. Gideon had talked of a governess too. A Mary Winston. Why wasn't she present? Why wasn't *she* helping the child with her homework?

Schoolgirls didn't do their evening homework alone in a formal drawing room—or, not in Prudence's experience.

The house was almost unnaturally quiet and there didn't seem to be any evidence of servants, except the chauffeur. There'd been a housekeeper when she'd come before. This was a puzzle beyond Prudence's unraveling, and as her astonishment at this surreal situation faded, annoyance took its place. Gideon was doing his surprise trick again, designed as always to throw her off balance. She looked up at the sound of the door opening.

"Prudence, forgive me for not greeting you the minute you arrived," Gideon said, entering the drawing room. "There's a particular moment with the eggs when one can't lose concentration. I hope Sarah has been entertaining you."

He wore impeccable evening dress, except that around his waist was a large and none-too-clean apron. Prudence stared at it.

"You forgot to take off your apron, Daddy," Sarah informed him.

"Oh, how remiss. I forgot I was wearing it." He untied the apron and threw it over a brocade chair by the door. He regarded his guest with smiling appreciation that went a long way to dissipating her flash of annoyance.

"My compliments," he murmured. "That gown has the unmistakable mark of Paris upon it."

Prudence, at her sisters' insistence, was also wearing the three strings of matchless pearls wound around her neck. They had originally belonged to their great-grandmother and the sisters trotted them out on suitable occasions. Constance had worn them for her wedding. Prudence had been a little reluctant to wear them this evening for what had, after all, been billed as a working occasion; but when she had seen how well they complemented the gown, she'd yielded without too much of an argument.

Prudence took off her glasses in the reflex that was always prompted by a moment of uncertainty. Sarah's presence seemed paradoxically to add to the intimacy of the moment while making it difficult to respond naturally.

Gideon smiled and resisted with difficulty the urge to lean over and kiss the tip of her nose. The soft glow of the gas lamps set deep fires ablaze in the copper mass on her nape and his fingers itched to loosen it. But his expression gave none of this away. He said calmly, in his low, pleasant voice, "I see Sarah gave you sherry." He went to the sideboard and poured himself a glass. "Did you manage the problem, Sarah?"

"Miss Duncan showed me how to do it, and then I did it myself," the child said with scrupulous honesty.

Gideon nodded. "May I see?" He took the exercise book and ran his eye over his daughter's work. "Nicely done," he commented, handing the book back to her. "Mary came in five minutes ago. She's waiting for you to join her for supper."

"Mary went to a suffragist meeting," Sarah said. "Do you believe in votes for women, Miss Duncan?"

"Most certainly I do," Prudence said.

"Do you belong to the Women's Social and Political Union? Mary does." Sarah's interest was clearly genuine.

"I don't, but my elder sister does. She often speaks at meetings."

Sarah's eyes widened. "Is her name Miss Duncan too? I wonder if Mary's ever heard her."

"My sister uses her married name now . . . Mrs. Ensor."

"Oh, I'll ask Mary if she knows her." Sarah stood up, clutching her exercise book. "I don't suppose you cooked extra quail for us, did you, Daddy?"

"No, I'm afraid not. Boning four quail is as many as I can tolerate," Gideon said. "But Mrs. Keith has roast pork and applesauce for you."

Sarah gave an exaggerated sigh. "Oh, well, I suppose that will have to do."

"The pork has crackling, I am reliably informed."

The girl's laugh was light and merry, and full of warmth. "We'll make do," she said. She gave Prudence her hand. "Good night, Miss Duncan. Thank you for helping me with the algebra."

"My pleasure, Sarah. Good night." Prudence sipped her sherry as Gideon kissed his daughter good night. Sarah responded to the kiss with a fierce hug. The bond between them was obviously so strong, so easy and affectionate it reminded Prudence of the bond she and her sisters had had with their mother. She watched the softness of Gideon's expression, the warm curve of his mouth. This was the side of the man that produced the laugh lines at the corners of his eyes, the easy way he had with endearments, the tenderness of the lover.

Sarah left with bouncing step and Prudence settled back against the corner of the sofa. "She's a delightful girl."

"Her proud papa certainly thinks so," Gideon said with a laugh, coming over with the sherry decanter. He leaned across her to refill her glass, and she inhaled the unmistakable, exotic, and earthy scent of truffles, mingled with a faint cologne that after a bare hesitation she decided was onion. Her host had been chopping raw onions.

"I seem to be getting the unmistakable impression that you cook," she declared.

"That would not be an inaccurate impression," he responded with a grin that was more than a little complacent.

"Just another one of your surprises?" She sipped her sherry, watching him with raised eyebrows.

"It's a hobby, almost a passion, really," he replied, sounding serious now. "I'm hoping you'll approve of the results shortly."

"An unusual hobby," Prudence commented. She could think of nothing else to say.

"It frees my mind," he returned, still seriously. "A man needs a break from dusty law books."

"Yes," she agreed. "I suppose he does. But I thought we were going to work this evening . . . I have something really exciting to show you." She reached for her handbag.

Gideon whipped the bag out from under her stretching hand. "Not now, Prudence. Later."

"It's evidence of Barclay's fraud," she declared.

"Good," he said, placing her bag out of reach on top of the mantel. "After dinner we will discuss it."

But Prudence was not to be put off. "We'll need to check into the records of a company calling itself Barclay Earl and Associates . . . whether it legally exists. Do you know how to do that?" She leaned forward eagerly.

"Yes," he said calmly. "I do. We will discuss it later."

Prudence stared at him in frustration. "They've got detectives asking all over town about us. And they sent a letter to the publication . . . oh, let me show you." She jumped up and went to the mantel, only to find her way barred.

"After dinner," he said, placing a finger decisively over her lips. "I have just spent the better part of four hours creating a masterpiece for your delectation and I refuse to have it spoiled. There's a time and a place for everything, and right now is the time and place for truffled eggs."

Prudence gave up. "What happens to truffled eggs?"

He shook his head. "Once you've tasted them I'll tell you. Let us go in to dinner." He took her hand and laid it firmly on his proffered arm.

All right, Prudence decided, if he wouldn't talk business then they would discuss something else. "Does Sarah live with you all the time?"

"Yes," he said, escorting her across the hall.

"It's somewhat unusual, isn't it? Girls tend to live with their mothers in such circumstances," Prudence persisted.

"That would be a little difficult in this situation, since I have no idea where Sarah's mother is." He ushered her into a square dining room.

"How could that be?" Prudence demanded, no longer concerned that she might be prying. She *was* prying, in fact, but in the face of these bland responses she had little choice.

"When Sarah was three, Harriet ran off with a horse trainer." He pulled out a chair for her to the right of his own at the head of the table.

"And you've not heard from her since?" Prudence couldn't conceal her shock at this cavalier explanation offered in a tone that was so matter-of-fact it sounded almost bored. She stood holding the back of her chair, looking up at him.

"Not since the divorce. She remembers Sarah's birthday, that's sufficient for me . . . and it would seem for Sarah too. Would you please sit down?"

Prudence did so. "Divorce must have been difficult," she persisted. He had to have some emotional response to this.

"Nowhere near as difficult as realizing that you hadn't noticed that your wife had developed interests elsewhere," he said aridly.

Prudence was quiet for a moment. However dry his statement, it had revealed some indication of hurt. If his noncommittal attitude earlier had been a simple defense mechanism, then it would be unforgivable to dig at a still-open wound.

Soft candlelight lit the room and a round bowl of the same red camellias that Sarah had put in the guest room formed a fragrant centerpiece. Again Prudence was struck by the feminine touches, the delicate lace edging to the table napkins, the silver bowl of potpourri on the sideboard.

"Sarah has a nice touch with flower arrangements," she observed. "At least I assume it's Sarah."

"With a fair amount of help from Mary," Gideon responded. "Mary, for all her suffragist leanings, doesn't disdain the gentler arts of her sex. You'll meet her soon, I'm sure. You'll like her."

"I'm sure I shall," Prudence said carefully. He was making some very broad assumptions, she thought with a prickle of apprehension. It seemed as if he was expecting her part in his life to become larger, as if it was going to be quite natural for her to become friends with Sarah's governess, as if it was quite natural for her to help the girl with her homework, or have a tête-à-tête dinner in his house. A dinner that he himself had cooked. As if somehow this was not in his eyes the brief fling she had so casually called it when talking to her sisters. And if it was more than a brief fling, then what happened to the bride hunt? Not to mention their working relationship.

If Gideon noticed anything unusual about her abrupt silence, he gave no sign. He rang a small handbell at his elbow before pouring champagne into two glasses, and said conversationally, "I think champagne works best with the eggs, but if you dislike champagne with food . . . some people do . . ."

"No, not at all," Prudence hastened to reassure him as the door opened softly and a maid entered with a tray.

"You gave them just three minutes in the bain-marie, Maggie?" the barrister asked, sounding uncharacteristically anxious.

"Yes, sir, exactly as you said." The maid set a small dish in front of Prudence and the second in front of Sir Gideon. "And the melba toast is just out of the oven, cooked nice and slow, just as you said." She set a toast rack between the diners. Her tone, Prudence thought, was rather soothing, as if she was accustomed to her employer's culinary anxieties.

"Will that be all, sir?"

"Thank you." He took up a tiny silver spoon. *"Oeufs en cocotte aux truffes,"* he announced. "The secret lies in getting them to set to exactly the right consistency." He dipped the tip of the spoon into the dish, and Prudence hesitated, waiting for the verdict.

"Ah, yes," he said. "Perfect."

Prudence took this as permission to taste her own. She dipped her spoon and conveyed its contents to her mouth. "Oh," she said. "Ah," she said. She gazed at him. "Unbelievable." Her tongue roamed around her mouth, catching every last elusive hint of truffle and caviar.

He smiled a most self-satisfied smile. "It will do." He passed the toast rack towards her. "Melba toast."

Prudence could not imagine that the astounding dish in front of her could benefit from toast but she bowed to the expert and took a fragile crisped piece. She broke off a corner and dipped it into her dish, following her host's example. *Oeufs en cocotte aux truffes* definitely needed melba toast.

She sipped her champagne and savored every tiny spoonful of the delicacy in front of her. It struck her that this was not a suitable moment for conversation of any kind, let alone of the business or personal varieties. This was a moment for awe and reverence. And it was over all too quickly.

She looked sadly into the empty *cocotte* and gave a little sigh that was part utter delight and part regret. "I have never tasted anything like that."

"Good," said her host, refilling her champagne glass. "The sole will be a few minutes." He smiled at her and laid a hand over hers.

Prudence twined her fingers in his. She hesitated, but without the distraction of culinary delight, her restless mind had turned back to the personal. She desperately needed to know the full story of his marriage. "How did you fail to notice that your wife had interests elsewhere?" she asked finally.

Gideon sipped his champagne and then gently but deliberately disengaged his hand. "I suppose you're entitled to ask, but in general I prefer not to talk about it."

"I'm sorry," she said. "But it seems very important to me to know."

He nodded. "I didn't notice for the same reason that Harriet found outside interests. I was too busy, too engrossed in my profession." He shook his head. "A barrister doesn't make KC without sacrifices, certainly not before his fortieth birthday. Harriet, with some justification, resented my absorption. She was—I assume still is—very beautiful. Very desirable . . . and the only man who failed to acknowledge that was her husband."

"But she had a child."

"Yes, but motherhood didn't suit her enough to substitute for the lack of a husband's attentions."

He looked across at her. "I blame Harriet for very little. She gave me a divorce without a murmur. I keep her in some of the luxuries that the racehorse trainer can't quite manage, and I prefer that her contact with Sarah be limited to birthday cards. Can we leave it at that now?"

He rose from the table, went to the sideboard, and took up a bottle of Chassagne Montrachet. "This will go very well with the sole. I have a fine Margaux for the quail. I trust you'll approve."

Prudence sat back as he filled her white-wine glass. "I didn't mean to open old wounds," she said, then fell silent as the maid reappeared to clear away the first course and place delicate fillets of Dover sole in front of them. She placed a sauceboat at Prudence's elbow.

"Champagne sauce," Sir Gideon said. "I can't take credit for this dish. It's one of Mrs. Keith's specialities."

Prudence dribbled sauce onto her fish. "I imagine you had your hands full with the cocotte and the quail." She took up her fish utensils and cut into the fillet. He had asked her to drop the subject, and without being insensitive to the point of discourtesy she could only accede. "To produce this in addition to a full day at work is impressive, to say the least." She smiled at him. "Were you in court today?"

"I was. Quite an interesting case. A property dispute. Usually I find them rather tedious, but this had some unusual aspects." He talked about the case, making relaxed and urbane conversation throughout the remainder of dinner.

"The quail were wonderful. And that gâteau basque . . ." Prudence set down her spoon and fork with a little sigh of repletion. "I have no idea how you could put something that delicious on a table."

"Cooking is not your forte, then?" he teased.

Prudence shook her head. "I'm afraid, unlike Miss Winston, that I lack many of the gentler arts of my sex."

He looked at her sharply, as if hearing a note of criticism in her repetition of his description of Mary Winston.

She continued, with an attempt at lightness. "My forays into the kitchen are usually only to discuss with Mrs. Hudson the cheapest way to put a meal on the table that will satisfy my father and not arouse his suspicions that we've cut corners. It's not easy to do."

"No, I can imagine," he said. He laid his napkin on the table. "Let's return to the drawing room for coffee." He pushed back his chair and moved behind hers, pulling it out for her.

"Can we talk business now?" Prudence asked as they entered the drawing room. She headed for the mantel and her handbag.

Gideon sat down on the sofa and patted the seat beside him. "Show me what you've got." He leaned forward to pour coffee from the tray set ready for them on the low table in front of the sofa.

"The good news or the bad news first?" She sat down beside him, opening her bag.

"Try me with the good."

She handed him the documents she had liberated from the safe-deposit box and began to explain, but he waved her into silence with one of his gestures that so exasperated her.

"Let me come to my own conclusions, Prudence. Drink your coffee and help yourself to cognac if you'd like."

"No, thank you," she said.

"Then pour me one, would you?" He didn't look up from his reading, either as he made the request or when she set the goblet in front of him.

Prudence took up her coffee cup and wandered over to the bookshelves. She felt dismissed as an irrelevancy, and although she now assumed that hadn't really been his intention, it was annoying nevertheless.

Chapter 17

Prudence remained with her back to the room, scanning the titles on the bookshelves, doing her best to appear nonchalant. It seemed her only defense against the feeling of being irrelevant to proceedings that touched her so nearly.

"Well," Gideon said at last.

Prudence turned very casually. "Well what?" She went over to the table and set down her empty coffee cup.

"I'll put Thadeus onto discovering the legal standing of this Barclay Earl and Associates first thing tomorrow," Gideon said, tapping the sheets that he still held on his knee. "You did well."

"Praise indeed," Prudence said with a sardonic little curtsy. "I'm overwhelmed to have satisfied the exacting standards of the most famous barrister in town."

"Wasp," he accused. "How did I just put your back up?"

Prudence folded her arms. "I suppose it didn't occur to you that I might have gone through hells of conscience getting that information. I had to falsify authorization from my father, deceive the bank manager, and then dig into Father's most private papers."

"But without it your case would have been lost," he pointed out. "Needs must, my dear." He tapped the papers again. "With this I can promise that the earl of Barclay will be squirming on the stand. I think you'll find the unsavory methods you had to use worth it then."

"So it will serve?" Prudence looked at him closely.

"I believe so." He put down the papers. "And it came none too soon. The trial date has been set for two weeks tomorrow."

"Two weeks!" she exclaimed. "Can we be ready by then?"

"We have no choice," he said. "I trust you can perfect the French maid imitation in that time."

"At least it doesn't give them too much more time for snooping," Prudence murmured, half to herself. Her stomach seemed to be turning somersaults, not a good response to truffled eggs and quail.

Gideon watched her for a second, guessing at her reaction. What had been a long-distance threat was now present reality. No wonder she looked a little green. He stood up. "Come here. I've been longing to kiss you all evening."

"You've been too busy eating to think of kissing," she retorted, but she allowed him to tilt her face up to his.

"There is, as I've so often told you, a time and a place for everything. Now is the time for kissing." He brushed her lips lightly with his own, tantalizing her with a sudden flick of his tongue into the corner of her mouth.

An instant before she was lost in the scent of his skin, the taste of his tongue, the firm yet pliable feel of his lips, Prudence pulled back her head. "No, Gideon. Before we get into this, what are we to do about the letter to *The Mayfair Lady* offering information for the case? It's so urgent now. Should we answer it?"

He frowned down at her, his fingers still closed over her chin. Then he shook his head as if in resignation and said, "I would suspect a trick."

"But supposing it *is* genuine?"

"You must do what you think best."

"That's not very helpful," she said, stepping back from him. "I need a better answer before we can move on to other things."

Gideon groaned. "How could I have fallen for a veritable Lysistrata?"

Fallen for? Prudence steepled her hands, pressing her fingertips against her mouth. There was no reason to be alarmed by such a statement, she told herself. Of course, he was not the kind of man to make delirious love to any woman who crossed his path. Any more than she was the kind of woman to fall into any man's bed. There was an attraction between them. The attraction of opposites, if nothing else. Silly to read more into it than that.

"Give me your answer," she demanded.

"Don't touch it with a barge pole. It's not worth the risk. Even if it is genuine and there is some information out there, we don't need it," he said crisply. "Now, could we go back to where we were, please?"

"Yes, sir. At your service, sir." Prudence moved into his arms, putting her own around his neck as she lifted her face imperatively. His mouth was wonderfully hard on hers, his lips at first closed then opened, pressing her own apart as his tongue drove deep into her mouth with a predatory possession that sent arrows of lust darting through her loins. In the still-sensible recess of her mind, she knew this would have to stop soon. There could be no logical conclusion to this kiss in Gideon's house, with his daughter asleep upstairs, but she was too hungry *now* to worry about the inevitable letdown to come.

The banging of the front door knocker, loud and imperative, broke their private, passionate circle. Gideon raised his head, frowning, running a hand through his already disheveled hair. "Who the hell could that be? I'm not expecting anyone. The staff have gone to bed."

The banging came again. He strode out of the drawing room. Prudence followed, standing in the drawing room entrance as he opened the front door. She couldn't see anything in the shadows of the hall, where all but a single lamp had been doused. There was a long silence.

There was a quality to the sudden silence that made her scalp crawl. Slowly she took a step into the hall.

"Harriet," Gideon said without inflection. "This is a surprise."

"I thought I'd better surprise you, Gideon," a woman's voice said with a little trill that sounded nervous to Prudence. "If I warned you I was coming, you might have refused to see me."

"Hardly," he said in the same expressionless tone. "You'd better come in."

Gideon's ex-wife stepped into the hall. She wore an opera cloak of black velvet. As she glanced curiously around, she raised a gloved hand to her black taffeta hat, adjusting one of the white plumes. Her eyes fell upon Prudence, standing now in the light streaming from the drawing room at her back.

"Oh," she said. "You're entertaining, Gideon. How inconsiderate of me not to have warned you of my arrival." She crossed the hall towards Prudence. "Good evening, I'm Harriet Malvern."

Prudence took the extended hand belonging to one of the most classically beautiful women she had ever encountered and shook it. "Prudence Duncan," she said.

"Oh, Gideon, could you find someone to take up my valise?" Harriet said over her shoulder. "I was sure you wouldn't mind if I stayed for a few days. I do so want to see Sarah. Where is she? She's not in bed yet?"

"It's nearly midnight," Gideon said in the same expressionless tone. "Where did you think she would be?"

"Oh, don't be disagreeable, Gideon," Harriet said. "I don't know what time children go to bed, and she must be almost grown up now."

"Go into the drawing room, Harriet," Gideon instructed. "I don't know what's going on here, and you're certainly not seeing Sarah until I find out."

Harriet pouted a little. "He's so stern sometimes, have you noticed?" she said in a conspiratorial undertone to Prudence.

This was not a conversation Prudence was about to have. She stepped around the elegant figure and said formally, "It's time I left, Sir Gideon."

"Oh, don't go on my account," trilled the visitor. "I'm so tired anyway. I'll just go up to my room. Perhaps Mrs. Keith—You do still have Mrs. Keith?—could bring me up a little soup."

"Mrs. Keith is in bed," Gideon said. "Now do as I say." His lips were very thin, his eyes hard. He turned to Prudence. "Would you mind waiting in the library for a few minutes? This won't take very long."

Prudence looked at him in astonishment. *Won't take very long.* He was intending simply to dismiss this woman, the mother of his child, who'd just turned up on his doorstep with bag and baggage. He was prepared to give her a few minutes of his time, and then presumably send her on her merry way.

"No," she said, shaking her head. "I'm leaving now. You have other things that require your attention."

"Daddy?" Sarah's girlish treble came unnervingly from the head of the stairs. "What's all that banging?"

"It's nothing, Sarah. Go back to bed. I'll come up in a minute," he called, laying an arresting hand on his ex-wife's arm as she made to move past him towards the stairs. "Not yet," he said through his teeth. "Go into the drawing room."

And this time she obeyed. Gideon turned back to Prudence. "Let me deal with this. It won't take a minute."

"What do you mean, it won't take a minute?" she demanded in an incredulous undertone, aware of Sarah now awake and curious upstairs. "That's your ex-wife, or am I mistaken?"

"No, you're not," he said wearily. "I just need to find out what she's doing here."

"Yes, you do," Prudence said, making for the guest room and her coat and hat. "And I cannot imagine how you can do that in three minutes. This is no time for me to be here." She picked up her coat from the bed and then stood in front of the mirror to put on her hat. Her hands were trembling and she hoped that Gideon, who was standing rather helplessly in the doorway, couldn't see them.

"Excuse me." She walked past him towards the front door, stepping around the pile of valises that seemed to indicate a stay of a more than transitory nature.

"Prudence." He came after her, catching her arm as she stepped out through the still-open door. "This is not your affair. It doesn't concern you at all. Leave now if you must, but nothing's changed between us."

"What do you mean, it doesn't concern me?" she demanded, trying to keep her voice low. "We've spent an entire night in bed together. That woman is a part of your life. The mother of your child. How could you possibly be so obtuse, so . . . so insensitive . . . as to dismiss her *and me* as somehow irrelevant to your own concerns? Are you suggesting we simply carry on as if nothing has happened?"

She shook her head in disbelief, shook off his arm, and waved at a passing hackney carriage, its driver nodding sleepily on the box. "Good night, Gideon."

The cab drew to a halt at the bottom of the narrow flight of steps. Gideon made no further attempt to stop her. He waited until she was in the cab, then turned back to the hall, his expression grim.

Prudence sat back against the cracked leather swabs and tried to sort out what had just happened. It wasn't Gideon's fault that Harriet had arrived, but how could he possibly think he didn't have to deal with it . . . that in a few minutes everything would be back to normal? *What kind of man was he?*

How was Sarah going to respond to her mother's abrupt reappearance? Surely he had to realize that that would take more than a few minutes to deal with.

It defied belief.

Prudence was as incredulous the next morning as she had been when she had finally fallen asleep. Recounting the incident to Chastity had not helped to clear her mind, and neither had the hours of restless tossing in hot sheets. She awoke headachy and as tired as if she had not slept a wink.

A bleary-eyed look at the clock told her it was barely seven. She rolled over and tried to go back to sleep, but without success. A knock at the door surprised her.

"Miss Prue?" Jenkins called softly.

"What is it, Jenkins?" She sat up.

The door opened, but instead of Jenkins, Gideon walked in, dressed impeccably in morning coat and waistcoat, carrying an attaché case. Clearly on his way to work, Prudence thought, even as she stared at him.

"What are you doing here?"

"I need to talk to you," he said, setting his attaché case on a chair.

"Sir Gideon insisted on coming up, Miss Prue," Jenkins said apologetically. "He said he would open every door until he found you if I didn't show him up."

"That's all right, Jenkins," Prudence said. "I know how very *persuasive* Sir Gideon can be. Could you bring me some tea?"

"At once, Miss Prue. Should I fetch Miss Chas first, though?"

"I don't need a chaperone, Jenkins," she said. It was a little late for that, but she kept that reflection to herself.

Jenkins left, leaving the door half open. Gideon closed it, then turned back to the bed. "Good morning."

"Good morning."

He swung a chair around to face the bed and straddled it, resting his arms along the back. "You don't look very refreshed," he observed.

"I'm not. Where's your ex-wife?"

"In bed and asleep, I assume. Harriet is not in the habit of greeting the day until the morning's well advanced."

"In bed in your house?"

"Where else?" he asked, sounding genuinely surprised. His eyes narrowed. "Not in my bed, if that's what you're asking."

"It wasn't."

"Just why did you run off like that, Prudence? I told you I had everything under control. All I needed—" He broke off as Jenkins came in with a tray of tea that he set down on the bedside table. He gave Gideon something approaching a glare and left, again leaving the door ajar.

Gideon got up and closed it.

"There seems to be only one cup," Prudence observed, taking up the teapot. "Jenkins does not look kindly upon intruders at any time of the day."

"No matter. I prefer coffee anyway. As I was saying, I needed to find out what had brought Harriet to my doorstep so that I'd know what I was getting into. Then you and I could have discussed it openly and we could at least have had a civilized good-bye. Why did you just up and run like that as if there was something to run from?"

Prudence took a sip of tea. It was impossible to have a conversation with someone so absolutely blind to another point of view. "I wasn't running from anything, Gideon. I was leaving you to your own business. I assume it's not every day that your ex-wife drops in on you?" Her eyebrows lifted. "I seem to remember you'd said she'd been absent for six years. Tell me, was Sarah pleased to see her mother after such a time?"

Gideon frowned at her tone. "I told you last night, it's no concern of yours. I have my own business well in hand." He passed a hand across his jaw, aware of her angry eyes, the set of her mouth. This was not going the way he'd intended, but she had to see reason. He made an effort to moderate his tone. "Sarah seemed puzzled by her mother's arrival more than anything," he said. "I would have preferred to have given her some warning. Harriet, however, doesn't think of other people when she's acting on impulse."

"How long is she going to stay with you?" Her voice was clipped, her expression unwavering.

He shrugged. "Until she finds somewhere else, I suppose. She's left her horse trainer and has nowhere to go at present."

She watched him over the rim of her cup. "You're not obligated to shelter an ex-wife, are you?"

"No, not legally. But ethically I think I am," he said. "Harriet isn't very good at taking care of herself. She doesn't have a practical bone in her body. But there's no reason why that should affect us, Prudence."

"Of course it affects us!" she exclaimed. "Either you're divorced or you're not, Gideon. I'm not having an affair with a man who's living with another woman, whatever the circumstances. How is Sarah going to make sense of it? Her mother has taken up residence again, but her father is seeing another woman?" She shook her head and set down her empty cup.

"Sarah's a sensible girl. She'll accept what I tell her."

"It's her *mother*," Prudence stated. "That's a relationship you clearly know nothing about. She's going to have a loyalty towards her just by the very fact of Harriet's being her mother." She held up her hands in an almost defensive gesture. "I'm not going anywhere near that, Gideon. It's not my business. It seems to me you have more than enough on your plate right now without complicating matters with a love affair. Let's just walk away from it, *now*."

"I'm not going to allow Harriet to interfere with my life," he said tautly, his mouth thinned. "Any more than she already has done. You are in my life, Prudence, and you're going to stay in it."

"Not at your say-so." She threw aside the covers and sprang to her feet, her nightgown swirling around her ankles. "I have had enough of your ultimatums, Gideon. I make my own choices, and I do not choose to be involved in your life at this moment. Or possibly at any moment," she added. "We're so different. You can't even begin to see my point of view." She shook her head, setting her hair swirling in a copper cloud against the white of her nightgown. "You're not even entertaining the possibility that I might be right . . . that I might know more about daughters and their mothers than you do."

He stood up, caught her shoulder, his fingers pressing through the thin cotton, feeling the sharp bone beneath. "If you insist, I'll send Harriet away."

"You're not listening to me," she cried, jerking away from his hold. "I don't insist on anything. Do you really imagine I would encourage you to throw a dependent woman onto the streets? Who do you think I am?"

She stalked to the window, unconsciously rubbing her shoulder where the warmth of his fingers lingered. She stood with her back to him, staring out at the dim light of dawn. "I am not involved in your life. I cannot be. As you so rightly said, it is not my concern. Only not the way you mean, it's the way I mean. I want no part of it . . . and no part of a man who thinks a simple statement that there's nothing to worry about is all that's needed to keep a nice little love affair humming smoothly."

She spun around to face him. "I am not a nice little love affair to be kept on the sidelines."

"Oh, for God's sake," Gideon said, his own anger now riding high. "You're not making any sense to me."

"No, I'm sure I'm not," she said bitterly. "That's exactly the point I'm making."

"I have to go to work." He grabbed up his attaché case. "We'll talk about this later."

"There's nothing to talk about," Prudence said. "Are you still prepared to be our barrister?"

He had his hand on the door. He turned and stared at her, a white shade around his mouth, a little muscle twitching in his cheek. "Are you suggesting I would allow my personal feelings to interfere in my professional life?"

Big mistake, Prudence realized belatedly. She'd forgotten that whatever else she chose to impugn, she should steer clear of his professionalism. "No," she said. "I was just thinking that it might be difficult if you had hostile feelings towards your client."

"Don't be ridiculous. I don't have hostile feelings towards you." The door banged on his departure.

And that was a piece of gross self-deception, if ever she'd heard one. Prudence flopped down on the bed again. Everything about that encounter left a sour taste. She had not expressed herself clearly and Gideon had in his habitual fashion tried to carry the issue on the tide of his own confidence and sense of superiority. They were not made to be lovers.

She lay back against the pillows, closing her eyes. She didn't blame him for wanting to protect Harriet—indeed, she applauded him. But she could certainly blame him for not beginning to understand that it might be a problem for her. Oh, it was all part and parcel of what was wrong with this relationship. Two people who had such vigorous differences of opinion and character were doomed as a couple from the start. Maybe it was good to break it off before they were in too deep. But she still felt hollow and disappointed, and in a strange way rather lost.

"I'm so confused," Prudence said to her sisters later that morning. "He talks about *falling* for me, about how much I'd like his daughter's governess, he takes it perfectly for granted that I should help Sarah with her homework, he cooks dinner for me, for God's sake, and then his ex-wife turns up and he tells me not to worry my pretty little head over it because it's none of my business, he'll take care of it all, and we should just carry on as before."

She refilled her coffee cup. "How could he not see the essential contradiction in that?"

Her sisters had run out of responses to a question that had been repeated in various forms throughout the morning. "I think from now until the case is over you have to see him only when it relates to the libel suit," Constance said, as she had done before. "It'll clear the way to keep things professional. Let him sort out his own domestic affairs, and when the case is over and his situation has been resolved, then you can decide how you feel."

"However it's resolved," Chastity said rather gloomily, "we can forget about finding him a bride. He's not going to be open to the hunt if he's got an ex-wife living in his house. I suppose we'll have to settle for the eighty-twenty split."

"Twenty percent is better than bankruptcy," Prudence pointed out. "Anyway, for all we know there may be no damages. We might just count ourselves lucky to manage a successful defense with no damages awarded."

"That is dismally true," Constance said. "But at least the barrister will get paid by the other side if that happens, so I suggest we let him get on with his work and Prue should put her feelings about the whole business aside until it's over."

Prudence sighed and flung herself against the sofa cushions. "I know how I'll feel," she stated. "It was a mistake ever to get involved with him, and I knew it from the word *go*. I just didn't listen to my rational self. We're totally incompatible, we see the world from opposite poles. So now I'll stop obsessing about it, it's just that—" She broke off. "No, I'm not going to say another word. Let's practice my French accent. Try to think up some really unpleasant questions about the publication, make them really aggressive, and see if I can hold up."

They worked until luncheon and Prudence forced herself to concentrate, but the image of Harriet Malvern would not leave her. Such an exquisitely beautiful woman. How could any other woman hope to compete? But she wasn't competing . . . of course she wasn't. She had no interest in extending her brief fling with Gideon. Particularly now.

She'd brought one thing away from it, after all. She'd discovered the joys of sex.

"Prue? Prue?"

"Oh, sorry. Where were we?"

"Your eyes were closed," Chastity told her.

"I must have been dozing."

"Dreaming, rather," Constance observed.

"Well, any luck?" Gideon asked his clerk as Thadeus came into the inner chamber.

"Oh, yes," Thadeus said. "I could find no records anywhere of the legal existence of a company called Barclay Earl and Associates. I checked with the solicitors who drew up the lien on Ten Manchester Square. They are, of course, not the same firm the earl is employing in his suit . . . the solicitors who have briefed Sir Samuel. Their reputation is, of course, impeccable." He coughed discreetly into his hand. "The other firm . . . from the shady side of the street, I would have said, Sir Gideon."

Gideon nodded and lit a cigarette. "Good," he said. "Go on."

"They were a little reluctant to be forthcoming, but I managed to convince them that my principal in this case would take a lack of cooperation amiss, that maybe there were aspects of their practice that might not stand up to scrutiny . . . I mentioned the faint possibility of a subpoena in the case."

"Ah. A useful stick, Thadeus." Gideon leaned back in his chair and blew a careful smoke ring. "Any holes in the document?"

Thadeus shook his head a little sadly. "Not exactly, sir. But if the company that holds the lien is not a legal entity, then . . ."

Gideon nodded. "Then the document is a fraud. Anything else?"

"I did discover that this particular firm had been involved in several previous dealings for Barclay Earl and Associates. They did have documents showing the establishment of the company, but, as I said, nothing to indicate that the company was legally registered." He laid a folder on the table in front of the barrister. "In fact, they as good as admitted that they had failed to register the company as a legal entity."

Gideon glanced down at them. "So, these papers were merely a blind to fool the unwary, or the unaware."

"That is my conclusion, Sir Gideon."

Gideon sat forward abruptly. "All right. That's good, Thadeus. It gives us what we need. Thank you." He opened the folder as the clerk backed discreetly from the chamber.

Gideon flipped through the documents, then he pushed the folder away from him with an impatient gesture. *Of all the intransigent, stubborn women.*

Maybe she did know more than he did about mothers and daughters, but from the mess the Duncan sisters were in at the moment, they all appeared to know remarkably little about what constituted a good relationship between fathers and daughters. Trust came to mind.

Of course Harriet's reappearance was a nuisance, but the fact that he both saw it and treated it as no more than that was no reason for Prudence to start prattling about the care and feeding of dependent women.

She had to be one of the most exasperating, opinionated women he'd ever met. Harriet seemed almost restful in comparison. One couldn't possibly contemplate living with a woman whom one disliked most of the time. Except that the rest of the time . . . and maybe it wasn't *most* of the time. And anyway, where had the idea about living with her come from?

With a muttered oath, he pulled paper and pen towards him. He was her barrister and at this moment that was *all* he was. And all he wanted to be.

"What does he say?" Chastity asked somewhat tentatively after her sister seemed to have been spending an inordinate length of time reading a one-page script. "It's from Gideon, isn't it?"

Prudence scrunched up the envelope and tossed it onto the hall table. "Yes," she said. "Just details about the trial."

"In that case, may we see?" Constance asked, turning from the mirror, where she'd been putting on her hat before leaving for home.

"Certainly," her sister said with a shrug. "There's nothing personal in it. He does stop short of calling me Miss Duncan and signing himself Malvern, but that's as personal as it gets." She held out the letter.

"That's good, isn't it?" Chastity asked, as tentatively as before.

"Yes, of course it is," Prudence said on a rather testy note. "It's business only, as we agreed."

Constance refrained from glancing at Chastity. Prudence would be bound to intercept the look and she was as sensitive at the moment as if she'd lost a layer of skin. Indeed, if Constance had been asked for her opinion, she would have said her younger sister was frightened out of her mind. And not about the court case. But then, she hadn't been asked for her opinion.

She perused the contents of the letter. "It looks promising, if you can decipher the legalese," she said. "Barclay's so-called company had no legal standing, and therefore had no legal basis for demanding payments from Father. Gideon seems to be saying that he's fairly confident he can go after Barclay on the stand and rattle him enough to get some kind of an admission." She passed the letter over to Chastity.

"Yes, that was my impression," Prudence agreed.

Chastity looked up from the letter. "He doesn't suggest seeing us again until the actual morning of the trial. Don't you need more preparation, Prue?" She looked anxiously at her sister.

Prudence shook her head. "I know what he wants, he made it very clear. A warmhearted, sympathetic woman who will appeal to the hearts and minds of twelve jurymen, and will absolutely refrain from offending them in any way. I'll have to bat my eyelashes and mutter of lot of *oo-la-la*s and *oui, monsieur*s."

"They won't see you batting anything under the veil," Chastity pointed out.

"No," Prudence agreed. "But I'll flutter my hands in a very Gallic fashion and wave a perfumed handkerchief around when I want it to seem that I'm distressed by the questions."

"You'll need some indignation," Constance said. "To be credible."

"Oh, I'm leaving that to Gideon," her sister stated, walking to the stairs. "His role is the fire and brimstone, mine is the honey." She turned, her foot on the bottom step. "I am not to come across as a bitter, ill-tempered, man-hating spinster, you see." Then she walked up the stairs before her sisters could close their mouths and marshal their responses.

Chapter 18

"You're up early this morning, Father," Prudence observed as she entered the breakfast room. Her father, in the most formal of morning wear, was already at the breakfast table, and judging by his empty plate had just finished his meal.

Lord Duncan regarded his daughter with a somewhat testy air. "Have you forgotten it's the first day of Barclay's libel suit? I'm to appear in court this morning."

"Oh, yes," Prudence said casually, going over to the sideboard. "It slipped my mind." She looked at the dish of kedgeree and her already rebellious stomach gave a queasy lurch.

"Well, it's a very important day," her father declared, setting aside his napkin and pushing back his chair. "I shall not be in for luncheon, you may tell Jenkins."

Neither would his daughters. But Prudence merely nodded agreeably and sat down, reaching for the toast rack. Maybe a piece of dry toast would ease the nausea.

"Good morning, Father." Chastity passed her father in the doorway. "You're up early."

"It's Father's day in court," Prudence said before her father could reply. "Did you forget?"

"Oh, yes, sorry," Chastity said. "Good luck."

"I can't imagine why you would think luck is necessary," Lord Duncan stated. "It's an open-and-shut case. By the end of today, that disgraceful rag will be off the streets and out of business. You mark my words." He gave a decisive nod and strode off.

"Oh, God, I hope not," Chastity said, heaping kedgeree on her plate. "How are you feeling, Prue?"

"Sick as a dog," her sister confessed. "How can you eat, Chas? This morning of all mornings."

"To keep up my strength," Chastity said. "And you should eat something more than dry toast, Prue. You're the one who's going to need the most strength."

Prudence shook her head. "I can't eat a thing. Even tea makes me want to vomit." She pushed away her cup and plate. "I'll go and get ready to leave."

Chastity glanced at the clock. It was only seven-thirty. "We have an hour and a half before we have to be at Gideon's chambers."

Prudence merely shook her head and left the breakfast room. In her bedroom she examined her face in the mirror. Pale and wan was about the kindest thing that could be said for her complexion at present. Her eyes were heavy-lidded and black-shadowed. Even her hair seemed to have lost some of its vibrancy. Not that her physical appearance was in the least important at the moment. No one was going to get so much as a glimpse of it beneath the thick black-spotted veil.

Gideon, of course, would see her unveiled when they met this morning. But then, her appearance was no concern of his. His sparse communications over the last two weeks had dealt only with the upcoming suit, and were implicitly addressed to all three of them. He never mentioned Harriet, or Sarah, or indeed anything personal. They had made the clean break she had asked for. She was heart-whole. Not hurt, not diminished in any way by that momentary flight of passion.

It was not at all surprising that the strain of the last two weeks of waiting should show on her face, Prudence told herself. They had been looking over their shoulders for spies and detectives, suspecting every piece of mail that came into the house. They had ceased publication of *The Mayfair Lady* for the duration. She and Chastity had barely shown their faces outside the house, and Constance had performed only those social duties that her position as Max's wife made necessary, even giving up her speaking engagements for the WSPU for these two weeks. They had sat for hours in the parlor, going over and over every detail of the case, anticipating hostile questions, as the barrister had demonstrated, Prudence practicing her fake accent until her tongue felt so thick and huge it barely seemed to fit her mouth anymore.

The door opened behind her and she spun around, feeling for some reason rather self-conscious, as if caught in an embarrassing activity . . . as if there was something odd about self-scrutiny. Chastity gave her a rather puzzled look. "Do you have any spare hairpins, Prue? I can't seem to find any and I need to fix this veil to my hat." She half lifted the black veil on her arm.

"Yes . . . yes, of course." Prudence rummaged through a drawer in her dresser. "I had a new pack in here somewhere."

"Father's just left," Chastity said.

"That's a bit early isn't it? The court doesn't even open until ten." Prudence found the pack of pins and handed them to her sister.

"I think he's as nervous as we are," Chastity said, tucking the pins into her skirt pocket. "I got the impression he'd rather walk around the square for an hour than hang around the house."

"I share the feeling," Prudence said. "Do you mind if we leave a little early? I'm going crazy just waiting."

"No, of course not. I'll be ready in ten minutes." Chastity whisked herself from the room and Prudence returned to her mirror, this time to put on her hat and try the effect of the veil for the umpteenth time.

They took a hackney to the Embankment and then walked up and down the Temple gardens, saying little to each other until it was time to meet Constance. It was a cloudy day, the river gray and sluggish, a sharp wind blowing the last remaining leaves from the trees. Prudence huddled into her coat, turning up the collar, but she still shivered.

"Are you nervous about seeing him?" Chastity asked suddenly.

Prudence didn't pretend not to know what she was talking about. "No, why should I be?"

"I don't know. I just thought you might be."

"He's our barrister, Chas. I'm only nervous that he won't succeed in defending us."

"Yes, of course," Chastity agreed. "Ah, here's Con." She gestured to where their sister was hurrying across the leaf-strewn, damp grass towards them.

"Am I late?"

"No, we were early. I couldn't stand to stay in the house another minute," Prudence said.

Constance looked at her sister. "Are you ready for this, Prue?"

Prudence knew she was not referring to the court appearance. "You're as bad as Chas. Of course I am. Gideon is our barrister. Other than that, he's nothing more to me than the memory of a brief fling in Henley-on-Thames that I've had two weeks to get over. And I'm sure it's the same for him. Let's go."

Big Ben chimed nine o'clock as they reached the street door to the barrister's chambers. They climbed the stairs in single file. The door at the top stood open and Thadeus was on his feet, clearly awaiting them, his eyes on the wall clock.

"Good morning, ladies." He bowed. "Sir Gideon is waiting for you."

But Gideon was already opening the door to the inner chamber. "Good morning," he said pleasantly. "Come in. Thadeus, bring coffee, will you?"

And Prudence knew that she was over nothing. The sound of his voice was all it took to bring memories surging to the surface. Unconsciously, she stiffened her shoulders and said neutrally, "Good morning, Gideon."

They filed past him and took the three seats awaiting them. Gideon went behind the table and took his seat, but not before he had given them all a swift, assessing glance. His gray gaze lingered for a minute longer on Prudence. She was aware of it and resisted the ridiculous urge to look away, instead forcing herself to meet his eye until he turned his attention to the papers on his desk.

He looked tired, she thought. Almost as tired as she felt.

Gideon thought that Prudence looked exhausted. He was weary himself, but she looked dead on her feet. The last two weeks had been the worst he could ever remember passing, and not only because of the chaos Harriet's reappearance had wreaked on Sarah's equilibrium. Prudence had certainly been right on that score. Keeping himself away from Prudence had been one of the hardest things he had ever made himself do. But she had made her wishes clear. Instead he had thrown himself into the libel case, working longer hours on it than he would normally devote even to a case that would guarantee him a substantial fee. Prudence would not have an opportunity to question his professionalism again.

"Forgive me for saying so, Prudence, but you don't look very robust this morning," he observed.

"It's been a stressful two weeks," she said. "I haven't slept well. And to be brutally honest, I'm quite sick with nerves this morning, as you might imagine." There was faint accusation in the last statement.

"That is only to be expected," he said so calmly, she once again had the urge to throw something at him. "Have you eaten this morning?"

"Not really," Chastity answered for her. "She ate barely a crumb of dry toast."

Prudence shot her sister an annoyed look. "So I have no appetite. That's no one's business but my own."

"Now, there I beg to differ," the barrister said. "If you faint in the witness box, it becomes mine."

"I will not faint," she retorted.

"Would you eat some toast and honey now?" he asked, his tone both conciliatory and sympathetic. A tone, Prudence decided, carefully calculated to achieve his objective.

She sighed, unwilling to appear petulant. "I'm not hungry, but if you insist . . ."

"No, I don't insist. I merely advise," he said, rising from the table and going to the door to make the request of Thadeus. He returned to his seat. "Now, let me explain what will happen this morning."

They listened as he gave them the order of business. Prudence was so absorbed that she had eaten most of a piece of toast and honey before she realized it, and rather to her chagrined surprise, she did feel stronger and less queasy.

Gideon wisely refrained from comment. "So, to sum up," he said. "Sir Samuel has notified us that he'll be calling *The Mayfair Lady* as a hostile witness. He's going to try to discredit the publication in the eyes of the jury before I get a chance to put on a defense. You can expect some very aggressive questioning, Prudence, but if he does any significant damage, I will have the opportunity to rectify it under my cross-examination."

Prudence, who was wondering what kind of damage he was anticipating having to rectify, merely nodded.

Gideon gave her an encouraging smile. "If I can damage Barclay's credibility sufficiently under my cross-examination, it's possible you might have a relatively easy ride."

"Unless they know who we are," Prudence said. "We don't think they do, but we can't be sure."

"They don't," he said.

"How do you know?"

He smiled. "There are ways in this business to find out certain germane facts."

"I suppose it didn't occur to you that it would have made life easier for us if we'd known that?" Prudence asked.

"I had to wait until the last minute to be certain. Things can change up until the eleventh hour."

"I see your point," Constance said, drawing Sir Gideon's attention away from Prudence. "But we've been on tenterhooks."

"I understand, but there was nothing to be done about it before." He lifted his fob watch and glanced at it. "We'll talk about how the morning's gone at the luncheon recess."

Prudence nodded, willing simply to be relieved that they didn't have to worry about their identities coming out. She found she had no thought now for inconvenient memory surges. "Should we go?"

He stood up. "Yes, we should. Constance, you and Chastity should sit in the gallery at the very back. Try not to be visible to anyone in the witness box, I don't want you to distract Prudence, even inadvertently. I'd prefer it if she almost didn't know that you were there."

"I will, though," Prudence said. "I couldn't possibly do this without them being there."

"No, I understand that. Nevertheless, you have to accept what I say. I do in this instance know what I'm talking about." He was putting on his gown and wig as he spoke.

There was the faintest emphasis on *in this instance* and Prudence wondered what it meant. It couldn't be a reference to anything personal between them, he'd given not the slightest indication this morning that they had any kind of shared history. And her own first reaction to seeing him had been an aberration, one best forgotten.

The libel case was being heard in a small courtroom in the Old Bailey, a location that limited spectators, which, as Gideon had told them, was all to the good. There were bound to be some press, some gossip columnists, maybe even some inquisitive members of London society, but there couldn't be too many of them. He did not tell the sisters that Thadeus on his principal's instruction had arranged this with his colleague, the clerk of the court responsible for allocating courtrooms.

In a small antechamber, the sisters donned their veils. The time for words was over now. They merely touched hands briefly and then Constance and Chastity left Prudence and went up to the gallery, which was already filled with a whispering, shifting crowd. They sat behind a pillar in the very back row.

Prudence waited for Gideon to come for her. She no longer felt sick. She no longer felt nervous. It was as if she had entered some quiet space quite separate from the bustling world around her.

"Are you ready to go in now?" Gideon had opened the door so quietly, she hadn't heard him, and she turned from the little window where she'd been standing staring at the blank wall visible beyond.

"Yes. How is my veil?"

"Impenetrable," he said. "How's the accent?"

"Thick," she said.

He nodded and smiled, hearing the attempt at humor in her voice. "Come." He put a hand on her shoulder and she was glad of the touch, of the sense it gave her of support. Gideon would not let her down. *Not in this instance.*

She banished the mental addendum. He would not let her down and she must not let *him* down.

The courtroom was busy and the people on the long benches turned to look at them as they walked down the narrow aisle to the defense table. Prudence heard the buzz of whispers rising to a low murmur but she looked neither to the right nor the left, merely took the chair Gideon held for her. He sat beside her, laid his papers on the table in front of him, and sat back, as calm and relaxed as if he were in front of his own fireside, except for the white curly wig and the black gown.

"May the court be upstanding."

The assembly scrambled to its feet as the judge entered and took his seat on the high dais. Prudence for the first time glanced sideways at the opposing table. Lord Barclay had an air that was both complacent and vicious, she thought, from a deep well of loathing. Sir Samuel Richardson looked rather older than Gideon, but in the same antique costume it was hard to distinguish them until they spoke. Then it was easy. Sir Samuel's voice was cracked and gravelly against Gideon's quiet, smooth tones. And they had quite different courtroom manners. Prudence was astonished to see that Gideon in his opening remarks was completely nonconfrontational, almost to the point of sounding conciliatory. He smiled, acknowledged his opposing colleague with a polite bow, and a murmured "My learned colleague" suggested that it was quite understandable that Lord Barclay should feel maligned by the publication in question, and sat down again.

Sir Samuel, on the other hand, ranted. His voice reached the rafters as he accused the publication of deliberate fabrication to dishonor the reputation of one of the most esteemed members of "Our society, m'lud."

"Like hell," muttered Prudence, and received a jab in the elbow from her companion. She looked studiously into her lap. Anger was now her friend. She had seen her father sitting in the row behind Barclay and his counsel, and at the thought of what had been done to him, her anxiety vanished. She could almost feel herself baring her teeth like a fox protecting her cubs. She could almost feel her mother's spirit on her shoulder. An absurd fantasy, she told herself, but she was willing to take any help she could get.

Barclay's testimony only strengthened her resolve. He was sanctimonious, hypocritical, and he lied through his teeth. And yet she couldn't feel the slightest reaction from Gideon, sitting so close beside her. He made the odd scratch on a piece of paper, but otherwise simply sat and listened.

Until Sir Samuel had bowed to the judge and the jury and stepped back with a nod to his learned colleague.

Gideon rose, smiling. He greeted Barclay with a bow. "Good morning, my lord."

"Morning." It was a surly response.

"You are under oath, Lord Barclay," Gideon said pleasantly. And from then on he was up and running. And this was the barrister Prudence had expected, the one she had herself experienced. Ruthless, brutal, letting nothing go until he had wrung the answer he wanted from the witness. There were objections from Sir Samuel, some sustained by the judge, but Gideon simply muttered a form withdrawal and swept on.

Prudence froze when her father's name first came up. She saw him raise his head higher with a jerk of surprise, and then she couldn't look at him again as Gideon exposed the fraudulent scheme, the lack of legal registration for the company, the demand for a huge monthly payment, and finally the lien on 10 Manchester Square.

And when the earl was a mere grumbling, muttering, sweating hulk in the witness box, Gideon reverted to his original smoothly charming manner and said, "May I suggest, Lord Barclay, that there was never any intention of building a trans-Saharan railway? I would ask you to consider how many other of your friends have been persuaded to invest in what now seem to be somewhat doubtful enterprises. How many other friends have been obliged to give your unregistered company a lien on their properties?"

"This is calumny, sir," the earl blustered. He looked up at the judge. "I appeal to you, my lord."

"Sir Samuel?" the judge suggested.

Barclay's barrister rose heavily to his feet. His gravelly voice was now rather weary and resigned. "I would ask for a recess and time to confer with my client while we examine the documents in question more closely, m'lud."

The judge banged his gavel. "We'll reconvene at two o'clock."

Prudence glanced up at Gideon as he returned to his chair. He had no expression on his face at all. His eyes were almost blank. And she realized with a chill that this was the face Barclay had been subjected to throughout his interrogation. It was enough to terrify the strongest, most righteous witness. And then it was gone, and he was smiling again, touching her hand lightly as he went around the table.

"That went well, I think," he said. "I'm afraid we can't go anywhere decent for luncheon since you can't take off that veil in public, but I've arranged a pleasant picnic in my chambers."

"My sisters?"

"Of course. Thadeus will bring them as soon as the court has cleared and there are no spying eyes around."

Prudence again refused to look anywhere but ahead of her as they walked out of the court. A few questions were shouted in their direction. Gideon ignored them and held her elbow until they were out in a street where a hackney waited. Not by accident, it was clear. Gideon gave no instructions to the cabbie and as soon as they were inside, the driver cracked his whip and the horse trotted off.

Prudence took a deep breath and put up her veil. "It's stifling behind this thing," she confided. "It is safe now, isn't it?"

"Safe enough." He turned sideways on the bench, examining her in the dim light of the carriage. "How are you bearing up?"

"Better than Barclay," she said with a shaky laugh. "You destroyed him."

"Only almost," he said gravely.

"But you can finish it?" she asked, a flutter of anxiety setting her heart racing.

"I need your father to finish it for me."

"Oh." Prudence understood now. Her father had to confirm that he had been inveigled by a man he thought his friend to invest in a fraudulent scheme designed purely to line the pockets of that so-called friend. If he insisted that he stood by his friend, that his friend had never led him astray, that he had always understood every nuance of the deal and had willingly given him a lien on his house, then their defense would crumble. It couldn't be called fraudulent if the one who was supposed to have been defrauded maintained that he was not.

Constance and Chastity listened in silence as their sister explained this. Gideon kept his offerings to dressed crab-and-lobster sandwiches, glasses of a Chablis Premier Cru, and comment when asked. But he watched Prudence closely and was glad that she took barely a single sip of her wine.

And finally he said, "Prudence, I'm guessing that Sir Samuel will call *The Mayfair Lady* as his next witness. He can't risk calling your father immediately after Barclay's breakdown."

"And with my testimony I have to get Father to switch sides." It was the flat statement of one who had already accepted this conclusion.

He nodded. He wanted to take her in his arms and kiss the lurking panic from her eyes. But if there ever would be a time again for a lover's gesture, this was not it.

"Very well," she said. She looked at her sisters, then back at him. "I'd like to talk to my sisters alone, if you don't mind."

"Of course." He rose from his chair and went to the door, then he hesitated. "You will need to tell me if what you discuss has anything to do with your testimony. You can't spring surprises on your barrister."

"We understand."

He nodded and went out.

The sisters sat in silence for a minute, then Prudence said, "We all know what I have to do."

"The question is how, without revealing your identity to the world at large," Constance said.

"I have an idea." Chastity leaned forward in her chair.

* * *

The courtroom that afternoon seemed hotter to Prudence than it had that morning. She thought she could detect a different, more alert note to the conversational buzz around her while they waited for the judge to reappear, and she was acutely conscious of the glances cast her way. Her heart was banging and the confines of the veil seemed even more stifling than before. She was sure her cheeks were scarlet, perspiration beading her forehead. Gideon, however, was as relaxed as ever as he sat beside her and she tried to draw some of that calm ease into herself by osmosis. It didn't seem to be working.

Her one glance at Lord Barclay had shown her that he too was crimson-hued, but that, she suspected, came as much from an excessively liquid lunch as anything. He was certainly huffing and puffing and having frequent vigorously whispered exchanges with his counsel. Her father looked paler than usual and was sitting very erect on the bench behind Barclay, staring straight ahead at the judge's dais.

"Please be upstanding."

The court rose, the judge took his chair, adjusted his wig, and looked out expectantly at the court below. "Sir Samuel?"

The barrister rose and intoned, "We call the Mayfair Lady to the box, m'lud."

"The publication itself?" The judge peered incredulously at the barrister.

"A representative of the publication, m'lud. A . . ." There was the barest hesitation to accentuate the insult. "A *lady,* as we understand it, m'lud, who prefers to be known simply as Madam Mayfair Lady."

"Unusual," the judge observed. "Can a publication take the oath?"

Gideon rose to his feet. "A representative of the publication can do so, m'lud. I would cite *Angus v. The* Northampton Herald, 1777."

The judge nodded slowly. "Do you have any objection to a representative, Sir Samuel?"

"No, m'lud. The witness is a member of the human race, I believe." This produced a titter around the courtroom. Prudence stared stonily ahead through her veil. Gideon didn't twitch a muscle.

"Very well." The judge nodded. "Call this Madam Mayfair Lady."

Prudence rose and walked steadily to the witness box. The clerk administered the oath and she sat down, folding her hands in her lap.

Sir Samuel approached the box. He looked like a malevolent crow, Prudence decided, with his black gown flapping around him and a look on his face that was almost a leer.

"You are responsible for this publication?" He waved a copy at the courtroom with an air of dismissive disgust.

"*Oui, m'sieur* . . . uh, yes, forgive me. I am one of ze editors."

"And you are from France, I gather."

"From *la France*, yes." Dear God, how was she going to keep this up? It was one thing in the parlor with her sisters at home, quite another here. For the first time, she looked towards the jury box. Twelve good men and true. At least they didn't look bored.

"Is it a habit of your publication to dishonor the reputations of members of our society, *madame*?"

"No," Prudence said simply. She caught the slight nod of approval from Gideon. His maxim had always been Keep it simple. Don't elaborate unless you must.

"And what would you call this article about one of the most respected members of our aristocracy, *madame*?"

"Ze truth, *m'sieur*."

"I would call it a deliberate attempt at character assassination," he said smoothly. "But, of course, citizens of your country are not unused to assassinating their aristocracy."

A ripple of laughter went through the spectators. Prudence glanced at Gideon. He was expressionless.

"We stand by our research, *monsieur*," she said. "And others have done so too."

"Others!" he boomed suddenly. "The *Pall Mall Gazette*, perhaps. And we all know the sensationalist penchants of that particular broadsheet. Your unfounded accusations, *madame*, have merely provided fodder for a known piece of yellow journalism."

"Zey were not unfounded, *m'sieur*," she stated. "We 'ad witnesses. Women who also spoke to ze *Pall Mall Gazette*."

"Women! Fallen women. Women of the streets! Has society come to this? We put the word of a woman no better than she should be against that of a peer of the realm?" He spun around with a swirl of his cloak and gesticulated at the jury, before continuing a circular spin back to face the witness box.

"Ah, Sir Samuel, that is what you call women who are abused by their so-called betters. Fallen women, harlots, whores, prostitutes—" She broke off abruptly, aware both that her accent had slipped and that she had broken Gideon's cardinal rule. She had let indignation rule her and shown her true colors.

"And these women are to be defended by harpies, it would seem," Sir Samuel said, turning again to nod at the jury, confirming her fears.

Prudence took a steamy breath behind her veil. "Revealing society's injustices, *m'sieur,* is part of our publication's mandate. I maintain that we 'ad ample evidence for our accusations against Lord Barclay."

"And these accusations of financial impropriety." He changed the subject with such an aggressive sweep of his hand that Prudence involuntarily flinched. "What could you, *madame,* what could this rag . . ." He waved the copy again. "What could you know of the intimate details of business between two friends . . . two very close friends of many years standing. I would suggest, *madame,* that you and your fellow editors for some reason known only to yourselves had a personal vendetta against the earl of Barclay and made up whatever facts suited you."

"That is not true," she stated.

"Is it not true that you made advances to his lordship? Advances that were rejected?" He put both hands on the rail of the witness box and peered at her as if he could see the pale frame of her face beneath the veil.

Prudence laughed. She couldn't help it, and even as she did so she saw her father's gaze swing towards her, his eyes vividly alert. She could not, of course, disguise her laugh. She hadn't practiced that. But in this case, all to the good.

"You find that amusing, *madame?*" It was clear that her laughter had discomfited the barrister. His accusation, however wild, had been intended to fluster her.

"Very much so," she said. "I was taught by *ma mère*—forgive me, my mother—to find male pretension . . . 'ow you say . . . amusing . . . ridiculous." She produced a very Gallic shrug and another careless laugh. It might not make her any friends among the jury but her father had gone very pale and his eyes remained fixed upon her.

Had he understood?

Sir Samuel, of course, had not. He was beaming now, certain that he had the jury in the palm of his hand. "Male pretension," he said, tapping the broadsheet against the rail. "Quite so, *madame.* Eloquently put. So you maintain that you have no personal knowledge of his lordship. So I ask you again, what could you know of the private business dealings between two men, friends for many years? Two men with whom you have had no dealings, whose characters you know nothing about."

He turned again to the courtroom. "Lord Duncan sits here, gentlemen of the jury, prepared to stand up as a character witness for his friend. Would he do so if that so-called friend had been dealing the cards behind his back? Would he give a man whom he distrusted a lien on his house? I ask you, gentlemen of the jury, ladies and gentlemen, isn't that a little far-fetched?" He turned back to the witness box, bowed at its occupant with a mocking flourish, and strode to his table with a nod towards Gideon.

Gideon rose. "I have no questions of this witness, m'lud."

There was a little collective gasp in the courtroom. The only witness for the defense had just been destroyed and her barrister was doing nothing to repair the damage.

Prudence rose and returned to her seat. Gideon touched her knee, a fleeting gesture, but it told her all she needed to know. She had not dared to look at her father during Sir Samuel's declamation, but Gideon had been watching him closely.

Sir Samuel declared, "I call Lord Arthur Duncan, m'lud."

Lord Duncan walked to the witness box.

Chapter 19

Prudence could barely watch as her father took the oath. His voice was controlled and courteous, and when he sat down his hands rested unmoving on the rail of the witness box.

Sir Samuel approached the box. "Good afternoon, Lord Duncan." He smiled.

"Good afternoon."

"You are here to testify on behalf of your friend Lord Barclay."

"I am here, sir, to testify in a libel suit against a publication known as *The Mayfair Lady*," Lord Duncan said steadily.

Sir Samuel looked startled. Then he recovered and said, "Quite so, m'lud. That is the business that brings us all here today. Would you tell the gentlemen of the jury how long you and Lord Barclay have been friends."

"I have known the earl of Barclay for close to ten years."

"And he is one of your closest friends." Sir Samuel was now regarding his witness much as a ferret might regard a rabbit hole from which a fox might appear instead of the rabbit.

"I would have called him so, yes."

Sir Samuel closed his eyes briefly and changed tack. "You and his lordship have shared several business ventures together, as I understand it."

"Only one of any significance."

"The matter of the trans-Saharan railway?"

"Yes. A venture that I was persuaded would bring a considerable return on investment."

"Such ventures often fail, unfortunately." Sir Samuel shook his head regretfully. "All the investors suffered losses in that instance, I understand."

"To my knowledge, the only investor involved was myself, sir. And, yes, I suffered losses of some magnitude."

Again the barrister shook his head. "As indeed did Lord Barclay himself."

"That I doubt, sir, since at the time of the apparent collapse of this venture, he held a lien on my house. That could not be called a loss."

Sir Samuel looked up at the dais. "M'lud," he began, but was interrupted.

"Testimony not going quite as you expected, Sir Samuel?"

"No, m'lud. I request a recess until the morning."

The judge shook his head. "No time for that. Dismiss the witness if you wish and call your next."

"I cannot dismiss the witness, m'lud, without making him available to my learned friend, Sir Gideon," the barrister pointed out in pained tones.

"No, that is certainly true," the judge said. He sounded as if he was enjoying himself, and Prudence decided she liked him even less than she liked Sir Samuel, even if he did appear to be ruling on their side.

Sir Samuel cleared his throat. "Lord Duncan, you surrendered a lien on your house willingly?"

"I did, because at the time I thought I had no choice. I was unaware, you must understand, that the company I had invested in had no legal standing. My *friend* failed to mention this." This emphasis was so slight and yet it rang through the now intent and silent courtroom like a peal of bells.

"No further questions, m'lud." Sir Samuel returned to his seat.

"Sir Gideon?" the judge invited.

Gideon rose. "No questions for this witness, m'lud."

"You seem to be having rather an easy time of it today, Sir Gideon," the judge remarked genially.

Gideon merely bowed and sat down.

Lord Duncan left the witness box and walked straight from the courtroom, ignoring the rising whispers, the interested looks that followed his progress.

Prudence half rose as if to follow him, and then resumed her seat when Gideon took her elbow.

The judge looked around the courtroom. "Any further witnesses, Sir Samuel?"

"No, m'lud."

"Then, Sir Gideon, the court is yours."

"I have nothing further, m'lud."

Prudence didn't hear the rest of the formalities. She paid no attention to the closing arguments to the jury before they were sent off to deliberate, and she registered only distantly the judge's advice that if they the jurors found the publication not guilty of libel, they could consider awarding *The Mayfair Lady* punitive damages for the distress caused by a frivolous suit.

Prudence could think only that for the last four years they had tried to protect their father, do for him what their mother would have done, and now in the most public and humiliating situation imaginable they had forced reality upon him. It had been Chastity's idea to use a phrase that their mother had used so often.

Male pretension. The phrase had always made her husband protest with one breath and laugh in the next. It had told Lord Duncan who was in the witness box. And, of course, it had explained exactly how his private shame was now public knowledge. Would he ever forgive them?

She became aware of Gideon's hand on her arm. He was ushering her out of the courtroom and into the small antechamber again. Chastity and Constance were already there. They hugged one another fiercely.

"Will he forgive us?" Chastity asked, echoing her sister's thought.

"How long could he go on living a lie?" The question came from Gideon, who still stood beside the door. They turned on him with livid eyes. He raised his hands defensively and backed out of the chamber. No man in his right mind would face the combined wrath of the Duncan sisters.

"It's true, though," Prudence said after an instant's silence. "How long could it go on?"

"It was already over," Constance pointed out practically. "Without his testimony we were going to lose and then he'd have to face reality, and with it . . . well . . ." She blew her nose vigorously.

The door opened and they all three spun to face it. Lord Duncan came in, letting it swing shut behind him. "That barrister told me I'd find you in here." He regarded his daughters in a silence that seemed to stretch like elastic. "How dared you?" he demanded finally. "My private papers? What possible right did you think you had?"

"We didn't think we had any," Prudence said. "But we *knew* that we had no choice. Any more than Mother would have had."

"*The Mayfair Lady* was Mother's publication," Constance said gently.

He gave a short laugh. "I realize that now. I should have known it all along."

"We couldn't lose it to a man who—" Prudence fell silent as he held up an imperative hand.

"I don't want to hear it. I've heard enough for one day. I'll see you at home. You too, Constance." The door closed quietly behind him.

The sisters gave a collective sigh, then Prudence said, "This may sound perverse, but I feel the most amazing sense of release . . . now that he knows, I mean."

"Yes," Chastity agreed soberly.

"I imagine Jenkins and Mrs. Hudson will feel it too," Constance said, just as a tap at the door heralded Gideon's return.

"The jury's coming back. Prudence . . ." He gestured to the open door.

"That was quick. Is that good or bad?" she asked.

"I prefer not to speculate. Come along." His tone was brisk and she sensed for the first time today that he was not as nerveless as he appeared.

The jury filed in. The verdict was read.

"We find the publication. The Mayfair Lady, *not guilty of libel, my lord.*"

Prudence went limp as if she'd lost her skeletal structure. She stared down at the table, at her hands intertwined on its surface. She barely heard the rest of it. The award to the defendant of all costs and one thousand pounds in damages.

Only when it was over did she realize that they were free and clear. All legal costs would be borne by Barclay's side, so Gideon would get his fee. Presumably. rather more than an eighty-percent share of a thousand pounds would give him, she thought as she tried not to stumble on their walk from the court. People crowded them, questions were shouted at her, but she was barely aware of her surroundings. Gideon's hand was under her arm, supporting her, and then they were outside in the gray afternoon, and once again a hackney awaited them.

"Get in," he said, thrusting her inside as a gaggle of newspapermen pressed close, shouting their questions. Prudence half climbed, half tumbled into the gloomy interior, and realized only when she was inside that her sisters were already seated. "How did you get here?"

"Thadeus," Constance said.

Gideon leaned in through the window and said softly, "The cabbie will take you to a hotel first. We don't want you followed home. I imagine your father is already besieged. When it's dark and they've given up for the night, Thadeus will escort you home."

"You think of everything," Prudence observed.

"That is part of my job. On which subject, if it's convenient I'll call upon you in the morning to conclude our business."

"Oh, yes," Prudence said. "Our bargain. Of course."

"Precisely." He closed the door on them.

"Not much of a bargain for the barrister," Constance remarked.

"Well, his fee's covered by Barclay's costs. I doubt he's concerned," Chastity said.

"No," Constance agreed. "But if not, why's he so anxious for his pound of flesh?"

"I daresay he wants to put the entire affair behind him completely," Prudence said from the darkest corner of the cab. "Once the last piece of business is settled, it will be over and he can get on with his normal life without worrying about three contentious and subversive sisters."

"You mean *one* contentious and subversive sister," Constance stated.

Prudence shrugged. "What if I do? I'll not be sorry to have it all over and done with, once and for all."

"I'm sure it will be a relief," Chastity agreed in soothing tones. Her eyes sought her eldest sister's in the dimness. Constance raised her eyebrows in silent comprehension.

Gideon went back to his chambers. He felt none of his usual euphoria after winning a case—in fact, he felt more as if he was about to start trying one. He discarded wig and gown, poured himself a stiff whisky, and sat down at his desk. He had a plan of campaign, just as he always had before starting a trial, but he had no backup plan. There was none to be had. It was a high-stakes throw. All or nothing. And there had been nothing in her manner to encourage making such a move at this juncture. He had hoped for something. He didn't know what exactly, but some small sign that she had missed him. But she'd given him nothing.

He reached for his cigarette box. He had to make allowances for the fact that she had had so much on her plate today, she probably had no mental or emotional energy for anything else. But all the same, he had watched her like a hawk when she'd first entered his chambers, and she'd given him nothing but that cool greeting. She hadn't looked well and she was clearly troubled, but that was hardly surprising. She was facing a courtroom and the possible loss of her livelihood and a great deal else besides. Her mind had definitely not been on matters of the heart.

He sighed and stubbed out his cigarette. He couldn't remember when he'd last felt this anxious.

"You look as if you could do with a sherry, Prue," Constance said when they were ensconced in a private parlor in a discreet establishment in a side street off Piccadilly.

"There seems to be everything here," Chastity said, turning from her examination of the sideboard. "There's tea, if you'd rather. Sandwiches and fruitcake . . . cheese and biscuits . . . sherry, wine, even cognac."

"It's a little early for cognac," Prudence said. "But I'll have a glass of sherry."

"You were magnificent, Prue," Constance said, tossing her hat and gloves on a console table. "I don't know how you managed to keep that accent going without it sounding like a Feydeau farce."

"I think it did," Prudence said, taking the sherry Chastity handed her. "It's the *ze* that always gets to me. I want to laugh every time." She took a sip of sherry. "Not this afternoon, however. I've never felt less like laughing."

"No, none of us have." Constance poured sherry for herself. "But it's over. We won. *The Mayfair Lady* and the Go-Between are safe. And no one knows us from Adam."

"Except Father."

"Except Father," she agreed.

"There's a pack of cards here," Chastity said. "How about we play three-handed bridge? We've got to do something to pass the time if we're not to fall into a slough of despond."

They had been playing for two hours when Thadeus came for them. "There are no newspapermen around the house anymore," he said.

"And Lord Duncan?"

"He had not left the premises when I came to fetch you," the clerk said. "He might have gone out since, of course."

"No, he's waiting for us," Prudence said, sliding the cards back into their silver case. "You're coming back with us, Con?"

"Of course," her elder sister said. "I'd hardly leave you to face him alone. Max will know what happened in court by now, so he'll assume I'm with you."

"The carriage is at the back door," Thadeus informed them. "I thought it best to avoid the front just in case anyone's lingering."

"You think of everything, Thadeus." Prudence smiled wanly at him. He merely bowed.

They sat in silence during the short ride to Manchester Square. "We'll go in the back way," Prudence said as they turned into the square. "Ask him to go to the mews entrance, Thadeus."

"I have already done so, Miss Duncan."

"Yes, of course you have," Prudence murmured.

"Sir Gideon wished me to give you this, Miss Duncan." Thadeus handed her an envelope as she stepped to the ground.

"Oh, thank you." She looked down at it, puzzled. "What is it?"

"The lien on the house, madam. He thought you would know best what to do with it."

Prudence tucked it into her handbag. "Yes, I think I will."

They went into the house through the kitchen. "Oh, my goodness," Mrs. Hudson said as they came in. "What a to-do there's been. Men ringing the doorbell, asking questions, Lord Duncan in the worst mood I've ever seen him in. Locked in the library, he is. What's been going on?"

"I trust the enterprise went in your favor, Miss Prue?" Jenkins appeared in the doorway, his face drawn with anxiety.

"Yes . . . yes, Jenkins, it did," Prudence said swiftly. "I'm sorry we couldn't get home earlier, but Sir Gideon thought we should avoid the newspapers. He was afraid the press would follow us here, even if they weren't already here trying to get at Father."

"They were here, all right," Jenkins said grimly. "Banging the knocker. I threatened to call the police. His lordship locked himself in the library. I tried to ask him what had happened but he cursed me to the devil. I thought it best to leave well enough alone."

"Wise of you, Jenkins," Constance said with a faint smile. "We did win the case, but in order for us to do so, Lord Duncan had to find out the truth."

"Ah," Jenkins said, "that explains it, then." Mrs. Hudson nodded gravely.

"It should make the house a little easier to manage," Prudence said. "If we don't have to pretend and cover up."

Jenkins shook his head. "I don't know about that, Miss Prue. Somehow I don't see his lordship settling for leftovers and inferior wine."

"No," Prudence agreed. "We'll still have to make shift, but at least we won't feel we're creeping around behind his back."

"I think we'd better go to him now," Chastity said. "We can't put it off much longer."

"There's no putting anything off," announced Lord Duncan from the kitchen door. "I assumed you conspirators would all be in here." He glared at the assembled group. "Don't pretend you didn't know about this Jenkins, or you, Mrs. Hudson."

"Father, it's nothing to do with either of them," Prudence protested. "You can blame us all you like, but Jenkins and Mrs. Hudson have only tried to help and make your life easier."

A dull flush mounted on Lord Duncan's cheeks. "For some reason my entire household seemed to find it necessary to shelter me from the consequences of my own folly. I do not find that a pleasant thought." He turned on his heel. "We will discuss this further in the library."

His daughters exchanged a look, shrugged in unison, and followed him. "There's no need to close the door," he said as they entered the library. "It's clear there are no secrets in this household from anyone but myself."

His daughters said nothing.

"How did you persuade Fitchley to let you examine my private papers?" he demanded.

Prudence sighed and told him. "You cannot blame Mr. Fitchley," she said at the end.

"Clearly not. Of all the deceitful . . ." He turned away from them and he seemed suddenly a very old man. "Go away, all of you. I can't face any of you at the moment."

They left him, closing the door softly. "He can't face us, or he can't face himself?" Constance muttered.

Prudence was staring at the closed door, then abruptly she said, "No, we're not bearing all this guilt. Come on." She opened the door and stalked in, her startled sisters behind her.

"I told you—"

"Yes, Father, and we heard you. However, you might want to burn this." She opened her handbag and took out the envelope. "I doubt very much that the earl of Barclay will be pursuing it after this afternoon." She held it out to him.

Lord Duncan opened the envelope, stared down at the lien on his house. "He has no legal claim, then?" he said, almost in disbelief.

"No," Prudence stated. "And he never did have. Since Barclay Earl and Associates is not a legal entity, they can't hold property in its name. Burn it, Father. *Now.*"

He looked at them as they stood in front of him, presenting a united and determined front. And he thought of his wife, and of how like her they all were. And he thought of how much he missed her, every minute of every waking hour. And he knew that his daughters missed her as deeply, if in different ways. And he thought how they were her living embodiment.

Deliberately, he tore the sheet in two, then turned and threw both pieces into the fire. He stood watching as the paper curled, caught, and fell into ash.

Lord Duncan heard the door close behind him as he remained staring into the fire, acknowledging his grief.

Chapter 20

"Prue, are you sure you don't mind seeing Gideon alone?" Chastity asked the next morning, standing on tiptoe to see in the high hall mirror as she adjusted the brim of her hat.

"Of course I don't," her sister said carelessly, sweeping into the palm of her hand fallen petals from the vase of fading chrysanthemums on the hall table. "We need to get *The Mayfair Lady* out on the streets again as soon as possible, and we haven't picked up the post from Mrs. Beedle in more than two weeks. Con's writing up the account of the trial this morning, so it's my task to deal with the barrister. It has been all along, after all."

"I suppose so," Chastity said, still sounding doubtful, but it was clear that her sister had her mind made up and it was the most sensible division of labor, since it would only take one of them to dispose of Gideon. "Very well, then, I'll be off. I'll only be a couple of hours, if that. It depends if Mrs. Beedle wants to chat."

Prudence waved her away and picked up the vase of flowers. She carried it into the kitchen to dispose of them and was returning with the empty vase to the hall when the doorbell rang.

"Shall I get that, Miss Prue?" Jenkins had appeared as usual as if by magic carpet.

"It'll be Sir Gideon," she said, smoothing down her skirts. "Show him into the drawing room."

Jenkins went to open the door and Prudence went into the drawing room, where she turned her attention to a bowl of late-blooming roses that seemed to require some rearranging.

"Good morning."

She turned slowly at the soft voice. "Good morning." She moved towards the sofa. "Do sit down."

"Thank you." He took an armchair and waited for Prudence to alight somewhere. She perched on the arm of the sofa.

"So, I take it you've come to settle our business?" she said.

"That was what I had in mind."

Prudence folded her arms. "You don't think it's a little premature?" she asked testily. "We haven't even received our thousand pounds as yet." She got to her feet abruptly. "I don't understand why this couldn't have been dealt with by letter. Presumably once the damages are paid the money will go to you. Why couldn't you simply subtract your eight hundred pounds and send us our two?"

"Well, you see, I don't think I could do that," he said.

"Well, I'm very sorry, but we don't have the money. I can't give you eighty percent of nothing, can I?" Her green eyes glared, and he could see dark emerald sparks in their depths. Miss Duncan was clearly rather irritated. He had the feeling that it had little to do with his supposed reason for this visit.

"Unfortunately, I find myself in dire straits," he murmured apologetically.

She stared at him. "What on earth . . . How could *you* find yourself in financial straits? Don't be absurd, Gideon. You can't possibly expect me to believe that. I don't believe for one minute that eight hundred pounds would make one iota of difference to your bank balance."

"Oh, it wouldn't," he agreed, shaking his head. "Not one iota."

"Then what the hell are you talking about?" She was growing more irritated by the minute, and his calm demeanor wasn't helping.

He rose to his feet, murmuring, "Since *you* won't sit down—"

"There's no reason to sit down. I've explained the situation, and that concludes our business. You will get your share when we get ours." She folded her arms again.

"Well, you see, I don't think it does quite conclude our business," he explained in the same slightly apologetic tone.

Prudence was suddenly wary. "What do you mean?"

"As I recall, there was another aspect to our business agreement," he said. He walked to the window and looked down at the winter-bare garden. "A bride, wasn't it? You—or rather, the Go-Between—were going to find me a bride in exchange for my defending you in the libel suit."

Prudence was now even warier. There was something palpably dangerous in the air. She reminded herself that this man was adept at the art of ambush. She'd seen him in court, and experienced it herself once or twice. Sudden moves on her part were not advisable. She said slowly, as if speaking to one a little short on mental acuity, "You were just toying with us, with the whole idea, Gideon. You remember that."

"Oh, no," he said, turning around from the window. "I was not toying with you or the bargain. I did, as I recall, say that I might prefer to find my own bride, but I was certainly open to suggestions that would widen the field."

"Oh," Prudence said, frowning. "Would you consider meeting Lavender Riley, then? I'm sure you would like each other."

Gideon crossed the room in three strides. "Never have I known you to be obtuse, Prudence. No, I would *not* under any circumstances consider meeting Lavender Riley."

"Perhaps Heather Peterson—" she began, and then said no more because it was impossible to do so when her mouth was suddenly otherwise and somewhat forcefully occupied.

"Have I made myself clear?" he demanded when he finally raised his lips from hers, his hands still, however, holding her firmly against him.

"I'm not sure," Prudence said. "You haven't really said anything yet."

He put his hands around her throat, lightly encircling the slender column. His eyes were dark as charcoal as he held her gaze, and she could feel his thumbs against the pulse in her throat, a pulse that was beating so fast, she could hear it in her ears.

"The Go-Between fulfilled its side of the bargain. It introduced me to the only woman who could possibly be my bride. Prudence Duncan, will you marry me?"

"Harriet?" It was the only word she seemed capable of uttering.

"Her horse trainer came back for her last week." He released her and ran his hands through his immaculately groomed hair in a gesture that expressed frustration. anxiety, and that flash of vulnerability that she found so endearing. "Sarah . . ." he said, "I need your help, Prudence. I was wrong—hell, I'm often wrong. I admit it. But I really need you."

"You're not the only one who's often wrong," she said softly, touching his face, moving her other hand up to smooth down his hair. "I admit it freely."

He grasped her wrists, held her hands tightly against his face, then turned his lips to kiss the inside of her wrists. "Will you marry me, sweetheart?"

She smiled. "I think you're supposed to produce a ring and go down on one knee."

"The ring I can do," he said, "but I'll be damned if I'm going down on one knee, even for you, sweetheart."

She grinned. "I didn't really expect you to."

"Do I have my answer?"

"Well," she said consideringly, "I suppose it would save us eight hundred pounds— No . . . no, Gideon." She danced away from him as he came after her with a look in his eye that she wasn't at all sure about. "I'll call Jenkins."

"Call him." He grabbed her arm, swinging her to his body. "You are a wasp and the most impossible woman I've ever met."

"Yes," she agreed. "And I dislike *you* intensely too."

"Then that seems like an equitable agreement."

It was an hour later when Constance and Chastity met on the steps of the house. "Well met," Constance greeted her sister. "Did you see Mrs. Beedle?"

"Yes, and a whole stack of letters. Did you write your article?"

Constance smiled. "Just wait until you read it."

"But you didn't hold Father up to ridicule?" Chastity asked with a worried frown.

"Chas!"

"No, of course you didn't. I'm sorry. I'm just so anxious."

"Prue? Did she see him alone?"

Chastity nodded. "I imagine he's gone by now. But you know how she tries to hide how she feels . . . if she's hurt, I mean. I really thought that . . ."

Constance put an arm around her. "So did I. But they aren't compatible, Chas. Prue knows that."

Chastity nodded as she put her key in the door. The hall was deserted when they went in, and they looked at each other in puzzlement. It was unheard of for Jenkins not to respond to the turn of a key, wherever he was in the house.

"I expect she's in the parlor," Chastity said, heading for the stairs. She stopped halfway across the hall as the stealthy figure of Jenkins suddenly appeared in the shadows of the stairs. He put a finger to his lips and beckoned with the other hand. Fascinated, the sisters followed him into the kitchen.

"Miss Prue is in the drawing room with Sir Gideon," Jenkins informed them.

"Still?" Chastity exclaimed. "He was supposed to come two hours ago."

"Yes, Miss Chas. But Miss Prue hasn't rung for anything."

"And you're certain Sir Gideon didn't leave . . . when you weren't looking maybe? Oh, of course he didn't," Constance corrected herself when she saw his outraged expression. "How could he have slipped past you?"

Jenkins nodded, appeased. "I thought it best not to inquire if they needed anything," he stated.

"Yes," Chastity said. "I would have done the same thing." She looked at her sister. "What do you think, Con? Shall we go in?"

"And risk in flagrante delicto?"

"Oh, don't be absurd, Con. It's the drawing room."

"Well, I think we'd better make a great deal of noise," Constance said. "Kettle drums. We need kettle drums."

"We don't have any," Chastity said through her reluctant laughter. "But we could try banging a couple of Mrs. Hudson's pans together."

"Oh, give over, Miss Chas, do," Mrs. Hudson said, although she, like Jenkins, was trying to stifle a smile.

"I suggest you knock upon the door, Miss Con," Jenkins said, once more his stately self. "And maybe wait a few minutes before you open it."

"Of course, Jenkins, the perfect solution," Constance said. She winked at him and he turned discreetly to one side, not quite managing to hide his smile.

The sisters returned to the hall. They walked around heavily for a few minutes, opened and shut the front door several times, and then approached the drawing room. Constance raised her hand to knock, but the door opened before she could do so.

"I could hear you from ten miles away," Prudence said. "Come in. We need your advice."

"Oh." That was unexpected, Constance reflected. "Good morning, Gideon. Are you still finishing up business?"

"No, I believe we're only beginning," Gideon said, coming forward with outstretched hand. "Good morning, Constance . . . Chastity."

They shook his hand and then turned as one to their sister. "Prue?"

"It seems," she said, "that Gideon has decided to take up the alternative to our bargain."

"Oh," Chastity said with a smile. "And did we find him a bride?"

"It would seem so," Prudence said. She moved her hand into the light. A circlet of emeralds threw green fire against the ray of sun piercing the window.

"The stones seemed appropriate . . . matched your sister's eyes," Gideon said, waving his hands in a slightly uncertain manner. He hadn't realized that he would think he needed the sisters' approval of his choice of gems. But he realized he needn't have worried. They were not in the least interested in the ring. They brushed their sister's hand aside as they embraced her in a hug so fierce, so all-encompassing, he couldn't help the slightest prick of jealousy.

And then they broke apart, and he found himself embraced by Constance and Chastity, and the prick of jealousy disappeared. He thought that perhaps it would be a good idea to talk to his soon-to-be brother-in-law about what he should expect of a life married to one of the Duncan sisters.

"You said you wanted our advice," Constance reminded them when the hugging was over.

"Oh, yes. I was thinking we should elope," Prudence said.

"The anvil at Gretna Green is not my idea of a wedding," Gideon said.

"But just think, we could take the overnight train to Edinburgh, it's wonderfully romantic, and then—" Prudence stopped. "You really hate the idea."

"I see no reason why we should hide in corners. Haven't you been doing enough of that?"

Prudence knew this was no ambush. He was facing her with such a question when she had her sisters around her. She could only commend his courage. "Yes," she said. "But something feels wrong about a grand spectacle at this moment. Constance's wedding was magnificent, but that wouldn't feel right now. We're all too raw." She looked at her sister for confirmation.

Constance said, "This is your wedding, love. Whatever you want to do, Chas and I will be here to support you. We'll leave you to talk it through." She nodded at Chastity, who nodded back and followed her to the door.

With her hand on the knob, Chastity turned back. "I do think Gretna Green is a really terrible idea, Prue." Then they left.

"If we could wait a year," Prudence began. "No, I don't want to either. How small . . . ?"

"As small as you like. Your family, Sarah, you and me."

"You don't have any family?"

"My parents are dead and I was an only child. If you wanted a big wedding, then I could produce a reasonable showing on my side, but only Sarah really needs to be there."

"And Mary Winston?"

"Yes," he agreed. "Mary needs to be there."

"Then we're agreed."

He took her in his arms again. "Sweetheart, we are going to agree some of the time, and disagree much of the time."

"Yes," she said against his mouth. "It won't be too difficult to remind myself that I dislike you intensely."

He moved his mouth from hers, brushed his lips along the line of her jaw, and then raised his head. "I'll get a special license. We can be married within the week."

"Yes," Prudence said. "Best to do it before I change my mind." Her smile gave the lie to her words.

"Wasp," he accused again, pinching the end of her nose. "I had better talk to your father now."

Prudence grimaced. "He's in the library. But bear in mind he's had more than his fair share of shocks in the last two days. He might not be exactly . . ." She shrugged.

"I can manage your father, if you can manage Sarah," he said.

Prudence nodded, all gravity now. "I'll do my best, Gideon."

"She's a little uncertain about things at the moment . . . after Harriet, you understand."

"I understand."

He nodded, ran his hands through his hair again, then kissed her quickly and left.

Epilogue

"Chas, are you ready?" Constance stuck her head around the door of her youngest sister's bedroom. "Prue and Father are leaving in five minutes."

"Yes, I'm quite ready." Chastity put down the letter she was reading. "I was only running through the last batch of mail for the Go-Between."

"Oh?" Constance gave her a rather quizzical look. "Strange thing to be doing on Prue's wedding morning."

"No, it's not." Chastity got up from the dresser chair. "You know how Mother used to say that a minute wasted was a minute lost forever. I'm ready, and I had a minute."

"Yes, of course," Constance said agreeably. "You look lovely."

"As do you," Chastity returned. "And Prue looks sensational. Let's give her the finishing touches." Constance nodded and left. Chastity hesitated for a minute before following. She picked up the letter she'd discarded on her dresser and looked again at the signature.

Dr. Douglas Farrell.

It seemed that the good doctor was in search of a wife. A helpmeet. A woman who would want to be involved in his work. Was it the same Dr. Farrell she'd seen at Mrs. Beedle's?

A question for another day. She grabbed her handbag, took a quick look in the mirror to make sure her hat was straight, and hurried to Prudence's bedroom.

"I don't know if I want this veil," Prudence was saying as Chastity came in. "It seems too bridal. I'm not walking down the aisle to the wedding march."

"Then wear it up," Constance suggested. "Lift it and put it back. Like so . . . then it frames your face."

"And you *are* a bride," Chastity chimed in. "It may not be the most conventional wedding, but it still has a bride and groom."

"I know. But I wish we'd gone to Gretna Green," Prudence said. She turned in front of the mirror. She could find no fault with her oyster-colored silk dress that had been refashioned from one of their mother's afternoon gowns. Something old. No fault with the mink pillow that Constance had lent her as a hat. Something borrowed. No fault with the diamond bracelet that Gideon had given her. Something new. And no fault with the turquoise earrings that her father had given her that morning. Something blue.

"You forgot the sixpence," Chastity said, dropping the shiny coin onto the dresser.

"Oh, yes." Prudence laughed, and much of her tension dissipated. She sat down, slipped off her ivory silk slipper, and slid the coin into the toe.

"Something old, something new, something borrowed, something blue, and a sixpence in your shoe," Chastity recited. "And now you're ready to get married."

"Oh, but am I?" Prudence asked, standing up, curling her toes around the sixpence. "*Am* I?"

"As ready as you'll ever be," Constance declared. "Gideon is the only man you could ever marry, Prue. If you don't know that by now, then nothing Chas and I can say will persuade you."

"Of course I know it." She smiled a little dreamily. "I love him, but sometimes I could pour boiling oil on him."

"That's normal," Constance said from the benefit of experience. "I don't see any way that Duncan women can marry men strong enough for them without accepting boiling oil and cannon fire as part of the bargain."

"I'm ready," Prudence declared. "Let's get married." She paused in the doorway and said with a slightly tremulous smile, "At least Gideon has Max to stand up with him. I'm sure he's as scared as I am."

Chastity looked at her anxiously. "No regrets, Prue?"

Prudence took a deep breath. "No . . . none. Let's go."

Gideon and Max stood at the altar in the side chapel of the small church in Westminster. Sarah and Mary Winston sat in the front pew. Constance and Chastity sat on the opposite side. Lord Duncan had insisted that he walk his daughter down the aisle.

The organist began to play. Gideon looked towards the door. Prudence, his bride, the woman who once upon a time he could never have dreamed of as a life's companion, was now the only woman he could imagine sharing his life. And she was walking towards him, her step as strong and decisive as always. And yet he could see the slight tremor of her lips, the hesitancy in her eye, and he knew she was as terrified and yet as certain of the rightness of this as he was.

He stepped forward as she reached him. Max touched his shoulder in brief masculine reassurance and then went to sit beside his wife. Lord Duncan kissed the bride's cheek and stepped back also to take his seat. Gideon took Prudence's hand and her fingers twined with his. The words were said. He put the gold band on her finger. He kissed her. And it was done. They went into the small registry to sign the book, and when they went back to the church, they were alone.

"Never," Gideon whispered, bending towards her ear, "will I let you go. *Never.* You understand that?"

"And that goes double for me," she returned in the same whisper. "Whatever happens, we belong together. Through boiling oil and cannon fire."

"I'm not going to ask where that came from. But yes, through boiling oil and cannon fire. We belong together." He kissed her again, and there was nothing formal about this kiss. It was an affirmation that ignored their surroundings, the incense-scented gloom, lit only by the altar candles.

Prudence looked around at the deserted church and Gideon said softly, "You wanted Gretna Green. I agreed with your sisters on a compromise. We'll have a family celebration tomorrow, but for now, there are only the two of us."

She smiled up at him. "Where are we going?"

"A bride is not supposed to know her honeymoon destination," he said. "You have to trust me."

"I do," she said. "Now and for always."

"Boiling oil and cannon fire notwithstanding?" he teased.

"Trust can withstand the occasional spark," she returned.